This is a work of fiction. Names, characters, places and incidents are either the product of the author's imagination or are used fictitiously, and any resemblance to actual persons, living or dead, business establishments, events or locales is entirely coincidental.

BUBBA 'N ME ON SULLIVAN'S ISLAND

Printing History
1st edition, 2013

Printed in the United States of America

ISBN: 9781494444365

Printed at Alphagraphics, Charleston SC

PROLOGUE

First of all let me say this book is a work of fiction. I say this because one of my severest and dearest critics, my mother, asked me after reading a certain chapter. "Y'all really do that?" My reply was, "Of course not, Mom. You know we were good little boys."

Way back in the midst of telling one of my many stories about growing up on Sullivans Island one of my beer-drinking buddies remarked, "Mike, you should write a book." I gave it some thought and well, some twenty odd years later here is that effort. But more than an effort or a chore it has been a love recalling fun times when my greatest worry was the threat of a new pimple or would Flash Gordon escape the clutches of Emperor Ming. And despite the long hours of trying to figure out how to put this on paper it has been a love of recalling just how lucky I was … and still am. Facts and faces had faded over time but the emotions of fun, acceptance, pain and pleasure are engraved deep in the canyons of my mind. Whether I can get these feelings down on paper sufficiently and clearly is a different matter. But I'm gonna try like hell because, to me, it's a story that I want to share with you the reader. I hope you enjoy the read half as much as I enjoyed the experience.

I grew up on Sullivans Island, South Carolina; a finger shaped Barrier Island just off the coast, not more than two good stone throws across the harbor from Charleston. It is bordered on the front by the Atlantic Ocean and on the back by The Intracoastal Waterway. We are connected to the mainland and the town of Mt.Pleasant by an ancient drawbridge. It was officially named the Ben Sawyer Bridge. Locals simply referred to it as "the bridge" and everyone knew what you were talking about. The two-lane causeway leading to the Island is no more than a mile long yet is a truly scenic and inspiring ride, at least, to a returning Islander offering marsh vistas and a panoramic view of the Island.

Sullivans Island is the same island used in the setting for the book entitled Sullivans Island written by the talented Dorothea Benton Frank who also grew up on the Island just up the street from me. She was always Dottie until about age twelve when she won a beauty contest (a beauty that she still retains) sponsored by the local radio station, WTMA. From that day on she was tagged with the moniker "Little Miss TMA." I still get a laugh from her when I refer to her using that title. It's OK because she is my cousin and I love her dearly.

The town of Mt.Pleasant that connects us to the outside world was once a sleepy village, forty years ago with no stoplights, no condominiums, and no traffic. That wonderful, oak-laden, moss draped community is now but a memory. Where you once drove for miles without stopping has been replaced by a traffic light every block highlighted by store after store in search of the almighty dollar. It is one of the fastest growing areas in the state complete with new and newer subdivisions, townhouses, strip malls, and the numerous gas stations and banks where folks gas up to take their haul to be deposited or go to the bank to secure a loan to gas up ... take your choice.

Sullivans Island is the opposite of Mt.Pleasant in size and lifestyle. It is much smaller, tiny in fact, compared to the immense spread of our immediate neighbor. Our lifestyle is unique in the modern world of hurry-hurry- let's- go. The pace here is laid back and easy, evidenced by the fact that there is not even one traffic light on the Island. If and when that terrible day comes when one is installed, many old-time residents vow they will move.

Island folks are friendly; the Island's natural beauty is unparalled and with one of the cleanest beaches on the East coast it makes for good living. Thank goodness our local politicians have had the foresight and the gumption to say "NO" to the Holiday Inns of the world and other commercial interests and not turn us into a concrete jungle. If you desire that, then go to Highway 17,turn right and go about a hundred miles. There you will run into Myrtle Beach.

Our little sanctuary is doing just fine as we move into the new millennium. It's not a perfect place but then again no place is. Taxes are higher (what's new?) and the crowds are larger in the summer on the beaches but that's tolerable. We have a few new businesses, which is all right, especially the new restaurants that give the Island a certain flavor, no pun intended.

Small, tranquil, and beautiful. That's Sullivans Island. Growing up on the Island was adventurous and exciting for two Island boys. There is a story somewhere that needs to be told. If I recall correctly, I remember seeing it something like this...

1
DOUBLE TROUBLE

It's June and it's hot. Real hot in the Lowcountry of South Carolina. A thick wall of humidity hanging like a curtain surrounds the Island blocking the cool ocean breezes. Baked sea gulls sit on the rooftops, gazing at the steamy air rising to form the cumulus clouds, which later will bring the cooling rains from the afternoon thunderstorms.

"Man, it's hotter than a well digger's butt in Alaska. Can't we rest a little while," I moaned and then wiped at the steady stream of sweat pouring down my face. I paused.

"Eah, did you hear me?" I yelled at my friend standing next to me ignoring my protests.

"Yeah, yeah, yeah. I heard ya, Mike." I'm not deaf, you know." He paused and stared at me and raising his voice said, "Will you shut up and quit complaining." He tossed another shovel full of dirt. "If you spent half the time digging that you do complaining we could have dug to China by now. You're worse than my little sister. You know that?"

"Eah, them's fighting words, boy," I said grinning, "you better watch your mouth." One look at my friend's tanned muscular arms and shoulders told me that skinny little ol' me was no match for him. But I didn't worry. He was my best friend and we had been through plenty already in our young lives and we weren't about to ever fight each other.

"Fighting words?" he exclaimed. "How about help me *fight* these oyster shells and quit running your mouth, OK?"

Even though we were wearing our summer "uniforms" consisting of a pair of shorts and tennis shoes, we suffered with each shovel full of dirt removed from the solidly packed dirt and oyster shell road hurrying to finish our task. Our victim will soon pass this way and we want to be ready. This is a one- shot deal and we don't want to blow it. It's hard work for a couple of twelve-year-old boys who are out of shape from sitting at a desk in school and doing nothing for nine months. Well, we had been doing *something* but it wasn't schoolwork. The only consoling thought I have is that we will be successful in our task and, of course, not get caught. And then we can celebrate with a cold Vanilla Coke at Burton's Drug Store, the local hangout of our crew, a group of Island kids and classmates. While enjoying the cool drink, we will brag to our envious friends who were dumb enough to challenge us to this caper thinking we wouldn't take on such a dare. The crew and me and my friend were a natural match, one as congenial as peanut butter and jelly. You see, they were full of dares and we were right there to take on any and every dare that came our way. *And* then they had the nerve to badger us saying we could never pull it off. Yeah, we planned to rub it in good.

Staring into the damp hole, watered with our sweat, my friend asked, "Think it's deep enough?" I took a quick look and decided that it was *not* deep enough and then thought again before I spoke.

"Oh yeah, it's plenty deep." I lied. " Plenty deep!" I didn't want to dig anymore. The sun was getting up high and by now it was so hot I could hear myself sweat.

He believed me.

The hole, three feet wide and two feet deep, was strategically placed in the right tire lane of the rutted road and its precise location was critical to our success or failure. This effort was the crowning touch of weeks of careful planning while pretending to pay attention in Sister Rosalind's Religion class at Saint Angela's School. We chose Religion class to do our planning because we were bored to death hearing about God and the Ten Commandments and how we were going to burn in Hell if we didn't straighten up. We figured God had given us Ten Commandments to live by and that was enough but our teachers must have added a hundred rules of their own making life truly miserable for us. Besides, Religion class met every day, giving us plenty of time to brainstorm.

I recall one such planning session that went wrong: "Psst, psst. Hey." I got my friend's attention while Sister Rosalind looked the other way. "How are we gonna camouflage the hole?"

"I don't know," he barely whispered, "we'll figure something out. Let me think about it."

"OK but don't take all day. We ain't got but a week left and I don't want to screw this up."

"Yeah, I know what you mean. You could screw up a one car funeral." His HA-HA came out a little too loud.

"Mister O'Toole *and* Mister Devlin!" Sister Rosalind who had been patrolling the aisles and, we thought, was out of hearing range, suddenly stopped and wheeled around like an attack dog. Putting the evil eye on us she strutted up to our desks. "Do you two have anything better to do than goof off in class and chit -chat anytime you fell like it?"

"No, Sister," we answered together quickly sitting up ramrod straight and looking straight ahead.

"No, Sister!" she exploded. "You mean to tell me you don't have something better to do than that?"

"Yes, Sister," we said again. We had learned many years earlier that when one of the nuns was in your face the best answer to give was either a "no Sister" or a "yes Sister" … nothing more, nothing less.

"And what is that, may I ask?" Sister Rosalind demanded with a scowl from hell. "Speak up," she yelled, "I can't hear you!"

"Yes, Sister," we repeated but from the disgusted look on Sister's face we had guessed wrong with our answer.

She paused for a few seconds, her eyes drilling holes in us. Sister Rosalind was a master at confusing us with her expert and crafty use of the English language, especially when it came to the use of the double negative. And today she sprung one on us: "Do you not think that you can not perform better in this class without talking when you feel like it?"

"U-u-u-h," … not understanding the question we didn't know how to answer so I just took a wild guess. "No, Sister," I said without much conviction as I waited for the wrath of God to pour down on me.

I must have guessed correctly because when I heard her say, "Do you two see this stick I'm holding?" I knew I was in the clear. It was her standard closing after a good tongue-lashing.

"Yes, Sister," I said with glee in my heart.

"Would you like for me to take to your backsides for about ten strokes each?"

"Yes, Sister. Uh, no Sister," we said quickly.

"Then that's your first and last warning. No more talking or else. Do you understand?"

"Oh, yes Sister."

And between the planning and passing of secret notes we said a few prayers to Saint Houdini, our designated Saint of Escape who we needed to help us escape from capture during our many escapades. And we thought it more appropriate to pray in Religion class whereas praying in math class just seemed so out of place. So far our patron saint hadn't come to our rescue, not once. My friend said he was probably busy somewhere else or sleeping or maybe going to the bathroom? Shoot, we didn't know what saints did in their free time. Whatever. We were not the originators or instigators of this undertaking. We were merely the executors, the doers, the risk takers and that's probably why the crew singled us out knowing that we would take on this bet.

Two prior events played their part in this episode, the bet with the crew, which we couldn't turn down without losing face and a statement from a beautiful girl, which in itself would have led me to this point and way beyond.

Carrying out pranks and tricks at school was a daily undertaking and not an hour passed when our busy little minds were not engaged in coming up with some sort of devious trickery. This Tomfoolery was strictly a male thing and we were a determined young group. Determined to prove our manhood and get into trouble. The girls, on the other hand, were way ahead of us on the maturity curve and they sat back and let us be our immature, silly selves. And we did not disappoint them as we continually made fools of ourselves trying to impress them.

I recall Susan Huggins sashaying up to my friend at recess, batting her eyes and in a tone dripping with honey say, "Bubba, I bet you can't climb to the top of the oak tree and sit up there for the rest of recess." I wondered why I couldn't find my friend at recess that day.

We also stayed in trouble with our teachers, the strict and unrelenting nuns of Our Lady of Mercy, our teachers at Saint Angela's Catholic School. If we had dedicated half the time we spent in trying to pull off stunts and tricks to our academic pursuits, life would have been so much easier. We would have spent less time being grounded due to poor grades, we wouldn't have to stay after school or in at recess and we would assure ourselves of passing to the next grade. Also, good grades would get our parents off our back. But in 1959, pranks and stunts came before studying and homework. And this particular undertaking was unique. It was in a league by itself, daring and grandiose. It was on a level with winning the World Series or making an "A" in Sister Roberta's English class. By taking on this challenge my friend and I thought we were in the big time compared to the small potato affairs of our classmates like Bailey Jones who slipped a live beetle down the back of Peggy Nickle's blouse scaring the dickens out of her and then strutted around for two days like he was the coolest. Or the time Lenny Swinton put Sister Ann Marie's chalk and erasers on top of the blackboard in plain view of the class. Everyone enjoyed a silent laugh watching the little nun attempting to jump up and retrieve her materials, only to miss by a mile. However, we held our collective breaths when she slipped and landed squarely on her butt luckily wounding only her pride. Lenny thought that was pretty neat until Mary Rogers, feeling sorry for the little red-faced nun, squealed on him and Sister gave him the big ruler treatment.

This particular escapade had its origin one morning, early at school on the playground.

"There they are, come on. We'll find out now." The crew led by Jocko and John cornered Bubba 'n me over by the swing set.

Jocko yelled, "Hey, Bubba, Mike! Y'all look here." We knew something was up the way our friends gathered around us, hemming us in, offering no escape.

"The crew here has been talking about doing something really cool on the Island instead of here at school. And we figured you guys might want to try it seeing that y'all live over there. We'll even bet you that y'all can't pull this one off."

When he said *bet* he had my attention.

"What you talking about, Jocko?" Bubba asked exhibiting great bravado. "Is it something you pansies can't do?" Yep, that was my friend.

Simple and to the point. Not always diplomatic, but to the point.

"A-a-a-w, we could probably do it but we don't live on the Island." Jocko folded his arms and stared at Bubba. "If the cops got after us it would be a long run home back to the Isle of Palms. You understand ... don't ya?"

Cops? Whoa, now he really had my attention.

"Here's the deal. All y'all have to do is stop the Island garbage truck somehow from picking up the trash for one day." It was John and he was smiling. "That's the bet. Simple as that." He turned to the crew who were nodding their assent but really they were egging us on. "Think you Island sissies can handle that?"

By this time a small group of admiring underclassmen had gathered and listened to the crew's latest stupid idea.

"I don't think it can be done. N-a-a-w, no way," pipped Bobby as he listened for the uh- huhs and yeas from the crew.

Shoot, what choice do we have? I thought but decided to let Bubba do the talking.

"How much y'all gonna give us if we do it," Bubba asked. "I know we can pull this off but we want some money for this one." He turned to me and I shrugged my shoulders.

"We're way ahead of ya, Bubba. We had Stinky steal $2.00 from the collection plate on Sunday and we took up a collection from the crew knowing you guys would bite. We have $3.75. Is it a bet?"

"You're on, sucker!" Bubba blurted out. "And after we're finished we'll come to Burton's and collect, just wait and see. Right, Mike?"

"Oh yeah. That's right, for sure." *What in the heck are we getting into this time* was what I really thought. But ...what the heck ... I didn't have anything else to do ... so why not?

My friend and I didn't give a hoot about the money. In our minds we were rich beyond anything money could buy. We lived on a playground in paradise, a place of swaying palms, a splendid beach, home of the Lowcountry marshes and creeks. We lived on Sullivans Island. It was the challenge that excited me, especially being told, "You can't do it." Tell *me* that and watch my dust!

Added to the dare was the innocent statement made by the girl of my dreams, the beautiful and bodacious Beverly Ann Johnson. Earlier in the school year she had told me, "I like boys who take chances and are successful at what they do." Well, I sure liked to take chances. Now all I needed to do was to prove to her that I could be successful at something other than getting into trouble. Besides, I had the help of my long time friend. *So,* I figured, *what could possibly go wrong? Stopping an old garbage truck ... a piece of cake.*

We smelt "Old Blue" before we saw it. Loaded with fresh garbage it came rumbling around the corner at Station 18, right on schedule, its rusted out muffler beating out a steady rhythm.

"Man, we just did make it. Quick get the screen." Bubba handed me the camouflaged screen and I put it across the hole while he sprinkled dirt over it.

"That looks good," he said, "let's go!" We scurried to the safety of our hideout in the oleander bushes. Serious thought had been given to digging the hole in the cool of the night, however, if our parents had caught us digging in the road at night we would promptly be attending a very personal funeral. And Chief William Perry, more commonly known as Bull Perry, but only behind his back, sometimes patrolled this road and in no way did I want to have any dealings with him or to obtain a criminal record for wrecking a police car. Also, my friend had this strange idea that someday he would be the police chief on the Island and he didn't think that getting caught in this caper would help him any in getting the job.

The clang of discarded garbage can lids signaled that Mrs. Kingman's house was being serviced, then one more stop at the Kramer's … then around the corner … down the road a little and into the hole. The sweat of anticipation mingled with that from the heat and formed a steady stream that ended in puddles in my shoes. Now that the moment of truth was near I began to worry.

"Do you think it will work? Will he see the screen and stop? What happens if he misses the hole?" I was thinking out loud, not seriously doubting our plan, because after all the planning we put into this it had to work. My friend wasn't standing for any talk like that. "Shut up, will ya," he said in no uncertain terms. "You're the biggest worry wart in the world."

So far our plan was working. Mr. Nick was driving today and in his usual hurry. The ever present Sambo was in position standing on the rear bumper looking like a Roman Centurion commanding his giant blue chariot ready to leap off at the next stop and take on the enemy leaving nothing but empty and defeated trash cans in his wake. Mr. Nick supervised from his command position in the driver's seat.

"Old Blue" came closer and closer, right on line for the hole. Just a little more, a little closer … almost there … and then BOOM into the hole!

The right front tire landed squarely in the hole shaking the whole truck for a second, throwing Mr. Nick forward in a rush. The tire immediately went flat and then the truck came to a sudden stop listing to the right like a sinking ship. When the tire had blown out, it sounded like a rifle shot, scaring the fool out of us. That's when the first feeling of fear hit us. Wide eyed we peeked through the branches and were startled by the enormity of the truck, just sitting there. We couldn't help but hear the prayerful pleas of Sambo, as he was thrown from the truck, and hurtled through the air yelling and screaming.

"Oh do Lord, Jesus, helps me. Oh Lordy, Lordy, please helps me!"

Mr. Nick leaped from the truck to attend to the disheveled Sambo who lay on the ground holding onto different body parts simultaneously. We exhaled a breath of relief when we heard the moans and groans from Sambo meaning he was still alive. *Man, I'm going to die young. Either Sambo or my parents are going to kill me.*

No more than a couple of minutes passed and we heard the blast of sirens, a bunch of them. Someone had raised the alarm signal. It was probably the widow Elliott who lived across the street. She might have been eighty-seven years old but she didn't miss a thing.

In less than ten minutes, the forces of rescue arrived: the Island Fire and Rescue Squad, Chief Perry, the ambulance, the fire truck, and several of the Island's finest volunteers joined by our neighboring community's Fire and Rescue Department from the Isle of Palms. They were led by their police chief. Everyone had their sirens blaring at full blast like it was a contest to see who could make the most noise and their flashing red lights added to the moment. Everyone jumped from their cars and trucks and ran here and there, back and forth, until they were practically stumbling over each other.

Chief Bull Perry, seeking shade under a tree no way large enough to shadow his rotund frame, stood with his hands on his hips with a small group of do-nothing, gawking volunteers. Each one trying hard to be a boss and get in the way. They were doing a good job.

With his trademark scowl firmly in place the Chief bellowed at a passing volunteer, "Over here. You! Get over here and check out the damage on the truck." He paused to frown. "No! Not you. Him!" He pointed and growled, "Yeah, you." The bewildered volunteer pointed at himself. "Who me?"

"Yeah, you!"

Obediently he ran frantically toward the truck, bumped into a charging fireman pulling on a hose, knocking the fireman to the ground.

"Hey, watch where the hell you're going, buddy!" he yelled dusting himself off. "Can't you see I've got to get this hose over there."

"Sorry, man. Sorry. By the way, why are y'all taking the hose off the truck?"

The fireman shrugged. "I don't know."

The Island firemen were pulling the thick, canvas hose off the truck like there was no tomorrow. For whatever reason, God only knows. There was no fire Maybe they thought one might start.

"Look out!" screamed the head hose puller. Too late as three Isle of Palms volunteers running by were swept off their feet by the thick hose like fresh cut wheat. Now they needed attention.

Chief Perry turned just in time to see the arrival of the Island ladder truck. *I guess they're going to crawl down to the ground and rescue*

Sambo? thought the Chief.

"Stop, you fool, stop!" the Chief screamed as he ran with his hands held up toward the truck. "S-T-O-P! … You're gonna ..." The driver came to a screeching halt about two feet shy of his intended destination crashing into the side of Chief Perry's car with a loud CRUNCH!

"Oh man! What the hell," the Chief moaned. "What next …"

Now he had a dent to match the one received during last summer's Fourth of July parade when a slightly inebriated fireman driving the fire truck rear-ended his car. That fireman is history but at least the dents matched in color, if not in size.

The Isle of Palms firemen not to be outdone by the Island firemen had pulled their hoses from their trucks overlapping those already sprawled on the ground creating a mass of white hoses running everywhere but nowhere. Then finally realizing there was no fire both groups began hauling their hose back to their trucks, overlapping each other's hoses until the tangle of hoses became a safety issue.

Lying flat on the stretcher Sambo groaned with pain, "O-o-o-h, my leg hurt. My arm hurt too. Me head hurt." Then suddenly he perked up and asked, "Where y'all taking me?"

"Over to the ambulance, Sambo. Just relax. You're going to be OK."

Trying to carry Sambo and dodge the fuss of humanity rushing about and attempting to walk through the minefield of hose was too much for Sambo's rescuers.

"Watch your step, Ed." Ed's partner paused and grimaced. He saw it coming. "Ed, look out!" Down went Ed and Sambo.

"O-o-o-wee! That hurt," Sambo yelled. "That be worse than the crash. What evers y'alls trying to do… kill me?"

"Sorry Sambo. Hang on," Bill said examining the twisted ankle of his co-worker. "Be with you in a minute." He paused and looked around. "Could someone, anyone help us over here?" His pleas fell on deaf ears.

Now things were *not* going like we planned, not at all. Our blueprint for success looked like someone had spilt water all over it, cut it up and then wadded it up and thrown it in the garbage. I think I saw it in the back of "Old Blue."

The rescue group continued their efforts as everyone ran around trying hard to find something important to do, looking and directing, but no one seemed to be in charge of this Chinese fire drill and matters only worsened when the tripping hose suddenly sprung to life deciding to do its duty and bathe everyone within twenty feet. Mr. White, the hose commander, had shouted "NO" in reply to " should I turn the water on" from old man Hagood whose hearing was on a par with Blind Bobby Benton's eyesight, who drove the fire truck whenever there was a fire. Island residents driving at the time of a fire would be warned by the sound of the truck's siren and the impending danger. Cars parted like the

Red Sea giving Blind Bobby plenty of room.

Taking the "NO" for a "GO" Mr. Hagood had proudly turned the handle wide open unleashing a hundred and fifty psi of water upon an unsuspecting crowd and an even more unsuspecting Mr. White. That hose jumped to life and was squirming like a snake run over by a lawnmower, just a swaying and turning, spraying water everywhere. Twenty wet men were chasing it, to no avail.

"Look out, I've got it," commanded the diminutive Johnny Antonelli. "I'll show you who the man around here is." That hose threw him like he was a rookie bronco rider. It took all three hundred and ten pounds of Buster Linhold to finally wrestle it to a halt waiting for it to make a turn his way and then diving through the air and landing belly flop style on the poor hose, dutifully doing its job.

Sambo continued to cry out for help from the Heavens as they finally placed him in the ambulance: "Helps me Lord, I's gonna die. Oh Lord, please helps me. Oh how I suffer!"

I looked at my friend and he looked at me. Neither one of us knew what to say and we both had a look of fear in our eyes. I knew my friend was scared the way he was rubbing his palms together very quickly while cocking his head to one side and looking up as for Divine Guidance, his signal of distress, while making funny little sounds. The sounds he made were something between a baby crying and a screech owl.

Hoping for the best, I closed my eyes and crouched lower for cover. I was already kissing the ground. Any lower and we would be married. The fatal flaw in our plan was that we had no escape route. And at the moment the overflow crowd of neighbors and rubberneckers hemmed us in. Our fate was sealed like a jar of Grandma's jam.

Why do kids pull stunts like this? It's anybody's guess and, if asked, a youngster's answer would vary from "I don't know" to "Well, we didn't have anything else to do." We certainly were not mean spirited kids trying to intentionally hurt anyone or cause any serious trouble. We were out to prove a point and impress our friends and, in this case, to win a bet. If there was some deep-seeded subliminal man versus machine theory involved, therein would lie the answer, but that kind of thought is reserved for performance-type contests where a man pits himself against a machine, like John Henry driving railroad spikes. That certainly was not the case here.

Boredom? No way. We had beaten that ugly rascal to death years ago with summers of endless fun enjoying everything Island life had to offer: swimming in the Atlantic Ocean, bike riding, playing baseball, fishing, crabbing, and enjoying the company of friends. In the winter we went clamming and oystering and fishing for the trout so abundant in the creeks. Life was so good I even enjoyed going to Church. Well … almost.

Accountability in our family was a big, big thing. My parents stressed it so much that our name could have probably been changed from Devlin to the Accountability family. It wasn't a complicated thing at all. There were only two things we kids were held accountable for: one was for what we did and the other was for what we didn't do. Being held accountable for our actions was self-explanatory. No one else could be blamed for something we did nor could we deny what we did. That part of accountability was easy. As for being held accountable for what we did *not* do was a little different but was viewed in the same vein of being accountable as a person. For example, we had chores and certain duties to do around the house and a certain job to do in school and in the community. If we didn't do them then we were held accountable. It was so simple that even I understood it. So if one of us got in trouble somewhere like at school when we got home we were in trouble again with our parents. Real trouble. Trouble two times. We Devlin kids called it double trouble. And the punishment dished out at home was usually harsher than what we had already received.

Well, I could see ol' double trouble coming on like a fast moving flood tide. I said a quick Hail Mary while all these thoughts ran through my adventurous little mind and was … Whoa! That's it, that's it … that's the answer! Adventure! Why do kids pull stunts like this? Adventure … fun … excitement … man's eternal quest for fun and adventure. Yes! That had to be it. And that quest was alive and well in 1959 on Sullivans Island.

"Man, you ever seen such a mess?" No answer. Silence. I was talking to the air. I turned and looked and my friend was gone. Now ain't that something. Being alone I became frightened and crouched lower, if that was possible, between the thin oleander branches hoping to disappear. I pulled the long green leaves in front of my eyes giving myself a sense of false security. The prayer must have helped as I breathed a little bit easier and then snuck a peek as the confusion across the street began to die down. The Isle of Palms group had finally untangled their hose and was gathering their materials and loading it onto their truck and helping the Island Rescue Squad roll up their hoses while the rest of the rescuers stood around with their hands on their hips shaking their heads. Sambo was resting in the back of the ambulance moaning slightly and somewhat overwhelmed by all the attention. Chief Perry was surveying the mess and scratching his head trying to figure out just what happened. Me? I breathed a sigh of relief thinking I *just* might escape this screw up?

Then I heard the rustle of leaves behind me and as the branches parted I caught a momentary glimpse of a thumb and forefinger a split second before they clapped onto my upper ear. It was caught in a vice-like grip, causing additional pain with each new twist. My mother had appeared magically from out of thin air as though she and my friend had traded places and she pulled me from my not so good hiding place.

My mother stood there with her hands on her hips and looking me sternly in the eyes with a possessed look and in a clear smooth tone said, "You better tell the truth because I'm only going to ask you once. Who did this?"

All I could say was "Bubba 'n me."

And all I could think was, *Uh- oh, I'm in trouble now. And not just trouble but double trouble.*

2

MY FRIEND

1953

It was a long time ago ... years ago. Bubba ... Paddy O'Toole ... Padraig Bryan O'Toole ... all the same person and he was my best friend.

My friends and I had the neatest sand box in the neighborhood. That's what the adults called it, a sand box. Us kids called it a dirt box because it was filled with the blackest dirt you ever saw. I remember watching my father sawing big wide boards and sweating in the heat as he nailed them together forming the high walls of the box.

"That's to keep out the critters that crawl around on the ground," said my father, "don't want none of you kids to get eaten up by some big old snake" and then he laughed.

"Hee-hee," I giggled. Not about the snake but because my father had laughed. We really didn't have to worry about such things because my mother or one of the other mothers always looked after us while we played in the huge dirt box making our delicious cookies and cakes and pies from the black dirt. We thought we were the world's best mud pie bakers. Today my mother had duty.

"See this one here." I pointed at a large unassuming shape. "Do you know what that is, Padraig?"

"That?" He answered turning his head from side to side looking at the mound of dirt. "I don't know."

After considerable effort and time I spent on this masterpiece and he didn't recognize the cake in the form of a ship. "You stupid." I gave him a short whack on the head with my plastic shovel telling him, "That's a boat."

"Don't hit me no more. Because if you do I'm gonna hit you back." Padraig moved away and began working on a spaceship.

"Yeah, Mike. Leave Padraig alone." It was Billy Scott, our neighbor. "He ain't bothering you."

"Let me see what you doing," I said inching toward Billy's carefully crafted mound of dirt.

"What's that?" I asked but I knew the artfully crafted structure was an airplane, complete with a tail section. Billy's little hand began to smooth out a wing.

When I turned back to Padriag I let my foot drag through the back half of Billy's airplane and then acted like it was an accident. "Oops! I sorry."

"I'm gonna get you." He had his shovel raised ready to hit me. "You messed up my plane," he squealed. "And you meant to!"

Messing up someone's cake or cookie under normal circumstances was no big deal but we had taken this activity a step further and had made a game out of it, really a contest, to see who could make the most original configuration. Whoever was watching over us that day would judge our efforts and even though no actual prize was presented the competition was spirited and stiff. In the end, however, we were usually told that all of us had won which never made sense to us but I suppose it was better than being told that we had all lost?

Billy, seeking revenge, flipped a shovelful of dirt on the back of my neck. I turned immediately with a handful of dirt ready to blast him when my mother stepped in. "Uh-uh … don't do that, Mister Devlin or you'll be in big trouble. Put it down!"

Even though my mother was the referee this day the home team wasn't getting any free shots and I was just as prone to correction as anyone else, maybe more so.

Sammy, Billy's younger brother by a year, sat in the corner by himself making mound after mound of round cookies. Never anything else. Just round cookies. When we asked him why he only made cookies he said that he liked cookies, round ones! They were his favorite food.

"Momma, can we have some more water … please?" The water hose was no more than ten feet from the box. A convenient mixer for our bake work.

"All right … just a little bit … wait a second." My mother retrieved the hose. " Here you go." She extended the hose into the box and turned it on.

Now was my chance to get Billy back. I grabbed the hose and put it on top of his head. He screamed, turned around and made a dive for the hose and missed it landing in the mud. I used my thumb to form a good hard spray and let him have it. While I was at it I thought what the heck might as well get them all. Sammy and Padraig were next!

"Wa-hoo! … Wa-hoo!" Billy yelled. He was about to yell again and I placed a perfect shot of water full blast into his open mouth. He unintentionally gargled and began coughing.

Sammy and Padraig were jumping around with their backs to me as I blasted away. I was king of the hose today.

Billy charged and jumped on me. We rolled over Padriag's spaceship obliterating it and my boat. There would be no contest winner today unless Sammy's cookies survived our wrestling match. It was not to be! I was up and tried to run from Billy but he tackled me and we both fell onto the many mounds of cookies.

"Gimme that hose!" Billy was yelling while pulling on it. "Let go, let go!"

Padraig and Sammy joined the fray by piling on top of Billy and me as we rolled in the mud fighting for control of the hose. When these episodes broke out, which was often, my mother allowed us a few minutes of dirty fun then she would calmly walk over and turn off the water. With no water we would quickly lose interest in the hose. As everyone unpiled I stood and looked at my mother with mud dripping everywhere from me hoping she would turn the water back on.
Even a desperate plea of, "Please Momma" was met with a firm, "No."

"P-a-d-r-a-i-g –g-g-g-g come home … P-a-d-r-a-i-g-g-g-g-g come home." It was Padraig's mother from next door and she really stretched out the "Padraig." So much it took almost ten seconds to call his name so there would be no mistake as to which neighborhood child was being summoned home.

"Come here, Paddy," said my mother. "You're a mess … look at ya. Mike, turn on the hose … please."

"Yes Ma'am." I ran to my chore.

Padraig stood at full attention while my mother turned the hose on him starting on top of his head and working down. That was why we wore our bathing suits when we played in the dirt box.

The Scott boys stood in line waiting for their rinsing.

When my friends were cleaned up my mother said to Billy and Sammy, "When y'all get home tell your mother to call me …right away … OK?" It was an unspoken rule amongst the families that when a child left your house or your care and was going back home that he was to have his mother call and let the other parent know that he arrived home safely. The Scott children were notorious for not letting anyone know where they were or had been. My mother was reminding them of their duty.

"Yes Ma'am," they answered heading out through Padraig's back yard. They lived four doors down. "Bye, Mrs. Devlin. Bye Mike."

"OK, mister, you're next."

I was wondering why my mother had referred to Padraig as Paddy so I asked her.

"That's a shortened way of saying his full name. Instead of Padraig … it's Paddy. Like with you. What's your full name?"

"Mike," I answered.

My mother rolled her eyes. "I mean your real full name." She paused. " Oh, never mind. What does Sister Caroline call you at kindergarten?"

"She calls me Michael and I don't like it."

"OK … see? We call you Mike, which is short for Michael. Well, it's the same with your friend Padraig. He can be called Paddy."

"He can?" I exclaimed. This was exciting news. Padraig could be called Paddy. Wow! I couldn't wait to tell him.

And from that day when we gave Padraig O'Toole his new name, *then* all the trouble started.

We had shortened all our friends' names unknowingly, of course. William was Billy and thankfully Samuel was Sammy and I wasn't a Michael. And now we wanted Padraig to be like the other kids in the neighborhood and not use his full given name, but our good intentions were for naught. More often than not our pronunciation of Paddy came out sounding more like Patty, a moniker the sensitive Paddy absolutely wanted no part of.

"Don't call me Patty." He would squeal. " I ain't no girl." This outcry went on repeatedly.

He was determined not to be called by that name feeling that people were making fun of him. So adamant was his resolve that when he was called Paddy he would bow up, push out his bottom lip and bawl up his fists ready to take on the tormentor. And he would have, releasing all sixty pounds of his pent up fury.

"You want us to call you Padraig?"

"No. I don't like that name either."

So that's when he took it upon himself to find a new name. If I recall correctly he gave himself the nickname "Bubba" at about age eight. The way he explained it was that it was easy to say and easy to spell and easy to remember. It stuck and from then on Padraig, our beloved Paddy O'Toole, became Bubba.

The modern Southern term "Bubba" has come to represent someone as a good ol' country boy, a hayseed type fellow, slow of wit, a kind of redneck laughable character wearing a straw hat, dressed in overalls with a toothpick sticking out his mouth. The Bubba I knew was not like that at all. He was a street-smart Irish kid like myself growing up on a barrier Island in the South. Some city people might have considered the Island country but it wasn't. It was a beach community and we were beach bums all the way.

By age twelve, Bubba 'n me were life long Island residents and knew everyone on the Island, all nine-hundred or so. Now the summer population brought the total to about twelve hundred. These extras were the folks from the city of Charleston who owned beach homes and came over for the summer for vacation and to escape the heat of the city. But the day after Labor Day the population shrank to nine hundred when the Charlestonians went home.

We were very active, to say the least, running freely about the Island, playing with our friends, bike riding, going to the beach, always outside and on the go. We had no computer to sit in front of all day, TV was a novelty, we had no soccer Mom to taxi us from one organized activity to the next, no video games, no mall to hang out in, why shucks, we were lucky to even use the phone in our own homes. Growing up in the 1950's forced us to create our own entertainment like everyone else of that generation and we did. We always had some type of activity or project ongoing or a new one on the horizon. Being on the outside and on the go presented a great opportunity to meet new kids, to form friendships, to establish a sense of community, and to learn about life.

We were both raised with the understanding that a person is responsible for his/her actions. It's a noble thought but the reality did not always sit well with Bubba 'n me because, you see, sometimes we got into trouble. The latest was the garbage truck incident and it was not going away any time soon without consequences.

"I ought to ground you for a month for pulling a stunt like that. You hear me? For a month."

Oh, I heard it all right. I was in the midst of a serious chewing out by my mother, the family disciplinarian. My father was too busy working six days a week or doing house repairs to try to keep tabs on six kids. Besides it wasn't in his nature to punish or reprimand. He was an easy going Irishman with a quick wit and a self styled humor that could turn a God awful affair into a laughing matter in a second given the chance. He chose not to find the humor in my latest adventure.

"What were you thinking?" My mother asked? "Oh, don't even answer that. For now you're grounded for a week. And do not even think of leaving this house … and no phone calls. There's no telling what you and Bubba will cook up next. And you will apologize to Mr. Nick and Sambo as soon as you get off restriction. Do you understand, young man?"

"Yes Ma'am." I dropped my head when I heard that awful word … "grounded."

I had learned early in life to answer "Yes Mam" to my mother's demands when she was angry, no excuses or explanations, just "Yes Ma'am."

"And you *will* help with the girls!"

"Yes Ma'am." That was the worst part of the punishment. I had four sisters and three were younger than me.

A couple of days of misery on my part had passed and then my mother finally relented giving me my freedom but assuring me that I was on a strict parole and the slightest wrongdoing would merit me a long, long grounding.

My mother looking exasperated and worn out had called me into the kitchen, sat me down and pointed her finger at me. "OK, you're free. Your restriction is over but you better keep your nose clean or else, you hear me? And don't forget about apologizing to Sambo and Mr. Nick." It was a command given in the form of a request. "And I'm serious about that. You understand?"

"Yes Ma'am."

My release had not come from the pure mercy of my mother. I had played my part to the hilt. The prior two days I had moped around the house sometimes just sitting in a chair staring at the ceiling and then at the floor or gazing off into space. At times I even mumbled to myself and every now and then let go with a strange off the wall comment like, "Here them come, look out." At other times I followed my mother around the house as she went about her chores. I was trying to get in the way as much as possible but without drawing the ire of a very busy mother. It was a fine line I was walking but it was my only chance for freedom. I gambled that she would tire of my antics and me and hopefully give in and run me out of the house. And she did. Her last syllable was barely out her mouth when I burst through the screen door on the back porch at full tilt headed for Bubba's. I ran across the yard past the infamous scene of our grounding and onto Bubba's back steps. WOW! ... FREE AT LAST, OH BOY! It was good to feel the grass on my bare feet and to know that my bike was waiting for a rider.

A rutted driveway ran right up to the back porch of the O'Toole's house. A driveway I knew so well I could have walked it with my eyes closed and stopped at precisely the spot leading up the faded and cracked concrete steps. The rusting screens on the back porch were full of holes, most of them filled with a tiny piece of cotton or in its place a wad of chewing gum in order to keep out the pesky mosquito that was always in search of a meal. And the cracked pieces of latticework holding down the screen were in dreadful need of repair. This shabby porch was in stark contrast to the rest of the neat and freshly painted house. I guess Mr.O'Toole didn't make repairing it a priority because it was on the back of the house out of sight from passersby.

"B-u-b-b-a-a-a-a ... hey! Where are you?" I yelled. I couldn't wait to see my friend again. "Hey, you home?"

He opened the back door and stepped onto the porch moving slowly with his head down. Almost whispering he said, "Yeah, I'm here. Where else would I be?" I couldn't tell if he was sleepy or sad.

He pushed open the sagging screen door with a depressed look.

"What's wrong?" I asked. "Man, you look terrible."

"A-a-a-w, I'm all right," he said but I knew better. "It's just staying in this house. I hate it."

He was rarely down in the dumps like this. He seemed really sad and out of sorts. Last time I saw him like this was at his puppy's funeral, which we held in his backyard last year, complete with a burial service when I read some prayers from a Missalette I swiped from church. At least, now, he wasn't crying like he did at Trixie's funeral. After we had tossed the final shovelful of dirt on poor Trixie I told my friend not to be sad because I had Mollie, our family dog, and I would share her with him. I placed my hand on his shoulder and said, "She can be your dog too." That's when I saw big old teardrops like the big raindrops that come from a thunderstorm trickle down his face. Then he ran into his house. Yeah, it took a lot to get my friend down … a lot. Today he was strangely quiet.

"Are you sure you're OK, Bubba. You ain't acting right."

"I'm grounded for seven more days. That's what's wrong. Can you believe that? Seven more days." Seven more days for someone who felt like he was locked in prison when he was in school for one day just as well have been seven more years.

"Oh man, that stinks," I offered, "why so long?"

"I dunno?" He shrugged his broad, tan shoulders. "Must be something I said? And Dad was pretty mad about us wrecking the truck."

I was elated with my newfound freedom and was trying to appear sympathetic about his extended grounding but it wasn't working. The tone of my voice gave me away.

"I just got out," I said trying not to smile. For an outsider listening in they might have thought we had been locked up in prison the way we were talking.

"Yeah?" Bubba gave a slight smile at my good fortune. "How'd you do that? Poison your Mom?"

"N-o-o-o-o. I tried the old bug 'em to death trick and she fell for it. Followed her around the house, getting in the way, acting stupid … the whole bit. Remember when you tried that at school with Sister Ann Marie?" I grinned recalling the incident.

"Yeah", Bubba answered with a bigger smile, "and she beat the fool out of me with the big ruler." He paused for a second like he was giving his next question some serious thought.

"Where you headed?" he asked softly. By the look on his face I could tell that he did not want to hear that I was going *anywhere.*

"To Burton's and see what the crew's up to and then probably to the beach."

The crew was a hodge podge, loose knit bunch of kids all about the same age that hung together floating from one cultural fad to the next in search of fun. It seemed that each person in the crew was on a separate journey except for a few of us who grew up on the Island and were close friends, like Bubba 'n me, having formed bonds early on when we were tiny tykes. Because the Island was so small you couldn't help but meet everyone as you grew up and many relationships blossomed while others faded. The members of the crew all got along, as well as could be expected, and enjoyed basically the same interests but there was lacking a real sense of closeness or togetherness like in a true friendship. I attributed this lack of closeness to the fact that we lived in three different communities: Sullivans Island, Mt. Pleasant, and Isle of Palms and, for example, at the end of a day of fun at the beach together when it was time to go home, everyone went their separate ways.

I was hoping to tempt Bubba enough so that he would come with me but I didn't want to seem too obvious about it. "I might ride up to the Breach Inlet later and see if anybody's catching any flounder and check out if anybody is catching any crabs. And then ride around for awhile ..."

Bubba almost groaned. "Don't tell me that, man. I'm going nuts here." His younger sisters, Mary and Patty, were driving him up a wall like mine had done me. Shoot, it didn't take much to get under the skin of a grounded twelve year old in the summertime. And my sisters, and his, were good at what they did. We believed it was part of a worldwide female conspiracy to torture all males. And they were succeeding.

Bubba said, "Do you know what it's like to be stuck in the same house with those ..."

"Yeah, yeah, yeah," I cut him short. "Eah, I've got to go, OK? I've been cooped up too and I want to ride my bike so I'll check on ya later. Tell ya what I'll do. I'll lie to the crew and tell them you're home reading your Bible getting ready for Sister Rosalind's Religion class. A- HA-HA! ... too bad you can't come."

"Yeah, me too but..."

"Don't look now," I said, "but two little faces just showed up. Oops, they're gone now." Mary and Patty, smiling broadly, had peeked around the corner from inside the house and then pulled back.

"Oh yeah," I said, "I almost forget to tell ya. Ed Wilson told me last week that the girls from the Isle of Palms will be at the beach today ... at the rocks. You remember?" I paused while Bubba rubbed his chin and furrowed his forehead, thinking. "The girls from Moultrie School that you like so much ... the ones with the big boobs," I added for emphasis.

Bubba's face took on an instant glow and he moved his head slowly upward smiling as though he were looking at the clouds, rubbing his chin again and slowly drawled, "H-u-m-m?"

Mary showed her face again followed by Patty, a good foot taller than her younger sister.

"What you doing, Mike?" It was Mary grinning her toothless smile. "I see you."

"Nuffin, Muffin," I answered smiling. "What you doing?"

"Nothing."

"She is so! She's talking to you." It was Patty, the eight year old and a pure terror according to Bubba. By now they had stepped onto the porch. "So she's doing something, not nothing."

"Get back in that house right now before I get after you," Bubba said unsuccessfully trying to shoo them away. "I mean it now." They stood their ground not flinching an inch. These girls weren't afraid of a tiger much less Bubba's weak attempt at scaring them.

They giggled and Mary asked me my name. It was a game we played every time I saw her.

"Pudding and tame. Ask me again and I'll tell you the same."

"What's your name?" Giggling louder.

"Pudding and tame … ask me again and I'll tell you the same." Mary squealed and started jumping up and down.

"Devlin, don't get them fired up … please. It took me all morning to settle 'em down … OK?" Bubba pleaded and turned quickly and made a rush at the girls. They jumped through the doorway yelling and hid behind the wall again.

"See. That's all you got to do to take care of those girls. You gotta show 'em who's the boss, Mike," Bubba announced proudly. I think it must have been the first time the girls had ever run from him? Then I pointed to the door.

Patty poked her head around the corner to inform me that my name was Mike, not "pudding and tame."

"T-h-a-t-`s right, Catbird," I answered giving her a big grin.

"I ain't no Catbird," Patty yelled, "and don't call me that."

"Devlin … p-l-e-a-s-e, man. Leave 'em alone. I gotta go back in that house, not you."

"OK … all right, all right," I said to Bubba and then I yelled at the girls hiding around the corner, "I got to go … see y'all later. Bye Mary … bye Patty."

"Oh … by the way …I almost forget to ask you. Why'd you run off and leave me by myself the other day? Remember in the oleanders?"

"Oh Yeah," Bubba said like he was recalling something he didn't want to talk about, " "I was going … uh … going to talk to you" …he cast his head down and lowered his voice… "Eah, I'm sorry about that. I really am. But when I saw Bull Perry and how mad he was I kind of … panicked. But I was with you in my mind and even said a prayer for you."

He smiled at me and just the thought of Bubba praying for me while I was hiding in the bushes made me smile.

"Don't worry it won't happen again. Not even if Bull Perry is right on top of us. I promise … OK?"

"O-o-h, all right. It's OK. Forget about it. But remember what you said. Eah, it was good seeing you but I gotta go."

I retraced my steps and got my bike from our backyard. I pedaled off and looked back over my shoulder and waved goodbye to my sad looking friend standing in the driveway. But I could tell that he was relieved that I wasn't mad at him for his running away the other day.

It sure felt strange, almost eerie, riding by myself. I caught myself getting ready to ask Bubba a question when I realized he wasn't with me. I even looked around to make sure I was by myself and as soon as I confirmed the fact a sinking feeling came over me. When was the last time I rode my bike by myself or had such a low feeling? I hadn't gone a block when that spooky feeling left me the second I heard that oh -so familiar voice.

"Hey! Wait up … where you going? To a fire?"

I slowed down a little as Bubba rolled up next to me wearing a huge grin, which made me feel better. My friend was his old self again.

"Was it my mentioning the girls from the Isle of Palms that made you decide to make your break from jail?"

He didn't say anything. He was just pedaling fast swerving all over the road and grinning, happy to have his freedom. Now we knew how James Cagney must have felt when he was released from prison in the movies.

"Couldn't stand it, huh?" I asked. "Being locked up?"

"Nope. A man's got to be able to ride his bike and feel the wind in his face and the sun on his back. Besides, Mom and Dad aren't home anyway … they're in Georgetown visiting Uncle Clyde." A long pause. "Girls from the Isle of Palms, huh?" he mumbled to himself but directed it at me.

I grinned not so much at what he said but at the thought of the Isle of Palms' girls.

"Eah, you know Patty's gonna squeal on ya?" She was the yakker in his family. We called her the mouth of the South. "What will your parents do when they find out?"

"A-a-a-h, I don't care. After grounding me, Dad sat me down and we had this long talk about taking responsibility for what I do and all that stuff. And he said we were on the honor system about me staying in the house and I agreed to it. The way I figure it he has the honor and I have the system. I'll think of something."

"Race ya to Burton's. Loser buys the Cokes," Bubba yelled, looking back at me after a lengthy head start. He had a big lead and I couldn't catch him.

As we sipped on our Cokes at Burton's, Bubba stared off in space barely saying a word.

"Eah, you O.K.?" I asked, truly concerned about my normally chatty friend.

Coming back to earth, he said, "Yeah, I'm fine. I was just thinking … trying to figure out a way I can get from being grounded. And … I think I found a way."

"Oh yeah. How?"

"You'll see … you'll see." Then he added, "I hope." He stood up, shoved his chair back in place and began to leave.

"You'll know by tomorrow. Gotta go. See ya later."
"Y-e-a-h … O.K. … I'll see you later." He was gone.

3
THE APOLOGY

Bubba 'n me were inseparable. Even though physically we did not have any brotherly resemblance most people mistook us for brothers, which was fine with me. Bubba didn't seem to care one way or the other and told me, "Shoot, anything is better than those two sisters of mine."

Sister Ann Marie, our very strict seventh grade teacher, likened us to The James Gang, of the old cowboy days, due to our rowdy behavior at school. I thought that label was kind of neat. I envisioned riding horses through the countryside, chasing the bad guys, hanging out in a saloon playing cards, not having to get up everyday and go to a boring and thankless job and then riding off in the sunset with a pretty woman. Not a bad life I thought. *And* I never saw a cowboy that had to go to school. Not Bubba. Oh no, he didn't want any part of getting on a horse.

"When I grow up I want to be the police chief right here on the Island. Yes sir, that's what I want to do."

"Police chief. Humph."

I asked him one day after we had escaped the clutches of Bull Perry. "Why would you *ever* want to be a policeman?"

"So I can arrest all those nuns and write 'em up, especially Sister Roberta," he said with a glitter in his eyes. "And then I can lock them up in a cell just like they do us in that classroom."

"Eah, you cant' just go around putting people in jail for the fun of it, you know that, don't ya? They have to break some law or do something wrong. What laws are the good holy ladies of Saint Angela's breaking?"

Bubba bowed up and spoke with the authority of a true small town policeman, "First, they would get a ticket for pure meaness, then one for giving us homework, and another one for beating me with the big ruler." I was not sure but I think he was serious so I egged him on a little more.

"Bubba, I'm following you about the first two things they do." I loved it when he went off on one of his tangents like this. "They are mean and giving homework is the pits but there isn't any law against hitting you with the big ruler. At least, I've never heard of one."

"Where you been, Devlin?" In the fog? Sister Roberta herself taught us The Ten Commandments didn't she?"

"So?"

"So! She and the rest of her gang are in direct violation of the fifth commandment."

"Oh yeah. And what's that?"

"Thou shalt not kill!" he said and stared at me with folded arms, his case rested.

I smiled and shook my head from side to side muttering a low, "O-o-o-h," amazed again by my friend's pure and exacting logic.

"T-h-a-t-s' right, Catbird." Bubba said in his slow southern drawl. "They're killing us, Devlin. Little by little they're killing us."

When Bubba had gotten home from Burton's the previous day, the first thing he did was corner Patty, the blabbermouth, and try to reason with her about not squealing on him for going out the house. He didn't need that infraction hanging over his head. However, with Patty there was no reasoning.

"And why shouldn't I tell on you," she demanded, "you always tell on me." Before he could reply she blurted out, "how much money you gonna give me if I don't tell. Huh?"

Oh boy. She wants money and I don't have any, Bubba thought.

So he played his ace in the hole and thought *here goes*. "Well, Patty," he said very calmly, "If you tell on me then I'm going to tell EVERYBODY" ... and he really emphasized "everybody" even pausing and giving Patty the eye ... "who you've been talking to on the phone. Seems like little Miss Bigmouth here has a new boyfriend."

Instantly Patty started screaming, "Do not. Do not. I don't have a boyfriend! That's a lie!"

"Oh yeah, just wait until I tell all your friends ... and ... what's his name? The boy you always flirt with down the street. Johnny ... yea ... that's his name."

Patty practically charged Bubba with balled up fists, ready to duke it out. "You do that and I'll ... I'll ... I'll ... do something. You better not say ..."

Bubba was smiling broadly because he knew he had pushed the right button. It was the button about the boyfriend and girlfriend relationship of kids the age of Patty. The little girls seemed to be super sensitive regarding the subject and wouldn't dare want anyone to know they even held the slightest interest in someone of the opposite sex. Bubba planned to play it to the hilt.

"So the something you will do is keep your mouth shut about me going out of the house today or I'll tell the whole Island about you and your new boyfriend. Is that clear?"

Patty mumbled, "Yea" under her breathe as she walked off.

Just to rub it in a little, Bubba said, "I didn't hear you" as he cocked his head to one side, cupping his ear.

"Yea," she yelled and ran off.

By the time dinner was over and the dishes had been washed, dried and stacked back on the shelves and everyone was settled, Bubba made his pitch to his parents. A pitch he had practiced since his lone and seldom victory over Patty.

As he began to speak about the garbage truck episode and his subsequent grounding, Bubba directed his eyes at both parents looking from one to the other, searching to get a read on which one seemed more vulnerable at the moment. *Mom is the one*, he thought. With his attention there, Bubba drew on all his powers of persuasion.

"… and because what Mike and I did was so wrong I figure I should apologize to Sambo for his getting hurt. It's the right thing to do. Right, Mom?" Then quickly he added, "Dad? Don't y'all think so?"

With nodding heads both parents agreed. His father added, "That's a good idea, son. A good idea."

And so Bubba successfully got off probation. Freedom was his now. Because once he got out of the house then that was it … viola … no more being grounded.

Man that was easy, he thought. *Maybe I should try using my brain more often. Think I'll call Mike and tell him the good news.*

The next morning I awoke with the same feeling of trepidation that I had gone to sleep with. My cause for concern was that when Bubba had called telling me he was no longer grounded we planned to find Mr. Nick and Sambo and apologize to them for wrecking the truck and hurting Sambo.

" Man, I'll sure be glad when *this* is over," I sighed as we pedaled down the Island looking for Old Blue and its occupants.

"Yep. Me too."

"Eah, I've been thinking and trying to figure out exactly what to say but … What *do* we say?" I asked. "Apologizing to garbage men? Humph." I shook my head. "Whoever heard of such a thing?"

"Well I guess we tell them we're sorry about wrecking the truck and hurting Sambo and all. That's all. Eah, it ain't like we're going to confession to Father Dawes or something."

"Yeah but what if they get mad and come after us?"

"A-a-a-w, don't worry. That ain't going to happen but be ready to leave in a hurry … just in case, OK?"

"Yeah, don't you worry. I'll be right behind you."

This was something entirely new for both of us. Not only was it rare that we had to make a formal apology to anyone much less to a couple of black men and garbage men on top of that. It seemed kind of strange and out of place but it sure beat whatever would happen to me if I didn't.

Bubba seemed apprehensive too. He was riding with no hands and doing his strange thing again: rubbing his palms together real fast, cocking his head to one side, and making those funny little wheezing sounds while looking up at the sky. I had given up a long time ago trying to figure out what he was doing or trying to make any sense of it.

"This way," Bubba yelled and pedaled off. "I hear 'em."

We heard "Old Blue's" rusted out muffler full of holes blasting out a tune.

"There they are. C'mon on."

We caught up with Mr. Nick and Sambo at a stop sign and hesitantly pulled up next to the truck, sitting on our bikes. We hemmed and hawed, stuttered and stumbled, our eyes cast down while Mr. Nick sat patiently looking down at us being kept from his work.

And then suddenly we exploded with apologies or at least what we had prepared in our minds.

"Oh, Mr. Nick we're so sorry for what we did, for wrecking the truck and we hope you and Sambo didn't get hurt real bad or anything. We were just fooling around and didn't mean nothing mean." We were rambling on like there was no tomorrow, both talking at the same time. "We hope y'all aren't mad at us or anything. And we promise not to do it again. We're so sorry."

Mr. Nick was very patient but had to put an end to this babbling. Interrupting he said, "What y'all is saying is that y'all are sorry for the trouble?"

"Oh yeah, we're sorry. Real sorry, we promise and …"

Mr. Nick stopped us with a wave of his hand. "That's all you has to say," he said blankly. "It's over."

He paused and then he gestured with his head toward the back of the truck and said,

"Maybe you should say something to Sambo?"

Sambo was standing guard silently on the back of the truck. Samuel Lott was his full name and he was an Island original, a true Island character, and a resourceful man of personality and unbridled happiness. He was a tall gangly man with l-o-n-g arms and hunched shoulders, giving him a hunchbacked appearance. It was jokingly said that Sambo's arms were so long he could pick up a quarter off the ground without bending over. When he walked he took huge strides that were in sync with his swinging arms. He had thick lips and big ears accentuated by his extremely short hair and he wore the same black boots everyday, size fifteen. His feet were so big that if he died standing up someone would have to push him in the grave. His physical appearance could not be mistaken but the defining characteristic of this man was his disposition. Whenever someone hailed Sambo, even a stranger, his immediate response was, "All right! All right! How you doing, buddy?" and he always gave a big smile and wave of the hand.

Seeing Sambo on the back of the truck gave me reason to recall a certain January day. It was a cold, miserable, drizzly, day with an east wind whipping in off the ocean, the kind of day when all you wanted was to be in a warm place. I was sitting in the house when I heard "Old Blue" coming up the street and I couldn't resist putting Sambo to the test. When I heard the clash of our garbage cans, I quickly stuck my head out the door into the wind and cold and yelled, "Sambo, how you doing?"

"All right, buddy! All right!", he yelled to me waving his hand. That particular day it came out more like A-l-l r-i-g-h-t, b-u-d-d-y. It was like he was singing. Even in the oppressive heat of summer you got the same reaction … it never varied and he was sincere. Island lore has it that the infant Sambo fell off a visiting watermelon cart and was picked up and adopted by a local Islander. No one knew his exact age or where he was born. Someone said that he was born in Saluda, S.C., a small upstate town. It really didn't matter because *everyone* on the Island loved Sambo. And Sambo loved everyone on the Island.

He was a hard worker and never got into trouble. His only known vice was taking a few too many drinks on occasion. But this only made him friendlier. His wardrobe consisted of hand-me downs from the locals who placed them on top of their garbage cans for him to collect. Someone of questionable character put a sweatshirt out for Sambo that became his favorite for some unknown reason He wore it practically every day … even in the oppressive heat of the summer. It was burgundy in color with big white lettering across the front that said: "HARVARD". Maybe it was a Yale graduate?

Near Christmas time Sambo received more presents than anyone on the Island. He wasn't formally educated and the truth be known, he probably *never* attended school but he was an expert when it came to playing to people's emotions. He skillfully let everyone know that he enjoyed Seagram's Seven whiskey and that if they would put a bottle underneath the garbage can lid, he would be most thankful and be sure to give them extra good service in the coming year. During the week preceding Christmas we would see Sambo in his HARVARD sweatshirt carefully lifting each lid and quietly looking in the can before he dumped it in hopes of finding yet another Christmas gift.

Bubba 'n me moved slowly toward the back of the truck where Sambo was standing on the bumper. He was a large man and standing high up on the bumper made him look like a giant.

"Sambo, we're sorry for wrecking the truck and you getting hurt," I said looking up. For some reason this time it came out easier and with more sincerity and Sambo sensed it.

"Hope you're O.K," Bubba added. "We really are sorry."

"All right, buddy." He gave us a big smile. "All right."

"Are you sure?" Bubba asked. "We really didn't mean to hurt you."
"Yeah, buddy, everything be all right. I just been scared mostly."
Then Mr. Nick turned his head and gave us a look that said we- gotta-go

Sambo was waving to us as Mr. Nick drove off. A gesture that I took to mean that everything was all right.

"Well," I said looking at Bubba, "that wasn't so bad, was it?" I asked wondering if Bubba felt the same relief I did. "But I don't want to ever have to do it again. Know what I mean?"

Bubba thought for a few seconds, grew serious, and said, "No, not bad at all. But I'll tell you one thing. If that had been me thrown from that truck because of two stupid kids digging a hole in the road I'd be mad as hell. And someone would be in real trouble."

We rode away in silence. And I wondered again like I often did at my friend's logic. After all it was Bubba and me who had dug the hole and were the cause of Sambo getting hurt in the first place.

Bubba 'n me's wood frame homes sit side-by-side in a row of modest Island houses with huge open porches and big grassy yards adorned with Palmetto tress and crape myrtles. The only thing separating our houses is a narrow dirt road full of potholes. The oleanders that grow abundantly all over the Island, line both sides of our yard like tall, open perfume bottles with their beautiful blossoms of pink, yellow, and white giving off their sweet fragrance. The landscaping is a complement of Mother Nature aided by the natural process of the many birds as they deposited their seeds at random over the years. A professional landscape architect could not have designed a more balanced and aesthetically pleasing setting if He tried. After all, who could compete with the Man Himself when it came to beautifying His own little piece of Paradise?

The Devlin house: That's what the old time Islanders called the place where I lived with my parents and four sisters and brother. It was called the Devlin house because it was where the Devlin family from my grandfather on down had been born and raised. My father's brothers and sisters had since moved away; however, two aunts and an uncle still lived on the Island. Shoot, I was glad that most of them had moved because that house would have really been crowded with them and all of us Devlin kids living in it at the same time. It was a big rambling one-story wood-frame house built like many of that era, a room added here and there when the need arose without much concern for architectural design in mind. It had two porches. Well, a porch and a half. There was the front porch cluttered with old weather- beaten chairs from ages past. They were the most comfortable seats and every time I sat in one, closed my eyes and daydreamed, a story from the past came to me telling me of others who had sat right there and telling me of the things they had done.

I often wondered if someone in the future would hear of my exploits?

The back porch, all screened in proper, was the half porch, which was really the back entrance to the house leading into the kitchen. The other half was the old storage room, now my bedroom having long ago been closed in. The back porch was nice and comfortable but we couldn't sit there and wave at passing neighbors or catch up on the latest Island happenings like we did on the big front porch, which faced the road. We would miss everything. In the corner on the front porch hung the hammock where survival skills were really pushed to their limits. A person took their life in their hands if they ever laid down for a snooze or nap. Two of my younger sisters, Emily and Katie, were expert at sneaking up on the poor innocent soul who didn't know their routine of flipping the unsuspecting, napping person onto the hard porch and then disappearing like a breeze. Anyone on the Island who lived within ten blocks of the Devlin house knew not to ever lie down in the hammock on the Devlin front porch and close their eyes. So as old as the hammock was it looked like brand new.

I was probably the luckiest in our family when it came to living space. I had my own bedroom, the only person in the family to be so honored. My father told me I wasn't lucky but had that room to myself because I was so special and special people need a room for themselves. Why I don't know? But I didn't argue. It was spacious, not so much because of its size, but because it lacked any real furniture to speak of. It had a bed and an old chest of drawers with four drawers and a cracked and faded old mirror balanced on the back edge of the chest of drawers. The mirror was so beat up and scarred I could barely see myself in it even when I stood a foot from it.

I remember my father telling me: "Son you take real good care of that mirror because that's an antique. You see, Julius Caesar used it in his house when he lived in Rome." And then he chuckled. I wasn't sure who Mr. Caesar was but I thank him for letting me have his mirror. Shoot, it was like a lot of things I had in life, it was a hand me down but better than nothing.

Hanging on the wall above my bed was a piece of faded cardboard about three feet by three feet with old and frayed pictures taped on it of my favorite baseball player that I had cut out of the newspaper. There were pictures of the great Mickey Mantle catching a fly ball after a long run or of him hitting another tape measure homerun with his bulging forearms rippling in the sunlight and the distinctive number "7" looming squarely in the middle of his back. He was the greatest player in the world and I swore that one day I would grow up and hit a ball just like him and then go into my famous trot with my arms bent at the elbows, bouncing up and down and with my head down, humbly rounding the bases. That would be the easy part because I had been practicing that routine for nearly two years. The hard part would be hitting the ball over the fence. Those pictures might have been faded and worn but their memories were as fresh as the new dawn.

My room held magical powers and was the launching pad for my many adventures that took me from Sullivans Island to places all over the world. I had already traveled the entire United States and was presently working my way through the Far East. When I was done with that trip I planned an expedition into outer space way past the sun to another whole world where there was no school and everyday I was on summer vacation. Yeah, I loved my room even though later in life I found out that it was originally a storage room of sorts and had been converted to make space for the growing Devlin clan. I always wondered why my room was on the backside of the house and kind of stuck out like an out of place Christmas ornament on the tree. It also explains why it didn't have a closet. But that was all right. My father suspended a stick from a worn out mop from the ceiling and I hung what few hang-up clothes I owned on it and didn't have to bother opening a door. I guess you could say I had a huge walk-in closet. The only other "person" who shared my room with me was Mollie, my faithful companion who was supposedly the family dog. But really she was mine and I considered her to be human, not totally human, mind you, but almost.

My four sisters shared one big room in the front of the house, which wasn't far enough away from me as far as I was concerned. They had two huge double beds, the size of an aircraft carrier. I think they were some kind of homemade type beds. All I know is they were big. But they had to be extra big in order to handle the squirming, pesky little Devlins: Sara, three years old, Katie, nine and Emily, ten years old. Those three were always moving. Even in their sleep I had noticed them wiggling around like a worm on a hook. Oh yeah, and there was Sissy. She was the oldest child, sixteen and the motherly guardian of all of us regarding everything from manners to pronunciation, to how we held our knives and forks at the dinner table whenever we weren't stabbing each other with them. In a way I felt sorry for Sissy having to live amongst those wild little people. No wonder she acted so strange all the time.

Ryan Devlin. He was my older brother by three years and his room was connected to the girls by a narrow passageway. There was no door, only a hanging curtain that you couldn't see through but you could hear through it. He had it rough and I prayed for him a lot. That's why I say I was the only child with my own room. Ryan knew all about cars and the N.Y. Yankees and crabbing and all that neat stuff. He even knew about girls but wouldn't tell me anything. I had been bugging him for about the last year to tell me about girls and what they liked and how to impress them … stuff like that. Man talk kind of things. Before this summer, girls didn't interest me very much but for some unknown reason lately I had more and more questions about them. He got mad at me once when I kept pestering him about girls and he told me to stay away from them because they weren't nothing but trouble. If that was true I asked him how come he was always after them? And then he really got mad! So I quit bugging him. I figured Bubba 'n me would figure out girls sometimes when we had some spare time ... like a weekend when we weren't real busy. That's what we would do and then I'd go and give Ryan the scoop.

As I grew older it dawned on me that our old house was just like the old people who grew up on the Island. She might not have retained her youthful beauty as the years went by and now had a few wrinkles, but she was solid, always there for me, and at last count all her parts were still working. And she had held up well over the years surviving the terribly hot and humid summers and, at times, the cold, cold winds of winter and even a hurricane or two. But her biggest challenge had come not from the elements of time and nature but from the Devlin children who tugged and pulled on her everyday. And like the old Islanders she was a survivor. I loved that old house.

The only drawback to our house was that it only had one bathroom like most of the houses built during that era and with eight people waking up each morning with the urge ... well ... it was every man for himself. You had to be quick. My father had threatened many times to build another bathroom, a really nice one with a shower and all but that never happened. I guess he couldn't afford the beer that would be required to complete the job. All the Devlin kids, later in life, of course, would get a good laugh talking about my father's building/repair projects, and the unique way he went about them. You see, my father would look at a needed repair job and judge its completion time by how many beers he would drink doing the job. For instance, to re-screen a door was usually a six-pack job, while painting a room was a twelve-pack affair. And there were the occasional short jobs where he consumed only two or three beers two. Like fixing a leaky pipe or hanging a new section of clothesline. His favorite job was cranking up the boat and catching a nice mess of fish at the jetties for the hungry Devlin family. That was a case job. And I witnessed my father sip through nearly a case of beer, Old Milwaukee his favorite, during a day of fishing and cleaning fish and *never* stagger or once slur his words, not once. It was like he was drinking water.

But as long as he continued to take me fishing, I was like him. Neither one of us cared if the new bathroom ever got built.

4
ESCAPE

It's early morning. As I lie in bed I was rubbing Mollie's head trying to decide between going to the beach or going fishing at the Point. Someone had told Bubba the flounder were running and hitting on small minnows and the locals were tearing 'em up. Of course, Bubba relayed that important piece of Island "gossip" on to me. *Oh goodness,* I thought as my mind wandered. *Decisions, decisions, decisions. Man. Life was getting too complicated.*

From down the hall I heard the unmistakable sound of small feet on the hard floor making their way toward my room. Closer and closer. Footsteps first then the muffled squeals of laughter.

My door creaked and inched opened slowly. *Which one would be it be?* I guessed. *Emily, Sara, or Katie?* Before I could answer my own thought, the door suddenly burst open with a jolt and Sara entered my room ending any peace and quiet that had existed.

"EEW-EEH, YEE-EEH, EEH-EEH!" She instantly headed for Mollie and me.

"Good morning. What you doing?" I asked but already knew what she would say.

"I hide. You help me, Mike? Hey Mollie. What you doing in the bed? Mommy gonna get mad at you."

All the while Sara was struggling with the sheet trying to get under it.

"Hide from who, Sara?" I asked while Mollie placed a super sloppy lick all across Sara's beautiful face. Sara opened her big, blue eyes wide, pushed back her long blonde hair, rubbed her face and said, "Come on Mollie, you hide too."

Heavier footsteps now. Pounding down the hall, coming through the kitchen, heading toward my room.

"Quick, Sara … here they come."

In her haste Sara couldn't manage the sheet, jerking and pulling in all directions.

"Sara, here." I rolled over and pointed. "Get under the bed. They'll never find you there."

"Huh?"

"Under the bed," I said and then helped her off the bed into her all time favorite hiding place no matter how many times they played hide-’n- seek.

“S-s-s-h.” Sara held her finger to her lips commanding my silence. She smiled and went into hiding. “Don’t tell.”

“OK… I don’t know where you are. How about you, Mollie? Seen Sara?” Mollie immediately leaped off the bed and stood looking at Sara, giving away her hideout.

“Oh Mollie. You’re just too smart. Get up here.” I patted the bed twice and Mollie was back resting in her spot.

I also went back to resting, acting like I was sleeping when the searchers arrived. I heard them creep slowly up to the bed.

“Is he sleeping?” I recognized Emily’s voice asking for Katie’s opinion. “Looks like it?”

“I dunno … I think so?” She paused. “Mike, you awake?” I heard Katie ask in a soft voice.

I lay still. No response. Another short pause. “Yeah, he’s sleeping … wake him up. Here...”

O-o-o-h no. I thought. But not quick enough. The plastic baseball bat came down right on top of my head … BOOP! Not a vicious blow but enough to wake up any human. Whenever I heard a Devlin girl say, “Here” or “Watch this” I knew from past experience that *something* with bad intentions was on its way.

I tried to snatch the baseball bat from Emily but she was too quick and the game was on. Sara giggled and rolled out from under the bed and jumped in the bed on top of me joining Katie and Emily who were trying to pin me. Mollie commenced to lick all three of the girls as they wrestled with me and, at the same time, tried to fight off the affections of Mollie. I dove under the sheet and held it real tight around me.

“If you don’t come out you’re gonna really get it,” Emily said raising the bat.

“Yeah, you’re gonna really get it, Mister Devlin.” It was Katie imitating my mother’s much used command: “You’re gonna be in trouble.”

I threw back the covers and jumped up yelling and growling like a maddened bear forming claws with my fingers. “ I’m gonna get y’all and eat you up! A-A-R-G-H!” All three squealed and tore from the room followed by a barking Mollie.

My morning wake up call was complete. Now to finally decide on going to the beach or go fishing? I lay back down and thought but couldn’t decide. I know. I’ll check first with Bubba and see what he’s gonna do today. Then while I was getting dressed it suddenly dawned on me.

Oh gosh. It’s Wednesday. I remembered. *I have a yard to cut today. I’ll check with Bubba later.*

I heard squealing and yelling from Ryan's room and knew that his wake up call had just begun.

A good deep breath told me breakfast was ready and we were having grits and eggs.

"What was all that commotion in your room, Mike?" my mother asked stirring the grits one last time and then lifting the pot to serve the waiting girls. They looked like angels sitting quietly in a row, all prim and proper. But I knew better. They were resting up for their next attack fortified by a big helping of grits and bacon and fried eggs.

"Who do you think, Mom?" I pointed across the table. " It was them."

"Not me," retorted Emily followed by Katie's denial.

Sara screamed, "It was me! I got Mike!"

"R-y-a-a-n, come on. Breakfast is ready!" My mother yelled, paused and hollered down the hall, "Sissy, you hear me?"

My father had long been gone to work. Shoot, he missed all the fun but I would usually fill him in the evening on anything he missed that was of importance.

How my mother did it I don't know? She fed us everyday, refereed our squabbles, bandaged our wounds and still held down a part time job. If you consider four days a week at the Laundromat part time. She did have the luxury of having Rebecca Washington, a black lady, helping two days a week with the house cleaning and washing the clothes, that indefatigable pile that never seemed to shrink. Rebecca also cooked a huge pot of beef stew on her two days, Tuesdays and Thursdays. And those were my favorite eating days. Sissy helped my mother around the house and did more than her share, which was mostly baby sitting the girls.

Ryan worked too. He had a part time job at St. Angela's Church where he did odd jobs like yard work and helping around the rectory. His latest job was learning to play the church organ so when the time came he could fill in for the aging Miss Brennan whose nimble fingers had about run their course over the last forty years, arthritis was setting in.

Sissy arrived while we slopped up our grits and gulped down our eggs and biscuits getting ready to fight over the last biscuit.

"Did someone say the blessing," she asked in a tone that reeked with arrogant authority.

"Yep … sure did." Ryan said grabbing for the biscuit only to be short-circuited by the fork of Emily, which landed squarely on the back of his hand.

"Owee! Emily, you fool." Ryan said pulling back his hand with four small indentations on the back. I oughta whack you one."

"Cool it, Ryan," my mother said, " if anybody does any whacking around here it'll be me."

"Yeah Ryan," Emily said with a big grin. "Cool it."

"When did y'all say the blessing?" It was Sissy, the ever-persistent one. "I did not hear one being said."

"While you were trying to get pretty," Ryan answered with a smirk. "Sissy, you didn't hear us, huh? Well, it's a new blessing. It just came down from the Pope himself and the church OK'ed it. You wanna hear it?"

"Yes, that would be nice. Wait a second. Let me bow my head and then you can say it again …OK?"

"Sure. Ready?" Ryan religiously bowed his head and demanded silence from everybody. My mother even stopped eating to have the meal blessed by her son. *That's so nice*, she thought.

When everyone was ready Ryan peeked up, gave me a wink and began the blessing: "In the name of the Father and the Son and the Holy Ghost." *So far so good,* I thought. *Why did he wink at me?*

He paused and then said, "Good gravy, good food, good meat. Good God, let's eat. A-men."

Ryan and I burst out laughing followed by the delightful squeals of Sara who was mimicking our pleasure.

"Ryan!" It was my mother and she wasn't any too happy. "Where did you learn that?" "And quit laughing," my mother ordered, "it isn't *that* funny."

"A-a-a-w, Mom it was just a joke."

"I realize that, son. But it kind of sets a bad example for the little ones. You know what I mean. Joking about God. Just don't say it anymore … OK?"

"Yes Ma'am."

"And besides," Sissy chimed in, "You could burn in hell for talking like that."

I gave Ryan a poke in the ribs. "Yeah Ryan, you could burn in hell."

"Well, that might be so, but I won't be alone." He gave me the eye and then a long look at Sissy. "That's for sure."

"Hey, everybody listen up. I've got to get to work. Sissy, help clean up please and watch over the girls … OK?" My mother looked around for me. "You have a yard to cut … right? And Ryan, you're going to the rectory?"

"Yes Ma'ams" all around.

"And one more thing. You boys, stay out of trouble … OK?"

"Yes Ma'am." We answered together. But I knew that last command was directed more at me than it was Ryan.

Sara giggled and pointed at me and said, "You trouble."

I excused myself and made for the door trying hard to remember how that blessing went. I couldn't wait to tell it to the crew at Burton's.

The Island was no more than two miles long and with its small population made it a community where everyone knew everyone. The Ben Sawyer Bridge, our creaking, rusty, drawbridge-friend built in the 1930's, connected us to the outside world and performed its job most of the time opening and closing slowly to allow the passage of boats using The Intracoastal Waterway. The bridge was located in the middle of the two mile long Causeway that stretched across a serene marsh expanse leading to the mainland and the town of Mt. Pleasant. If you lived on the Island, you belonged to one, singular community as opposed to a city, which was usually made up of many different sub-divisions or boroughs. The Island was the Island. It offered a peaceful existence and was regarded by some of the younger generation, mainly the teenagers, as boring but overall it was a tranquil and safe place, not much different from any small town during the 1950's.It wasn't the perfect place to live, mind you, but close. One slight drawback to life in a small community was that we were not spared the "conversation"of the little minded people, the gossipers, who wanted to mind everyone else's business but their own and were always eager to stir the pot. However, they were few in number, thank goodness.

Mrs. Adams, gossip queen extraordinaire, said that the Island was the original Peyton Place and did not take a backseat to anyplace when it came to good old gossip laced with a dose of backstabbing. Being twelve years old that opinion meant nothing to Bubba 'n me as we roamed the Island in search of fun and adventure.

Being a small, well-knit community gave way to adults looking after each other's kids. And if something was needed, whether it was food or a building project or whatever, neighbors pitched in. We helped each other and nothing was asked in return. With all this attention we kids had lots of "mothers," which most of the time proved beneficial as far as our safety and well being went. But sometimes over cautious adults could unintentionally spoil some of our *fun.* In the long run I'm sure it was reassuring for our parents to know that other families took an active interest in our welfare, bandaging us up when injured, giving us a ride home after dark, correcting our manners, and helping us make right decisions. It was a reciprocal gesture carried out throughout the Island.

It was the previous summer when my mother had come to me and told me, "Mike, you're eleven years old now. You're growing up and you're getting pretty tall and strong too."

I was a bit stunned, not used to such statements from my busy mother and wondered, *What is she talking about?* Of course I answered most respectfully, "Yes Ma'am."

She cleared the kitchen table, pulled out two chairs and said, "Sit down and let's talk some business while we have a few minutes of peace and quiet."

"Sure Mom, what's up," I asked as I sat erect with my hands folded and resting on the table.

"Son, I'll come right to the point." She looked me in the eye and said, "It's time for you to get a job, make some money, and start saving it."

At first I thought, *Wow! A job. Making money.* Then the reality of working a job hit me. *No more school. No recess. No more playing basketball. No more girls. No more going in the creek whenever I wanted to. And I'm only eleven years old. O-o-o-h NO!*

"A real job?" I blurted out. "Like you and Daddy have? One that pays money and all." I know I must have looked frightened as my mother reached across the table and reassuringly patted my hands.

"Oh no, Mike. Not a full time job. No. You're not old enough for that. Just something in the summers. You see, your father and I don't have much money what with all you kids to feed and the house payment and bills and …" Her voice was shaky and rising. "Oh forget all that." My mother paused and collected herself.

"Mom, if y'all need money to buy stuff I don't mind getting a job and helping but I don't know if …"

"Mike!" She interrupted me. "Mike, listen. Here's the plan. Any money you make with your summer jobs will go to help pay for when you get ready to go to college, which is coming sooner than you realize. I know, I know … you think college is way, way off but it isn't. Believe me it'll be here sooner than you think."

"But Mom do you think I can make enough money to pay for college? Doesn't it cost a lot of money?"

"Oh no, we don't expect you to pay for it all by yourself, Mike. Look, here's the deal your father and I came up with. For every dollar you save we will match it. We figure if you start saving now … what are you in the sixth grade?" I nodded. "Then by the time you graduate from high school you'll have enough for the first year or so and then after that you will be on your own."

I frowned at that last statement.

"Hey mister, don't give me that look. You aren't the only child around here. There's Sissy and Ryan ahead of you and then … then we have the girls to worry about coming up behind you. Do you understand?"

My smile and nod of approval answered her but all this talk about saving money and college seemed so very far away. All I wanted to do was go outside and play.

"OK. Good." My mother smiled which made me feel good. Then she said, "Now what kind of job can we find for a growing young lad like you?"

I rubbed my chin and thought and immediately said, "I know. How about being a bagboy at Owen's grocery?" I was thinking about Julie, the shapely, flirtatious daughter of the owner, who was the cashier. My hormones as of late had been working overtime.

"At Owen's." My mother read my mind. "Son, you would be dropping eggs on the floor and putting the bread at the bottom of the bag while ogling Julie. Uh-uh. And besides it doesn't pay enough. Think of something else."

"How about at the movie theater or the skating rink? James and Stinky worked there last summer."

"No way. I said a job, not someplace where you can go and play."

"How about …"

My mother interrupted. "Your father and I talked about something and because the Island is so small and you know so many people we think you're big enough to handle a grass cutting business. Not only will you make some decent money but you get to be your own boss, which might not sound like a big deal to you but, believe me, it makes working a whole lot easier when you're doing it for yourself. Whatta you think?"

"Grass cutting, h-u-m-m." I paused and envisioned myself pushing a lawn mower, something I did on a weekly basis in our yard. "Well, that doesn't sound too bad."

"And besides," my mother added, "most people can't stand working in the heat in the summer so you should be able to find plenty of customers."

Shoot, I thought, *I'm young and full of energy and I need the money … so why not even though college was the last thing on my mind.* My interests were along the lines of boating, the beach, sports and girls … in that order. However, girls, as of late, were quickly moving up the list.

"Yeah, I can do that Mom."

"Good," my mother said pushing herself up from the table. "I'll tell your father, he'll tune up ol' Red for you, and you'll be in business. Tell you what you need to do. You need to round up a few customers to begin with, which shouldn't be hard for you and then when other people see what a good job you do then they'll be calling you."

"But Mom," I exclaimed, "how do I get customers?"

"Easy, Mike. Go from house to house and knock on people's doors and ask 'em if they need their yard cut?"

So I did. And this summer I had about ten yards I mowed on a regular schedule with a twenty inch gas powered push mower that smoked like a locomotive, which I pulled behind me on my bike with a piece of rope as I went from job to job.

My faithful helper, helper of morale that is, was Mollie who normally accompanied me and today I was headed to the Kerr's who lived on the front beach row and had a beautiful, huge lawn running right up to the sand dunes. It looked like a miniature football field with its soft, even green grass and no obstructions. Because it was what I called a big yard, I charged them a whole seven dollars for each cut.

My father had taught me how to cut a yard so it looked really neat when finished.

He said, "Always pick your longest run and start there and go back and forth and don't ever cut across those rows. Then you'll have one row that is darker than the other and it will look really good."

"Yes sir," I said, " but do I have to cut our yard like that?"

"No. You can practice on our yard but always cut your customers that way."

When I got to the Kerr's it was early morning and already getting hot so when I was about half finished I decided to take a break from the heat. I sat in the shade underneath the raised house admiring the long, even, alternating stripes of cut grass … *not bad, not* bad*,* I told myself as I sipped cold water from my jug. I was hot and sweaty and was thinking, *Now if I just had a helper. I could finish quicker and get out of here and go to the beach and go swimming.* Previously, I had thought about Bubba helping me and I had mentioned it to him but he kind of shrugged off the idea, mumbling something about the heat and too much work. The crew? N-a-a-w, they seemed too busy with other stuff. Then a really good thought hit me: *What if I had a free helper, someone I didn't have to pay. Yeah, that would be even better ... a free helper.*

H-u-m-m. I took another swig of water, looked at Mollie, I looked at the idle lawnmower, and then looked at Mollie again and looked at the lawnmower again and thought … *well ... maybe?* I had an idea that *just* might work? I figured *Eah, nothing ventured, nothing gained.* I ran to my bike parked in the backyard and grabbed my rope.

Yep, just the right length and I ran back to the front yard and called for Mollie, my unsuspecting new helper. First, I secured the rope by wrapping it around the motor and then got Mollie to back into position in front of the lawnmower and stand there real still. Much like a farmer rigging up his mule in preparation for plowing a field. Mollie was more than cooperative thinking it was another game we were playing as she stood there smiling and wagging her tail while I tied the rope to her collar and explained what we were going to do. When I cranked up the lawnmower, she jumped at first startled by the sound of the engine but when I hollered, "Let's go" Mollie took off pulling the lawnmower with me right behind her. Of course, I didn't let her do all the work. I pushed and guided the mower but it was almost effortless as compared to me doing all the pushing. Turning around at the end of a row was a little tricky to begin with but Mollie was so smart it wasn't long before she sensed when to make the turn and after about ten minutes we were happily working as a well-trained team until … until … that durn rabbit showed up and spoiled the day. It came out of the bushes lining the yard, stopped, and looked at Mollie and me. More at Mollie I think? Guess that rabbit had never seen a dog pulling a lawnmower? It didn't move for a few seconds and neither did Mollie. But when that rabbit took off running so did Mollie. The chase was on before I could free Mollie from the lawnmower or do anything. Whoosh! It happened so fast. They were outtta there. Mollie jerked the lawnmower right out of my hands. That rabbit was bouncing all over the yard running from one side to the other and back again with Mollie and the lawnmower, still cutting grass, in hot pursuit ... all three being chased by a screaming twelve year old.

"Whoa, Mollie. Stop. Stop!" It seemed the more I yelled the faster she ran.

Shoot, I thought, *she probably can't hear me over the noise of the engine?*

Once she got into the chase that was one determined dog. Around and around and from side to side we went.

I even tried yelling at the rabbit: "Hey, you stupid rabbit. Stop! Get out of here!" And every time I screamed at that rabbit to go away it would stop dead in its tracks for a second and just look at me as to ask, "Would you repeat that please?" Then ZOOM ...he was gone again.

Finally, the rabbit took to the high weeds by the sand dunes and when Mollie paused to pick up the scent I grabbed the lawnmower handle and shut the engine off.

PHEW-EE, man. I didn't think they'd ever stop. And when I turned Mollie loose she bolted into the bushes with her nose to the ground looking for that dumb rabbit.

In five minutes that beautiful yard had gone from looking like a Homecoming queen to the wicked witch with long, green warts on her nose. My perfectly laid stripes now had zigzag cuts through them and the rest of the yard looked like a blind person had mowed it.

Well, so much for Mollie helping mow the grass, I thought. *Nope. Won't do this again.*

I remembered what my father had told me one time: "Son, there ain't no use in crying over spilt milk." So I cranked up ol' Red and put the Kerr's yard back together best I could.

Riding back to the house with Mollie trotting along side of me and smiling up at me when I called her name made me smile and I also recalled something my mother had once told me: "Mike," she said, " there isn't any such thing as a free lunch." Today I think I learned what she meant by that statement.

I had done some extra, unwanted, work that day but I was sure of two things: I had some good parents and a willing helper in Mollie even though she did like to chase rabbits.

Whenever I finished my chores or the yards I had on any particular day then it was playtime. And I would go in search of the crew, which was usually at the beach or hanging out at Burton's Drug store. And that's where I would find my best friend, Bubba, if he wasn't home watching

TV.

There was no formal recreation department or playground on the Island so we kids adapted to our surroundings. And it was this adaptation, which sometimes led us to trouble. As we got older and more observant, we began to see a whole new world right in front of our eyes, a vast new arena to play in and have fun. There were the creeks and the beach and the forts and the hill compound. Why, we had a natural playground right beneath our feet all this time. We just hadn't taken the time before to look around. Another attraction and possible source of adventure that caught my eye that spring was the Ben Sawyer Bridge.

I was riding in the car with my father coming back from Mt. Pleasant one day when the bridge caught us and we sat watching the sailboat leisurely move toward the opening bridge. It was a swing span bridge that went in a circle reminding me of a merry go round. And, as always, I relayed this thought to my father.

"Daddy, the bridge moves around almost like a big slow merry go round, huh?"

"Yeah, it sure does," my father answered upon closer inspection of the slow moving span as it came to a stop midway through its cycle. "Yeah, I never thought of that."

Then the thought came to me. *A merry-go-round. Right here. Just like at the fair.*

H-u-u-m-m, I thought. *I bet that would be a fun ride and it wouldn't cost a penny.*

My father glanced over at me, catching me smiling. "And what are you so happy about, young man?"

"Oh nothing … I was just daydreaming …"

Shoot, I couldn't wait to get home and talk to Bubba about him and I taking a ride on the Ben Sawyer Bridge. That would be so neat! I was even betting that no one else had ever been on the bridge when it opened except for the man who operated the bridge.

At first Bubba was skeptical. "You mean ride the bridge around while it opens and shuts. I don't know … that's kinda tricky … don't you think? What if we get caught?"

"Eah, that's the good part. Who can catch us? We'll be the only people on it." I was beaming. "Don't you see?"

"Yeah, that's right. Yeah, we'll be the only ones there. Man, you so smart, Devlin." Bubba smiled and patted me on the back. "Eah, I'm sorry I called you stupid last week."

"You called me stupid when?"

"Last week."

"Yeah? How come I didn't hear you?"

"Oh." He paused and said, "Because I said it to myself."

"Well, I think it's stupid that you would call me stupid. So there, stupid."

"Well, thanks, stupid."

"And why did you call me stupid to begin with?"

"Eah, just forget it OK? You done got me mixed up. Let's make up a plan for this bridge ride, OK?"

It was springtime and the annual parade of boats running from their northern berths, as far away as Massachusetts, headed southward showcasing themselves in the waters of the Intracoastal Waterway, which runs directly under the Ben Sawyer Bridge. On any given day, especially the weekends, sailboats with their tall protruding masts and power yachts, the huge ones, would stall traffic while the bridge opened for them to pass. Bubba 'n me agreed that was when we wanted to be there.

"C'mon slow poke. Let's go." We were headed for our lookout spot, not at the Ben Sawyer Bridge, but at the Breach Inlet Bridge. Bubba, usually ahead of me, was lagging behind me on a Saturday morning, a busy day for bridge openings. "What's wrong? You got lead in your shoes?"

"T-h-a-t -'s right, Catbird. I got lead in my shoes. Watch this." Bubba stood up and pedaled hard and fast and flew past me. "Take that, lead in your head!"

We raced until we got to the Breach Inlet Bridge and there we sat on our bikes catching our breath, resting one foot on the rail of the bridge. Here we had an open view of the Intracoastal Waterway, which ran behind Sullivans Island and the Isle of Palms in a line as straight as an arrow. And we sat and waited for a tall sailboat to come along headed south that would cause the Ben Sawyer Bridge to open. We took in the views around us, mostly the beach area fronting along the Brach Inlet.

"Look at that. There must be ten guys down there," Bubba said pointing to the beach by the Breach Inlet where fishermen were lined up, casting their lines.

"Wonder what they're fishing for," I asked. "Flounder you reckon?"

"I'll tell you in a minute. Soon as I can see what kind of bait they're using." Bubba eyed the nearest fisherman making a cast.

"Yep, flounder," he said as he pointed. " See the minnow on the end of the line?"

"Yep, you're right. Eah, there's lots of crabbers there too. Wonder who catches the most? The fishermen or the crabbers?"

"Get serious, Devlin." Bubba gave me the eye. "You know the crabbers do!"

Just to pass the time I figured I'd egg Bubba on a little more. "Oh yea, then how come there are more fishermen than crabbers there?" I asked without grinning.

"Because they're just like you … stupid!"

"Bubba, look here." I pointed toward the beach. "Look at that. See what I see?"

"What?" he said, surveying the beach. "Nothing but a bunch of stupid fishermen."

"Uh-uh. Over there." I pointed out a group of arriving beachgoers, all set for a day in the sun and a nice beach picnic. "That bunch with the blanket and all."

Bubba looked at the lily-white group with cameras draped around their necks and sporting the latest fashion statement of black lace up shoes with white socks, all wearing funny looking hats.

Bubba gazing skyward spotted a flock of approaching seagulls and said, "Oh boy! Here we go again." He pointed toward the seagulls. "This oughta be good but remember we gotta kind of keep an eye out for the sailboat."

"Don't worry, O'Toole. Remember I'm the one in this group that can do two things at once …OK!"

"Yeah, right. The only two things you can at the same time is maybe walk and chew gum."

"T-h-a-t-'s right, Catbird and I'm w-a-a-a-y ahead of you."

Overhead the patient circling gulls were making plans for their morning meal.

"See him," I said pointing at the gulls. "That big one, right there. He's the leader. Wanna bet?"

Bubba squinted his eyes, moved his head back and forth studying the gulls and agreed, "Yeah, he kind of looks like the daring type."

The happy beachgoers had claimed their particular section of the beach, spread their blanket and set up camp, and were standing around admiring their accomplishment when our pre selected leader of the seagulls made his move. He separated himself from the flock, soared down effortlessly, and landed gently near the tourist's blanket of goodies. From past experience Mister Seagull knew he couldn't just walk up and help himself to anything he wanted.

Bubba poked me in the side, grinned, and said, "This should be good. Right?"

"Oh yeah!" said Bubba. "R-e-a-l good."

The timing of the sea gull was perfect. Most of the beachgoers had moved to the water's edge, some electing to take a stroll down the beach. The kids were already in the water, splashing about.

"Oh look, John. Look at the cute little seagull," Mrs. Tourist said with sweetness as Mister Seagull waddled toward them. "I wonder if the poor thing is hungry?"

"Oh lady, if you only knew," muttered Bubba, "if you only knew."

"Come here, nice bird. C-o-m-e on," pleaded Mrs. Tourist coaxing the wary seagull to eat a potato chip from her outstretched hand. Mr. Gull, however, only stared. He had his sights set on something other than a durn old potato chip. As she took three steps toward Mister Gull, he took four steps backwards. Three steps for the lady. Four back for the gull. And on it went. Slowly they were leaving the vicinity of the blanket.

"No honey. Like this," John lectured as he literally began to crawl on his knees toward the ever backing up gull. He then tossed bits of bread in front of the gull that for some unknown reason ignored them.

"Humph. Must not like bread," John said, "Maybe he'll eat some cookies. Here try these, sweetie."

Honey poured from Mrs. Tourist's mouth and then she begged for Mister Gull to take some free food from her hand as he slowly moved himself and these tourists further and further from their blanket.

"Bubba, watch 'em." I gestured toward the circling flock of hungry and anxious but patient seagulls overhead. "Man, they're smart."

"John, I think he's going to take it. Watch." The wily seagull's deception was complete. Then he backed away some more, followed by the determined feeders.

"Ever notice how quiet they are when they go in for the kill?" Bubba asked. "No squawking or anything. Watch. H-e-r-e they go."

Mr. And Mrs. Tourist learned a lesson that day, a bit too late.

Minutes later. "Oh no!" gasped Mrs. Tourist with her hands over her face. "Look John!"

John turned to witness the flock of twenty or so seagulls on their blanket helping themselves to anything that wasn't nailed down. Those gulls had themselves a feast and downed everything except the cold sodas.

Bubba jokingly said, "Eah, I bet they would have opened the sodas if they'd found the opener. BA-HA-HA-HA-HA!"

I was enjoying a good laugh too. "You got that right. Oh boy! What a mess."

The seagull show was cut short by the arrival of a sailboat. "Hey look! There she is!" Bubba pointed, looking out over the marsh expanse toward the Intracoastal Waterway. "There's our boat. Boy, she's a big one and moving fast."

It was a three masted schooner in full flight slicing her way through the calm Intracoastal, her hull so white in the morning sun that it reflected like a mirror.

"Let's go," I yelled. "Time to go for a ride on the Ben Sawyer Bridge!" Race ya to the Causeway."

"Gotta quarter says I beat ya," Bubba responded looking for some easy money and took off like a bat outta hell.

It was about a ride of a mile or so back down the Island to the Causeway where we would turn right and then ride out to the Ben Sawyer Bridge, which was another half mile off the back of the Island.

Not wanting to miss our opportunity we pedaled like demons

and when we got on the Causeway we looked out to the Intracoastal Waterway and saw the approaching sailboat in the distance chugging toward the bridge. In our haste we had beaten the boat by a long shot and were so early we had to take cover in the thick overgrowth at the foot of the bridge in order to hide from the bridge tender perched high up in his little hut in the middle of the bridge. What we were getting ready to do was not some normal- everyday-as- you- please- fun- thing. Being on the bridge when it opened and circled around was trespassing and against the law. We knew that. And that's what made it so much fun!

Crouching in the bushes, I eyed the bridge tender carefully as he took the last drag off his cigarette, flipped it off into the water below and went back inside the small hut and prepared himself for the mechanics of the opening. I had somewhat of a plan. A plan more thought out than the garbage truck disaster but I had not let Bubba in on the details yet. His job for now was to follow my lead.

"Get ready … OK …Now! Let's go … no cars are coming!" There was a sense of urgency in my voice. We darted across the road, pushing our bikes. "Come on, hurry!"

Bubba followed and about halfway across the road asked, "Why we going to the other side?"

"Don't worry, you'll see later … maybe?"

"All right," I said, "get ready." Bubba frowned and must have thought I'd lost my mind when I said, "We're going back to the other side. Get ready but leave your bike here."

"What? I hope you know what you're doing," Bubba said. "Because I sure don't."

We darted back across the road to the safety of the bushes.

"Eah, have no fear. Your fearless leader is here," I said and then asked Bubba trying to relieve any fears he might have, "What does Buckwheat say?"

Bubba smiled real big showing clenched teeth, opened his eyes wide, threw his head, pushed his chest out back and said, "Everything is O-O-O-O- TAY."

I laughed and told him he looked just like Buckwheat. He gave me a friendly punch on the shoulder and told me that if he was Buckwheat then I was Alfalfa. We both chuckled trying to take our minds off the hungry horseflies that we swatted at and constantly missed. We were roasting in the sun hoping the sailboat would hurry up. Then we heard the long horn blast coming from the waterway and knew she was getting closer We waited patiently and had a contest seeing who could kill the most ants crawling up our bare legs. Bubba won again. Then we lay back in the grass and stared upward and played the what-do-you-see-game with the clouds. We were both kind of drifting with the clouds when the ding- ding-ding of the warning bell awakened us from our sun induced slumber and spooked the seagulls resting on the bridge railing not fifteen feet from us as they let out a collective squawk and flew away. The wooden arm used to block the cars swung down like a guillotine in slow motion. It was our cue to make a break for the bridge … it was ready to swing open. We scurried along the walkway to the sounds of the bridge as it creaked and moaned, sounding like an old man getting out of bed in the morning. We were real close to where the bridge connects to the roadway when the bridge began to move very slowly. It had moved just enough to show daylight and the marsh below when we jumped onto it and ran like the dickens towards the middle not quite sure where we were headed but knew we would go for a ride like never before.

The bridge tender, a crusty looking old man with a stubby beard and gray hair, spotted us immediately and yelled at us.

"Hey, you two! Whatta ya think you're doin." He was pointing his finger. "You boys are gonna be in big trouble! You hear me." I guess he thought we hadn't heard him because we just kept on running toward the end of the bridge as it continued on its circular orbit. "You better …" he ducked back inside his hut.

"Yeah right, mister. What ya gonna do … come and get us?" Bubba screamed back with a big smile followed by a hearty laugh.

"Eah, what's he gonna do. Tell our parents? A-HA-HA," I said giving Bubba a friendly slap on the shoulder. "Let's go."

Bubba 'n me had this pact that if we were ever in trouble and anyone asked us our name and told us they were going to call our parents we always answered, "Tommy Wade." We'd used it many times in the past without getting caught and planned to keep on using it but I suppose the Wades were tired of receiving calls about the mysterious misbehavior of their favorite son?

While the bridge was swinging open we were running from side to side peering over the sides at the moving water and waving at the people sitting and waiting in their cars behind the barriers. We were jumping around and hollering, just having a big time. The tourists must have thought this was some kind of promotional welcoming them to the Island because some of them were waving back.

As the bridge came to its midway point it slowly coasted to a stop. This resting position made for the opening that allowed the tall sailboat to come through. We raced to the very end, right to the edge of the bridge, and dared each other to see how close we could get without falling some fifty feet into the Intracoastal Waterway. I was on my knees crawling to the end and decided to lie on my stomach and peek over the edge. Bubba was right beside me. It was quite a spectacle lying there seeing only the water. It was a feeling of being suspended in mid air. We waved and hollered at the passing sailboat whose passengers gave us a surprised look yet waved back. And then there was a sudden jerk, which startled and scared us, and the bridge moved slowly, starting its return journey to the closed position. We laid there staring at the water not being able to see anything around us as we moved slowly, which gave us the sensation of floating through space. It was a surreal experience and made me want to come back and do it again, however, the spell was broken by the loud shouts of the bridge tender who had come out of his hut and was really letting us have it.

"Who do you think you are? Coming out on this bridge like this. Are y'all crazy? Just wait 'till I close this bridge. I'll take care of you two!"

I couldn't wait for him to ask me my name. Shoot, you would have thought it was his very own bridge the way he was carrying on. But we weren't here to cause any trouble so we kept our big mouths shut … well, almost.

"Hey mister, go fly a kite will ya." Bubba screamed. "That is if you got enough brains to know how. BA-HA-HA-HA-HA!"

I chimed in, "Yeah, what ya gonna do? Come and get us? A-HA-HA-HA!"

Leaning against the rail and staring down at us the angry bridge tender retorted, "Y'all are trespassing and in trouble, big trouble. When this bridge closes I'm gonna take care of the both of you. You hear me?"

I shouted back. "We got news for you, mister. We ain't gonna be on your stupid bridge when it closes."

He really got mad then and stormed back into his hut. We would have probably been out of trouble at this point but we decided to give one parting shot so when Mr. Bridge Tender stuck his head out again we stuck our thumbs in our ears and wiggled our hands at him while sticking out our tongues giving him the "N-a-a, n-a-a,n-a, n-a-a, naa- Y-o-u c-a-n-t c-a-t-c-h us" chorus. We figured all we had to do was walk off the bridge when it closed, get on our bikes and ride home but we forgot the bridge tender had a radio and so did Chief Perry. The bridge tender, however, hadn't forgotten and had called Chief Perry five minutes earlier and, little did we know, that our favorite nemesis was pulling off the shoulder of the road at the foot of the bridge at this very instant chopping at the bit because he figured he finally, at last, had two of the infamous, law breaking crew cornered on the Ben Sawyer Bridge.

As the bridge slowly swung shut occupying the bridge tender, we made our way toward the end of the bridge to make our escape and then we caught sight of Bull Perry, not trying to hide his fat old self but standing tall and large, feet apart with his hands on his bulging hips on the other side of the wooden barrier. He then began to walk confidentially toward us grinning in anticipation of collaring Bubba 'n me and finally getting that dreaded monkey off his back … the fact that he had *never* caught any kid trespassing anywhere at anytime in ten years. The barrier was still in place and traffic was lined up bumper to bumper with eager drivers ready to continue their journey. DING-DING-DING went the bridge's warning bell. It reminded me of the beginning of a prizefight but the opponent on the other side of that barrier was in the wrong weight division and all the dieting in the world would never have reduced him to the bantamweight division, which we were in.

Bubba looked at me trembling. I knew he was terrified of Bull Perry and he was on the verge of tears when he asked, "What are we gonna do now?"

"Hey, Buckwheat, calm down. Remember, everything is O-O-O TAY. Just follow me … all right?"

"Eah, who else am I gonna follow?" he said bravely. "You the leader, Alfalfa!"

Chief Perry picked up his pace and his rounded frame was looming larger and larger by the second. I began to back up slowly step by step watching the wooden barrier rise and Bull Perry getting closer at the same time. With some luck and good timing we could get out of this mess if the Chief would unknowingly cooperate. He went for the bait following us until the three of us were about in the middle of the closed bridge when the wooden barrier lifted completely allowing traffic to begin to flow. Chief Perry was no more than fifteen feet from us and then he stopped, put his hands on his hips, and looked us over, not saying a thing. Bubba suddenly froze, his eyes locked onto the steady gaze of the Chief's penetrating gray eyes, completely mesmerized. Bubba was calling back a memory from years ago when he must have been three or four years old and had wandered out the backyard into an old abandoned warehouse near Back Street. He became scared in the unfamiliar surroundings and darkness. The wailing siren from the approaching police car had scared him even more. He retreated to the safety of a corner with his face pressed against the wall and his little arms hugging the flatness of the two walls. The loud shouts from the big man made him close his eyes over the wetness now on his face. The big man with the penetrating eyes, finding the child huddled in the corner came to its rescue. A face the child would never forget … the same face that stared at Bubba now.

"Bubba!" I screamed. "B-u-b-b-a!" I grabbed a handful of tee shirt and yanked hard. It worked and we bolted.

"Now!" I yelled. I jumped into the road in front of the oncoming traffic racing for safety to the other side. Bubba was right beside me. Chief Perry hesitated for a split second and that was our margin of escape as the first car barely missed us and an angry driver shook his fist and blew his horn at us. Chief Perry stood looking, not daring to chase after us into the traffic. He was way too slow. We ran down the bridge while his face showed the same dejected look of a child whose favorite toy has just been snatched from him. He began a slow jog bouncing and giggling like a walrus, stopped, drew a few deep breaths and began walking. He had covered about twenty feet while we were nearly off the bridge. We hopped on our waiting bikes and rode like the wind toward the Island zipping past the cars still lined up waiting to get started.

After a fast and furious ride we reached the safety of Bubba's backyard, sweating like pigs in South Georgia.

"O-o-o-h man," Bubba said as we dismounted and headed for the shade of the giant hackberry tree. The one with the exposed roots that had been pulled from the ground by Hurrricane Gracie in 1957. I plopped down on my favorite root, leaned back against the tree resting my head, feeling relief not only physically but also emotionally. Coming that close to the human dogface of Bull Perry had been a surreal moment.

Bubba sat down and broke the silence: "I see why we put the bikes over on the other side now … I see, I see."

"Yeah, that was our safety get away plan. Got to always have that."

"Yeah, good idea but … if that's so … how come we got caught when the garbage truck wrecked?"

"Because we didn't have a way out, that's why. And there's another thing I learned from that."

"Yeah, what's that?"

"Don't ever try to hide in oleander bushes." We both smiled. Our smiles were not ones of happiness at outrunning Bull Perry again but were smiles of approval of each other, smiles of friendship.

"Eah, I'm hungry," Bubba said as he got up, "let's get something to eat. Come on."

I didn't need much encouragement. The bike ride and the encounter with chief Perry for some reason gave me a tremendous appetite. "I'm right behind you, my friend. What ya got to eat in this house?"

"Well, … let me scout around a little and I'll tell ya," Bubba declared as he opened the frig, took a peek inside and then shut it. A quick look in the cabinets and then he announced, "You can have either peanut butter and jelly sandwiches or jelly and peanut butter sandwiches." He grinned and then said, "Which will it be?"

I rubbed my chin, gazed upward, paused and said, "I think I'll have the peanut butter and jelly sandwiches. They sound delicious."

"Good choice, good choice!" And we both laughed.

As we grabbed our plates and began to head outside to eat, bubba stopped and said, "Go ahead. I forgot something. I'll be out in a minute."

I was hoping he had momentarily forgotten my favorite beverage, which was always plentiful in the O'Toole household. A nice cold Nehi grape soda.

As I was sitting down under the tree, Bubba appeared on the back porch carrying his plate of sandwiches. We each had two huge sandwiches. In his other hand, much to my delight were two Nehi grape sodas.

"Here you go," he said, extending the soda to me. "Bet you thought I had forgotten?"

"Well," I joked, " … you did have me worried there for a minute.

"Talk about being worried. Man … that was something else with Bull Perry. He scared the you know what out of me," Bubba said. He took a big bite of his sandwich and shaking his sandwich at me for emphasis added, "Mike, I was so scared that if he had grabbed me I probably would have fainted right then and there. Boom … right out."

I gave Bubba a sincere look. "Eah, I'm sure glad that didn't happen, my friend. Oh man that would have …"

Bubba interrupted, "Gosh that's nice of you to say that about me. I didn't know that you cared that much."

I broke his smile when I shot back. "Yeah, because if Bull Perry had caught you then I wouldn't have these sandwiches and this cold grape soda right now. A-HA-HA-HA!"

"A-a-a-h," Bubba replied waving his hand at me. "You're so funny," he mumbled and then got real quiet and stared off in space.

When my friend got like this I knew something serious was on his mind so I just sat and ate my sandwiches enjoying the cool shade and refreshing breeze. When he was ready to return to this world he would announce it in no uncertain terms. After a minute or so Bubba had that deliberate look on his face. He was back.

"Mike?" He called my name but it was more in the form of a question. "Do you think Bull Perry will come and get us?"

I was taken back for a second, not fully comprehending his question. I stumbled, "You mean … right now?"

"Yeah, right now. Why doesn't he just drive up in his car, get out and come get us? I mean … we are just sitting right here like ducks on a pond."

"A-a-a-h, that ain't never gonna happen," I said, "So don't worry about it … O.K."

A long time ago I had figured out that line of reasoning. Chief Perry knew who we were, he knew where we lived, and he knew our parents and could have easily placed a phone call squealing on us about what took place today or come by our house to pick us up but there was an unwritten code of honor between us and him that said he had to actually physically catch us during one of our escapades. No phone calls or tattle telling or anything short of an actual arrest. That was against the rules.

He was determined to catch us. We knew that much. And today he was very close.

But like my father used to tell me, "Close is only good in two things, son … horseshoes and hand grenades."

I finished off my lunch and said good-bye to my friend. I felt relieved after our little talk and was tired after all the excitement of the day. A good nap was in order.

Bubba waved good-bye and told me he would see me in the morning.

I yelled across the street to Bubba just as he was headed in the house, "And don't worry. That's my department."

He laughed and shot back, "Eah, I won't and you're right … you old worry wart!"

5
THE HILL

In addition to the many Island "mothers" watching over us we had the added protection of the Island police, Chief Perry and his assistant, Lumus Mc Farland whether we wanted their attention or not. They were constantly on the lookout for us and the crew, waiting for us to screw up. We were considered thorns in their sides and a constant reminder that they were unable to catch such brash young lawbreakers who openly defied them by trespassing on government property, such as the forts on the Island and especially the hill. The hill's official name was Battery Logan. It was part of the coastal defense system built by the federal government after the Spanish American War consisting of four huge gun pits, minus the guns, and was about ninety feet tall with slanted sides about two hundred feet long. This was one of a series of forts on the Island, but the only hill and had been abandoned some fifteen years earlier. It sat there as a monument to our government's concern for our country's welfare and as a huge temptation for us Island kids. The locals simply called it "the hill" and by the end of the winter the grass on it had become brown and slippery … perfect for us to slide down on using a piece of cardboard as our sled. Chief Perry, more so than Lumus was out to catch us or should I say catch someone, anyone. Shucks, it must have been a living hell for tough old Bull Perry, the Army sergeant who had helped capture hundreds of Germans in WWII, but couldn't catch any of the trespassing kids on the Island. As for the crew we thought it was great fun to be chased by Bull Perry, however, we thought it even more fun every time we outran him and Lumus and escaped. We treated the whole idea of the police chasing after us as more of a game than anything else. On the other hand, there were a few of us if the truth were known who were terrified by just the thought of Bull Perry. Of course, this kind of thought would never ever become common knowledge to the crew. That would be a sign of weakness, which was the complete opposite of the bravado we always displayed in public.

The Island Police Department was a simple place. There was no jail or sophisticated police equipment or even a real headquarters to speak of. For one thing there was no money for a large staff or elaborate surroundings. And in reality there was no need. The Island was a peaceful place almost devoid of serious crime. The Department's means of communication was a radio at the station linked to the Chief's patrol car and an old Jeep used mainly by Lumus. This arrangement was a testament to the Island lifestyle, laid back and trusting, where residents still came and went without the worry of being robbed and even slept with unlocked doors and open windows. If someone were going to run a few errands and be away from their house for a while they normally left their doors unlocked and everyone knew it. Neighbors looked out for each other keeping a keen eye peeled for anything out of the ordinary and were quick to question a stranger should they wander into someone's yard and they reported anything of a suspicious nature. Gertie Evans and her group of gossip queens, known as Gertie's Gang, were scattered throughout the Island and were especially adept at keeping tabs on anything and everything that went on. If you were a stranger on the Island, the ever-savvy Gertie would know it.

The police chief was William Sherman Perry, affectionately known by the locals as Bull Perry, a retired, grizzled World War II veteran who had been highly decorated for the courage and valor he displayed while fighting his way across Italy into Europe and finally engaging the Germans in hand to hand combat during the Battle of the Bulge. When the war ended he returned to the States, retired as a Sergeant, sat down one day, and asked himself, "What in the hell am I going to do now?"

Doris, his wife, answered that question for him: Her family was from upstate South Carolina and her desire had always been to live on the seacoast so through her persuasion and with the help of local contacts the Perrys made their way to Sullivans Island. Law enforcement was right up his alley. *Another war to fight,* he thought. He was thinking about crime. Little did he know that his main enemy would be a bunch of kids? Influenced by friends he took the job as Chief on the Island. His monthly retirement check added to his pay as Chief took care of his modest needs, his only heavy expense being his penchant for food … and a lot of it. He had already fought one Battle of the Bulge and was engaged in another on a daily basis and judging from the size of his waistline he was losing this one. His physical appearance was indisputable, short in stature, wide in girth with huge shoulders supporting a tiny head adorned with a GI haircut. His beady gray eyes only rendered a peek at his soul.

His gruff, no nonsense demeanor often drew criticism from overly sensitive residents not used to dealing with an ex-sergeant. The Chief's patented response was, "If they had wanted a school marm for a Chief then they should have hired one."

However, Bull Perry the quintessential bulldog of a man who took no prisoners, the sour puss who only loved his doughnuts, this cantankerous old Sergeant had a hidden agenda. He had a big heart. Often he went out of his way to help others but always gave credit to someone else or simply kept his mouth shut, never one to heap praise on himself. The way he figured it, this job was just like the war: he had a job to do and he would do it.

Doris and he lived modestly enjoying the pleasures of the Island: the beach, the quiet beauty, tending their vegetable garden, and hanging out with friends on their big open front porch where many "happy hours" took place. Chief Perry did a good job of "watching the peace" and except for a few squirrelly little Irish kids had no serious problems … that is … until the summer of 1959.

Chief Perry's only assistant was Lumus Mc Farland, a happy go lucky, twenty-five year old bachelor, who loved sailing and owned a disposition as laid back as the seagulls on a Sunday afternoon. He was from Mc Clellanville, a small community north of the Island, twenty-five miles as the crow flies, population two hundred.

Mc Clellanville was not a town but rather a village with a few family owned shops, a hardware/general store with the Post Office in the rear of the store. There was only one road, no gas station, no traffic light, and no police. The only sidewalk in town was rolled up at 6:00 every evening. The village owed its very existence to the shrimping fleet that docked on Jeremy Creek adjacent to the Intracoastal Waterway providing jobs for the locals thus generating a cash flow that kept everyone happy, if not rich. The people of Mc Clellanville were friendly and in no hurry to go anywhere or do anything. It was rumored that life was so slow and easy going that if the folks in Mc Clellanville moved any slower they would be moving backwards.

Lumus' family had been there forever and it was assumed that when he came of age Lumus would follow his brothers, all five of them, into the family farming business. If you were a Mc Farland you were a farmer and there was no discussion about it. But Lumus had other plans and shocked the family his junior year in high school when he announced that when he graduated he planned to attend The Citadel, the military college in Charleston. His father's initial response was negative but Lumus explained that he wasn't cut out for farming and that if he couldn't go to The Citadel then he would just move out and find a job other than farming. Eventually his father came around and it was with his and the family's blessing and money Lumus earned on the shrimp boats that he entered The Citadel, the first Mc Farland to ever attend college.

Lumus' common sense, country-boy approach to life and its problems did not serve him well at The Citadel. His frustrations grew daily. His adaptation to the military was like trying to mix water and oil. The plebe system at The Citadel was notoriously demanding both physically and mentally, not akin at all to Lumus' straight forth, aw shucks mentality.

Lumus wasn't dumb or stupid by any means … he just went about things in a different way than most folks. However, at the Citadel it was their way or the highway … no in between. When he questioned an upperclassman about what a "knob" was on the first day he received fifteen automatic tours (marching once around the parade ground constituted one tour) and was ordered to perform a hundred pushups.

This don't make no sense a'tall to me, thought Lumus. *All we do is walk tours, stand at attention and get yelled at and shine shoes. This ain't what I thought it was going to be. No sir-ree, this here stinks.*

And with that attitude, unbeknownst to Lumus, he was on his way out of The Citadel. Adding to his problems was his thick Southern drawl and his physical appearance, which made him a constant target for the unrelenting upperclassmen who thrived on inflicting mental and physical torture on their unsuspecting classmates. And why not? They themselves had suffered the same humiliation the year before so why not return it. Lumus was tall and gangly with a large protruding nose matched in size by his ears. He looked like a taxicab going down the street with the back doors open. Somehow he managed to endure all of two years while making respectable grades and many new friends and then he quit. His eyes had been opened to another world other than Mc Clellanville and he had the urge to travel. His final thoughts were that there must be a better way to get an education and besides, there aren't any girls here to look at … only all these hard asses.

So broke as a church mouse, he took off for Europe telling his family that he heard there was another world on the other side of the Atlantic and he planned to see some of it. And that he did. He worked his way through thirteen European countries in three years by doing odd jobs while gaining an experience of a lifetime. When asked about his European travels, Lumus said that it was fun but more of an education that he ever received at The Citadel. The irony of the whole situation he remarked was that it was the lifestyle of the Citadel that drove him to his travels and for that he would always be grateful.

His true passion was sailing, a pastime he learned growing up in Mc Clellanville, so when the job opened up on Sullivans Island he decided to kill two birds with one stone … making a living and enjoy plenty of sailing. He applied, interviewed with the Chief who appreciated his honest approach to life and down to earth personality and was hired. Lumus had been on the force three years and was comfortable with all aspects of his job … even dealing with Chief Perry.

It was Lumus who answered the Chief's call and came to his aid one Saturday in mid June at the hill.

Bubba 'n me met the crew at the hill that morning, played a few games of tag in the tunnels inside the mound, went to Burton's Drug Store for a Coke and rested, and then returned to the hill for an afternoon of sliding. We considered it part of our playground and met there often even though we knew it was government property and to be on it was trespassing. Of course, in the back of our minds was the special appeal that Bull Perry would add some excitement to our day and try to catch us. Chief Perry had been trying for ten years to catch *anyone* trespassing on the hill but so far hadn't been successful.

Chief Perry had driven to the back of the hill and sat in the car waiting for the hill to full up with happy sliders. Then he called Lumus hoping his youth and athletic ability would help lead to the capture of at least one of the culprits who always laughed at him during their many escapes. When Lumus received the call he knew what the Chief was up to and realized the futility and waste of time involved in chasing those kids. They'd done better chasing lightning bugs blindfolded … but … he was the Chief's assistant … and he was on the payroll.

There had to be a better way of going about this ongoing battle between the kids on the hill and Chief Perry, Lumus thought and besides, *it was the Chief's problem.* Lumus could care less if those kids slid on that hill until their butts wore out. His only concern was of one of them getting seriously hurt by falling into one of the deep gun pits but in fifteen years of play on the hill no one had fallen it yet.

As Lumus came to a stop by the Chief's car he knew he'd already been spotted by one of the slider's lookouts probably lurking in the thick cane bamboo that grew on the west side of the hill.

Lumus greeted the Chief, "Afternoon, Chief." He hoped he did not sound too condescending. "What's going on?"

"Hi Lumus, sorry to disturb you. I know you were doing some paperwork but it's those kids again. There's a whole bunch of 'em on the front of the hill. I just ran 'em off Thursday and dag-gone-it, they're back already. What's wrong with these kids now days? Don't they have any respect for authority? Next thing you know they'll have their driving license and be running stop signs and who knows what."

Lumus subtlety attempted to defuse the whole situation with a touch of humor. "Yeah Chief, they're a regular bunch of Al Capones … that bunch … yes sir." He chuckled at the stone-faced Chief who glared back at him.

"Well, I tell you what. I'm gonna nail 'em this time because I got a plan. It came to me in the middle of the night, Lumus. Right in the middle of sleeping. Even woke me up so I know it's gonna work."

The Chief was out of his car pacing back and forth, looking around, pointing here and there, rubbing his hands together as though he were about to address the troops … all wired up for action.

Damn, no wonder those Germans didn't have a chance. Lumus thought as he listened to the Chief map out his strategy.

"Now here's what we do, Lumus. You listening?" Lumus nodded but didn't mean it.

"I'll go through the main tunnel, come out near the front, and go up the steps by the front pit and spook 'em from the top. Now you … you … you sneak around to the front going through the cane and wait at the bottom. Don't go all the way to the front … wait on the side over there where the cane is real thick. Know where I'm talking about? You'll hear 'em coming, hooting and a hollering and carrying on."

"Chief, excuse me a second …OK?"

"Yeah. What Lumus, did I leave something out?"

"No, no, Chief. That sounds like a good plan but …before we go blasting off here … u-u-u-h … let me ask you just one thing … O.K?"

"Sure Lumus, what is it?"

"I was just wondering. Is this that bunch led by the Devlin and O'Toole kid?"

"Yep, that's them all right. And you can bet those two skinny little Irish kids will be right there with `em."

"Well Chief, I hate to be the bearer of bad news but there ain't no way you and me gonna catch them. We'd need a battalion of troops and a bunch of back up. And I say this … just between me and you Chief … we don't have much of a chance of catching them. They're just too dog gone slick."

With that said Lumus headed for the Jeep. "Tell you what, Chief. I've got an idea that just might work. You go ahead like you planned and spook 'em but I ain't gonna be in the cane waiting on 'em."

"Where you going then?"

"Give me ten minutes and then you go. I'll catch up with you later at the station …trust me, Chief."

Chief Perry shrugged, scratched his sweaty head and mumbled, "All right, all right, Lumus. Hope you know what you're doing?"

The Chief waited a few minutes giving Lumus time to do whatever it was he was going to do and then set off down through the main tunnel which exited in the front pit. He took the stairs leading out off the pit to the top but halfway up was spotted by a lookout. Well, it wasn't exactly a lookout who spotted the Chief but Robert Dunlap who was in the bushes … u-u-u-h …how you say … tending to nature's call. He hurriedly raised his zipper and the alarm signal. When the Chief appeared on top of the hill the crew scattered like flies from a watermelon. Billy Scott was spooked so bad he went down the hill head first, then feet first, and over again, and again, and again, finally settling in a heap of dust and grass at the bottom looking a little worn for the trip. The Chief, looking down the hill, felt sorry for the poor, dishelved kid almost to the point of apologizing for scaring him so badly.

He yelled down the hill, "Eah, you all right?"

Billy dusted himself off, looked up the hill and realizing he was safe jumped up and screamed, "G-r-e-a-t-t-t God, it's B-u-l-l-l-l Perry!" and did a little dance, waving his arms over his head, turning in circles and at the precise moment stopped, bent over and shot the Chief an imaginary moon.

"Why you little"… muttered the Chief.

Bubba 'n me were leading the pack as we high tailed it to the safety of Burton's Drug Store just down the block with the crew in tow. After our all out sprint and breathing heavily, we gathered outside the store.

"Is everyone here?" I looked around checking to make sure everyone escaped the clutches of the law. "Where's Billy?" someone asked.

"He went home," Timmy said, "he has to go to town with his Mom or something."

"Then that's everybody. Shoot, let's go." Bubba said as he opened the door to Burton's. "I want a cold Cherry Coke."

We were a happy lot. We had outfoxed the police again and it was time to celebrate.

"Could you imagine being caught by Bull Perry? Man, he's so fat he can't even bend over to tie his shoes," John chuckled, then added. "You would be the first person in history to be caught. Your family name would live in shame for generations to come. You hear me, Devlin?"

"Yeah, yeah, yeah. I hear you, John. Next you're gonna say, "And you would be branded for life as a failure to the crew and society as a whole. Right?"

"Eah, how'd you know?"

"Because I'm so smart. That's why." Bubba and Timmy laughed and I playfully slapped John on the shoulder. It wasn't very often I got ahead of John, the brain.

"Eah man," Bubba said, "old Bull Perry was so close to catching me that I could smell his breathe and feel his fingertips on the back of my shirt but then I hit my after- burner and ZOOM …I was gone."

"Really Bubba? And what did his breath smell like?" Timmy asked. "Not that I really want to know but I'm curious."

"It smelt like" … now Bubba is really searching hard for an answer … "like … u-u-u-h … stale doughnuts mixed with old coffee. Yeah, that's exactly what it smelled like." Bubba paused. "There. You satisfied, Timmy."

"Yeah, sure. I was just asking. Don't get bent out of shape … come on let's get something to drink."

Bubba smiled broadly and said, "T-h-a-t-'s right, Catbird."

Burton's Drug Store was more of a general store than a drug store offering Island residents anything from food items to cosmetics and beach apparel. The owners realizing the potential, had converted the right side of the store into a soda fountain, and additions, such as tables and chairs, a pool table and a jukebox were added piecemeal through the years.

For the crew it was *the* place. It served as a meeting place, a sanctuary, and a social club, all rolled into one. It was a place where we could relax and just sit around talking over the accounts of the day, like today's escape from the police, or lay plans for the future. We also shared many a laugh sitting at those tables.

The jukebox was on the far wall and stocked with all the hit songs of the day from Elvis to Jerry Lee Lewis to Fats Domino and we about wore them out. Situated near the jukebox were eight blacktopped tables with small cane chairs and red cushions, four chairs to a table. The pool table was conviently located just off the wooden dance floor and away from the tables. This whole area was in the back corner of the store away from prying eyes and nosey parents who sometimes feigned buying a soda while attempting to eavesdrop on our conversations. When this happened we just clammed up and waited them out … we usually won.

There was a long soda fountain complete with high- backed swivel chairs, which we pushed aside when we placed our orders. None of the crew sat at the fountain. We gathered at the tables in the pool table area leaning back on two legs of the chair like we were some big shots. We had figured out how to play free pool games by lifting the end of the table about six inches off the floor and dropping it, thus tripping the switch which allowed the balls to "freely" roll out. We were still trying to figure out how to play free music on the jukebox but 20th. Century technology was ahead of us there.

Our classmates and friends who made up the crew met here, usually impromptu, just to share our thoughts and dreams and be together. The boys met to talk about the girls while the girls met to talk about the boys talking about the girls. The girls were always a step ahead of us. We played pool and sat around listening to music. However, only the very brave got up and danced. And when we tired of hatching new plans of adventure we just hung out. Today was extra special … we came to celebrate our escape from the police … again.

Bubba 'n me had plopped down at a table in the back and were about to take a sip of our celebratory Coke when out of nowhere I felt a slight tap on my shoulder, a three tapper, that said, "Here I am." I turned my head and none other than Lumus was standing over me, smiling.

Oh my God! What's he doing here? And at our table!

Startled, I looked at Bubba for an answer but his head was down staring at the floor. I thought, *That's right, good buddy ... when the police show up and I need you ... look down at your shoes. Whatcha doing? Counting your shoelaces?*

"Hello boys. How y'all doing?"

"U-u-u-h…pretty good … OK … I guess, Mr. Lumus," I answered nervously. "How you doing?"

"That's good." He looked around. " Nice hangout y'all got here … pool table, music and all. By the way, you don't have to call me Mr. Lumus … you boys can call me Lumus."

"Well, my father always taught me to call adults Mr. or Mrs. because …"

Lumus raised his hand to cut me off. "I'm telling you it's OK to call me by my name … Lumus. Believe me, it's all right." He paused for a second to let what he told us sink in. We nodded still wondering what this was all about.

"H-u-u-m, looks like you boys been running … kinda sweaty there, aren't ya?"

"Yeah …we've … u-u-u-m … been running a lot," I said. "We're … u-u-u-h … trying to get in shape for … u-u-u-h … football tryouts. Yeah, football tryouts. They start in August. We're gonna try out for the JV team … right Bubba?"

"Oh yeah," Bubba said quickly … "that's right. Getting in shape. We've been exercising and running and all … maybe we can make the team," he said nodding his head up and down way too fast.

"That's good, fellas … real good. Y'all keep up the hard work." Lumus turned to walk away. "See y'all later."

"Yeah, see ya later Mr. Lum … uh, Lumus," I said, feeling relieved but puzzled by this strange visit. I looked at Bubba and the baffled look on his face matched mine.

Lumus took a few steps, stopped, turned around and deliberately looked down at our feet, examining our shoes.

"That clay on y'all's shoes … looks just like the stuff over at the hill. Ain't that something?" He paused … looking back and forth at our shoes, which no matter how hard we tried, we couldn't hide.

"And those grass stains on your pants. Those look pretty familiar."

Before we could offer up some lame excuse, Lumus smiled and walked off. Bubba 'n me were looking at each other with open mouths and blank stares.

Lumus stopped again, turned around with a raised finger and said, "Uh … one more thing. Do you boys really want to get in shape for football?"

"Oh yeah," we answered in unison. "We sure do."

"Good. Good. I thought y'all did. Then running up the hill after you've slid down might be some good exercise?" Lumus smiled, gave us a wink, and left.

6
RETRIBUTION

Bubba 'n me left Burton's and spent the rest of the afternoon messing around at the Breach Inlet checking on the crabbers and fishermen and looking for lost fishing riggings lodged in the rocks from fishermen who had gotten hung up and were forced to pop their lines. We didn't find any which was a rare occurrence. Someone, who needed them worse than us, had beaten us to them.

We were still a little shaken by Lumus' strange and completely unexpected visit at Burton's, still not sure what to make of his talk with us. Did he really know we had been on the hill? If so, why didn't he do something? Or was he telling our parents about it right now? We agreed to think about it for a while, like we did everything we did not understand, and then talk about it later, which we never did.

It was getting late, near suppertime at the Devlin household so we started back home. I had built up a really good appetite playing on the hill and pedaling hard in a spirited bike race with Bubba from Station 23 to our houses at Station 18. Bubba, as usual, won again. That boy ought to go out for The Olympics in bike riding. He had strong legs that never seemed to get tired.

We were winded as we rolled to a stop in his backyard. Our normal, lengthy conversation summing up the day and laying plans for the next day was cut short to a wave goodbye and a "see ya tomorrow."

O-o-o-h, I didn't want to be late for supper … or else. No, I wouldn't get punished. A far worse ordeal awaited me if I were late, far worse. I wouldn't get anything to eat. When my mother said, "Supper's ready," she meant it and it was time to eat. And if you were late then too bad. At each meal our mother gave the group gathered around the table two choices concerning the meal. They were: Take it or leave it.

Of all the talents us Devlin children possessed the one most evident on a day in day out basis was eating. We held a backseat to no one, mind you, no one. And any stragglers to the table could moan and groan all they wanted about there not being any food left but it was not going to bring back the meal resting comfortably in some one else's full stomach or relieve the growls of the empty stomach of the one who was late. We kids kind of looked forward to one of the family missing a meal. It meant for an extra serving to be fought over.

As I crossed the back porch I could not help but notice a ghostly silence in the house and at first I panicked. Durn, they're already eating. It was one of the few times the Devlin clan was quiet, when their mouths were full. Then I heard a loud cheer, the signal to begin eating, and knew they had been saying grace. PHEW! That was close ... I had just made it.

Before I even opened the door I could tell what was for supper. My nose told me it was beef stew over rice, a staple we ate two, sometimes three times a week without the first complaint. It was a balanced meal full of carrots, onions, meat, and potatoes and was delicious, melting in your mouth. The aroma of homemade biscuits added to the culinary delight. And it was a cheap way to feed a crowd. You see, money was an issue in our house and with six kids to clothe and feed on a daily basis on a limited income ... well, we were grateful for all we had.

I was the last Devlin to the table, as usual.

"Where you been? Didn't I tell you we would eat at six? You hungry? Wash up and come on."

It was my mother and I didn't know where to begin so I said, "Yes Ma'am," hoping I covered all bases. Eight people gathered at the worn and beaten old table every evening ... eight! That's a lot of people to feed everyday but some how, some way, we ate and ate well, never going hungry. The TV was in the front room, silent, like every evening at this time. We gathered, gave thanks and ate as a family. Not always as an agreeable family but still as a family. And following the meal when everything was cleaned up, dishes washed and dried, then and only then, was the TV turned on, much to our delight.

The four girls lined up like combatants on one side of the table while Ryan, my older brother, and myself defended the other side. My parents sat at opposite ends acting as referees during our frequent skirmishes.

On a rare occasion a piece of round steak was left after everyone was about finished eaten.

"I'm gonna eat that last piece," yelled Emily, stabbing at it with her fork.

"Sorry Charlie," countered Ryan, "but that's mine." He made a move for Emily's fork with his own.

I spotted an opening. "Uh-uh, neither one of you. It's mine," I replied and made the mistake of grabbing for the delicious piece of meat with a bare hand.

Katie whacked me on my outstretched hand with a spoon and screamed, "You done ate enough, you old pig. That's mine."

"That's mine! That's mine!" screeched baby Sara. "That's mine!"

"OK, OK," I relented just to shut up the wining Sara. "Good grief you would think it was gold," I added. "Go ahead Sara ... you can have it ... it's yours."

Immediately Emily and Katie folded their arms and went into their pout mode.

"Tell y'all what I'm gonna do." It was my father speaking. "I'm gonna buy a whistle and wear it around my neck just like the referees do in a basketball game and I'm gonna blow it everytime there's an argument. Are y'all listening? I'm gonna make my ruling so we can move the meal on in peace … I hope."

"Well, Mr. Devlin." It was my mother's turn. "If you get to have a whistle then I get one too, only bigger."

"Oh yeah," my father said and then asked, "why bigger than mine?"

"Because I cooked the meal. That's why," my mother said in no uncertain terms. "Am I clear on that?"

"Very clear. It's true you might have cooked the meal but I bought the food so that entitles me to make any call I want. How about that?"

"Well, it's my kitchen" came the reply from my determined mother. " How about that?"

We kids sat back grinning and elbowing each other in the sides, trying hard to stifle our giggles as they began to argue over ownership of everything from the chairs to the toilet. I think in the final analysis my father ended up with the boat and the motor, which was fine with him … and me too.

Today's meal began with the normal taunting from the girls toward Ryan and me. They were clever little rascals and would lean across the table and whisper their provoking words, laced with acid and rolling from a spiteful tongue.

"Who's your girlfriend now, Mike?" Emily asked with a sneer. "I bet it's fat old Betty Big Bottom." Emily nudged Katie who giggled. Little Sara did too.

"N-o-o-o." Katie chimed in. "I bet it's ugly old four-eyed Cecilia. That's who. Huh, Mike?"

I did not say a word. Ryan gave me a glance and a small smile.

There was a noticeable pause and then they tried to get a rise out of Ryan.

"Ryan," Katie said softly, "you don't have a girlfriend, do you?"

"No. Not a girlfriend, Katie but he's got a boyfriend," Emily said sarcastically and I know who it is."

"Oh yeah," Katie asked, "who?"

"Sambo. That's S-A-M with the big B-O." And they laughed and pointed their fingers at us.

Ryan gave me another smile and did not say a word to the girls.

"Hey, Mike. Gonna take Big Betty or Cecilia to the movies," Emily mumbled. She paused and then added. "You better take Cecilia because you don't have enough money to feed Big Betty. She would eat all the popcorn and candy. A-HA-HA-HA!"

Katie checked to see if Mom was watching then stuck her tongue out at me and said, “You don’t have to worry about taking anybody to the movies because you’re too ugly. Nobody would go with you except stupid old Bubba.”

“Yeah,” Emily agreed. “The Two Stooges. That’s what y’all are. Right Katie?”

Katie did not hear Emily’s plea so she looked at Sara and asked, “Right, Sara?”

“Yeah, you right.” Sara said. “You right.”

Ryan and I had figured out a long time ago that if we clammed up and ignored the girls which was hard to do in light of some of the sharp insults hurled our way, then they would eventually lose interest in us and would attack their own. And that’s what happened as Ryan and I silently ignored their taunts and ate our stew.

“Leave me alone!” Katie yelled at Emily. “What do you think you’re doing?”

“I’m not doing anything to you,” defended Emily. “I’m eating my supper, dummy.”

“Yes you are … you’re looking at me. Quit it.”

Sissy, the oldest, tried to make peace. Big mistake. “Why don’t y’all look at your plate when you eat?”

“Why don’t you shut up?” It was Emily the instigator. “Look at your own plate.”

“Yeah, who asked you?” chimed in Katie. “Ain’t none of your beez-ness.”

Baby Sara entered the fray, “Yeah, shud up.”

“M-o-m-m-m,” Emily pleaded, “tell Katie to quit kicking me.”

I could tell by the smirk on Ryan’s face it wasn’t Katie who was kicking Emily.

Then I cut my eyes up at Ryan and smiled and he gave me the OK. I gave Katie a good kick in the shin as I looked down at my plate and took another bite of my beef stew.

“Emily!” shouted Katie, “ I’m gonna kill you up if you touch me again … you hear me?”

Ryan jumped at the chance and let Katie have another one. That’s when Katie reached around Sara and grabbed Emily by the hair and pulled her over backwards out of the chair spilling onto the floor. Katie was on Emily like white on rice or you might say ugly on a gorilla. Emily was yelling and carrying on, struggling to get Katie off of her, the whole time making vile threats while taking a licking from her little sister.

Sara started squealing, “W-A-A -H… W-A-A-H.”

Ryan and I sat back grinning.

Sissy was trying to get Katie off Emily. “Now Katie, you know better than to fight at the table. Katie quickly let Sissy have a fist right on the nose ... BOOP!

Sara, still screaming, then threw a spoonful of stew at Emily who was wrestling with Sissy. Emily had managed to get Katie off of her and was beginning a comeback. She had a handful of Katie's hair and was pulling her across the floor.

My father, the wise man that he was, had pushed back his chair when the ruckus started and without saying a word retired to the front room seeking a sane place to read his paper. He knew better than to get in the middle of this.

My mother stood up and yelled: "That's it!" And it was over as quickly as it started.

Ryan and I grinning from ear to ear poked each other in the ribs, happy as clowns. We gulped down our last bites of stew, excused ourselves, and ran outside while the girls were ordered to clean up and do the dishes. Ryan and I had a good laugh about starting the trouble with the girls because it was not often we got one over on them. Usually it was the other way around. The girls were smart and would wait until Ryan or I were alone then go into their act. Just being in the same room with them when they started playing and screaming and yelling got under my skin. And they constantly rummaged through our possessions taking whatever they wanted and usually ended up breaking it. If we dared to lift a finger against them, then they would go yelling and hollering to my mother claiming that we were picking on them. Then my mother punished us. That was bad enough but the worst part was enduring the smirks and laughs from the girls while we were being punished, which was usually confinement to our room, for the rest of the day.

While we were rejoicing about Emily and Katie fighting it reminded me of an incident at school that was just as funny as pulling one over on the girls. It had been the final week of school and the crew was aiming for a grand finale, something spectacular to end the school year with, something outstanding to leave the good nuns of O.L.M., something that would stick in their memory for the entire summer, if not their entire lives. Earlier in the school year Bubba 'n me and the crew had pulled off the Ex-lax incident and it had gone over great but lost a bit of its luster and proved not to be so spectacular or monumental when I learned later from Ryan that the Ex-lax trick was as old as Sister Roberta. It turned out that every eighth grade class for the past five years had at least tried it with moderate success.

Ryan told me, "Shoot, those nuns had drank enough Ex-lax to clean 'em out for a lifetime. Why don't you guys get together and come up with something *really* new?"

"Like what?" I asked. We thought we had tried every trick in the book.

"I don't know. Why don't you check with your dumb One Stooge friend across the street? I bet he could come up with something good." It sounded like more of a dare than a suggestion.

"Eah, watch how you talk about Bubba. He's my friend and besides, he's really a smart guy."

"Smart. That boy. Why he's about as smart as a load of bricks… that's how smart he is"

"Humph! Look who's talking … Mister Geometry."

Ryan put on an angry scowl and walked away. I was making reference to his failing Geometry, an extremely sore spot with him.

In a way Ryan was right. Not about Bubba being dumb but about talking to Bubba and coming up with something spectacular to do. It was a Sunday morning and right after Mass I planned to get together with Bubba and see if we could come up with an idea.

My father yelled from the yard, "Come on, boy, hurry up. You gonna be late for your own funeral."

"I'm coming, Daddy, just a minute. Now Mollie, you stay here and I'll be back in a little while". Like always she gave me that hangdog look whenever I left without her. "Tell ya what I'll do, Mollie. You listening? I'll check with Father Dawes again about bringing you to church. How's that?" Her ears perked up for a second and then she plopped down and closed her eyes. "You ain't never gonna get to heaven with an attitude like that, girl."

"M-i-k-e … let's go."

"Bye, Mollie."

This Sunday my father decided to take the Devlin children to church in the company laundry truck. Our car, he told me was sick. " Had a mild heart attack," he joked, "and it needed to rest." Everyone minus my mother was piling into the truck and Ryan grabbed my hand helping me aboard. The big green truck was one of those with the sliding side doors, like a modern day UPS truck, but this one was empty of cargo and had two steel bars, one on each side, running from the back to the front acting as racks for the dry cleaning my father delivered. I rode sitting on the engine cowl next to my father. Ryan rode shotgun standing in the open door making sure none of the bouncing and screaming little Devlins fell out the truck. The girls, except for prissy Ms. Sissy, would swing on the bars banging into the side of the truck with their Sunday- best shoes, sounding like sledgehammers and then drop to the floor of the truck, run around in a circle and jump up onto the other rack with extended arms and do it again. Yelling and screaming, as usual. They looked like the monkeys at the zoo except they were dressed in what were once neatly pressed clean dresses that my mother hoped would make a good impression at church. With all the racket and noise going on, thank goodness the church was only a three-minute drive away.

Of all the unlikely and improbable places to develop an idea for our last escapade at school, it would turn out to be at church. Who would have ever thought it? Not me. Not in a million years. But … it was during Father Dawes' sermon that I noticed a peculiar but recognizable, unwanted odor as it silently made its way up and down the rows of pews amongst its captive audience, invisible but noticeable and deadly. Shoot, I knew immediately what it was. Its odor was so bad a dead person would have noticed it. The crew were experts at spreading this form of deadly fumes but they weren't in church at the moment, however, they were in my thoughts as my little brain started to work on an idea. As I breathed the vile air, I watched several of the adults around me twitching their noses and making feeble attempts at erasing the stench by rubbing their noses. It didn't help. The gas in the air was like a cold and had to play itself out. And like a cold there was no cure for it as it spread throughout the congregation. Someone had let go a real whopper but we would never know who it was unless the guilty party stood up in front of the congregation and announced, "Yep, it was me, I did it … I dropped it … stinks huh?" It was a Silent But Deadly of the boiled egg and beer variety. I looked up and down the pews searching for the culprit and narrowed it down to Mr. Jennings or Mr. Kiler. The ladies seated around me looked too dainty and saint- like to be dropping deadly gas at Mass. Probably old man Kiler? He was known to hang out at Chippys and drink beer. But I don't know if he ate boiled eggs? Because it was so bad I think Father Dawes cut short his sermon. And the coughing from the rear of the small church wasn't from a winter cold. A good ol' SBD … that's what it was … right there in church and that's when the thought hit me about what we could do at school for our grand finale. Right there when Father Dawes said, "To do unto others as they have done unto you" or something like that?

I couldn't wait to see the crew at school. Early Monday morning I rounded them up and told them of my idea. Everyone was excited and thought it a good idea especially Bubba. He loved the idea of stinking up the class and giving one of Our Ladies of Mercy a faceful of nasty farts without her knowing who to blame. He said it would be *a gas* and we all laughed at his clever yet unintended double entendre. All that day we were serenaded by Bubba's prophetic jingle: "Beans, beans, the musical fruit … the more you eat the more you poot."

But we left most of the planning up to John, the brainchild of the crew. The big problem or question was: When will we do this? In what class? By the end of the day he came up with the details of a plan of how we could carry out this most devious of attacks. And maybe, just maybe, pull it off without getting caught.

I had always thought the older a person got the smarter they got. Well …that certainly was not the case with the crew, uh-uh. It seemed to me that we were getting dumber because after a heated discussion of the inner circle of the crew we decided to target none other than Sister Roberta with this latest attack. She was about the meanest white woman on two legs and taught us English *and* was the principal. No one ever messed with Sister Roberta … no one! Yes sir, we were going for the downs, swinging for the fence. We planned on hitting a grand slam. Being the smart young Einsteins of the world we decided that we would pull our little trick on the last day of school, which was about the only smart part of our plan because that way if we got caught, well… so what? What could Sister do?

The big finale. To tell the truth there was not much really to plan. It called for everyone to eat *all* the pork and beans they could possibly stuff in themselves the night before and then pack an extra can or two in their lunch bag for the next day as backup material. English class met right after lunch and by that time we figured we would be loaded with ammunition and ready to blast off. That Thursday night I snuck a can of pork and beans into bed with me, pulled the sheet over my head and commenced to fill myself with that powerful potion.

Ryan showed up in my room and jerking back the sheet asked, "What in the world are you doing? Didn't you eat enough supper?"

"U-h-h-h, yeah" …Ryan was eyeing the can of beans. "Oh … that," I said, … "that's for Mollie."

"For Mollie, huh?" Ryan reached down and picked up the spoon. "And since when does Mollie eat with one of these?"

"Oh … u-u-u-h … all right." I knew I had been caught. "It's mine," I said and then I proceeded to tell Ryan about our plan and what we were going to do at school and he laughed silly.

"Eah, that's pretty good … pretty good. Tell you what you do if you really want to stink 'em up. Eat some boiled eggs too. "W-o-o-o-e-e … bad." He was holding his nose.

I pulled the sheet off me and was ready to eat a dozen eggs right then and there.

"No, not now … in the morning at breakfast. Give 'em time to settle in and then do their work later."

"O-o-o-h … I see. How come you know about all this? Y'all done this before at school?"

"Nope. I promise. We haven't ever done this before. Good luck … goodnight."

H-u-m-m, I thought, *boiled eggs and beans?* Sounds like a good combination to me. "Goodnight Mollie."

"Boiled eggs? What are you talking about?" The tone of my mother's voice told me I was not going to be getting any boiled eggs for breakfast.

"The only time you ever ate a boiled egg was at Easter. What's with you? Besides Mike, you don't want to eat those things … they'll give you gas, O.K? Eat your oatmeal and get out of here."

"Yes Ma'am." I didn't argue. Besides, I had eaten the whole can of beans the night before, down to the last bean fighting Mollie away the whole time.

Ryan peeked up over his fork from across the table and smiled at me. And when my mother turned around he lifted his leg and mockingly let go a fart.

Katie squealed, "Ryan's pooting again."

"Am not," Ryan said. "Why don't you eat and shut up for once?"

"I saw you … you was pooting at the table."

Sara giggled, stuck out her tongue and tried to make a farting sound ending up slobbering oatmeal all over the front of her dress.

"Oh you kids. You're gonna be the death of me yet. Sara! What are you doing?" She wiped Sara's face and shooed us from the table telling us we would miss the bus if we didn't hurry and run.

Our gas-filled crew met at recess and finalized our plan over our last cans of beans. All but Jocko who had a certain urge to go to the bathroom and couldn't hold it back. He showed up just before recess was over and proudly announced that the beans were taking effect and if what he just experienced was any indication of things to come he might just cut school and go home right now.

"Bad huh?" Timmy inquired.

"Bad? How's that conjugation go … bad, worse, worse? Well, that was the *worseest*! I almost got sick. That smell would gag a maggot."

"Maybe we should call this thing off if it's that stinky?" Bubba halfway suggested, without giving it much thought. "Whatta you think?"

"Bubba, think for a second, will ya. How you gonna call it off?" John shot back. "Talk to your ass and say, "Eah, look don't pass no gas today while I'm in English class, OK? Mother Nature is gonna take her course whether we like it or not."

We all nodded, not so much in agreement that we wanted to carry this out but in agreement that Mother Nature would take her course.

Jammed in the doorway after recess we reminded each other to drop only SBD's, don't cut no noisemakers. That was part of the master plan. That way Sister Roberta wouldn't know who was doing what.

At precisely 12:35 the classroom door swung open and the frowning Sister Roberta, the one who was never late and never failed NOT to smile, strutted to the front of the class, opened her text and began class. We had forty-five minutes to do our thing having agreed to begin our assault when Timmy raised his hand and asked to be excused already knowing the answer would be an emphatic "No" followed by "Why do you think we give you thirty minutes for recess?"

Well, things got off to an auspicious beginning. *Somebody* jumped the gun. It came from nowhere and like a good SBD it did its job thoroughly, engulfing you, surrounding you with its smell like a low hanging, thick cloud. My first reaction was, "It must have been someone close to me because it was deadly, a lingerer. I waved my hands at it but it just wouldn't go away. I even thought for a second about breathing through my mouth but the very thought of inhaling that stinking gas stopped my breathing all together. And then I had to take a deep breath through the nose … oh man, o-o-o-wee.

I looked around for the gun-jumper and sure enough there sat Bubba stone-faced as a granite statue. Our eyes met for a second and I asked him if it was him and his look said, "Yeah … couldn't hold it … sorry."

I suppose Timmy thought what the heck, "It's not time but somebody has let" … so … he raised his hand and received his answer from Sister Roberta.

Bubba's original silent blast was but a pittance of what was to come: ten of the crew, nine without Jocko (who we later found out still had it in him to participate slightly) began our attack. People would put their hands on the top of their desk, push up slightly, lean to one side to allow the escape of the deadly gas, ease back down, give it a quick fan with the hand when Sister wasn't looking and then smile broadly. Within minutes the room was completely saturated with a smell so offensive I thought for sure someone had missed a good chance at going to the bathroom to really relieve themselves. O-o-o-o-h … me –oh- my … it was terrible and I immediately began to have second thoughts about having come up with this stupid idea. Most body gas odors might remain for a minute or so and then it's over like the one in church Sunday. Not this smell, uh-uh. It hung around like a lost puppy that had just been fed.

Our poor unsuspecting classmates, those not in on this caper, had their fingers over their noses looking around the room for the culprit or culprits. All they saw were serious looking members of the crew sitting up in their desks following Sister Roberta's lesson word for word. John even had the nerve to raise his hand and ask a question about the lesson in hopes of deflecting the blame from himself.

I did a quick survey of the class to see how they were holding up under this horrendous barrage of some of the worst SBD's ever to gain entry into the world of fresh air. The crew seemed to be coping all right but some of the girls weren't faring so well. Their eyes were watering and then the coughing began sounding like a tuberculosis ward. The boys, maybe because they were more accustomed to the odor from passing gas all the time, were breathing heavy but nothing like the poor girls from whom we would get an earful later about this nasty caper.

And when I noticed Tiny Mulhaven, all three hundred or more pounds of him, lift his fat leg slowly, hold it there for a second and then ease it down and smile I knew it was all over but the crying. What we had been forced to sniff up to this point was perfume compared to what Tiny let loose in *that* room *that* day. It was so bad it chased all the other smells completely out the room … they couldn't stand it. *Why, he was not even in on the plan,* I thought? *How did he know what to do?* We learned later that he *wasn't* in on the deal at all. He was just dropping one on his own. One he said that he had been holding the whole school year and being the last day of school and being in Sister Roberta's class … well, it was all the reason he needed.

And Tiny's emittance did it for poor Mary Rogers who sat directly behind Tiny. After a few whiffs of what Tiny had let pass, she freaked out. She jumped up out of her desk with watery eyes and began fanning the air with her English book.

Violating Sister Roberta's most strict rule of silence in the classroom she shouted out, "I can't stand it. No more. It's awful! Not one more second!" Her eyes rolled up in her head as though she was praying to the Almighty and she wailed, "Ahhhhh!" As she frantically ran up and down the aisle trying to escape the deadly fumes, she yelled and hollered like a person possessed by some kind of demon. She even scared me. I ducked and hid behind my notebook as she ran by. She was gasping for air and when she inhaled deeply after a scorching, lengthy tirade directed at us "awful, nasty, nasty, boys" she looked as though she was going to keel over. She stopped, got quiet and stood still. Her eyes had a blank look like she was gazing out into space. Appearing completely exhausted and white as a ghost, she shook her finger at Jocko who couldn't keep a smile off his face. She then wobbled back to her desk in time to sit down and faint dead out, sliding out of her desk onto the floor.

Jocko said, "Mary, I love you too, honey" in his best Elvis voice "and I'd marry ya today but you smell too bad." The class howled.

Sister Roberta who had put up a brave and stoic front to this point agreed with Mary and gave us a piece of her mind while trying to pick up the sprawled-out Mary Rogers and at the same time waving her hand, trying to clear the air in hopes of some relief. The crew sat where we were and thoroughly enjoyed the moment. It was the first time Sister Roberta did not know who to blame for the trouble and we could tell she was flustered, which made the whole scene even that more enjoyable.

Sister Roberta, seeing that she was not going to get any help, stood up and yelled, "All of you! Get out of here now! Go home … and pray!" All the while she was dragging Mary into the hall in search of breathable air. We cheered loudly and patted each other on the back as we headed for the door. The crew could not get out of there fast enough.

And by that afternoon we had gathered at Burton's to celebrate our victory. Oh man, we sang to Elvis' records, even dared to dance, guzzled down our Cherry Cokes, and had a good old time. We smiled and laughed the afternoon away. What a way to start the summer.

Ryan and I laughed again as we sat under the tree recalling the passing gas episode and vowed hopefully to come up with something as good for the little Devlin girls. We agreed to give it some thought. As we started back inside, we could hear the girls even though we were still on the back porch. They were racing through the house, yelling, slamming doors with tremendous enthusiasm. They were probably playing their favorite game again, tag. We called it The slamming –the-doors game.

I heard Emily scream to no one in particular, “Where’s Mike and Ryan?” I froze when I heard my name. Ryan did the same. We just stood still looking hopefully at each other, hoping not to be discovered.

I then recognized Katie’s screaming voice. “I don’t know”? But when I find them I’m gonna get ’em”

O-o-o-h no. I thought. *“Not again.”*

7
THE GIRLS

When I was forced to stay inside the house, which only happened when my parents were punishing me, I felt like a prisoner in a jail cell. A person with no rights or opinions or options. My whole psyche, even my soul, was at the mercy of the unrelenting wardens who roamed the halls of the house as they roamed the halls of my mind in search of mayhem and persecution. My wardens, my tormentors, the affable, sweet little Devlin girls, had control over me physically and worst of all mentally. The only part of me that they had not stolen yet was my spirituality but they were working hard on that. My failure as a grown adult to be able to stay indoors for an extended period of time without experiencing an anxiety attack, I believe, had its deep and sad origins from those bleak days in the Devlin house when I curled up under a sheet and prayed the girls would not find me, which was a stupid thought on my part but it lent credence to just how desperate I had become. The darkness under that sheet was as false a piece of security ever invented by a twelve- year-old but it was all I had. Even when they would charge into my room hollering and yelling and rip the sheet from me I would hold my eyes shut tight, retaining the darkness, and hope by some miracle from God that when I opened my eyes they would be gone.

Today I was not being punished by my parents but was restricted to the house because of the weather. It was raining cats and dogs with no relief in sight. A stalled low-pressure system hovering over the Lowcountry meant my life was stalled for a day, stuck in the house, my prison. I had nowhere to go, no place to hide, nowhere to escape from their endless questions, their bountiful playfulness and their beautiful innocence. I was trapped and knew it. Worse was that I was trapped and *they* knew it. Males, even little boys like me, when put in a situation out of their element and placed in one of isolation can find things to do to occupy themselves or, if push came to shove, find something to do to amuse themselves. Females, on the other hand, if they cannot find something to do then they create something. And my three younger sisters, age three, nine and ten, created havoc from the time they cracked their eyelids open in the morning until they exhausted themselves and succumbed to the demands of sleep, usually late at night. My sisters were a spirited group that was constantly on the go having fun and they always laughed a lot. I guess they were happy kids.

Emily, the oldest of my younger sisters, had a distinctive hardy, deep laugh like a HA-HA type. Katie, age nine, was more of a squealer, a high-pitched squealing laugh like a baby pig. And Sara, three years old, giggled all the time no matter the occasion.

As I lay in bed half awake rubbing Mollie's head I heard their advance down the hall toward my room. The rise in concerted laughter drowned out their heavy footsteps as they approached my door, the door with no lock. I told Mollie to get ready. Here they come. Mollie jumped off the bed without hesitation and dove for cover underneath the bed. She had been privy to the morning wake up call from the Devlin girls before and did not need much encouragement.

They burst into my room like a gang of gung- ho firemen going through a door into a smoky house with pick axes. Thank God the girls didn't have any pick axes. All three rushed the bed and piled on top of me as I hustled under the sheet and got into a crouching position holding my arms over my head. They played ride -'em -cowboy, pin the tail on the donkey except they pinched me instead of using a real pin and then they performed their rendition of the Saturday Night fights using me as the punching bag. Once they managed to pull the sheet off me then I had a fighting chance … well, somewhat. I would wrestle and fight with them trying hard not to hurt their fragile little bodies and in the end they would pin me and make me holler "uncle", which thrilled them to death.

After unpiling it would always be Katie the wildcat who would holler, " Let's do it again."

They would all agree with a big laugh, retreat outside and regroup in the hallway and charge again. I would be waiting under the sheet and go through the same routine with the same ending. This process continued until all three had given the command "let's do it again" and they never got tired, only more energized. And I dutifully played my part as their object of affection. What else could I do? Shoot, I had no choice.

Following the third and final charge of the morning commanded by Sara who said, "Do agin," my mother stuck her head in the door and delivered the bad news: "Sissy is going to work with me today and Ryan is helping Father Dawes most of the day so you will have to look after the girls until we get back."

"Oh God," I thought, "What will I do? No. No. I must have misunderstood what Mom said."

"You mean me?" I pointed at myself. "You want me to watch the girls …but what will I do, Mom?"

"Yeah you. Look after the girls, that's what."

"Yeah, look after us, Mike," yelled Emily picking up my pillow and delivering a perfectly placed blow up side my head. "Didn't you hear,

Mom?" she added.

I fell back on the bed like I was knocked out, not moving a muscle.

"Good shot, Em," Katie said inspecting me carefully. "I think you knocked him out?" Then she squealed and jumped on me full force landing on my stomach. Sara followed and then Emily.

"That's good, Mike. Just keep playing like that and everything will be OK." My mother chuckled and left. She hollered back as she and Sissy were leaving, "And don't forget to feed the girls. We gotta go. Call me if you need anything. Bye."

"All right, ladies. Up! Y'all get up. I gotta get dressed and let Mollie out. Then I'll fix y'all some breakfast."

"Mike, can we fix breakfast," Emily said with a hopeful gaze. "We've watched Mom plenty of times. Please … let us … p-l-e-a-s-e?"

"Yeah," Katie chimed in. "It's easy … please … OK?"

"What you think, Sara?" I asked bending over and tweaking her cheek. "Can y'all cook breakfast?"

Sara looked down, put her finger in her mouth and gave it some thought. Looking up with those big beautiful blue eyes she said, "Peez?"

"OK …y'all go ahead. I'll be there in a little bit," I said against my better judgment. "I gotta get dressed …now y'all get."

It didn't take long to get dressed and let Mollie out. And it didn't take the Devlin girls long to start the day with a bang. The smell from the kitchen was familiar. It was that of pancakes. However, the trail of smoke coming from the kitchen was my first real clue that something was not right. And the sight I encountered was not what I expected as I ran into the kitchen. The pancakes were black and getting blacker by the second. I caught Emily just as she was about to dose the whole frying pan with a big glass of water she had tilted over the skillet.

"N-o-o-o," I yelled. Emily, give me that!" I grabbed the water from her and at the same time grabbed the skillet and pulled it off the burner. I turned off the stove then.

I looked around the kitchen and pancake batter was everywhere: a steady stream was on the floor where it had dripped from the table across the room, batter was dripping from the ceiling, it was all over the stove and even in Sara's hair. She stood motionless staring at the stove, wiping her face smearing more of her potential breakfast all over herself.

Katie was grinning, pointing at Emily who was grinning too, pointing at Katie.

"I know, I know," I said looking at both of them. "She did it … right?"

No one answered. And Sara was still staring at the stove.

"C'mon. Let's clean up this mess." I began searching for some rags. "Thought y'all said this was easy? I bet y'all never saw Mom cook pancakes like this?"

They leaped into action. Emily appeared with a towel from the bathroom while Katie grabbed a mop and started wiping the floor. Then I noticed the smoke billowing from the oven.

"O-o-o-o-h no! Y'all didn't?" I pulled open the oven door and was engulfed with smoke from a plate of burning pancakes resting in eternal peace, burnt to a crisp. It dawned on me that they were the concern of Sara and without my asking she pointed and said, "Mine."

I gave Emily and Katie the look.

"Well, Sara wanted to help too, Mike," Emily said in a voice of sincere innocence. "Those are hers."

Sara looked at me and agreed whole-heartedly. "Mine!" she said and then giggled.

"Have y'all got anything else cooking in here?" I asked and pulled the pancakes from the oven. "Here Emily, take all of these outside and give 'em to the birds."

"What we gonna eat?" Katie asked looking around for something else to cook.

"Nothin' for right now … nothin'. You hear me? Y'all just go to your room and … and find something to do. I'll tell you what. Y'all go clean up your room. I'll clean this up. Man, y'all are a mess."

"Yeah, let's clean up our room," Katie yelled. They laughed and bolted for their room.

After making the kitchen as presentable as possible I decided to clean up my room too, a good rainy day job.

Peace and quiet was restored for a while until I heard small giggles and laughter coming from the girls' room. Light banter, nothing loud. They must be OK I thought. I'll check on 'em later. Leaving my room to let Mollie in from the rain I heard shouts and yelling of the loud variety coming from the girls, which meant only one thing … trouble!

I opened their door and made a quick assessment. Clothes pulled from the dresser drawers were strewn all over the room, their beds were a mess, and a layer of feathers from two busted pillows blanketed the room like a fresh fallen snow. Emily and Katie dropped the torn pillowcases and made a dash to hide under their beds. Sara, as usual, stood looking at me giggling.

"Emily! Katie! Y'all come here right now!" I demanded. "Come here!" I looked under the bed.

"We ain't here." It was Emily wanting to play. Then Katie mocked Emily.

Sara tugged at my shirt and serious as a heart attack said, "They ain't here, Mike."

"They're not, huh Sara? Tell you what little one, you come with me and help me clean up my room and I'll give you three dollars … OK?" I spoke loud enough to make sure Emily and Katie heard me.

Within seconds Emily and Katie rolled out from under their beds and offered profusely to help me clean my room.

"Not until y'all clean this room up spic and span. And then maybe I'll think about it."

They leaped into action.

I had no intention of paying them any amount of money to clean my room. And besides, I was so poor I didn't even know what a five-dollar bill looked like. "C'mon, Sara let's go."

I had learned a long time ago that trickery, mixed with an occasional lie, had to be a part of my arsenal if I was to have a chance to stay a step ahead of this trio. And my devious little mind would be pushed to its limits today.

"Here Sara, you sweep and I'll make the bed and clean the rest … OK?" I said handing her the broom that towered over her like a flagpole. She looked so cute and innocent, which deep down she was, trying to manage the tall broom and be helpful. Her swaying long blonde hair matched the back and forth motion of the broom head as she made her way around the room in a childlike dance of perfect proportions. What a cutie.

"Sara, you stay here. I'll be right back. I gotta go check on something … OK?"

"OK … I sweep eberyting. Mollie too." Then she giggled. "OK?"

"All right, just don't hurt Mollie."

The something I had to check on was Emily and Katie. I tip-toed down the hall and peeked in on them. They were sitting in the middle of the floor picking up the feathers one by one and depositing them in a wastebasket, probably hatching some wicked plan of what they were going to do with them when they were finished. A damp cloth or rag would have been much easier and quicker but leaving well enough alone was something else I had learned over the years about dealing with my sisters. So I crept silently back to the safety of my room. Sara was not there. My heart jumped, did a little dance, and then sank.

"Oh God! Where is she?" I glanced around the room. "Sara!" I yelled. "Where are you?" My room was small enough to check with a glance or two and it was obvious she was not in the bed or hiding behind the chest of drawers, which was jammed against the wall. Under the bed. It's the *only* place she could be if she were in the room. I flipped the overhanging spread and to my complete relief there she was cuddled up with Mollie, both fast asleep. Again I left well enough alone and continued to clean my room.

By lunchtime I knew the girls would be starving having gone without breakfast but I decided to wait for them to make the call for food. After picking up ten thousand feathers I guess Emily and Katie were ready for something to eat when they came to my room seeking fuel to energize

their fading bodies.
Sometimes their innocence and absolute desire to do what was right was not always perceived as such. Like when they sincerely offered to make lunch assuring me they were quite capable and had watched Mom do it a hundred times.
I flat told Emily and Katie that from now on when I was babysitting I'd be the one making the meals. No more burnt pancakes for me.

"A-w-w, you won't let us do nothin'," Emily pouted and then sought assurance from Katie. "Right, Katie?" Katie was about to back up her sister until she saw me giving her the look. She shrugged her shoulders, looked down at the floor and shuffled off to the kitchen.

"T-h-a-t-'s right, Catbird." I told Emily. "Y'all can't do nothing." Then I remembered the sleeping Sara. "Sara, wake up. Let's eat! Sara! Wake up!" Mollie stirred waking up Sara who looked surprised about her whereabouts.

"All right, ladies. I'm gonna fix y'all's lunch. Y'all have a choice today. You can have either peanut butter and jelly or jelly and peanut butter sandwiches. Which will it be?"

Katie was pondering the choice by looking at the ceiling. Sara with wide eyes was thinking about her preference with her finger in her mouth. Emily had just about figured out there was no difference in what I offered and was about to let her sisters in on my deceit when Katie suddenly spoke up, "I want peanut butter and jelly."

"Me too," Sara yelled.

"How about you, Emily? I asked with a silly grin like I was mocking her.

Emily looked at me with a straight serious face and said, "I want both." Then it was her turn to grin. *Durn, duped again,* I thought. *And by a ten year old.* But I didn't flinch. I took her rightful indignation and asked Emily, "Which one would you like first?" *HA*-HA *got you back*, I thought.

"Either one … it doesn't matter to me … should it?" Emily said and smiled.

I gave up and made the sandwiches. Meanwhile Sara had stuck her whole tiny little hand down inside the peanut butter jar and was thoroughly enjoying her pre- meal snack. Half of the peanut butter was in her mouth and the other half spread across her face. Yep, and she was giggling.

I stepped onto the back porch to check on the rain and it was steady coming down like a waterfall. Huge pools were forming in the low spots in the yard. I went inside and turned on the TV to check with our favorite weatherman, Charlie Hall. He said that the low-pressure area would hang around all day and through the night. The rains he said would be of the frog- strangling type so carry your umbrella with you if you planned on going outside. Well, at least it might clear out by tomorrow I thought. One more day of babysitting and staying in this house and somebody might have to baby-sit me after I cracked up.

All was quiet. Too quiet. Oh gee whiz! What are they up to now? I eased down the hall and eavesdropped outside their room. They had a game of Parcheesi out and were playing a game or Emily was trying to explain to Katie and Sara how to play? I kept hearing Emily raise her voice about something. It didn't matter. They were quiet and occupied. I figured a short nap was possible.

Before my nap started it ended when the girls, bored with Parcheesi, came to my room looking for something to do.

"Eah, how about y'all's coloring books? Y'all wanna color?" I suggested hoping they would because they were always quiet when they colored.

"Yeah, let's color, Em." Katie rushed from the room followed by Emily and Sara.

Hey Mike, you're getting pretty smart, boy, I told myself. "Right, Mollie?" Mollie looked at me like I was crazy. Now for that nap.

I quickly dozed off and dreamed of a faraway place with exotic people dressed in funny- looking costumes who chased me through an endless maze of alleys and streets lined with bad people with swords and clubs who tried to kill me only to be outsmarted by my physical prowess and quick moves. Finally, the bad guys had me cornered in a dead -end alley and were moving in for the kill with raised clubs, which were about to smash my head like a melon and would have had I not been awakened by the girls tugging and pulling on me.

"Wake up! Wake up, Mike! Guess what?" They asked together. "You'll never guess what."

"Oh?" I rubbed my eyes and felt relief that the people in the funny looking costumes weren't bashing me to death. "It's y'all. What'cha doing?"

Emily stepped forward and acted as the spokesperson for the group. "Mike, we want to tell you we are sorry for causing trouble today." She turned and glanced at her cohorts in crime. "Right, Katie?" Right, Sara?" Katie and Sara smiled their angelic smiles and answered softly, "Yeah, we sorry." I surveyed them for a second and thought, *Well, they sure look sincere?*

"To show you we really are sorry we wrote you a letter, Mike," Emily continued. "And we all signed it."

"Why thank you, Emily," I said looking around for the letter of appreciation. "Thank you," I said again. I paused and still no letter appeared. "Well, that's nice, Emily but... u-u-u-u-h ... where is the letter?"

"Oh," she started. "It's in our room. C'mon we'll show you."

They proudly led me down the hall and into their room and stood tall by the door and pointed.

"There it is, Mike" Emily announced. "Your letter."

She was pointing at the wall and sure enough there it was. It was a message written in red crayon: " To Mike. We luv you." They had drawn three stick figures accompanying my letter and at the end they signed off with their names in huge letters. The first stick figure I took to be Emily … it was the largest of the three. The middle figure must have been Katie because it had oversized feet just like Katie's in real life. And the third had to be Sara because of its long hair, which ran from their drawing all the way down the wall to the floor representing her long flowing blonde hair. Their spelling of the word "love" might have been in error but there was no mistake in their sentiment. It was as clear as a Sullivans Island summer night. I'll never forget how proud I felt at reading their "letter" and witnessing their feeling of accomplishment. I tried hard to fuss at them for messing up the wall but looking at those innocent, smiling faces made it impossible. So I pretended to fuss as much as possible.

"Y'all know when Mom gets home she's gonna make y'all wash that off the wall?" I said as sternly and gently as I could. "I wish y'all could leave it up there. It's neat but we don't want Mom to get mad … do we?"

Katie looked at me and said, "N-o-o-o." I could tell she meant it so I made a suggestion. "Let's wash this off and then color in your books some more, OK?"

Emily tapped me on the shoulder and announced in no uncertain terms, "We can wash it off but later we can write you another letter. Next time it will be longer … OK?"

"Sure, Emily. That's fine," I said. "But not on the wall … all right?"

Emily smiled and said, "We'll see, Catbird. We'll see." And we all laughed.

After the wall- cleaning session we were all settled and watching the Mouseketeers sing and dance their way through our hearts and the Devlin house when we heard the front door open and my mother sound her greetings. The girls scrambled for attention grabbing and hugging my mother's arms and legs, Mollie barked, and I let out a huge sigh of relief that my mother, the true guardian of my sisters, was home and now in control.

8
THE MEETING

Every small town has its own special, informal meeting place where everyone comes together, a place everyone acknowledges as the social center or gathering place. It is a spot where they gather either by accident or design to discuss and complain, reminisce or plan, or just chew the fat and catch up on recent happenings and it is a place where you can find answers to life's everyday problems. It could be a restaurant, a doughnut shop or even a gas station. The Island's meeting place was the Post Office where you went to pick up on the latest did you hear news. However, you had to be careful as to what you said because the Post Office was the central command post of Gertie's Gossipers and, believe me, they didn't miss much. Gertie and her troops were on twenty four hour alert with an ever present, finely tuned radar system second to none. They made the rounds in the grocery store, the bakery, the drug store, the churches and the Post Office. They were everywhere with their ears open and their eyes searching. Their motto was: "Any gossip is good gossip." Locals swore that Gertie Evans, the head gossiper, could read lips from a hundred yards and hear a pin drop from further than that.

I heard old man Kennedy tell Sergeant Walker, "I've done took to holding a piece of mail in front of my mouth whenever I'm talking to someone at the Post Office. Shucks, ain't even a whisper safe from old Gertie."

And he was right. If you did not want any dirty laundry hung in public then you best be real careful about what you say around Gertie. Many a juicy story began with Gertie speculating, "Well, he was probably thinking that" or whispering, "I'll tell you but don't say anything to anyone else, O.K?" And once the process began it moved faster than a woman with a credit card at a Macy's Thanksgiving Sale.

More sins were transmitted over the phone lines on the Island than were confessed in the confessional at Saint Angela's Church at Easter. Whether there was any truth to any of these rumors was inconsequential. If it were true then it would not be gossip and would be no fun. Gossip was alive and well and despite its negative overtones it did, however, serve a useful purpose because it kept many a person from giving in to temptation in fear that Gertie might get a whiff of any wrongdoing and run with it, thus ruining their life.

Any trip to the Post Office was not complete without receiving a friendly greeting from my Uncle Schroeder, my father's older brother. They had been born and raised on the Island. He was the original Wal Mart greeter except he was not paid a penny and he loved every minute of his "job." Positioning himself by the entrance he made sure not to miss any approaching "customers."

With a deep baritone voice and a bobbing head, he gently touched the tip of his gray fedora and repeated verbatim that wonderful greeting, "H-e-y, how *you* f-e-e-l-i-n-g?"

Most people responded with, "Good. How about yourself?"

"O-o-o-h, *fine* and *dandy*, "he would answer, dragging out the "oh" … and emphasizing the "fine" and "dandy." All the while he did a little two-step shuffle with his feet that matched perfectly the bobbing head and the waving of his hand clutching his ever-present cigar. The Tampa Nugget gave off white curls of smoke that seemed to rest just above his head forming a halo, lending to him a saintly appearance. This perfectly synchronized choreography was as natural to him as breathing and it never varied. When not greeting someone, his cigar remained lodged securely in the left side of his mouth and he would fold his hands behind his back, smiling broadly and doing his little two-step shuffle while his head bobbed up and down. The man never had a bad day.

Uncle Schroeder greeted two gentlemen, no more than ten seconds apart from each other. One was older and a more distinguished looking gentleman than the other who was a scruffy looking younger man in Bermuda shorts. Both gave a nod of acknowledgement to Uncle Schroeder and walked inside the Post Office.

Thomas Poe had lived on the Island all his life. He was a local. And like most of the locals he dressed like one: A plain tee shirt. Worn out, threadbare Bermuda shorts and sandals. The two men stood by the trashcan discarding junk mail. Thomas noticed a familiar publication that the older gentleman was not trashing but clutching in his right hand. It was "The National Coin Registry," kind of a What's-What in the world of coin collecting. He couldn't help but inquire.

"Excuse me but I couldn't help noticing "The National Coin Registry" you have there. Are you into coin collecting?"

"Why yes, I sure am. Have been for over forty years and still get a kick out of it … gives me something to do now that I'm retired. How about yourself?"

"Oh yeah," Thomas replied eagerly, "it's a passion with me but I've only been at it for about twenty years. Got a long way to go to catch up with you."

"Well, it's not how long you've been at it that makes a difference. It's how lucky you are. You know what I mean?"

"Oh yeah, that's so true. Lady Luck is sure needed." He paused a second. "My name's Thomas Poe," said Thomas extending his hand.

Dr. Steven Jenkins reciprocated, "Steven Jenkins, a pleasure to meet you," shaking hands with Thomas. "So … how long have you lived on the Island?"

"All my life practically. I was born in Charleston and we moved here when I was five. Our family vacationed here every summer and come September we would move back to the city and then during the rest of the year we would come back and visit the locals we had met during the summer. My father loved the beach and fishing so much that he decided one day to move. Didn't even talk it over with my mother. He found a place, bought it, and here I am. How about yourself? From Charleston?"

"Oh no, I'm from Georgia. My wife Peggy and I moved here about a year ago from Atlanta. I kick myself for not moving sooner but Peggy had been sick for quite awhile. Heart trouble and she needed specialized treatment that was only available in Atlanta so we stayed there until there wasn't much hope and … well" … his voice faded away.

Steven Jenkins cast his head down for a few seconds, composed himself and said, "It's been over six months since she died and it's still difficult to talk about."

"Yes, well …that must be hard on you," Thomas said not able to find the appropriate words. "Sorry about your loss." He quickly decided to try to change the mood of the conversation. "What line of work were you in?"

"I was a surgeon at Atlanta Memorial for more years than I can remember." "Atlanta, huh? Why leave Atlanta? I hear that's the place to be."

"Oh no, not for me. When it was smaller it was a great place to live. Peggy and I had some wonderful memories, but the building boom after the war was unreal. Every day a new office building or conference center went up and people moved in like there was no tomorrow. I guess they're trying to become the New York of the South? That's when we decided to look for a place with a relaxed, slower pace. You see, basically I'm an ol' country boy. We looked up and down the East coast but couldn't find anywhere better than this Island. It's got everything … nothing. You know what I'm saying, don't you?""

"Oh yeah. Small and charming, that's the Island all right."

"Anyway, I retired and here I am. Poor Peggy only got to enjoy the Island for a short time but at least she died happy, if there is such a thing as a happy death. I've seen people suffer while they hang on for years with what she had and it's terrible."

Again Thomas did not know how to reply. "That must have been quite an ordeal?"

"Yes, but life goes on," Steven said giving Thomas an out.

"You must have quite a coin collection," Thomas commented, "if you've been collecting for forty years … that's a long time."

"Yes, that is a long time and the collection has grown to be quite substantial. My father got me started as a kid and I loved it. When I was little the kids at school used to tease me and called me "The Coin Boy." I still enjoy the search. Started a new collection just last month for dimes. If you subscribe to" The Registry, "then maybe you have read about my early American fifty cent piece collection, the Walking Liberty Half Dollar. They were struck from 1916-1947 and are a rare find. I'm right proud of it, not because of what it's worth, but because it took eighteen years to complete. And you wouldn't believe where I found the last coin … in a laundromat in Marietta, Georgia, of all places. How about your collection? Is it …?"

The instant Dr. Steven Jenkins made mention of his owning the acclaimed Walking Liberty Half dollar collection, a serious but devious thought struck Thomas like a bolt of lightning. *What if I had his collection to go along with mine?* And in the same instant the thought vanished as quickly as it had appeared.

"Your collection? I was saying. What about your collection? How extensive is it?" Dr. Jenkins inquired of the man who seemed adrift at the moment.

"Oh, my collection? Oh, it's… uh… nothing much. Nothing to write home about. That's for sure." He paused and lied again. "It's just some rare coins I've collected over the years here and there. But it's growing."

"Do you subscribe to any publications?" asked the doctor.

"Oh yeah, over the years different ones," Thomas said. "Right now I get "Coin World" and "The Coin Collector's Guide" trying to keep up with what's going on." He feigned unfamiliarity with Dr. Jenkins' collection but he was lying again. Anyone at all who collected coins had heard of the famous Jenkins' Walking Liberty Collection. He told Dr. Jenkins, " Your collection sounds awfully familiar. I know I've read about it somewhere … but I can't recall exactly where."

"Yeah … oh yeah … it's been written up over the years in different publications. Who knows? Maybe I'll read about one of your collections someday."

"That would be something, wouldn't it," Thomas said with a slight chuckle.

"Well, it was nice meeting you, Mr. Poe, but I need to get going … lots of errands to run."

"Thomas, call me Thomas, and it was my pleasure. Hope to see you around the Island, Dr. Jenkins."

"And call me Steven. In that case Thomas, why don't you come over sometime?

Bring your collection and we can swap some stories. I live at Station 10, front beach, the one-story tan house with the green shutters … you can't miss it."

"Thanks, that sounds good. I'll give you a call sometime ... you are in the phone book?"

"Yea ... I look forward to hearing from you ... so long."

I just might have to visit the good doctor, Thomas thought *and check out his collection. Yep, I think I need to check out his collection.*

Thomas Poe was the younger of two boys. His brother, Warren, never cared much for Island life and what it offered so when the time came he headed north to attend college, eventually settling in Ohio. He and Thomas were never close. Maybe it was the age thing, Warren was ten years older.

Thomas, forty-two, lived a quiet, unassuming life trying to raise twin daughters the best he knew how. He gave them love and understanding, trying not to over-parent but still give them enough affection to show that he cared for them. He worked hard at his job in Charleston at Fisher and Lee, an established advertising firm, where he worked in the accounting department. It was a job that paid the bills and Mr. Lee was a decent man to work for. Thomas' real love, however, was collecting coins. It was almost a passion with him and he invested endless hours of reading and researching. If there had been a way to make a living collecting coins then he would have been a truly happy man. There was a story behind each coin: it's birth, travels and final resting spot. "Just like a human," Thomas thought. And Thomas practically treated his collection as though it were human to the point of talking to it, hugging it, and on occasion kissing it.

Life had had its ups and downs over the years but he and his wife, Mary Helen, had been able to weather them by communicating their true feelings and talking things out. Usually he gave in to her feelings and demands just to keep the peace.

Overall he was satisfied with his lifestyle and had planned to live out the rest of his life on the Island. The twins were in their freshman year at U.S.C. and doing well academically and otherwise. Mary Helen enjoyed gardening, the beach, and her small circle of friends who seemed to always have an ongoing project where she was desperately needed. The latest craze was the "Save the Birds" project sponsored by the Ladies Garden Club, a group of true fanatics. *God knows we need more birds on the Island*, Thomas thought. *Pretty soon the grackles will take over and we'll have to start a "Save the People" project.*

Then the bottom fell out of his life. Not all of a sudden but it was more of a gradual spiral downward brought on by the disease he had contracted. It came upon him from out of nowhere, no warning, nothing, like a bad dream. The moods of depression were slight in the beginning and he just wrote them off as strain from the job or not eating properly of which he was guilty. *A-w-w, it isn't anything to worry about. A life change, that's all.*

He felt anxious and depressed for no reason at all, there were strong mood swings too and then he realized he had a problem. It had gone on for more than six months and he had been able to cope with it mostly through sleep, a form of denial that he finally accepted. As of late the sessions of depression lasted longer and came about more frequently. Now they were his constant companions like a shadow and the feeling of hopelessness was becoming harder to disguise. Co-workers noticed the change but he shrugged off their inquires with a lame excuse about working too hard and a laugh: "Been putting in overtime at home for the good of the company. The company first, that's what I say." They weren't buying it.

At home it was a different story. His illness was like an open book. It was impossible to mask or hide his worsening condition from Mary Helen. She knew him far too well. At first she made an attempt to help him work through whatever the causes of his depression might be but as time went on, her patience dwindled to the point of apathy, and then came resentment. She felt like she was carrying the load of the family and it was too heavy. Small disagreements, which normally amounted to nothing in the past, now flared into full-scale arguments.

After a year of constant bickering and fighting she decided enough is enough and told Thomas during their latest spat, "Why don't you check into The Hoo Hoo Hotel or just blow your brains out! One of the two, O.K? I can't go on like this any longer. Make a choice."

"For God's sake, I'm doing the best that I can," Thomas pleaded. " What more do you want?" he asked as he sensed the end coming.

"A life, Thomas. That's what I want ... a life," Mary Helen sneered. "Is that too much to ask for?"

Shortly after this last round of bickering, which lately was one of many, Mary Helen packed up the girls and headed to Florida, her family's home.

For Thomas it was a relief. All the screaming and fighting and name-calling were making matters worse for him, to the point of his becoming more and more depressed such that he began to worry about his sanity. He figured her leaving was bound to happen. Mary Helen never was good at handling adversity. He recalled early in the marriage when she freaked out over the sudden death of her Uncle Ray.

"What will poor Aunt Wilma do? How will she survive? I don't know what to do." She lamented for months over nothing and before she could finish her hysterics, Aunt Wilma met and married a rich widower and lived happily ever after.

Besides, Thomas didn't have time to worry about Mary Helen. Another storm was brewing on the horizon, a bigger problem. Thomas

Poe was in deep financial trouble. Plus he had the well- being of the twins to think about. The wolf was at the door and peeking in. He was desperate and desperate men do desperate things.

The divorce had gone quickly and peacefully, if peacefully is a way to describe losing practically everything you own including your dignity. His financial woes began when Fisher and Lee decided to restructure and Thomas became dispensable. Out of the goodness of his heart Mr. Lee demoted Thomas to part-time rather than laying him off. Thomas, of course, didn't see it that way and blamed it on his depression but not openly. For the first time resentment set in at the office and tensions between him and his co-workers mounted. The final nail in the coffin was losing his health benefits now that he was part-time. It only deepened his depression. *How will I afford the doctor visits or the medication? Think man, think.*

The business world of Charleston was a small close-knit group of good ol' homeboys who grew up together and scratched each other's backs on a daily basis. Thomas Poe wasn't privy to that group's coddling and with his sickness was considered "persona non grata." His chances of making a job switch were nearly impossible. The bills mounted resembling the mountain of paperwork he faced every day at work. The mortgage payment, college tuitions, doctor bills, car payments, taxes, insurance, and daily living expenses flowed in like clockwork and his hour was almost up.

Maybe I should take Mary Helen's advice and bite the bullet?

His savings account had been wiped out by the latest tuition payments for the girls. Selling the house was a thought but Mary Helen years earlier had insisted on a second mortgage thus putting a halt to that idea. Besides, where would I move to? Plus it would be another payment. Will it ever end? This was all so unfair and with no end in sight, that Thomas was ready to run naked through the streets screaming. *Maybe they would lock me up and I'd get some peace and quiet. "Go to sleep, now!* He told himself. *Sleep, yes, my good friend, a peaceful sleep!* That had been his only relief to this point. Waking up was the hard part; things seemed to have gotten worse while he escaped for a while.

The only salvageable item of value from the divorce was his coin collection. The one he had held back telling Dr. Steven Jenkins about. It was a complete set of quarters in very good condition called the Standing Liberty collection and had been minted from 1916-1930. So many precious years had been put into completing the collection that he felt he couldn't live without it. And now he had the added worry about the possibility of losing it should the courts get involved in his financial affairs and confiscate it as a means of paying off some of his many past due bills. *Can't let that happen. I've put my life into that collection. I'll die before anyone gets their hands on it.*

Thomas was determined to find a way out of this mess and in his deepest mood of darkness he began to devise a plan so sinister that even he couldn't believe it. His rationale, flawed from the start, was that he had *nothing* to lose and when people like him begin to think like that then they usually have *everything* to lose.

He went to the library and did some research, learning a great deal about Dr. Steven Jenkins' coin collection. Turned out, Dr.Jenkins was a modest man. His collection was world famous, the only one of its kind and very, very valuable. It could be the answer to a lot of problems. And what more could he hope for? The good doctor himself had issued him a personal invitation to visit. *He probably has the collection right there in his house?*

Thomas' reasoning was that a complete coin collection by itself maintains a certain market value but when coupled with the right partner can gain tremendous value. And the perfect match was here on the Island, not three blocks away. If it were combined with Thomas' collection of Standing Liberty quarters, then he would have enough money to write his own ticket. *Head South. The Caribbean ... St.Kitts? Aruba? Martinique?*

The ringing of the phone jolted him from his thoughts. *Why can't they leave me alone?*

"No, he is not here. Yes, I'll be happy to tell Mr. Poe to call you as soon as he comes in."

Why do they keep calling? Don't they have anything better to do! Stupid finance company. They will be the first to receive a postcard from Aruba. Need to act before the courts do. Soon ... real soon.)

Thomas Poe began to devise a plan, a sinister and evil one. He was hopeful that Dr.Jenkins kept his collection at home even though it was very valuable, which would be an important and key element of his scheme. After his conversation with Dr. Jenkins at the Post Office, Thomas came away with the feeling that the collection was at the doctor's house. He also knew that serious crime was a rarity on the Island and many people felt secure enough to sleep with unlocked doors and windows.

"First things first, however," he thought, "What I need to do is take the good doctor up on his invitation to visit. Yes, that's exactly what I will do."

9
CRABS IN THE CREEK

It was near the end of June and the heat wave continued without a hint of relief. The sea oats on top of the sand dunes hung lifeless on their branches like wet sheets. Sun worshipers lay motionless on their beach towels hoping to catch even a hint of a breeze from the flapping wings of the low flying pelicans who themselves were in search of shade. The tomatoes in my mother's garden were ruined, so shriveled up they looked like red prunes, useful only as food for the grackles. This hot weather was fine with Bubba 'n me. The heat meant great beach weather and it meant the waters in the creeks were warming up, providing more food for the many crabs.

"Them Jimmies oughta be getting fat and sassy by now, what'cha think?" I asked.

A frown of doubt was on Bubba's face." You mean they gain and lose weight?"

"No man, do you think they are fat enough? Got some meat in 'em to eat? Cause we're going crabbing."

"Oh yeah, yeah, they're ready if you are," Bubba yelled out confidently and then issued his challenge: "Look out you big ol' Jimmies. Here comes me and Mike and you guys ain't got a chance. Y'all are going in the pot."

The seemingly endless marshes and winding creeks that bordered the back of the Island were abundant with wildlife and provided an endless supply of food for human consumption: clams, oysters, fish, shrimp, and the tasty crab, more commonly known as the Atlantic blue crab. There were two kinds of crabs: the female, which was called a "she crab", and the male, known as a "Jimmy." The thick succulent meat could be made into crab cakes, soup, or salad; however, our favorite way of eating them was right out of the shell at a crab crack in somebody's back yard.

A crab crack was not normally announced nor were invitations sent out but it just kind of happened when someone in the neighborhood caught a nice mess of crabs and decided to cook them in the backyard over an open fire in some type of big pot. The word got out that there were crabs to eat thus a crab crack was created and everyone showed up. All over the Island could be seen old, smoke charred washtubs hanging on the side of a garage or sitting on top of cinder blocks from a recent cooking. These tubs held up to four or five dozen crabs at a time. A picnic table was covered with newspaper, butter knives were thrown in a pile, and if you wanted to be fancy, water bowls would be set out, to use to rinse the body of the crab after the claws and "feet" were removed. The butter knives were held by the blade while using the handle to crack the pinchers or claws. It was an informal affair, shoes optional, with neighbors drifting in and out, eating a little, drinking a little, talking, listening to the music or just stopping by to visit. The only invitation was an open one. Some crab cracks, fueled by an abundance of alcohol, mainly beer, got out of hand and turned into regular parties that lasted long into the night … those were the fun ones! Someone, obviously not a local, once asked what made a crab taste so good? The old Islander told 'em, "Because they're crabs … that's why." Rarely were there any leftovers after a crab crack.

This marshland was a heaven-made playground of pluff mud, oyster banks and shallow streams that offered two Island boys unlimited fun and adventure. And we accepted that offer with great enthusiasm. We tromped in the mud, swam the creeks, fished and crabbed and learned about boats while gaining a tremendous appreciation for one of God's great creations. Many a day Bubba 'n me would come home smelling like pluff mud, totally exhausted from a day at our playground. Our parents in the beginning used to scold us and make us shower and clean up before they would let us in the house. That routine grew old, they relented, and finally accepted the fact that we were a couple of marsh rats.

The Island had few businesses, about five total: a bakery, gas station, grocery store, Burton's Drug Store and for the many Irish folks on the Island … a liquor store. There were not any family restaurants or retail businesses to shop at like in a larger city, however, our growing neighbor, Mt. Pleasant, offered many new shops and stores, even a new Piggly Wiggly food store, a supermarket they called it, full of every imaginable food product under the sun.

It's funny how rituals and traditions get their beginning. Something that started out as a reward for the Devlin childrens' good behavior during the week, led to a family tradition. This was the weekly trip to the Milk Bar in Mt. Pleasant, a neat drug store with a long white Formica counter and spinning stools with red cushions. It was there that we would be rewarded with the best homemade milkshake in the county, if not, the whole state. On Friday evening about 6:30,all my father had to do was put down his newspaper, pick up his car keys from the tray on the table and say, "Would anyone like …" The whole troop of us had been innocently lounging around or near the front room awaiting those magical words from my father. Before he could finish the sentence we were half way out the door piling into the backseat of our '49 Ford, one of those big black ones with four doors. Ryan and I would fight for the honor of riding shot-gun but seeing that he was older I usually gave in, sitting in the backseat with the squealing girls, occasionally ducking down to hide from friends so as not to suffer the embarrassment of being seen riding in the same seat with my sisters. It was a guy thing.

Oh boy! You would have thought we were going to the circus the way we carried on bouncing around like cats on a hot tin roof, yelling out the window at anyone we saw, "Milk Bar, Milk Bar! We going to the Milk Bar!" Folks who were aware of our routine must have asked themselves, "I wonder how poor Mr. Devlin handles those kids once they get their bellies full of a Milk Bar shake loaded with all that sugar?" We were generally being rambunctious, a term my father used so many times on those trips that I had memorized it by age seven even though I never knew its meaning.

My mother usually stayed behind savoring the peace and quiet that she so richly deserved. My older sister, Sissy, also preferred to stay at home offering the excuse that she had better things to do. What? We never figured out?

The Milk Bar was just over the causeway in Mt.Pleasant. It sat off the road in the midst of a grove of century- old, massive oak trees with moss that hung like a gray beard attesting to their age. Picnic tables had been set out under the protective canopy of the oaks to be used by the patrons. We took advantage of these, especially when the weather was nice, much to the delight of the owner, Mr. Wiggins, who didn't have to put up with a bunch of screaming Devlin kids inside his store. There was always a race for the stools as we bolted from the car and crashed through the front door, heading for the counter. We would kneel on the small red cushions peeking over the countertop, carefully observing Mr. Wiggins preparing our shakes scoop by scoop. Sometimes we would plead for more ice cream with our father standing guard right behind us. I think he was worried about us falling off our stool as we spun each other at supersonic speeds .It was a game we played when we got bored watching Mr. Wiggins. I'm sure he never had a boring moment when we were in his store.

" More ice cream, more ice cream," the Devlins chanted.

"Say please," our father reminded us.

"*Please* more ice cream, *please* more ice cream," we screamed, being obedient children.

Three year old Sara couldn't get the words to come out: "Peas mo I creme," she yelled. It didn't really matter because only us older kids could finish a Milk Bar shake. We would try to drink the leftovers from our siblings remembering the starving kids in China but after getting sick on one occasion, one milkshake was enough for me. These shakes were so thick you could stand a baseball bat up in them and the portions were more than generous. I don't where we got the idea to plead for more ice cream? And they only cost a quarter.

When we were riding home from one of our recent trips to the Milk Bar, I noticed a sign in the window at Simmons Seafood that read, "Crabs for Sale---Caught Fresh Daley". I wasn't sure what the sign meant and I made a mental note to ask my father about it later. I do know one thing though, and that is whoever wrote that sign with the misspelled word better not let Sister Roberta see it or he was going to get the big ruler treatment.

That evening after supper I remembered to ask my father about the sign at Simmons Seafood. He simply told me that you could buy crabs there if you wanted to.

"Dead ones or live ones," I asked like a dummy.

"Oh, they're alive … kind of … but probably dying. But you wouldn't want any dead ones, you know that."

"Well, how do they keep 'em alive?"

"Oh, they have a big swimming pool out back full of salt water and let them swim and sun bathe and dive off the diving board and…"

"A-w-w, you're funning me now," I said. My father laughed his hearty laugh.

"Why would anybody buy crabs when they are free … I mean if you can go catch 'em?"

"I guess because some people don't know how to crab," my father said.

"Don't know how to crab," I shouted in total disbelief. "Who doesn't know how to crab?"

"There are lots of people that don't know how."

"Well, I never heard of that. Wait till' I tell Bubba."

"Mike, when did you learn to crab?"

"Uh?" I had to think on that one. "About three years ago? Remember when you took me."

"Yeah, but it was longer ago than that but the point is that you had to learn. Do you understand what I'm saying?"

I was doubtful but nodded my head anyway.

"Good," my father said, "I'm glad we got that cleared up."

"One other thing …OK?" I was being persistent and my father knew what I was driving at but he let me go on. "How much do they sell the crabs for?"

"I'm not sure. I've never bought any." He yelled toward the kitchen, "Alyce, how much are the crabs at Simmons?"

"Why? You plan on buying some when the creek is full of 'em?"

"No, Mike wants to know."

"I don't know … about a dollar a dozen, I guess? What you got planned, boy?" mother asked, poking her head around the corner.

"Oh nothing." When my mother's head disappeared, my father smiled at me and whispered, "Talk to Bubba tomorrow. Y'all can make a killing."

"Yes sir," I whispered and gave my father a thumbs up sign.

My mother was concerned because I already had a summer job mowing lawns on the Island. It wasn't a full time job but was the beginning of what my mother called my college fund and she probably didn't want some half-baked crabbing scheme interfering with my saving money for college. Money was tight around the Devlin household. The deal between my mother and me was that for every dollar I put in savings she would match it. It was like double trouble but the opposite.

Many of the older Island residents could not physically get out in the creek and catch their own crabs. And like I had learned from my father, a lot of people did not know how to crab. In my mind those kinds of people must have been from Columbia or Greenville. The locals had been spoiled since childhood, eating fresh seafood thus the demand for crabs fresh out of the creek was there *and* the crabs were there. And that's where Bubba 'n me come in. I couldn't wait to talk to him about us going into the crabbing business.

Beverly Ann Johnson again … "a successful boy."

I must have overslept. Mollie woke me up with juicy licks in my ear.

"What you want, girl?" Mollie sat up, looked toward the door, leaped off the bed, and stood patiently by the door.

"OK, OK … hang on." Then I leaped from the bed remembering I had to see Bubba and go over my crabbing brainstorm. No time to eat. Mollie and I ran across the yard. I was yelling for Bubba who was just getting on his bike.

"Wait up … wait a minute!" Catching my breath I told him about my idea. We agreed that we needed to come up with a plan … a real plan. And it had to be something better than the garbage truck disaster plan.

"Eah, ride with me up to the gas station. I gotta get my father a newspaper then we can go to the rocks," Bubba asked already rolling out the driveway. "It won't take long."

"OK … good idea. Let me get my bike," I said. This would be good because for some unknown reason I always did my best thinking when riding my bike. "Let's go, Mollie."

We rode in silence for a few blocks and I thought to myself, Now *if Bubba will just listen to what I've got in mind then everything will work out.*

Bubba was thinking to himself, *Now if Mike will just listen to what I have planned then everything will work out.*

I pulled up even with Bubba and asked, "What did you say?"

Bubba looked surprised and answered, "I didn't say anything."
"Well, you didn't exactly say anything but you were thinking something. Weren't you?"

"How'd you know?"

"Because I could just tell. Kind of feel it." I paused. "A-a-a-w, I can't explain it." I paused again. "Just forget it."

"Hey man, cool it will ya. I thought I heard you say something too. Tell you what, the best thing we can do is let the crabbing gods take care of this one, OK?"

I followed Bubba as he pedaled off ahead of me and turned into Chippys. "What crabbing gods?" I was thinking. "That boy sure is smart … sometimes."

Chippys Pure Oil gas station was located in the middle of the Island at the corner of Station 22 and Middle Street across from the grocery store and the bakery in the business district. The highway beside it connected to the causeway, which was only a couple of hundred yards down the road.

Chippys served as a meeting place for a different group of locals. We kids hung out at Burton's, the adults hung out at Chippys. We drank Cokes and looked at girls; they drank beer and looked at each other. In the last year an addition had been added on the side of the building and was now home to a pool table and a bar, which sold only beer, no whiskey. There were about six tables in the bar area. The homemade bar was a huge, smooth, shiny wooden oak plank that reflected the different colored lights from the cheap flashing neon lights hung on the walls.

The Island was home to many of the military that had served on the Island during WWII and retired here and considered Chippys as a place where they could come and relax with the guys. It was their "palace of freedom" as one old- timer called it. Each evening they would shuffle in, pull back their favorite barstool, sit down and begin to retell those wonderful war stories that only men like them could while sipping beer from a frosty mug.

On this day Bubba 'n me would hide our bikes around back and sneak into the bar area but not too secretively. We didn't want the patrons to know this place was off limits for us. We would swagger up to the bar, pull out a stool, sit down, and wait for the bartender. We were underage and everyone there tolerated us as long as we did not get loud or cause any trouble.

"Same as usual, boys?" Mr.Bollinger asked. "Coca Cola?"

"Yes sir", we said together.

"Two Cokes coming up. Y'all want straws?"

He asked us that every time and every time our response was the same. "No sir."

Oh, we thought we were the cat's meow, sitting up there at the bar like a regular beer swilling grownup as we sipped on our Coca Cola, trying to copy the way the grownups threw their head back and then let out a nice a-h-h-h after a cold sip. I couldn't wait until I was old enough to sit here and drink a real Pabst Blue Ribbon, right in front of everybody. Maybe I would drink two or three? Yeah, we thought we were hot stuff until one day when we approached the pool table for a game and were quickly brought down a notch.

"Nope. No pool for you boys," Mr. Bollinger said sternly. " The pool table is for adults only. If y'all want to shoot a game, go to Burton's. Hearsay it's free down there?"

"Yes sir. Free pool, how about that," we mumbled to ourselves as we headed for the door. We knew when not to push our luck.

In the evenings and especially on the weekends, there was usually a good crowd at Chippys, relaxing, having a few beers, and talking over events of the past week. It was amazing there wasn't more trouble with the amount of alcohol that was consumed daily. The empty fifty gallon oil drums, used for trash cans, stayed full of beer cans, sometimes overflowing onto the sidewalk, giving the outside of the station a certain ambiance. Chippys probably sold more gallons of beer than it did gas.

There may have been two fights a year at Chippys resulting from some silly disagreement or someone having one too many and losing control. These were usually fist-a-cuffs with no real blows being exchanged or anyone getting seriously hurt. The latest scuffle had been between two retired Sergeants: Walker and Henry. It started when Sergeant Walker accused Sergeant Henry of being a slacker w-a-y back when and added the insult that he hadn't carried his share of the load during the war.

"Shut up, Walker! Or I'm gonna shut you up once and for all. For thirty damn years that's all we've heard … your big mouth!"

"Oh yeah, you and whose battalion is gonna shut me up? You stupid lazy infantry couldn't shut up your Grandmas." Walker edged closer. Henry stood his ground.

"Don't get too close old man," Henry said, "or you might eat some of this," he gestured with a balled-up fist.

"Henry, I ain't afraid of you," Walker retorted and made a bull rush at the taller Henry who took a mighty swipe and nearly fell over, losing his balance.

Both had a few beers in them and were in no state to stage a fistfight.

Walker, hanging on to Henry's shirttail, went around and around trying to grab Henry. "I've got you now, you son of a bitch. You're all mine, Henry. You're a dead man!"

"Oh yeah, you dumpy little paper-pusher. Bring it on!"

They ended up in an embrace more suited to a waltz than a fight. Everyone at Chippys got a huge laugh out of this because, you see,

Sergeant Walker was eighty-four years old at the time and Sergeant Henry was eighty-six.

As we drank our Cokes, we talked about going into the crabbing business and we both had theses grandiose visions of lots of money without doing much work. And by the time we left the only thing we could settle on was how to split the profits, if there were any: Fifty-fifty. We rode down to Station 20 and checked out the rocks but the crew was nowhere in sight. I had chores to do at home and Bubba had to take the newspaper to his father so we headed back. When we made the turn at the Coast Guard Station our traditional bike race to Bubba's house began. Of course, Bubba would win, by pulling ahead of me little by little until he got a sizeable lead, then he would look back at me and yell, "Race ya to my house." Like I didn't know what was going on. I might have been just a kid but I didn't come in on the last load of turnips.

"Well, I won again. How many Cokes do you owe me now, Mike?"

"About a hundred, I guess."

"Yeah … Well …When you gonna pay up?"

"Tomorrow."

"Yeah, you always say that. Huh?"

I ignored his question. "Eah look, when are we gonna make some plans about the crabbing thing?"

Bubba looked at me and smiled and said, "Tomorrow."

"Yeah. Tomorrow. I'll see ya then." I pushed my bike toward home and stopped to yell back, "And we need a good plan, OK? A good plan … so give it some thought."

"Yeah right, Einstein. I'll think about it all night."

10
BUSINESSMEN

It is 6:00 in the morning. I am dreaming of Beverly Ann…again. These reoccurring dreams were soothing and pleasant, more real than dreamlike. Then I heard a voice so real it seemed like it was in my room that very moment.

"Wake up, sleepy head. It's late!" I rolled over and looked toward where the sound had come from, by the window, expecting to see the beautiful face of Beverly Ann. Not so. Instead, there was Bubba at the open window, bugged-eyed as a squashed bullfrog, all excited and ready to go with a huge smile on his face. He held the look of a very determined young crabber on his first day at work as he climbed through the window with his trusty crab net in hand.

"Come on, get up, Mike!" he exclaimed loud enough to wake half the Island, " let's go or we'll miss the tide."

"Afraid not," I said. " And if you don't quiet down right now and you wake up my father the only place we're going is to the hospital."

"Afraid not? Did you say *afraid* not?" Bubba was half laughing. "Man, what are you so serious about, my friend? What's with the "afraid not?" It's like this …you mean, "F-r-a-y-e-d not." Bubba had assumed the proper stance like the eighth grade boys at school standing erect with his arms held straight down by his sides and his hands cocked out at the wrists. The "afraid not" was to be drawn out with emphasis on the word "afraid" …but coming out sounding like "frayed." While this was spoken the head was shaken vigorously in little short negative motions and the hands were held in their position and shook just as quickly as the head. Another guy thing we were into. And anytime us seventh graders tried it at school the girls just laughed at us and walked away. Bubba, however, was getting pretty good at it but was still a long ways from the cool way the eighth graders performed it.

"OK, OK … frayed not," I said then asked "By the way, Chief Rising Sun, where are we going at this hour?"

"Crabbing, man. We're going crabbing! Catch those big 'ol Jimmies."

"Calm down some. Will ya," I said.

Bubba suddenly got real quiet, cocked his head to one side, put his hand behind his ear and whispered, “S-h-h-h, listen. Hear them bad boys taunting us, Mike?” (“Taunting was a big word Bubba had learned from Sister Roberta one day as she had described his action toward the fifth graders.)

“Hear ’em? Catch me if you can. Bet you can’t. I’m too fast for you two little Island boys. C-a-t-c-h me if y-o-u c-a-n.” Now he was singing.

“Eah, not so loud, man. What did you eat this morning … a bowl of sugar?”

A serious look came over Bubba’s face. “Mike, I really do hear ’em calling me. The crab voices … I heard ’em all night.”

I stared at him thinking, *Oh gee whiz. The boy is finally cracking up.*

Then he gave me that big grin of his and slapped me on the shoulder and laughed.

Thank God, I thought.

“Bubba, slow down a little. And eah, didn’t we agree to come up with a plan about going crabbing and all?”

“Yeah, we sure did.” He jumped back a space and glared at me. “You don’t get it do you, Devlin? This *is* the plan. You *are* looking at the plan. Here’s what we do: You and me go to the rocks at Station 20 with my net here and we just scoop those rascals up. It’s that simple if you’ll ever get your lazy bee-hind outta bed. And the neat thing is we don’t even need any bait, just the net and a bucket. Maybe we’ll catch ’em two at a time and …”

I quickly interrupted, “WHOA, W-H-O-A slow down, slow down. That sounds great, Bubba. Just great. I hope we do catch a bunch of crabs … maybe a hundred. But think about this for a minute: Suppose we catch a nice mess of crabs. OK … you with me?”

Bubba nodded as he leaned on his crab net.

I was waking up by now and my mind was coming to life too. “Let’s say we have all these crabs. Then what are we going to do with them?”

“U-u-u-h?” Bubba’s face had a quizzical look. “I’m not sure … guess I didn’t think about that. Maybe we could …”

“See, what you’re doing Bubba, is letting your emotions rule your actions without proper forethought,” I said repeating something I’d heard on TV and thought it fit the situation. “Your thought process is improper and not flowing in the correct sequence. Therefore, your logic is flawed.”

“Eah, don’t get smart with me or you can find another partner. I’m just trying to help and catch some crabs, my fancy talking friend. If I want a sermon, I’ll call Sister Ann Marie.”

Despite his rugged exterior, Bubba was sensitive to a fine degree so immediately I apologized.

“Hey, I’m sorry partner. Without you this whole thing won’t work. You’re the best dog-gone crabber on this Island … I need ya. OK?” I said this as I slipped on my khaki shorts and my black high-top Converse tennis shoes.

Bubba accepted my apology with a smile. The last thing we needed was an argument on our first day at work.

"Is it gonna be hot today?" I asked.

Bubba gave me a dumb look and asked, "Is the Pope Catholic?"

"I mean do I need a shirt?"

"Good grief, Mike, we're not going to church. Come on let's go."

"Eah, first of all let's ride up to the Breach Inlet and see if anyone is catching any flounder," I suggested. I figured a nice long ride would give me time to think and come up with a good plan for our crabbing business. Something better than Bubba's idea of going to the rocks at the front beach, which was usually crowded with crabbers who practically fought with each other just to catch a dozen or so small ones. We would need to catch not just a lot of crabs but a lot of big crabs a lot of big crabs if we wanted to make a name for ourselves and make some money.

The Breach Inlet was at the eastern tip of the Island, a gap of water no more than three hundred yards wide and was a popular spot for the fishermen. It was spanned by a two-lane bridge, which connected the Island to our neighbors on the Isle of Palms. The waters of the Inlet were treacherous with extremely fast running currents and undertows. Coupled with a drop-off that went from ground level to twenty feet in the blink of an eye made this a dangerous place for swimming or wading. It was the only other place off limits to me other than Chippys.

With a little tact and diplomacy I convinced Bubba that if we crabbed in Miller's Creek out of a boat we could catch more crabs in less time than crabbing at the rocks on the front beach. This would cut our labor time while increasing our profits. I did not exactly word it that way. What I said was, "Don't you want more free time to goof off and hang out at the beach?

"Oh yeah, that's neat, man." Bubba wholeheartedly agreed. "Mike, you so smart. But … there's *one* other thing?"

"What's that?"

"Whose gonna buy the crabs?"

"Our customers, of course … who else?"

"And where are we going to get them?"

"Follow me and you'll see." I was hoping there was someone who wanted to buy crabs. Shoot, there had to be. If the seafood store was selling crabs then why couldn't we? Now all we had to do was find them and convince them to buy them from us, which should be easy because I had thought of a sure fire offer that our future customers could not turn down. First, we would undercut the seafood market's price drastically *and* second, we would deliver right to the doorstep.

We began knocking on doors in the neighborhood. The same as I had done in establishing my grass cutting business. We started with our parents, which was an easy sell. They gave us an order for two dozen. When Mrs. Reilly followed that up by readily agreeing to buy a dozen, we figured, "Shoot man, there ain't nothing to this crab business."

Then we hit a lull in the action, getting a "No, no thanks" … "Maybe next week" …and a "Not today" from crab eaters who must not have been very hungry. We just knew that what we were offering was a deal and a half: big fresh crabs delivered to their house for only twenty-five cents a dozen. Shoot, who could turn down that offer? Of course, we could have settled with our order for three dozen from our parents and Mrs. Reilly but splitting seventy-five cents two ways was too much arithmetic for us. Trying to divide up that amount of money was too much like schoolwork.

The tide was going to be right in a while so we gave it one last shot with the widow, Ms.Kingman.She was a retired librarian and about a hundred years old who was in failing health and she lived just across the street. Bubba's attitude was we better sell her some crabs today because she might not be here tomorrow. Being the honest con man that he was Bubba tried to convince the ailing Ms.Kingman that eating crabs would add years to her life.

"I know it's true, Ms.Kingman," he said, "we learned it in school."

"Oh yeah", remarked the skeptical Ms.Kingman, "and in what class did you learn that, Bubba?"

"Religion class," came a quick and positive reply. "Right, Mike?" I wanted no part of this discussion so I just nodded my head, as I looked the other way.

"How so?" she inquired. This lady was a tough sell but Bubba was up to the task.

"Well, we learned that we should put our trust in God's will in our lives."

"Yes," Ms. Kingman agreed. "That's right … go on."

"And well, I trust that part of God's will is that by helping us catch these crabs they are going to make you more healthy."

Ms. Kingman smiled and said, "In that case put me down for a dozen."

"Thank you, Ms.Kingman," we said together, … "see ya later." As we rushed away Ms. Kingman gave me a smile and a wink

Now the arithmetic became simpler. Our total order now was for four dozen crabs at twenty-five cents a dozen, which came to one dollar. Even our limited Math skills told us that. So we were able to quickly figure out that each of us would earn fifty cents. That's hardly any money in today's market but back then we could go to the Island movie theater and not only cover the cost of admission but also buy a Coke and a bag of popcorn … and still, believe it or not, have fifteen cents left over. Or if we decided to splurge and go to the skating rink right across the street from the movies, strap-on skates were only twenty-five cents for the whole night, leaving us with an extra twenty-five cents. We would be in high cotton. First, however, we had to deliver on our orders and one small obstacle that just might present a problem was in our way. We did not have a boat.

"Where are we gonna get a boat, where in the world can we get a boat? Let me think," I was thinking out loud, just loud enough for Bubba to hear me.

Bubba looked at me with that gleam in his eye and the beginning of a smile then he said, "Don't you worry one little bit about that, my friend."

I did.

"You see, Devlin, your problem is that you worry too much. Way too much about everything. Shoot, getting a boat is easy."

"Oh yeah, how?"

"No big deal, we borrow one." He was serious and I thought here we go again. Just like the garbage truck fiasco that I had tried to talk him out of it … kind of. I played along with him on this one. "And who do we *borrow* this boat from?

Bubba stopped his bike, which meant he was serious about something. You see, he could not think or talk seriously and ride his bike at the same time. He leaned down on his handlebars and explained to me that there were three or four boats anchored in Miller's Creek that just sit there all the time doing nothing but going up and down with the tides and we could help ourselves. We use the boat and then put it back. Nobody would know the difference.

I thought about it for a second and he was right. Several of the old-timey creek people like Charlie Tapia docked their boats permanently in Miller's Creek and when it was needed he would pull it to shore by the anchor line which was attached to the anchor lying on the shore. These were old, wooden affairs, rarely used, about twelve feet long and rotting away from neglect. Most leaked like a colander. *We would need something to bail with,* I reminded myself.

I still was not committed one hundred per cent to the idea of "borrowing" a boat without an owner's permission and needed just a little push. Bubba was good at giving that little push.

"Won't we get in trouble if we get caught … I mean"… a long pause … as I thought of the worst thing that could happen to us … "couldn't we be put in jail or something?"

"There you go again, worry wart."

"Well, shouldn't I worry a little?"

"No, no, don't worry. You see, we're not stealing" … a pause while he thought …   "Just borrowing a boat for a while. Know what I'm saying?"

"Kind of?"

"You know, like the story of Moses and The Ten Commandments …

how he borrowed them from God."

"No, I don't know. If I remember correctly, Moses was given The Commandments. Where were you in Religion class? Trying to look up Ellen Bagley's dress?"

In a loud voice Bubba shot back, "For your information The Commandments were *given* to all of us and if Moses had kept them then *he* would have been stealing." He paused and then added. "And ... and ...because we aren't keeping a boat we aren't stealing either just like Moses. Don't you see?"

I scratched my head, looked at Bubba and thought if Moses got away with it then it was all right with me. "Yeah, that makes perfect sense," I said rolling my eyes. Bubba grinned and was happy that I saw the light.

"Look, we aren't getting anywhere standing here flapping our jaws," Bubba said "Let's get the stuff together we need and go catch them Jimmies."

I nodded. That made more sense than anything we had done so far.

Now that the boat problem was temporarily solved we needed oars, an anchor line, an anchor, bait, some string for lines, and something to bail water with. Bubba already had a net, one he had found at the dump that had a cracked handle but at least it did not have any holes in it. We made a bailer out of a discarded coffee can by simply flatting out the top of the can a little so it would slide along the bottom of the boat. Anchors were plentiful. We would use a cinder block, the kind with the hole through the middle, making it easy to fasten the anchor line. My father had a set of oars hanging in the shed and I was sure he wouldn't mind us using them. The search for an anchor line proved fruitless and then Bubba suggested we cut down some of Ms.Kingman's clothesline.

I disagreed and sarcastically asked, "And where does Moses fit in there?"

"Oh, he doesn't but Jesus once said that..."

"No, no!" I quickly cut him off. "No more, cool it! There's no way Jesus is going to get dragged into this. He has more important things to do."

"All right, come on then," Bubba said dejectedly because I wouldn't let him tell me about Jesus. "Let's go to the Scott's and look around for an anchor line."

"Good idea. If there ain't no rope there, then there ain't no rope nowhere."

The Scotts lived three houses down, the home of Billy and Sammy Scott. They were an old Island family and their father, Willie Scott, was my father's childhood friend. And their backyard was the Mecca of the junk world. Discarded items, from God knows where, littered the whole backyard and it was a big backyard. Stoves, furniture, car parts, lumber, old tires, refrigerators were all stacked so high we labeled it "Junk

Mountain." More than the sight of Junk Mountain I loved its smell, which invigorated the most basic instinct of survival in me. The rusting steel of discarded appliances came to life and the odor of lumber long thrown out and considered useless by its former owners held no price. I treasured the whole pile and spent many an afternoon roaming that area of the Scott's yard trying to figure out what role each piece of treasure had played and would still play in its existing life. Bubba 'n me loved going there and combing through the endless piles of stuff that seemed to take on a life of its own and grow daily. It was like stepping back in time, like a museum, except far better. Here you could pick up anything you wanted to, examine it and throw it back on the pile. It was like hands-on window-shopping. Mr. Scott didn't mind a bit even if strangers came by and rummaged through the mounds, taking whatever they wanted.

"Be less for me to have to throw out," he said.

Throw out? I thought. *He had not thrown out anything in twenty years.* He even drove around the Island pulling an old rickety trailer behind his beat up old car in search of more stuff to add to the mountain of junk. The modern day Flea Market had its origin right there except everything here was free.

Bubba 'n me needed an anchor line. Tougher work than we thought as we dug through the mounds of debris. Some stuff was buried under vegetation so deep that a machine hadn't yet been invented that could cut through it. I thought maybe that was why Mr. Scott let this junk pile grew to such enormity… now he wouldn't have to mow as much grass?

Billy Scott was our age and a member of the crew but he was nowhere in sight. When Sammy appeared from out the house we inquired about Billy's whereabouts.

Sammy, a couple of years younger than Billy and the official keeper of the junk pile, told us, "He went in the creek with Ryan. They are gonna try to catch some crabs at Station 26 at the landing there, wading out using crab lines."

"Ain't no crabs up there," Bubba said like a crabbing authority. "Even Sambo knows that. They're so dumb."

"Yeah, I know but you can't tell them knuckleheads anything," Sammy said as he tossed an old chair onto the pile. "What y'all looking for?"

"Anchor line," Bubba answered. "We need about ten or twelve feet."

"Shoot man, why come up here? There's plenty right down the street … all you want."

"Oh yeah. Where?" I asked eagerly.

"Ms.Kingman's. Right there in her backyard."

"Oh, no!" I said. "We ain't cutting down somebody's clothes line."

Sammy grinned. "OK, OK … just a thought. I'll help y'all look around … give me a second. Y'all going crabbing?"

"Yep."

"Yeah. I hear they're running real good now."

After a twenty- minute empty search, none of us could find a long enough piece of rope in all that junk. We were about to give up when Sammy held up his finger and said, "Ah- hah. I just remembered where there's an anchor line."

"Oh great. Where?"

"Right here." And Sammy took out his pocketknife, waved us toward his father's car, opened the back door and promptly cut the seat belts out of the car.

"What in the world are you doing?" I lamented. "Your father is going to kill you." Sammy proudly handed me twelve feet of sturdy seat belts tied together.

"A-a-a-w … he won't miss 'em. He never uses 'em anyway."

"Man alive." I thought to myself. "And Sammy is the smart one in the family."

"Eah, now that's real thinking," Bubba whispered to me.

"Yep, real thinking." I shook my head and groaned, "Well, at least we got an anchor line."

The tide waits for no man and we were no exception. And sure enough we missed it by fooling around at the Scotts.

"Well, we done missed the tide." I looked at Bubba. "What do we do now, Moses?"

"Have no fear, my son. We call upon the Almighty to make it go back out and then … Bubba grinned and then said, "Actually, we plan on going tomorrow."

"Right and let's not forget our seat belt anchor," I said holding up Mr. Scott's former seatbelts.

"Yeah," Bubba exclaimed excitedly, "and besides, that will give them Jimmies one more day to fatten up!"

We quickly rode to Mrs. Reilly's and Ms. Kingman's to ask them if it would be all right if we were a day late in our delivery hoping and praying they would say, OK." Some businessmen we were… Humph!

"Sure, no problem," Mrs. Reilly said. "But don't forget me tomorrow."

Ms. Kingman was just as understanding and added, "And besides, that'll give them old Jimmies one more day to fatten up."

By 1959 improvements had been made on how to catch crabs in abundant numbers through the marketing of crab traps rather than using the old-fashioned hand line. Crab traps had been modernized and mass-marketed to the general public so that anyone could *trap* crabs as opposed to catching them on a line, using a net. Bubba 'n me preferred the old-timey method of a chicken neck on a string line with a sinker attached, which was the way taught to my father by his father and then passed on down to Bubba ’n me.

My father fished and crabbed these very creeks where he trained me and where his father had trained him. My father started me crabbing and fishing at a young age and by the ripe old age of twelve, I was no longer considered a rookie, the term my father used for anyone new at something, but neither was I a master crabber.

My Dad was more than a father to me. He was my friend as we shared equally in the enjoyment of outdoor Island life, his being fishing mostly. I was more than happy to be a part of whatever we did together. We had fun but I’m sure in the early stages of my tutelage it must have taken all of my father’s resolve not to tie me to a tree somewhere and leave me there. I recall whining and complaining in the boat when the fish weren’t biting or when it was too hot. I must have asked a thousand times, “When are we going home?”

Physically my father was a powerful man, especially in the arms and shoulders. Those muscles were developed early in life by his part-time job as a teenager rowing customers out to the jetties in the entrance to Charleston harbor from off the beach on the Island. Round trip was about two miles. He could cast a net, pole a boat through the thickest marsh, and row like a collegiate champion.

“Why didn’t you use the motor like the one you have now,” I asked one morning while we were loading the boat for a trip to those same jetties in hopes of catching supper.

“Son, we didn’t have motors back then.”

I didn’t understand. “You mean you paddled all the way out to the jetties just to take some people fishing?” I was full of questions and my father was full of answers. We made a great team. At least, I thought so.

“Yeah, but I didn’t paddle. I had oarlocks and oars and I got $2.00 for the day sometimes $3.00 if we hit the blackfish good and I got a tip.”

I shook my head in agreement but my father knew there was doubt. It would be later that I would learn how to row and what a tip was. My father was talking about 1929- 1932, and stuff like The Great Depression and feelings of hunger were foreign to my young mind. Maybe that was why he was so generous with the little bit he had, always giving and sharing with others. It was one of the most valuable lessons of life that I ever learned. What I found strange was that many from his era who were now well- off financially were stingy, giving little to their own families, much less strangers. I witnessed the greed constantly and can only thank God for my father. He also taught me how to fish and crab. What else can you say about a man whose generosity was exceeded only by his kindness and patience?

If you wanted to catch a bunch of crabs at once then a folding trap was used. The trap, triangular in shape, and made of steel opened as it descended to the bottom, remaining open in a flat position with bait attached in the middle. Its sides closed upward as you pulled it to the surface thus trapping the crabs. These traps later became common among those who were too impatient to crab with a line or didn't know how to crab properly.

Commercial crabbers had a different type of trap and would set out as many as fifty traps in a day, returning to check them in a couple of days. These traps were worked from a large boat, tossed overboard and sank to the bottom from their own weight and baited with dead fish, a delicacy of the crab. These crab traps or "pots" as they were commonly called were made from wire mesh and marked with a large cork tied with an identifying mark on it. They were tied to a rope. This type of trapping mechanism was simple but highly effective. In two sides of these traps were openings designed to allow the crab entrance but no exit. The outer opening was larger than the inner part, it simply narrowed down. These traps were about three feet by three feet in size and could hold up to fifty to sixty crabs. It was pure irony that a crab eating a meal became a meal in its capture and death. These trapping methods were so impersonal that they never held any interest for Bubba 'n me.

Crabbing from a boat was loads of fun. Once you got to your favorite spot in the creek and anchored, the lines, usually three to four per person, were lowered to the bottom of the creek where the crabs fed. A fancy crab line had a store-bought sinker on it like fisherman use to give it weight to get it to the bottom. Because we did not want to waste what little money we had on store bought sinkers, Bubba 'n me used small pipe fittings found in the Scott junk pile like an elbow through which the string could easily pass through and be tied, along with the bait, a chicken neck. Each crabber was responsible for his lines and it was an unspoken rule you didn't check or mess with anybody else's lines while crabbing. Each crabber checked his lines for the feel of extra weight or a tugging sensation, which announced that a crab was on the line. The crab or crabs were gently raised to just below the water line about a foot to eighteen inches and promptly scooped up with the net. Normally each person was responsible for netting his own crabs but in the case of a rookie being onboard the veteran would help with the netting so as not to unnecessarily lose crabs. The all time record for most crabs pulled in on a hand line at one time was five by my father one day crabbing in a spot he called Grandfather's Hole because the crabs there had barnacles on their backs attesting to their age. I was with my father that particular day. That one catch was a meal in itself and I looked around the surrounding area memorizing distances and angles, looking for landmarks and checked the time of the tide to assure myself that when the time came I would be able to find my own way back to Grandfather's Hole.

A couple of years earlier my father had taken me crabbing at

Station12 in front of Saint Angela's Church at the rocks. We were crabbing off the beach on the edge of the rocks that extended no more than a hundred feet into the harbor. It was a beautiful summer morning, the kind with a breeze just weak enough to move a few hairs on your head yet strong enough to keep the gnats at bay. The harbor was as slick as a baby's butt, my father's term, and shined like a mirror, giving the appearance of two worlds of clouds. It was so flat it looked as though you could walk on it. Only the diving gulls disturbed this stillness as they breakfasted on schools of fresh menhaden. The gulls' plunges sent out perfectly formed ripples in an endless circle.

My father noticed me watching the gulls at work and staring at the ripples. He told me that life was like that circle of ripples.

"What do you mean, Daddy? We go around in circles?"

"No, no," he said and then patiently explained. "It's like this." He paused and I could tell he was thinking hard about something. "Well, how do I tell you? Anyway, something that you say or do can have an effect on someone and then they in turn do something resulting from that effect and have an effect on someone else and it goes right on down the line. It's called the ripple effect and keeps on going forever. That's the best way I know to tell you." He smiled, placing his hand on my shoulder. "You understand?"

I nodded "yes" with a very doubtful look on my face.

"Don't worry it'll come to you," he said. "You'll see. Eah, let's go catch some crabs."

That day we enjoyed the crabbing almost as much as we enjoyed the company of each other as we hauled in crab after crab. We were using the chicken necks on a line and casting our lines out no more than six feet.

"You ever use one of those steel traps to catch crabs, Daddy?"

"Uh-uh, not me. Never have and never will. If I did I'd have to go to church immediately."

"What for … to give Father Dawes some crabs?"

"Oh no, son, to confess a mortal sin," my father said as he laughed his wonderful laugh.

As the morning progressed a few crabbers appeared along with the usual mix of beachgoers and sun worshipers. However, I couldn't help but notice a young man watching us crab. He couldn't seem to take his eyes off us as he carefully watched our every move and what we were doing. The distance between us shortened. Every few minutes he edged closer and closer to us until his curiosity got the best of him. With an accent that had New Jersey written all over it he asked, "What are those?" He was pointing in our bucket. I almost started laughing and looked to my father who gently shook his head from side to side. (*I wish Bubba were here now because he would not believe this.)*

My father patiently explained to our visitor what a crab was and gave a crash course on the ins and outs of crabbing. I could tell by this man's intent, bug-eyed expression and the way he was jumping around and acting all excited that he was hooked before he even caught his first crab. He listened carefully and was very thankful for the lesson and seemed to be in a hurry to leave as he dashed off.

No more than thirty minutes later our Yankee rookie was back ready to set up shop and do some serious crabbing. He had a bucket in hand with store bought lines, a net, sinkers, and "bait." All still had the price tags on them from Owen's Grocery. We watched in total amazement as this young man crabbed for the first time attempting to pull in a big one. Over and over he failed, his efforts in vain. But he would not give up. He would pull in an empty line, rebait it, and toss it back in the water. Momentarily he would have a crab on the line only to lose him as the bait and crab seemed to disappear. For bait this rookie had unbelievably selected a pack of hot dogs, the kind you eat at the ballpark. The sharp and powerful claws of the crabs were cutting through them with one bite like a steak knife through hot butter providing the crabs with an endless feast. The frustrated crabber continued to tie on hot dog after hot dog. When we left our Northern brethren was scratching his head and mumbling in despair, while he wiped away the pouring sweat.

Walking back to the car, my father asked me, "Do you know why that guy didn't catch any crabs with those hot dogs?"

"No, Daddy.Why?"

"Because he didn't put any mustard on 'em, that's why," he said grinning.

It took a second or two for me to catch on and then I laughed … and laughed … and laughed … the whole way home.

11
UP THE CREEK

This was the big day. The day Bubba 'n me would officially begin our crabbing business. I was awake before the chickens next door cracked an eyelid. Not up but awake. I was lying in bed visualizing Bubba 'n me hauling in crab after crab; then I heard Rudy, the Brown's rooster, greet the new day. I had been all keyed up since last night when I went to bed thinking about going crabbing and had barely slept a wink. Shoot, I was still excited about going in the creek with my friend and catching crabs on our own … and then selling them! It was kind of like the feeling a kid gets when he goes to bed on Christmas Eve. Anticipation. What a great feeling. The only feeling better is the fulfillment of that anticipation.

Bubba 'n me had agreed to get up extra early because we wanted to make sure we caught the morning tide just right without wasting time rushing around looking for this or that, like old ladies searching for their gloves before going to church.

I had learned two basic rules of the creek from my father who not only taught them but he also lived by them. One was the tide waits for no man. If you are late … it's too late. You cannot pray or wish it back. It's gone and you have to wait for the next one… it's like missing the train. The other rule was do not *ever* tell anyone the location of your favorite crabbing or fishing spot, not even your mother. If you do it will become public knowledge, regardless of how many promises were made to you by someone that they would never reveal your secret spot. And you can assure yourself that the next time you go to that spot to haul in a nice mess of crabs or fish you won't be alone or so many people have already been there that it will have been fished out. This was especially true among fishermen more so than crabbers. With crabbers there was more or less room for everyone, crabs were plentiful and roamed the whole creek but Bubba 'n me weren't taking any chances. We decided as part of our master plan that we would abide by these rules thus the early start and we would be careful not to tell any of our friends about any good crabbing spots, if we found any. Not even our mothers.

I had heard my father say that the crabs do not fill out good until July and that if we have a real hot summer then come September they are so fat you can hardly lift 'em into the boat. We had our crabbing stuff ready:

net, lines, basket, bait and, of course, our seat-belt anchor line which I hid under the back steps so that my father would not see it and wonder what kind of creek person I was. We were all set to confirm my father's claim about the size of the crabs because it had been a hot summer so far, and if what he said was true, then we would be in for a good day. You see, we did not plan to catch little baby crabs even though it was impossible not to. They were everywhere, always tagging along with their parents. You couldn't blame 'em for biting our lines, they had to eat too and besides, they would grow up and someday become a meal. We planned to deliver the big crabs, the male Jimmies, the ones with barnacles on their back, which was an indication of old age and usually meant they were full of meat … the old timers, the Grandfathers. That's what we were after. But don't think we were prejudiced against the female crabs. No sir-ree, not one bit. We would toss a nice size female crab in the bucket in a New York second.

This would be our first solo attempt at putting into practice the crabbing skills we had learned from my father who had been a patient and excellent teacher and a fun crabbing partner. He had been crabbing these very waters for over forty years and never failed to bring home a fine mess of big crabs. Oh, Bubba 'n me had messed around some at the rocks on the front beach with a net scooping up a stray crab every now and then but had never attempted anything like this. As far as we were concerned this was serious business. Crabbing from a boat and getting paid for it was different than just messing around in the creek. We had to produce. There could be no excuses. The real pressure came from the fact that we had people, our customers, depending on us, which was a big change. Now the shoe was on the other foot.

Bubba had become somewhat of a fixture in the Devlin household and had practically been adopted by my father who included him in most everything we did. We were as much brothers as non-kin could be. There was a line, however, that Bubba refused to cross for whatever unknown reason and at times he decided not to become a part of particular outings, especially sporting events. Maybe he just didn't like sports? Or maybe he was like his father who was not into the outdoors or sports or boating and fishing. The only time I ever saw Mr. O'Toole outside was when he mowed the grass when Bubba failed to do his job because he was at the beach or in the creek or someplace other than cutting the grass. Lately Mr. O'Toole cut the grass a lot.

I considered myself the lucky one having a father who took me not only crabbing and fishing but also to the football and basketball games at The Citadel, the local military college in Charleston. I remember the young and slender Paul "Sticky Fingers" Mac Guire, split end, who also punted and later had a successful pro career. In basketball I fell in love with Dick Jones and the Whiz Kids who showed the rest of the

Southern Conference how basketball should be played. We went to high school basketball games and talked sports all the time, especially college football. I learned from an early age that there was only one special team in college football … Notre Dame! And don't ever bet against 'em. Sports was my second passion behind the pleasures and adventures of the creek. It was the glue that formed and held together many a childhood friendship and, in my case, helped cement a father-son relationship that lasted a lifetime.

My father's teaching technique was simple and straightforward, just like him. He would tell me how to do something, like when I learned to cast a net, he would demonstrate, and then let me try. When I did it wrong he would patiently show me again and let me try again. And it usually worked but not without its trials and tribulations. Because of his willingness to let me tag along on fishing and crabbing trips, when really he was seeking some quiet time for himself, I got a lot of hands on practice. Early in my training I probably lost more crabs than I caught if someone had bothered to keep count. Getting a crab on the line was easy; netting him was the hard part, especially in a swift moving current. When I would knock another one off the line with the net or miss by being too anxious, my father would just look at me and ask, "Do you know what that crab's name is?"

I'd answer, "Yes sir."

And he would ask, "What?"

And I would answer, "Lucky."

We would laugh. It was a routine we never got tired of.

His method of teaching was known as the K-I-S-S rule … the anagram for Keep It Simple Stupid; however, we had modified it to mean Keep It Simple Son… more appropriate for a young boy and his father-teacher.

Miller's Creek ran along the back of the Island its source at the western point of the Island across the harbor from Charleston, and ended at Station 19. It was no more than a mile long. It was a typical Lowcountry salt- water creek winding its way through the thick marsh grass, never more than ten feet deep at high tide; and it offered the possibility of new excitement at every turn, weaving its way to an unknown destination. Its width varied from five to fifty feet thus providing many different spots from which to fish or crab.

The greatest thing about Miller's Creek that Bubba 'n me liked, other than it was full of fish and crabs, was that it was a three-minute walk from Bubba's backyard. This day we were excited as we walked from his backyard at a brisk pace, almost running. After all the preparation of lining up our customers, all the planning, gathering everything we needed: the net, lines, basket, bait, anchor and anchor line, we both silently hoped it would be worth all the effort. I felt as though we had completed a heavy task already and now it was time to rest and that's what brought on the apprehensive thoughts. I was thinking about all that could go wrong instead of thinking about all the good we had accomplished.

"What you thinking about, Mike?" Bubba asked me as we neared the landing. "Why you so quiet?"

"A-a-a-w nothing. I was just thinking. Just being the ol' worry wart."

"You mean about going out in the boat and crabbing and all?"

"Y-e-a-h."

"Eah, don't worry we're going to have a good time catching Mister Jimmy and his family. Maybe they'll have some relatives visiting for the summer. Like some fat aunts and uncles or cousins from up North?" He was trying to lighten the moment.

"HA-HA, you should be a commodeian" ...our term for a comedian whose humor is so bad it should be flushed.

"But you know ... you're right, Bubba. What could be the worst thing that could happen ... we don't catch any crabs? Just waste a lot of time? Get sunburned?"

"N-a-a-w, the worst thing that could happen is the boat sinks and we drown," deadpanned Bubba. What he said held a certain amount of truth but I decided to keep the moment on the light side. I thought for a few seconds and said, "Eah, that wouldn't be so bad. Know why?"

"Why?"

"Then we wouldn't have to go back to school." I smiled at that thought but Bubba was frowning. Maybe the heat was getting to him.

Bubba then stopped and looked me straight in the eye, real serious like and said, "Devlin, let me tell you something. If the boat sank and we died today, when school started Sister Roberta would dig us up, take us right over to school and set us up in our desks, and demand that we pay attention and behave, the whole time shaking that bony finger at us and waving the big ruler." And then he let go a thunderous laugh.

"A-HA-HA-HA", I laughed too. "I can see her now whacking the hell out of you with the big ruler and you just sitting there dead as a doornail with a big smile on your face."

"Oh yeah, why would I be smiling while I'm getting the big ruler treatment?"

"For one thing you're smiling because you are dead and don't feel a thing but the real reason you're smiling is because you died crabbing in Miller's Creek with your best buddy and all time friend ... me!"

"And what will you be doing?"

"Smiling too because I'd be dead and not have to do any more homework."

"Eah, you never know?" Bubba said chuckling. "The Devil might hand out homework assignments every day?"

"Humph," I said. "Don't even think like that. Eah, enough of this jaw flapping … let's go crabbing."

We put our gear on the ground, stood on the bank, and checked out the available boats at anchor, pitching and bobbing with the current. I couldn't help but admire the beauty of the huge marsh expanse that stretched all the way to Mt. Pleasant, over two miles away to the north. It looked like a giant green lawn complete with the perfectly placed ornamentation of egrets, sea gulls, and pelicans. Looking to the east it stretched as far as the eye could see, way up the Intracoastal Waterway toward the Isle of Palms. It was a magnificent sight that gave me a chilly feeling even under the warm sun.

"Eah, you all right," Bubba asked. "You're not still feeling funny are ya?"

"No, I'm good to go … just looking around that's all."

"Whatcha think? Wilson's boat, it's bigger or Graham's boat … it's smaller but would be easier to row. And look over there. There's Mr. Scott's leaky tub … HA-HA." Bubba's remark took the Scott's boat out of the running.

We chose to borrow Bobby Graham's boat, not because it was smaller, but because Mr. Graham was an easy going, nice guy who would probably be more lenient with us if we got caught using his boat without permission than old man Wilson who was mean as a wart hog and twice as ugly. The only other choice, Mr. Scott's, leaked like a running faucet. When Sammy and Billy went out in it they spent more time bailing water than crabbing, they must have felt like they were taking a bath while crabbing. When asked why their Dad didn't fix the leaks Sammy said that his father sometimes missed the crab bucket after catching a crab and the water in the bottom of the boat gave the strays somewhere to play and plus it kept 'em fresh. He said he went with his Dad once and he thought he was missing the bucket intentionally they had so many crabs running around the boat.

"What'd you do?" I asked.

"Nothing. Waited till we got back and scooped 'em up. Man, that was easy crabbing."

"Here", I said, handing Bubba the rope securing Mr. Graham's boat. "Pull 'er in and I'll get the basket and lines," which were on the bank behind us.

"Aye, aye, captain."

Bubba pulled the boat toward him working the line hand over hand coiling the rope at his feet until he got a secure hold on the bow and pulled the boat about two feet onto the edge of the bank.

Just before stepping into the boat a flashback of an old Island tale hit me. In the late 1920's a famed creek-man named John McAlister went crabbing in this very creek hoping to catch food for his family.

Many people during The Depression fed their families from the creek and vegetable gardens in their yards. The story goes that the crabs of Miller's Creek held a particular grudge against old John because he had taken so many of their friends and relatives to the pot over the years and they vowed to exact their pound of flesh someday. With the help of some healthy and strong crabs from neighboring Swinton's Creek they all got together, laid their plans and waited. The fateful day arrived when a scout recognized John's trademark, a double- chicken- neck bait, and quickly sent out the alarm. Oh, John thought he was doing really well and into a good mess after netting a few sacrificial crabs until he felt the boat moving against the current toward the harbor. Those big neighbors from Swinton's Creek helped make the day with their huge pinchers which gnawed through John's anchor line and with the Miller's Creek gang they grabbed hold of the anchor line and towed John McAlister, boat and all, from Miller's Creek to the harbor, and then all the way out to sea where he was never heard from again. This story was called the Payback of the Crabs and was told to me by my father but only as a reminder to be careful … I think?

"Hey you!" A loud yell from Bubba woke me up. "Are you gonna crab or look around all day?"

He held the boat while I climbed in carrying the straw bushel basket, home for the not so lucky ones, and the lines and net. I began squaring things away, setting up space for us to sit and clearing out an open area for us to crab in without crowding each other. Lastly, Bubba passed me the oars, and in his eagerness to finally get going, put the anchor in the boat and at the same time pushed off from the bank and jumped in the boat, without any warning to me. And before I could bat an eye we were launched.

"Oh yeah," he yelled. "We're finally going to catch 'ol Jimmy … I'm ready. How about you?

Before I could answer we were quickly in midstream, caught in the swift current, moving backwards downstream at a good clip. I threw Bubba an oar and told him to grab an oarlock.

"Hurry," I said. Hoping to right the boat we frantically tried to get the oarlocks set in their holes but they kept slipping out; we were moving even faster now and sideways. Finally, it seemed like forever, we got the oarlocks in place and set the oars in them and I yelled to Bubba, "You get over there" pointing to the port side. "I'll get over here… we gotta slow this thing down."

"What if I don't want to sit on that side?" Bubba said in a way reminding me of my little sister Katie when she whined. "Maybe I like your side better?"

"Do you want to fight or crab?" I said in a very serious tone giving Bubba the look. "Which is it?"

"Right here, oh yeah, that's fine," Bubba said apologetically. " I'll sit right here. Yeah, this a great seat."

"Good. Now let's work together and maybe we can crab sometime today." I knew Bubba did not like confrontations of any kind and at this moment I needed his help, not a bunch of mouth about where he wanted to sit. Whether he realized it or not, but with this fast flowing ebb tide we could easily end up in Charleston harbor or at the jetties in a heartbeat.

We pulled on the oars with all the might the Good Lord had given us and it was a total waste of energy. The current was way mightier than the strength of any two skinny, little Irish kids but we didn't know that. After a couple of futile minutes, we jerked the oars out of the oarlocks and tried standing up and paddling but kept bumping into each other and slipping around, something we didn't need. We even got on the same side and tried to muscle the boat around but didn't possess the brawn to do it and, in the process, we nearly tipped over the boat with all our weight on one side. We put the oars back in the oarlocks and sat down to catch our breath as we drifted aimlessly with the outgoing tide.

Finally, we tried solo. Each of us taking a turn at rowing the boat into position by our self. We would have done better trying to do brain surgery. Then Bubba mercifully suggested we rest ... I was all for that. We sat glum-faced looking at each other wondering what to do next? We were floating down the creek at a steady pace headed for Charleston harbor, a mile or so away.

"I thought you knew how to row a boat?" I asked Bubba disgustingly.

"Yeah, you know what," he said disgustingly. "I was just getting ready to ask you the same thing, Einstein."

We grabbed the oars and tried again. The only progress we made upon our return to the oars was that we were able to keep the boat in a sideways movement. I thought that if we could only get it straightened out then we might have a chance of rowing to the side of the creek by the marsh and escape the main thrust of the current. Right now we were at its mercy. If we were swept out of Miller's Creek and got into the open flats, which weren't that far off, then the harbor was next and we definitely did not want to end up there because after that it was the open sea.

Here we were, two rookies drifting the wrong way down Miller's Creek, caught in an unforgiving ebb tide that said, "You boys are going to sea whether you like it or not."

All I could envision was us ending up in the nether world of lost mariners, face-to-face with the ghost of John McAlister who would ask, "H-e-l-l-o b-o-y-s, y'all wouldn't be from Sullivans Island now would ya?" in a slow, deep Southern drawl. "Welcome to my world."

"Oh no, A-H-H-H," I yelled, frightened by my own thoughts.

"What's wrong with you?" Bubba asked. " Looks like you've seen a ghost."

"Well yeah, kinda… ah, forget it."

I was looking for someone to blame for this screw up and Bubba was the nearest victim. "Why'd you push us out? I wasn't ready."

"I thought you were ready to go… shut up and row … OK?"
I gave a mighty stroke of the oar, slipped, hitting Bubba on the shoulder, nearly knocking him out the boat. He returned the favor with a dirty look.

"O-O-P-S, sorry," I said.

"You better be!"

"Row more even, Bubba. I mean more level like. A-A-A-H, you know what I mean, more …" (long pause) "quit being so spastic," I blurted out. It was more of a plea than a command but Bubba was having none of it. He quit rowing, stood up, threw his oar down and bellowed, "If you don't like my rowing then I'm going home… right now! OK, Mr. Smarty. Just because you think you're the captain doesn't mean you can order me around."

"Oh yeah," I grinned, "and how you getting home?"

"I'm swimming that's how."

He was serious and I barely got hold of the back of his bathing suit a split second before he went overboard. I held on for dear life pulling him back in the boat.

"Eah look here, man. Your rowing is good. No, it's better than good it's great, it really is … it's me that's messing up," I pleaded. "Don't go home, not now. Sit down … OK?"

The way he was looking at me I could tell he was thinking it over. Oh, a-l-l right … just don't be blaming me for this screw-up or I'm outta here and quit grinning … I mean it, Devlin."

"OK, OK," I said, "I'm sorry. Let's try again. We can do it." I handed him his oar. "Here. Come on and help me … please." I was thinking I did not want to meet John McAlister alone.

We tried our little hearts out but rowing was not our cup of tea. Meanwhile we were all over the creek, still heading for the harbor and I'm thinking, "Gee whiz, things ain't going too good."

One thing we were not were quitters and we continued to row hard and steady, making a little headway almost getting control of the boat. But about the time we thought we had it straightened out either the current or the wind would pull us off course and it was sideways again we would go. On my next stroke I put all I had into it, barely missing the water, skimming the surface and with no resistance went backwards sliding off the seat like a shot banging my head on the forward seat … PHOW YOW! I was lucky I hadn't busted open my head open. I was stunned and layed there. And nothing was seriously hurt but Bubba didn't know that so I lay there real still playing possum, cracking one eye to check Bubba's reaction. He tossed his oar down and quickly came to my aid with a worried expression.

"Mike, you OK? Hey, can you hear me? Wake up, man, you all right?

I gave my best Hollywood groan, "O-o-o-o-h. … O-o-o-o-h."

"Oh no," Bubba said with a pitiful look. "Hang on …I'll pick ya up. You OK? Mike, talk to me … say something." He tried to lift me but I was dead weight so he eased me back down. He stood up looking out over the creek and back down at me looking like he might have an anxiety attack right then and there. His face was all screwed up and his eyes were darting from the land back to me so fast I thought for sure they were going to pop out of his head any second now. "You OK?" He tried to move me again, then sat down with his hands over his face. I thought he was going to cry.

I figured enough was enough and I was barely able to hold it back any longer so I let go with a loud, "A-HA-HA-HA …A-HA-HA" and jumped up. "Gotcha good, huh?"

His face showed anger but his eyes were thankful.

"You know Devlin, someday that crap is going to backfire on you. Sister Rosalind is going to be beating you to death with the big ruler and you'll be screaming for help and we won't do a thing thinking you're faking it again, how you gonna feel then?"

"I don't know but I'll feel better now if we ever get this boat from going all over this creek. C'mon we can do it."

We fought the current and the wind, which had picked up steadily and offered us some relief from the morning heat but otherwise was as relentless as the current. Little progress was being made and we were wasting valuable crabbing time with a task that looked so easy when my father glided across the water in a straight line, stroke after stroke. I kept slipping on the now wet seat from all the splashing we had done, bumping into Bubba's elbow.

"O-O-P-S, sorry."

"Eah, stay on your side Devlin, and maybe we can get somewhere," Bubba said giving a powerful stroke.

Anyone but real friends in a situation like this could lead to deathblows. I knew Bubba was getting mad because he called me by my last name. I hoped he was madder at the boat than at me. Once at school he asked Sister Ann Marie her last name after receiving a good paddling and I knew something bad was on his mind. Good thing Sister Ann Marie didn't know what he was thinking. It was rare that Bubba 'n me got mad at each other and if we did it was usually over in a minute. Neither one of us believed in holding a grudge or was so set in our ways that we couldn't give in when it was called for. Now was the time for patience and understanding and some know-how. That is … in how to row a boat.

Bubba had once told me in all sincerity after a heated argument, "You might be a jack leg sometimes Mike, but you're still my best friend." Eah, what else can a man ask for? The dilemma we were in now was testing our friendship and nerves so we did what the good nuns at St. Angela's had taught us best …we prayed. And, I mean mightily we prayed. It was time for one of those if- I- ever- get- out- of- this- alive -I'll- be- good- the- rest –of- my- whole- life type prayers.

I prayed long and hard, throwing in an extra plea that the Yankees win the pennant this year. Bubba's prayer was shorter than mine and more to the point: I heard him say, "God, please get us out of this mess, will ya?"

I asked him, "Could you pray just a little bit more, I mean…"

"Nope, God's too busy with more important stuff than to listen to a long prayer."

"Yeah, like what?"

"Like trying to figure out how to save your sinful soul, Devlin." There was the last name again. Time for me to shut up.

"Man, this would piss off the Pope," Bubba mumbled to himself as he slipped again on the wet seat. He was getting madder by the minute. Not me, I was too scared to be mad. If we end up in Charleston harbor, the highway of the huge freighters making their way to the docks on East Bay Street, we would be in a fix. I could see it now. I'm sure some nice, considerate captain would stop his ship in mid-harbor should we drift into his right of way, and wave us through thinking, "I'll just let these two boys go on by, looks like they're out for a nice afternoon of crabbing."

Yeah right. If one of those monsters hit us, it would take a year and a day to find the splinters.

We went from one side of the creek to the other, back and forth, sideways. Why we even did a three hundred and sixty degree turn at one point. We looked like a sparrow in a hurricane.

I could hear my father now, "Mike don't plan on going anywhere this Saturday about 5:00 because you need to go to church and make a confession."

"For what, Daddy?"

"I heard about you and Bubba in the creek the other day in the boat. Shame, shame, shame," he would say with a smile so I knew he was only half serious.

"Yes sir." If not a mortal sin, it certainly was a venial sin … a Devlin not being able to handle a boat.

Then it finally dawned on me that part of the problem was either Bubba's over powering strength or my weakness. His powerful stroke overwhelmed my efforts thus turning the bow more with each pass of the oar. I would yell for him to quit rowing and by my continuing to row I then became guilty of the same mistake. We were unknowingly fighting each other's stroke. What we needed to do was stroke the oars at the same time and with equal velocity in order to keep the bow on straight. It sounds easy but up to this point it had been a two- man Chinese fire drill. It hadn't taken all that long to figure this out but when you're caught in a fast moving tide it doesn't take long to cover a lot of creek.

We were at least three-quarters of a mile from the landing and the only hope in sight was the thick marsh grass lining the creek. We settled down, got the correct motion and power into each stroke and mercifully we were able to get the boat headed toward the marsh, which brought us to a stop, finally. We reached out and grabbed a handful of marsh grass and held on, holding us in place. Another five minutes and we would have been in Charleston harbor with the big boys and in real danger. I could see us now whooping and hollering, waving the oars for someone to come rescue us before we drifted out to sea. In reality we would have probably been crying like newborns and praying like saints. Lodged safely in the thick marsh grass I just wanted to sit and rest awhile.

Our shoulders and little arms were burning from the unfamiliar exercise and sweat soaked our bathing suits.

"Oh boy! Wasn't that fun? Hey, wanna do it again," Bubba said in a true mocking tone. Then came *his* laugh and *his* laugh only … BA-HA-HA-HA, BA-HA-HA! It was like no other laugh in the universe. Bubba would toss his head back and coming from his toes he would bellow this rhythmic sequence very loudly and always the same in tone and sequence. Its meaning was that "everything is OK". It was used many times later in life and carried us through many a difficult situation.

"Funny," I replied. " Real funny, huh?"

"Eah, who taught you how to row anyway, Mike? …Sambo?"

"At least I had a lesson, mister-don't –know-jack-about-rowing," I said. "You don't know your bee-hind from third base, you know that?"

"Yeah, yeah, yeah. Let's sit here and rest." Bubba breathed heavily. "I'm tired…OK?"

"Good idea, Bubba. That's the only smart thing you've said today." I stretched out across the seat and stared at the circling gulls as they searched for a free meal. *Ain't this great? Sitting in the marsh sweating like a tourist from Cleveland while all those crabs are getting away. I'll never make enough money to take Beverly Ann to the movies. Shoot!*

12
CRABBING

My mother used to say that God worked in "strange" ways and for the longest time I did not understand what she meant. So I guess if I did not know what it meant I should have kept my big mouth shut. What I did know was that I should have never said anything like that around Sister Rosalind, implying that God was "strange," because she called me a "hair-a-tick" or something like that and threatened me with the big ruler treatment if I ever said it again. I didn't.

God was working in his strange way at this very moment. We just didn't know it. Here we were sitting in the boat up in the marsh grass, looking dumbly at each other, missing the tide again, and with an order of four-dozen crabs hanging over our heads. Neither of us knew what to do.

"Whose big idea was this anyway … to go into the crabbing business? Huh, Devlin?"

"Eah, I didn't twist your arm to be my partner … now did I?"

"I didn't twist your arm to be my partner," Bubba repeated in a sarcastic tone, mocking me. He paused and then said, "No you didn't but I wish I was home right now watching TV. This stinks."

The bad part wasn't listening to my friend complain. It was the fact that we hadn't even wet a line yet. Yet it was in this deep, dark moment we made the discovery of a lifetime, which was not ten feet from the bow of the boat, behind Bubba. It was in the form of a huge rusty pipe almost two feet in diameter coming from the back of the Island which was no more than two hundred yards away. This pipeline, which we had never noticed before, ran straight across the top of the marsh about a foot above the tip of the marsh reeds all the way to Miller's Creek. It was an eyesore that spoiled an otherwise beautiful view of the green pristine marsh that stretched for miles reflecting greenish yellow sparkles of light.

"What in the world? I mumbled to Bubba. "Where'd that thing come from?"

"Some kind of drain pipe …I think." Bubba eyed the pipe suspiciously.

"I don't know, but just maybe…"

We paddled over to the pipe until we became pinned against it by the current, which was not running nearly as strong here as in the creek because of the thick marsh grass, but it was strong enough to hold us in place.

"Got an idea," I said.

"That's great," Bubba said. "I've got plenty. Hope yours has something to do with getting us out of here."

"Eah!" I practically yelled. "Tell you what, if you don't want to hear it put your thumbs in your ears, close your eyes, and smile … at least, you'll look smarter."

"You've been watching too much of the Three Stooges, my friend," Bubba replied like a scolded child. He paused, looked around at the great marsh expanse and said slowly, "OK what's your big idea?"

"Why don't we grab the pipe and pull our way back out to the creek."

"You know what, Mike? And you probably won't believe this, but I was just thinking the same thing," Bubba said giving me a big smile that I did not return. I wanted to crab and make some money and not next year.

"There's nothing to grab hold to," Bubba said balancing himself in the bow and grabbing at the pipe.

"Wait a minute, got another idea," I said quickly before Bubba could get the chance to disrupt my "idea thoughts" again. "Get the anchor line ready."

"What for?"

"Don't ask questions, OK? Just hold us right here for a second and watch, will ya?"

"What ya doing?"

"I'm getting up on the pipe, Einstein. What does it look like I'm doing. You know you sound just like Tommy Wade."

"Eah boy, watch your mouth. Them's fighting words."

I managed to scramble up onto the pipe. Standing there I looked down at Bubba and told him, "Well, I'll see ya later, alligator." I took a couple of steps back the other way. "I'm going home… have fun."

"If you leave…" Bubba froze momentarily … "I'll wring your …"

"Just kidding man, just kidding," I quickly interrupted. "Hand me the anchor line." I leaned over and extended my hand. " No! … Not the anchor … the anchor line!"

"Well, the anchor's tied to it," Bubba said in obvious frustration.

"Then why don't you untie it and … oh man," I thought, "What is going on here?" Finally, I got Bubba to toss me the anchor line.

Walking the wide pipeline was easy. I held the anchor line in my hand and pulled the boat while Bubba did his part by keeping the boat from rubbing against the pipe using the oar to fend the boat off.

"A-W-O-O-P, W-H-O-O-P, W-H-O-O-P, KNUCK, KNUCK, KNUCK… look Moe, look Larry, see Mike on the pipe," Bubba said doing his best Curley imitation.

I came back with my much-practiced John Wayne: "This town ain't big enough for the four of us partner, and if you Stooges aren't outta town by sundown I'm g-o-n-n-a kick your butts." Much needed laughter spilled over the marshland.

I stopped at the end of the pipe, which was on the edge of the creek. At the pipe's end, a steady dribble of brownish water trickled into Miller's Creek giving off a peculiar yet familiar odor, but we couldn't place it. Not wanting to venture back into the creek and do battle with the current, we decided to drop anchor and try our luck here at the end of the pipe. Bubba looked like a man who was just told by the doctor that his severe heart attack was just a gas attack. I felt relief too now that we were at least going to crab. Six lines with warm juicy chicken necks anchored with two-ounce sinkers went to the bottom along with a prayer.

We crabbed for awhile getting a few nibbles from smaller crabs but not landing any prize Jimmies, each left to his own thoughts which was relaxing after the war with the current.

And this relaxing was one of the unsung pleasures of boating, having the peace and solitude and time to think that went with it. On the contrary, if you ever had the misfortune to end up in a boat with a chatterbox whose only goal in life was to see how many words they could speak in a minute, the whole day, then you were in for one miserable time. Being stuck with someone who talked incessantly was a bummer wherever it may occur but in a small boat its absolutely the worst scenario because of their mere proximity and you have no way of avoiding them or any other activity you can turn to as an escape. I really believe these types of people were responsible for us not catching crabs on occasion because the crabs got an earful from below and moved on. My father once experienced such a person and remarked, "When he was born he must have been vaccinated with a phonograph needle."

Bubba 'n me were the perfect crabbing partners, talking just enough, teasing when necessary, and if I got long-winded he would look at me and say, "Shut up, will ya?" And I would. Also, Bubba's laugh was only a second away if the tension needed easing.

"Ain't this something?" Bubba said. "Not catching a durn thing and now I'm hung up."

He tugged at his line just a fussin' and fumin'.

"The sinker's probably just hung up in some oyster shells," I said trying to calm him. "Let it sit a minute."

"There it goes. It's moving some, a little bit… maybe it's … there we go… it's loose now, I think," he said. "It sure feels heavy. Must be some shells on it?" Nearing the top of the water he caught a glimpse of the distinct blue streak of a claw and let out with a yell, "Great day! Looka here, looka here! Mike, hand me the net, quick."

I casually tossed the net to the back of the boat.

"Holy mackerel!" Bubba was definitely excited about something. I looked toward the stern of the boat as he slipped the net under three big crabs, lifted up and dumped them in the basket all in one smooth motion.

"Mike, these things are huge. And heavy too!"

"Yeah, I see," I said with obvious envy.

"WA-HOO!" Bubba screamed, "we are in crab city!"

Within three minutes Bubba did it again …landed three more. Two hat tricks in a row. "YOW-EE! We done hit the jackpot!"

"Neat man, neat," I said. Red with envy.

Bubba was grinning like a jackass eating briars as he lowered his line.

Within a minute my line got tense and felt heavy. "Easy now, easy," I told myself. "Don't rush it or you'll spook 'em." The tension in my fingers matched that of the taunt line as I slowly pulled it upwards. "Come from under with the net like Daddy taught me. Lift up and scoop under."

"Two more," I announced proudly. "Two more Jimmies!"

"Yeah, your first two, slow poke," Bubba remarked. " I got seven. O-O-P-S, make that eight" as he netted a huge rusty looking crab with a green slime growing on its shell.

"Hand me the net, hurry up!" My other line was running under the boat, something taking it and it wasn't the current. A quick check of my third line told me it had crabs on it. More crabs, more money, Beverly Ann and the movies… oh boy. I was smiling enjoying my thoughts.

"Quit thinking about that girl and crab, will ya?" Bubba said as he hauled in two more keepers. Our agreement with our customers was for big crabs and there was no way we would cheat them by slipping in a few babies at the bottom of the basket so we agreed to keep only the large ones, the keepers, and threw back the smaller ones. So far no little ones.

Bubba passed me the net from his position in the stern of the boat, always the best spot in the boat because it offered unlimited space and without the annoyance of getting tangled in the anchor line, which was at the bow of the boat. *(Big crabs, the Payback of the Crabs. The thought hit me.)* Thank goodness we didn't have to worry about that because we had our "Scott Safety Belt" anchor line. If there was a crab down there big enough to gnaw through that seat belt, then I didn't want no part of crabbing, no more.

"The net, hurry, the net," Bubba commanded. Within five minutes he added six more monster Jimmys to the highly agitated mess in the straw basket. A crab is called the buzzard of the sea because they will eat *anything* and evidenced by their death-like grip on each other they would eat *anything* on land too. There was always a big ruckus when a new crab joined his fellow captives in the basket. They moved around all agitated, fighting for a certain spot. Once their powerful pinchers locked up with another crab then they would calm down, still maintaining their grip on each other, barely moving as to say, "Gottcha now, I'm gonna rest." The whole process would start again when the next crab was added to the catch.

The net went from bow to stern in a dizzying pace with no letup. Back and forth, back and forth we passed it to each other. We were catching crabs and sweating and having the time of our lives.

"Why didn't we bring two nets?" I asked." Make things a lot easier."

"Eah, I can't think of everything. Next time we'll… speaking of the net, let me have it got number twenty- one coming right up."

"Twenty- one? You sure? I think it's twenty-two? You been counting?" I hadn't bothered to count. I was having too much fun catching 'em. I just wanted to mess with Bubba by questioning his count.

"Yeah, how else we gonna know when we got forty- eight?"

"Yeah, well"…I stammered, " I … u-u-u-h … thought we had twenty- two." I thought I knew what was coming.

"Twenty- one, twenty- two. Shoot, who knows how many we got?" Bubba remarked and without any further discussion quickly grabbed the basket and dumped all the crabs onto the bottom of the boat. Jailbreak! Those crabs had a sense of newfound freedom and planned to make the best of it. They scurried under the seat, under the oars and anchor line … anywhere… looking for a hiding place.

"WHAT are *you* doing? You gone nuts?"

"Gonna count the crabs, that's what Einstein."

"O-o-o-h … I see. Hey, I got a better idea, Mr. Smarty. Why don't you stand up, put one hand on your hip, and shake your finger at 'em with a big frown on your face and then yell at 'em to line up straight and march back in the basket like we do after recess at school. If they don't, tell 'em they'll get the big oar treatment … and oh yea …no talking! Who knows you might even get them to say a little prayer while they're in line?"

"Very funny … HA-HA," Bubba said sarcastically. "Tell you what though, I bet if Sister Roberta were here and told those crabs to get back in that basket they would run like hell into that basket and there wouldn't be any crab-back-talk either."

Bubba took the net handle, placed it on the back of the nearest crab, pinned it securely, reached down and with his thumb and forefinger placed on the separate joint on each side by the back flipper, picked up a big Jimmy and put him in the basket and said, "One."

"How'd you do that?"

"Easy, I thought for a second about where to begin and said, "one."

"Man, you're full of yourself today. No, how'd you pick up that crab without getting the fool bitten out of ya?

"Easy. Watch." He repeated the process and said, "Two."

"Where'd you learn that?"

"What? How to count? At school, dummy."

I gave Bubba the look and he laughed and then said, "Mr. Scott showed me."

"When?"

"Couple of weeks ago. I was over at the Scott's helping Billy clean up the yard and Mr. Scott came in from the creek with a mess of crabs and Sammy knocked them over fooling around. Those crabs acted like it was the Fourth of July… freedom…
and took off running all over the yard. You should have seen Mr. Scott chasing Sammy and the crabs. I don't know for sure but I think Mr. Scott might have been drinking a few beers out there in the creek. He kind of wobbled when he was chasing Sammy and fell over once when he bent over to pick up a crab. So I tried to help and picked up the net and went after a few but there ain't no way you can scoop up crabs in the grass."

Mr. Scott told me, "No, no, like this."

Bubba said it was kind of scary at first, seeing those big blue claws open up wide ready to bite and those twitching eyes watching his every move. He would try to run around behind a crab but ol' Jimmy had three- hundred- and- sixty- degree vision and would move quickly to any danger whether in front or behind him. Bubba said that he finally got a stick and held 'em down like he was doing now.

"Let me try one."

"Help yourself. Ain't but about twenty of 'em running around. There goes another one under the seat… see 'em… right there". Bubba was pointing them out from his lookout in the stern. He was right. It was scary at first but once I got the hang of it I was slinging crabs back into the basket like I knew what I was doing.

Meanwhile, Mr. Crab and his family below were feasting on our unattended line. Who says there's no such thing as a free lunch?

"Twenty- two, twenty- three. Do you think you can keep count now?" Bubba asked putting the last crab in the basket. Some quick arithmetic told me we needed twenty-five more crabs to fill our order.

Messing with Bubba, I said, "Yeah, we're doing all right. Only need twenty- six more, right?"

Not missing a beat, Bubba replied, "You moron, don't mess with me or I'll tell Beverly Ann just how dumb you are."

"Whatcha mean?"

"Can't subtract, that's what I mean, any idiot knows we only need twenty- four more… BA-HA-HA-HA-HA!"

At the rate we were catching crabs, we figured that on a normal day, one where we didn't spend half the time figuring out how to row the boat, we could catch about two hundred and seventy-five crabs, and at twenty-five cents a dozen that would come to … o-o-o-h, somewhere around… that's when we gave up. Addition and subtraction, OK … multiplication no way.

Then like a parade it suddenly ended, the crab catching. No more bites, nothing, not even a nibble from a little baby crab… no more crabs and we were eight crabs, I think, shy of our goal. We continued to crab hard with great enthusiasm and said many prayers but no crabs bit. It was as quiet as a nun at confession. We sat there astounded, sweating in the hot sun, which was getting up high enough to send us his beams of ultraviolet rays, the ones that burn you up. Sweat rolled down our tanned bodies adding to the puddle of water on the deck of the boat. Neither of us knew what to say or do. Shoot, we figured once we started catching the crabs then they would continue to bite and bite until we were ready to leave. It never dawned on us that it was the crabs' choice about when the crabbing was over.

"Is it over? Did we catch all the crabs in the creek?" I thought.

We were wary about trying another spot because that meant we would have to fight the current again, something neither one of us ever wanted to do again, and it was still running strong carrying loads of seaweed and any floatable item with it toward the harbor. Rowing in that mess would be like trying to rake leaves in a windstorm. Besides, if we moved would we be guaranteed to catch more crabs?

Bubba broke the silence. "Let's move back toward the landing … that way," he said, pointing upstream.

I nodded at my friend's idea.

"We can stay on the edge of the marsh and kind of paddle, not row, and pull the boat using the marsh if we have to." Considering our rowing ability, it sounded good to me.

"You sure you don't want to get out in the middle of the creek and we can row back," I joked.

"You get funnier and funnier every day, you know that?"

"Yep, just trying to keep up with you, my friend, let's go."

And by accident we learned a basic rule of crabbing and fishing: if you aren't catching anything where you are, then *move* and keep moving until you get on 'em. There is a major difference, believe me, between crabbing and catching crabs. We needed to catch crabs. By using this method at the end of the day you could say you at least you tried if you happened to come home empty- handed. Yet I've seen people sit in one spot all day and catch nothing. I wondered if their anchor was glued to the bottom.

We set up thirty yards upstream and this time Bubba lowered the anchor gently, not throwing it with all his strength three feet and splashing both of us, even though I must admit the temporary bath was some relief from the heat. Our lines were neatly coiled on the deck beside us, not tangled and all messed up or caught on something, ready to do their thing. Once we got the rowing part down we might, just might, become first-rate crabbers or at best stay out of the marsh.

Immediately our luck changed and our smiles returned along with the crabs. It was like before … crab after crab was hauled in, non-stop. We were sweating again and loving it.

It wasn't long when Bubba yelled out, "And under the J, for Jimmy … forty-eight!" as he netted a nice one.

"Bingo," I screamed. "Let's go!"

We did it. We rounded up some customers, we got all our stuff together, borrowed a boat and caught forty-eight crabs. Now all we had to do was deliver 'em. I don't know if I was more relieved or happier but it was a good feeling and Bubba 'n me were all smiles and grinning at everything, even the mean old current that had threatened our day earlier.

"Ya done good Mike, even though you row like Annette." He was referring to Annette Funnicello, my favorite Mouseketeer.

"Thanks, at least, I don't row like Curley … HA-HA."

We decided to pull anchor and head in but not before I suggested we dump the whole basket and count the crabs again… "Just to be sure," I said jokingly in a serious tone.

"If you touch that basket, just once, I'll break this oar over your hard head, Devlin. BA-HA-HA-HA-HA."

Two proud young boys returned to the landing as we clung to the safety of the marsh grass and kind of half rowed, half poled the boat. We felt good about ourselves for accomplishing all that we did: crabbing on our own from a boat, making some money, and getting back safely. But the most important lesson to come out of this venture was that we earned a respect for the creek. There had been some scary moments when we felt totally helpless against the current, and the uncertainty of how or where we would end up was frightening. It was a lot for a kid to comprehend on short notice. Next time we would do things differently but hindsight is always twenty-twenty and three hours earlier we didn't have that luxury. We came away, not with a fear of the water, but a healthy respect and an understanding that when we got into a boat again we were at the mercy of Mother Nature and had to play by her rules. However, we also understood that the creek was a place to have fun and enjoy ourselves. We might not have been the brightest kids on the block but we weren't stupid either and realized that boating was a lot like life itself. It was a trial and error process, and that day we were learners as on our many subsequent trips to the creek.

My mother liked to say, "Everybody makes a mistake but only a fool makes the same mistake twice." Our mistake was going on the wrong tide. We learned that we would never go crabbing again on an ebb tide.

We pushed the handle of the crab net through the wire handles of the basket, each of us grabbing hold of one end sharing the load of forty eight crabs and lines with chicken necks still attached, piled on top of our catch. We began our walk home feeling like victorious conquerors with our prisoners intact.

"Looka there," I said, "those suckers are going to town on those chicken necks."

Bubba looked in the basket and said, "Yeah, kind of reminds me about something Jesus said …"

"What's that?" I asked in anxious anticipation of another of Bubba's wild Biblical exhortations.

"Remember, when He said something about those who are first will be last and those who are last will be first. You remember in Religion class?"

"What are you talking about?"

"The crabs here… the last ones caught getting a free meal first. You see what I mean."

"Bubba, are you serious?" I knew he wasn't. "All of these crabs are headed for a pot of boiling water."

"Yeah, I know but these guys will die happy on a full tummy."

"Forget it, will ya." I had more important things on my mind like Beverly Ann and having some money.

We hadn't gone far when Lumus interrupted our conversation rounding the corner at Back Street slowly coasting to a stop near us, resting his tanned arm on the car door, the window all the way down.

"Uh -oh, we're in trouble now. " Bubba whispered with trepidation in his voice. And Bubba wanted to be a policeman when he grew up? Humph! How was that possible when every time he saw a policeman he thought he was in trouble?

"E-a-s-y Bubba," I said calmly, "we haven't done anything wrong."

"No, nothing except steal a boat."

"Borrowed the boat Moses, remember? Borrowed." I was telling myself that too… we borrowed the boat. I didn't need any double trouble.

"Hey there, my little hill buddies," Lumus said in a friendly tone. "What y'all up to?"

"Been crabbing, at the landing," we answered together. Sweat was pouring off our foreheads and it wasn't from the heat. "Yes sir, been right there at the landing, catching crabs."

"Do any good?"

"Yeah, got a good mess," I said moving closer to the car so Lumus could get a look in the basket and to prove we had been crabbing at the landing.

"Hey, y'all done pretty good for a couple of rookies. Caught those at the landing, huh? What you gonna do with 'em, have a crab crack?"

"Uh, yeah... I mean no ...yeah, we caught 'em at the landing but we're gonna sell 'em... no crab crack." I was hoping my indecision didn't give us away.

"Good way to make some money. Why I hear them boys over in Mt.Pleasant get fifty cents a dozen for 'em, all day long. How much y'all getting?" I felt some relief because the conversation was leaving the issue of the landing.

"They get fifty cents," Bubba practically shouted. "We only ..."

I quickly interrupted. "Yeah, we get fifty cents too," I said calmly covering Bubba's outburst. I don't think Lumus believed me but before I could say anything else Lumus said, "Good seeing you boys, gotta go ... see ya later."

"All right," said a relieved Bubba then he added, "Hey Lumus, let me see ya scratch off."

"Oh no, not in the Chief's car," Lumus answered, "he'd skin me alive."

"A-a-a-w come on," Bubba begged, "just once ... please."

"Oh yeah," Lumus said, "there's one other thing. There's been a report of somebody taking boats from the landing and using 'em without the owner's permission and then putting them back. It could be trouble. Y'all do me a favor and if you hear anything about that, I'd appreciate you letting me know ... O.K? When we catch those crooks we gonna lock 'em up for twenty years."

Before we could say anything Lumus punched the gas in the Chief's old Ford and popped the clutch scratching off leaving a trail of dust much to Bubba's delight.

"Hey, hey! You see that. Lumus really did a good one. WOW!"

"Now I know why you want to be the policeman on the Island. So you can go around scratching off and all. Boy, you are something else."

"A-a-a-h, you don't know what you're talking about, Devlin. I've told you at least ten times I know. I want to be the policeman so I can lock up all those nuns ... and that's the truth." Suddenly Bubba grew serious, departing from his joyful glee of Lumus' hot-rodding the Chief's car. "Eah, you think Lumus knows?" Bubba asked.

"About what?"

"The boat, us, you know..."

"Oh yeah, Lumus knows," I said. "He knows all right."

In Bubba's backyard we sprayed ourselves with the hose and then we sprayed the crabs. When we made our initial deliveries to our customers, I wanted to look somewhat presentable, not like we just finished a mud fight and smelling like a chicken neck. Bubba didn't share my thoughts about being neat and clean and making a favorable impression.

"We might get more business," I lectured, "If we are at least clean. Right?"

"Eah, you want to go delivering crabs looking like Fred Astaire or something. Want me to get my Dad's new tie for you? Remember we're crabbers and have a certain dirty dress code to live up to."

"Yeah, it's just that… oh, never mind."

"Never mind what?"

"Then why are you spraying the crabs?" I asked trying to follow his logic.

"Because they're dirty, that's why."

"Oh, I see. I understand now." Bubba was my best friend but durn if I could understand him at times. Clean crabs but dirty us? It didn't make any sense. Maybe at twelve years old that was the way it was supposed to be?

We delivered to Ms.Kingman's, Mrs. Scott, the Reilly's, and a dozen at our house, saving the fat ones for our house, not being partial at all, just smart. I couldn't wait for the Sunday mid-day meal when we would feast on my mother's deviled crabs, a true delicacy! It was an old Island recipe handed down for generations and far better than what could be found in the fancy restaurants in Charleston and didn't cost an arm and a leg. My father referred to a deviled crab as "a $2.OO New York snack." These were real deviled crabs loaded with crabmeat, not bread, and would just about cause a fight at the dinner table over who got seconds. Combined with a *big* sheepshead fish, caught that morning by my father, we had a meal fit for a king. We might not have had much by way of material things but we sure ate well. The local blacks had a unique way of summing up such a meal. They said, "Da food be so good 'e make yo tongue slap yo teef."

"Mike, make sure that fire is out when you're finished," my mother shouted from the back steps, "don't want you to burn down the Island."

"Yes, Ma'am."

Bubba 'n me had built a fire and filled a washtub half full of water and set it on concrete blocks and waited for it to boil. We debated whether it was cruel or not to put the crabs in the water before it reached a full boil and have them die a slow death.

"I think it's cruel and they suffer if the water isn't boiling hot. How would you like to be put in warm water and have someone watch you suffer," I said presenting my side.

"These stupid crabs don't know what's going on," Bubba countered. "If they were that smart they wouldn't get caught by eating some nasty old chicken neck tied to a string."

"Sure they do. They have feelings just like me and you," I shot back.

"In that case, I'm so sorry, Mister Jimmy if I ruined your day," Bubba said as he dropped another "stupid" crab in the pot.

We didn't use any salt or pepper or add any fancy seasoning to our pot of boiling crabs. We stirred them occasionally with an oar and kept an eye on the fire which gave us time to talk about the events of the day and make plans for tomorrow. When we got older we would do the same thing except over a cold beer or two. We knew they were ready when they began to float to the top and a thick, whitish, foam appeared across the top of the tub. Mother Nature had seasoned these creatures perfectly along with their fellow creek mate, the oyster, with the right consistency and just enough salt. Over the years I would eat many a crab in a nice restaurant but none ever tasted as good as those in our backyard.

"Man, I'm pooped. All that rowing whipped my you know what," I said, as we poured off the used water.

"Me too. What time we going tomorrow?"

"Let me check the tide table. We don't want to catch that ebb tide again," I said, "and I'll call you later. Oh yeah, I just thought of something. Today out there in the boat when we were going down the creek, why didn't we just throw the anchor out and stop the boat?"

"Cause we're stupid… that's why," Bubba said with a faint smile. Then he headed home.

I wasn't in the house two minutes when the phone rang.

"What time we going," came the excited voice from across the street, so loud I barely needed the phone to hear him.

"I haven't checked the tide yet, I'll call ya back later, OK?"

"Whatever, I'll be ready at 6:00 anyway. And another thing … we can get fifty cents a dozen, you know?" He quickly hung up.

After supper that evening I cornered my father in his favorite chair with his open newspaper. I sat on the floor, resting my head against the soft arm of the chair, almost asleep. My father instinctively asked," What's wrong? Yankees lose again?" He knew how I acted after a Yankees' loss.

"No, sir, I don't think so. It's not that. It's about crabbing … I was just thinking."

"Crabbing? You and Bubba had a good time today didn't you?"

"Yes, sir."

"And you made some money too?"

"Yes, sir."

"Then what's the problem?"

"Oh, I don't have a problem," I said reassuringly, " It's the crabs … they have a problem."

"Son, what in the world are you talking about? Can't you see I'm trying to read the paper."

"Well, we were doing real good catching crabs like crazy, big 'ol Jimmys too, and then all of a sudden they quit biting. We didn't catch anymore until we moved. That ever happened to you? I mean not catch any all of a sudden like?"

"Sure. Plenty of times. See, crabs travel in groups or packs like dogs."

I felt relieved to hear that. "Like fish in a school," I added.

"Yeah, that's right. You and Bubba happened to hit a bunch of 'em at first and y'all probably caught 'em all from that spot. Then when you moved y'all found some more."

"Oh-h-h-h … I see."

"Don't worry there's more crabs in Miller's Creek than you can shake a stick at."

"Good … because we're going tomorrow."

"Where were y'all crabbing?"

Uh-oh, should I tell him about the boat? What the heck … he probably already knows. A person can't keep nothing secret on this Island.

"Mike … Hey … Wake up. Where were y'all crabbing?"

"Oh sorry, Dad. I was thinking. Oh yeah, we were in Miller's Creek."

"I know that. But where in Miller's Creek?"

"Oh, down by some old pipe sticking out the marsh, it was real big."

A grin growing into a laugh spread across my father's handsome face.

"What's so funny," I asked.

"Nothing, not really."

"What'd ya mean, not really?"

My father confessed: "You and Bubba were crabbing at the Island sewer pipe, Mike. It comes from the treatment plant, the brick building on Back Street.

His explanation accounted for the peculiar smell and the brownish water and stuff trickling into the creek.

"I don't care. There's big 'ol Jimmys there and we're going back again. Daddy, would you do me a favor?"

"Sure son, what?"

"Don't tell any of our customers where we crab, O.K?"

"I won't, that's just between me and you and Bubba and…"

I finished the sentence, "the crabs."

"Right. And will you do yourself a favor next time you crab there?"

"Yes sir, what's that?"

"Anchor down wind," he said with a smile.

"Yes sir."

Upon learning the source of our crabs' meals I suppose that made Bubba 'n me the pioneers of recycling.

13
THE VISIT

Thomas Poe, hoping not to arouse the suspicion of Dr. Steven Jenkins, had waited two weeks since his conversation with the doctor at the Post Office … then he took action. He made a phone call.

"Hello, Steven, it's Thomas Poe, your fellow coin collector. How are you? … Good, good, that's good news. … Yeah, I thank God every day for my health too. … Oh, everything is fine on this end. … No, I haven't found any new coins, at least, not anything of value. How about yourself? … Yeah, yeah, I see … time sure does get away.
I was fooling with my collection the other day and I thought about you and figured I'd take you up on that invite… it was an invite wasn't it? … Yeah, I thought so… I'm calling to see if you wanted to get together sometime? Tell some war stories over a few beers, shoot the breeze … Yeah … and you can bring me up to date on the latest gossip if you've been to the Post Office."

"I don't see why not," Dr. Jenkins replied. "Sounds good to me, I'm looking forward to seeing your collection. Any time would suit me, Thomas. It would be nice to have some company. I've been piddling around doing nothing for the last week or so."

I know I'm pushing it, but here goes. "Would this evening be O.K. with you?" Thomas asked trying hard not to sound too eager. "If not, please just tell me and…" *Oh, shut up Thomas and let it be,* he told himself.

"No, no, not at all," Dr. Jenkins readily agreed. "It would be my pleasure. What time would suit you?" There was a pause. "Around 6:30 … Great! I'll see you then. Oh, and don't forget your collection. OK, see you then."

Dr. Jenkins pondered for a minute. "Thomas sounded kind of edgy, a little nervous or something. A-a-a-w, it probably wasn't anything. Must be me … I'm just getting old."

Thomas hung up feeling relief. *Maybe this will be easier than I thought? The good doctor is so accommodating.*

Now to do a little rearranging. Thomas went into the den, opened the huge cedar chest and pulled out his coin collection.

Time to do some separating, he mused to himself. *Let'see. Dimes over here, nickels over here, and you pennies and half dollars can go over here.*

He stared dearingly at the Standing Liberty quarter collection, sighed and said, "Sorry ladies but you can't go. Gotta keep y'all under wraps for a while longer."

He looked at the coins he had assembled and was satisfied that it would credit him as a serious coin collector, maybe not on the professional level but enough to satisfy Dr. Jenkins' curiosity.

Dr. Jenkins had errands to run and a sick dog on his hands. "Dodger," the runt of the litter, was named after a Brooklyn Dodger great, the diminutive shortstop, Pee Wee Reese. "Dodger," however, was now a full grown ninety-pound Black Lab and could easily have had his name changed to "Moose," after the N.Y.Yankee's muscular first baseman Bill Skowron. Steven knew something was ailing "Dodger" who had hardly eaten in two days and was moping around the house, lifeless, not even wanting to go to the "b-e-a-c-h."

Let's see, drop "Dodger" at the vet, then to the Red and White and pick up a few groceries, and then pick up my suit from Richter's. Oh yeah, get some beer ... Thomas Poe is coming over.

These weekly trips to Mt. Pleasant were a necessary evil as far as he was concerned.

Let me stay on the Island, go to the beach and sit on the porch and relax, that's not much to ask for he thought as he turned onto The Causeway. *A-w-w-h, what the heck, it won't take that long for these few errands and besides, "Dodger" really needs to be looked at.*

All the Islanders were forced to do their shopping in Mt.Pleasant or Charleston unless they wanted to pay the "beach price" and there weren't too many of those folks around. The few businesses on the Island were not set up for volume type traffic. They were mostly small Mom 'n Pop type places, like Grannie's Bakery and Owens Grocery. The Island certainly was in need of some new stores but there was a group of old Islanders dead set against any new businesses and the debate, heated at times at City Council meetings, had gone on for years. The problem was how many new places should be allowed to open? And to whom do you issue a license and to whom do you not issue one without showing partiality? Recently the Town Council had decided to designate a small area near Station 22 as the commercial or business district allowing only those existing businesses to stay there and not expand the business zone. It was a somewhat Solomonesque solution and for the time being and the locals and business owners alike accepted it.

Driving to Mt. Pleasant wasn't such a chore; it was no more than six miles both ways and the traveler was given a free scenic view of the marsh vistas on both sides of The Causeway, complete with the invigorating aroma of the low tide pluff mud, a reminder that you weren't far from home.

Miller's Veterinary Clinic was located across from Shem Creek, whose winding waters cut through the heart of Mt. Pleasant, a stone's throw from the many shrimp boats that called this creek home. Dr. Jonathan Miller was a second-generation veterinarian who prided himself on giving excellent service and not gouging his patrons. Whenever he wasn't too busy, Dr. Miller would greet his customers at the door upon their entrance, today business was slow.

"Good morning Dr.Jenkins, and hello to you, "Dodger." They both returned a smile.

"How's everything over there in paradise?"

"Wonderful, except for the heat."

"Well, it is summer," he reminded Dr. Jenkins. "It's supposed to be hot."

"That's right, I shouldn't complain. I could be in Atlanta right now. Ever spend a summer there, Doc?"

"Nope and don't care to. What's with "Dodger"? He knelt down and rubbed "Dodger's" long black ears. "He looks healthy enough."

"He's not eating like he should and is listless, kind of dragging around. I thought it was the heat at first, but when he wasn't eating I figured something was wrong."

"Let me take a look-see. Come on "Dodger," let's go."

Obediently "Dodger," wagging his huge tail, followed Dr. Miller toward the examination room in hopes of getting a rub from Ms. Littles, the pretty assistant with the magic fingers.

Dr. Jenkins grabbed a magazine from the nearby rack, sat down, and tried to get comfortable.

Dr. Miller was gone for a lengthy spell. *Longer than it took for just a look-see* Dr. Jenkins thought. *Gosh, I hope there's nothing seriously wrong.*

Dr. Miller reappeared without "Dodger."

Not a good sign. "Is he all right?" Dr. Jenkins asked anxiously as he stood up.

"Nothing serious, I don't think … but I'll need to run some tests. Can "Dodger" spend the night?"

"Sure, he would love that. What kind of tests?"

"He probably has some kind of "bug," and it's something that I can't pinpoint without running some tests. We'll do that right away, let him rest, and by tomorrow I should know more. Don't worry, "Dodger's" a strong boy … he'll be OK. Like I said, I don't think it's anything serious, but I want to be on the safe side."

Dr. Jenkins began to make his way to his car. "Sounds good," he said. "Thanks doc, and I'll call tomorrow morning."

"Good, talk to you then," Dr. Miller said ducking back inside.

Upon completing his errands, Dr. Jenkins started back to the Island, alone and in thought. *What a quaint little town Mt. Pleasant is. Clean, beautiful, especially the oak trees, no serious crime, good schools. It just needs a beach.* With his attention elsewhere he almost noticed the light turn yellow too late. *Punch it... I can make it.* He did and the big Oldsmobile V-8 jumped to life as he zoomed past Choppys and soon had Page's Thieves Market in his rear view mirror. Out on The Causeway he let his mind drift off again. *With "Dodger" at the vet I haven't been this alone in a long time. Time sure does fly. It seems like yesterday Peggy died, but come October it'll be two years. And it doesn't seem that long ago I finished my residency and...*

His thoughts were interrupted by the red taillights of the car in front of him braking to a stop on the Ben Sawyer Bridge, the drawbridge that connected the Island and Mt.Pleasant. It was opening for a sailboat in the distance. He was fourth in line as the black and white striped, wooden arm on the bridge dutifully fell from its upright position blocking both lanes while the foot high steel barrier on wheels appeared from the side of the bridge. It rolled into position and stopped with an attitude that said, "You might get by old wooden arm there, but there's no way you're going over me."

Different personalities handled the inconvience of the bridge opening in different ways. All one had to do was sit in their car and observe. The curious got out of their car and inspected the marsh and its surroundings looking here and there as if to make sure everything was in its proper place and then got back in their car. The laid- back, worry-free listened to the music on their car radio thumping out the rhythm of the music on the steering wheel or on the top of the car with their fingers. The impatient souls repeatedly stuck their heads out the window glaring at the open bridge as though their determined gaze would make it close quicker and this silly and unwanted inconvience in their hurry-up-and-go life would be over. There had been a time when being caught by a bridge opening was a pain in the neck for Dr. Jenkins who would sit anxiously and wait while one inconsiderate boater brought the universe to a stop. For these "hurry-uppers" of the world it was an event equal to personal torture. And Dr. Jenkins had been one of them dreading to see the red flashing light and descending arm until he finally realized he had no control of when the bridge opened and closed. That was when his attitude changed for the better. *Maybe*, he thought, *it was God's way of saying, Slow down Steven, slow down, you're going too fast.*

And with that idea in mind he emerged from his car and headed for the bridge railing like a tourist checking out the waterway for the first time. Resting his folded arms on the warm steel railing, he gazed westward towards the end of the Island in the hazy distance. The cause of this opening showed its face, slicing through the ripple-free waters of the Intracoastal Waterway pushing matching swells from its white bow. It was a handsome sailboat in full flight urged on by a steady westerly wind. As close as he could guess she was about a fifty-footer, named "Sea Ya Later," out of Wilmington, Delaware, and headed north.

The clear skyline of the Island from the Point, the western end of the Island, to Station 23, where the causeway entered the Island was a low one interrupted only by the distinctive tower of Saint Angela's Church at Station 12. On top of this ninety-foot rectangular steeple stood a statue of the Blessed Mother adorned with a light that had served as a beacon for many a returning mariner over the years. The only other tall structures on the Island were the eye- wrenching but necessary water towers (there were two of these eye-sores) that had been painted and repainted so many times over the years it was hard to tell what color they truly represented. Presently they resembled a gosh- awful green.

Scanning the length of the Island Dr. Jenkins noticed it looked like a forest ... green everywhere ... a distinction he had not noticed before. The trees on the waterway side had grown uninterrupted for centuries, and oaks reaching a height of eighty to a hundred feet were common. The Island was flooded with vegetation... wax myrtles, pine trees, crape myrtles, cedar, pecan trees, and the ever present Palmettos ... combined with the abundance of wildflowers such as buttercups, black-eyed-Susie's and blue bells ... complimented an already pristine setting. Wisteria and honeysuckle vine were so abundant in the spring their seductive scent made the Island quite the tempting lady. These scents permeated every fiber of the Island with the help of the ocean breezes.

On the ocean side sea oats lined the top of the dunes, their oval-shaped granules set in perfect symmetry, waving their greetings to all visitors entering on the footpaths that ran through the dunes, making for an exquisite entrance to the beach whose backdrop was the Atlantic Ocean.

With the first light of day came the pelicans soaring effortlessly in formation over the creeks and ocean in search of food. Their meal of choice was the finger mullet or menhaden schooling on the surface hoping there was safety in numbers as they attempted to escape the jaws of the bigger and hungry fish below. Lifted by thermal heat and utilizing its massive wingspan to its maximum, the pelican could glide for extended periods of time while carefully searching out its meal with eagle-like vision. And when he dove for food, very rarely did he miss his mark. Their graceful dance across the sky never grew old and each day's opening act surpassed that of the day before.

And then there was the seagull, a totally different bird. He was overly aggressive and very bold in his attempts at getting something to eat, bordering on disrespect as he invaded any unattended plate of food whether at the beach or in a backyard. They were scavengers and would eat anywhere at anytime *and* anything. And when the screeching gulls arrived, you better be on guard if you had food and especially watchful after their meal because the sky was the limit with their not so nice "droppings."

The Island was also home to flocks of smaller birds such as sparrows, mockingbirds, robins, cardinals, blue jays, doves and the infamous grackle, first cousin of the raven. These huge black rascals were everywhere getting into everything. Nothing was sacred with them, pillaging anything they could get their sharp little beaks on. If they were to take on human form, they would certainly become Huns. It was a daily battle of epic proportions between them and the seagulls to see which could wreak the most havoc. At last count the grackles had a substantial lead.

DING, DING, DING, DING! Dr. Jenkins was jolted back to life as the warning bell told the wooden arm and steel barrier to let everyone pass and go home.

An early lunch, a nice nap and ill be able to stay up late with Mr. Poe.

Dr. Jenkins turned into his driveway feeling alone without the company of "Dodger."

Thomas Poe had gone over his plan so many times that he had it memorized to the point where he could recite it backwards. *Can't be too careful, no time to screw up now*, he said to himself, as he prepared to leave for Steven Jenkins's house.

Driving slowly up the driveway at Dr. Jenkins,' he counted each tree and was attentive to the location of the footpath leading to the beach. His mind was acting like a camera, taking pictures of every detail as he made a mental note of the overall lay of the land. Each door and window was referenced ... all possible entrances or exits.

Dr. Jenkins, hearing the familiar crunch of the oyster shells in the driveway headed for the porch.

"Hello, how are you?" He waved at Thomas. "Welcome to my humble abode." Dr. Jenkins was standing by the screen door leading onto the front porch clad in khaki shorts and a snug golf shirt that accentuated his trim, athletic build.

"Hello," said Thomas, "good to see you." *He's in pretty good shape for a man his age. But if matters ever came to a physical confrontation it would be no contest,* thought Thomas.

Thomas switched his collection to his left hand and extended his right hand in the gesture of a handshake that Dr. Jenkins quickly acknowledged, adding a friendly pat on the shoulder.

"How you doing?" Thomas said, "and thanks for letting me come over on such a short notice."

"I'm fine and hey, no problem about the short notice. I'm glad you called." Dr. Jenkins pushed open the screen door. "How about you. Haven't seen you at the Post Office. Thought you might have moved back to the

Holy City," Dr. Jenkins joked. "You wouldn't do that, now would you?"

"No, no. Just been busy at work and messing around with my collection," Thomas replied holding it out in front of him.

"Come on in, let's sit on the porch. There's a nice breeze and we can take in the view… sit down, please, take a load off. How about a drink," offered Dr. Jenkins, rising and heading toward the kitchen. "What'll you have? Cold beer, bourbon, vodka? Got some iced tea or Coke. Name your poison."

"A cold beer would hit the spot, thank you," Thomas said as he subtly followed Dr. Jenkins into the kitchen again making mental notes of the house arrangements.

"Let's see," Dr. Jenkins said looking in the refrigerator. "How about a cold Pabst Blue Ribbon?"

"That's fine, thanks," Thomas said accepting the cold can of beer from his host.

In an attempt to take a much-desired tour of the house Thomas said, "You've got quite a place here … lots of space, nice and open. And the way it's furnished … and the view … wow!

"Thank you. I wish I could take some credit for all this but I can't," Dr. Jenkins replied extending his arm in a sweeping motion. "My wife did all the decorating, choosing the furniture… everything, right down to the floor plan."

He isn't biting. I need to see the rest of the house. Be patient. The night is young.

"She did a great job," Thomas offered. "A great job."

"Let's go back on the porch, catch that breeze."

Thomas followed the doctor's lead.

Walking through the dining area Thomas glanced around, mentally taking in what he could yet trying to keep up a conversation. "We've had a hot summer, especially this month with the humidity as high as it's been," he said. "Last week it was so thick you could cut it with a knife."

"You got that right. In Atlanta we used to get some of this "mug," I call it. Oh, it made life miserable."

"Yeah, that was probably humidity that left here looking for a cool spot," Thomas said at an attempt at humor.

"Well, it followed me here."

"Speaking of the heat …got a good one for ya … ready?" Thomas said.

"Sure."

"Do you know how hot it was today?"

"No, how hot was it," Dr. Jenkins said playing along.

"It was so hot I saw a dog chasing a cat and they were both walking."

Both men roared with laughter … the doctor's sounding more sincere.

"How about this one," Thomas said. "It was so hot when we were fishing that the fish we caught were already cooked."

A mild laugh from Dr. Jenkins who added, "I like the other one better."

"Me too," Thomas agreed as he mentally took a picture of the living room-dining area and the thought hit him: *It's a shame I have to rob this decent, friendly man. Under different circumstances we could be friends and...* Thomas was snapped from his thoughts by the sound of Dr. Jenkins, "Yep, if all we have to complain about is the weather then we're doing pretty good... don't you think?"

"Oh, absolutely, absolutely," Thomas said but was thinking, *if you only knew.*

"Let me see your collection, Thomas. I've been quite anxious to see what you have."

Thomas handed his collection to Dr. Jenkins who opened the case and sat it gently on the table, oohing and aahing at the brilliance of the shiny coins. "Wow! It's magnificent," Dr. Jenkins said. "Absolutely magnificent. And how long did it take you to find all of these?"

"Close to fifteen years," said a beaming Thomas. "Off and on as you well know. Yeah, I'm proud of what I've collected even though I don't have a full set of coins ... yet."

"Oh, it doesn't matter, Thomas. What you have here is outstanding. Outstanding!"

They spent the rest of the evening sipping beer, chatting about families and careers, talking a little sports and a lot about coin collecting. They showed a mutual respect for each other's efforts and results as far as coin collecting went; however, both knew that what Dr. Jenkins had accomplished in the world of coin collecting was just short of phenomenal, something very few people achieve. Dr. Steven Jenkins was a big fish in a big pond whereas Thomas was still trying to get out of the small pond. And Thomas appreciated Steven Jenkin's humility.

Will I ever get to see this collection? Maybe it's not here? At the bank in a vault? Safety deposit box?

As the evening grew longer Thomas began to question his plan more and more. He was about ready to give up and call off the whole crazy idea and go home when ...

From out of nowhere came the invitation he had been waiting for all since arriving at Steven Jerkin's house: "Thomas, would you like to see my collection?"

"Yeah," Thomas answered as calmly as possible, "I sure would. Hope we don't have to go to Atlanta." He gave a slight chuckle.

"No, no, I mean right now." Dr. Jenkins rose from his chair. "Sit tight, I'll be right back."

He went down the hall, which adjoined to the living room, and then he disappeared into the first room on the right. Thomas noted the doctor's movements and added the information to everything else he had seen tonight. *The room at the end of the hall must be the bedroom* Thomas thought *because of its size and location. The other smaller room on the left is probably a spare guest room?*

Dr. Jenkins reappeared with a handsome leather case with two buckles holding in place his valuable collection. The case folded in half. As he cleared a spot on the dining room table, Dr. Jenkins deftly unbuckled the buckles, then opened the case with the ease and precision of a surgeon.

"Come closer, Thomas, take a look.'

"Oh, wow. My goodness," Thomas exclaimed at the thirty or so shiny coins. "They look like brand new. They're in mint condition. So shiny."

"Yes, I clean them about every other day it seems like. It's an old habit."

Thomas now felt relief and ready to go ahead with his plan, but guilt feelings began to fill his thoughts. He was in awe of what he was looking at and knew it was the lifelong work of this considerate man standing beside him but ... he had no choice. There was no other way out.

They stood admiring the old but very valuable coins that sparkled under the overhead light like new stars. Thomas was dreading to hear the litany of each coin that he was sure Dr. Jenkins would launch into any second, describing where each was found and how he came upon it, its particular significance, where it was minted, and so on. However, he was wrong, absolutely wrong. Dr. Jenkins neither boasted nor went into any kind of long-winded explanation. On the contrary he was quite proud of his collection but also very quiet.

A humble man thought Thomas.

Dr. Jenkins closed the case, and just as deftly as he had laid it out he then folded it, buckled it back, and headed back toward the same room. "Excuse me, I'll be back in a minute."

After the viewing of Dr. Jenkins' collection the remainder of the evening's conversation was anti-climatic, to say the least. Both men were aware of the somewhat forced conversation, which was beginning to take on the tones of torture and when the discussion turned to the weather again, it was the unspoken signal it was time to call it a night. Dr. Jenkins was as relieved as Thomas when his guest suggested that he had to get on home and get some sleep. Something about a big day tomorrow at the office.

"Thank you for an enjoyable evening Dr. Jenkins, I enjoyed it," Thomas said as he his exit. "And thanks for showing me the collection ... it's unbelievable."

"Thank you for coming, it was my pleasure. You'll have to come back soon."

"Oh, I will," Thomas said with purpose. "I will."

Thomas closed his car door, thought for a second, smiled and then drove home satisfied that he had seen enough.

14
PLAYING GAMES

The crew was made up of a diverse group of kids with different backgrounds, interests, and personalities. Contrary to public belief, and especially that of the nuns at St. Angela's, we were not *always* getting into trouble. Many of the crew were quite talented, regardless of the fact that they might not display their talent. Timmy was the musician of the crowd, an accomplished piano player while John was the academian making straight A's since first grade. And Stinky Johnson might have been a stinker but he could sing like a bird and was in the church choir.

The athlete, and one of the most envied of the crew, was Rusty. He was blessed with natural talent and the athlete's build. Not too tall, not too short. He was wiry with strong legs and long lanky arms. He was built for speed and agility and knew how to use them in whatever sport he was participating. Shoot, he just looked and even walked like an athlete. He also practiced all the time honing his skills making himself go through the repetitious and often boring drills that made a person a better player, which in itself called for a lot of self-discipline. The endless hours of practice paid off because he made the All- Star team for every sport he participated in for three years in a row: baseball, football, and basketball.

This summer he was playing for the Giants, the Island team, in Little League baseball, doubling as their ace pitcher and when not on the mound playing left field. He could pitch and hit with the best of them. His overall stellar play both in the field and at the plate had taken his team deep into the playoffs and tonight they were playing for the league championship. It was also a big rival matchup. Most of the boys on the opposing Cardinals were from Mt. Pleasant, the Island's rivals in everything from sports to crabbing to girls. And so the bragging rights for the championship were at stake along with the attention and praise from the girls, something we Island boys desired desperately.

The crew had left the beach a little bit early today and gathered at Burton's with most everyone agreeing to show up at the big game and cheer Rusty on to victory. The game that evening was on our home turf so the odds were more in our favor and, we thought, if we could hassle our opponents enough maybe they would become distracted and commit a few unforced errors or strike out a few more times.

As soon as I gulped down my last piece of carrot from the beef stew I excused myself, went to my room, got my hat and headed for the door. I was hoping my mother was too busy scraping dishes and cleaning up after supper to notice my absence. My hand was on the door when I heard: "And where do you think you're going, young man?" My mother, it seemed, was never too busy.

"Oh … I was just getting ready to check with you about going to the game tonight down at the field. Is it O.K. if I go?"

"The field down by the Waterworks Building?"

"Yes Ma'am. Rusty's pitching … it's the championship game."

"Yeah, that's OK. But you have to do something for me … all right?"

"Sure, Mom, what?" I was hoping it wouldn't take long. The game started in a few minutes.

"You have to take the girls with you."

The who? With me? Where? I just knew I did not hear what I just heard. Still in shock I asked, "You want me to take the girls where, Mom?"

"To the game. With you to the game. Understand?"

I felt like a balloon you blow up and then let go of it. I was at the flattened stage.

"M-o-m-m-m … why do I have … what am I gonna do with them, especially Sara. She's so wild and all."

My mother reflected for a second. "You know," she said smiling, "you're right. Sara's too young, and she is a bit wild sometimes. Tell you what. How about take just Emily and Katie? That's not too much to ask, is it?"

In my mind it was a ton too much to ask. *Imagine showing up at the game to meet the crew with my two sisters with me. Oh man, I'd never hear the end of that. How uncool could that be?* I knew I could never explain this line of thinking to my mother so I decided not to even try.

"Well" … I said putting on my best sad-sack face … "I guess I won't go then. I'll just stay here and do something … I guess."

"That's fine with me, …suit yourself." A short pause. "Here dry these." My mother tossed me a dishcloth and I started on the pile of damp dishes.

As soon as I finished helping with the dishes, I immediately sought out the only source of help I knew of to find a way to go to the game without dragging my sisters along with me. He was my only chance.

"Daddy?" He was sitting in his normal spot reading the paper. "Can you help me?"

"If I can. What's wrong, Mickey?" He sometimes called me that because he knew Mickey Mantle was my favorite player. "Having trouble hitting that curveball?"

"N-o-o-o, it's Mom. She wants me to …" I wasn't sure how to present my plea. "Well … I want to go to the game tonight and watch Rusty's team play. It's the championship and all. The crew's going to be there but Mom wants me to take Emily and Katie with me. Can't you just tell Mom No

… I don't have to take them with me?"

My father suddenly perked up."Hey, you really are trying to stir up a hornet's nest around here, aren't you?" How old are you now … twelve?"

"Yes sir."

"And how many females are there in this house. That is, how many live here?"

"Well … there's …" I paused and counted in my mind. "There are five all together if you count Mom."

"Oh let me tell you one thing, young man," he said quickly, "you better count your mother. You see, there are only two of us, males that is. We are hopelessly outnumbered when it comes to any kind of us versus them thing. And besides, you know the rule in this house. Both parents have to agree to where you're going at night." He paused for reflection and said, "So I'm not going to get in the middle of this one. Uh-uh, not me."

"But Daddy … it's the last game and everybody's gonna be there and …"

"Are you sure about that?" He gave me a serious look. *"Everybody's* going to be there?"

I nodded and he chuckled, "I don't think so. I know one person who's not going to be there."

"Who?" I asked.

"You." he answered. And smiled.

"Yeah, you're right. I'll be the only one who's not going to be there. Couldn't you just this once talk to Mom and …"

He held up his hand stopping me and asked, "How badly do you want to go to the game, Mike? Kind of bad? Real bad? How bad?"

"Oh, real bad," I said perking up. "Real bad!"

"Well, here's the question you have to ask yourself. Do I want to go to the game bad enough that I'll take my sisters with me or do I just stay home? I mean after all what is your goal or objective here? Isn't it to go to the game?"

"Yes sir."

"Mike, sometimes in order to meet a goal or objective we have to do things we don't want to do. You understand?"

"Yes sir. If I want to got to the game then I'll have to take Emily and Katie with me."

"You got it. Now go think about it and let me read the paper … O.K. Mickey?"

"Thanks Daddy. See ya later." I turned to head to the kitchen to find my mother.

"Where you going?" My father asked, already knowing the answer.

"To the game … with Emily and Katie."

I found my mother on the back porch going through a pile of dirty clothes separating the darks from the whites. "Mom, I'll take Emily and

Katie with me. Where are they?"

"Thanks, Mike. You know sometimes your father and I need a little break from you kids? They're in their room getting ready."

"Getting ready? Ready for what?"

"To go to the game. You know how little girls are about going out and all?"

"No, I don't Mom. We're just going to a baseball game. We're not going to church or something … gee whiz." *And how did they know I would end up taking them to the game in the first place?* It was getting late so I didn't bother to ask.

"Well, get the girls and get going. And be careful crossing that street."

"Yes Ma'am."

I placed a quick phone call to Bubba checking to see if he wanted to go to the game. He told me he had to baby sit. I told him I did too but was taking Emily and Katie to the game with me. Then I suggested he do the same with Patty and Mary. His response was, "What! Are you crazy? Take those two wild Indians to a baseball game, out in public! You must be kidding … I wouldn't take them to a dogfight."

I understood and hung up.

I ran down the hall toward the girls' room calling for them when suddenly Emily and Katie came bursting out of their room out, all decked out in their fashionable best for an evening out on da Island. Emily looked like a street person and Katie, well … she looked like the street person's sister.

Emily had on a pair of baggy shorts that must have belonged to Sissy. They were so big they looked almost like a dress of some kind. Her blouse was the top to her one-piece bathing suit … I think? On her feet were her black Easter shoes, shiny as a new penny. And her head was covered with a big straw hat with a purple band. Something Minnie Pearl would wear on TV.

Katie had chosen to go more fashionable and somewhat with the theme of the evening … sports and baseball. She had a Cubs baseball cap with the distinctive "C" on the front pulled down around her ears looking as though she was trying to hide from someone. Her flowing jet-black hair was adorned with small yellow barrettes in the shape of butterflies. She too had on her bathing suit top but, at least, she had on a pair of shorts that almost fit. She chose the blue ones, she told me, to match the hat. Katie's big feet were covered with a pair of worn out, black, high- top basketball shoes, Chuck Taylor style. They were a pair I thought I had thrown out years ago.

On man! What a sight. I thought. "Y'all, are going looking like *that*?" I asked with my hands on my hips and an expression of disbelief.

"What's wrong with this?" It was Emily looking herself over. "Don't we look good?"

"Yeah, what's wrong?" It was Katie bent over tying her shoelace.

"O-o-o-o-h nothing … nothing. Let's go. We're gonna miss half the game," I said hustling out the door. "Come on, Mollie. Let's go."

Mollie jumped from her resting spot by the front porch and began to bark and growl like I'd never seen before.

I turned to find the cause of her attention. There stood Emily and Katie at the top of the steps looking like they were heading out on Halloween night. Mollie was spooked and let 'em know it.

"Mollie, look it's us. Mollie it's me." Katie took off her cap. "See, girl … it's OK." Emily did the same and much to Mollie's relief stood the Devlin girls and not a couple of wayward strangers coming to rob us.

It was a three-block walk to the ball field and with every passing car I turned my head and looked the other way hoping not to be noticed by anyone I knew with these two strangely dressed girls. And I almost escaped recognition until Stinky Johnson and a carload of the crew spotted me and yelled out the car window as they went by: "Devlin … hey Devlin! Don't try to hide." They were headed to the game. "We s-e-e-e you!"

A-w-w what the heck, I thought. *I've been through worse than this many a time. And shoot, I was getting to go to the game.*

"Who was that?" Katie asked adjusting her cap so she could see. "Somebody you know?"

"Some of his stupid friends," Emily said, nodding her head. "Wasn't it, Mike?"

"Yep… some of my stupid friends." I was only twelve but had already learned not to argue with the opposite sex. "Y'all will probably see them at the game."

"Do you have any smart friends?" Katie asked, and gave a silly grin. "Are they all stupid?"

"Nope. Not a smart one in the group."

"Why not?"

"Because they're all stupid, that's why."

They thought that was funny and giggled their cute giggles.

The lights were on at the field giving that part of the Island a strange look, a glow that brightened the dark sky, showcasing the ball players as though they were in full sunlight.

The Giants had taken the field about twenty minutes before we got there. They were quite a spectacle in their white uniforms with the red trim while the Cardinals, their counterparts in apparel, were wearing their red uniforms with white trim. Both teams looked magnificent as the nighttime gave them an almost magical look. Each player was assigned to a particular position and expected to perform a certain job giving the game such a wonderful sense of purpose and an orderliness not evidenced in everyday life. They were miniature professionals.

I realized we were late when I heard a huge roar go up from the crowd at the ball field. Not wanting to miss any action, I tried to hustle the girls along as best I could. Katie with her big feet kept tripping on the cracks in the sidewalk. Emily, meanwhile, kept trying to shove her floppy hat up so she could see where she was going. What a sight! I looked like I was escorting two orphans to their new home.

As we got closer to the field we could hear the distinct hoots and jeers coming from the crew while the team from Mt. Pleasant tried hard to block out the insults being hurled at them. I hurried the girls along even more, dismissing their complaints as girly stuff. They weren't old enough to understand that a male couldn't be late for any athletic event. The crew was doing their job and doing it well. They were lined up on the visiting team's side, close to their dugout, clutching the wire fence, which separated the players and spectators by only a few feet with their fingers sticking through … perfect for taunting and yelling at the visiting team, something the crew was good at. Rusty and the Giants, however, didn't need the crew's help. Not right now anyway.

As the girls and I walked past the small bleachers where the adults gathered, Mr. Barber informed me that Rusty had struck out the side in the top of the first and then blasted a two-run homer in the bottom of the inning, clear over the center field fence.

"It was a thing of beauty, Mike. A thing of beauty, I tell youse."

"It went that far, huh?"

"Mike, it went so far they'd have to get a jackass and a lantern to find that ball." He laughed and then turned back to thy game.

A jackass and a lantern. I'd never heard that one before. Then I chuckled to myself.

Rusty didn't have much when it came to a fastball, it was average at best, but his curve ball was wicked. No one had ever seen a curveball like that in Little League. It broke like it rolled off the top of a kitchen table. Opposing batters had been seen to jump back from the plate at the approaching curve only to be called for a strike while they stood there shaking their head with the unswung bat resting on their shoulder.

I knelt down in front of the girls. Of course the kneeling position was most appropriate because instead of telling them what to do, which it seemed like I was doing, I was secretly praying that they would heed my instruction. "Now y'all behave," I said to the girls, "and be good … OK?" It probably sounded more like a plea than a command. "And don't leave the ballpark area." Their little heads were bobbing up and down. "Because if you do, Mom will kill me."

"OK, we'll be good." Emily said sounding sincere but I knew I had to watch them like a hawk. She looked at her sister and said, "Right, Katie?"

"Yeah, I promise." Already she was looking around, taking in the territory, scoping things out. "We won't get into no trouble … honest injun, Mike." Then she giggled.

We approached the noisy crew who were really giving it to the Cardinals. And when I turned my head to tap John on the shoulder, Emily and Katie took off running like jackrabbits over to the other side of the ballpark.

"Hey, Emily! Katie! Where y'all going?" I yelled. They didn't even look back.

A-a-a-w heck, let 'em go. I thought. *I'll check on `em later.*

"Who was that?" John asked between jeers at the batter.

"My sisters. I had to bring them or stay home so …"

"Oh? One of them deals, huh? Glad you came. Man, we're whipping them good so far. Rusty's throwing that curve by 'em like they were blind." John paused and then yelled at the batter. "Hey batter. You swing like a washwoman! Look out here it comes … yeah that's it. H-e-y, h-e-y, h-e-y, swing batter!"

Stinky Johnson and Timmy and Jocko were adding their two cents worth. They had a chant going: "One, two, three looka me … strike out! One two three …" It wasn't near as catchy as it was annoying not only to the poor batter but to anyone within hearing distance.

"Where's Bubba?" Stinky asked and then spit through the fence. "We could use his big mouth."

"Home … he had to baby-sit."

"H-e-e-e-e-y, swing batter!" He screamed and then asked, "Who were those kids with you?"

"You mean the cute little angels?" I joked without getting a laugh from Stinky. "They're my sisters."

"Oh? They dress kind of funny … don't they?"

"Well … yeah … you know, they're just kids. But I wouldn't mess with 'em. They're mean as snakes." I chuckled and Stinky smiled for a second, turned around and began yelling at the batter again.

"Hi, Susan. Hey, Timmy … Jocko. How y'all doing? Oh … hey Billy, Sammy … how y'all doing?"

"Oh hey, Mike. Didn't see ya." It was Jocko. There he stood, his pearly whites contrasted against his wave of black, wavy hair, always combed perfectly. With just a hint of envy I couldn't help but think how much he resembled Elvis, especially from the side … the way his nose turned up and his lips stuck out.

"Jocko," Timmy yelled, "Davenport's batting next. You ready?" Jocko immediately pressed his face right up next to the fence and broke into song: "You ain't nothing but a hound dog" pointing at the star player for the Cardinals, a fellow classmate at St.Angela's.

Davenport turned his head: "Is that the best you can do, Jocko?" he shouted, as Jocko was finishing up with "and you ain't no friend of mine."

"What'd he say?" Jocko asked above the yelling. "Did he say anything about my singing?"

"He said you sound just like Elvis," Susan said laughing and then telling me hello.

"Yeah, that's what I thought he said. Hey, hey! Swing batter."

As soon as the inning came to an end, the crew changed sides moving over to the home side to cheer on the Giants as they went to bat. Emily and Katie saw us coming and ran back to the visitor's side giving me a quick wave as they zoomed by. Now the cheers from the crew were more of a positive nature: "Hit that sucker! Home run time, baby! You better back up centerfielder because it's going over your head."

It was the same old cheers and taunts we had learned years earlier from our older brothers until Jocko took center stage. "Eah, stick a fork in that pitcher," he screamed, "he's done." The crew howled at that one.

"Hey first baseman! You couldn't catch a cold." The crew hooted again. "And you dummy, at second base … how can you play a game that you can't even spell?" Oh, the crew loved that one!

About that time Emily and Katie came roaring around the corner of the concession stand and slid to a stop at my feet.

"Nice … real nice," I said. "The Cardinals could use y'all."

"Cardinals. B-O-O-O! We don't want to play for them. We want to play for Rusty's team. He's good. Right Katie?"

"Right Emily."

Stinky Johnson turned around and checked out the girls, especially admiring their attire. "There's that little girl with the funny hat," he said as Emily looked up at him.

"It ain't a funny hat," she told him edging closer, "It cost five whole dollars."

"Then that makes it a stupid, funny hat," Stinky said grinning. "Because anybody would be stupid to pay five dollars for a hat like that!" Stinky looked at me and smiled, obviously seeking my approval. I gave him a blank stare.

"Stupid?" Emily stated. "I'll show you what's stupid." She had edged up real close to Stinky.

"And what's that little girl," Stinky remarked sarcastically.

"You … that's what!" And Emily kicked Stinky hard, right in the shin with her pointed Easter shoe. It made a popping sound like leather against bone.

"Yeah you," Katie added and quickly kicked Stinky in the other shin. "Take that, stupid!"

"O-o-o-w-e-e! Ouch!" Stinky yelled and grabbed for his shins. "Why you little brats … I'm gonna …" He reached out and grabbed nothing but air. Emily and Katie were gone.

Stinky grimaced looking up at me, "What the …"

"Eah, I warned you didn't I?" I chuckled. "You OK?"

"Wait till I get my hands on them," he mumbled to no one in particular. "I'll show 'em a thing or two."

"Won't happen, Stinky. They're too fast." I paused. "Let's watch the game."

It wasn't ten minutes later when Emily and Katie raced by again. This time they were each carrying a baseball bat with them.

Oh God! I thought. *A bat! They could kill somebody.* I took off after them and caught them hiding the bats under a car down near the third base line.

"Whoa, young ladies. Hold it right there!" Katie's eyes were looking for a way out and she moved just a step. "Uh-uh Katie," I yelled, "Stay there. I mean it!"

They were trapped and knew it and stood still, looking down at the ground as though by averting my steady gaze I might not see them.

"What are y'all doing with those bats? Look at me! … And where did you get 'em?"

Emily slowly raised her head. "We're hiding 'em." she said. "See. Under here."

"And … ?" I said.

"And we got 'em from over there." Katie pointed at the rack of bats lined up on the fence by the visitor's dugout.

"How'd y'all do that?"

"Easy, we just slid 'em through the hole in the fence."

"What? Come show me. And bring those bats with you."

We walked toward the fence. "If y'all don't mind me asking, young ladies. Why in the world would y'all steal their bats?"

"Cause we want Rusty's team to win," Katie answered giggling. "And if they don't have no bats then they can't hit the ball, Mike. And if they can't hit the ball then …"

"Whoa, whoa, whoa! Stop right there!" I interrupted. "I get the picture. Katie. And what you say is *true* but that's stealing. Taking something that's not yours. You know that … don't you?"

"Yeah but we wasn't gonna keep 'em," Emily said. "We were gonna give 'em back … honest."

Because their intentions were so pure, it was hard to stay mad at them and accuse them of actually stealing. My curiosity as to how they got the bats got the best of me. "Whatever, now show me how you did that. How'd you get the bat from there to here?" We were at the fence. "Wait a minute," I said, "just take this one and put it back where you got it from."

"OK. Katie, gimmee that one." Emily grabbed the bat out of Katie's hand and began to slide it through the hole in the fence just like she had told me. I stood there watching. And when it was back in place she slipped her thin little hand through the hole in the fence and adjusted it so it was sitting at the proper angle. "There," she said. Satisfied that it was back in its proper place.

Amazing, I thought. *That's slick.*

"Why you little bugger, you," I said, "Y'all are something else."

They put their hands over their mouths innocently trying to stifle a laugh looking up at me with their big beautiful eyes.

"Y'all get outta here before I call Bull Perry to lock you thieves up. Go on. Git." They ran off laughing.

I found the crew behind home plate, still doing their thing. Judging from the moans and groans coming from the Cardinal's dugout, the Cardinals were still baffled by Rusty's curveball as they continued to strike out. And the crew was still doing their job letting the Cardinals have it at every opportunity. When a batter would strike out, the crew would march him back to the dugout by counting out in a loud, unified voice the number of steps the poor soul took in order to get back to the safety of the dugout. When the player slowed down, then the cadence slowed down. The crew had this form of humiliation down pat. After whiffing on another of Rusty's curves, one Cardinal tried to alter his footsteps by speeding up his walk only to be met with a loud and quickened cadence from the crew that matched his attempt at deception. And then they slowed down when the player did. Even the crowd howled on that one.

"Mike, come here." Billy grabbed me by the arm. "You gotta see this. You won't believe it."

"What?" I asked.

"Wait a minute … you'll see." Billy turned toward Jocko.

"Eah, Jocko," Billy asked, "there's two outs, right?" He pulled me closer to the fence. "Watch this."

"Yep … two outs," answered Jocko.

"Mike, check out Mr. Mac at the end of the inning."

Mr. Mac was the home plate umpire. Billy seemed awfully excited about something so I played along with him. When we heard "strike three" from Mr. Mac signaling the end of the inning, Billy elbowed me in the side and pointed at the ump. "Just watch," he said, "you'll see." *With all this buildup,* I thought, *this better be good.*

As the team were changing sides after the inning, Mr. Mac walked from the back of home plate all the way to the fence, stopped facing the fence, looked around for a quick second, and then reached into his back pocket pulling out a bottle of whiskey, which he promptly threw up to his mouth.

"See! Right there." Billy pointed at the whiskey sipping ump. "Ain't that cool? Man oh man … drinking while umpping!"

It was no secret on the Island that Mr. Mac had been known to carry his little half pint in his back pocket and sneak a sip between innings every now and then. But tonight was different. In honor of it being the championship game and being a BIG game, he had a BIGGER bottle, about a pint size, and it was nearly empty.

"How long has he been sipping?" I asked Jocko.

"The whole game, man. The whole game!" Jocko answered. "He's gotta be getting a little tipsy by now … wouldn't you think?"

"I don't know? Maybe he can drink a whole bunch. You know like Herman."

Well, there were three more innings left in the game and we were definitely going to wait around and find out if the whiskey-sipping ump would make it through the game. I left the crew to go check on the girls as the crew continued to harass the poor Cardinals who were down 6-0 by now. Thankfully, Emily and Katie had sat down for a while and were in conversation with Mrs. Barber who gave me the OK sign, a thumbs up and a smile, when I caught her eye. I waved and returned to the crew still glued to the fence.

Then we heard a loud "ball *tree*" come from Mr. Mac.

"What did he say? Timmy asked. "Ball *tree*? What's a ball *tree*? Is the ball stuck in a tree?" He laughed looking around.

"Yep, ball *tree*," Billy answered. "That's what he said."

Rusty reared back and let go of one of his sweeping curves. I could have sworn it circled around the back of the batter and into the catcher's mitt, which was right over the middle of the plate. Then Mr. Mac yelled, "*Trike* two."

"Are you sure, Mister Ump that wasn't *strike* two?" Jocko screamed and then turned to the crew. "Now we got *trikes* … next thing you know we'll have bikes and then mikes … huh, Mike?"

"HA-HA! Jocko, you so funny," I said. "So funny. It's a good think you look like Elvis or people would mistake you for Mo or maybe Curley?"

A little later we heard Mr. Mac call "Ball *foo*." and then stumble back a step or two.

"*Foo*? What is a *foo*?" Sammy asked. "Is it something like the flu when you're sick?"

"Looks like it won't be long now, guys," Billy said with a big grin. "I think the old whiskey is starting to kick in r-e-a-l good."

WHAM! One of the Cardinals got lucky and made contact with one of Rusty's fastballs It was a line drive, which was fielded on the fly by our first baseman who quickly stepped on first doubling up the runner who had taken off for second base. As the inning ended Mr. Mac returned to his spot by the fence and took a tremendous swig from his bottle. We heard a long "A-a-a-h" come from the depths of his big round stomach. And to our amazement the bottle was nearly empty.

We sensed trouble when Mr. Mac staggered a couple of steps going back to home plate. And when he attempted to lean over and dust off home plate he nearly fell flat on his face. At that point anticipation gripped the park. Nerves were on edge. Excitement hung in the summer air. Because of the game? Of course not! Everyone was sitting on pins and needles, not knowing what Mr. Mac's next move would be. We all waited. Everyone knew what the outcome of the game would be.

"*Hatter* up," the ump slurred as he steadied himself.

The confused batter stood there for a second looking at Mr. Mac and then pointed at himself with a look of "you mean me?" Mr. Mac stumbled and then motioned the batter into the box accidentally bopping the catcher on the head who turned to see what the ump wanted.

Mr. Mac yelled, "*Hay* ball!"

The first two pitches were right down the pike, obvious strikes. However, Mr. Mac judged them to be balls as he slurred out "*hall* one" and then "*hall* two."

Before the crowd and the crew could get on him for making the wrong call, he raised his right hand on the third pitch, yelled "*trike* one" and then slowly began to fall over backwards like a tall tree that had just been cut down. He landed with a loud thud on his back and with his arms spread out. The whiskey, it seems, had struck out the ump.

The coaches from both teams rushed to home plate while the crew howled with laughter. Bewildered players from both teams stood gawking at the prostrate umpire. The players then slowly joined the coaches, gathering around Mr. Mac who was completely oblivious to this world. Fans rushed from the bleachers onto the field forming a circle around home plate.

Mrs. Banks, the prim and proper local librarian, gave the crew a dirty look as she walked by and shouted, "What are y'all laughing at? That poor man might be dying."

"He's had a heart attack," screamed the always-hysterical Mrs. Rivers after she had bent over Mr. Mac and checked his breathing. "Oh my God! He's had a heart attack!"

"Someone call Lumus or the Chief," Mrs. Banks yelled to no one in particular. "Quick get the Rescue Squad. He's dying!"

Mr. Barber jumped in his car and blasted out of the parking lot headed for the police station.

"Oh my God! He's bleeding too … he's bleeding!" Mrs. Rivers yelled. " Look!"

A pool of blood trickled from under Mr. Mac, coming from his backside, near the pocket where he kept his whiskey.

The sound of sirens filled the otherwise quiet night. Lumus arrived just ahead of the Fire and Rescue fire truck. A loud shrilling sound could be heard coming from up the Island. It was the distinctive sound of the ambulance. In the far distance I thought I heard the Isle of Palms crew's sirens. *Oh no!* I thought. *Not another garbage truck fiasco?*

The crew had grown silent, re-thinking their original cause of Mr. Mac's sudden departure from the game. The sight of the blood had gotten their attention.

Lumus arrived and rushed to the fallen ump. He crouched over Mr. Mac with the crowd gathered over him watching and waiting for Lumus to do something. He carefully rolled Mr. Mac onto his side exposing the cause of the cut and the flow of blood. The Rescue people were jumping off their truck hurrying with a stretcher and a bottle of oxygen. Lumus then gently and carefully produced the broken bottle that caused *all* the bleeding. It was what was left of Mr. Mac's pint of Bourbon, which was smashed from the fall, cutting his rear end.

Mr. Mac, in a stupor, woke up for a second, raised his head slightly, and tried vainly to call "strike three" only getting out t-r-i ... and passed out again. Lumus with a disdainful look turned his head away from the breath of Mr. Mac.

"Everybody calm down," Lumus said, "I think we found out the problem ... he's going to be all right. Let's just let him rest a few minutes."

Lumus looked up at the Rescue squad and tipped his hand by his mouth a few times indicating that Mr. Mac had one too many. They nodded in agreement.

"Let's wrap up that cut. But first let me get the broken glass out of his pocket." Lumus went to work on Mr. Mac. "There we go." He paused. "Mr. Johnson, bring me the first-aid kit from the car ... it's on the back seat of the jeep ... thanks."

Oh my gosh! I thought nervously glancing around. *Where are Emily and Katie?* In all of the excitement, I had completely forgotten about them. *Oh God, where are they?*

I looked in the bleachers. I scanned the area around the concession stand. I didn't see them. Panic was about to set in and then out of the corner of my eye I caught a glimpse of Emily's hat, just enough to calm me down. I should have known ... they were right in the middle of everything ... at homplate with the crowd. "There y'all are," I yelled to the girls who were squatting down just behind the group. As the girls looked up at me I waved for them to come on, indicating that it was time to leave.

A gentlemen's agreement was reached between the two opposing coaches, and the game was called to a halt with the Giants winning 6-0. I don't think the Cardinals wanted anymore of Rusty's curve anyway. They'd seen enough to last them a lifetime. In six full innings he had struck out fourteen batters and had given up only two scratch singles. "Come on ... Emily ... Katie. Y'all hear me!" I called and waved my arm. "Come on ... let's go. We're going home."

"A-a-a-w ... do we have to," Emily whined, "can't we stay longer?"

"No," I declared, "the game's over and it's getting late. Mom will be wondering where we are."

"What about the umpire?" Katie asked, "Will he be O. K.?"

"Yeah, he'll be all right," I said as we walked across the street.

"Where will they take him, Mike?" Emily asked. "To the hospital?"

"No." I thought for a second and then told the girls to reassure them. "They will probably take him home where he can rest. And then he will be all right."

As the lights of the field faded in the background I became lost in thought: *Just another episode of Island happenings,* I mused. *Then it dawned on me. Shoot, somebody should write a book one day about all the stuff that goes on. Humph ... I doubt it ... no body would want to take the time.*

Just before we got home, Katie asked me what happened to the umpire man? I told her he was sick from something he drank and fainted.

Miss Emily still adjusting her Minnie Pearl hat immediately corrected me. "No. He was drinking whiskey Katie, and he got drunk and fell down just like Mr. Herman did that time. Remember, Mike?" Her hat was now cocked to one side giving her a lopsided look.

"I'm not sure, Emily?" *Man, these kids don't miss a thing,* I thought.

"Well, he looked like he was sleeping to me," Katie said, "because I heard him snoring."

"Right Katie," her sister said, "that's what you do when you drink whiskey and fall down … you go right to sleep. Ain't that right, Mike?"

"T-h-a-t's right, Catbird."

"Oh, be quiet … don't say that," she said. "I ain't no Catbird."

I felt a tug on my sleeve. I bent down as Katie whispered, "If Emily don't wanna be a Catbird then I will … OK?"

I whispered back, "OK, Catbird."

Katie showed her beautiful smile, grabbed my hand, and held it the rest of the way home.

My mother was waiting on the porch, relaxing in the rocker looking tired. "I was worried. I heard the sirens headed down that way. Is everything all right?"

"Oh yeah, everything's O.K." I said, "everything's O-O-O-TAY."

"Mommy," Katie exclaimed, " Guess what?"

"What, Katie?"

"I'm a Catbird!" She turned, grinned and looked at me and giggled, "H-e-e, h-e-e."

"A what," asked Mom?

"It's what Mike calls me … you know …"

"No, I don't know. Mike, what's she talking about?"

"Oh nothing, Mom. Nothing … believe me."

"Mommy, mommy," Emily interrupted. "The umpire man got drunk and fell down and Mr. Lumus came and they fixed him up."

"What are you talking about, Emily?" Before Emily could answer my mother directed her attention to me. "Mike, what happened at the game … with the umpire?"

"Mom, I think I'll let Emily and Katie tell you all about it. I'm sleepy … I'm going to bed." I waved a good night. As I opened the screen door I yelled at Mollie, "Come on girl, let's go."

"Mommy, the man fell down and couldn't get up and …"

"No Katie, let me tell her," Emily said. "He tried to get up but he couldn't and then Mr. Lumus put a bandage thing on his bee-hind."

The girls put their hands to their face and giggled.

I stuck my head back outside the door and said to the girls, "Eah, y'all don't forget to tell Mom about Stinky Johnson *and* the part about the baseball bats … OK? … good night."

Katie squealed, "Mike!" And when I turned around she said, "Good night, Catbird" and smiled.

15
THE INFERNO

The beach was our favorite place to enjoy ourselves in the summer. It offered more than a beautiful place to swim and have fun ... it offered freedom. A lot of freedom to roam and let our imaginations take over and carry us to many different places. And there weren't many days when Bubba 'n me and the crew were not on the beach enjoying such freedom.

The beach at Sullivans Island occupied two miles of the serene Atlantic Ocean back dropped by smooth, brown sand and rolling white sand dunes that reflected the first slivers of light with each new dawn. Preceding the dunes were grassy footpaths worn smooth from decades of happy travelers whose migration was as eternal as the sun that beckoned them to this paradise of nature.

"Stations" rather than the common term "block" as in a city marked the Island. The term had been retained from the streetcar days when the streetcar would start and stop at each station, ferrying its passengers from the Point, the western end of the Island, to the Breach Inlet at the eastern end. Wax myrtle trees that grew wild all over the Island emanating their distinctive fragrance, something between new and stale perfume, flanked the footpaths leading to the beach at each Station.

As the summer day progressed, the sand dunes and the flat area from the end of the path that allowed entrance to the beach would absorb the sun's radiation like a sponge and generate terrific heat, especially on a windless day. The distance through this hot dessert- like zone was no more than a hundred feet but you could feel the rising heat even on your face as you walked through this area, which was the *only* access to the beach itself. To walk through this scorching area some kind of protective footwear was not only wise but a necessity.

On occasion, like when we did not have anything to do, Bubba 'n me would camp out on our bikes with a cold Coke and a square meal (cheese crackers in a pack) resting our forearms on our bike's handlebars and awaiting the unfortunate rookie, usually a tourist or visitor, who would unknowingly enter this scorched piece of earth barefooted. I called it "The Inferno." Bubba called it "The Run Through Hell."

A typical routine went something like this: a few steps into the hot zone followed by a yelp, run back to the cooling grass, assess the situation, and usually with a running start, take off for the beach at full speed. Naturally, the faster runners suffered the least amount of pain but *no one* who entered the hot zone barefooted got away without experiencing some degree of pain. Olympic sprinters didn't hold a candle to these tortured folks as they raced to the water to soak their burning feet. Sometimes steam rose from their feet as they sighed in relief … "A-A-A-A-H."

Bubba 'n me thought it an amusing sport to watch; however, at times, the pain overshadowed the humor when some of these sprinters could not make the hundred-foot dash before the heat and pain overtook them. Realizing their predicament and for some unknown reason, they invariably stopped, looked back and forth, all the while hopping from one foot to the other with a pained expression on their lily-white face, which matched their lily-white feet now turning red. I guess it's kind of hard to think clearly when your feet are on fire? The precious time wasted trying to decide whether to go back or head for the beach only worsened matters, each additional second added to the pain. Sometimes these trapped victims simply sat down in order to relieve the pain of their burning feet. And this tactic offered momentary relief until the heat bore through their bathing suits and now they had to deal with a burning bee-hind. There was usually a leader of the pack and often his or her indecision of whether to continue on or go back led to gridlock while everyone hopped around in pain looking for guidance. If there were children in the group, however, they were usually intuitive enough to make a quick decision and usually bolted like jackrabbits to the ocean and its cooling waters.

Bubba 'n me had first-hand knowledge of "The Inferno." On a family beach-outing some years earlier, we were nearing the end of the footpath, and being the hard heads that we were, took off running to the beach ahead of my parents and against their protests. And we were barefooted. Not only did we end up in the hot zone but also we charged directly into a patch of giant "stickers," the big brown ones, called sandburs or cockleburs. They were nothing like the small green burr found in a yard … these were twice the size And because they stuck like needles we always called 'em stickers. We couldn't hop around with the stickers in our feet so we did the only thing we could do. We sat down in the hot sand to pull them out and in doing so scorched our young butts in fine fashion. Getting up from the butt- burning, we attempted to run and again we loaded our feet with stickers. They hurt our tender little feet and the sand was burning us too but nary a peep came from our mouths because I already knew what my parents' reaction would be and it wouldn't be one of pity. Bubba, I think, was following my lead and by the pained expression on his face I could tell he wasn't enjoying this family outing.

From that day forward we *always* wore our old tennis shoes, flip-flops, or some type of footwear that we didn't mind getting wet or abused: our sticker shoes we called them.

It was a Saturday morning and Bubba was watching the end of his favorite, educational TV program on their new television … the Three Stooges Comedy Hour. I yelled through an open window, "Come on let's go … to the beach!"

"I'll catch up in a little bit," he screamed, "meet ya at the rocks … KNUCK, KNUCK, KNUCK!"

Not much was happening at the rocks, except for Mollie in her endless but hopeless pursuit of seagulls. Bubba arrived and we decided to ride our bikes up the beach checking the footpaths for people coming to the beach. We didn't have anything special planned that day and we thought it would be fun to watch the tenderfoots in the hot zone. Everything was quiet, not much beach activity but we knew sooner or later the crowds would show up. It was too beautiful of a beach day for them not to. We decided to wait at one of our special spots where there was usually a train of beachgoers, plus it offered a nice view of the beach and the harbor. We parked our bikes, and climbed our favorite dune, which was the highest on the beach … we called it Mount Sullivan's even though it wasn't near the size of a mountain. Perched up high we had a panoramic view allowing us to see all the way up to the Breach Inlet to our left, in front of us we could see the beach and the entrance to the harbor and off to our right was the city of Charleston silhouetted with its many church steeples. Also up high we could catch a little breeze. It was a typical June day, hot and hazy, the humidity and temperature both around ninety heating up the sand in the hot zone. We could tell it was getting hot by the barely visible wavy lines coming from the sand. It was rising heat.

We sat for a short time enjoying the view of the ocean and the harbor with the protruding jetties sticking out of the ocean in a long curvy line giving the appearance of a walled fort rising from the water. The ocean was "laid down," a local term referring to its flat surface because of the lack of a strong wind. White sprays of water systematically bounced off the ocean surface from the bows of the swift sport fishermen boats headed out to the open sea far beyond the jetties. The gulls and pelicans soared effortlessly overhead headed toward the beach. They were lucky. They didn't have to deal with the hot zone … ever.

The silence was broken by the sound of footsteps, very heavy and loud footsteps … CLOMP, CLOMP, CLOMP … it sounded like a herd of horses but we knew horses did not come to the beach Or did they? Then we heard the squeal of young children. We looked down the pathway and there they were: the biggest and fattest people we had ever seen in real life. What a sight. The mother reminded me of The

Fat Lady in a funny little costume on a poster tacked to a telephone pole advertising The Circus. This family of culinary delight made their appearance at the end of the footpath at Station 19, laughing and grinning and loaded down with food, ready for a fun day at the beach. And they were all *barefooted*!

"Oh boy! This oughta be good … real good," Bubba said as he sat back, crossed his legs, and folded his hands behind his head. He was smiling and shaking his head from side to side."Yep, this should be quite a show."

"Eah, I don't know if I can stand to watch this?" I said. "These people can barely walk and they're s-o-o white."

"A-a-a-w, you'll watch, Mr. Worrywart. Sit down … relax. Ain't nothing but a bunch of fat people going to the beach." Sometimes Bubba had a warped perspective on life. But a lot of times his perception was right on target. And this time he was correct. I agreed and sat down. And another thing he was right about … *I was* a worrywart.

"Yep, they sure are fat," I said to myself, *"no doubt about that."*

To add to these folks' misery was that the "run through hell," was longer here than anywhere on the Island, about fifty feet longer. There were five of these obese people: Mom, Dad, two girls and a boy. I laughed to myself as I thought, "Yep, the family that eats together stays together."

The mother was so fat that if she were to sit on a concrete bench it would squeak. The father was no slouch himself, all three hundred and something pounds neatly rounded on a five-foot frame with a bathing suit that was the size of an open parachute.

I stared at what I saw and could not believe my eyes. I thought the heat must have been playing tricks on me.

"Bubba," I said rubbing my eyes … I couldn't believe what I was seeing so I asked Bubba, "Eah, do you see what I see?"

"Yep," came a quick reply "You're talking about the walk they …u-u-u-h … walk … right?"

I nodded.

"They don't walk … they kind of like… they u-u-u-h… they waddle, like ducks. I wonder if they quack?" he asked grinning. "Want me to give 'em a quack or two and see if they answer?"

"Eah, not so loud," I warned, "they might hear you."

"So what?" he said. "We could say anything we wanted to those people and not have to worry. Shoot, they could *never* climb this sand dune … could you imagine? … BA-HA-HA."

Bubba 'n me were normal sized twelve- year- olds, but their son, who looked to be about eight or nine, must have outweighed me by at least fifty pounds. This kid did not miss a meal, that's for sure. He was short and round with rolls of fat that hung over and practically hid his bathing suit. *Call him anything you want, just don't call him late for dinner.*

The girls were a little older and a lot heavier. Their bathing suits lent new meaning to the term "two piece." They each wore a "four-piece" and they had obviously been on a seafood diet, which meant any food they saw, they ate. They all had jaws like pumpkins with noses like buttons. How any of them could see was amazing because they had no eyes, only slits in their place. Pudgy kids, to say the least, but kind of cute. One of the girls was wearing a Donald Duck inner tube around her huge waist. The rolls of fat smothering poor ol' Donald to death. His twisted face made him look like he was trying desperately to get out of there but today he wasn't going anywhere … he was locked in.

Here they come, Mom and Pop waddling along, decked out in their Hawaiian shirts with tacky straw hats perched on their big ol' heads and wearing those God-awful mirrored sunglasses. Everyone had a king-size Pepsi in one hand and some kind of sweet snack in the other except for Junior. Both of his hands clutched chocolate bars … a Snickers in one hand and a Baby Ruth in the other.

"Humph, like these people need to be eating candy bars," I said for no particular reason.

"Eah man, how do you think they got so fat?" Bubba replied smiling, "by eating oatmeal?"

Dad, leading this happy tribe of mounds of round, stepped into the hot zone first and instantly feeling the heat decided to back up, letting out a medium size, "Ouch!"

"What's wrong, Honey?" the overweight wife asked as the words literally rolled off her. "What ya yelling for?"

"Hot … the sand … it's hot," he managed to say with a mouthful of candy. Big Daddy stood there gawking at the sand. The corpulent clan gathered around their leader.

"A-a-a-a-w, you're just a big ol' sissy," Big Momma said stepping off the grassy path into the sand. *She got the "big" part right,* I thought.

"YOW-EE! OUCH!" Big Momma quickly agreed with her food mate, "Yeah, it's hot all right" as she looked from side to side surveying the situation. "Nope … can't cross down there or that way either," she gestured pointing to one side of the path to the other … the flabby skin hanging from her huge arms just a flapping from side to side.

"Earl!" … *E-a-r-l-l-l* ... Momma yelled. "Whatcha doing?"

"I'm going to the beach, what's it look like? Just leave me alone, will ya," Big Daddy said as he placed one towel on the ground, stepped on it, placed another ahead of it, stepped on it while picking up the other towel, repeating the process.

"I didn't drive all the way down here from Clinton with you and them screaming kids to stand here and look at the ocean. I'm going swimming … ya hear?"

Shaking his head from side to side Bubba said softly, "Sorry, Mr. Earl but it ain't gonna work." And Bubba was right. We had seen this scenario played out before.

I was already feeling sorry for Earl and his family so I asked Bubba, "Should we say something to 'em or not?"

"No!" Bubba shot back. "Not a word, you hear?"

"Man, you're a regular saydin… ah, saydint… a-a-h, what's that word?" … You know someone who likes pain and all," I said shaking my head from side to side.

"You mean sadist. And where were you in English class?" Bubba smiled broadly spelling out the word for me. "S-a-d- i-s-t." He was thrilled whenever he had the chance to correct my English.

"Yeah, that's it."

"I'm not a sadist. I'm just an observer of life. And right now I'm getting ready to observe some fat people burn their feet up. You have to understand Mike, this is nothing more than God-given entertainment. It's just like television except it's live."

On cue Earl completed his trip across the blazing sand using the towels as stepping-stones and stood triumphant on the other side, his fat little hands on his big fat hips, and his chest pumped up like an overstuffed peacock. Smiling and grinning with outstretched arms he acted like Moses after the Crossing. Now he decided to return the towels to Momma and the waiting kids so they could get across. He bundled up the towels as tightly as possible and with a mighty heave sent them a flying. The group watched in horror as the wad of towels opened about half way back and parachuted softly to earth, lying in the scorching sand. Meanwhile Earl had run to the water's edge to soak his chubby feet and then returned to the edge of the hot sand to urge his now stranded family to join him on the beach.

"Betty, whatcha waiting on? Kids, y'all come on, the day's a wasting, let's go."

"The towels, Earl. We only have two left. Whose gonna use 'em?"

"U-u-u-h, you use 'em. Then let the kids run across."

"We ain't running across no hot sand barefooted," the mutinous crew of little big people protested, "we'll just sit here all day if we gots to."

"I know what," said an excited Betty, "I'll get a running start and go through that sand in no time." *Then after I'm across the kids will see how easy it was and they'll run across. That'll solve everything,* Betty thought.

Bubba nudged me in the side with an elbow, "O-o-o-o-h boy! This I gotta see." I felt the same way. I threw my worrywart attitude away and sat back.

Shoot, this was far more suspenseful than waiting for the garbage truck. Here was this three hundred pound woman, completely out of shape, whose top speed downhill with a gale force wind behind her might be two miles an hour, and she was going to blitz a hundred feet of scorching sand in "no time?" This lady was so big and slow there wasn't anything she could do in "no time." However, we had to hand it to Big Betty. She was, at least, willing to give it the old college try as she slowly backpedaled step-by-step, steadily eyeing the spot where the cool grass ended and Dante's inferno began, her take off point. She looked like an Olympic long jumper preparing for the jump of his life except Betty wasn't going to jump … thank God.

"She looks like a 727 getting ready for takeoff except I don't think Betty's gonna fly too far," Bubba said grinning, "what you think?"

"I think this is going to be terrible. That's what I think."

Five, four, three, two, one and off she went down the pathway, huffing and a puffing. With some white circles of smoke coming from the top of her head, Betty would have looked like a human train the way she approached the takeoff spot, grimfaced and with teeth bared. This was one determined Momma. She must have had tremendous leg strength to be able to lift those huge fat feet. They looked like smoked hams attached at the ankles.

BOOM-BOOM-BOOM! Betty's feet pounded out a rhythm as she gained momentum. Her huge breasts flopping up and down matched the rhythm of her feet. A-FLOP, A-FLOP, A-FLOP. Her breasts were so big that Betty's whole face was lost for a second on the upswing portion of this cycle. BOOM- A-FLOP, BOOM, A-FLOP, went Betty. With arms pumping like pistons on a Mack truck, Betty entered the sand and immediately commenced to a hollering! " YOW-EE, WHOA, YOW-E-E-E-E-E!"

She made it about halfway across. No, she didn't stop or quit. Not this business-like big person. She inadvertently tangled her red, scorched feet in one of Earl's discarded beach towels causing her to go down in a heap like a sack of potatoes. Then the wailing and gnashing of teeth became that of a serious nature.

"O-O-O-W, OH-WEE, Y-O-W-W!" Poor Betty rolled from side to side like a beached whale trying to upright herself, which only added to her misery, exposing more of her tender skin to the hot sand. Her whole body began to fry like a burger at the Milk Bar.

"Oh dear God, help me!" she screamed. "Earl, help me, please somebody help me. I'm burning up!"

"Bubba, we gotta do something man," I said, "this ain't funny no more."

Bubba's perspective stepped in. "Eah, the only way we gonna help that lady is to get a crane and lift her up." That statement was as real as reality gets. "What you gonna do Hercules, go down there and pick her up? Humph, I doubt it." It was a statement of fact, not meant to be demeaning or hurtful.

But still ... I thought, *that lady needs help. Maybe she'll get up and everything will be O.K?*

Betty was trying her best to get up, still hollering and pleading for help, and just when she would almost make it, then gravity would rear its ugly head, and down she'd go in a heap onto the hot sand. Somehow she managed to get to one knee and begged Earl and the kids to help her. It looked like she was praying. The kids stood like statues, eating their snacks, hands deep in potato chip bags and gawking, either too lazy or too hungry to help. Junior shared the sentiments of the group when he asked, "Will ya let me have another candy bar if I help?"

"Oh yeah, yeah," Betty quickly shouted between screams, "three more if you want… four, five … whatever … just help me."

"O-h-h-h … all right," Junior said as he waddled into the sand licking the chocolate from his fingertips. Earl and the rest followed. They were hopping around trying not to touch the ground with their feet. But that was impossible. Now the whole family was screaming and a yelling and carrying on. You'd have thought they were at an Arkansas dogfight.

It was a family effort but they finally got Betty to one knee and then they spread her short flabby arms out to help maintain her balance. The kids had hold on one arm and Earl had the other. Now they faced the unenviable task of raising this huge woman to her feet.

Bubba was chuckling and shaking his head from side to side. "Ain't no way they're gonna lift Betty. Wanna bet?"

I tended to agree with Bubba but my emotions had gotten swept up in the thrill of the moment so I said, "Eah, you're on … a Coke and pack of nabs. I think they'll do it." Now Betty had a true supporter even though it was backed by a bet.

Bubba looked at me and said, "S-u-c-k-e-r."

Deep down I wanted this poor lady to find some relief more than I wanted to win some stupid bet. I silently began to pull hard for the fat lady named Betty.

The group gave a mighty tug but Betty's sweaty, slippery arms prevented them from getting a good grip and whoosh, their hands slid off. They tried again, this fat family of fried feet, and just when they thought they had her up … she was about half way up … Betty began a slow slide back toward the ground. Then she fell sideways landing on the leg of the slow moving daughter, Missy, trapping her beneath the sweaty, sand-coated, massive woman.

"Miss-e-e-y", Earl yelled, "You OK, honey?" All he could see were Missy's arms and legs, the rest hidden by Betty.

"I think so?" came a muffled sound from under Betty, "but it's real hot."

When little Missy disappeared under the folded skin of Betty that did it for me. The situation, which had been going downhill for a while, had now gone from a game to something serious. And I think Bubba realized it was time for us to act too because I saw that look of fear, almost fright on his face. We didn't say a word. At the same time we jumped up and both bolted down the hill in hopes of helping Betty and her trapped daughter.

"Quick Junior, grab your Momma's leg and pull." Earl had hold of an arm. They could have made a Thanksgiving wish right then and there.

Just as we were arriving on the scene I heard Earl scream, "Pull, Junior. Pull, boy!"

With Earl and Junior's mighty effort, Betty more of less slide off the squashed little girl named Missy. Everyone then turned their attention back to Betty, still sitting and frying in the sand.

Earl looked surprised when he saw Bubba 'n me.

"We were over and saw y'all. Looks like y'all need some help," I said, "that is if you need us?"

"Oh yeah, yeah. Please," said Earl and then he smiled at Betty and added, "Looka here, Momma. Here's some boys to help us. Ain't that nice?"

You would have thought we were angels sent directly from the heavens right then and there the way Betty began to talk. "Praise God … Hallelujah … Amen … Thank the Lord! They have come to save me from this Hell on earth."

Bubba 'n me didn't know whether to take a bow or help get Betty up or what?

We heard Earl yell to us, "Boys … just a hold of a leg … each one of ya grab one and pull for everything your worth … O. K?"

Following Earl's instructions we pulled and pulled with all our might and maybe … maybe … budged big Betty three inches.

"U-u-u-h, uh," I said between breathes. "She's too …" I caught myself getting ready to say she's too fat. I stopped. "Won't work. Let's try to roll …" and I stopped again. What was I thinking? Roll her? That was dumb.

Bubba had an idea: "Let's get behind her, grab her arms and pull her. With all of us we might can … before he finished Earl and Junior had grabbed one of Betty's arms and were tugging on her like they were trying to pull her arms out of her sockets. The two daughters stood off to the side jumping up and down and yelling and screaming exactly like cheerleaders. Bubba 'n me noticed a slight movement and became encouraged that this tactic just might work. We jumped in and joined the "pull Betty train" and grabbed her other arm but were of little help. Betty's sweaty, flabby skin made it hard to get a good grip. We gave a mighty tug and losing our grip we quickly slipped backward and plopped down backwards onto the hot sand.

"OUCH!" yelled Bubba. "Man! That sand's hot."

I stood up, looked at Bubba and with as sarcastic a tone as I could muster said, "Oh really, Mr. O'Toole. Aren't you the smart one."

"Eah," said Bubba, "we ain't time for all that right now … O.K?"

Out of the corner of my eye I saw a beach pale, a small bucket but it was still something capable of holding water. I grabbed it and quickly presented it to the exhausted fat man standing over his wife as he wiped sweat from his brow.

"Mr. Earl," I declared, "take this bucket and fill it up … quick … and then … Mr. Earl was reading my mind and took off in a shoot, bucket in hand. I heard him yell back as he neared the water edge, "Aw shucks! Why didn't I think of that sooner?"

Because if you were that smart in the first place then you wouldn't be in this predicament ... now would you? is what I thought. Of course, I kept my mouth shut. I had been told that exact phrase so many times by the nuns at school that I had memorized it in hopes of someday using it on someone. And that day had come. How sweet it was!

When Earl returned with the bucket full of water he attempted to pour the water on Betty's head. To cool her off I guess? I stopped him immediately saying, "No … no. Here … pour it under her."

"O-o-o-h," cooed Earl, "I see." After pouring the water under Betty so she could sit in the cooling mud, Earl stepped back admiring his handiwork with a big smile on his face.

Before I could remind Earl to go fetch more water, Betty took over: "Well, Earl. Don't just stand there like a damned fool. Go get more water!"

I think Earl got the message. When he tired out after six or seven runs to get water, his son relieved him and they continued to pour water under and around Betty. By this time poor old Betty could have almost swam away from her dilemma.

Now that Betty had cooled down and wasn't sweating a stream and everybody was rested, Earl decided that all of us, Earl and his kids and Bubba 'n me, could pull Betty to her feet. Our combined efforts were successful as Betty rose from the sand like a mighty warrior who had gone into battle, been wounded, and now stood tall, ready to fight again.

"W-H-O-O-O-E-E," she hollered, "Thank God! And thank you two youngun's" as she looked at Bubba 'n me …. "Thank you!"

Earl slapped Bubba 'n me on the back. "Without you two fellows … *fellars* … there ain't no way we'd gotten Betty up … thank you."

As the "thank yous" and well wishes were being handed out, all of us made our way to the cool grass at the end of the path.

"You're welcome, Miss Betty," Bubba 'n me chimed in unison. "Nothing to it" and then we laughed. "Well … we got to get going," I said

"Oh no. Wait a minute. Can't we repay you somehow for helping?"

"Oh, no thank you, Ma'am," said Bubba, "we were just glad to help."

Betty wasn't having any of that. She waved us off and then yelled to Junior, "Bring these boys a Coca-Cola." She looked at us and asked, "Y'all do drink Coke, doesn't you?"

"Yes Ma'am," we replied.

"And bring them a Snicker bar or some kind of candy too," added Betty.

"Does I have to?" Junior pleaded as he pillaged through a cooler full of assorted candies and cookies, all being chocolate.

"Boy!" screamed Betty, "don't make me have to come over there … *thare* … or else there's gonna be big trouble."

I nudged Bubba in the side and gave a nod of my head as to say, "let's get out of here."

Bubba's silent response was, "You got that right."

As we accepted our reward … the Cokes and candy bars … I said as politely as I could, "Thank you." A slight pause. "Well … we have to be getting home now. Got chores to do. I thought, *they'll excuse us immediately upon hearing we had chores to do.*

That little bit of deception seemed to work. There were no protests.

"See ya'll later," we said, as we sauntered off, a little bit for the worse after the hot encounter of trying to lift a fat lady out of the sand.

As we got back to our bikes I overheard Earl in a cheerful tone say, "Now we can all go to the beach."

I looked back to see if they were about to enter The Inferno again and saw the boss of that outfit, Betty, shaking a finger in Earl's face and saying very clearly, "We're going home, Mister. That's where we're going. Back home to Clinton. And I mean right this minute. Let' go!"

They gathered themselves and their belongings, brushed themselves off, checked for broken bones, and stood gawking at the cool Atlantic Ocean with its tempting waves gently breaking, sliding up the beach and back out. The family's final look was one of lost dreams and hot memories.

Fading words about a never-to-be- picnic, towels, and burnt feet drifted away with the big people as they slowly made their way to their car.

Bubba 'n me retrieved our bikes and began walking them toward the path.

"Man oh man, that was something else … huh?" said Bubba.

"Got that right." I replied. Bubba had a huge grin on his face. I asked, "What? … "What's so funny?"

"I was thinking. That whole thing … that whole …" he was searching for a word… "that whole … "episode," he blurted out. "Yeah, that's it … episode. It reminded me of the times at the boat landing but this beats all."

Bubba was referring to the boat ramp at the Point, another human nature observation point where we camped for hours learning how *not* to launch a boat.

"Yep, that was something else," he said to himself, shaking his head.

"Yeah, more family involvement and without all the cussing," I said, "and we even got involved this time. How about that?"

"Y-e-a-h," Bubba said softly. Not an agreeing "yeah" but an affirming one. What he was affirming I didn't know. Then he continued, "Mike, you know what that lady was?" said Bubba giving me a serious look. He need not have given me that look because I knew he was serious about something when he called me by my name.

"What's that, Bubba?" I asked thinking he was going to say she was a fat woman who couldn't get up. But he fooled me ... again.

"She was a big problem ... that's what ... a big problem."

I reflected for a second and then from out of nowhere ... I mean from way out in left field ... this crazy, deep, thought came to me. "Yeah," I blurted out, "just like big problems we have in life." Bubba gave me a quizzical look. Then I realized why I had said that. In the back of my mind, hidden away deep in my subconscious was lurking a big problem: the problem of how I was ever going to get Beverly to be my girlfriend.

I must have been staring off in space again because Bubba yelled, "Eah ... eah, you!"

"What?" I retorted angrily because he had disturbed my lovely thought process. "Well ... what?" I repeated.

"Eah, don't get all bent out of shape, Devlin. I was just going to agree with you about what you said about big problems in life ... that's all ... O.K?"

"Yeah, yeah. I'm sorry. I didn't mean to yell at ya like that." I gave Bubba a friendly love tap on the shoulder. "I was just thinking ..."

Bubba stopped, looked at me and said, "Thinking about what?"

I couldn't dare tell him the truth. That I was thinking about Beverly. No way! Over the past six months he told me on several occasions that he "had heard enough about that girl to last a lifetime."

"About what?" I mumbled. I paused. "About big problems." Before he could ask me about specific problems I changed the whole direction of the conversation. I did a quick three-sixty. "And you know what I figured out?" I spoke again before he could reply. "The best way to solve problems sometimes is to simply walk away from them."

"Yep, that's exactly right," said Bubba. "Just like we did with the fat lady a little while ago ... just walk away and let somebody else deal with it."

"Whoa, what ya mean ... walk away. Didn't we help her?"

"Help her?" Bubba said. "Oh yeah. We helped her get up out of the sand but the problem is still there ... isn't it? She's still fat as an elephant and problems will keep coming up because of it. So did we really solve a problem or just put it back on its feet again?"

WOW! I was amazed at my friend's logic and deep understanding. I was so stunned I didn't know what to say. So I simply mumbled, "Yeah, you're right. I didn't even think of it that way."

We walked in silence for a minute or so and as I did I sneaked a peek at my best friend and felt proud to be his buddy. Here was the guy I had known all my life … my best friend and confidant … and I thought I knew everything about him but realized that I was only now beginning to really know him. Then a slight smile broke across my face as I realized it took a fat lady stuck in the sand to bring this out of me.

The thought of Beverly was still there, lingering in its little special place in by mind. It would be much later in life that I would learn that Beverly, during these happy-hopping-hormonal times of mine, wasn't a problem at all. As a matter of fact, she was probably the solution to a lot of my problems.

We reached the hard part of the path where we could now ride our bikes. Bubba was pushing his bike, getting it up to a speed where he could leap on it, which he did, landing squarely on the seat. He looked much like the cowboys we watched on TV leaving town in a hurry as they mounted their horses.

"C'mon, slowpoke," he yelled, "let's go!"

As usual, I pedaled hard trying to keep up with my friend and lost another race to Burton's.

16
MOLLIE

Mollie was the family dog but in reality she was *my* dog because of the bond she and I had formed from the time she was a pup. And if she could talk she would tell you the same thing. We went practically everywhere together. Like most kids I was definitely prejudiced and thought she was the greatest and smartest dog in the whole world except for Lassie, of course. My Uncle Homer gave her to the family but Mollie and I, for whatever reason, hit it off right from the time we met and it's been that way ever since.

My Uncle Homer was a retired country gentleman who lived in Rock Hill, S.C., a small Upstate town where he led the easy life. He was always pawning off a dog or chicken and an occasional cat to his Lowcountry relatives. I was sure glad he gave us Mollie.

We did not know exactly what kind of breed Mollie was.

"She's a Heinz 57, son," my father told me and laughed.

I didn't understand what he meant and it didn't really matter. The best I could figure was that Mollie was part Border Collie, part Shepherd and part something else. But what I did know was that she was as loyal to me as she was smart. Shoot … she was so smart she could even spell. And that was doing a lot better than some of my friends. If I spelled out E-A-T or B-E-A-C-H she would know right away what I meant. Why she was so smart she did everything except help me with my homework and from the looks of my grades maybe I should have gotten some help from her. My father used to say that she was smarter than most humans he knew. Now I don't know if that said much for the type of humans my father knew or made Mollie real smart? All I know is that I loved Mollie and Mollie loved me.

I enjoyed having her tag along with Bubba 'n me when we rode our bikes all over the Island. She scouted ahead, always on the lookout for mean dogs or any kind of trouble, raising her tail and the hair on her back as a sign that danger lurked nearby. She went everywhere with me except to church and school. As for going to school … well, as smart as she was she didn't need to go to school. Now church was a different matter … with me anyway. I had often questioned why dogs, especially

Mollie, couldn't go to church with their masters as long as they, the dogs, were clean and well behaved. Shoot, if they were like that then they were already in a higher class than a lot of Sunday churchgoers. I didn't understand this and presented my case to about everyone I knew and no one could give me a satisfactory answer. Finally, Bubba who was tired of listening to my griping about not being able to take Mollie to church suggested I ask Sister Roberta about it: "She's smart and knows about the church and religion and all that stuff. She could probably tell you."

"Well, when we go back to school I just might do that. Nobody else knows why."

"Yeah, right. And she'll think you're nuts and whoop you upside the head with the big ruler."

"No she won't, Curley. KNUCK-KNUCK. She's saving all her strength to give you a good licking for all the trouble you've been in this summer."

"Oh yeah! That's stupid, Devlin. How does she know what I've done this summer, huh?"

"Because I told her, that's how, smarty."

"Yeah, yeah, yeah. I hear you talking."

"Well, she calls me once a week to check on what you're doing and I tell her."

"Really?" Bubba exclaimed not knowing if I was kidding or not. "What did you tell her?"

"O-o-o-h just things." I had him going now. "But eah, don't worry. I don't tell her about none of the nasty stuff."

"Devlin, I'm gonna ..." He moved toward me with his hands in the choking position but he was smiling.

"Eah, don't get bent out of shape. I'm kidding ... just kidding. You know that don't you?"

"I don't k-n-o-w. I'm not so sure about you sometimes," Bubba said and then let go a thunderous "BA-HA-HA-HA-HA ... BA-HA!"

Bubba had given me a good idea about my unanswerable question as to why Mollie couldn't go to church when he mentioned Sister Roberta, a holy person, but I was not planning on asking her. Instead I gave it some thought and I decided to go to the main source ... the man himself ... Father Dawes, our parish priest. If anybody would know why Mollie couldn't go to church it would certainly be him because it was his church and he ran it and besides, he was a priest and knew about all that holy stuff and all. I laid my plans that week and the following Sunday after Mass I hung back near the back of the church rather than racing out of church and heading to the car as usual.

My father spotted me. "Come on, Mike," he yelled, "I've got to get home and get the boat loaded. I want to catch the low tide ... the flounder are biting at the Point."

"Just a minute." A long pause. "I need to see Father Dawes."

"What for?"

"I got to talk to him about something."

Our new priest, Father Dawes, was fresh out of the seminary on his first assignment, a true rookie. Being a young priest, I felt as though I could talk to him, or at least, I wasn't afraid to try like so many of my classmates at St. Angela's who viewed a priest as some kind of holy demon who would condemn you to hell for anything short of perfection. Father Dawes seemed nice enough and besides, I liked his short sermons, which got to the point and made sense. Not a bunch of senseless rambling.

"Can't it wait?" My father was getting jumpy already. "Tide's low in an hour."

"No, sir." I was determined. "I need to ask him something."

By this time my father and I were closer to each other, no longer shouting across the parking lot. Mr. Devlin was thinking. *(Oh gosh! What's that boy done now?)*

"OK … I'll wait in the car with the girls. But hurry if you can. You know how antsy the girls can get."

"Yes sir."

Maybe the boy is thinking about becoming a priest? N-a-a-w. Ryan maybe, but not Mike.

I caught Father Dawes trying to make his escape to the solitude and peace of the rectory across the street. It was difficult for him to hide or blend in amongst the still dispersing parishioners. His full mane of bright red hair stuck out like a fire in the night.

"Father! Father!" I yelled. He turned around, surprised. "Can I see you for a minute?"

He smiled and said, "Certainly, young man."

As he approached he gave me a funny stare while tapping his finger to his temple and then he asked, "You're one of the Devlin clan … right?"

"U-u-u-h … yes Father." I thought for a second. "There's lots of Devlin clams … I'm Mike."

"Yes, yes. I thought I recognized you. Saw you at school this year. Remember?"

First he calls me a clam and now he wants me to remember seeing him at school. I don't know about all this?

"U-u-u-h … kind of," I stammered. "It must have been a long time ago?"

"Yes, yes. It was. It was the beginning of school if I recall correctly." He paused and looked down at me. "What can I do for you, Mike?"

I guess he thinks I need another blessing the way he's holding his hand? Maybe he's been talking to Sister Rosalind?

"Father, there's something that's been bothering me for a long time and I'd like to ask you about it. I've already asked a bunch of people and nobody knows the answer."

"OK, I'll try." He gave me his full attention. " What is it?"

"Why can't dogs go to church? Like when I came to Mass this morning … why couldn't I bring Mollie … my dog?"

"Dogs?" His eyes were as wide as saucers. "In church?" He looked totally surprised but that didn't bother me. I was used to that look. "You mean dogs, like animals?"

"Yeah dogs, like Mollie, my dog. Do you know her?"

"Well, no I can't say that I've ever met Mollie but …" he was searching hard for an explanation. "Uh- hum." Father cleared his voice. "Well, Mike … you see. The church is God's house and it's considered holy and sacred, a blessed place, a place of worship."

I thought he was finished so I blurted out, "You mean God doesn't like dogs?"

"No, no," he said emphatically. "It's not that. God loves all his creatures but there is a place for them and the church is … u-u-u-h … how do you say … u-u-u-h …" Father Dawes was really searching *now.*

He managed to continue. "It's like this, my son. Dogs don't have a soul like you and me and are therefore considered by the church not to be in need of salvation. Does that make it clearer, Mike?"

"I'm not sure?" I gave Father a quizzical stare. I paused and really put on my thinking cap. "Does that mean Mollie can't go to heaven? Is that what you're saying?" I asked politely.

In an effort at total placation and with mistaken innocence Father Dawes said, "Well Mike, I'm sure there is a dog heaven somewhere in God's plan where Mollie can rest in peace when her time on earth is up."

"A dog heaven." I almost yelled and would have if I weren't talking to a priest. So as calmly as possible I replied, "Can't dogs go to regular heaven?"

"Well, a-hum." Father cleared his throat again and said, "Not really. Heaven is reserved for humans, a place for the soul. God's spiritual creatures live there."

I didn't like the sound of this one bit! If Mollie and me couldn't be together in regular heaven then I don't know about all this church stuff.

Father Dawes had had enough of Theology 101 with one of the Devlin children and before he could bless himself out of this situation my father came to the rescue. Coming around the corner my father said, "Oh, there you are. Excuse me, Father. But we're running late and …"

The relieved priest eagerly spoke up, "Good to see you Mr. Devlin. Good to see you. It's all right. Mike and I were just finishing up." He turned toward me and asked, " I hope I answered your question, Mike?

Anyway, think about it and if need be we can talk next Sunday. OK?" He didn't sound very sincere but, at least, he had taken the time to talk to me.

"OK, and thank you Father," I said as my father and I headed for the car.

"What was all that about?" My father asked quickening his pace. "It must have been important? Father Dawes looked kind of worried."

"Oh nothing. I just had a question about dogs and church and heaven. That kind of stuff."

"Did Father help you?"

"Yes sir." I was hesitant in my answer. "Kind of ... I guess."

As we rode home I was still searching for an answer. The part that bothered me the most was what Father Dawes said about Mollie not being able to go to heaven with me. Well, I'd have to give that some thought when I found the time, that's for sure. My father sensed something was on my mind but being the good father that he was left me alone to figure it out knowing that if I couldn't I'd come to him for help. It was one of the many ways he said, "I love you."

By the time we pulled into the back yard I had thought about showing up at Mass next Sunday with Mollie, after she had a bath of course, and see what would happen. On second thought that would not be such a good idea. Father Dawes might tell Sister Roberta and then I'd be in trouble at school even before it started. So I dropped that idea.

Mollie, the center of my attention, was dutifully waiting for me by the back steps, curled up under the leafy Fatsia plant seeking a cool spot.

"Hey, Mollie! How you doing, girl?"

She gave me the I'm OK look, wagging her tail as she got up.

"Wanna go to c-h-u-r-c-h?" At that very moment I could have sworn that she knelt down, bowed her head and began to bless herself. I roared with laughter.

My father trailing behind asked, " What's so funny?"

"Oh nothing, Daddy ... nothing. Just something about church."

I stepped onto the back porch smiling, stopped, looked back at Mollie and she was smiling too.

I told her then, "Don't worry Mollie. Don't you worry one bit. You and me will be in the same heaven someday."

17
THE TABLE

It's been said that time flies when you're having fun. It's so true. We had been having fun … more than fun … a great summer … and before we knew it the month of June was gone. Durn! Why couldn't school go by that quickly? I had often asked Bubba that question and he always answered, "Because it's school, stupid. It's supposed to last longer."

The air was filled with excitement along with the July humidity. It was July 2 and in two more days we would celebrate the most fun-filled day of the year, except for Christmas, of course. Islanders took great pride not only in their little beach community but also in America and in being called Americans. American flags on just about everybody's porches waved proudly in the slight breeze, announcing the day to be celebrated much like a Christmas tree does at Christmas. World War II was still fresh in the minds of many adults particularly the men who served and served well, especially overseas in Europe and in the Pacific theater. The Fourth of July was celebrated with special events, cookouts and parties galore. Patriotism ran deep in the Devlin family and we were always part of the celebration on this special day.

About two weeks before the Fourth, I had overheard my father talking with my mother one evening about an argument he had with Mr. Scott about where the 4th of July cookout would be held this year. Willie, or Wee Willie as my father called his life- long friend, insisted on hosting the party while my father disagreed and wanted to have it at our house. Mr. Scott said that it was his turn to have it at his house, even as a courtesy. My father tried to counter Wee Willie's argument by telling him that first of all, Willie didn't have a picnic table for everyone to eat off of nor a grill to cook on. Wee Willie's counterpoint was that he could *get* a table and a grill. He said that his yard had bigger trees, which offered more shade and comfort to the people at the cookout, especially the older folks. And he had a good selling point. While we had more trees in our yard they were spaced too far apart to offer sufficient relief from the heat. And no one, in their right mind, enjoyed a party in July in the direct sun. Besides, Willie told my father that the Devlins always had the party at their place. Why couldn't someone else have it at their house? My father told my mother that Willie had him there and Willie, despite his propensity for screwing things up, was right. So, my father reasoned, why not? … and gave up his argument. Deep down my father's reluctance to letting Wee Willie plan and have the party stemmed from the fact that Willie was notorious about his messing up anything of importance he tried to plan. My father had given up on going fishing with him after Willie had ruined more fishing trips by missing the tide or forgetting to bring the bait than anyone on the Island. He even ruined his wife's surprise birthday party by getting the wrong date, which in the end turned out to be a real surprise for all involved. So the great debate over where the 4th of July celebration would be held was finally settled after a series of phone calls and much discussion. It would be held at the Scotts' house. And in the end no one's feelings were hurt, just a few feathers ruffled.

Shoot, to the Devlin kids it didn't matter where the celebration was held. It could have been on the moon and it would be all right with us as long as there was good food, good company, and fireworks.

Sometimes I rode my bike with no real purpose or real direction just like I led my life. I was spinning not only the wheels of my bike but also the wheels of life and not really going anywhere in particular. I always had a starting point but never seemed to have a destination. But today was different: I had a purpose, a goal, and better yet a place to go as I pedaled my way up the Island on my mother's instructions. I was headed to my Aunt Cele and Aunt Christle's house and then to Uncle Schroeder's to invite them to the Fourth of July cookout. My friend Bubba was with me as we rode up the Island.

"Why didn't your Mom or Dad just call them?" Bubba asked wiping the sweat from his brow. Before I could answer he yelled. "Looka here! No hands," as he let go of his grip on the handle bar and extended his arms straight out from his shoulders for balance. He was riding down the middle of Central Avenue. "I can ride like this all the way to the Post Office, Mike … wanna bet?"

"No bet." I pulled up even with Bubba, riding with no hands and pedaled hard to race by him and would have had it not been for oncoming traffic, which forced us to grab our handlebars and move to the side of the road.

"And to answer your question, Aunt Christle is real old and doesn't hear so good. I think she's mostly deaf."

"She's the gray- headed one who wears the glasses, ain't she?"

"Yeah, anyway she sits by the phone all day and once she gets on it she won't ever hang up. You have to keep yelling the same thing over and over like a broken record. So Mom asked me to just go tell 'em and make sure they got the message."

"Eah, that's OK with me. Hope we take all day. I was supposed to cut the grass today … now I have a good excuse not to."

"Yeah right." I looked at Bubba like I was real surprised. He looked back and knew what I was thinking. "If the sun came up this morning you would have a good reason not to cut the grass." I paused to check Bubba's reaction to my comment about his laziness when it came to mowing their yard. He just smiled and said, "So …?"

"Eah, let's stop by the Post Office first and I can tell Uncle Schroeder. Won't take but a minute."

"T-h-a-t-'s right, Catbird!" Bubba said. "Race ya to the corner … no hands … GO!"

A small group of town workers were pushing a set of bleachers, the same one used at the baseball field, into its place in the corner of the parking lot at the Post Office. A podium had already been set up near the front of the Post Office from which the mayor would speak his words of patriotism on the Fourth. After his speech he would officially declare the Fourth of July festivities to begin, which was the signal for the parade to start. A long blast from the fire truck would let the Islanders know it was time to celebrate the Fourth and to be extra careful about starting a fire because the fire truck was the lead vehicle of the parade and wouldn't have time for putting out fires and celebrating in a parade too.

I heard Uncle Schroeder's deep, familiar voice greeting people by the front door of the Post Office.

When I walked up he hailed me with a big smile and said, "Hey, how you feeling?"

"Oh… fine and dandy," I answered in the deepest voice I could muster.

"Hey, you're stealing my line now. What you trying to do? Get my job?"

"Oh no sir, no sir. I was just trying to talk like you do. It sounds neat."

"Yeah? Why thank you, Mike. You've made this old man's day."

"I just stopped by to tell you that you are invited to the Fourth of July cookout on Saturday, and it'll be at Mr. Scott's house instead of ours."

Uncle Schroeder smiled, took off his hat and wiped the sweat from his bald head. "At Wee Willie's, huh? What happened? Your Mom won't let Bernie have it at yawl's house?"

"Gosh, I don't know about all that. Mom asked me to tell you where it will be. And it starts about 4:00."

"Besides a bunch of beer what else should I bring?"

The question sounded more like a quiz than a concern about bringing beer.

I frowned and thought for a second and then looked at him. The sly grin on his face gave away the answer. "Oh yeah, and bring Aunt Simmie too. Daddy wouldn't want you to get in trouble." We both chuckled.

"OK … beer and the wife. Sure hope I don't forget to bring the beer."

"Well, I've got to go to Aunt Cele's and Aunt Christle's now. I'll see ya later. Bye." I ran to my bike and the impatient, squirming Bubba who had been waving at me the whole time.

"OK, see you on Saturday," Uncle Schroeder said and then opened the door for another customer and tipped his hat.

"What's your hurry, boy?" I asked Bubba. "Thought you wanted to get out of cutting the grass. Remember?"

"I do but it's hot out here. Let's ride and get some breeze going."

"OK. To Aunt Cele's and that's it," I said as we rode out of the parking lot. "Maybe we can go to the beach later?"

"Eah" Bubba paused. He looked over his shoulder at me. "Haven't you forgotten something?"

"N-o-o-o, I don't think so? What?"

"We can't go to the beach. Remember Billy and Sammy asked us the other day to come by and help 'em out."

"Oh yeah, that's right, that's right. I'd forgotten all about that. Man, I'm glad you remembered."

"That's what friends are for." Bubba was in the middle of the street again riding with no hands. "All the way to Chippys … no hands … bet ya a dime."

"OK … it's a bet." I let Bubba get going and then eased over in front of him and slowed down until I was barely moving. "One dime coming up!" I yelled.

"Hey, man. Get out the way." I knew he needed speed to maintain balance. "No fair. You're cheating, Devlin."

I glanced back and Bubba touched the handle bar to keep from falling.

"Gottcha. You touched. That's one dime. Wanna go for another one?"

"No because you cheat." Bubba paused and studied the approaching car. "Look out … clear the way. Here c-o-m-e-s S-a-r-g-e Henry," he drawled. "Never know where he's going."

We pulled to the side of the road giving Sergeant Henry, the blindest of all the Island drivers a wide path. We watched him go by, his head practically on top of the steering wheel squinting hard just to see the road.

"Did you hear what he did last week?" I asked Bubba.

"No what?"

"He ran into Mrs. Taylor's car when he was pulling into Owen's store. And Mrs. Taylor really got mad even though he barely scratched her car. You know how slow he goes. Anyway, Mrs. Taylor jumped out of her car and was screaming and yelling and carrying on and all. And then she asked Sergeant Henry if he was blind or what? Know what Henry said?"

"Uh-uh … what?"

"No, I'm not blind. I hit you … didn't I? A-HA-HA-HA."

"BA-HA-HA-HA-HA … that's pretty good … pretty good."

"Turn here. We'll take the short cut through Swain's yard," I said, "we're almost there."

We sat on our bikes out by the fence at Aunt Cele's for at least five minutes yelling to Aunt Cele and Aunt Christle who were nowhere in sight. We got no answer.

"I was afraid this wasn't going to work. Want to go in with me?"

"N-a-a-a-w. I'll wait over there in the shade. And Mike, don't take forever … OK?"

"Yes sir, right away sir. Yes sir. You can come in too, you know. They don't bite."

"Eah, that's not what I heard. Stinky Johnson said he saw Christle last week at the school getting her rabies shot. HA-HA."

"Boy, you better shut up talking like that about my aunt."

"Why? Whatcha gonna do. Beat me up?"

"N-o-o-o. What I'm gonna do is sic my aunt Christle on you, that's what. A- HA-HA-HA!" And then I grinned at Bubba laid out in the cool blanket of clover waving good-bye to me.

"Be right back." I walked across the yard, stopped at the bottom of the steps, and yelled for Aunt Cele and Aunt Christle. Still no answer. I knew they were home because the car was in the driveway.

I walked to the top of the steps, shaded my eyes and pressed my face against the screen. I was about to yell again and then I saw the figure of one of my old maid aunts sitting in a rocking chair, not ten feet away. It was Aunt Christle just sitting there staring blankly straight ahead.

"Aunt Christle." I said and then paused. No movement. Louder. "Aunt Christle!"

She stirred slowly and looked my way. "Hah?" A long pause. "Who's that?"

"It's me … Mike." I pulled open the screen door and walked in. "Hi, Aunt Christle."

She gave me a look of disbelief. Like I was a Martian or something.

As I got closer I think she recognized me? "Aunt Christle, it's me Mike. How are you?"

"Hah, what'd you say?"

I yelled, "How are you?" I wasn't five feet from her.

She moved her head back, cocked it on an angle and took a long look at me. "I guess I'm OK." She paused for the longest time and then asked rather authoritatively, "What you want?"

"Oh, I don't want anything. I just came by to tell you and Aunt Cele about the cookout on the Fourth of July."

"Hah … Aunt Cele? I think she's in the house somewhere but I'm not sure."

I practically shouted, "No! About the cookout on the Fourth … y'all are supposed to come."

She turned her head and cupped her ear, staring at me and said, "Hah?"

I heard Bubba out by the fence, laughing.

"The cookout, the cookout," I shouted. "You know the cookout on the Fourth of July."

"Yeah, uh-huh. The Fourth. That's two days from today … so what?"

"Oh boy," I thought, *this ain't working."* I was about to scream again when Aunt Cele appeared at the door. " Hello Michael, what's all the yelling about?"

"Oh … hi, Aunt Cele. I was telling Aunt Christle about the cookout on the Fourth."

Aunt Christle heard her name and asked, "Hah? Want you want?"

"Nothing Christle," Aunt Cele said. "You want to sit for a spell, Michael?" She motioned to a rocker. "Now what's this about the Fourth?" she asked taking a seat.

"Well, y'all are invited to the cookout. Mom asked me to come by and tell you. But this year it will be at the Scott's house."

"O-o-o-h, the Scotts. Not yawl's house, huh?" Aunt Cele asked and then she paused analyzing my statement as though it were some grandiose announcement. "At the Scotts. Oh, I see, I see. Hear that, Christle?" Aunt Cele looked toward Christle. "The Fourth of July cookout will be at the Scotts, not at Bernie's."

"Hah?" Aunt Christle said, then asked, "what did you say Cele?"

Aunt Cele turned her attention toward me ignoring her sister.

"Yes Ma'am," I said. "And it will start about 4:00."

"Hah? What'd he say, Cele?"

"Nothing, Christle," Aunt Cele yelled. " Nothing."

Aunt Christle took on the impression of a scolded child, closed her eyes, and dropped her head. I heard her mumble her all time favorite saying, "Always yelling at me. Oh, how I suffer."

It was time to leave. I was out of my chair and edging toward the door, ready to make my escape. "Well … it was nice to see y'all but I've …"

"Don't go yet, Michael," Aunt Cele said, "I've got some cake for you. Sit down and rest your bones. You're just like your father … impatient."

I put up my hands in protest.

"Oh no thank you, Aunt Cele." It wasn't that her cake wasn't delicious because it was. But sometimes these food-gathering episodes went on for what seemed like an eternity. "Really, I'm not hungry," I pleaded and lied.

Simply because she had a heart of gold she insisted and took forever as she pulled herself up from the rocker and moved slowly back into the house.

"Cele!" Christle shouted suddenly coming awake. "You better bring two pieces of cake." She pointed at Bubba lying in the grass. "Isn't that Bubba O'Toole out there by the fence? Hah?"

"Yes Ma'am," I said, "that's him."

Bubba 'n me gulped down the fresh pineapple cake on the way to the Scott's house.

"Mike, you should have stayed longer at Aunt Cele's. I bet she would have brought you some cookies and Kool Aid. Shoot, man, you don't know. Maybe a whole meal?"

"Yeah right! And by the time I got out of there it would have been midnight."

We headed to the Scotts to help Billy and Sammy with whatever it was they were doing.

"Hey, Billy! Hey, Sammy!" Bubba yelled as we coasted into their backyard. "Have no fear, your help is here. What you want us to do?"

"Hey, glad to see y'all. What took you so long to get here? You only live down the street."

"Oh we had to go by Aunt Cele's for a little while," I said, "tell 'em about the cookout."

"O-o-o-h, I see. Eah, you ain't gotta say no more," Sammy replied. Then he added with a chuckle: "Glad you could make it today."

Billy and Sammy were standing by a pile of scrap lumber, hands on their hips and sweating. They were sorting through the pile looking for good pieces of wood they told us so they could build the picnic table for the party on the Fourth. They said they had already found a really neat grill in Junk Mountain and as soon as they patched the holes in the bottom of it and cleaned it up a little it would look like new. It would be used at the cookout. What they wanted was for us to help them in building the picnic table. We agreed to help but I thought I had a better idea:"Eah, why don't y'all just borrow somebody's picnic table?" I asked. "Wouldn't that be a lot easier?"

"Borrow? You mean like how you "borrow" Bobby Graham's boat all the time?" Sammy asked grinning. "N-a-a-a-w man, we gonna build us a table. A really nice one."

"No," I said. "Like really borrowing … just for one day."

"We tried, Mike. But everybody's using their table for the Fourth and all," Billy said. "And besides, if we build one then we'll always have one. It won't take but a little while. Y'all gonna help, aren't you?"

"Yeah sure," I said. "I don't have anything else to do and hey, it oughta be fun. How about you, Bubba. Gonna help?"

"Oh sure, sure. I'm a great carpenter. Watched my father build a birdhouse once. That makes me an expert on building stuff."

"Good." Sammy said. "Good … then you can get us a hammer and some nails 'cause we ain't got any."

"Hammer? What's that?" Bubba deadpanned. Billy gave Bubba the look.

"Eah, just kidding, guys. Just kidding. I'll run to the house and get 'em right now … be right back."

"Sammy, y'all got a saw?" I asked looking around the yard.

"Yeah, it's here somewhere. And we got all this wood. All we need is something to measure with like a ruler or tape measure or something."

Billy headed for inside. "I know where there's a ruler. Be right back."

Bubba returned with a hammer and an old coffee can full of nails. Billy came out the house with a school ruler. One of those twelve inch deals made of wood.

"A-l-l right!" Billy yelled. "We're in business now." He looked around the yard and pointed to a spot under the big oak tree. "Right over there. That's where we will build it."

"Why over there? Sammy asked. "Why not right here?"

"Because it's gonna be a big table and pretty heavy. And when it's finished we don't want to be dragging it around. And, besides, that's where the shade is."

We didn't argue. We just shrugged our shoulders and nodded our heads. Billy seemed like he knew what he was talking about.

"OK, get me a long board, a real long one. And straight too," Billy ordered, "it's gotta be straight because it's gonna be one of the boards for the top."

"How about this one?" Sammy was pulling a long board from Junk Mountain.

Sammy put the eye on it and declared it perfect. "Now cut it," he said.

"Cut it where?" Sammy asked. He held a rusty, dull handsaw.

"U-u-u-h … let's see? About right here," Billy said. He paused and looked again. "No … right here maybe?"

Bubba made a suggestion: "Billy, maybe we should look at another table and get an idea about how long we want to cut the boards for the top. Don't ya think?" Everyone nodded.

"Hey, O'Toole. Good idea. Where's the nearest table?"

"We have one but it's real small and it's in the shed under a bunch of junk," I said. "Let me think … I saw one somewhere not long ago." Then it came to me. "Oh yeah, Mr. Barber has a nice big one out in his back yard. You remember don't ya, Bubba?"

"Yeah, it's out back by his driveway. And you know, it is bigger than most tables."

"Mike, why don't you ride down to Mr. Barber's and measure how long it is," Billy suggested, "so we'll know how long to cut these?" He handed me the ruler.

"Sure!" I said eager to help. "Be right back."

"Hey!" It was Bubba. "Want me to ride with ya?"

"Yeah, sure. Come on."

For the second time today we sat on our bikes and yelled without anyone answering us. This time we were at Mr. Barber's house, sitting at the end of his driveway eyeing the picnic table.

"Come on. Let's measure the thing and go," I said pedaling toward the table, "Mr. Barber won't mind."

"You put the ruler down," Bubba said, "and I'll mark the spots where it is." He held his finger while I moved the ruler from mark to mark. "Got it … eight feet. Let's go."

"Eight feet!" I yelled riding into the Scott's driveway, handing Billy the ruler.

"Eight feet exactly?" Billy asked. "You're sure now?"

"Yep, eight feet," I said. "Right, Bubba?" He nodded.

"Sammy, hand me that long board. That one over there." Billy laid the board on two sawhorses, measured eight feet, made his mark and began sawing. "Y'all find some more long ones like this while I'm sawing."

"There we go. That wasn't too bad. Now we take this one and use it to measure the next one we cut. See? Simple ain't it?" Billy was proud of his newly sawn board but already doubt was creeping into my mind.

"Billy? How many more are you gonna cut?" I asked. "How many eight foot long ones, I mean?"

"As many as we need, Einstein."

"Well … what I mean is… u-u-u-h … how many more do we need exactly?"

"That depends on how wide the table is," Billy answered. "Y'all did measure how wide it was too?" He could tell by the look on my face that we didn't get the width measurement. "A-a-a-w, come on, man. Don't tell me y'all didn't?" Billy said in an exasperated tone.

"Bubba?"

"Eah! Don't look at me. I was just going along for the ride."

"Hey, Billy. Don't get all bent out of shape. I'll go back and get the width measurement … OK." I said. "And Bubba … you can stay here!"

"Dag gone Scotts! Get their planning smarts from their Daddy," I thought heading back to Mr. Barber's.

Still no one was home at the Barber's so I got my measurement and headed back to the Scott's. Billy was sawing away.

"Thirty inches across," I announced. "Exactly thirty, Mr. Carpenter." I was looking at Billy.

"Good," he said, "now we're getting somewhere."

Sammy grabbed the cut boards and placed them together to form the top, spacing them so they came out close to thirty inches. "Is thirty-one inches too much?"

We all shook our heads from side to side. I surveyed the scene and we looked just like the Little Rascals during one of their infamous construction projects. I only hoped ours would turn out better.

"OK … let's see. We've got the length and the width," Billy stated. " Now we need to build a frame of some kind with some legs to put the top on … right?"

We just stood there dumbly looking at the top.

"Well … that's right isn't it?" Billy demanded. "What's wrong now?"

We recognized the obvious. Billy didn't. Bubba spoke up. "Billy, we know the table has to have some legs but … u-u-u-h … how high will they have to be?"

Billy stepped back and thought for a second and held his hand off the ground and said, "About this high."

"N-a-a-a-w. That's too high," Sammy said. "About like this," holding his hand a little lower.

"Uh-uh," Bubba said, "more like this. Right, Mike?"

In a matter of minutes my friends had gone from being Spanky and Our Gang to The Three Stooges and I told them so. "Larry, Moe and Curley," I said and pointed at Bubba when I mentioned Curley. "You guys should be on TV. You know that?"

Billy was about to speak but I beat him to it. "I know, I know. Mike, why don't you go back to Mr. Barber's and measure how high the legs are … right, Billy?"

"Yeah," he said, "how'd you know?"

"Just a lucky guess, I suppose. I'll be back in a little bit … why don't y'all find some boards for the legs while I'm gone."

Down to the Barber's and back again.

"OK, the legs are thirty inches too," I said returning and telling myself that was my last trip to measure the table.

"You sure?" Billy asked. " You didn't measure the width again did you?"

"No! I measured the legs. If you don't believe me then go measure them for yourself."

"Hey, cool it. I believe you. I just want to get this thing right … that's all … OK?"

"OK, OK… I don't mean to be a jackleg or anything. It's just that I'm getting tired of riding back and forth."

"Well, don't worry. We got everything we need now. So let's … u-u-u-h … get all the boards and let's kind of set it up before we begin nailing anything."

"Good idea, Billy," Sammy remarked, "that's the smartest thing anybody's said yet."

"Yeah, you so smart brother," Billy said, "you take after me … HA-HA."

We pre-assembled our picnic table and the top was the right width and length and the legs were the correct height but one thing was missing. There was no place to sit, no bench for anyone to sit on. It looked like a table all right, the kind you set something on, not a table to eat off of.

"I know what you're thinking, guys," I said, " but forget it. I ain't riding all the way back down to the Barber's again and measure for the bench. Somebody else can go."

They all stood looking at the ground, no one speaking or making an offer to make the trip.

Then Sammy lit up like he'd been shocked. "Eah! I got it! It's what we should have done to begin with. We'll all go to Mr. Barber's and get his table and bring it here." He looked around for approval. "Then we'll have it right in front of us and we can't go wrong."

"Oh yeah, how we gonna carry Mr. Barber's heavy old table all the way up here?" Bubba asked shaking his head as he started walking away. "I think I'm going home. At the speed we're going … we won't get this stupid table built until Christmas."

"Eah! Wait up, Bubba. We won't have to carry it. I know what we can do. We'll take Dad's car and put the table in the trunk or something and bring it up here."

"Hey, hey, now ya talking," Billy, said. "Yeah, that's so simple. Why didn't we think of that before?"

"I think it has something to do with brains," Bubba answered and then laughed.

"Shoot, let's go. Get the keys, Billy … they're in the kitchen," Sammy said. "And I'll drive."

"How can you drive?" I questioned. "You don't even have a driver's license."

"Oh, that's easy … we'll go down Back Street and then turn at Station Fifteen and be right there," Sammy said. "Bull Perry and Lumus never go on Back Street." Then he patted me on the shoulder and told me not to worry. I did.

"And Billy," he yelled. "Bring the periscope!"

"Periscope?" Bubba asked. "What's that for?"

"A-a-a-w nothing … just in case we need it."

"Periscope in a car?" Bubba persisted. "Where we going? In Miller's Creek?"

"Hold your horses, O'Toole … OK? You'll see …maybe."

Billy came racing out the house, tossed the car keys to Sammy and jumped in the front seat. "Let's go. Time's a wasting." He was clutching a homemade periscope about three feet long.

"Where'd you get that," I asked from the backseat. "That's cool."

"Oh, the periscope? I made it last year for the Science Fair. You remember don't you?"

"You kidding. I have a hard time remembering my name sometimes."

"See, I told you there wouldn't be anybody on Back Street," Sammy assured us. "We got us a straight shot."

Bubba 'n me held on tight as we bounced from pothole to pothole on the unpaved road called Back Street. It ran along the marsh on the backside of the Island and Sammy was right. It was seldom used by anyone. The only paved road on the Island was Central Avenue, the main drag that ran the length of the Island.

"What if Mr. Barber still ain't home?" Bubba asked. "What then?"

"We'll just borrow the table and then bring it back," Sammy said. " He won't miss it … I don't think? Right, guys?"

"Just like we do the boats," Billy added turning around to give us a grin. "Right, my friends?"

"Whatever," Bubba said. " I ain't been arrested for stealing yet." He poked me in the ribs and smiled. "But there's always a first time, huh Mike? … BA-HA-HA-HA-HA!"

"T-h-a-t-s right, Catbird," I said. "There's always a first time." I was hoping it wouldn't be today.

Sammy pulled into the Barber's driveway and laid down on the horn, which gave one little beep and drowned out like it had a heart attack.

"Stupid thing! Never did work right," Sammy fussed and then yelled out the window. "Mr. Barber, you home?" No answer. Immediately Sammy cut the engine and was out the car and at the table. "Come on, guys. Let's move your butts. This thing's heavy."

"Wait a second. Let me open the trunk," Billy offered. "Where's the key, Sammy?"

"Key ain't no good… trunk's broken … it won't open."

I looked at Bubba and Bubba looked at me. And we just shook our heads from side to side. *"Here we go again,"* I thought.

"Why don't we put the table on top of the car?" I suggested. It was an idea made in jest. "You know flat side down and just let it ride up there?"

"Hey. Great idea, Mike." Billy smiled at me. "You so smart. Just like my brother."

"But I wasn't serious about …"

"Everybody grab a corner and kind of turn it when we get it high enough." Billy was back to giving instruction. … "then we can slide it."

The table cooperated and we headed back to the Scott's with *all* the measurements we would ever need.

"Go slow, Sammy." Billy ordered, while we each had an arm out the window and held onto any part of the table we could grab from inside the car. "Nice and slow. Take it easy."

"Eah, Sammy. I've got an idea," I asked hoping someone would take me seriously. "Why don't we call Mr. Barber and tell him we borrowed his table so he won't think it's been stolen?"

"Yeah, sounds good," Sammy said looking at me in the rear view mirror. "You call him when we get back to the house." Sammy paused and his eyes suddenly widened.

"Uh-oh," he exclaimed with fear in his voice still looking in the rear view mirror. "Don't look now guys, but guess who is behind us … B-u-l-l Perry."

We turned quickly to look and the fear emanating from Sammy's voice jumped on us like a robin on a june bug.

Sammy yelled out, "Dive, dive!" And he started making the sound of a horn on a submarine. "Ougaa! Ougaa! Dive, dive," he repeated. "Everybody duck down real low."

"Do what?" Bubba asked seriously not understanding what was going on. "Duck down?"

"Get down now! And stay down!" Sammy ordered as he disappeared onto the floorboard. Billy was already there. Bubba 'n me hit the deck looking at each other wondering just what the heck was happening.

"Eah, who's driving the car?" Bubba asked, "if you're on the floor."

"I am," Sammy said. "Don't worry … we've done this before."

"Thanks, Sammy," Bubba said with a frown. "I feel better already."

"Up scope," Sammy ordered sounding just like a submarine Captain.

"Aye, aye sir," Billy answered. "Scope up."

"Distance?" Sammy asked.

"About one hundred feet and closing," Billy answered and then turned the scope forward to view the road and act as Sammy's eyes. "A little to the left … easy. Right there …a little back to the right … steady. There you go." Sammy was working the gas with one hand and the steering wheel with the other while he crouched in the floorboard. "Don't worry, guys! I can tell by the potholes we're still on the road," Sammy said. "Darn things."

"Good news, guys." It was Billy, the navigator, announcing that it was Lumus behind us and not Bull Perry. A collective sigh of relief rushed from the car. And Lumus was keeping his distance … about fifty feet back. "Hold what you got Sammy. You're doing real good. The corner is a good ways up … just keep going slow."

"What about the table?" Bubba asked. "Won't it fall off?"

"N-a-a-a-w …it ain't going nowhere it's too heavy." It was more of a statement of hope than assurance.

"Lumus is coming up closer … he's right behind us. Go to the right some, Sammy … easy … right there … now hold it there."

"What's he doing?" I asked and shouldn't have.

"He's driving the police car, Einstein." Billy could be a sarcastic thing at times. "What do ya think he's doing?"

"Well, I don't know. I thought he might be singing a song or knitting or something. I was just asking," was my sarcastic reply. "You can see … I can't."

Bubba shook his head. "I should have known … another grounding coming up," he whispered, " I can see it now. Man, oh, man."

"What the heck are we in anyway?" I asked. "A car or a submarine?" Bubba shrugged his shoulders and rolled his eyes.

"He's getting real close now, guys … real close. Don't make any noise," Billy ordered trying to sound like Captain Sammy. "H-e-r-e he c-o-m-e-s. Be quiet everybody."

Lumus had decided to escort the Scott boys home safely and then deal with them. But first he was going to put a little fear into them. He hit his siren switch and turned on the red light.

"There." A loud blast flowed over the marshes. "That ought to get their attention."

"Whoa! What's that?" Sammy yelled while Billy shh'd him and turned the scope to look at Lumus.

"The siren. And the red light is on. I guess he wants us to stop?" Billy asked without really thinking. "How can he do that? He can't even see us."

"Brilliant, Billy." Bubba said looking at me and moving his finger in a circular motion on the side of his head indicating that Billy might have a screw or two loose. "You're so smart."

"Little to the right, Sammy … good. Hold it … good," Billy said and then he added, "Aw shut up, Bubba."

Before Bubba could answer Billy a sharp piercing noise filled the inside of the car startling all of us. Lumus had pulled alongside of us and hit the siren one more time, a long loud one and then he smiled.

Then his radio came to life."Lumus, this is the Chief!" It sounded urgent. "Where you at?"

"I'm on Back Street … about Station 18 … what's up?"

"I've got a missing child report. I'm at Breach Inlet right around the turn in front of the James' house. You know where I'm talking about?"

"Gottcha, Chief."

"Some lady can't find her kid. Seems he just wandered off and it's pretty crowded up here. The child didn't go in the water … she's sure of that. Anyway, come on up and help us look around. You get all that?"

"10-4. Chief. I'll be right there."

Lumus stopped, turned around on Back Street and headed toward Breach Inlet in a cloud of dust.

"Eah, Lumus just stopped and is going toward Central Avenue," Billy announced proudly like an expectant father heralding a new son. "H-e-'s going, going, gone."

I whispered to Bubba, "Yeah, Billy probably scared him off with all his smarts." Bubba burst out with a thunderous, "BA-HA-HA-HA!"

"What's so funny?" Sammy asked as we all sat up and stretched our cramped muscles. "Y'all don't like my driving or something?"

"Nothing, Sammy. It was nothing," I said, "we were just kind of discussing the situation here and found it kind of funny. Don't you?"

"Yeah, yeah, yeah." He stopped the car, got out for a second and then proudly announced that the table was OK but we had missed our turn by a block. He gave Billy the look. "Station 19 is way back there, Mr. Navigator!"

"H-u-u-m, guess I'll have to adjust my periscope, huh?"

"Either that or your brain," Sammy said taking the words right out of my mouth. I wanted to go home right then and there but I also didn't want to chicken out at this stage of the game. What to do? So I did what any normal twelve year old would do. I went along with the group.

When we pulled into the Scott's driveway with the picnic table still on top of the car I was wondering, "Am I gonna be grounded for the Fourth of July? Will I miss all the fun after going through all this trouble to build a table for the cookout? Durn, I hope not!"

I got my answer a short while later.

We had taken Mr. Barber's table off the car and set it under the tree and proceeded to measure and cut boards like busy little beavers. Our table was actually beginning to take the shape of Mr. Barber's, which was one of those store bought fancy ones, from Willard's Hardware. Ours might not have been as steady but it sure looked good. We were completing the benches and putting the final nails in place when Lumus pulled up. He got out of the car and walked over to our project. He just stood there not saying a word and looking at us and then at the table and then back at us. We sneaked a peek at Lumus but mostly we kept our heads down, acting as though we were busy working on the table.

"Uh- hum," Lumus cleared his throat, as a form of announcing his presence and when he got no response he cleared it again. This time with emphasis: "Uh-hum!"

Sammy spoke first, " Oh, hi Lumus. How you doing? Nice day, huh?"

No response from Lumus.

Billy tried, "How ya been doing, Lumus?"

Still no response. Now we were getting nervous.

After Bubba spoke I didn't have to say a word. He said, "Well Lumus we haven't been on the hill today." Never a more brilliant yet baffling statement from a twelve- year- old. It was some of Bubba's unintentional gibberish.

Lumus not understanding Bubba's logic shook his head from side to side like he was clearing it of what he just heard. Then he said, "No. I didn't see y'all up there today. Y'all must have been somewhere else?"

Lumus paused and walked around to the side of the table, put his foot up on the seat of the table, rubbed his chin and said, "Boys!" We jumped. "If I'm not mistaken I saw this same car right here." He pointed to it. "And it was on Back Street not more than an hour ago and it had a table on top of it." He pointed at the table. "AND the car was moving." Lumus paused again. "Am I correct so far, boys?"

Seeing that he said "boys" I didn't dare say a word and, looking at Bubba, put my finger to my mouth.

Billy in his almighty wisdom blurted out, "Are you talking about this car?" This time it was premeditated ignorance.

"Billy! And you too Sammy! I have a sneaking feeling that y'all were in the car Billy just referred to. Am I right?"

"Well … we …"

"Driving without a license is one offense and stealing a table is another," Lumus interrupted. " So I can write y'all up for driving without a license and stealing and haul you down to the station unless y'all want to come clean?"

"Lumus," Sammy pleaded with begging eyes, "all we were doing was …"

"Wait a minute, Sammy. I'm not finished." Lumus thought for a second and said, "You boys have exactly fifteen minutes to get this table." He pointed to Mr. Barber's table. "Back to its rightful owner and all is forgotten. And … don't drive the car to take it back. Y'all understand?"

"Yes sir," we exclaimed in unison and feeling the mercy of God. "Yes sir. Right now!"

"OK, then get to it but next time there's going to be trouble." Lumus turned to walk away.

"Lumus, you didn't see anybody in the backseat of the car, did you?" It was Bubba who wanted to know what Lumus knew.

"No. I didn't, Bubba. No I didn't. But … never mind. Y'all just get that table back and soon."

"We will, Lumus. We promise. Right, guys?" Billy said grabbing Mr. Barber's table and trying by himself to get it out of the yard. "Man, this thing's heavy … y'all help me!"

Lumus was sitting in the patrol car and about to pull away when he stuck his head out the window. "How were y'all able to drive the car when no one was at the wheel?" Then shaking his head he quickly added, "A-w-w never mind … forget it! I don't want to hear it."

The three-block walk toting Mr. Barber's heavy old picnic table was no easy job even though there was one of us on each corner of the table. We'd take little bitty steps and pop our shins on the table's legs. We'd stop and rub our shins and then repeat the process again. All the way back to Mr. Barber's house. And we sweated, stopped to complain, went a little further then stopped again and complained some more. We must have stopped ten times and complained and then sweated some more. Oh man, we were soaked with sweat looking liked we just stepped out of the ocean.

This had been a close one and all I could say to myself was, "Thank you, Lumus. Thank you. I can still go to the Fourth of July celebration.

Thank you, Lumus …and thank you God."

18
THE FOURTH OF JULY

The Fourth of July arrived like a firecracker … hot and with a bang. Without the high humidity and mug that hung in the air it wouldn't have been the Fourth. As far as we Islanders were concerned it was great weather for a great day in America and a great day on Sullivans Island! I was up early and out the house. And I could feel the Island coming to life in anticipation of a day that was sure to be full of fun and celebration. I couldn't help but notice the many birds that lined the treetops like a feathery crown led by the talkative grackles. The sea gulls were more numerous or so it seemed as they floated overhead. The ocean even had a different sound to it … that of an inviting, gracious host welcoming all to its cooling and refreshing waters.

I was in the backyard checking to make sure everything was in my father's boat: life jackets (one for each person), oars, anchor line, anchor, gas lines were OK, gas in the tank, the plug was in, and the straps holding the boat on the trailer were secure. It was my father's sixteen-foot wooden Halsey and he was going to take the Devlin kids for a boat ride right after breakfast. What a great way to begin the Fourth of July. After the boat ride we would come home, pack up and be off to the beach for a day in the sun and ocean. And then late that afternoon the cookout at the Scott's would begin. It was a full menu but I was up to the task.

Everybody in the family went on the boat ride except Sissy and my mother who stayed at the house to prepare casseroles for the cookout and make sandwiches for the beach outing. The six of us, Ryan and I and my three younger sisters, took turns riding in the boat because my father was overly cautious about overloading the boat, the cause of many boating accidents. It was exhilarating to fly across the glass-like Intracoastal Waterway, which ran along the whole backside of the Island with small creeks branching out here and there to add to the overall marsh vista effect. We chased low- flying sea gulls that managed to stay just a tad ahead of us and in the end always won the race. Now the pelicans were a bit slower and sometimes we passed them only because they often went into their glide pattern as they searched for food. What was especially exciting was my father letting each one of us, even little Sara, have a turn at steering the boat … for a minute or so under his direct supervision, of course. The only nerve-racking part of the whole ride was when Katie, the nine- year- old, was given a chance to steer the boat. Ducking down and cupping his hands to form a shield against the wind, my father was attempting to fire up one of his favorite Pall Malls. In his moment of distraction Katie took it upon herself to aim the boat at one of the huge pilings supporting The Ben Sawyer Bridge. She had us on a head on collision. With bulging eyes I turned and checked to see who was running the boat. Katie was grinning profusely. She thought it great fun to scare us. Typical Katie. I nervously glanced back at my father who exhaled a large cloud of smoke, then gently but quickly grabbed the steering wheel and eased us back on course, and then smiled like nothing had happened. He would take us up the Intracoastal, under the bridge, and make a run through Long Creek that curled its way to Breach Inlet and then back out to the Intracoastal Waterway and returning to the Point. Emily and Sara would be at the landing at water's edge jumping up and down and yelling all excited because it was their turn to ride. I had been in the boat many times before, even out to the jetties just off the front beach. And now that I was older and a seasoned sailor, at least I thought I was and played the role, I was to act as a helper for my father getting the girls in and out of the boat and helping them put on their life jackets. Ryan, my older brother, was real good about not interfering with my job as the second in command or pulling rank on me because he was older and more experienced than I in a boat. And when he called me "Skipper" it made me feel good.

I think part of my parent's plan on the Fourth was to get us kids up early and keep us on the go all day in hopes of wearing us down and sapping our energy so we wouldn't be so wild at the cookout that evening thus allowing them more time to relax and enjoy themselves. But it wouldn't work. Not with the Devlin kids. The more you threw at us the faster and stronger we went at it. Then after a particularly long day, when bedtime came we would be out like a light … but not until then. I think my parents came to this realization way too late in life to do them any good as far as relaxing went.

Many families treated the Fourth of July like Christmas or Thanksgiving Day or a holiday, using it as a focal point for a celebration and a family gathering.

At the beach that day in our group were our immediate neighbors: the Scott family, the O'Tooles, the Johnsons and the Wades. I could tell it was the Fourth of July by all the white skin and the smell of suntan lotion filling the air. People like my mother and father who worked and raised a bunch of kids rarely had time to go to the beach and the whiteness of their skin was almost blinding in the direct sun. This was their day to relax, have fun, go for a swim and fry in the sun. No matter how much suntan lotion they applied they invariably got cooked … lobster red. Shoot, us kids were dark brown almost black.

All the families laid out their beach blankets and towels with one oversized towel designated for food only. Coolers loaded with ice and sodas were set up for the kids. The adults had their special coolers just as cold as ours but loaded with cans of beer. The kids swam, played on their inner tubes, body surfed and later in the day participated in the annual mud castle building contest. The mothers played mother hen and watched over the kids while the men wandered over to the rocks, told stories, mostly lies I think, and drank beer. Mr. O'Toole had brought a set of horseshoes and soon a spirited game began and got even more spirited as the afternoon went on and the flowing beer began to take effect, especially in the hot sun. The mothers finally canceled the game when Mr. Scott let go a toss way too late and the horseshoe went straight up in the air. He stood looking around for the lost horseshoe and everyone held their heads and breaths and then cringed as it dropped right beside him missing his head by inches. And these were the old timey horseshoes made of steel and were plenty heavy. The adults figured it was time to go and no one argued. Our little tummies were full of peanut butter and jelly sandwiches, Oreos, and Kool Aid and we were thinking about the cookout this evening and the fireworks.

My younger sisters seemed edgy about something. They kept bugging my mother and Sissy about getting home and practicing. Practicing what I don't know? I was afraid to ask.

Tradition had it that whoever hosted the Fourth of July celebration was responsible for putting on the fireworks display that night. Billy and Sammy had assured me that they would be ready and that they had a special fireworks surprise never before seen on the Island. God only knows what they had cooked up? I couldn't wait to find out. They told Bubba 'n me that their father had spent a ton of money on fireworks: lots of bottle rockets, sparklers, shooting stars, and some cherry bombs. But they wouldn't let us in on their secret firework surprise no matter how much we chided and eventually threatened them. Usually they would give in but not this time. It must be something special.

After the boat riding and the beach I was feeling tired and tried to sneak in a quick nap. Mollie joined me looking tired too. She had done everything I had except go for the boat ride. But there was no quiet. I could barely hear the girls led by Sissy down the hall in their room singing. They weren't loud loud but made enough noise to irritate me. They kept going over the same verse over and over followed by laughter and the familiar squeals of Sara. All of a sudden things got quiet. Then I heard Sissy tell the girls to work on their shirts. *Work on their shirts?* I thought. *What's going on? Maybe I need to investigate?* But I didn't have a chance. With the sudden quiet, Mr. Sandman paid me a visit and sleep quickly overtook me.

The ringing of the phone woke me up. My mother yelled, "It's for you, Mike. It's Bubba."

"Coming!"

"Hello," I answered.

"Hey, it's me. What ya doing?"

"What am I doing?"

"Yeah, what ya doing?"

"If I tell ya … you promise not to tell anybody."

"Yeah sure."

"You promise?"

"Yeah!"

"I'm talking to you … that's what I'm doing, Curley."

"Hardee har har. You are so funny. You know that."

"Thought you'd like that … what's going on?"

"Billy called me and wants me to come help him and Sammy move the picnic table … how about come and help?"

"Move it where?"

"I'm not sure. Something about it's not in the shade enough. C'mon it won't take but a minute."

"All right then. Meet ya there in a few minutes."

"Mom," I yelled, "I'm going to the Scott's for a little while … be right back."

Before I could get out the door my mother stopped me in the kitchen."OK, but do me a favor while you're out. Go to Owen's and get a pound of hamburger meat and a package of buns for tonight. Here, take this. It should be enough and if you run short tell Mr. Owen I'll see him next week."

"Yes Ma'am."

"And some cheese," Katie yelled, "for the cheeseburgers."

"Cheebuga," mocked Sara.

"*And* some cheese," my mother added … for the cheeseburgers. The kind in the pack."

"What color cheese?" I asked Katie. "Red or black?"

I smiled at Sara.

"You know, Mike, yellow!" Katie yelled. "*Yellow* cheese!"

"T-h-a-t-`s right, Catbird," I said. "Anything else, Mom?"

"No, that should do it. And don't be all day."

"Yes Ma'am."

Billy was right about the table. It was partly in the sun, just enough to draw complaints from one of the adults, probably one of my aunts. After we moved it not a drop of sunlight hit it and, I must admit, it did feel better in the cooling shade. Bubba `n me pestered Billy and Sammy trying to get them to tell us about the surprise fireworks they had planned for tonight. But those Scotts, a testament to their mentality, were stubborn as mules and wouldn't tell us much of anything. The only hint they revealed was that it involved a lot of gunpowder. *Oh boy,* I thought, *Billy and Sammy Scott and a lot of gunpowder ... man oh man ... this should be good.*

"Bubba, ride up to Owen's with me? I gotta get some stuff for the party."

"N-a-a-w, I'm going home … take a nap."

I grinned and said, "Julie's working … I think?" I paused to let that little seed take root. "Sure you don't want to go?"

Julie was Mr. Owen's shapely nineteen-year-old daughter who worked part-time at the store. She *always* wore tight clothing whether it be sweaters in the winter or short low cut tops in the summer. And her shorts were as short as they were tight. We weren't sure what we were looking at but we did a lot of looking.

"Oh… in that case … then. Well, y-e-a-h, I think maybe I'll ride with ya." Looking at Julie Owens for even just a few minutes was worth way more than a nap and Bubba knew it. "The nap can wait." Bubba was smiling.

Arriving at Owen's Grocery we parked our bikes and made haste toward the entrance. Our eyes were alert and our necks strained eagerly as we peered through the huge plate glass window at Owen's Grocery hoping to be the first to catch a glimpse of the curvaceous Julie. Much to our dismay Julie wasn't working today. Talk about two deflated young boys. I looked at Bubba who looked as though he were about to cry. *Well* …I thought … *at least I was on a mission, getting some food for the party.* But that didn't hide my disappointment. I was just better than Bubba when it came to masking my feelings. So, needless to say, my shopping spree was much quicker than if Julie had been there. When she was there, bending over stocking shelves or stretching to pull an item from the top shelf, I took my time and took in the sights while I innocently moseyed through the aisles like a window shopper. Today was different. Bubba 'n me were in and out in a flash, then headed home to get ready for the big cookout.

The people of Ireland have proven historically that they know how to have a party. Not that they had a patent on partying or having a good time by any means. Many of my non-Irish friends could down a pint with the best of them. The Irish of Sullivans Island following their ancestral habits knew how to party and drink. Or drink and have a party … whichever way you looked at it. All they needed was an excuse for a gathering. And it didn't have to be a large gathering. Many Irish parties consisted of only two people. And what better excuse than a Fourth of July coming together of families.

Why old man Flannigan who lived down the Island used to say that the sun coming up was reason enough to have a drink and spread some merriment.

Neighborhood families, many of whom were not of Irish descent like the Scotts and the Johnsons, would attend this year's Fourth of July party and they would have a good time, for sure. But let me be clear. It would be the O'Tooles and the Devlins who would set the tone and pace for the party. And that tone and pace would be "full speed ahead."

Card tables had been set up under the big oak tree in the Scott's huge backyard. They would hold the many and varied dishes of food brought by each family. Casseroles still steaming from the oven, plates of freshly sliced ham, fried chicken that melted in your mouth, corned beef for the die-hard Irish, fresh garden vegetables and a plate of sliced tomatoes straight from my mother's garden. The main course, however, for the kids was the hamburgers, cheeseburgers, and hot dogs that would be cooked on the grill. There would be an unofficial hot dog eating contest, which would start off innocently enough when someone made note of the fact that he or she had eaten four hot dogs and might go for five. Then, a response of "Well, I've eaten four too" would be interpreted as a challenge. And then the contest would be on. Stinky Johnson was last year's winner after somehow managing to swallow sixteen hot dogs, buns and all, without getting sick. And Stinky was here today ready to defend his title.

Then there was the table for desserts only. Cookies, brownies, cakes, homemade sweet things we'd never seen before, even candy, was there for the taking and all afternoon kids playing would invariably run by the dessert table and snatch a handful of added energy. That sugar jolt is what kept them going all day and into the night.

By 5:00 the yard was filled with adults gathered in groups chit-chatting and laughing and drinking their ice-cold beers. Kids ran everywhere just being kids. My sisters along with Bubba's sisters were in the thick of any and all action. Right now they had a game of tag going on … their own version. The person who was "it" was blindfolded and running around trying to tag someone while the others ran by and poked and pinched the poor tagger. They thought it was great fun.

Mr. Scott, along with help from Uncle Schroeder, had gone out of his way to make this cookout extra special for the kids. They had set up several booths offering games and prizes for the youngsters. Most were made from huge pieces of cardboard … the kind used to pack refrigerators. A few booths consisted of nothing more than a stack of concrete blocks with a board stretched across forming a counter where the person running that booth stood. These were primitive affairs but highly effective. The kids loved them. Just participating won you a prize … granted it wasn't much of a prize but the gesture is what mattered. A booth where a small wooden ring was tossed to a crate of empty Coca Cola bottles sitting on the ground to circle any of the bottles was a challenge. Bubba 'n me would spend an hour tossing ring after ring with no success and then along comes baby Sara, curious as to what we were doing. She watched for a minute and then asked if she could try. And yep, that's right. On her first toss … bingo. She circles a bottle. Then to rub it in she walks away in huff acting as though it was too easy and boring.

A piece of plywood had been put up with balloons attached to it. The object was to stand behind the rope, toss a dart, and pop a balloon. This was one of the more popular games with all the kids. But I had warned Mrs. Johnson who was running this booth about the dangers of letting any little Devlin people get a dart in their hands. She nodded and gave me a wink assuring me she knew exactly where I was coming from.

The other booth involving skill was the "knock down the cans," a game where you were given one chance to toss a softball and knock down all three cans, which were stacked two on the bottom with one on the top in the shape of a pyramid. For the smaller children Mr. Taylor stacked the cans one on top of the other. And then there was the bobbing for apples in a tub of water. And the day would not be complete without the sack races across the Scott's backyard. All the games were fun and all the kids participated fully.

The adults had set up the same horseshoe game they had at the beach putting it way over in the corner of the yard for the safety of the kids. Mr. Scott was bound to play and drink beer, so the far corner seemed to be a logical place where he could exhibit his exemplary horseshoe- throwing skills.

Everyone stopped whatever they were doing when they heard the loud distinctive wail of the Island's fire truck siren getting louder and louder as it headed our way. There was then a mad dash to go see the parade. The kids bolted for the road in front of the Scott's house while the adults leisurely walked around. Even Aunt Cele and Aunt Christle made the effort to get out of their rockers they so comfortably rested in. Mr. Scott had put the rockers out especially for them. Nobody wanted to miss the parade. Believe me, this was an event. Not everyday did you get to see a parade on Sullivans Island. As a matter of fact you only got to see a parade once a year, on the Fourth of July.

WOW! This year there were seven vehicles in the parade, a growth of three from last year. Leading the group was the Island fire truck wailing its siren with a big American flag on top held by Mr. O'Connell who alternated his grip between holding the flag in one hand and taking a sip of his beer from the other. The mayor was next in his shiny red Cadillac, sitting proudly and waving and smiling at everyone like he was campaigning for office. All he needed to complete the scene was a baby he could kiss. Then came Chief Perry and Lumus who added to the excitement by hitting their siren between blasts from the fire truck's siren. Three unidentified cars with individuals who looked as though they had begun their celebratory drinks early this morning were next in line trying hard to stay in line. My father called 'em "the weavers" as they slowly went from one side of the road to the other. The highlight of the parade was bringing up the rear. It was the garbage truck, Ol' Blue, spitting and sputtering adding its own distinct sound from the muffler that had died many months ago with Mr. Nick at the wheel and the irrepressible Sambo on the back bumper. Sambo was lending his usual greeting of "All right buddy" to all. Today he added a joyous "Happy Fourth," much to the delight of the crowd. He too was coddling a beer, a tall Falstaff and hanging on with the other hand.

As our party stood on the side of the road admiring the parade, Emily walked up and tugged at my shirt from behind.

"What you want?" I asked. She looked awfully worried for a ten-year- old at a parade.

"Why's Sambo got a rope tied around him?" She asked after giving the passing Sambo a big wave and yelling, "How you doing?"

"Oh that? That's tied around him and to the truck so he won't fall off the truck if he drinks too much. You know what I mean?"

"Yeah," Emily said half nodding, "I think so?"

"Come on I'll show ya." Emily followed me as I raced to find my father. "Daddy, can I get a beer to give to Sambo?"

"Yeah sure. Look in the red Styrofoam cooler by the tree. There should be a few left in there."

"Thanks." I raced to the back yard. Emily was still with me. "What you doing, Mike?"

"Follow me … hurry. They're getting away," I said running back around the house with an unopened can of beer in my hand. "Just watch, Emily."

I ran up to the back of the garbage truck and yelled above the sirens for Sambo. He turned and immediately broke into a huge grin when he saw the can of beer I was holding up for him. His huge hand encircled the can and in one deft move he took it and deposited it in an open cardboard box that was brimming with unopened beers with his name on each one given to him by Islanders along the parade route.

"All right, buddy!" he exclaimed, "all right!" and went back to working the crowd.

Emily told me that she understood now why Sambo was tied to the truck.

I thought about the parade, which by now was long gone, and we were back in the Scott's yard. I thought *whoever organized the parade should be told that a parade is supposed to have a beginning and an end.* Our parade, it seemed, only had an ending to it.

Nightfall was fast approaching. But that was OK because it meant it was almost time for the big finale … the much-anticipated climax … the finishing touch to our day of celebration … it was almost show time … time for the fireworks! There was a noticeable edginess among the kids as they quieted down somewhat in anticipation of something they got to see only once a year just like the parade. *Hopefully,* I thought, *the fireworks display will last longer than the parade did.*

The adult's silence came more, I think, from a fear that somebody might get blown up or maimed by some act of stupidity. As everybody found a place to sit in the grass and began to settle in, Mr. Scott announced that the fireworks would begin in a few minutes. Most of the kids were sitting on the ground while the adults kicked back in their beach chairs, popped another cold one, and waited for the show to begin.

"But first, folks …" Mr. Scott began, paused and took a huge sip of his Schlitz.

Mr. Scott continued, "Before we wind up today's wonderful celebration we have a special presentation tonight and after that we will start the fireworks show." Pause for another sip. "So sit back," he announced with great gusto, "and welcome the Devlin Dancers." He stepped aside and with a flourish threw out his arm in a grand sweeping motion.

Bubba elbowed me in the ribs. "The who? You're not in this … are ya?"

I shrugged and looked around for my mother to find out what was going on. And then I saw at Emily, Katie, and Sara coming out of the Scott's house and down the back steps in homemade costumes and each was carrying two unlit sparklers. Their costumes displayed the theme of the day. Matching shorts, somewhat the same color of blue, were topped with white tee shirts. On the tee shirts they had drawn small red, white, and blue American flags. It was an impressive logo coming from such youngsters. The words "Forth of July" were spread among the three. The only obvious mistake was in their spelling, certainly not in their show of patriotism. Emily stood proudly smiling with the word "Forth" written in large red print above her flag, followed by Katie with "of" and Sara with "July." Each wore white flip-flops colored over with blue crayon. (Oh yeah, I remembered now Sissy telling the girls to go work on their shirts.) They approached their audience backwards, stopped to straighten up their line and have Mr. Scott light the two sparklers each one held. When the darkness was lit up from the waving sparklers of the Devlin Dancers, they turned around in unison and began their dance. It was a cross between an operatic swan dance and an old fashioned clog but everyone understood its meaning. Sara, the youngest, was watching Emily and Katie and came in a beat too late on every step, which only added to their majestic performance. The sparklers circled above their heads and then low to the ground, to their sides, up and over and back again. They must have practiced because they were actually in sync and drew an impromptu applause from the onlookers. They smiled broadly. Just before their sparklers died out they stopped, facing the audience. Emily, the oldest, stepped forward, and acting as spokesperson asked everyone to participate with them in the singing of "America the Beautiful." There was a slight pause as Emily looked back at her sisters. And then they opened their mouths. The voices of angels floated through the clear warm night ascending through the branches of the oak tree as Emily, Katie and Sara sang from their true innocent little hearts. Everyone there couldn't help but join in, even the unsteady Mr. Scott and my father who had put his beer down and placed his hand over his heart just like Emily, Katie, and Sara were doing. Spontaneously, the crowd stood up for the ending of the first verse and the ending of the Devlin Dancer's performance. "From sea to shining sea" could be heard blocks away, I'm sure. Even Bubba 'n me had joined in … the first time we ever sang a song in public in our lives.

Everyone applauded wildly and the buzzword throughout the crowd was, "Who taught them that?"

Emily, Katie, and Sara dispelled any rumors about where they learned their act when they raced for Sissy who was standing in the last row of the crowd beaming like a proud mother. The girls ran up to Sissy and clutched her waist and hugged her. Sara was holding onto a thigh. They were as overwhelmed by the reaction from the adults as the adults were by their performance.

"Oh wow! How about that, ladies and gentleman! How about that!" Mr. Scott stood in front of everyone. There was no response. No one heard him. Everyone was still excited and talking about the girls' performance and offering congratulatory hugs to the girls. I heard my father yell to Mr. Scott, and when I looked around he was giving Wee Willie the finger across the throat motion. Wee Willie shrugged and walked away headed for the beer cooler.

For a moment everybody had forgotten about the fireworks having been overwhelmed by the girls' song and dance. But the fireworks were ready and waiting. Billy and Sammy had retreated to the back of the yard and were awaiting their father's cue to begin the show. Wee Willie, now in front of the crowd again, shouted for everyone to get ready because the fireworks would go off in five minutes.

"Time enough to grab another beer and get that last hot dog," he said laughing. And the adults did just that. Everyone settled back in to their spots and gazed high into the night, waiting for the first blast of fireworks. Striking a match and at the same time screaming, "Here we go!" Billy got things started with a "bang." And the display we had all anxiously waited for began with a lighting of the sky in the shape of an umbrella- on- fire drifting slowly toward earth, followed by a thunderous BOOM! The crowd OOHED and AAHED when the second blast came whistling down from the sky and exploded just over our heads. Then a group of bottle rockets set off by Sammy and Billy whished their way toward the heavens. Firecrackers, which we later learned were taped to the bottle rockets for added effect, popped on the ground like an afterthought. The umbrella display again splashed its brilliance and the crowd OOHED and AAHED again. Immediately, three rockets were launched at the same time, which really got the crowd buzzing. From each flash of the rockets, smiles of glee could be seen on all the uplifted faces in the crowd. The kids, especially the Devlins, were squealing like stuck pigs at the slightest display, clapping their hands and hollering for more. The fireworks lasted about fifteen minutes, which in my mind went by like a minute. *Too bad school didn't pass that fast* I thought.

Just when everyone thought the fireworks were over and started to stand up and gather their belongings, Mr. Scott jumped up and announced that there was one more special thing for us to see. "Hold on to your hats, everybody. The biggee is coming."

He then turned and yelled across the yard to Billy and Sammy, "Let `er go!"

Now … finally at last … we were going to see what Billy and Sammy had kept such a big secret. I hoped it would be good. Later we learned it was their super rocket loaded with firecrackers and it was supposed to fly far into the sky before the firecrackers went off. They said that they had cut open about a hundred firecrackers and drained the powder from them to use as extra fuel in order to boost the rocket way up into the sky. It seems there was a miscalculation somewhere along the way. Maybe in the math? Neither one of them could add worth a darn.

The crowd anxiously looked toward the backyard where they saw the movement of Billy and Sammy and the light from a burning match. And then there was an enormous sa flash of fire like a rocket taking off from Cape Canaveral. It lit up and sat there for a few seconds burning and then in a super flash it whooshed upward, got to about tree top level and made a ninety degree right turn and disappeared. There were no OOHS and AAHS for this display … only doubt.

"What the … what was that supposed to be?" I asked Bubba as we stood up brushing ourselves off. "Was that Billy's big secret thing?"

"I dunno. Guess so?" Even though we were disappointed we didn't show it. We were too tired. "That's it, huh?"

I was helping my mother gather up her empty dishes and round up the girls when we heard the siren from the fire truck. "Still parading, huh?" It was my father commenting to himself.

Then the sound of the siren grew louder and louder and was coming on faster and faster like it was getting closer to us. Then we realized it was just down the street and headed our way. Everyone dashed to the front of the Scott's house like we did earlier in the day for the parade. "Maybe the party is just beginning," I heard Mr. Scott tell Mr. Joyner.

The fire truck roared by us with its siren at full blast. This obviously wasn't part of the celebration. Bubba 'n me ran after the truck following it down the street. Three doors down from the Scott's it slowed down and began to turn into the Lowe's driveway. As it disappeared behind the Lowe's house, we followed it and watched as three firemen fully clothed in fire fighting attire leaped off the truck. By this time a crowd was gathering. Once the firemen had pulled the hose off the truck and were in position, they turned on the water and began fighting the raging fire in the Lowe's back yard, which was headed toward the house. We stood and watched as the firemen dosed the potentially dangerous fire before it could get out of control.

Our crowd from the Scott cookout, looking drawn and beat from a long day at the beach and the party, began to drag themselves back to the Scott's.

"Man, that was close," I remarked to Bubba as we walked back to the Scott's. "Eah, I wonder how it got started?"

"You don't think maybe that … n-a-a-a-w … it couldn't," Bubba said rubbing his chin and in deep thought. "That rocket went way too far. Right, Mike?"

"I d-u-n-n-o. And I ain't saying nothing.' It's been a fun day and I don't feel like arguing with Billy and Sammy. I'm going home and goin' to sleep."

"Yep, you're right. It's been a fun day. Let's go … I'm tired too."

We joined the dispersing crowd and headed home.

19
OUR TRUE LOVE

It's another beautiful day at the beach as the sun peeks over the horizon giving first light to a darkened beach. Within minutes the huge, orange ball would rise out of the ocean giving off instant heat while soaring upward as being drawn by some cosmic magnet. The dance of the Universe begins. Sometimes Bubba 'n me went to the beach early in the morning, experiencing the solitude of a deserted beach and enjoying the friendship of each other.

The beach was like the perfect lover: seductive, beautiful, and always there. And Bubba 'n me loved our beach. She was not only pleasing and gentle to the eye, but as we walked each step, we landed in a perfectly balanced segment of nature, each grain of sand perfectly placed in its individual spot, giving us the feeling of being in a special place. Upon arrival early in the morning it was like the beginning of time, a totally pristine world that we hated to spoil with our footprints.

Bubba 'n me, accompanied by Mollie, were performing our ritualistic beach walk early on a Saturday morning before the throng of sun worshipers made their weekend invasion. Each summer, more and more people were showing up. The beach itself was plenty spacious and roomy, but parking was beginning to become a problem, along with the litter a few inconsiderate beach-goers left behind.

"Which way?" I asked, "toward Breach Inlet" (which was to our left) "or to Station 12."

"Let's head down to the rocks at Station 12. We'll see if anybody is catching any fish or crabs."

"C'mon, Mollie," I yelled, "this way!"

I stopped for a second and stared at the ocean, in awe of its sheer size, which stretched thousands of miles. Today it was calm and smooth. "Man. Look at that, would ya. Just think. That water goes all the way to Europe. I wonder where we would end up if we took off from here and went straight across?"

"I'm not sure but I don't think it would be Europe. More than likely somewhere in Africa." Bubba thought for a second. "Yeah, somewhere in Africa."

"Africa, huh? Shoot, I don't want to go there. We might get eat up by some lion or tiger or something."

"T-h-a-t-'s right, Catbird."

I still stared at the huge expanse of water and became mesmerized by its calming sound. "Hear that, Bubba? Listen to the waves. They're talking."

"Oh yeah." Bubba rolled his eyes. "And what are they saying?"

"They're saying that if you go to Africa you don't have to worry about being eaten by a lion or tiger."

"A-w-w really. That's nice but I didn't plan on going any time soon."

"They say that before a lion or tiger can get to you, the cannibals will eat you up. A-HA-HA!"

"Man, it's too early for you. That's about the dumbest thing I ever heard you say. I hope you're not trying to be funny." Bubba looked at me and I was still grinning. "And look. Even Mollie thinks that's stupid."

"Forget it. You have to have some brains to understand really funny people, my friend."

A group of early rising seagulls squawked overhead, looking down and swooping in close for a hand -out that we didn't have. Mollie, the protector, promptly chased them away.

"Look at all that … a-l-l the way down." I was pointing toward the end of the beach, more than a mile away. "It's perfect, *every* grain of sand in place. Perfect."

"How do you know?" Bubba asked somewhat sarcastically. He was more than likely looking for an argument … no, not an argument … a debate. We often debated as a test of our powers of logic and thought. If not for any other reason … just for the fun of it.

"Isn't God perfect?" I quizzed Bubba, "Right?"

"Yeah, we learned that in Rosey Rosalind's class."

"Didn't God make the whole world?" I continued, "and everything in it?"

"No Sambo did in his spare time," Bubba joked then he said, "Yeah, God made the world."

" If that's the case then…"

"Whoa, wait a minute," Bubba interrupted me. "Then what about you and me and everybody else in the world. God made all of us and we're not perfect."

"That's the point. Man is not perfect even though he was made by a perfect God."

"Why?" Bubba interjected." How can that be?"

"Because man has free will and chooses to do wrong … to commit sins."

"What's that got to do with a perfect beach?"

"Simple. The sand doesn't have a free will, therefore, it can't choose to sin or not to sin, therefore it's perfect."

"O-o-o-h, I see. That makes sense," Bubba said warming to the occasion. "But let me ask you this. What if man comes along and messes with the sand or let's say the rocks, for example, at Station 20 … he moves 'em. Would they still be perfect?"

This is getting too deep for me, I thought ... *time to bail out.*

"To answer your question, I'd say it depended upon how sinful the person was who moved the rocks," I gave as my final answer, I hoped. "You understand?"

Bubba continued, "In that case what if …"

"Hey! Hey you guys. Hey!" I was saved by the shout from Tommy Wade, running toward us from the pathway at Station 16. Bubba frowned at me and then looked at the ground like he hated it. Tommy was *not* Bubba's favorite person. More likely his favorite enemy.

"Hey, what y'all doing?" It was his trademark question. No matter the circumstance or the place or time of day or night. You could be eating, playing baseball, singing, riding your bike, whatever … and always the same question came from him: "What ya'll doing?"

Bubba slipped me a sly wink and I nodded.

"Oh, hi Tommy. We were just talking about philosophy," Bubba said very slowly and distinctively.

"Phil Osophy?" Tommy looked puzzled. "Who's he?"

Another wink from Bubba. "The new kid from Florida," Bubba said quickly, "he just moved here a few weeks ago."

"Oh yeah, you mean the skinny guy with the sister who has the big tits?" Tommy remarked.

What in the world is he talking about? I thought. *Typical Tommy Wade.*

Bubba didn't need any help or encouragement. "Yeah, yeah, that's it. The big tits!" Bubba said extending his hands out in front of his chest with a broad smile.

Tommy smiled generously and nodded his head.

"Tommy, look here. We're… u-h-h-h … going over to their house later. We thought you might wanna go with us?" I said. "What ya say?"

"N-a-a-w, I don't think so. I gotta go down to the creek and check my crab trap."

He better enjoy his crab trap because his and a whole bunch more would soon be history. More and more were showing up in Miller's Creek and it wouldn't be long before you couldn't throw a rock without hitting one. Bubba 'n me had plans for those traps.

"Oh, by the way," Tommy asked, " What's Phil's sister's name?"

Bubba couldn't resist: "Shirley," he yelled, " Shirley Osophy."

"Yeah," I chimed in, "Shirley Osophy with the big tits."

"Well, tell her I said, "Hi!" Tommy yelled back as he sauntered up the path.

"Shirley Osophy?" I asked grinning, "Where in the world did that come from?"

"I don't know." He was chuckling. "Did I ever tell you that boy only has one oar in the water?"

"Yeah, you did. And did I ever tell you that he's as dumb as a sack of hammers?"

"You just did." And we both laughed. "Eah, let's go, we got a lot of perfect beach to cover," I said.

"And after we walk this perfect beach," Bubba said in a serious tone suckering me in, "you know what we need to do?"

"No," I asked being serious, "what's that?"

"Me and you need to find this Shirley Osophy." Bubba paused being just as sincere as he could, then added, "Hear tell she has big old tits. BA-HA-HA-HA-HA!"

Bubba 'n me enjoyed life on the Island, the creek, the beach, hanging out with the crew, without the worries of adulthood … but it's not to say that there was not doubt, even conflict, in our young lives. We were going through the pains of adolescence like generations before us, but it was all new to us. We knew it was right to help and look out for the needs of other people, which was something we had been taught and observed in the behavior of our parents. However, the conflict arose in that we were also concerned about how other people perceived us.

"Mike, you ever notice how Tommy Wade is always talking about other people? Running 'em down and all."

"Yeah, funny you mention that. Last week at school I got so mad at him I almost hit him. He was running his big mouth about everybody and I thought I heard him mention your name and I was about to whack him upside his ugly old head. But I didn't."

"Really?" Bubba asked seeming surprised. "You would do that for me?"

"Sure."

"Thanks, man. Thanks."

"No problem. You'd do the same for me, wouldn't you?"

"More than that. I'd done whomped him upside the head if I heard him talking bad about you. And that's the truth!"

"Can't nobody say nothin' bad about you, Bubba. Because they don't know you. Not like I do."

"Yeah, I know what you're talking about." Bubba paused and gave me a big smile. "I know exactly what you're talking about." He slapped me on my shoulder and then moved toward a big pile of debris and started poking his stick in it.

"Eah, when we going crabbing?" Before he answered I asked, "How about fishing? Wanna go?"

"N-a-a-w, too much trouble getting bait and the rods and everything. And besides, we never catch anything anyway. When we go crabbing we always catch something."

"OK, if you don't want to go fishin' then let's go girlin.' "

"Go girlin.' What in the world are you talking about?"

"Girlin'? It's like this. If we go fishing to catch a fish or crabbing to catch a crab then doesn't it make sense we would go girlin' if we wanted to catch a girl?"

"Y-e-a-h, that makes sense but let me ask you just *one* thing. What would you do if you went girlin' and by some chance or miracle you caught a girl? I mean what would you do with her?" Bubba had stopped and had his arms folded waiting for an answer.

I stammered, "I … u-h-h-h … don't know."

"Just what I thought, Einstein," Bubba said shaking his head. "Maybe we ought to think about girlin' sometime later. I think we should stick to talking about somethin' else." He paused and grinned and added, "like somethin' we know about."

The passing ships in the harbor reminded us of other parts of the world, faraway places we had seen only on TV or looked at in National Geographic magazine.

"Mike, I wonder what kids do for fun in other countries like Japan or China?"

"I dunno. Just play and mess around like we do, I guess?"

"Y-e-a-h," Bubba drawled. "I bet they even go crabbing."

I nodded and then he asked, "What kind of school do they go to? I sure hope it ain't nothing like what we go to."

"Don't worry. Their school couldn't be that bad. I guarantee you that."

"Mike, do you think their parents fuss at them about cleaning their room and making good grades and all that stuff?"

"I guess so?" I didn't have all the answers and my question was, "Do you think the kids in other parts of the world are thinking about other kids in other parts of the world, like us?"

"Eah, man you got me there," Bubba said. "Who knows?"

"I know, Bubba. When you get to Africa and before the cannibals eat you up, you can ask their kids. Send me letter and let me know. A-HA-HA!"

Not only did I wonder about kids in other parts of the world, I often thought about kids in the United States.

I asked Bubba, "Do you think kids our age in other states act like we do? You know what I mean. Do they have a place to go to and have fun like the beach or a creek to go in and all?"

"Have fun? Well, yeah, if they're normal kids then they probably act like me and have fun and all, but if they're kind of whacked out or crazy then they probably act more like you and I doubt if they have much fun. BA-HA-HA-HA-HA!"

Evidently my friend had heard enough of my rambling mind so I kept my most important question to myself: *"I wonder if they had a special friend that they shared everything with like my friend Bubba and I did?"*

The beach was also a wonderful place to let our minds go free and dream. The fresh air and the smell of the salt air stimulated the senses to depths I never thought existed. At times I got completely lost in my dreams, so caught up in them I lost all contact with the real world, and magically floated through the air soaring over the beach barely inches off the ground, and with the twist of my hand, just like Peter Pan, soared high over the Island taking in the total view feeling as though I were the sole protector of this marvelous kingdom with my super powers. I had this experience, this fantasy, more than once, but had never given it much thought. Actually, I had dismissed it as some corny dream of a stupid twelve- year- old until one day while walking on the beach I noticed Bubba with a faraway look on his face put his hand up and twist it just like I did in my dreams.

"Eah, what you doing? What are you twisting your hand for like that?"

Reluctantly he said, "Well, I was kind of daydreaming and …" his voice trailed off.

"Don't stop. Keep on," I pleaded, "tell me."

Bubba cast his eyes down and said in a low tone, "I was … u-h-h-h flying."

"Flying!" I blurted out. Flying! WOW!" I paused and looked Bubba in the eye. "Over the Island I bet."

Bubba froze momentarily:"Yeah, how'd you know?"

"Just a real lucky guess, I suppose … just lucky."

These walks on the beach complemented with dreams and talks were wonderful escapes from everyday life, but reality has a way of rearing its ugly head. The reality was that we were middle- class kids barely getting by in school, and our only chance of securing any kind of decent career later in life would be by means of a college degree. For us that thought had not yet made its way into our fantasies. In my case, there were six siblings, at the latest count, and my mother and father worked hard just to put food on the table and clothe us. College cost money.

Bubba had two sisters and both of his parents worked providing nicely for his family. His chances looked better than mine, financially anyway.

I recall one afternoon coming home after a game of baseball in Bubba's backyard when Ryan grabbed me with a gleam in his eyes.

"Come here, Mike! Come on. I want to show you something." Incredibility was in his voice. And I was getting excited as to what he was talking about as he led me toward the bathroom.

"You will not *believe* this!" He pointed to the toilet. "Look!"

I looked hard expecting something of magnificence and greatness but was sorely disappointed. All I saw was the toilet and a roll of toilet tissue sitting on the back of the toilet.

"So?" I said looking at Ryan hoping for an explanation. "A roll of toilet paper?"

"You know what that means don't you?" he asked with a big grin reaching for the roll of toilet paper. "Do you understand the meaning of this?" holding the roll in front of my face.

I thought hard for a second frowning. "U-h-h-h … I'm not sure, Ryan … what?"

"It means company is coming," he blurted out, "somebody is coming to visit. We can throw away the newspaper. Get it?"

"O-o-o-h," I said, "so that's what you're talking about. Toilet paper … company. Gosh Ryan, I'd never have figured that out. Who's coming anyway?"

"I don't know. Probably the Devlins from Columbia?" Then that gleam returned to his eyes. "And you won't believe what I'm about to show you! You just won't believe this."

He reached for the door beneath the sink, swung it open as to present some unknown artifact from another world and yelled, "Look. Look at that!"

I peeked inside the cabinet and lo and behold was a twelve pack of new tissue paper minus one roll. A sight not often seen in the Devlin household.

"Yep, we are definitely having company," I agreed. "Maybe they won't use it all up and some will be left for us? What ya think?"

Ryan smiled and said, "Ain't no way they're going to use that much. Yeah, there will be plenty left for us." He was actually holding the twelve pack and fondling it like some million dollar diamond he had just found.

It wasn't that we were poor. It was just that we did not know that we were poor. Not poor-poor like people without the basics of life. Let me put it this way. Extra money? Well, there was no such thing as anything "extra" in the Devlin household unless it was "doing without" … there were a lot of those "extras" floating around. The wolf was not actually lurking at the door, but he was constantly in the yard eyeing the house. And only through dogged determination and a strong work ethic did my parents manage to feed, clothe, and house us. Along the way they taught us how to work at an early age and the value of a dollar. They were survivors of the Depression and figured they could make it through anything if it dealt with scrimping and scrounging and working. And they did. And so did the Devlin kids.

Often people who did not live on the Island remarked, "That living on Sullivans Island was like living in a fantasy world." Their sarcasm was as clear as its intention.

"Reality," they said, "begins when you cross the Ben Sawyer Bridge onto the mainland."

Upon first hearing such statements, I felt offended, but after giving these judgments some thought … well, I suppose we were living in a fantasy world and I was dog gone glad I was. As a matter of fact, in the summer of 1959, the only time I crossed the Ben Sawyer Bridge was to go to the Milk Bar for a chocolate milkshake. Yep. I loved living in my fantasy world. It was wonderful.

Seriously, however, reality for Bubba 'n me began when we left the beach and set foot on the pathway leading home. I might have only been a kid, but I recognized jealousy when I saw it and anyone talking bad about life on the Island and of reality and a fantasy world were simply trying to put down our Island and home. And as far as we were concerned they were nothing but a bunch of jealous, small-minded people. And if they were to ask Bubba 'n me we'd tell them, "Yeah, we saw Tinkerbell and Peter Pan just the other night and we had a nice long talk with them about people like you. And do you know what they told us to tell you? Up yours, buddy!"

It was near the end of one of our beach walks that the Lord works in strange ways experience struck again and always seemed to when least expected. Down near Station 12 there are three sets of jetties protruding from the beach into the entrance to the harbor, built many years ago for the control of beach erosion. They were formed from huge granite rocks brought by barges from quarries in the upstate by way of connecting lakes. It was kind of neat the way they built these jetties before the onset of modern equipment. Barges were loaded and set in place and then rocks were added until the barge sank. And then the process continued until a set of rocks literally rose out of the ocean. It was definitely the theory of "the straw that broke the camel's back" in action. They became good fishing spots, especially for flounder and sheepshead, which fed on the minnows and smaller fish that fed on seaweed and other sea life near the rocks. And where there are fish, crabs are not far behind. These jetties were no more than a hundred fifty feet long and eight feet wide.

Bubba 'n me found ourselves at the Station 12 rocks (jetties), tide was low, and we had our usual probing stick in hand when Bubba spotted a big crab retreating under a rock on the edge of the jetty. Bubba instinctively bent down and began probing a little bit behind where he imagined the crab would be hiding and sure enough Mr. Jimmy came scurrying out from under that rock like the goosed crab he was. Of course, he fled immediately under a neighboring rock and found safety.

I had been the silent observer up to this point: "Where'd you learn that?"

"Nowhere."

"Nowhere? I just saw you get that crab outta there."

"Eah, I didn't learn it nowhere. Some things I just do." He looked at me, began to smile, broke into a huge grin, jumped from the rock onto the beach, and said, "Let's go!

"Where?" I asked and before I knew it, he was halfway up the beach headed toward the path.

"Home, man. Gotta get my net. Is the basket still at your house?"

You didn't have to slap this Island boy in the face with a wet mop to know what was on Bubba's mind. He couldn't stand for a crab to get away from him.

"Let's cut up by the fort and bum a ride with Lumus or somebody," Bubba said now well ahead of me. "C'mon slow poke!"

"Wait up will ya?"

That evening my mother and Bubba's mother received free of charge a dozen crabs each already cooked by Bubba 'n me in the backyard. We had gone straight back to the rocks armed with nothing more than a net and a basket, and collected supper.

Whenever the weather did not cooperate for us to crab out of a boat, or the tide was not right and we had orders to fill, we would head for the rocks at Station 12 or Station 20 in order to meet our quota. And that whole summer we never failed on a delivery promise. Bubba became so expert at this type of crabbing, "poking-'em-out" we called it, that he would crawl all over those slippery rocks like a lizard, seeking the tell-tale blue streaked claw which gave away the crab's secret hideout. He had dispensed with the usual probing stick and instead used the handle of the crab net to run 'em out with and then he would quickly use the net for its intended purpose and scoop 'em up. It was like watching a ballet, just not quite as graceful. He rarely missed a crab and when he did I could hear him grumbling to himself, "Don't worry, Mr. Jimmy I'll see *you* later because I know where *you* live."

20
SCHOOL

We were having a good time experiencing all the joys of summertime: No school. Hanging out with the crew. The beach. Going in the creek. However, not *everything* in our young lives was fun and adventure. Life is like a coin … it has two sides. There is the good and the bad, the up and the down, the positive and the negative. Life is also much like a roller coaster ride: one minute you are up and everything is going your way and then in a flash … WHOOSH … and you are down in the valley and then back up again thinking everything is OK now and then it's back down again. Maybe life doesn't present its peaks and valleys so quickly but they were bound to show up. In 1959 I didn't understand this up and down cycle. It would be many years before I figured that out and many more before I came to grips about how to deal with it. The upside of life for the crew and me was obviously spent at the beach, at Burton's, going to the movie theater simply riding our bikes while roaming the Island. A-a-a-h it was summertime … it was wonderful … and we made the most of it. It was a shame life could not have just stopped then, for at least a few years anyway. The other side of that coin, the bad part, was attending school at St. Angela's and pursuing an education, which was a horse of another color. Not that we did not try, and try hard we did, to have fun and enjoy ourselves at school but there was the obstacle of dealing with Our Ladies of Mercy … or them dealing with us. Either way it was a hurdle we never quite got over. And they were a force to be reckoned with when it came to discipline. There was no doubt about it … those nuns were on us like holy on the pope.

There are two forms of the word discipline: discipline, the verb. It's an action word, meant to be used by one person toward another person to either alter certain behavior or punish the person for a certain behavior. Then there is self-discipline, the noun. It's a more subjective form, which implies training and control of oneself and one's conduct.

The Catholic nuns of O.L.M., our teachers at St. Angela's School in the 1950's were not seasoned in the art of teaching self-discipline to us, nor were they interested in it. It would be just something else they had to teach or be bothered with along with eight other subjects they taught plus their many other duties. However, when it came to dispersing and handing out punishment, disguised in the form of "discipline," these women held a backseat to no one. And they were strict, to say the least, almost to the point of "killing the spirit." We were held accountable not only for our actions but also for our *thoughts,* which I found amusing because the only way you could be punished for what you were *thinking* was to reveal your thoughts to your tormentor. And anyone that stupid probably needed a reminder to keep quiet anyway. Many a time at school I answered, "I dunno," when asked, "What were you thinking?" Especially when the person asking you was a red-faced nun waving a big stick in your face.

Years later I asked myself the question: "What prompted or motivated these teachers to be so strict and one-sided in their dealings with us? Were we really that bad and out of control?"

Two answers came to mind: one, the family standard of living under which they were raised in the 1920's was a rigorous and strict one. Also many of these nuns were children raised during The Depression and it had its tough, just-do-it, carry-over effect on them, which eventually trickled down to the classrooms at St. Angela's. The other was the monastic atmosphere of the convents where these nuns were trained with its insistence on strict adherence to rules and routine, with little or no room for variance, which they brought with them and preached daily to us. Also, the Catholic Church's emphasis on living a Christian life and the Sisters' belief in performing their vow of "poverty, chastity, and service to God" did not transfer well to the daily lives of high-spirited 7th graders.

We were not taught self-discipline. We were force-fed discipline at every turn until we were ready to explode. What we could never comprehend was that if these ladies had learned and applied self-discipline to their own lives, which to their credit they had to have done in order to complete their training, then why didn't they teach us about self-discipline instead of wasting time inflicting a severe form of discipline/punishment upon us? Maybe they thought they were teaching us self-discipline. Maybe it was all they knew to do.

By 1959 Bubba 'n me had somehow managed to make it to the seventh grade in one piece … physically anyway. Mentally we were bouncing around. Old enough to know that things around us and within us were changing, but still young enough not to figure out what these changes were, and immature enough to want to revert back to the safety of our parents when things went wrong. Yet we cried out for our freedom and to be left alone while at the same time craving the security of family and of being told what to do. Yep, we were mental yo-yos.

Added to our mental woes was the calling of the tribe, our classmates. The peer pressure was always there to be reckoned with. And our crew was no different than any other group during this era. How we dressed, walked, talked, and even combed our hair was predicated upon the approval or ridicule of the crew. So when the crew at school declared war on the Our Lady of Mercy Order, Bubba 'n me enlisted happily, determined to do our duty for God, country, and all seventh graders. We were dumb enough to think we had a chance against those "old ladies." Shoot, what did they know? We were much smarter and too clever for them. Plus we easily had them outnumbered. That's what we thought. Yeah right! We had about as much chance against them as that proverbial snowball in hell. But we did not know that and all the wisdom in the world could not have convinced us otherwise. Oh, we won a few skirmishes here and there and came close in a few battles but overall it was a mismatch of gigantic proportions. If this had been a boxing match it would have been stopped in the first round. We came out scarred but alive and learned the difference between discipline and self-discipline and a lot about punishment.

At school a well-defined pecking order had been in place for years. It was understood but not obeyed by all. Our Ladies of Mercy were at the top of the heap fueled and energized by their fearless leader, the frail, determined, could- hardly-walk principal, Sister Mary Aloysius Roberta Flaherty. Everyone knew her as Sister Roberta. She was everywhere and everything at once. Nothing got by this woman, not even time.

Within our ranks, the eight graders ruled the roost, but us seventh graders, not that far from the top, were well- trained on how to treat the underclassmen having been ourselves in the system the previous six years while enduring the persecution of the upperclassmen.

Of course, we did not let our attention drift toward the younger grades, like the third, fourth, or fifth grades. Like our tormentors before us, we upheld an unspoken tradition of regulating mainly the grade directly below us. For example, it would be considered out of order and downright cowardly, say for a fifth grader, to pick on a second or third grader. Thus, the sixth graders were considered to be fair and open game when it came to any kind of harassing or menacing behavior from us seventh graders. On occasion a member of our own class would be singled out for special treatment, if need be. We boys demonstrated all of this juvenile, childish behavior on a constant basis. We would take a "dare" in a second and bet you the moon would fall out of the sky if the odds were right. The girls, on the other hand, were way to smart to be playing the fool. They sat on the sidelines cheering us onto even more bizarre and foolish behavior. And we went right along like a puppy on a leash with our teachers right there, especially Sister Roberta, watching us and ready to discipline us into being good little Catholic boys.

Within a part of the school yard there stood a grove of about thirty persimmon trees whose fruit went unpicked, ripened to a beautiful orange-red color, and then fell from the trees thus creating a huge area of ground covered with rotting persimmons. I have yet to see a twelve-year-old boy constantly walk past a throwable object on the ground within his reach and not stop, pick it up, and throw it at someone or something. We had walked past these persimmons many times on our way to recess without incident until one day Bubba stopped and began to gather a few nice soft rotters. He was smiling as he carefully made his selections. The odor of the rotting persimmons barely overpowered the smell of trouble.

"Eah," I said, "if you're that hungry I'll share my peanut butter and jelly sandwich with you. You can have the jelly side…HA, HA!"

Bubba failed to see my humor. He had a serious look about him. "What you smartin' off about, Devlin?" After that remark I knew something was bothering him but I had not made the connection between his problem and the gathering of rotting persimmons. I should have.

"The persimmons," I asked, making another effort at humor, "you gonna eat 'em?"

"Eat these? You gotta be kidding. These are for my good buddy and friend Tommy Wade." Judging from the sarcasm dripping from Bubba's mouth, I knew Tommy Wade was in for trouble.

"O-h-h-h, I see … he's gonna eat 'em?"

"T-h-a-t-'s right, Catbird. He's gonna eat 'em all right but not because he wants to."

"Oh yeah? And what's he done this time to deserve such a treat?"

"I saw him talking to Susan this morning in the hall and he was giggling and pointing at me and acting all stupid like he does. So later I asked Susan what was going on and she said that Tommy told her I was a queer."

"Well," I said as straight-faced as I could, "you do act like a little fairy sometimes and…"

"Eah, knock it off right now Devlin, unless you want to eat some persimmons too," Bubba shouted halfway mad. I was his best friend but when it came to remarks about a person's sexual preference … well, all joking went out the window.

"I was just kidding, man. Just kidding." I held up my hands in self-defense. "I promise … you ain't no fairy!"

"Yeah right! And you remember that!" This wasn't Bubba's first run-in with Tommy Wade and I could sense something bad was brewing. Bubba continued, "First of all, I don't like him and now he tells a girl I'm a queer so he thinks it makes him look like Mister Cool. Well … these nice juicy persimmons will be a little reminder about who ain't queer."

We were big into deductive reasoning and I was feeling brave so I gave it a shot. "So if you are not a queer, that means you can throw persimmons really good?" I asked casually. "Is that what you mean?" Bubba was too busy gathering persimmons to argue with me. "What are you talking about?" he demanded. Then he stared at me and said, "If you're calling me a fairy again… I swear Devlin you're gonna eat a dozen of these." He had the look and two handfuls of persimmons so I backed off.

"Nothing," I said, "nothing at all. I was just mumbling to myself."

"Yeah, right! I thought that's what you were doing," Bubba said as he stalked off in search of his prey.

Tommy Wade didn't exactly eat any persimmons that day but he did go back to class after recess with persimmon stains all over his shirt, front and back, and I'm sure some in his hair. Bubba had surprised him and peppered his back when he made a run for it and then proceeded to chase him down and really unload on the slower Tommy who might have escaped had his feet been as fast as his always running mouth. That payback was the beginning of our personal persimmon persecution period … the "4P Club" we called it … fun time of splattering those in need of punishment for any social mishap or classroom goof like smarting off with a teacher, especially Sister Roberta, and getting the whole class punished, which was usually in the form of a recess detention. I believe the reasoning behind a teacher's action was to bring peer pressure down on the violator in hopes of him improving his behavior, not for the poor soul to be bombarded with persimmons by our vigilante group.

The only drawback to our fun and games at school was the chance of getting caught and facing the wrath of Sister Roberta, which was usually the big ruler treatment or, in my mind, an even worse punishment, the dreaded after-school detention. Whenever we came home late from school, our parents knew we had been in trouble so we were punished again. Old double trouble. On one occasion after getting home late from a detention my mother asked where I had been? I told her I stayed after school to do some extra studying in the library. A phone call to the school presented the truth and I was given a double punishment, which amounted to triple trouble and put a quick end to any future fibbing.

It was one of those hot and steamy days late in May and the persimmons were soft and plentiful. We couldn't resist their calling and there were a few boisterous sixth graders who needed to be brought down a notch or two after giving Bubba 'n me some lip about how tough they were and how they were not afraid of any seventh graders. Bubba 'n me along with Bobby and Jocko surrounded the rude big mouths during recess and gave 'em a bombardment of persimmons they wouldn't soon forget. But the ever-present Sister Roberta caught us and I mean caught us in the act, while we were laughing and splattering the fool out of those poor sixth graders. She taught the eighth grade and being the resourceful woman that she was she didn't feel like she had the time to punish us and be away from her class so she decided to do both, at the same time. To our utter humiliation she had us line up on the front lawn of the school just outside her classroom in full view of her class. She stuck her pointed little head through one of those foldout windows and yelled her orders at us and at the same time kept an eye on her class and taught her lesson. We were told to stretch out our arms straight from out shoulders and then hold them there without talking or complaining. Well, the first couple of minutes were not that bad as we looked at each other grinning. We asked silently, *"What's the big deal? This is easy."* Bubba was even smiling. Then the pain came. Slowly at first until the intensity grew to a point that was unbearable and our skinny little arms began to sag slowly until they were in full descent. That's when Sister Roberta beat on the window with the big ruler and screamed, "Get those arms up! Don't make me come out there with this ruler!"

Instantly we jerked our arms back up but they only stayed there momentarily and she yelled again. This repetitive torture went on for what seemed like an eternity but actually lasted about ten minutes. As hard as we tried it was impossible to hold our arms out like that once the pain began.

"Get those arms up or I'm coming out there!" Sister Roberta hollered. "You'll regret it. You hear me?"

How could we not hear her? For an old lady she could yell. I think God could hear her.

The beads of sweat outnumbered the flies that were having their way with us because we weren't able to swat them away. After a few more minutes of intense pain, she relented and ordered us inside where we received a tongue lashing in front of her class who seemed to be enjoying our misery. We dutifully answered, "No, Sister" to every question she asked regarding us doing anything wrong ever again. My arms and shoulders ached so bad I was just babbling. Bubba stood back and was silent.

Physical pain only hurts for a while and then its over. That day on the lawn my arms and shoulders could not have hurt any more than they did. Pain reaches a certain level and then it doesn't matter after that. It can't hurt anymore. The real and lasting pain came from being humiliated in front of other students, which was the case that day in front of Sister Roberta's class.

It was one thing to get caught and be punished. We went through a lot of that at school and accepted our punishment without complaint. After all, we were in the wrong and deserved to be punished. But sometimes things were not so cut and dry and when our teachers misused their authority either directly or indirectly it became an issue with us and we fought back the only way we knew how. By breaking the rules again.

Take for instance the case of Andy Clark. It was part of the standard classroom procedure to raise your hand when you wanted to speak. Once acknowledged you would rise and stand by your desk and state your business. So no one in class gave it a second thought when Andy Clark raised his hand, rose and asked if he could go to the bathroom and was promptly turned down by Sister Ann Marie. "No! Sit back down and do your work. There's no time for that."

About an hour passed and finally recess time drew near. We knew when it was time for recess because we constantly watched the clock and being the good Catholic children we were, we prayed for the hands to move faster. We had become expert clock-watchers sneaking a sideways peek every couple of minutes at the hands … a trait we learned after receiving warnings about the fury of God from Sister Roberta about how sinful it was to look at the clock and not pay attention to the lesson. You would have thought that the clock, one of those big, ugly, black and white deals, was the Holy Grail itself there on the wall only to be bowed down to but certainly not to be used to tell time by.

When the recess bell rang announcing a few minutes of freedom we stood by our desks waiting for Sister Ann Marie to excuse us. We bolted for the door. Everyone except Andy Clark who sat motionless. The class emptied in less than a minute but my friend still sat in his desk facing the front of the room. I hung back sensing something was very wrong.

"Andy," I said. "Andy, come on let's go," I now pleaded. "It's recess." Something had to be wrong? Andy was one of the crew and like the rest of us loved recess.

No movement. I moved a little closer. "Andy, let's go," I urged him, "time's a wasting."

Then I heard the sobs. His head dropped and slowly his hand went for his face. I moved quickly toward him and just before I reached his desk Andy rose pitifully from his puddle-soaked desk revealing his soaking wet pants. I'll never forget the look of absolute humiliation of Andy Clark that day as the tears trickled steadily down his face.

After the class learned of Andy's disgrace, the crew got together and we vowed revenge for our friend's sake. And for weeks we went on a rampage of breaking rules and generally acting out and being disobedient. However, it was all to no avail as we were punished again and again. It seemed like an endless, vicious cycle.

I'm certain none of our teachers desired to intentionally hurt us either physically or psychologically but punishment does carry with it a certain stigma. Through corporal punishment the nuns were showing us who was in control and were attempting to use such punishment as a deterrent but, of course, at twelve years old we did not see it that way and continued to buck the system. The psychological damage done was nearly irreparable and some students from that era still today carry not only scars but open psychological wounds.

Every now and then someone in our class would become brave

enough or brash enough to come out in an open display and challenge the authority of one of our teachers. Big mistake. Maybe they were stupid ... or were just seeking attention? My friends in the crew ... uh-uh. We liked to be way more discreet with hopes that we wouldn't get caught. But there was one brazen individual in our class who had displayed from the time of kindergarten a certain outlook on life that reeked with disdain for everyone and everything. His name was David Hopkins. He was an accident looking for a place to happen. His surly attitude along with a you-can't-tell-me-what-to-do approach to life, was a lethal combination at St. Angela's, and especially when dealing with Sister Rosalind, the diminutive nun who rarely spoke or smiled. If ever there was a poster person for the Speak-Softly-and-Carry-a Big-Stick group, then she was the person.

A showdown between her and David had been brewing since the beginning of this school year when David would do little annoying things like refuse to stay in line or not raise his hand to speak and he constantly attempted to sleep in class. It was always something with him and it was always directed toward Sister Rosalind.

"I don't have to do what she says. If I don't then what's she going to do? Hit me with the ruler? Big deal." And on and on he went. Even the class was tiring of David's antics and truthfully we could hardly wait for sister to lower the boom. We had given some thought to confronting David ourselves but he was a big kid with a big "attitude" so we figured it wasn't worth the trouble. Being mischievous and pulling off pranks was one thing but being rude and disrespectful to an adult, much less a nun, was another thing. On and on it went ... a tit for tat ... until Sister could not take it any more. David was talking out of turn again bothering the class and when reprimanded by sister he gave her a dirty look and said arrogantly, "What if I don't want to be quiet, huh?"

I couldn't believe my ears. A student talking back to a teacher like that right in front of the class. *Has he lost his mind,* I thought. *Maybe he wants to die?* I glanced around the class and took a quick inventory of the class' reaction. Everybody was sitting on the edge of their desks with their mouths open in disbelief. Bubba gave me the finger sliding across the throat movement.

Sister Rosalind, the quiet one, backed up and stood near the entrance to the coatroom, not saying a word, just looking at David with her small clear eyes. She raised her hand and motioned to David to come to her moving her beckoning finger very slowly. When her face turned red it signaled that you were in trouble and right now hers was as red as Rudolph's nose. The coatroom had no doors. There was an opening at each end and it was at the very front of the room and consisted of two shelves for our books and shiny hangars bolted to the wall for hanging our coats on. The class had front row seats and we held our breath in anticipation of the long-awaited confrontation between the ever-arrogant student and the determined little nun. If I could have placed a bet right then and there I'd have taken Sister Rosalind in a heartbeat. She entered the coatroom followed by the strutting cocky David who had the nerve to turn and grin at the class. He was swinging his arms back and forth like he was taking a stroll in the park. They disappeared around the corner. There were no loud voices or yelling. No sounds of voices at all came from the coatroom. Only the sound of a scuffle. A very short scuffle at that because momentarily Sister Rosalind reappeared, red-faced as ever. She gave a quick stare at the class, opened the door and stormed out of the classroom. The class sat in silence. As silent as the coatroom still. We were listening for any clue as to what happened behind the wall. We heard what sounded like the scraping of feet as against a wall. We continued to sit silently not daring to move. No David. No noise. For a second I thought, *Did she somehow kill him? Maybe strangled him? Surely not.*

Billy Hill got up, motioned Bubba to cover the door and be the lookout should Sister Rosalind come back, and then he moved slowly toward the coatroom like he was stalking a deer. The rest of us were literally on the edge of our seats, easing ourselves out ever so slowly, wanting so badly to investigate the coatroom, but our fears held us back.

Shoot, let Billy check it out, I thought. *I don't want to get caught being out of my desk if Sister comes back.*

Billy slowly peeked around the corner into the coatroom and immediately let out a loud, "Oh my God!"

It was all we needed to hear. We dashed from our desks and raced to the coatroom. And there he was in all of his suspended glory. The cocksure, brash David Hopkins hanging from one of the hooks with his feet about five inches shy of the floor, dangling in the breeze like a puppet. The back of his shirt was securely attached to the hook and his weight pulling down acted as his keeper. The bugged out eyes and look of shock on his face said it all. Although no one said it, the class felt relief from the tension caused by David's poor attitude and I could sense a round of applause was in order … for Sister Rosalind, that is. David was frantically trying to unhook himself and finally with some help the now not so brazen David Hopkins' feet again found earth. For the first time in seven years at school David was speechless.

None of us from that day on, especially David Hopkins, ever said more than was necessary to Sister Rosalind.

21
PAYBACK

If there was one consistent trait among all the nuns at St. Angela's School, year in and year out, it was that they were consistent. Let me explain. They never let up in their discipling of us. And when I say never I mean *never.* Every day they watched us and scolded us and watched us some more and scolded us again. Their demand for excellence was unrelenting. And we were just as consistent in our misbehavior so I suppose in that regard we made a good team. It seemed all that mattered to them was: keep 'em in line, don't give up, watch 'em like a hawk, and then bear down a little more. There was an old adage we must have heard a thousand times from Sister Roberta that said, "You can't squeeze blood from a turnip." But let me tell you the good Sisters of St. Angela's sure tried their best to find some blood … ours. Their other favorite saying from that era and I can still hear it as clear as day was: "You can lead a horse to the water but you can't make him drink." Well, they sure as hell tried to make us drink … I can tell you that.

As the school year grew older it became clear that *someone* would have to pay the price for our pent-up frustrations for being squeezed day after day after day. Besides the demand for perfect behavior, we were saddled with an academic load St. Thomas Aquinas would have shied away from.

Retribution was unknown to us but somebody was going to feel our wrath sooner or later and it was near the end of the school year when our little minds and nerves were frayed and at the breaking point. Unloading our anxieties on our parents was out of the question; however, much of our disruptive behavior at home could probably be traced back to our repression at school and unknowingly taking out our resentment for authority on our parents.

The venting of anger … The relieving of frustrations … We desperately needed an outlet or surely we would explode. Well, it just so happened that our sacrificial lamb appeared right on schedule in the form of a substitute teacher who was to take over for the departing Sister Agnes. Here was someone we could unload all of our frustrations on. Sister Mary Joseph, the cross-eyed nun. She stepped in as our new Math and Science teacher looking very much the part in her newly starched penguin outfit with shiny new Rosary beads rattling at her side. She even carried a new big ruler and exhibited a certain swagger that was all too familiar. God, was this woman a cousin of Sister Roberta's? I hope not. Most of the time we could get a "read" on a new teacher right away but because of this woman's defect in vision we couldn't get a clear vision on any of her intentions. Actually we couldn't get a clear read on anything from her. No one could tell where she was focusing. She was so cross-eyed she could stand in the middle of a room and see all four walls at the same time. Something deep down inside of me told me our new teacher could be trouble.

Sister Roberta had taught or rather demanded that we look whomever we were talking to in the eye when engaged in conversation.

"The eyes," she said, "are the windows to the soul and it's there you will find the truth."

Well, we were not finding any truth in the soul of Sister Mary Joseph. The only thing we found was the undaunting task of trying to look her in the eye when addressing her. Whenever I talked to her I found myself switching from one of her eyes to the other in an attempt to focus in on where her gaze was at the moment. This switching from eye to eye made me feel, not only self-conscious, but also uneasy. Did she recognize my confusion? Should I say something? Of course I didn't. I had no idea what to say. I would focus hard on her left eye, hoping to gain some perspective but it only led to my following it to her right eye and then it was back to her left eye. Back and forth it would go until I decided to settle my sights on the ceiling. At least it wasn't moving around. This offered momentary relief … then the whole process would begin again. My gazing at the ceiling was a sure sign that I was having trouble keeping up with her unusual visionary status so Sister mercifully and discreetly cut short her direct conversations with us.

When she addressed the class for the first time, and not knowing our names, she corrected a talkative Mike Hart by looking in his direction and telling him to be quiet and stand up. Mike and two other puzzled classmates on his side of the room stood up. Also two other students on the other side of the room stood up with everyone looking perplexed. We snickered and I thought, *Oh boy, ain't this something?*

Only by pointing was Sister Mary Joseph able to relay her true intent and so over and over she would point to whomever she was talking to earning her the nickname, "The Pointer." In the beginning the crew felt kind of sorry for "The Pointer" with her visionary problem but that sorrow quickly faded. On her third day she proved to be more than adequate with the big stick, proving that her eyesight might be flawed in its direction but was still twenty-twenty when it came to punishing a rear end. Bubba was her first customer having been caught landing a huge spitball on the side of Tommy Wade's face.

"I thought she was looking out the window," lamented Bubba. "I swear she was."

And Bubba was just the first of many victims of the cross-eyed nun. This all-seeing nun who seemed to take great pleasure in our mistakes continuously caught us dead-to-rights and she showed no mercy. We thought her arm would wear out from paddling us so much but we were wrong again and the unfair competition went on. We complained to each other that she was taking all the fun of us trying to get by with some kind of mischief or breaking of the rules. Shoot, this game was about as unfair as throwing the Christians to the lions. It wasn't fair, we moaned, that she could be watching one side of the room (so we thought) and catch us doing something wrong on the other side. We just did not know where she was looking and proved to be a lot tougher adversary then we ever imagined. Shucks, most substitute teachers were patsies. This time we were outgunned and outmaneuvered at every turn, never before experiencing a teacher quite like this. There was only one thing to do. Get rid of her but it was going to take an awfully good and well thought out plan. That much we were sure of.

So four of us put our heads together figuring four of us could come up with a decent plan to rid ourselves of "The Pointer" but in reality it took four of our pea brains to match wits with any one nun and we knew it. We just didn't want to admit it.

"I know. I've got it," Bubba said, "let's refuse to go to class. Do a-a-a-h … what do you call it? A boycat?"

"You mean a boycott," Fred corrected him. "Not a boycat, that's an animal, you jackleg."

"Yeah, that's it. A boycott!" Bubba was smiling. "Then we won't have to go to school and do no more homework. And no more paddlings from "The Pointer."

"It won't work. She would go to Sister Roberta and she would call our parents and then we would be in real trouble." We all nodded our heads. It was John talking and just by the tone of his voice and the look in his eye we could tell he was trying hard to come up with a good plan. "I've got an idea but …"

Bubba was itching to get his two cents worth in. "How about locking her in the kitchen like we did Sister Ann Marie that time?"

"N-a-a-a-w. Already been done," I said. "We need something new." Bubba gave me a hard stare. I stared back at him even harder giving him a quick "KNUCK- KNUCK- KNUCK." He smiled.

"OK, listen up. Here's what we do." Fred seemed dead serious. "We grab the old bitty, tie her up, and put her in top of the oak tree with a big sign around her neck that says, "I hate Sister Roberta." Fred grinned and we howled with laughter.

“Seriously, guys. I’ve got it,” John said. “But this is going to take some work and good timing but I figure between the four of us we can pull it off.”

“Excuse me,” Fred interrupted, “you mean among the four of us?”

“What?”

“The correct English is “among” when talking about three or more people.”

“Fred!” It was Bubba who said, “Who gives a big buffalo’s butt about whether we say between or among? This ain’t Sister Roberta’s English class. Now get with the program or we’re gonna tie you up and put you in the top of the tree with a sign up your …”

“All right, all right! Fred said holding up his hands like he was surrendering. “Don’t get your bowels in an uproar, O’Toole.”

I played the peacemaker. “Both of ya. Cool it, OK? We’re trying to get something done here. Go ahead, John.”

“Like I was trying to say. It’s going to take some good timing to pull this off but we can do it.” John had our attention as he outlined a scheme that only his honor roll mind could come up with. And it was so simple that it might actually work.

“Now I’m not sure if this little plan will get rid of Sister Mary Joseph but it will make her think twice before messing with us seventh graders anymore. And we can kill four birds with one stone.”

“Excuse me.” It was Fred again. “I’m not correcting your grammar, John. But don’t you mean kill two birds with one stone?”

John was more patient than Bubba. “No, Fred. I meant to say four birds because with this plan we’ll get four teachers.”

“O-o-o-o-h. I’m sorry. Go ahead.”

“All right. Here’s the deal. All we need is a box of super strength Ex-lax and some scouting of the kitchen during lunchtime the next few days.” John looked around for volunteers.

“I can get the Ex-lax,” Fred exclaimed. “There’s some in the medicine cabinet at home.”

“The kitchen, John?” I asked. “What’s with that?”

“That’s where the teachers eat lunch and during our recess period Sister Roberta, Ann Marie, Rosalind and Mary Joseph eat at the same time. The other teachers eat during the lower grades’ recess.”

“How you know all that?” Bubba asked. “You don’t eat with them do you?” Before John could answer Bubba shouted, “Yeah, that’s it! That’s how you get all those “A’s.” You’re down there in the kitchen kissing butt all the time. A-HA-HA-HA!”

“Now that your brilliant mind has spoken its bit and I mean a *little* bit, may I continue?” John paused. “Milk duty. That’s how I know, Bubba. Where you guys are too lazy to help. I go to the cooler in the kitchen for our milk and Mrs. Kennedy is there everyday setting the table for the fabulous four. Is that word OK, Fred? Fabulous?"

"Stupendous, my young scholar. Absolutely stupid-endous," Fred said smiling.

"Tell you what," I said, "it's beginning to sound like we've been in this school too long."

"Anyway," John continued, "they drink milk every day just like us. Out of the carton and …"

Bubba lit up and said, "And that's where the ex-lax comes in. Right?"

"Excuse me again," Fred said, "but that's where the Ex-lax does not come in but is poured in. Am I correct, John?"

"You just hit a grand slam, my man."

Being the ol' worrywart I had a question about this whole plan. Maybe that's why I was included in the group? "John, all that sounds great. But let's say they drink the ex-lax and it makes 'em have to go to the bathroom … so what? You know what I'm saying? They'll just go. What's the big deal about that?"

"Oh yeah?" Bubba said. "Not if they don't have a place to go."

John had obviously given this plan some thought. "Right, Bubba. And we can do something about that."

"Like what?" I asked.

"We'll get to that a little later but first we have to figure a way to get Mrs. Kennedy out of the kitchen for about one minute so I can pour our favorite teachers a little pick-'em- up-and-sit-'em-down-drink."

I had an idea. "John, give me till tomorrow and I think I can come up with a way to get Mrs. Kennedy out of the kitchen. Bubba will you help me?"

"Sure. When?"

"Tomorrow morning."

Fred hesitantly asked the most important question. "When are we going to do this?"

John answered, "Today's Monday. Let's see? By Friday everything should be ready. And please guys, keep your mouths shut, especially around you-know-who."

He was referring to Tommy Wade. What –You- Doing?- Motor –Mouth- Tommy -Wade. Bubba remarked that Tommy ran his mouth so much that he could talk underwater with a mouthful of marbles.

Early the next morning Bubba 'n me were staking out the entrance to the chapel at school trying hard to act inconspicuous but we were as out of place as a goose in a ten- cents store. We were awaiting the arrival of Mrs. Kennedy, one of the many volunteers who kept St. Angela's running smoothly on a daily basis. Right on schedule she arrived with her daily bouquet of flowers from her home garden and she was bound for the altar in the chapel, which was located next to the main office and the kitchen, connected by a short breezeway. The flowers were so fresh we could smell the sweet aroma of roses in the air as she approached. Mrs. Kennedy took great pride in her homegrown flowers and never missed a day decorating the altar. Mrs. Kennedy was also a creature of habit. Bubba 'n me stuck our noses in our Math books in a feeble attempt at espionage but I don't think we fooled anyone but ourselves. Maybe? Mrs. Kennedy who was normally very friendly and talkative breezed by without a word.

"Ah yeah," I smiled. "Our little plan just might work? Mrs. Kennedy with her flowers. Same time everyday. Do you think she's the same way in the kitchen?"

"Mrs. Kennedy with flowers," Bubba said, "so what?"

"Keep still. You'll see. Let's see how long it takes for her to go from the chapel to the kitchen door." Mrs. Kennedy exited the chapel and we stuck our faces back into our books. She headed directly for the kitchen. I began counting, "One Mississippi, two Mississippi …Yeah, about thirty seconds in and thirty seconds out. That ought to be enough time. One full minute."

"Enough time for what?' Bubba asked.

"For John. See, he needs to know how long it will take her to walk to the chapel and then back to the kitchen."

"Oh, I got it!" Bubba was getting excited about the plan. "We're gonna get Mrs. Kennedy out of the kitchen so John can do his dirty work. Cool, man. Cool."

"T-h-a-t-'s right, Catbird. And the flowers Mrs. Kennedy brings every morning …"

"Yeah, what about them?"

"Well, Fred will rush into the kitchen and tell her someone stole them off the altar. And then she will go to check on them."

"But they weren't stolen."

"Not yet," I said grinning. "That's where you come in. You old flower thief! And that ain't all."

The next three days we spent fine-tuning our masterful plan of ex-laxing our favorite teachers. John took careful notice of the exact layout in the kitchen and the precise arrival time of each teacher noting when they began eating and when they finished. Like Mrs. Kennedy they too were creatures of habit. Fred practiced his part until he had it down like a Hollywood actor ready for a final take. Bubba 'n me checked daily on Mrs. Kennedy and sure enough she was a lady of schedule. She brought flowers the same time each day.

The much-anticipated day had arrived, Friday. And to our credit all of us had kept the plan under our hats thus giving us a better chance of success. Failures in the past had been mostly due to someone's big mouth ruining a lot of planning and mental preparation, something we were not used to. Not being quiet, the mental part. Success or failure hinged on several things happening like they were planned but one crucial element was getting Mrs. Kennedy out of the kitchen while John poured the Ex-lax, which had been proudly supplied by Fred and it was one of the "super strong" varieties. The only time anyone was allowed out of class at this particular time of day were the milk people who went to the kitchen with their count and loaded up a plastic crate and carried it back to their respective classroom to be distributed just before recess. On Friday prior to the recess bell, John, as usual, got ready to make his milk run. This time he asked Sister Mary Joseph if it would be all right if Fred helped him with the milk today? This too was a critical element of our plan. Bubba 'n me held our breaths praying for a "yes" so Fred could accompany John and then go into his act and get Mrs. Kennedy out of the kitchen.

"I don't know about that, John?" Sister Mary Joseph said. Our hearts fluttered. "Why do you need Fred to help you?"

John was a quick thinker and responded immediately, "Well, Fred told me he wants to do the milk run next year and I figured some training now might help him for next year."

Sister mulled over his answer and the said, "In that case, OK."

"All right." I thought. "The rest will be easy."

I looked at Bubba who had a serious look about him but I knew on the inside he was celebrating.

John entered the kitchen and headed for the milk cooler, eyeing the table set for four, complete with the usual four open milk cartons awaiting their thirsty patrons. Mrs. Kennedy was in the process of taking a delicious smelling casserole out of the oven when Fred burst into the room shouting, "Mrs. Kennedy! Mrs. Kennedy! Come quick! Hurry! Some kid just ran out of the chapel with all the flowers. Quick! Come on!" He was holding the door open and glancing quickly back and forth from the chapel to Mrs. Kennedy who hesitated for a long second, set the casserole on top of the stove and then followed Fred out the door.

"Fred, what in the world," Mrs. Kennedy said, "is going on with *these* kids nowadays?"

"It was a little boy," Fred told Mrs. Kennedy, "and he ran right past here and then down there and around the corner. I saw him."

Mrs. Kennedy stopped, put her hands on her hips and looked in the direction of the running child and then back to the chapel. She opened the chapel door and walked toward the flowerless altar to check on her roses. It was all the time John needed. The distraught Mrs. Kennedy and Fred left the chapel with Fred assuring her that he would catch the culprit if it were the last thing he did. He then offered to help John carry the milk back to class, which John gladly accepted. Upon distribution of the milk John gave Bubba 'n me a much anticipated wink, the signal that everything went as planned.

Now for some private work of my own. Bubba had the same idea though not the same task so when we parted ways at recess each offering some lame excuse about having something to do neither of us gave each other much thought.

John was so animated and funny at recess telling about the act Fred put on for Mrs. Kennedy and how Fred had set the flowers down on the floor on the side of the altar, out of sight. Fred planned on "finding" them after school and taking them to Mrs. Kennedy and playing the role of the hero. He wondered if he should hold out for a reward? John said that he had more than enough time so he gave each carton an extra shake or two mixing in the Ex-lax beyond recognition.

Upon returning to class after recess there was a glaring absence from the room. Bubba was not in his desk. As a matter of fact I hadn't seen him since he said he had to go to the office and see Mrs. Trucksis for something. Sister Mary Joseph noticed Bubba's absence right away and looking at the whole class by focusing her gaze on the back wall our cross-eyed Lady of Mercy bellowed, "Where's Bubba O'Toole?" Then she felt a certain twinge in her stomach. *Must be that second helping of casserole*, she thought.

She yelled again, "Where's Bubba O'Toole?"

Again no answer. Because no one knew.

Louder. "Where's Bubba O'Toole?" Are you people deaf?"

The class sat in dumbfound silence while John and Fred and I sat in anticipation, waiting for the ex-lax to kick in.

"If someone does not answer me the whole class will have an after school detention. Do you hear me?" Sister was yelling. A churning sensation deep in her stomach made a noise. *The lima beans?* she thought.

"But I can't stay after school, whined Susan Wilson, the reigning world champion whiner. She had a whiny whine, the kind that made your skin crawl. I'd almost rather face an after-school detention than listen to her.

Here she went again, "I've got recital practice."

"Young lady, I don't care what kind of practice you have. Shut your mouth and all that whining or you'll get two! Understand?"

Yahoo! Go Sister, you tell her! I thought.

"You boys!" She glared around the room and, I think, she was looking directly at me? "Listen to me. If one of you doesn't speak up then I'm going to ..."

Oh my gosh! Sister thought. *I feel like I'm going to pop.*

Sister Mary Joseph's eyes widened like she had seen a ghost, her head snapped back and her back straightened while her shoulders shook quickly as though she were dancing the Watusi.

"Excuse me class. I'll be right back." Sister Mary Joseph made a beeline for the door while John, Fred, and I smiled broadly.

Sister Mary Joseph never made it back to class that day.

We sat in silence for a while posted a lookout, and then chit-chatted with our classmates for about an hour and had a good old time walking around the room talking with whomever we wanted to enjoying our newfound freedom. But we were smart enough to keep the noise level to a minimum because Sister Roberta's room was two doors down the hall. No one questioned the sudden disappearance of Sister Mary Joseph and even if they had John and Fred and I knew nothing and would say nothing.

Just before dismissal at 2:30 Bubba came strolling back into class with a tale from The Twilight Zone. It seems that Bubba was going to guarantee that our ex-lax drinking teachers did not have a place to rest themselves when the time came. He went to the teacher's bathroom and managed to slip in unnoticed when the secretary went to lunch and he locked himself in the bathroom from the inside. And then he waited. We were gathered in a circle around Bubba as he gave us a blow-by-blow account of what happened.

"You mean to tell us," Fred asked, "that you've been in the teacher's bathroom all this time?"

"T-h-a-t-`s right, Catbird!"

"What'd you do?" I asked. I couldn't imagine someone just sitting in a bathroom for two hours. "Just stand there?"

"No. I sat down for a while and then I ate my lunch."

"Ate your lunch in the bathroom?"

"Well, where else was I gonna eat it, Einstein?"

"Well, I guess …" I didn't know what to say.

"It was kind of hard to eat in there. I could hardly tell what I was eating," Bubba said. "It was so dark."

"You were eating in the dark?" Fred asked. "Why didn't you turn on the light?"

"O-o-o-h, the light. I … u-u-u-h … Well, I was hiding and well … I didn't think of that."

"Eah, why were you in there to begin with," I asked.

"So they couldn't get in to use the bathroom. I had the door locked."

I looked at my friend and smiled. "Bubba you are something else, man! You are something else." Then I gave him a big pat on the back.

"A-a-a-a-w, it was nothing," he said almost embarrassed.

"Let me ask you this. How'd you get out?"

Bubba lit up like a Christmas tree. "Oh man, that's the best part. Well, I was in there for a long time but I knew somebody would be coming sooner or later to use the bathroom. You know with the Ex-lax and all. Finally, I heard someone pulling on the doorknob and then I heard 'em ask Mrs. Trucksis if anyone was in there. Then whoever it was started knocking on the door. I think it was Sister Ann Marie because of that high-pitched squeal of hers. She kept asking, "Is there anyone in there?" I kept answering "yes' but I guess she didn't hear me because I was answering to myself. HA-HA!"

"What happened then?"

"Hold your horses. I'm getting there." Bubba paused for effect and studied the gaze from the group assembled around him. "Next thing I heard was Sister Rosalind talking to Sister Ann Marie and then Rosalind started beating on the door. Real hard like. Bam, bam, bam! Rosalind was trying to break in front of Ann Marie but Ann Marie said no way and they started arguing. They were yelling at each other and when Ann Marie told Rosalind to get the hell out of there or there was going to be real trouble I almost busted out laughing. Rosalind told Ann Marie to go use the girls' bathroom. That's when Ann Marie got mad and threatened to hit Rosalind."

"What were you doing?" Fred asked Bubba.

"Me? Oh, I was standing there with my ear to the door listening about to laugh my butt off."

"Were they still banging on the door?"

"Oh yeah! They really had to go bad. Now here's the good part. Sister Roberta shows up and all hell breaks loose. She tells Rosalind and Ann Marie to get back to their classes and now! I knew that wasn't going to happen. They must have been pushing and shoving each other because one of 'em fell down and I heard Mrs. Trucksis yell. "Sister, are you all right?"

"It sounded like Ann Marie was the one who fell. I'm not sure. Anyway I'm just standing there listening and after a few minutes I hear this sound in the lock. It was somebody with a key."

"What'd you do?"

"Nothing. There was nothing I could do. So when Sister Roberta opened the door she found me asleep, sitting on the toilet seat. Of course I wasn't really asleep."

"Asleep on a toilet seat! Hey, hey!" John said. "If that ain't the coolest thing in the world!"

This was getting to be too much. And we were laughing our heads off.

"Bubba," I asked, "what did she say?"

"Oh, she started yelling for me to get out of there. Right now! Go back to class and all that. Man, those nuns had it so bad they wouldn't have cared if Frankenstein was in that bathroom. They just wanted to go to the bathroom." Bubba paused, looked around and asked, "By the way, where's Sister Mary Joseph?"

"U-h-h-h … we don't know." I said. "She left here about two hours ago and never came back. She wasn't down there at the teacher's bathroom?"

"Nope. I didn't see her."
I nudged Bubba and whispered, "I'll tell you later."

I couldn't tell Bubba or anyone else for that matter about Sister Mary Joseph for fear of getting caught and also because I had violated one of the strictest unwritten rules among us males. I had gotten help from a girl. One of the girls in class, Ellen, had stood as a lookout during recess that Friday while I snuck into the girls' bathroom. I locked two of the stalls from the inside and climbed over the top and then left the third stall open. It was the only available one left. Ellen stayed the rest of the recess period just standing in the accessible stall to prevent anyone from using it. That particular seat was reserved for Sister Mary Joseph who, in my mind wouldn't be too choosy when she began her run for the toilet. Besides, the teacher's bathroom should be full by then.

Her throne was special and would become a place of permanence. Well, at least permanent for a good while. I had given the toilet seat a healthy coating of glue. Not your cheap Elmer's type glue used in school to hold paper items together that felt sticky but didn't have any real bonding power. I used an all-purpose cement, which was clear and blended in nicely against the white background of the toilet seat. My father had used it for plumbing purpose when working with plastic pipes so I borrowed what he had left. It was as dastardly a deed as I had ever done but at the time my real concern was that someone else other than Sister Mary Joseph might use that toilet from the end of recess until Sister Mary Joseph went in search of a seat. When she did not return right away after leaving class I felt relief and a little remorse not because of Sister Mary Joseph's plight but because I couldn't share my story with the class.

It was a day we would remember as fun and a battle that went our way but we knew we could never win this war and that when we returned to school Monday there would be hell to pay.

Sister Mary Joseph meanwhile had found her relief and plenty of time on the throne to think and pray. "Dear God, please give me the patience not to kill that Devlin and O'Toole kid. Thank you, God. Oh me. I guess the cleaning crew will find me?"

22
ROBBERY

Thomas Poe sat on the beach taking in what he thought might be one of his last looks at the ocean, which he had enjoyed over the years. His thoughts wandered from the past to the present and back again replaying the events that led to his predicament and finally to what he thought was the final answer. He envied the stillness and serenity of the calm waters, wishing his life could be the same. The weather, at least, was cooperating with his plan he mused, little or no moon tonight. It's the middle of the week. Fewer eyes around. Perfect.

He was in the final stages of a much-thought-out plan. He realized this was a one shot deal that could turn ugly or go smooth with no hitches. "God, I hope so," he whispered. He figured all he had to do was get in and out of Dr. Steven Jenkins' house without getting caught. *I'll be as quiet as a whisper. No, even quieter,* he thought. *I'll be as quiet as it is right now. I won't make a sound.* Either way, he had decided, it was his savior, the *only* way out. Just last week he had spoken with a middleman contact in Chicago who would be taking the real risk of making the money payment to Thomas in exchange for the goods. Then Thomas would do his part and get the money safely to the bank in Charlotte, which would wire it onto Miami and eventually it would make its way to an unmarked account in the Bahamas. For now all Thomas had to do was to obtain the collection and make good on his delivery promise.

He went over his plan again, visualizing his movements: I can walk the beach, cut through the dunes, and make my way alongside the myrtles, coming out near the driveway on the oceanside. Simple. Getting in the house should be easy.

Upon leaving Dr. Jenkins' house last week, Thomas carefully made a mental note that Dr. Jenkins used only the latch to secure the front screen door on the porch. Also, the windows were *not* secured. One of them could be used as an entry if he had trouble with the screen door. During the evening Thomas had spent at Dr. Jenkins' house he was led to believe that Dr. Jenkins was not overly concerned about the security of his house. A small slit in the screen would get him onto the porch and from there all he had to do was gain entrance to the inside of the house, which should be easy enough. Should something go wrong like Dr. Jenkins suddenly waking up, subduing the older man in the dark with the element of surprise on Thomas' side should pose no problem.

Thomas waited until nearly 3:00 in the morning before leaving his home. It was no more than a ten- minute walk to Dr. Jenkins' house. *The Island is peacefully at rest with its residents sound asleep, including the police* Thomas thought.

He headed straight to the beach and turned right, headed toward the path at Station 10. From the beach, streetlights on the Island served as beacons marking the Stations. The path at Station 10 was easy to find. A fifty-gallon barrel that served as a trash container, compliments of the Fire and Rescue Squad, marked it. Slipping from the thick wax myrtles alongside the beach path, Thomas approached the house in a low crouched position, sometimes almost crawling, scooting along quietly and swiftly, a few feet at a time. Just as he had imagined, several windows were open with only a screen providing protection as they filtered the cool ocean breezes. Dr. Jenkins' house was situated on a small rise no more than two hundred yards from the beach with the closest neighbor a block away. He was isolated.

No floodlight. No moon. Good.

He made his way to the screen porch and to Thomas' surprise he didn't need the sharp penknife to cut the screen on the door. It was unlatched as if to say, "come on in." He eased himself onto the porch being extra careful not to disturb any porch furniture. As far as he could tell, everything was in its normal place, his eyes still adjusting to the dark. He slowly approached the front door, sliding sideways along the wall, ducking under the only window on the porch until he reached the front door. He slowly grasped the doorknob and gave it a try. He couldn't believe it. It turned. The door was open.

Moving like a cat stalking a sparrow, Thomas entered the house, leaving the door cracked just a tad. He stopped for a moment to gain his bearings and picture the layout: living room to the left, dining area to the right, kitchen in the right corner and the hallway off the living room leading to the bedroom and the collection.

It better still be there. It has to be.

He was aided by a small night light in the hallway, which eased his tension somewhat as his eyes made the necessary adjustment.

He breathed out ever so slowly. *So far so good. Go slow.*

He inched toward the hallway at a snail's pace being careful not to disturb anything. He felt his leg rub against something hard and smooth.

Stop, freeze. The coffee table?

He eased his leg away slowly, feeling with his hand ... it was the coffee table. *The big easy chair, the one Dr. Jenkins had sat in, should be across from the table.* He moved quietly with one arm outstretched in front of him. *Got it. Now go around easy.*

The nightlight in the hall was now of tremendous help as he entered the hallway itself and was just about to the bedroom with its door open when he heard a growl, a long, deep, low one, not some whining poodleish type whimper but a *real* growl. Thomas knew it came from a big dog. The sound came from the bedroom at the end of the hall, Dr. Jenkins' room, and the sound slowly moved closer, still low but growing in intensity.

He strained his eyes but couldn't see the source of the growl. *Oh hell. What now? Don't run ... keep calm ... think Thomas, think!*

Then he saw it. The large black head appeared first through the open door, teeth bared and hair raised on its back with a snarl that had "don't mess with me" written all over it.

What was needed *now* was some good quick thinking, and Thomas rose to the occasion like a Presidential candidate caught in a bind in a serious debate.

There's no way I'm gonna tangle with that dog.

Thomas knelt on one knee, extended an open hand, palm side up and in a whisper dripping with sweetness and brimming with prayer whispered, "Here boy, nice doggie. Good doggie. Wanna go to the beach?"

To Thomas' utter and complete surprise, "Dodger" quit growling, perked his ears, wagged his tail and headed directly for the screen porch. Thomas felt his heart begin to beat again as he backtracked, following "Dodger" and obligingly opened the screen door for the waiting dog who took off for the beach.

Where did he come from? Wasn't here last week.

Thomas stood where he was, took a couple of deep breaths, and listened. No noise. He made his way back down the hallway and carefully peeked around the corner of Dr. Jenkins' bedroom at the sleeping figure, presumably of Dr. Jenkins. Feeling relieved at seeing Dr. Jenkins still asleep, Thomas stealthfully moved to the other bedroom, the same room from which Dr. Jenkins had brought the collection last week. The ever-so-slight sound of his tennis shoes on the hardwood floors sounded like bombs going off to Thomas. He tried to walk on air realizing he was getting close to his goal.

Don't get jumpy now... Easy ... You're almost home.

The search ended quickly. The second place he searched … on his knees, and reaching under the bed … he felt the soft leather case.

All right! Got it. Now to get out of here.

He raised slowly, collection in hand when…

Thomas was startled by the click of the light switch and momentarily blinded by the immediate brightness in the room, but recovered quickly, turned, and to his dismay saw Steven Jenkins standing in the doorway with a pistol pointed directly at Thomas' head.

"Hello again Thomas. I've been expecting you but you're late. I thought you might have been here two or three days sooner."

" I … uh … uh… I don't understand. How did you know I was …"

"Was going to be here," said Dr. Jenkins finishing Thomas' statement. He added, "Later Thomas, later. We can go over all that. Relax. You don't have to say anything. I think the circumstances speak for themselves. And please take off that ski mask. You must be suffocating … and the gloves … nice touch," Steven Jenkins said in a calm but stern voice. "Now, just do as I say. Understand."

"Why Steven, what a surprise!" Thomas finally managed, trying to match Steven's aplomb. "Who invited you?" Thomas quickly surveyed the room looking for any avenue of escape.

"I live here. Remember?"

"Well," Thomas said half heartily, "I was just leaving." He couldn't believe the situation he found himself in.

"You're not forgetting something, are you?" Steven said indicating the collection.

"Oh that? I was going …" He tried to edge close enough to Steven so he could use the collection as a weapon.

"Whoa! Hold it right there. Not so fast, Thomas. Do exactly as I say and you might live until tomorrow. First, put the collection on the bed … very slowly … and then come with me," Steven ordered as he backed out of the room and clicked on the hall light. He was eyeing Thomas like a Momma duck. "That's good. Now move slowly and let's go to the front room and don't get cute."

Obediently Thomas went down the hallway toward the front room. Upon reaching the front room Steven ordered Thomas to lay on the floor on his stomach and extend his arms completely out in front of him. Steven turned on the table lamp and began his body search of Thomas.

"And don't move." Steven stood over Thomas and felt each pocket for any kind of weapon. Satisfied that Thomas had none he told him to sit on the couch.

"That's right, nice and easy, right there," Steven commanded. "Now, let's talk."

Again Thomas obeyed, warily eyeing the pistol, hoping for a chance at escape but Steven sat across from him in the rocking chair, just out of reach.

Steven began the discussion. "We have some business to discuss … shall we say, a little quid pro quo? You have something I want and I have something you want."

Thomas nodded knowingly and said, "Yeah, we both have coin collections."

"You're very quick to answer Thomas but that's not exactly what I had in mind. That's not what I'm thinking even though it's true … you have a collection and I have a collection …and we want each other's. But you're only half right. You have a collection that I want, but the thing I have is way more valuable than my collection. Know what it is?"

"No," Thomas asked hesitantly. "What?"

"Your life, that's what. Right now it's in my hands to do with as I please. The way I figure it I have two choices: one, I can shoot you right now and be completely within my rights, especially since you were sporting a ski mask, wearing rubber gloves, it's the middle of the night, *and* you were caught inside my house. What's a person to think running into someone dressed like that? Or two, I can let you go under the condition that you hand over your collection to me. It's your choice, Thomas. Your life or your collection. What will it be? And Thomas I must add that I want your *real* collection. You know the one I'm talking about?" He paused and studied Thomas' reaction.

Thomas did not flinch and said calmly, "And what collection are you talking about other than the one I showed you a couple of weeks ago?"

"I'll tell you this, Thomas. I'm not talking about that bunch of old coins you brought around here. I'm talking about your Standing Liberty Quarter collection, which will be a perfect complement to my collection. Now do you understand?"

"But … but …Thomas asked haltingly, "How do you know about my collection … I never said anything …"

Steven held up his hand to silence Thomas. "Never mind that. Let's just call it a lucky guess and leave it at that."

Thomas was in shock realizing that he was about to lose his prized collection.

"I … I … I don't know what to say." Thomas looked down, put his face in his hands and then slowly looked up and sighed, "I suppose I don't have much of a choice, do I?"

"No, you don't. But you know what … you brought all of this on yourself by being greedy, Thomas." Steven paused and smiled. "Greed, my good man, it'll do you in every time."

That's the last thing I need, Thomas thought ... *a damn lecture on greed.*

"Shall we go?" Steven gestured waving the pistol toward the door. "Nice and slow."

"To where?"

"Come on, Thomas. Get serious. To your house of course."

Thomas rose slowly with every intention of making a move for the gun but again Steven was cautious, keeping a safe distance. *If I can just get close enough ... I know I'm faster than he is,* Thomas thought. Steven led him to the driveway.

"My car, you drive and I'll sit in the back. If you try anything silly I'll shoot you and swear you were stealing my car. Understand?"

No answer.

Louder, "Understand?"

"Yeah."

"That's better. I always thought we communicated very well, didn't you Thomas? Never mind, don't answer that, just drive."

The doctor's talking was distracting Thomas as he tried to think. It was a short ride to his house and time was running out to do something. A real sense of urgency was coming on. *Don't panic, don't panic. Think,* he kept telling himself. *I've got to do something ... anything to distract him ... this nut might shoot me.*

"Steven," Thomas said evenly, "what do you say we combine our collections and sell `em. We split seventy-five/twenty-five and, of course, you get the seventy-five percent. That way we both come out OK, no one gets hurt or goes to jail. What do you say? A deal?"

Steven's quick reply bothered Thomas. Not so much the answer but its quickness like this man already had things planned out. "Forget it. Besides, I already made an offer to buy yours, remember?"

"You mean the night I was at your house? Thomas asked. "I didn't think you meant it."

"A-a-a-w, come on Thomas, be serious. How could you possibly have considered my offer when you had all of these other plans on your mind ... like tonight."

They were approaching the driveway at Thomas' house and he needed to stall for time. It was all he had left.

If we can't get in the house, he can't get the collection and the longer we stay out here the better chance someone might happen by or the police...

"What will I do without my collection?" Thomas asked. "It's the only valuable thing I own."

"The same thing I was going to do without mine, I guess," Steven said as he began to laugh. "I bet that thought never entered your mind now did it?"

Thomas caught a glimpse of Steven's smiling face from a passing streetlight and the evil he saw sent a chill down his spine. Thomas rolled to a stop still racking his brain for some way to distract his captor and make a move for the gun.

As they stepped from the car Thomas mockingly said in a loud voice, almost yelling, "I fail to see the humor." He looked to see if any of his neighbors' lights came on. He knew it was a feeble attempt because his nearest neighbor was nearly a block away. But it was his only hope.

He was about to try again when Steven interrupted, "Easy Thomas, not so loud. We wouldn't want to wake up anybody, now would we? And there's humor everywhere, my good man. All you have to do is look for it," Steven said with the same maniacal look on his face.

"Yeah right," Thomas said sarcastically. "I can't find a damn thing funny about any of this."

Steven stared hard at Thomas with wide bulging eyes. "You mean you can't find something funny about this situation? After all that planning and plotting and now you end up like this. You don't think that's funny? Thomas, if you take life too seriously it can kill you." He then smiled broadly waving the gun motioning Thomas to move.

"In that case, ha-ha," said Thomas, and for the first time tonight he feared for his life. "I can't find my keys," he said digging into his pockets, attempting to stall for time hoping Steven would make the mistake of trying to pat him down.

"Thomas, if you don't open that door in the next ten seconds I will shoot you. Do you understand?" Steven said in no uncertain terms. "I will shoot you dead."

Thomas pulled the jingling keys from his pants and began to unlock the door.

"That's better, now push the door open slowly and step inside," Steven said, "and don't try anything foolish."

Once inside Steven ordered Thomas to lay on the floor in the same way he did at Steven's house. Belly down and arms stretched out.

"Now," Steven said, "where are the lights?"

Once the lights were on, Steven instructed Thomas to walk to the kitchen in the rear of the house and secured him in a kitchen chair tying his hands behind him and his feet so tight he practically cut off the circulation.

"Nice place you have here, Thomas. Nice and cozy," Steven said. The evil look returned and Thomas simply dropped his head, afraid to look.

"Where's the collection?" Steven asked walking behind Thomas with a crazed look. "Where is it, Thomas? You damn thief."

No answer.

"Do you want to live? If so, you better talk and right now!"

"In the den," Thomas mumbled.

"Where in the den?"

"Over by the big chair, there's a cedar chest, look in there."

"Remember … no funny business." Steven headed quickly to the den, located the cedar chest and removed the collection, checking its contents on his way back.

In the couple of minutes of Steven's absence, Thomas struggled mightily, to no avail.

Steven reappeared carrying the collection in one hand and a sofa pillow tucked under his arm.

"Decision time again, Thomas. Do I let you go and live in fear …

or should I say in anticipation … of your next move, or do I kill you?" Steven didn't have to mention killing, his intentions were written all over him.

"Don't kill me, please. For God's sake don't do that. Whatever … don't shoot me. Please … I don't want to die … p-l-e-a-s-e don't …"

Steven Jenkins looked through Thomas, not hearing a word.

"I won't say a word. I promise," Thomas begged. "Don't shoot. Whatever, please don't shoot."

Steven circled behind Thomas positioning the pistol barrel no more than six inches from Thomas' head.

"Oh Thomas, Thomas, Thomas. The irony of life. Born a child, die a child. Come into the world with nothing, leave with nothing. And now a man's last words are that he promises not to talk."

He placed the pillow, acting as a silencer, next to Thomas' head, placed the gun firmly against the pillow, and gently squeezed the trigger, squeezing the life out of Thomas Poe.

The cleanup was thorough, everything was wiped down, especially where any prints could possibly be, and everything was put back in place, the den was checked just to make sure nothing was out of place. The kitchen floor took awhile to clean, but Steven was satisfied that after it dried it would appear normal. He even remembered to take the other matching sofa pillow from the den, not wanting to leave just one which might be a small clue but nevertheless a clue. He carefully laid the body in the newspaper-lined trunk of his car. Everything, except the body, in the trunk would be burned tomorrow in a pile of leaves waiting in his yard. Steven drove calmly to the landing.

High tide going out, no moon … everything on schedule … even Thomas had been so predictable.

He stopped, looked around, took Thomas from the trunk, waded out a few steps and with a shove let the current do the rest. The body floated for no more than a minute and sank into the darkness of Miller's Creek. Steven Jenkins felt relieved. He now had what he needed and there were no witnesses to Thomas Poe's death. He drove home slowly thinking only about destroying the remaining evidence. *I can't forget to burn the ski mask and the gloves,* he thought.

23
DISCOVERY

A loud drawn out ERK-A-ERK-A-E-R-R-R echoed from the backyard the moment the sun peeked over the horizon. He rested his vocal cords and let loose again … ERK-A-ERK-A-E-R-R-R … to let the whole Island know that a new day had begun.

"Rudy, I'm gonna wring your neck," is what I wanted to scream but could only manage a low groan, "Oh Rudy, whatcha doing? I was sleeping s-o-o-o good."

Rudy, the rooster, belonged to the Browns, a long-time Island family, who lived directly behind us. They were good neighbors. They still retained a country style of life from their backwoods' ancestors … unassuming, hardworking, and abundant in manners. They also retained a familiarity for farm animals. Our houses were separated by a huge grassy yard adorned with crape myrtle trees, enormous oleander bushes, palmetto trees and one solitary pecan tree. All of these trees and shrubs were placed exactly where they should be. The landscaping was perfect, compliments of Mother Nature just like the rest of the Island. The boundary line between our yards was a natural ten-foot tall barrier of honeysuckle vine and wisteria growing on an old wire fence, giving off a fragrance angels fought over.

Rudy had a harem of a dozen or so hens, which lent a certain barnyard flavor to the neighborhood. Recently four goats … Matthew, Mark, Luke and John … so named by Mrs. Brown who held a certain high affinity for the Lord, had been added and, as far as I could tell, for no obvious reason other than protection. They sure looked mean. But when Mrs. Brown wanted to add some pigs and casually mentioned it to my father, he drew the line, "Oh no! No pigs! Those smelly goats are enough." Being the neighborly folks that they were the Browns gave up on the pig idea.

In the springtime I would line up my grass-cutting customers the same way Bubba 'n me approached our crab customers, going door to door using the time-tested sales approach of asking and receiving a "yes" or a "no.' I learned quickly that a "maybe" or "let me think about it" was the same as a "no." I had pretty much cornered the grass- cutting market in my immediate neighborhood but had intentionally avoided approaching the Browns because their yard was huge and the smell of the goats was … well, it smelled like goats. On a windless, hot, summer, day things could get good and ripe in the Browns' yard and I didn't want to be trapped there in the boiling heat and humidity, holding my nose trying to mow the grass. My mother, however, insisted that I at least ask Mrs. Brown out of courtesy because Mrs. Brown knew I was in the grass-cutting business and they were our neighbors. Seeing that I presently had nine yards and adding one more would round out my rotation nicely, so I figured what the heck? It won't hurt to ask.

I caught Mrs. Brown one afternoon sweeping her porch. Not wanting to be too direct in my approach about cutting the yard I decided to make a little small talk with her. Kind of "loosen 'em up for the kill," like Bubba used to say.

"Afternoon, Mrs. Brown. How you doing?"

Mrs. Brown turned slowly toward me, looked up from her sweeping, stared at me and said, "I's fine. And you?"

Her slow and deliberate movements made it look like a real effort to even notice me. I was wondering how this almost hundred-year-old lady was going to be able to carry on a conversation? "Good, real good. I wanted to ask you something … if that's OK?"

"Goes right aheads. I's listening."

"I've been wondering. Why you got all those goats?"

The aging Mrs. Brown, stooped and bent, leaned heavily on her broom, looked up to heaven as for divine inspiration, then down at me from the top step and replied, "They is my friends. Theys keeps me company and you sees whats they doin'?"

I glanced in the yard and gave a quick examination of what the goats were doing and felt like I was in school answering a question.

"Yes Ma'am."

"What's they doin'?"

Mrs. Brown must have been a schoolteacher, I thought. She caught me off guard. I paused and looked at the goats again. I answered then, "They're eating the grass?"

"Xacly, that's wat goats do. That's they job."

What is she talking about, I thought. I knew humans had jobs but I'd never heard of goats having one. So I asked her, "The goats have a *job*?"

"Sho de does. They eats da grass sos I's donts has to pays nobody to cut it. Now you sees?"

Well, there goes my tenth yard but that's OK. Nobody else got it. I was beat out by goats, I thought. "Yes Ma'am," I exclaimed smiling, "like a lawn mower with legs."

A quizzical expression showed on her brown wrinkled face. "What you say?"

"Oh nothing, just trying to be funny."

"Oh," Mrs. Brown said with absolutely no emotion.

"I guess you save a lot of money not having to pay to have your grass cut?"

"Thas right, Mike." She bent over and squinted her eyes at me. "You is Mike ain't you? Be so many of them Devlin chillin' I's have a hard time keepin' ups wit 'em."

"Yes Ma'am, I'm Mike."

"Like I's sayin.' Saved a buncha money and I's gives it all to da church right chere on da Island. You knows what da good Lord says don't ya?"

Again I felt like I was in school. "Yes Ma'am, most of the time I think I do," I said nodding my head.

Mrs. Brown acted like she didn't even hear me, looking heavenward again, and yelled, "Wat goes round, comes round, dats wat da Lord say. Yes sir- ree! Glory Hallelujah!" She now had both hands up high swaying back and forth. "Whats you gives in life is whats yous gets back! Hallelujah!"

I could sense the mood of the conversation changing drastically.

"Well, it's been nice talking to you Mrs. Brown." I was looking for an excuse, even a lame one, to make a getaway before she launched into one of her legendary fire and brimstone sermons, which sometimes lasted for thirty minutes or more.

"I gotta go, Mrs. Brown. I gotta go do my chores … talk to you later."

"Y-e-a-h … sees ya later. Betta gets dem chores done fo yo Momma whips you beehind." She chuckled to herself, closed the screenless door and mumbled, "Dat boy donts know wat a cho'e is iffin it set on eh head."

One good thing about Rudy's daily repertoire was that he was a reliable alarm clock, but, of course, if Rudy overslept there was always my backup alarm…Bubba. And if I wasn't out the door in ten minutes he would be at the window, yelling and a carrying on.

I jumped out of bed and … *OOPS! My prayers.* I knelt down and began my daily ritual.

"Dear God, please bless the Devlin family. Thank You for all the things You give me. And please help us to catch some crabs today. Hail Mary full of grace … now and at the hour of our death. Amen. And please bless my friend Bubba … and Mollie too. Thank You, God. Amen."

I stepped into my threadbare khaki shorts and began to search for my lucky tennis shoes. Last time in the creek I hadn't worn them and that's probably why we had all that trouble. Not under the bed. Not in the pile of dirty clothes in the corner. *H-U-M-M. Where could they be?*

"Mollie, where's my shoes?" Mollie looked up and then plopped her head back down, not interested one bit in my lucky shoes.

"OK just wait 'till you want a bone. See if I get you one." She perked up for a second when she heard the word "bone" but when one didn't appear she flopped back down and went back to sleep.

Finally, the lucky shoes … white Chuck Taylor low cuts …appeared in the corner of the closet where I had thrown them after my latest bike crash, a really bad spill coming down the incinerator ramp full speed and clipping a low hanging tree limb with my face. Bubba thought it was funny and roared with laughter until he saw the blood gushing from my nose and cut lip. And the lucky tennis shoes still had little red stains all over the top of them.

We rarely wore a shirt because of the heat and lack of air-conditioning. About the only time we put a shirt on was when we went to church and at the dinner table, which was a requirement at our house.

"You boys will not only dress decent at the dinner table but you will also display good manners," my mother said. I heard that statement so many times it became ingrained in my consciousness.

In late spring when the temperature began to rise and we were seeking relief from the heat, the shirt came off when we got home from school everyday and didn't return until after Labor Day. By mid-June, Bubba 'n me were so darkly tanned we could almost pass for people of color, well, maybe not that dark, but certainly Hispanic.

Shoes were optional and were usually worn out of necessity, like today. We needed protection against whatever lay on the creek bottom … broken glass, rusted-out tin cans, or razor-sharp oyster shells. Or even a loose crab in the boat, which could do considerable damage to a naked foot. Crabs loved toes. However, if there were a formal meeting of the crew at Burton's we would wear *shoes* and a *shirt.* A formal meeting was one in which pretty girls were present.

It was embarrassing to wear new tennis shoes in public. The whiteness and newness was a symbol of prissiness indicating the wearer was somehow less of a man. Immediately, after the purchase of new shoes, usually in the spring, Bubba 'n me would slip down to Miller's Creek and perform our annual mud dance in our sparkling white shoes thus guaranteeing our manhood. We would go at low tide, wade across a knee- deep shallow, find a nice undisturbed section of pluff mud, and step right in sinking up to our knees. Many a time a shoe would slip off, left deep in the soft mud. The only means of retrieving it was to lean down sticking your arm up to your shoulder in the mud and feel around for it. If it hadn't been for the distinct odor of the pluff mud, something between fish and marsh grass, we would have stayed for hours because beneath the surface it was cool, almost cold and refreshing, and it was a challenge to try to walk in it without falling. When five or six of us got together to go bogging, a mud fight invariably broke out, and then the real fun began.

After the mud bath and a good rinsing with the hose, our shoes looked better and felt better. Besides, the smell of the pluff mud only lasted a few days. After a month's wear mine were perfect … stained dark from the dirt with a small hole worn above the big toe on each shoe. Of course, my shoes for social outings like bike riding, going to the beach or Burton's were my black, high-top Converse tennis shoes. I didn't have to worry about dirtying up those. I put them on right out of the box and wore them until they literally fell apart.

The final piece of my Island uniform was my frayed and faded New York Yankee baseball cap with the distinctive NY in big white letters embroidered on top. It was like Mollie … it went everywhere with me except to school and church. With my cap pulled down squarely just over my eyes, I was ready to go.

Bubba was waiting for me on our steps, net in hand and looking anxious.

"What took ya so long?" he asked. "I've been out here for five minutes."

I rolled my eyes at him. "Five whole minutes, huh? Eah, I had to say my prayers, man. Had to pray for you too. Don't want you to end up in hell. You couldn't go crabbing there … too hot … know what I mean?" I picked up the basket with the lines in it inspecting each one carefully without saying a word.

"Yeah, yeah, yeah," he said grinning. "It might be too hot in hell for crabbing but you know what's going to be the really bad thing about hell is Sister Rosalind chasing us around with the big ruler."

"Eah, you better watch your mouth, Padrig.Talking about a holy lady like that could get you a ticket to hell real quick," I said speaking his given name in a mocking tone. "And you know what else? She might be listening and hear you? Those nuns are everywhere, you know?"

"Enough of that, OK?" Bubba answered with a scowl. I could tell he was serious about not wanting to be teased about his name.

"OK, BUBBA!" I said with emphasis. "No more with the Padrig."

"Good," he said, then smiled at me. "Let's go. You can walk and talk at the same time … can't you Michael?"

"Yea, Pad …" I cut myself short not wanting to get into an argument with him about names… "Bubba," I said.

We walked across my backyard, into Bubba's yard when suddenly he stopped, looked at me and said, "S-h-h-h, listen, hear 'em?" as he cocked his head toward Miller's Creek while cupping his hand behind his ear.

"Yeah, yeah, I know, … they're taunting you again … right?"

"No man, they're saying we surrender, we surrender, we give up."

"Yeah, well good. Shoot, we'll take all the prisoners we can. Before we forget, we need another net."

"A net? Net?" he said, "Oh, we can get one from the Scotts."

"Aw right, let's go."

"Anything else, Mike?"

"Yeah, now that you ask. Something's been on my mind. I've been meaning to ask you. It's about Mollie."

"And what's that?"

"Can she go crabbing with us?"

"Mollie? You mean Mollie, Mollie … your dog?"

"Yeah that Mollie."

"A quick "No! Ain't no dog going crabbing. Not with me. Shoot, that would be worse than a girl going."

I understood completely my friend's feelings and agreed with him because I had only been kidding about taking Mollie crabbing.

"And besides," Bubba said smiling, "we don't have any crab lines that would fit her paws." And then he let out a huge laugh that set the tone for the day.

As we neared the road leading to the landing, I decided to do my latest imitation I had been working on. And who better to try it out on than my best friend? "Listen to this," I said and stopped to grab hold of the crab net to use as my prop. Grasping the end of the crab net handle like a microphone, clearing my voice, and acting like I was reading from a script, I launched into my best Curt Gowdy imitation. And now, ladies and gentleman, we come to you live from beautiful Sullivans Island, S.C. We are here covering the first ever-annual Island Open Crabbing Tournament. And before we go any further … the score is (a pause) Bubba 'n Mike … Forty-Eight! (A long pause.) Crabs …Z-z-z-e-r-o-o-o-o."

Bubba roared, "BA-HA-HA-HA-HA …BA-HA!"

Earlier I had noticed something different in the basket and had been waiting for Bubba to tell me what it was. Evidently he wasn't going to offer any explanation so as nonchalantly as I could I asked pointing in the basket. "What's that? Right there … that rope."

"Oh, that?" Bubba answered with a question.

"Yeah that."

"Oh, it's our new anchor line," he said as though he were noticing it for the first time. "Us real crabbers can't be using no old seat belt … know what I mean?"

"And I wonder where you got it?"

"U-u-u-h … I borrowed it from a nice old lady."

"Ms. Kingman? You mean you stole …"

"No, no, you didn't hear me. I said I borrowed it and hey, it's only about ten feet … she'll never miss it."

As usual I just shook my head and walked on.

After our initial embarrassment of not being able to handle the boat in the creek, we decided to try again with a modified plan, which meant we would paddle the boat instead of trying to row using the oarlocks. But first we needed an order for crabs, so we asked Mrs. Kimbrell who lived just down the block. She said, "Yes." And even though the order was for only two dozen, which wasn't much money, it would give us some more practice time in the boat to work on our rowing skills. As we were pedaling off from Mrs. Kimbrell's, we noticed Mr. Barber, her neighbor, emptying his trash.

Bubba circled back. "Come on Mike, there's Mr. Barber, maybe he wants some crabs?"

"N-a-a-w, he's from New York. He don't know nothing about crabs."

"Eah … you never know, man. Let's ask him. And besides," Bubba said as he poked me on the shoulder … "the worst thing he can say is no."

We coasted to a stop by the garbage cans. "Hey there, youse guys, whatcha up to?"

Even though he was one of those people from up north … "them damn Yankees" the locals called them … I liked Mr. Barber because he was friendly and always had a big smile on his face. Plus he pulled for the Yankees, my team.

"Oh not much, just riding around," Bubba said. "How you been? Where's Pete?"… His son and our classmate.

"He's in the city with his Mom."

"Yeah, ain't nothing like going into the city with your Mom. I do it all the time myself," Bubba said obviously lying.

Mr. Barber acknowledged Bubba's remark with a nod, looked at me and asked, "What did Mantle do yesterday, Mike?" (referring to only the greatest player ever and my favorite, the legendary Mickey Mantle)

"Two for four, homer and a double, and three runs batted in." I answered a lot quicker than I ever did in school.

"Just checking," he said with a smile. "How about you Bubba, what'd you do yesterday?" Mr. Barber joked.

Not being a baseball fan Bubba was momentarily stumped like he was stumped in school all the time."U-u-u-h… u-u-u-h…" then he blurted out, "forty-eight to nothing … yeah, forty-eight to nothing."

"Forty-eight to nothing? Wow!" Mr. Barber said. "You must have hit a lot of grand slams?"

"Oh yeah, hit a whole bunch of grand slams, a whole bunch." He paused for a moment, grew serious and said, "Mr. Barber, Mike 'n me are trying to earn some money and save it so we can go to college someday and we are selling crabs that we catch for twenty-five cents a dozen. It's our only way of making money and I was wondering if you would want to buy a dozen from us?"

My friend had been watching too much TV. That was the only thing I could think after hearing all that baloney. I wondered just how far Bubba would take it so I just folded my arms, sat back, and listened.

"That's nice Bubba, youse guys working to save money for college and all but what would I do with a bunch of crabs? I don't even know how to cook 'em and I know the wife doesn't want to mess with 'em."

"Eah, Mr. Barber don't worry, I'll show you how to cook 'em. Tell you what. If you buy 'em not only will I help you cook 'em, I'll show you how to pick 'em. I know I won't have to show ya how to eat 'em." Bubba laughed. "How about it? We'll bring 'em by this afternoon, OK?"

Mr. Barber looked at us and we smiled wishfully.

"O-o-o-h, all right, I'll try 'em. Put me down for a dozen."

"Oh, thank you, Mr. Barber. Thank you. Well, we gotta go … see ya later," I said amazed at Bubba's salesmanship.

"Yeah thanks." Bubba added. "Bye."

Just as we started to ride off Bubba stopped and yelled at Mr. Barber retreating into the yard. "Mr. Barber!" Mr. Barber turned around and Bubba said, "I didn't really hit all those grand slams. Their pitcher was real wild and walked in all those runs."

Mr. Barber waved us away with a big smile.

On the ride home I was curious and asked Bubba, "Are you serious about showing Mr. Barber how to cook crabs and all? That's a lot of trouble."

"Yeah man, and with you helping … you will help … won't you?" Bubba gave me the hangdog look hoping for a "yes" which I signaled with a nod of my head. "All right now! With the two of us it won't be any trouble at all. Shoot, we can fix him up with a pot of crabs in no time. Just like that." He clicked his fingers real loud. "And after he eats a few he'll love 'em. Next thing you know he'll be wanting some more. And then he'll tell a neighbor and then they'll call us and we got ourselves another customer."

"Got it all figured out, huh?"

"No not everything, just the part about crab customers. It's kind of like girls, Mike. You get one girlfriend and she tells another girl how nice you are and then …"

"I know, I know. And the next thing you know you she calls you up for some crabs? A-HA-HA-HA-HA!" I said. "Lets go Curley, the crabs are hungry and waiting."

"See ya later alligator," Bubba said as he wheeled ahead of me. "KNUCK- KNUCK-KNUCK!"

My father always used a checklist before going out in the boat just to make sure we had the essentials once we got on the water.

"If you leave something home and get in a fix out on the water there's no store you can go to and buy what you need," he told me as part of my training.

Bubba 'n me had set up a similar system whereby I was the checker and he was the checkee.

"Let's see," I asked, "got the basket?"

"Check."

"Six lines?"

"Check."

"Sinkers and bait?"

"Check. Do we gotta do this?" Bubba moaned.

"Anchor and new anchor line stolen from Mrs. Kingman?"

"Check. Check."

"Nets?"

"No check. Only have one net. Got to go to the Scotts and get the other one. Billy said he would leave it outside by the shed."

"Need anything else?" I asked.

"Nothing but your brains. Got those in there?" Bubba asked looking in the basket.

"Check. Got mine but I don't see yours."

"Of course you don't. They're in my head not in a basket with smelly chicken necks, BA-HA-HA-HA!"

After picking up the net in the Scott's backyard we headed for the landing at Miller's Creek.

Bobby Graham's boat was right where we left it last week, untouched it seemed, bobbing in the refreshing westerly breeze, water lapping against its side, sounding like the clippity-clop of miniature horses.

We were intentionally a little early for the tide, not wanting to rush and hurry into another mistake in our haste to catch crabs. We would take our time launching. It also gave me a chance to admire one of my favorite scenes … the marshland. This setting was nature at its purest with the winding creek and green marsh grass extending for miles. Its backdrop in the west were the tall church steeples of Charleston, the "Holy City," and at sunset there was never a more glorious setting. To the east the marshland ran right up to the tree line of the Island making the trees look like they were emerging from the marsh. And just as glorious as the sunset was the sunrise illuminating through the trees sending split light rays across the marsh.

No matter how many trips I made to the creek it never looked the same twice, each time it was more awe inspiring.

Bubba snapped me back to reality. "Let's go, boy! Them Jimmies are waiting."

"Yeah, OK, I'm coming. And today," I announced, "We will *paddle* the boat, no rowing. And don't push us off until I say so. OK?"

"Yes sir, Captain Fartingsnot," Bubba said standing at attention mocking a salute. "Anything else, sir?"

"Yeah, you learn to salute better or you'll get thirty lashes with a wet noodle, you-u-u-u dir-r-r-t-y r-a-a-t." It was my best James Cagney imitation.

"Whoa, that's bad, man. Real bad. Eah, you better stick with the Curt Gowdy, my friend, OK?" Bubba remarked pinching his nose with his fingers. He was my truest critic.

The single most important thing we had learned from our atrocious maiden voyage of last week was that you do not go crabbing on a flood (outgoing) tide. If trouble did arise, like it did with us, we could have easily been swept out to sea. From now on we would go crabbing on an ebb (incoming) tide. If something went wrong now, at least, the tide would carry us back toward the landing and safety. Also, I found out from my father that an incoming tide brings more crab *in* than an outgoing tide takes *out*. Made sense to me.

Without having to contend with a boiling ebb tide this time and fueled with the added confidence we had gained in our infamous first outing, we made the transition from rookie to novice seaman a much smoother one. Also, we were paddling the boat together, not fighting each other's strokes, like when we tried to row.

"Paddling sure beats rowing, huh?" I commented.

"Yep, sure does. By the way, guess you'll have to go see Sambo soon?"

"Why? What for?"

"To get back the money you paid him for your rowing lessons. BA-HA-HA-HA-HA!"

"V-e-r-y funny, I said with a sneer. "Har-dee, har, har."

"Eah, wanna try the same spot by the pipe?" Bubba asked, not sounding very convincing.

"Yeah," I said in the same tone, "and if they're not biting there we can try over there by that pole," gesturing toward a tall wooden pole sticking out of the water like some kind of homemade channel marker. It looked like the work of one of the Scotts. We paddled up to it and Bubba grabbed hold of it, giving it a few good tugs, and announced that it was firmly anchored, like in concrete.

"Let's just leave it there," I suggested. "We can use it as a marker."

"Good idea."

I had yet to tell Bubba about the pipe being part of the sewage drainage system and so after we had anchored upwind as my father had suggested. I figured it was as good a time as any to tell him what the crabs were feeding on.

Bubba casually remarked, "Eah, man. It don't matter to me what they eat as long as we catch crabs." A few silent minutes passed.

"Mike?"

"What?"

"Do you think we can find another sewer pipe?" Bubba asked smiling.

"I dunno. I think there's only one but I'll ask Dad tonight."

It wasn't long and we were anchored, set up, lines out and ready for some serious crabbing. Within five minutes the action began, fast and furious again, but now we had two nets and didn't have to pass the one net back and forth or wait to use it. My three lines were straight out from the boat and it wasn't the current carrying them. We had hit a hot spot. Bubba was hauling 'em two at a time and his other two lines were under the boat, pulled there by some big Jimmy hoping to enjoy his meal in the shade. Shoot, they probably had a big picnic table set up down there loaded with refreshments and now with a smelly chicken neck to gnaw on, they thought they were in high cotton.

"Come on Jimmy, that's it, nice and easy, hang on just another second, there you go," Bubba said as he slipped the net under another one. He liked talking to his catch as he pulled 'em in and when I asked him about it he said, "Cause they don't talk back like some people I know." He grinned.

"Two more. That makes eleven," I said loudly and defiantly in a response to a previous lecture about keeping the correct count.

"Eah, leave the counting to me, OK?" Bubba said. "You done failed arithmetic twice."

"All right, if that's the case, then leave the talking to me cause *you done* failed English every time since… let's see, u-u-u-h… since kindergarten, right? How bad is that?"

It was a sensitive subject with Bubba and I knew I was on shaky ground.

Bubba lashed out, "Let me tell you one thing about speaking right." There was a long pause. "Eah, what's wrong with you? You listening to me, Mike? You all right?" Bubba was staring at me. "Eah, I'm talking to you. You hear?"

I was staring at Bubba. My mouth was open but no words were coming out. I did manage to point behind him and mutter a jumble of words that should have said, "There's a dead body floating behind you" but it came out as gibberish and totally incomprehensible.

"What? What'd you say?" Bubba asked tentatively. I scared him with the way I was acting and with the look on my face. "Hey, Mike," Bubba asked sincerely, "Are you all right?"

I took a deep breath and told myself to calm down and I added a quick, "Dear God, help us." Then I managed to stammer, "B-e-hind y-o-u

… look." I was pointing in the water near the bow of the boat.

Bubba turned and saw the crab-infested body of Thomas Poe half floating, half bobbing face down, no more than ten feet away.

"WHOA! What the hell!!" Bubba screamed. " OH MAN! I ain't believing this!"

"Let's go! Let's get outta here," Bubba yelled and then scrambled from the bow to the middle seat. "Come on, Mike, let's go!" Bubba reached for the anchor line.

"Wait a second, wait a second. Hold on, don't get all shook up." I was trying to think. "Bubba, we got to do something, man." I shot a quick look at the body and decided it was a man judging from its size and the short hair. "We can't just leave him here."

"Oh yeah, why not?" Bubba said like a frightened child. "Look he moved. Let's go!"

The body of Thomas Poe bounced with the current several times in a life-like attempt at rescue, then floated closer to the boat.

"I know." Really I didn't but I had an idea. "Throw a crab line on him and … u-u-u-h… u-u-u-h …" I stuttered, "and maybe we can pull him closer to the boat."

"Then what?" Bubba said in jest. "Net it?"

"No." But Bubba did give me an idea. "Get the net ready, OK?"

"P-H-E-W-E-E … the smell …man, he stinks." Bubba was holding his nose. " Get the net and what?"

"Use the net to hold him still and maybe you can tie the anchor line on him?"

"What? Me? Uh-uh.You mean, maybe *you* can tie the anchor line on him. I ain't touching no dead body. You hear … no dead body!" Bubba said emphatically. "Uh-uh. Not me."

"OK, OK, scaredy cat. Get the net and … no, never mind use the oar and pull him over this way and I'll tie the anchor line on him."

"Now you talking, Daddy-o!" Bubba said quickly.

"Here goes nothing." Bubba stood up and stretched as far as he could with the oar making contact with the corpse's leg.

"Oh no, I can't do it. I can't touch a dead person … it's nasty," Bubba said trying to pull the half submerged body toward the boat. "I don't think this is gonna work, Mike."

"Wait a second. I know what we'll do." I couldn't believe how clearly I was thinking at a time like this. "Let's tie him to the sewer pipe and then go get help. Find Lumus or somebody," I suggested. "Untie the anchor from the anchor line and we can use the rope." I paused. "Wait a minute. Better yet." I handed Bubba the knife we used for rigging lines. "Just cut the anchor line down by the anchor. Understand?"

"Yeah, yeah. I gotcha."

Bubba began cutting. "Good idea, my friend. Good idea. Are *you* still gonna tie the rope on him?"

"Yeah, yeah, yeah. If you can hold it right there with the oar for a second I'll tie the anchor line around the sewer pipe first?"

"OK, I'll try to hold it … P-H-E-W-W-W-W. But hurry … Oh man, this guy stinks."

I looped the anchor line around the pipe, tightened it, and pulled out the slack

"Hang on Bubba … almost done."

"You gonna tie the rope on him?" Bubba pleaded again. "You said you would, remember."

"I told you I would. Just calm down, will ya? Good grief. It ain't gonna bite you." As I got closer I inhaled the smell of death. "You're right … he stinks."

I managed to slip the rope around an ankle without touching the body (just the thought scared the hell out of me), and tightened the line on the soft flesh and then tossed the line in the water very quickly. We watched for a second as the body bobbed up and down with the rope on his ankle. We didn't say anything except for a few grunts and groans originating somewhere from between shock and disgust as we paddled back to the landing.

Just as the bow of the boat touched land Bubba jumped on the bank, turned, looked at me and asked, "Mike, did you see what I saw?" I knew exactly what was on his mind.

"Yeah," I said slowly and disgustingly, "all those crabs eating on him."

24
THE SEARCH

"Stay here with the stuff and I'll go get somebody!" I said jumping from the boat. We were both scared but I wasn't going to give Bubba the chance of going for help and leaving me behind at the landing alone. I had visions of dead people rising up out of Miller's Creek and coming after me.

"All right but hurry," Bubba said hesitantly. Then added, "Eah, what about the crabs …"

His words faded quickly. I was gone in a flash.

I made a beeline up the dirt road. My feet flew across the dusty road as I headed for Back Street leaving a whirlwind behind me like the roadrunner on TV being chased by Wiley Coyote. I ran down Back Street and in a flash tore through Mrs. Brown's back yard ducking wet towels and sheets hanging limply in the July heat. I did not know exactly where I was headed except in the direction of home and ran mostly out of fright now that what we had discovered began to sink in. A dead man in Miller's Creek. And he was all puffy looking and smelled and… o-o-o-h… it was bad.

What am I gonna do? Call the police, I guess? I thought as I neared our house.

Luckily Sissy happened to be home. She was the self-appointed guardian, disciplinarian and peacekeeper amongst the kids in the family. She was on the back porch, doing her thing: setting up small tables and chairs in the form of school desks, getting ready to teach her imaginary class. We often teased her referring to her as Sister Sissy as in nun, but she didn't seem to mind and would simply go about her business with her towel adorning her head representing a nun's habit. Of course, she held a long stick in her hand she used to point at and whack her invisible students with. I scrambled up the steps completely out of breath, pointing back toward the landing and trying to formulate my words in my mind and talk at the same time. Nothing came out.

Sissy practiced her nun look on me and asked sternly, "In trouble again? Who's chasing you this time … Chief Perry?"

I managed an emphatic, "No, no, oh no! Nobody!" I paused. "Bubba

’n me found a … we found a …”

I took a deep breath and tried to slow everything down. But I’m thinking, “ain’t no way she is gonna believe this.” Finally, I blurted out, “Bubba ’n me found a dead man in the creek.”

Sissy stared at me just like Sister Roberta. It’s a look somewhere between disbelief and I’m gonna wring your neck, you little troublemaker.

“What did you say?” she demanded. “You found a what?”

“A dead man,” I repeated. “You know, somebody who ain’t breathing.”

Sissy stood rigidly, hands on hips looking down at me hard. “I know what dead means. Now what are you talking about …When? Where?” she asked.

“A little while ago. Bubba ’n me were crabbing. Where’s Mom?” I was jumping around and nervously glancing from Sissy back to the door. I wanted to get back to the landing as soon as I could. *Why I don’t know?*

“She’s in Mt.Pleasant. Now calm down and tell me exactly what happened.”

“OK, here’s what happened.” It was beginning to seem like I spent half my life explaining things that happened. “Bubba ’n me were crabbing in Miller’s Creek and a body floated up … by the boat … we were in Bobby Graham’s boat.”

“OK, then what happened?” Sissy was skeptical. I could tell because I had seen that same look on many adults’ faces before.

“We, well Bubba did, he used the net and kind of moved it so we could tie it up. I did the tying to the end of the sewer pipe. The one in the creek back by the landing.” I was talking fast, not sure if I was making sense or not. Sissy was nodding her head but still not fully convinced that I was telling the truth.

“Where’s Bubba?”

“At the landing,” I said, “He’s with the boat and guarding the crabs.”

Sissy gave me a deadly stare and said, “Let me get this straight. A dead man floated up in the creek by you and Bubba and you tied it to the sewer pipe. Right?”

I nodded.

She went on, “You’re not telling me another one of your wild tales, are you? Putting me on like the story of the wrecked cars last year? Remember?”

I was kind of mad that she didn’t believe me but I couldn’t much blame her because too many times she had been the butt of me ’n Bubba’s pranks.

“No Sissy, this is for real … Scout’s honor … honest Injun!” I held up three straight fingers together making the Boy Scout salute even though I wasn’t in the Scouts.

"OK, OK. I believe you, but if you're lying you're in for double trouble. You understand? This is a serious matter." She paused giving me a long look and said, " I'll call Chief Perry."

"Okey-dokey, slow pokey," I answered, knowing she hated that kind of talk.

"Don't start that …" She headed for the phone.

"OK … I'm going back to the landing," I yelled bolting off the back porch, taking four steps in one leap.

Now that the initial shock of the gruesome discovery began to wane, this tragedy was becoming an adventure. I envisioned the headlines in tomorrow's paper as I retraced my steps to the landing. " Island Boys Discover Body" or maybe "Bubba 'n Mike --- Local Heroes." Hey. This was heady stuff for a young Island boy.

Bubba was sitting on one of the big rocks at the water's edge that formed a kind of seawall, glancing nervously over his shoulder down the creek as if the dead body were suddenly going to come to life, sneak up on him and grab him.

"That was quick," he said, "who'd you talk to?"

"Sissy," I said between gasps for air. "At first she didn't believe me but then she did."

"Man, let's hope so." Bubba said between bites on his fingernails.

I breathed deep and tried to calm myself down and then tried to calm Bubba who seemed more upset than me by this whole ordeal. He was beginning to rub his hands together real fast and a couple of those weird sounds slipped out. I didn't go into detail about the conversation with Sissy but slipped up when I said that she called Chief Perry and he would be here anytime now. I had planned to wait and let Bull Perry show up rather than alarm Bubba ahead of time. When I mentioned Chief Perry's name, the hand rubbing and noises accelerated and his face took on the appearance of someone about to have serious root canal work done by a rookie dentist.

"Whatta we gonna do?" he asked. "Whatta we gonna do, huh?"

"Gosh Bubba, I don't know? I've never found a dead body before. I guess we just …"

"No, no, not that. The crabs and stuff and the *boat*, I mean. When Bull Perry and Lumus show up. Man, we could get in trouble about the boat and …"

I interrupted him, "Bubba. Eah, look. We tied a dead body to the pipe, remember? Lumus and the Chief got other things to worry about other than an old boat … like a dead man! You understand? Lumus doesn't care if we used a boat. But I know what you mean, my friend. It's Bull Perry I'm worried about … that man scares me too."

We were sitting on a big rock throwing the smoothest flat rocks we could find along the flat surface of Miller's Creek. It was an unofficial rock-skimming contest. However, it was not near enough activity to break the tension gripping us so I decided to try some humor on my friend to ease his worriment and mine.

"Eah, if you look up the word "mean" in the dictionary you know what you'll find?"

"No, what?"

"A picture of Bull Perry." Bubba didn't share a laugh with me. I tried again. "He's so mean I heard that when he was in the war he killed ten Germans with only five bullets," I said hoping to get a rise out of my friend.

"Oh yeah, how?"

"He shot five of 'em and then looked at the others real mean like and scared 'em to death. A-HA-HA-HA!"

"Yeah, that's right, that's right. They got other stuff to worry about like a dead man," Bubba was mumbling trying to reassure himself. He wasn't even listening to me.

We heard the faint sound of Chief Perry's siren in the distance as it screeched and hollered like a crying baby trying so hard to sound official. It was coming from the business district near Station 23. I didn't even know he had a siren. Never heard it before. I guess this is as serious as it gets.

We stood up and looked toward Back Street anxiously awaiting the arrival of Bull Perry.

"Eah, tell you what," Bubba said, "when I get to be the police chief I'm gonna blow that siren *all* the time."

"What for?"

"I don't know … just am. Wanna bet he was at the doughnut shop?" Bubba wagered.

"N-a-a-w, I'd lose that one for sure."

We both knew Chief Perry had a thing for food. I guess it was more than a thing. It was more like a love affair. And his main lover was the doughnut. The man had never met a doughnut he did not like. My father said that Bull Perry loved 'em so much he even ate the hole out of the doughnut and one look at his well-rounded stomach said that there was some truth to that statement. The Chief single-handedly kept Frannies, our local bakery, in business but who could blame him. The sweet aroma of freshly baked cinnamon buns coated with a gooey sugary glaze and the smell of fresh baked homemade bread permeated the Island every morning like clockwork. It was rumored that Chief Perry opened and closed Frannies licking the tips of his fingers.

My older brother, Ryan, in a very earnest tone and with a straight face, once told Bubba 'n me that we shouldn't tease about Chief Perry, calling him Bull Perry and all that, because the poor man probably didn't have much longer to live due to his illness.

"What's wrong with him," Bubba asked.

As serious as a heart attack, Ryan said, "You didn't know he has Dunlap disease?"

"Uh-uh. Dunlap disease, what's that?"

Ryan deadpanned, "He's so fat, his stomach "Done Lapped" over his belt," and then he let out a hearty laugh.

"Very funny, HA-HA," I laughed sarcastically not wanting Ryan to know he had gotten us again … he was good at that.

"Bull Perry …Dunlap disease," I said to myself. Actually, I couldn't wait to use that line on the crew at Burton's someday.

The police car was a surplus WWII Ford, black with four doors and officially marked on one side in white lettering with the word POLICE. It was the old three-speed on the column model but as slowly as Chief Perry drove I don't think it had seen third gear in ten years and the only thing holding it together was a hope and a prayer. It turned the corner at Station 19, making good time, crossed Back Street and fought the good fight against the many potholes before stopping by us at the landing in a cloud of dust. Maybe it found third gear today.

The Chief was driving with Lumus riding shotgun, which was rare. Lumus usually worked the night shift. Chief must have needed help polishing off that last dozen of chocolate covered doughnuts.

We overheard the end of the Chief's radio conversation as he gave us the eye. I immediately looked the other way, not wanting to look at Bull Perry eyeball-to-eyeball. I had always thought Sister Roberta had the evilest of the evil eyes until last summer when I had the unfortunate circumstance of meeting Bull Perry face-to-face in an eye-to-eye encounter at Owen's Grocery. It was purely a chance meeting in the grocery line as I waited to pay for the bread. He wasn't mad at me, couldn't have been, because I hadn't even spoken to him. He just glanced my way for a second making eye contact and spooked me so badly I jumped backward five feet. Some people refer to eyes that chill you as dead eyes. Not his, uh-uh. They were very much alive eyes that said, "I'm going to get you." Small and beady but intense.

"No, no, I repeat no! Don't bring the cavalry and for God's sake leave the fire truck at the station," Bull Perry barked out in a loud voice. "There ain't no fire. You hear me… there ain't no fire!" He paused for a second. "Yeah, we'll call if we need ya. Humph, damn idiots." Then he frowned and slammed the radio handle back into its holder.

He rolled out of the driver's seat with a pained look as his stomach fought with the steering wheel for space while Lumus strolled around the front of the car giving us a more comforting look. Bull Perry grabbed his slouching pants and tugged mightily to get them over his stomach. He failed. Then he adjusted his hat as though he were going into combat and with a jaw set as firm as stone marched toward us. I couldn't help but notice the similarity between Chief Perry and Lumus … and Laurel and Hardy on TV. The only prop the Chief needed was the black derby that Ollie wore and if Lumus were a tad shorter they would come real close to being look-a-likes. It was to be my last humorous thought of the day.

In a harsh voice that matched his gruff personality Chief Perry stared at Bubba'n me and growled, "What's this nonsense about a body?"

God, I pray we hadn't interrupted a meal?

"Well, don't just stand there," he commanded. "Speak up!"

It was one of those moments suspended in time and burned into the memory. All I could see was Elvis Presley on a stage somewhere, grinding his hips and swaying back and forth and just a singing his heart out … "Shaking like a leaf on a tree, I'm all shook up, Mm mm mm, mm, yeah, yeah!, I'm all shook up."

Bubba nudged me in the side hoping I would speak and handle this situation like I'd done many times before. Shoot, I was afraid to talk and Bubba didn't know what to say so we just stood there, looking down at the dirt, which we were nervously kicking at. Subconsciously we were probably hoping to dig a hole deep enough to crawl into and hide.

Lumus sensing our apprehension attempted to lighten the mood, "Just tell us what you saw, the best you can, that's all."

What the heck, I thought, *we haven't done anything wrong. Well, at least, not this time.* And that's what was preying on our minds: all the mischief we had gotten into and all the trouble we had caused in the past had caught up with us and now we might have to "pay the piper" as my father always said. "Well shucks, if that's the case then … here goes."

I spoke up, "We found a body … a dead body. Down there in the creek … down by the big pipe," pointing in that direction.

"Yeah, he was dead," Bubba chimed in. "Kind of floating."

"How long ago?" demanded Chief Perry. This man didn't talk. His words came out in a gravely sequence with a menacing tone like a baby volcano erupting.

"About ten, maybe fifteen minutes ago, sir, Mr. Perry." *Kiss butt, maybe that'll work?*

"Well which was it son," he bellowed "ten or fifteen minutes ago?"

So much for butt kissing. "Ten. It was ten minutes ago," I answered shooting a glance at Bubba. *Come on Bubba. Jump in anytime, my friend.* I looked at Bubba again and knew I was whistling in the dark.

Then came the voice of Lumus, quiet and matter-of-fact as if in general conversation. "Where did you first see the body?"

Bubba, the smart one, decided he was brave enough to talk to Lumus. "Well Lumus, sorry Mr.Lumus. You see, we were in Mr. Graham's boat with his permission, of course." Bubba paused to see if his lie was accepted and breathed out when Lumus said, "I see, go on."

"And well, this dead body just came floating up to the boat. It stunk real bad and …"

"Wait a minute," Lumus broke in, "you said floating up. Did it come off the bottom of the creek and pop up all of a sudden or did it come floating down the creek?"

"I don't know," Bubba said looking to me, "Mike, you saw it first … right?"

The Chief looked at me and began to speak but I took a big risk and cut him off before he could get a word out. "It was kind of like it came from the bottom but real slow. I mean it didn't pop up real fast like WHOOM and it was there."

"I see," Lumus said rubbing his chin and in thought.

"And where is it *now*?" barked Bull Perry.

"It's at the end of the sewer pipe," Bubba said. "We tied it there."

"Tied it how?" Lumus asked.

"With the anchor line," I said. "We tied it to the pipe."

Lumus told us, "Good work, boys," as he walked over to huddle with Chief Perry.

Bubba 'n me thought we were finished so we grabbed our basket and net and started to walk off. Finished or not we just wanted to get away from Bull Perry.

"Eah, hold it right there, boys. Where you think you're going?" the Chief yelled. "We might have some more questions for you. Stay right there!"

"Uh, nowhere … we were just … u-u-u-h … checking our stuff … yes sir," I answered giving Bubba the eye to set the basket down. The way he was clutching the basket handle I think he was ready to make a run for it.

Chief Perry frowning said to Lumus, "Damn! I hate like hell to have to do this but how about call the Coast Guard and wake those people up. Tell 'em we need the fifteen- footer, the one with the motor over here now. And to move their butts! If they want to know what for don't tell 'em anything. Just tell 'em to get over here and don't take all day about it either."

Bubba whispered to me, "Eah, what are we gonna do with the crabs?"

"The crabs? I don't know," I answered in a tone that said I-don't-really-care. "Why don't you eat 'em?"

"Well, they're going to die soon … we gotta do something."

"Eah, do whatever you want. I don't care."

Bubba walked over to the car, poked his head through the open window, and asked Lumus, "Would it be OK to let the crabs go? They're almost dead."

"Sure, dump 'em back. Maybe y'all catch 'em again sometime?"

"Thanks, Lumus," Bubba then whispered very quietly to Lumus, "hey, what's with Chief Perry? He seems a little ticked off about something."

Lumus looked toward the Chief to make sure the coast was clear, raised a finger to his lips, and said quietly, "S-h-h-h." Bubba nodded. He understood completely.

"What was all that about?" I asked, "with you and Lumus."

Bubba winked at me, raised his finger to his lips, and said, "S-h-h-h."

The U.S.Coast Guard Station was no more than three blocks away, situated on the front row overlooking the beach and staffed with a crew of ten full-time U.S. Coastguardsmen. It was a large two-story building with its own machine shop, warehouse, living quarters, and a beautifully manicured lawn, which stretched all the way to the sand dunes. The whole complex was immaculately maintained according to Government regulations and was, it seemed, never without a fresh coat of paint. The young men serving there had unconsciously and luckily drawn a duty that most servicemen only dreamed of. Their work hours were minimal, when they worked at all; they had their own room, and three good meals a day, including all the ice cream they could eat which was kept in a big cooler in five gallon containers, all flavors. They also enjoyed the Island's best vantage spot for girl watching. While on guard duty in the tower high atop the station, overlooking the Atlantic Ocean, which they were supposed to be protecting, they spent more time searching the beach for eligible young ladies than eyeing the coast for any potential dangers. Not only did they have the use of binoculars, they had access to a powerful telescope, the use of which I'm certain, its inventor Mr. Galileo had intended for viewing other celestial bodies. At the end of their tour of duty many re-upped specifically requesting to be stationed on Sullivans Island. Some even re-upped after re-upping. Most were from out of state and from big cities, and landing here was a pleasant surprise. They were a happy and friendly lot and got along with all the locals … well, *almost* all the locals.

Two baby-faced Coastguardsmen, not a minute over twenty, came bouncing down the lumpy landing road in a new U.S. Jeep, complete with a radio and a new top with a fifteen footer in tow. There was a visible aura between the Coastguardsmen and Chief Perry and it was not one of friendliness. The new equipment of the Coast Guard was just another reason for the Chief to show his displeasure for them. They were wearing Government Issue bluejeans that they had cut off and made into shorts. They wore these frayed shorts with white tee shirts rolled up with a pack of Luckies secured snugly in place under the shirt at the shoulder. They wore their bleached white sailor hats cocked on the back of their heads James Dean style. And their sunglasses and tennis shoes really set off their appearance. They really looked cool.

Recognizing each other we waved "hellos" while greetings and smiles filled the humid air except for the frowning Chief Perry who stood silent, arms folded like a statue, which has just been abused by a dog. As usual, he was all business and had gone against every fiber of his being in calling for their help.

"What's happening, youse guys?" Danatagilio asked in his thick Brooklyn accent. "Hey Lumus. Who's that? Bubba and Mike? Hows youse guys doing?"

We nodded and smiled. He paused and said, "Hello, Chief."

Danatagilio was talking fast and we had to listen hard just to keep up with him. He was one of the more outgoing of the group, always flashing a wide smile and talkative as a magpie. It was amusing to hear him talk because Allie, Alberto Danatagilio, wanting to fit in, tried so hard to sound like a Southerner but there was no way he'd ever fool anyone, not with his heavy accent. It would be like Bubba or me trying to sound like a New Yorker …coming out something like "Eah, y'alls guyse," but only in a slow drawl.

Chief Perry stood just looking at Danataligio, not saying a word, contempt showing on his face.

Helping Danatagilio was Matthew Jorgensen from a place called Minnesota. He was the quiet one, not so much out of choice but it was hard to get a word in edgewise with Danatagilio around. Jorgenson was tall, blond hair, blue eyes, and athletic, the typical Swede. And the heartthrob of the young ladies on the Island. Jorgensen's good looks and athletic build only added to the Chief's dislike of the Coast Guard. For the Chief it was a reminder of days long gone by.

Bull Perry often referred to the Coast Guard crew as "the Momma's boys on vacation" and didn't care for them no matter how friendly or helpful they tried to be and went out of his way to avoid them at all costs. Police matters were police matters and belonged to the Chief and he didn't want to share his business with anyone much less "those pretty boys." But in this case they had him over a barrel and he knew it and they knew it. He needed their boat. Citing a lack of funds Town Council had repeatedly turned down the Chief's request for a small boat with an outboard motor for emergencies, such as this, and for helping in rescue operations. His disdain toward the Coastguardsmen was open and public knowledge, as many of the Chief's feelings were; however, the feeling was mutual amongst the Coastguardsmen. If it wasn't food, Southern, or U.S. Army Issue, Chief Perry didn't much care for it and wasn't bashful about expressing his opinion. To a degree, the Chief had a legitimate gripe concerning the local Coastguardsmen. The scars they carried were broken hearts from failed romances. The Chief's scars were from German guns. And no Coastguardsman on the Island had died yet from a broken heart.

The Chief's contempt was summed up when he talked about being in action during the War. "Humph, the only action those boys have ever seen is in the backseat of a '57 Chevy on a Saturday night."

Jorgenson's comment when asked about Chief Perry's feelings was, "I'll put it this way. None of us were invited to the Chief's birthday party and we don't have him over for afternoon tea. Know what I mean?"

"What youse need the boat for Chief, going fishing?" Danatagilio jokingly asked. He wasn't intimidated by Bull Perry and knew the Chief needed the boat for something important.

It must have killed the Chief's soul to call us for help, Danatagilio thought as he acknowledged Lumus with a nod of the head and waited for the Chief's reply.

"No, no fishing," Chief Perry answered very businesslike. "We've got a body out there in the creek somewhere."

"Oh yeah? How about that. Now that ain't an everyday happening around here, not on this Island anyway," Jorgenson remarked in a failed attempt at conversation.

No reply. The Chief stared blankly at Jorgensen.

"Whereabouts?" Danatagilio asked looking at Lumus then the Chief.

"Down by the sewer pipe," the Chief grunted, pointing down the creek, no more than two hundred yards away. "That way."

Danataligio spoke up, "Jorgie, youse back the boat down and I'll get the life jackets and call the station and let them guys know what's going on." He reached for the two-way radio on his hip.

"Just don't bring any more people over here," Chief Perry grumbled, "We got enough now. Understand?"

"Yes sir," Danatagilio said mockingly. "Yes sir!" He gave a quick salute. "I'll make sure no mores volunteers come running over here to help."

Chief Perry scowled, turned, and walked over to the car where he propped himself up against the fender.

"I'll go with them," Lumus offered. "If that's OK with you?"

"Good idea," the Chief said. "I'll wait here."

"Bubba, you say the body is at the end of the pipe, right?" Lumus asked. " On the creek end?"

Bubba looked at me for assurance. I nodded. "Yeah, it's on the end of the pipe. Go there, at the end." He pointed. "You'll see it."

It wasn't long before Lumus, Jorgenson, and Danataligio were motoring toward the sewer pipe, just a hop and a skip in a motorboat.

"Who told youse guys about the body," Danatagilio asked as they neared the pipe. He put the motor in neutral and slowly eased the boat next to the pipe like an expert .So gently you could have had your fingers on the outside of the railing and barely felt the contact.

"The boys," Lumus said, " the ones at the landing."

"O-o-o-h, Bubba and Mike ... Yeah, we know them. Dose guyse always getting into something. We caught 'em last summer putting firecrackers in the exhaust pipe of the truck at the station."

Lumus grinned recalling the incident.

"Is this the only sewer pipe out here?" Jorgenson inquired looking over the marsh expanse.

Lumus nodded as he stood up to get a better view. He put his hands on top of the pipe, steadied himself, leaned over and looked up and down the other side of the pipe for a body. No body in sight. He thought for a second about jumping up on the pipe for a more thorough search but decided it wasn't worth the risk of falling into the water.

"Then where's this body?" Jorgenson asked, "because I sure don't see anything."

Lumus was thinking out loud more than answering Jorgenson. "They said they tied it to the end of the pipe but I don't …"

"See anything?" It was the voice of Chief Perry. He was probably the only person in the county who could yell from that far and be heard.

"Not yet." It was an attempt at a reply by Lumus, which no one on shore heard.

"It's got to be here somewhere. We couldn't miss something that big," Lumus thought.

"Maybe it sank?" Danatagilio suggested shrugging his shoulders.

"Maybe? But the rope would still be here."*…If those boys… think Lumus, think.*

"Tell you what," Lumus ordered, "head back to the landing. There ain't no body here, that's for sure."

"O-O-O-K," Danatagilio said and he knew that Chief Perry was going to be plenty pissed off if they came back without a body.

Bubba 'n me were relieved to see them coming back so soon. We had kept our distance from Chief Perry who stood near the water's edge glaring down the creek. Trying to be helpful we reached out to hold off the bow as Danatagilio cut the engine and the boat coasted slowly toward the bank. And then our hearts sank to our toes. I know because I stepped on mine when I jumped back realizing there was no dead body in the boat. There was no dead body behind the boat or anywhere to be seen and the look on Lumus' face spelt trouble.

The Chief could also tell by the expression on Lumus' face that something wasn't right. "What's wrong?" Bull Perry demanded. "Where's the body? Then he turned and gave Bubba 'n me the eye.

"No dead body …no nothing … that's what's wrong. We looked everywhere real good," Lumus said with an irritated look directed at Bubba 'n me. "Which one of you tied the body to the pipe?" His face took on the look of his boss.

"I did, why?" I answered. The "why" came out wrong and was taken wrong. Lumus walked up to me looked me directly in the eye and said very slowly and clearly, "Because we didn't find a body … that's *why*."

"Well, it's gotta be there," I pleaded, " I know. I tied it to the …"

"Yeah," Bubba added," I saw it and Mike tied it up."

"All right then, let's go," Lumus said giving Bubba a hard look.

Oh no, my worst fears were realized ... I'm going to jail.

Lumus paused and then turned and looked at me. "You! Get in the boat and I want you to show me exactly where you tied *this* body." The way he said "this" made me wonder if they believed us. "Oh man. What if they don't and what if we don't find the body? It's got to be there," I told myself. " Dead people can't just swim away."

"Just me?" I innocently pointed at myself. "In the boat?"

"Yeah, just you."

I saw Danatagilio and Jorgensen sitting in the boat with their heads down moving 'em slowly back and forth. Not a good sign. Then Jorgensen got up and got out of the boat deciding to stay at the landing.

Bubba grimaced. "Want me to go too?" he offered. It came out more as a plea.

"No. You stay right there with the Chief." You would have thought someone murdered Bubba's parents by the look on his face.

"Hey partner, I'll be right back," I said trying to relieve my friend's misery.

"Yeah, hurry up," he said only loud enough for me to hear.

Danatagilio was running the boat, Lumus was quiet and I was nervous.

"Surely they must have overlooked it?" I thought. "Yeah, that's it. They just didn't see it. When we get there that body will be right where I tied it."

When we got to the end of the pipe I showed them exactly where I had tied the rope and explained everything. We searched and searched but couldn't find the body or the rope. Things weren't looking real good for the home team. I must have gone over what happened ten times but there was no body and I was without words or an explanation. I threw my hands up and said, "I don't know. I don't know where it is?"

Lumus finally called off the search and he didn't seem none too happy about riding around in a boat in the heat looking for a dead body. I had a good idea what was on his mind but when I tried to make a suggestion that we look farther upstream he cut me short.

"Enough of this," said an exasperated Lumus, "let's go … head on in, Allie."

I didn't say a word. I put my hands over my face and thought, *Where could the body be? Surely Bubba 'n me hadn't dreamed or imagined this whole thing like some crazy person? Could we?*

Chief Perry, wiping his brow with an even sweatier hand, replaced his hat and asked, "What you think, Lumus?"

Lumus answered quickly, "I think we need to go to the station and have a good talk with these boys."

Elvis again. "C'mon an do the jailhouse rock with me... let's rock..."

"Come on boys, this way," Lumus said gesturing toward the car. He opened the back door. "Get in. We're gonna take a little ride."

Oh no, not to jail, I thought. "Hey … uh Lumus … I can't go nowhere I've got to get home and baby-sit. My Mom is expecting me." I was hoping for a miracle.

"Yeah, me too," Bubba said. "My Mom *and* Dad are expecting me. We're supposed to go see my aunt in the hospital. Can I just stop by the station tomorrow maybe?"

I wanted to say something to Bubba and remind him about how he left me alone once already this summer during the garbage truck incident. Was he trying to do it again? So I gave him the if I'm going you're going stare. He shrugged his shoulders and whispered, "Can't blame a guy for trying."

"The *only* place you two are going right now is to the police station!" declared Chief Perry. "And I don't want to hear anymore about it. Is that clear?"

He was so clear we jumped into the backseat quickly.

25
GROUNDED

I had two things on my mind as I rode in the backseat of the patrol car headed for the police station. One was that my parents were *really* going to be upset with me, which would lead to another grounding, a serious one this time and probably a suspension of privileges, such as using the telephone and watching TV. All that I could somehow handle. Shoot, I'd had so much practice at groundings over the last few years that staying at home was almost becoming a routine but it was still and would always be a torture for me not being able to run free. However, the other thing that seriously bothered me was that we were going to be in trouble, in my opinion, for doing nothing wrong. In the past it was different. Bubba 'n me deserved our punishment for all the screwups and silly pranks but this time we did what we thought was right and here we were in the backseat of a police car probably headed for jail. This did not make much sense to me.

I nudged Bubba who was looking intently over the front seat inspecting the contents of the car, which was a set of handcuffs dangling from the dashboard with rust grown all over them, the car radio, and a baton of sorts probably used by Chief Perry to hang his doughnuts on. I could tell by the look in Bubba's eyes that he was imagining himself in Chief Perry's place someday taking two innocent kids to the station. Bubba seemed more than content, almost happy.

"Ain't this a drag?" I moaned staring out the window at the passing Palmetto trees.

"What?" Bubba was actually smiling. "What are you talking about?"

"In the back of a police car, being taken to the station for doing nothing … that's what I'm talking about. Man, I'm in *big* trouble now."

"It's neat," he whispered, "look at all that stuff."

"Are you crazy? I know you want to be a cop someday but this ain't right and what are you gonna do when your parents …" A-a-a-h, he wasn't listening to me so I shut up. *Why ruin his fun?* I thought.

Another negative thought snuck into my mind … *Beverly. Oh no! What will she think? And the crew? Oh God, I can hear them now.*

The Island police station was a converted office from the old military base, Fort Moultrie, given to the town by the government after WWII. Judging from its size, which was three rooms, one of them huge, it might have been an officer's quarters. There was a large open area in the front with a desk and an old filing cabinet standing alone in the corner and two smaller rooms. One room in the back had a small cot for whomever had night duty and another room was equipped to serve as a small kitchenette with a sink, small stove, and a table. Army green covered the walls and the floors were faded tiles. A huge, buzzing overhead-fan stirred the hot air. Staring down intently from underneath a cracked piece of dusty glass was ex-President Harry Truman with a caption that read: "The Buck Stops Here." It hung directly over Bull Perry's head.

When we stepped into the station, the gravity of the situation finally dawned on Bubba evidenced by his slow, fearful entrance. I had to give him a little nudge in the back to get him inside. He stopped, looked around the room suspiciously, glanced back at the door, gave thought to making a break for it, and then let out a long sigh and dropped his head. The excitement of riding in a police car, and his promising images of himself at the wheel of the car, had worn off quickly and completely.

Chief Perry gathered all of us around his gray steel desk and got right to the point.

He demanded, "Do you boys want to tell us anything … anything different, that is, from what you've already said? Or are y'all sticking to your story?" He eased himself into his chair while Lumus stood guard over us.

"Sit," Chief Perry barked at us, motioning at two chairs.

Bubba 'n me looked at each other like lost tourists. I threw my hands up. "Chief Perry, there's nothing else I can say," I said. Then I looked at Bubba again.

With his head down and barely audible Bubba said, "No … nothing." Then he buried his head in his chest.

"OK," the Chief said as he reached for the phone, "what's your phone number, Mike?"

"TU-33784," I answered.

He jotted the number on a pad.

"And yours?"

"TU-33262," Bubba said.

Oh no! Was I in big trouble now or what? I had imagined a lecture from Chief Perry and a ride back home. I figured my parents would probably hear about this from someone else before I told my story, and then the grounding would come. It was one thing to bring home from school the "whipping" note or have my parents learn of some misbehavior from another parent or through the Island grapevine but a phone call from Chief Perry himself was like a life sentence. I'd be stuck in that house with my sisters until school started. Maybe I'd really go crazy and have a breakdown or something and my parents would pack me up and send me off to Columbia where all the wackos lived on Bull Street. Nope, on second thought, Columbia would be too much like a vacation. I'd probably be a grounded babbling idiot tied up and tortured daily by my little sisters.

Bubba 'n me looked at each other and the pitiful expressions on our faces told it all. In this moment of dire circumstance when we were about to lose our deeply loved and most precious thing of all … our freedom … I leaned over close to Bubba and whispered, "Give me a big BA-HA-HA. Come on, man … just this one time … I need one."

He raised his head slowly and sadly said, "Ain't got one right now." Then he dropped his head and went back to counting the dirty square tiles on the floor.

We could hear half the phone conversations as we sat and only imagined the other half. Both of our fathers were at work slaving away for the welfare of their families … two of whom were jailbirds. There would be no quick thinking and talking our way out of this one because this was the most unique situation we had ever been put in. We had not done anything wrong; therefore, there was not anything of substance to talk our way out of. What a mess. Chief Perry and Lumus were convinced we were making up this story just for the fun of it and putting them on, and all the pleading in the world was not going to change that, so we had no choice but to face the music and see what happened.

Just before hanging up the Chief said, "Yes Ma'am, we'll drop him off at the house in just a few minutes."

"Let's go, boys." Chief Perry growled. "I'm taking ya'll home."

Bubba 'n me jumped into the backseat of the big black Ford and overheard Lumus, poking his head through the open window, tell the Chief that he was going to take the Jeep, the other war surplus vehicle of the department, and go check on some things. As we pulled away we looked out the back window at Lumus standing on the sidewalk waving to us and smiling. Or was he sneering?

Bubba 'n my quest for activity and love of life, our freedom to roam and search for and take part in adventure was as natural to us as breathing. The few minutes we spent sitting in the police station was excruciating, not the time spent there but the feeling of hopelessness and being cooped up, our freedom taken from us. It was as though we were in prison, locked up in a cell or a cage like the many dogs we saw year after year crammed into the back of the dog catcher's small truck as they sat there sadly behind the screen bars of their prison. Which reminds me …it so happened in the springtime when all of life renews itself that we decided we had seen enough and planned to do something about our fellow creatures from God who were denied their freedom only because they were dogs. We decided that this spring they too would have new life.

As far as we were concerned the most unpopular man on the Island was Mr. Grunting, the dogcatcher. That wasn't his real name. We didn't know what his name was and didn't really care. Chief Perry was a barker, a bellower, and a loud person who was used to being in command. The dogcatcher, whatever his name, was a grunter, a groaner. Grunting and groaning his way through life with unintelligible sounds, barely making conversation with anyone. I once heard him trying to tell a dog something but neither the dog nor I could understand him. Bubba 'n me even confronted him one time and tried to ask him why he caught and locked up innocent dogs, someone's pet, but all we could make out was an occasional grunt that sounded like a dying man's last breath. Then when he went on to moaning and groaning about something or another we just hopped on our bikes and rode away wondering if the man spoke English. That was the day Bubba gave to Mr. whatever-his-name-was the label of "Mr. Grunting."

I suppose Mr. Grunting was only doing a job he was paid to do and I felt kind of sorry for him in that respect but I also felt way more compassion for the animals. I loved dogs. To see them caged up in the back of Mr. Grunting's truck on a hot day suffering and whining for their master made me as angry as I was sorry for their ordeal. And goodness knows their final plight? I know one thing: If that man had ever gone after Mollie he would have one heck of a battle on his hands and not from Mollie but me. I sometimes thought he sensed just that because he never made a move toward Mollie even though she roamed freely and the opportunity to go after her must have presented itself at one time or another. My problem was with the small town politicians who created the job of dogcatcher in the first place by passing some unneeded law calling for the seizure of peoples' pets. Where was the need? There was no rabies problem on the Island, no pack of dogs roaming the streets attacking innocent women and children. It was unheard of anyone ever being bitten by a dog. The dogs that ran loose, like Mollie, were docile, easy going and pleasant like most of the population of the Island. Shoot, the dogs would have been more justified to have gotten together and elected a people-catcher to round up some of the local undesirables and haul them off, beginning with Mr. Grunting.

Being locked up whether you're human or animal has to be a terrifying form of punishment but, of course, laws must be enforced and humans, at least, have a choice in life and the opportunity to be responsible for their actions and be held accountable. What about the family pet? Should a dog be imprisoned for straying from his master's yard and taking a leisurely stroll through the neighborhood and going to the beach or meeting down the block with a group of fellow canines for a little fun and games? God forbid that he would ever answer Nature's call in an untimely manner or place. Oh my goodness, how terrible. To some it was a crime whose only suitable punishment was a life sentence in the house or total exile from the neighborhood or the dog pound.

Bubba 'n me had watched from the sidelines over the years the treatment dished out to the Island's dogs and we didn't like what we saw one bit. Now that we were a little older and a little dumber, actually a little more brazen in expressing ourselves, we decided it was time to take action on behalf of the dogs and if our plan worked maybe, just maybe, Mr. Grunting would be fired. That way the Island dogs would have some relief until a new dogcatcher was hired or better yet maybe the mayor or somebody would decide not to hire a new one. To fulfill our plan we needed an accomplice of impeccable integrity, unmatched wits, and complete obedience to help us with our plan of freedom. We needed Mollie. That's right, my Mollie, the wonder dog. The friend of all friends. I would have a talk with her concerning our plan hoping for her total commitment of which I was confident.

So late one morning I got the chance when the Devlins had cleared out of the house. Most had gone to Mt.Pleasant with my mother and Ryan was at the library again. I often wondered what that boy did there.

I called Mollie to my room, got her situated on the bed, sat down beside her and with her full attention went over Bubba 'n my plan for Mr. Grunting and his captives.

As I went over the plan step by step she looked up at me nodding her head up and down or from side to side at all the appropriate times giving me the impression that she indeed understood what I was saying. Maybe she did? I do know that she sensed something was up when I mentioned the word "Mr. Grunting" because her head went down and she cut her eyes up at me as to say, I don't like him.

"Who you talking to?" It was Sissy sneaking up and poking her head around the corner.

"Who does it look like I'm talking to … Mollie."

"Mollie … humph! Is she talking back to you?"

"What!" And I grinned. "Are you stupid? Dogs can't talk. Leave us alone. We got business to take care of."

"You're a strange little boy, do you know that? Alone in your room, sitting on your bed, talking to a dog."

"Oh yeah, I'd rather talk to Mollie than some of your friends like that stupid Joanie. She's as dumb as a box of rocks."

"Hey, you better watch your mouth, boy."

"Why? What you gonna do? Keep me in at recess, S-i-s-t-e-r Sissy?"

"Humph, you…" She wheeled and walked off. I could tell she was going to be a good school teacher by the way she threw her hands up in the air and tossed her head back.

When I was finished going over the plans I asked Mollie if she understood what was to happen and did she have any questions? She cocked that beautiful head of hers, stared at me and went into her stretch routine, which meant no questions but will you take me to the beach?

"Why not," I said, "let's go to the b-e-a-c-h!" She jumped off the bed and was at the front door before I could put on my hat.

If given sufficient time Bubba was a great planner of schemes and pranks; if not he was less than adequate, not good at spur of the moment thinking or improvisation. I was the opposite and performed best in an impromptu situation. Therefore, Bubba 'n me made a good team as long as we had plenty of time to sit down and talk and plan. Then if we got caught it would be my job to talk us out of trouble. For this caper we had enough time to plan and even go over details. We took several bike rides that served as scouting missions to iron out any rough edges to help ensure success. We learned two things about Mr. Grunting: he had a routine or schedule that he followed religiously on certain days, and he had the habit of leaving the door to the cage on the back of the truck where he imprisoned his captives unlocked once he made his first seizure of the day. Whether leaving it unlocked was by design or out of laziness we didn't know but it became the major part of our plan.

We chose a late Friday afternoon to carry out our rescue. Everyone was in place: Bubba 'n me on our bikes ready to intercept Mr. Grunting, Mollie was sitting at my side and Billy Scott's dog, Beau, was sitting by Mollie. Neither Billy nor Beau knew anything about our plan. Billy wouldn't know until after the fact that Beau had taken part in the great escape serving as Mollie's accomplice. We sighted Mr.Grunting's truck at Station 20 turning toward Back Street following his Friday schedule and we pedaled furiously to take up our positions on Back Street at Station 18, keeping ahead of the sound of the barking dogs in the back of his truck. Mr. Grunting must have had a busy day … the cage was loaded. Learning from the garbage truck fiasco, this time I had chosen something thicker than the thin-branched oleanders to hide behind, something offering absolute cover. I was at the base of a huge hackberry tree surrounded by an overgrowth of wisteria vines. I was hidden so well I could hardly see myself. Bubba was no more than twenty feet from me up the road crouched behind a remaining section of an old wooden fence engulfed in vegetation. I looked his way and couldn't spot him. We hollered a final "OK" signal to each other and waited as Mr. Grunting approached slowly down the pot-holed dirt road called Back Street.

Mollie and Beau were in position on Back Street perpendicular to me, both lying in a separate pothole like it was their normal resting place. I whispered to them," Stay" for the second time as assurance that they would lay there and not move. The added commands really weren't necessary because Mollie had been trained to "stay" on just one command and Beau … well … he mostly followed Mollie's lead in pretty much whatever they did, plus Billy had trained him to "stay." They heard the approaching truck and the beep-beep from Mr. Grunting but there was no way Mollie was going to disobey her master even if a train was coming. Shoot, ol' Beau, not only ignored the sound of the horn, he defiantly plopped his head down as though he were going to take a nap. Mollie and Beau were set and so far the plan was working beautifully and Mr. Grunting performed his part to perfection by slowing down for the stubborn Devlin and Scott dogs. Now the rest was up to Bubba 'n me and the timing had to be on the money. When Mr. Grunting was no more than fifteen feet from Mollie and Beau and his truck barely moving, I made my appearance from the bushes carrying on in a search mode, looking around and calling for Mollie, acting surprised to see Mr. Grunting. "Oh, there you are, Mollie. Good girl, let's go. You too, Beau. Wanna go home?" Mr. Grunting had rolled to a stop and stuck his head out the window frowning at the dogs and me. For a second I thought he might, just might, come after the dogs but he didn't move. He didn't even grunt. He lacked the nerve to pick up someone's dog when the owner was right there.

We had counted on Mr. Grunting being his lazy self and sure enough he just sat in the truck staring at the dogs and me, looking agitated. I briefly glanced his way as I led Mollie and Beau out of the road stopping momentarily to give Mollie a pat on the head and a hug for her performance while Beau licked my ear.

I was killing time and the distraction of me and the dogs was just long enough for Bubba to slip from his hiding spot and dash to the back of the truck and deftly lift the lock off the cage door, which held ten, yapping, hot, dogs. The sound of the whining and barking dogs muted any noise Bubba may have made coming out the bushes and his quick retreat back into the bushes. He was like a rabbit … there one second and gone the next. By the time I finished hugging Mollie and wiping my ear dry it was a done deal. Freedom! No dog pound! Now the group in the cage needed to cooperate and they did just that. When old man Grunting began to pull off, all the dogs began to jump from the back of the truck, one at a time, as though their escape was planned. Zeke, the Jones' Boykin Spaniel whose feet didn't seem to hit the ground as he raced for Station 23 and hugs from his owner, led them. What a great sight! Here was Mr. Grunting riding down Back Street looking ahead attentively for more guiltless dogs to put in his little cage while his catch for the day was leaping out the back of his truck to freedom. They took off like rockets, each one destined for the safety and comforts of home. Bubba, grinning from ear to ear, appeared from the bushes. "Hey, hey, we did it.! We did it. Hope the ol' grunter gets fired today."

"Good job, Bubba. Man, you were so fast. It was like… zoom, zoom and you were gone."

"Yeah, almost as fast as those dogs. We oughta do this every day!"

"When do you think he'll find out he doesn't have any dogs?"

"I dunno. Guess whenever he gets where he's going," Bubba said and then laughed. "Looka here," he said showing me the lock from the cage. Then he tossed Mr. Grunting's lock about a foot in the air, caught it, and with a mighty heave threw it way out into the marsh.

I was smiling thinking about the sight of those dogs running free and returning to their home and being with their families when I felt a sharp nudge in the ribs.

"Hey wake up, dream boy. Looka there. You got a bunch of people waiting for *you*."

I snapped awake to find myself in the backseat of the police car as Chief Perry brought it to a stop by the front gate and sure enough there was a committee of Devlins waiting for me on the steps of the front porch. There was Ryan, Katie holding Sara in her arms, Sissy, Emily, Aunt Cele and Aunt Christle who wouldn't have missed this for anything, especially Aunt Christle who was in the inner loop of Gertie's gossipers.

Man, I thought, *word sure does travel fast on this Island.*

Clearly absent was my mother, which was not a good sign for me. The group was lined up on each side of the steps forming a small entranceway up the steps, just standing there looking at me not saying a word nor did they say anything as I trudged up the steps like a condemned man headed for the gallows. Their eyes bore into me like a woodscrew into balsa wood reaching my very soul. Their silence was killing me. They followed me into the house and when the door slammed they lit into me like a pack of hyenas on a fresh kill.

Sissy began the harangue, "I told you but you wouldn't listen, would you. And you promised. Remember, honest injun? Boy, you're in trouble now!"

"But I was …"

Ryan's turn. "A dead person, humph! Couldn't you and Bubba come up with something better than that?"

"There was a …" I tried to defend myself but was outnumbered and outgunned.

Aunt Cele and Aunt Christle both just "Tsshed, Tsshed", shaking their gray heads from side to side and looking down. Finally, Aunt Cele spoke, "Shame on you," pointing her finger at me. Aunt Christle was rolling her eyes so badly I thought they might get stuck in her head?

Emily yelled her opinion, "You stupid." followed by little Sara's "Th … tupit."

I think Katie was trying to tell me I was stupid also but Ryan out-shouted her. "A dead person in the creek." he said, "What's next? … Martians running around on the hill?"

My mother swept into the room from the kitchen and cleared the room with one loud word: "Out!" She looked at everyone but me.

As the group grudgingly departed I could barely hear Aunt Christle mumbling something about how she had never heard of such a thing or something like that. The only words I could make out clearly were "sinner" and "confession." She was obviously disappointed that she couldn't hang around and gather more valuable information for her gossip-queen friends.

My mother used the finger-in-the-face treatment sparingly, but when it appeared you knew it was serious business and I was getting it big time and double time!

"I can't believe … why would you… what in the world …" she was so agitated she couldn't get a sentence out.

"Mom, I can explain everything if …"

"No. Sit down and listen." She calmed herself, sat down, and quit wagging the finger in my face. "First, there was trouble at school"… I tried to interrupt, "But that wasn't my fault and …"

"Hush, and let me finish," she declared firmly holding her hand up. "OK?"

"Yes Ma'am."

"… the trouble at school, then the firecrackers at the Coast Guard Station, the mess at the movie theater and skating rink, then the garbage truck, and now some story about a dead body. It's one thing after another. Where does it end? What's going on with you, Mike?"

I didn't realize mothers had such good memories with everything else going on in their lives like working, taking care of a household, cooking, shopping, and keeping track of six Devlin kids, but there she was with a list of the past and she was right. I was guilty of all those shenanigans, there was no questioning that; however, *this* time I was innocent. But my past reputation was too much to overcome. However, I wasn't going down without a fight.

"Mom," I blurted out, "there was a body … I swear … I mean (there was no swearing in the Devlin house) there was a dead man. Bubba 'n me saw it and tied it to the sewer pipe and then I ran to the house."

"Mike, I had a talk with Chief Perry and he told me that the Coast Guard and Lumus and even you couldn't find this body. And with all the things that have happened in the past … do you understand what I'm saying?"

"No Ma'am," and I was risking a longer grounding and maybe more but I went ahead, "But Mom, how can a dead man swim away?"

"O-o-o-h." My mother rising from the couch, threw her hands up in despair, looked at me and told me "when your father gets home we'll talk again. Until then get in here and help me with all these dirty clothes."

"Yes Ma'am. But first can I call Bubba?"

"If I were you, I'd wait and call Bubba later. It's Mr. O'Toole's day off and I don't think Bubba will be talking to anyone for a while or able to sit down for a while. You know how mad Mr. O'Toole can get sometimes?"

"Yes Ma'am."

After supper and when quiet finally found its way into the house (only after the Devlin children were safely tucked away storing up energy for the next day's assault on humanity) did my parents sit me down for a Sunday-come-to-meeting-discussion. For the umpteenth time I recounted the same story almost word for word. There was nothing new or different to add and each time I told someone the story I received the same stares of disbelief. I was hoping with all my might that my father would understand, believe me, and take my side assuring me that everything would be all right. He had been my savior so many times in the past. This time, however, it was not to be as he gave me the same stare of disbelief that everyone else had given me. And I was crushed beyond my wildest dreams. Now I had no one to turn to. I had no one to talk to about this whole deal, which was not about the dead man anymore, as far as I was concerned, it was about my credibility. What could I do?

"OK here's the deal. Your mother and I have decided to ground you for two weeks. There will be no phone privileges and no nighttime TV and you will help your mother around the house with chores. Do you understand?"

"Yes sir," I said trying not to show my utter and absolute disappointment that my father did not believe me. "Do I …" I was about to make a feeble attempt at earning *some* freedom or concessions when I decided quickly to drop it.

"Go ahead," my father said.

"Never mind. Forget it," I answered looking up.

"Oh yeah, Mike." It was my mother. "And you will help baby-sit Katie and Sara and help Sissy."

"Help Sissy? What does she…"

"Hush, right now. You hear me. You're in no position to be making the rules. Do you understand? And don't try that worrying me to death trick again. This time you're in for the duration."

"Yes Ma'am."

"But what about the lawns I have to mow?" I had played my last trump card.

"Ryan will take over for you," my father said, "so you don't have to worry about that."

My head dropped and I was counting the white spots on the green linoleum tiles. Then I looked up and started counting the boards in the old tongue and groove ceiling.

"Mike," my father said in a stern voice, "Don't give me that hang-dog look. You got yourself into this. Nobody else."

"But ..."

"No buts, mister. If what you tell us is true within two weeks this matter will resolve itself. But until then you're grounded. If there's a body it will be found and if not then ... well, it means you weren't telling the truth."

"Yes sir," I said apologetically.

"Now get to bed," my father said.

"Yes sir," I said about as downcast as I had been in a long time. "Come on Mollie, let's go."

I lay in bed trying to make sense of this mess but I was too tired to think clearly. When I thought about my father not believing me, my eyes began to water and my chest tightened but with all my resolve I refused to cry. A sob or two managed to fight their way to freedom but I promised myself that was it. But I was fighting a losing battle with my emotions. My own father, my best friend. That can't happen. Why won't he believe me? Somehow I had managed to almost doze off when I heard soft but familiar footsteps enter the room. My father sat on the edge of the bed reaching out to me in his best fatherly manner.

"Mike?"

I tried hard to mask the sobbing and gave the manliest response I could muster. "Yes sir." He knew I was hurting.

"I want to ask you just one thing, OK son?" He paused. "Are you telling me the truth?"

"Yes sir," I answered with tears welling up in my eyes. "It's the truth, I promise. You know I'd never lie to you."

"OK fine, fine." He gently rubbed my shoulder. Then a long pause. "But if you aren't, there are consequences you will have to face and I'm not talking about being punished." Pause. "It's something far more serious and longer lasting. Are you listening to me?"

"Yes sir."

"If you aren't telling the truth then you will be a liar and no one wants that. And also that will be the burden you will have to carry ... the fact that you're a liar and know it. That's a tough burden to carry around, son ... a tough burden. Understand?"

"Yes sir," I nodded and wiped my nose on the pillowcase as my father gave me a hug and left. I dozed off trying to think of a way Bubba 'n me could find out what happened to that body.

And I gave a lot of thought to what my father said about people who go through life knowing they are liars.

26
COVERUP

Dr. Steven Jenkins had been a busy man for the last two days detailing the interior of his car, even washing and waxing the exterior hoping to eliminate any possible traces of evidence that might have somehow been left behind the night of Thomas Poe's murder. He was leaving nothing to chance. The newspaper from the trunk of the car had been burned along with the clothing he wore that night, the rubber gloves and tennis shoes, including the rope he had used to bind Thomas Poe. And the ski mask and gloves Thomas had worn the night of the murder. *Everything.* Even the cushions from Thomas Poe's home had been reduced to ashes.

He knew he could not be cautious enough concerning the destruction of possible evidence and repeatedly he retraced his movements of that night carefully recalling the smallest detail just to reassure himself that he had covered his tracks. Everything involving the car, his clothing, and anything he handled at Poe's house had been disposed of.

Now he had to decide what to do with two vital pieces of evidence, which he knew could tie him to the crime and possibly lead to his arrest and conviction. They were Thomas Poe's coin collection and the murder weapon.

He decided that if he were caught with Poe's collection he could claim he bought it and the authorities would have a difficult time proving otherwise seeing that the former owner was dead. But, on the other hand, when he got rid of it there could be no possible link between him and Thomas Poe and the only motive would vanish. And that was what he had planned to do all along.

A group of clandestine businessmen based in Canada had been negotiating with him for over six months about acquiring his collection and their interest peaked immensely when they learned he might have access to a valuable addition to his collection. That being Thomas Poe's collection. Evidently these people knew their coins and what they were after. Their implications were that they wanted both collections but would consider purchasing his alone but at a greatly reduced price. Negotiations with this secretive group thus far had been handled by a man known only as The Collector, a "gopher" for this group thought Steven, not even a middleman, just an errand boy. Steven didn't know the name of this group nor did he care to. As a matter of fact, he had never met The Collector personally. Their correspondence had always been by phone but he was assured that the buyers were "well connected and financially able and would be in contact periodically." This arrangement was fine with him. His only concern was the money. Would they pay the price now that he had Thomas Poe's collection to add to his?

The Collector, true to his word, had last made contact two months ago and made Steven an offer for his collection that was very tempting. However, when he had told The Collector of the possibility of adding another collection to his, The Collector hesitated for a second, telling Steven that he would have to check on things and get back with him soon. And, he added, "Don't do anything until you hear from us."

And then there was the question of the other piece of evidence linking him to the crime, the gun. What to do with it? It too was part of another valuable collection of Steven's, which consisted of early American rifles, and pistols and discarding it would be kin to destroying the whole collection, at least, in his mind. It had taken over thirty years to assemble the gun collection and parting with any of it would be extremely difficult from an emotional standpoint. Steven had often wondered which he was attached to more … his coin collection or the gun collection?

I've enjoyed collecting the guns as much as the coins he often thought. *They have so much character and personality about them.*

All of his guns had been meticulously maintained and kept in immaculate condition and each was as operable as the day it came down the assembly line. Thomas Poe had met his death from a Colt .45 caliber, six-shooter made in 1898 by the Colt Arms Company in Baltimore, Maryland. Steven had purchased it for $40.00 in 1929. On today's market it would bring nearly $1,500.00; however, he wasn't interested in selling any of his guns. When the deal was finalized for the sale of the coin collections he would be set.

Common sense tells me to get rid of the pistol. Then he rationalized, *what harm can there be in my owning a pistol that's part of a collection? I have that right. And besides, no one will ever know I own it or ever see it.*

The following evening the phone rang at exactly 7:00 P.M. Right on schedule.

"Hello, this is Steven Jenkins."

"Hello Dr. Jenkins. How are you? Do you recognize my voice?"

"Yes, yes I do. You sound very close like you're next door. Are you in Charleston?"

"Oh no, no," The Collector said. " I'm much farther away than that.

Do you have the merchandise we talked about last time … the complete package … that is?"

"Yes, I do."

"And both are fully intact?"

"Yes, in mint condition."

"Excellent Dr. Jenkins, excellent. However, I must tell you there has been a slight change in plans concerning the original offer made by the group."

Oh no! Don't tell me they're going to back out. Not now ... they can't.

"What kind of change?" Steven Jenkins asked trying hard to sound nonchalant.

"You'll be happy to hear, I'm sure, that the offer has been upped to $100,000." A slight pause. "A nice increase, you might say?"

"Yes, I should say so." Feeling a great burden lifted off his shoulders, he sat down and put his forehead in his palm and thought. *Thank God. It's going to work. Everything is going to be OK.*

"Do you accept the offer?"

"Yes, it sounds more than fair to me."

"Good. Then we have a deal and now you must follow my instructions very carefully and do not write anything down, no written notes. Do you understand?"

"Yes, I understand."

"Come to Atlanta on Delta flight 146, August 8th and check into the Airport Holiday Inn where you will then be contacted with further instructions. Of course, bring both collections. Repeat these instructions to me, please."

"Atlanta, Delta flight 146, August 8th check into the Airport Holiday Inn," Steven repeated.

"Good. I will call you back at this same time on August 7th to make sure your booking went OK. Until then, good evening and goodbye."

Everything was falling into place. Steven Jenkins felt so confident about the upcoming sale that he decided to call his daughter who lived just outside Atlanta and plan a short visit with the grandchildren while he was there.

These people are very secretive and don't take any chances but that's good, I suppose, because I can't afford a slipup now. I wonder if they know about Thomas Poe?

Let's see ... gloves, clothes, cushions, shoes, rope ... all burned. Car cleaned, gun cleaned, spent casing destroyed. I'll clean the gun again.

Steven pulled the Colt from inside the velvet laden chest, admired its craftsmanship, took out his oil and rags *(must remember to burn these rags)* and very thoroughly cleaned the Colt, rubbing oil all over it giving it new life and then placed it back in the case and then decided to take "Dodger" for an early evening walk.

"Dodger," wanna go to the b-e-a-c-h?" Dodger ran for the door.

Steven stopped at the door and stared at the ocean. The waves washing ashore reminded him of the guilt building up in him. Would it come crashing down on him eventually like the waves on the beach totally engulfing and drowning him? For as many times as he wiped oil on the Colt pistol, Steven Jenkins still could not wipe away the memory of Thomas Poe's slumping head and knowing that he had taken another human being's life.

27
YOUNG DETECTIVES

This was my second restriction within a few weeks. No one in their right mind enjoys being punished. And I was having a hard time with this particular confinement. Punishment comes in all forms, shapes, sizes and degrees and is normally meted out in proportion to the offense committed but to me this grounding was excessive and oppressive and I darn well voiced my displeasure loud and clear in no uncertain terms. This was America and I still had the freedom to speak my mind and I did and often. And in a brazen manner to my captive and attentive audience of one. Mollie was a good listener and heard every word of every legitimate complaint and agreed with me one hundred percent. It was a ritual I performed behind closed doors, which acted as a sort of cleansing of my mind and soul. Thank God Mollie listened, otherwise I would have felt like a complete idiot standing there talking to the wall.

Whoever came up with the idea of grounding a person, as a form of punishment must have had a direct descendant in The Spanish Inquisition. It was torture, pure torture for me to stay in a house all day with nothing to do but sit around wasting time or laying in my bed looking at the ceiling and thinking and trying to figure out how I got into this mess. I had rather take a spanking any day. It might hurt for a while but at least it was over and done and I could be on my way. My parents, however, did not believe in inflicting pain just for the sake of it. Rather, they believed in taking away something we kids enjoyed as a form of punishment and they had definitely succeeded by taking away one of my most precious possessions … my freedom. I knew right then and there I would never turn to a life of crime or even take the slightest risk of losing my freedom and end up locked away in some jail cell. Uh-uh not me! Being locked up was the ultimate form of punishment for this young boy.

After a day or so of being grounded and laying around and doing nothing I'd about run out of things to think about and Mollie was tired of my griping and complaining indicating she had heard enough by putting her front paws over her ears and peeking at me between them whenever I launched into another gripe session. I was so desperate I was to the point of taking imaginary bike rides and talking with Bubba, walking on the beach alone and staring into the mirror and carrying on conversations with myself … not a good sign. But maybe that was the goal of the grounding, to give me time to think about my wrongdoing, to get my act together and mend my ways. Maybe it was time for reflection and adjustment? And that was fine with me but in this instance I had not done anything wrong and that's what made this whole matter so frustrating because there was no logical answer as to why I was being punished. It made no sense to me no matter how many times I ran it through my little mind. But I suppose a dose of the real world every now then was not going to kill me so I decided to hang in there and stick it out. Added to my displeasure were my sisters who ruled the house, constantly on the go, running around with boundless energy that carried over into my room and getting into everything, including my head. I might have a real breakdown if these kids don't calm down for just a little while and just leave me alone. There's no quiet, no peace.

"What we gonna do, Mollie?" I reached down and scratched her head as another little Devlin flew by. This time it was Superwoman on her way to Mars being chased by Wanda the Witch.

"W-A-A-H-O-O!" Zoom and they were gone.

I know. My baseball cards. Yeah, I'll go through them and figure out who I'm going to trade and who I want to keep. Rusty and I and a circle of friends had an informal baseball card-collecting group. And every so often whenever the mood hit us we would get together and trade players/cards. I pulled the chair over to the closet, stepped up on to it, moved the pile of clothes hiding my shoebox of cards nestled securely in the corner of the shelf and lifted out the greatest players of this era. I enjoyed messing with my baseball card collection almost as much as watching my heroes play on the Saturday game of the week with my father whenever he had that rare Saturday off. There was some kind of personal magic feeling generated through those cards as I adoringly and reverently held them in my hand. I could almost feel the smooth leather of Willie Mays' glove and the newness of the stitches on the ball he held as "The Say Hey Kid" smiled up at me.

"Don't worry Willie … I'll never trade you," I quipped, "or you Mickey, as I rubbed the smooth wood of the Louisville slugger resting on the muscular shoulder of Mickey Mantle.

As I walked through the front room with my shoebox of cards under my arm, Sissy asked, "What are you smiling about? You're on restriction, remember?"

I answered with an even bigger smile. She couldn't stand it when I walked around smiling. I guess I was supposed to be the unhappy, frowning brother. Not me. I might be on restriction but I had my baseball cards and Mollie. So even though I was about as miserable as I could be from my lack of freedom I had still put on a big fake smile just for her over the last two days, which really got under her skin. And another thing she couldn't stand was when I didn't answer her. It drove her nuts, so I didn't say a word as I walked by.

"Hey, 'dead man,'" the new nickname she had come up with to irritate me, … "you hear me? I'm talking to you, 'dead man.'"

"Come on Mollie," I said looking around completely ignoring Sissy, "let's go count some cards" as I headed for the porch. "There seems to be a draft in here."

Bubba had received the same punishment as me. A two-week grounding except he had daytime TV privileges, which had to lessen the pain somewhat. The no phone rule was strictly enforced under the watchful eye of Sissy who noticed me looking in the general direction of it and told me quickly, "Don't even think about it." That didn't bother me because I had rarely been one to use the phone under normal circumstances. Normally I was outside and came in the house only to eat and sleep. Now Bubba was different when it came to a phone. He loved to talk on the phone and would sometimes stop at a pay phone when we were bike riding, put in a nickel while still sitting on his bike and call somebody … anybody just to use the phone. So the no phone rule for him must have been excruciating. But leave it to Bubba to get around whatever obstacle was in the way. And if he really wanted to talk to me he'd find a way.

He liked to tell me, "Devlin, there's more than one way to pick a crab."

Bubba sent his little sister, Mary, over with a package for me. A small brown lunch bag with a sandwich, an apple and a Hershey bar with the message: "It's some leftovers …thought you might be hungry."

Sissy made the delivery to me, throwing the bag at me. "Here's a care package from Bubba. Enjoy."

The second I spotted the Hershey bar I knew something was wrong. I hated Hershey bars and Bubba knew it … I liked Snickers. Was Bubba trying to tell me something? Now I wished I could use the phone but a quick survey of the front room told me no way. Sissy was guarding it like a mother hen, practically sitting on it. Maybe Bubba was just being nice and really did think I might be hungry. I took the bag to my room and began to search through it with some skepticism but there was only food in it. *That was nice of Bubba. I'll have to remember to thank him twelve days from now.*

The thought of not being able to talk to my friend for twelve whole days saddened me even more.

I tossed the bag on the bed and headed back to the front porch, plopping in the nearest rocker, Mollie at my side. I reached over and rubbed her head and ears while she gave me a sympathetic look.

"Yeah Mollie, this is something else, ain't it? Can't go to the beach (her ears straightened up immediately). No girl, I said, "can't go." No bike riding or crabbing or nothing. And nobody except you believes me that Bubba 'n me found a dead man in the creek."

Dwelling on the situation only made matters worse so for relief I decided on a nap. My care package from Bubba was where I left it and being near lunchtime I figured what the heck I'll eat it and then take a nap, except for the Hershey bar. As I bit into the sandwich I felt something crunchy, not food, but crunchy like paper and upon opening the sandwich I found a piece of aluminum foil topped with mayonnaise covering half the sandwich and partially hidden under a piece of ham.

"What the heck is this?"

I took out the aluminum foil, cleaned it off, and upon unfolding it found a small piece of paper with a message scribbled in only Bubba's distinctive handwriting … chicken scratch Sister Ann Marie called it. It read, "Meet me behind the cistern at 10:00 tonight. Your friend, Bubba." I read the note again and smiled because I wouldn't have to wait twelve days to see my friend. I also wondered what he wanted.

Sneaking in and out of my room was easy, especially in the summertime with all the windows in the house open welcoming any stray breeze. By 10:00 it was quiet in the Devlin household, except probably in the minds of my little sisters who ran and jumped and screamed in their sleep, practicing up for the coming day. I got out of bed and tiptoed across the room, balanced myself gingerly on the window ledge, gave a slight push and landed in the soft grass with barely a sound. I had tried unsuccessfully in the past to sneak out by using the back porch. Big mistake. Its old wooden floor creaked like Grandma's joints. About this same time, I figured, Bubba should be tipey-toeing across their back porch like a thief in the night.

The old, abandoned water cistern was a block away in an unoccupied and overgrown lot, a popular meeting place for secret rendezvouses like this. I was almost there when I heard Bubba. "P-s-s-t, p-s-s-t, over here." He was half crouched down behind the wall of the cistern not taking any chances of being seen by anyone other than me.

"Man, am I glad to see you," I said greeting Bubba with a friendly pat on the shoulder.

"Yeah, it's good to see you too, my friend." He was smiling from ear to ear.

"This being grounded thing is for the birds, especially in the summertime. It's like being kept in at recess but not ever getting out. How's it going at your house?" I asked.

"A-a-a-w man, it's the pits. Can't go nowhere, nothing to do and Mary and Patty won't leave me alone. They're pestering the fool out of me. And, you know, girls don't *think* like us. You know what I mean?"

I nodded eagerly.

"So. How you doing?" he asked.

"About the same except there's four of them. I just hang out in my room and ..."

Bubba excitedly interrupted me. "Look, I've got this great idea! It came to me the other day. That's why I sent the note. Of course, I wanted to see you too. By the way, how ya like that note ... in a sandwich."

"Pretty coo," I said, "Where'd you get that idea?"

"From TV. I was watching this old movie the other day and this guy in prison gets a saw blade ... one of them hanck, hack, ... u-u-u-h?"

"Hacksaws," I offered.

"Yeah, that's it, hacksaw. His girlfriend slipped it to him and he saws the bars on the window and escapes."

"Why didn't you send me a hacksaw blade?"

"V-e-r-y funny ... because I'm not your girlfriend? BA-HA-HA-HA"

"Eah, not so loud. We're in enough trouble now."

An intent look came to Bubba's face lit by the full moon. "Seriously, I ..."

Uh- oh, whenever he used that word it was lookout time.

"I think I know where the body is," he said, "well, I've got a good idea."

"Oh yeah." I said excitedly. "Where, man? Where?"

"In the creek," Bubba said matter of factly. Then he smiled.

Just as matter of factly and without contempt I said, "No hock Sherlock, where'd you park your squad car?" It was something I had heard one of the older teenagers say.

"Seriously Mike, listen. What was the tide doing when we found the body?"

"H-u-m-m, let me see ...it was about two hours after low and incoming ... I think?"

"Right. So here's what I figured happened. After we left, the rope must have slipped off the pipe ... OK? It had to." Bubba looked intently at me. "Are you with me?"

I nodded and Bubba said, "OK, then the body would drift away ... we know that." He thought for a second and said, "The thing is which ... which way would it drift?"

"Well, if the tide was coming in then it would drift upstream," I said beginning to follow his logic. "Upstream. Yeah, upstream. It had to go that way."

"Right again, my well educated, young Saint Angela's scholar ... upstream, toward the landing. And where was Lumus and them looking for the body?" Before I could follow up on my thought he said, "all around the pipe, which is *downstream*."

"Hey, you've put some thought into this, Bubba. I didn't know you had it in you."

"Yeah. Either that or go crazy."

"So you think the body was right there near the landing the whole time?" I asked.

"Yeah … somewhere around there …or maybe further upstream."

A thought exploded in my mind. My brain was racing with questions about current speeds, undertows, wind speed and direction … anything that could affect the movement of a dead body in water.

"Gotta go," I said hurriedly, "I've got an idea."

"What! Where? Why so fast?" Bubba looked dejected. "We just got here."

"Tell ya tomorrow." I hopped on my bike and took off. "Same time, right here." I yelled back.

"OK," Bubba said softly, "I'll see you …"

Earlier that same afternoon Delta Flight 146 left Charleston on time and arrived on schedule in Atlanta.

Stepping from the coolness of the air-conditioned cabin into the Atlanta heat and humidity, Steven Jenkins felt mugged by the mug. *And people think Charleston is humid. These poor folks here don't have the luxury of an ocean breeze ... oh goodness.*

Steven settled into his room at the Airport Holiday Inn and waited for the phone call, which came early that afternoon from the Collector with exact instructions concerning the transfer of the collection and the money leaving no doubt as to what was to take place. He thought these people were almost paranoid in their planning and preparation. Why? Maybe he wasn't going to live long enough to enjoy spending the $100,000. Did they have some other well- thought- out plan for him?

It had been another short conversation.

"Hello, Dr. Jenkins."

"Yes, hello."

"Listen carefully, please. Tonight at precisely 9:00 go to room 108, which will be unlocked. The lights will be off. As soon as you step into the room you will find a briefcase on the floor in front of you, it's about three feet from the door. Pick it up, take it to your room, and make sure everything is there. Don't rush … take your time. Then return to Room 108 with the collection, place it in the same spot, shut the door and leave. Do you understand?"

"Yes."

"And it's been a pleasure doing business with you. Goodbye."

Steven Jenkins realized he wasn't very good at handling stress by sitting around and doing nothing so he decided to visit Cathy, his daughter, and Tom who lived just outside town. Tom would probably be at work but Cathy and the kids should be home.

Should I call her? No, I'll surprise them. I wonder if I'm being followed?

After an enjoyable visit with Cathy and the grandchildren, Steven returned to the motel and rested and surprised himself by being able to take a long nap despite the anticipation of tonight's business.

The transfer that night went smoothly, too smoothly he thought. Everything was where it was supposed to be and as far as he knew there was no one in the room when he picked up the cash and returned with the collection. He didn't notice any people in the hallway on either trip. It was as if only he and The Collector were involved. But in his mind he knew better. These people planned everything and surely someone was watching everything.

The weight of the briefcase securely in his right hand outweighed any regrets of giving up his collection as he boarded his plane for Charleston.

Leaving Bubba alone at the cistern was a purely instinctive move. I hopped on my bike on the run like a cowboy saddling up in a hurry and pedaled off like there was no tomorrow. I was on a mission of immense importance. The Palmetto tress on the roadside became a blur and the oleanders were like greenish meteorites passing through the clear night as I headed to the police station with hopes of redemption running wildly through my head. I prayed a little, big prayer that Lumus would be on duty and be at the station. I was going so fast I wondered if my prayer had a chance to get to God or would it be lost in the wind?

I breathed a huge sigh of relief when I rounded the bend at the Baptist Church and saw the distinctive green Jeep parked on the side of the station three blocks away indicating that Lumus was on duty and Chief Perry was home full of doughnuts and fast asleep. If the Jeep was there then Bull Perry was not. The Chief was too fat, Dunlap and all (I grinned) to get in and out of the Jeep … it was way too high.

Well, here goes something, as I banged on the door with my nose pressed against the screen as though that would speed things up.

I yelled softly, "Lumus, you there? Hey, Lumus … Lumus, you there?"

Lumus appeared from out of the backroom looking as though he might have been sleeping. He was scratching his head and tucking in his shirt.

"Hold your horses for Pete's sake, I'm coming."

Before he opened the door I went into my unrehearsed spiel, letting the words fly. "Lumus, I'm so glad you're here. You just don't know. Bubba 'n me were talking and I gotta talk to you about the body, I …"

"Whoa there. Slow down a little bit, Mike. Slow down, you're gonna have a heart attack. By the way, what you doing out this time of night? Kind of late for you isn't it?"

"Yeah, I guess so? But Bubba 'n me had some special business to take care of and this was the only time we could do it."

“There you go. That’s better, now you can breathe. Wait here, I’ll get us a Coke and we can sit out here.” He pointed to a bench under the oak tree. “Be right back.”

The two-minute wait of anxiety seemed like an eternity.

“Here you go,” Lumus said, handing me a cold bottle of Coke, “now what’s on your mind?”

As I told him Bubba’s theory about where the body might be Lumus listened intently. And when I was finished, I was certain that he would say, “OK, let’s go get it right now.”

Instead Lumus asked softly, “Mike, how many tides are there in one day?”

I thought for a second. “Two, a high tide and a low tide.”

“No,” Lumus said in a gentle tone not like Sister Roberta’s blunt “no” at school. Then he calmly explained, “There are four tides … two high and two low.”

“Oh?” I thought for a few seconds. “O-o-o-h yeah. That’s right. I see.”

“Now, how many days has this body been out there?”

“U-u-u-h,” I said out loud, “Thursday, and Friday … two.”

Another soft “No.”

I quickly defended my answer. “Yeah, Lumus. We found it on Thursday and today is Friday. So that’s two days, right?”

Lumus calmly looked at me and explained that I was correct in saying that we found the body two days ago but we didn’t know how long it had actually been in the creek before we found it. “It could have been in the water for a week or two or whatever. Right?”

“O-o-o-h … I see.”

“The point is Mike is that there have been many tide changes and with the creek bed in Miller’s Creek being full of oyster beds and, God knows what else, there’s no telling if the body is hung up on the bottom or what. It could be stuck in the marsh somewhere.” Lumus paused and looked at me and then said, “And there’s one other thing” … he gave me a gesture of doubt, eyes wide and his hands held up in the air, palms facing me. “If there really is a body” and then his voice trailed off.

“Lumus, there’s a body. I promise. Don’t you believe me?”

Lumus had been doing some investigating on his own since the “no body” incident that day at the landing. After Chief Perry had dropped Mike and Bubba off at their respective *jail cells,* he waited at the station for Chief Perry to return figuring two heads were always better than one.

“Chief, wouldn’t you agree that if there is a body, then it’s more than likely a local rather than someone from out of town? I mean it doesn’t add up to murder someone, say over in Charleston or West Ashley, and then take the trouble to haul the body all the way over here and dump it in a creek on the back of the Island. Besides, not too many people even know about that creek."

"Makes sense to me, Lumus."

"I thought so," Lumus said, as he stood up, stretched, and put on his gray straw hat with the badge pinned squarely in the front. "I gotta go."

"Where you headed?"

"Going to check on something. It would be helpful if we knew the name of the dead man, don't you think?"

Lumus knew Mike and Bubba well enough from past encounters to understand that they might pull some immature stunts and pranks, but to lie to the police and to their parents about a dead body was not their way of having fun. There definitely was a body and the place to begin looking for answers was with the one man on the Island who knew everyone and mostly their business too. That man was Norman Keenan, the Postmaster.

Uncle Schroeder greeted Lumus at the entrance to the Post Office with his familiar greeting.

"I'm doing good, Mr. Schroeder," Lumus said with a tip of his hat, "and how about yourself?"

"Oh fine and dandy," he answered and then turned to greet Mrs. Hawkins.

Lumus held the door for the exiting Miss Kitty, the ageless beauty and classic flirt of the Island.

"Why thank you, Lumus. You're such a gentleman." She never missed a chance to bat her big brown eyes and flash her million-dollar smile. "You sure look sharp in that uniform. Those are the cutest Bermuda shorts … and those legs … oh me, makes a woman my age wish for younger days."

"Thank you for noticing, Miss Kitty … the shorts that is."

"I'm surprised old Bull Perry would let you wear shorts on the job?"

"Yeah … well. I had to do a *lot* of talking … I'll tell ya that."

"Or a lot of doughnut buying?" She laughed. "Take care Honey, and come see us at the diner. I'll load you up with some extra mashed potatoes … put some meat on dem bones. Bye now."

"Thanks and I'll try to get over soon. Goodbye, Miss Kitty."

Lumus held the door for three more people before making his entrance. *This sure is a busy little place,* he thought. *They ought to charge admission ... they'd make a fortune.*

"Afternoon. Hello. Hey, how ya doing." Everyone always had a friendly word for each other and Lumus was no exception.

Norman greeted Lumus warmly with a friendly smile like he did all his customers.

"Good afternoon, Lumus. How you doing?"

"Hi, Norm. Fine. How you doing? Leaving any fish in the creek for the rest of us?"

"A-a-a-w, what you talking about … I haven't been catching

anything."

"That's not what I heard. Last week you had a string of flounder long enough to feed half the Island."

"Oh yeah. From who?"

"Old Man Kennedy."

"Him? Why that old buzzard would rather climb a tree and tell a lie than stand on the ground and tell the truth."

"Ha. Wait 'til I tell him you said that."

"Don't bother … he already knows it. What can I help you with, Lumus?"

"Well, Norm I got a little favor to ask. I was wondering if you could take a quick look at the mailboxes and tell me if you have any full ones?"

"Lumus, without even looking I can tell you there's plenty of 'em like that."

"Well, not just full, I mean like overflowing." Lumus paused. "What I'm getting at is anybody's box that's real full or overflowing because they haven't been checked in a while. Like a week or so."

"Oh, OK, sure. Let me take a look … just a minute." Norman disappeared behind the wall of mailboxes while Lumus inspected the FBI mug shots on the wall wondering if they ever caught any of those people?

"Lumus, I've got about ten or twelve boxes that are more full than usual but that's normal this time of year with people on vacation. They'll go off for a week or so and it just piles up."

"H-u-m-m, I didn't think of that. Vacation, huh? Well thanks, Norm. Appreciate your help. See ya later."

"Anytime Lumus, take care."

A dejected Lumus sat in the Jeep outside the Post Office muttering to himself. "Vacation. Let me think… out of town … out of town, huh. I wonder? Well, there's more than one way to skin a cat."

He called The News and Courier, the Charleston newspaper, the only one in town, which served the Charleston area and asked if they would mail him a list of subscribers on Sullivans Island, which they agreed to do. When he received the list, which would be a day or two he planned to compare it with the count he was about to make. It took him the rest of the day to complete his inspection of the Island doing what he normally did on patrol. He combed the Island street-by-street, Station-by-Station, giving each house a quick yet thorough glance. This time instead of being concerned mainly with possible security breeches such as open doors or open windows on unoccupied houses, he was performing another kind of check. This was a newspaper check, a simple working formula, whereby he would determine almost to the day how long someone had been away from their residence. He simply counted the number of old newspapers in the yard or on the porch and made a note of those houses and how many papers were in their yard. The dead person in the creek obviously could not collect his daily paper. The only things left to chance Lumus thought were: (1) that the dead person he was trying to identify did not subscribe to The News and Courier thus negating any evidence lying in the yard, or (2) a member of the dead man's family was collecting the paper each morning. But that was a chance he would have to take. It was a start and who knows he might get lucky. And since the overflowing Post Office box idea had backfired he had to do something.

By mid-afternoon he had narrowed down his original list of twelve possible candidates who had numerous newspapers lying in their yard to five solid prospects. The first four he checked on by questioning their neighbors and found out they were on vacation and due back within the week.

Then came a break. Upon questioning Mr. Pickett, Thomas Poe's neighbor, he learned that Mr. Poe had not been seen since Wednesday morning, which according to Mr. Pickett was unusual. Mr. Poe was a man of habit and had a regular schedule of coming and going. And not seeing or hearing from him was very unusual, according to Mr. Pickett.

"Yeah, I distinctively remember it was Wednesday because that's trash pick-up day and he put his garbage out that morning.

"Did you talk to him that day?" Lumus asked.

"No, I saw him through my kitchen window when I was having breakfast.

"And about what time was that?"

"O-o-o-h, about 8:00. Is there something wrong? I mean with Mr. Poe?"

"No, no. Just a routine check. Thanks Mr. Pickett. Have a good day."

Lumus left wondering, "Could be? Could be? It's worth a follow-up."

Lumus glanced at his watch …10:30 … as he tried to get comfortable on the bench.

"Yeah Mike, I believe you. I got to thinking about what y'all said happened and I figured y'all were telling the truth. Shucks, I know you and Bubba get into a lot of stuff but I don't think y'all are liars, especially about finding a dead person. By the way, how'd you get off being grounded? And, I know I asked you this earlier but … what are you doing out so late?"

"Well, uh … I'm … u-u-u-h… kinda still grounded … you know what I mean?"

"Yeah, I know. I was a kid not so long ago and I had my share of groundings. I ain't forgot."

"You was grounded, Lumus. I'd never thought that. The policeman being grounded. Man, that's something."

"You just don't go telling anybody now, O.K?" Lumus smiled and took the last swig of his Coke.

"Oh no, I won't say a word, honest injun." I paused and thought about the best way to present my case to Lumus. "Lumus, the reason I snuck, I mean came out, was to tell you that I know a way we can find that body."

"Hope you got a good plan because that's a lot of water to cover out there. Tell me. What's on your mind?" Lumus kicked back, locked his hands behind his head, and listened.

I finished off my Coke and said, "Well, you know when you're coming out of Miller's Creek how it winds around down near the flats and then turns back by the old Coast Guard dock?" Lumus was frowning. "You remember," I gestured, "down behind the Olsen's house?"

Lumus' eyes widened and he grinned."Yeah, yeah, I remember now. I just haven't been back that way in so long."

"Well anyway, the creek there is kind of … how you say? Skinny?

"Narrow," Lumus offered.

"Yeah narrow," I accepted … "not so wide there. Anyway, all you have to do is run a seine net across right there on an outgoing tide. It would block the whole creek and I'll guarantee you it'll catch anything coming out of Miller's Creek, including that poor dead man if he hasn't already drifted into the harbor. That's what I think."

"By the way Mike, I've been meaning to ask you this before but how do you know that dead body is a *man*?"

I answered quickly, "Come on, Lumus. I'm only twelve-years-old but I know the difference between what a man and a woman look like … gee whiz."

"OK, OK," Lumus said with a big grin, "just checking."

"You know kid, you might be on to something?" Lumus said in a reassuring tone. "Yep, you just might be on to something. It's worth a try anyway. Yes sir, it's worth a try. Eah, Let's go."

"Where?"

"You're going home and I'm going to get the seine net. It's up at the Fire Station and I can drop you off on the way. Throw your bike in the back of the Jeep."

"Can I go with you to get the net?"

"U-h-h-uh. No sir- re, bobtail. You get caught with me riding around at 10:30 at night and I'll be in trouble with you know who … Mr. Bull."

"Mr. Bull?" I chuckled. "Is that what you call him?"

"Not to his face … that's for sure." Then we shared a laugh.

"And what would your parents do if they caught you out tonight?"

"Oh man, I don't even wanna think about that."

28
FREEDOM

The morning sun was slicing through the curved, green fronds of the Palmetto trees sending out splintered rays that danced on the calm, smooth water of Miller's Creek like baby minnows in a frenzy. The sound of flopping mullet awoke all below and the creek began to come to life. The squawking seagulls and boisterous grackles did their duty of awakening those on dry land. Fiddler crabs played joyous tunes on their fiddles and the dance of all the creatures throughout the marsh began. The loud extended cackle of the marsh hens made it impossible for any creek animal to slumber any longer. It was the final alarm beginning a new day in Miller's Creek.

Lumus, Chief Perry, Danatagilio, and Jorgensen had gathered that morning in Miller's Creek where it narrowed enough to allow a seine net to be placed across it.

Using the Coast Guard's boat again and with the help of Danatagilio and Jorgenson, Lumus set the seine net just before the tide turned to outgoing. It was right where Mike had suggested, by the turn near the Olsen's house, and it covered the width of the creek. Nothing of size could escape its clutches. And again Chief Perry stood on the bank supervising, beginning another new day with his arms folded and frowning.

"Make sure ya drive them stakes down good and deep," the Chief bellowed. "Don't wanna lose that net else those jokers at the Fire and Rescue will raise hell. You hear me, Lumus?"

"Yes sir," Lumus yelled across the creek, giving Danatagilio and Jorgenson a wink. "He likes to hear 'Yes sir' … makes him think he's still in Europe somewhere leading the Army."

"Yeah, know what yous mean," Danatagilio said. "We do the same thing at the station with Commander Wright. Makes them old guys feel wanted."

"Eah, thanks for the help, guys," Lumus said as he jumped from the boat onto the bank. "I hope this works."

"Anytime. Just give us a call," Jorgenson yelled from the departing boat. "And let us know if you have any luck."

Lumus turned to the Chief who was walking toward his car and told him, "I'm gone. Got patrol duty."

"OK. But let me know if you catch anything," the Chief said, "I'll be at Grannie's for a while and then at the house."

Lumus planned to go about his normal patrol of the Island and every twenty or thirty minutes come back and check the net. He would be looking for a significant bend in the net indicating something large and heavy had been caught, preferably a body. The position of the net couldn't have been better. The creek narrowed and with the tide boiling out of Miller's Creek it was like water going down a drain and anything floating had to pass this way. Lumus had given thought that maybe the body had already washed out to sea but there was always the chance that it hadn't.

That afternoon Lumus stopped and got out of the Jeep and spotted a large bulge in the net. He eased down the bank, tugged on the net and then spotted what looked like a human leg come to the surface. He scrambled back up the bank and immediately radioed the Fire and Rescue Squad. Within minutes they arrived and pulled a decaying, badly decomposed body from Miller's Creek.

While the body was being placed in the Rescue's pickup for transport to Mt. Pleasant, Lumus noticed a sizeable hole at the base of the body's skull and a ten-foot section of rope attached at the ankle with a perfect slipknot still in place at the other end.

"Where y'all taking him?" Lumus asked as he untied Bubba and Mike's anchor line and placed it in the back of the Jeep.

"To Mc Swain's Funeral Home. Why?"

"Just curious that's all ... j-u-s-t curious."

Lumus was understanding about my distress at having been grounded and was nice enough to place a call to my mother with the news about finding the body. I wonder if he told her about my sneaking out and meeting with him? I hope not but on the other hand it would show a certain resolve on my part, a certain I-can-do-attitude about wanting to resolve what, in my mind, was an unjust grounding. On second thought disobeying my parents by sneaking out would more than likely overwhelm any resolve or attitude I might have exhibited and lead to another grounding. So, for now at least, I decided to keep my mouth shut and leave well enough alone. I would, however, check later with Lumus about whether or not he said anything.

Before I could manage to get out of the house I heard a familiar singing voice, a deep one full of Gullah, on the road beside our house. It was a deep, guttural call familiar to all Islanders, a voice like no other.

"V-e-g-g-g-g-e-t-a-b-l-e man!" came the pleasing tune and he really stretched out the word "vegetable".

His cadence was so long a vegetable practically had time to grow to maturity before he finished, I thought.

He sang out: "I gots okra, corn, squash, tomatoes and fresh w-a-t-e-r-m-e-l-o-n. Gots some c-a-n-t-a-l-o-u-p-e too. V-e-g-g-g-g-e-t-a-b-l-e man!"

"Mike … where are you?" It was my mother. "Get in here." She reached for her pocketbook and pulled out two dollars and began to place her order. "Get me some corn, tomatoes and …"

"I know," I said interrupting her, "lima beans … right?"

"Yeah and don't forget …"

"Yes Ma'am, and don't forget to check the corn and don't get soft tomatoes and just a few pieces of okra."

"That's right," she smiled, "how'd you know that?"

"C'mon Mom! I ain't done this but about a million times."

She grinned and hurried me out the door.

None of us knew exactly where the Vegetable Man really came from. Probably somewhere in Mt. Pleasant? But he was like clockwork. Every Saturday morning he was singing out his wares to the Islanders and we came a running. And why not. He sold freshly grown vegetables for a pittance. And he had a bountiful variety to choose from. He drove a beat up, old, rusty, pickup truck that was way past a paint job with a homemade top made of leftover two by fours and a couple of pieces of plywood, which conveniently leaked droplets of rainwater through its cracks onto the vegetables. There was an old and worn scale swinging in the breeze from the back of the truck for weighing and pricing the vegetables.

I ran up to the truck as Ms. Kingman was ambling off toting a large bag of vegetables. And there he stood. The Vegetable Man. A kindly old gentleman who had for countless years been selling his vegetables on the Island and he knew all his customers by name. I often wondered if he plowed his field with the Vegetable Truck, hooking up a big steel plow and having a helper drive slowly up and down the furrows while he walked behind guiding the plow. N-a-a-w, he probably had a mule. A big brown one, strong and healthy in order to plow enough fields to grow all these vegetables. The Vegetable Mule … yeah, that's who helped him.

When he spotted me coming across the yard, he stopped, went to the side of the truck and took a brown paper bag and began to fill it with corn wrapped securely in their green covering. I stood and watched the strong, nimble fingers lift each ear and carefully slide it in a bag in an almost sacred movement. Those strong fingers and hands that had planted this very corn, which we would eat for nourishment, now reached for the tomatoes and gently squeezed each one testing its firmness.

"Nots too soft … right? … my little succotash man."

I nodded and smiled.

"And jes a lil bits a okra un' somes lima beans," he said putting just the right amount in another bag. We had been through this routine so many times he didn't even bother to weigh or price anything. He took a puff off his cigar, looked at me, and asked, "You doin' OK?"

I answered, "Yes sir" and asked, "How you doing?"

He gave his standard reply, "I thanks God for da breath a life." Then he smiled and handed me the bag.

I gave my standard reply of "Thank you" and handed him the two dollars. As I ran back to the house I could hear the call half a block away …" v-e-g-g-g-g-t-a-b-l-e man" as he made his way to another happy customer.

Obviously, I was the official succotash kid of the family and that night for supper my mother would cook up the best tomatoes, corn, lima beans, okra and onions flavored with a piece of fat back that even the Devlin kids would eat, ignoring their disdain for vegetables.

I threw the vegetables on the kitchen table, hollered for Mollie and took off for Bubba's.

Now that we were off the hook and free again Bubba 'n me headed directly to Burton's to check in with the crew and bask in the glory of being a local hero for finding a body and reporting it to the police and then offering up an idea that led to the actual discovery of the body. This kind of drama never took place on the Island and here we were, two of the main characters, right in the thick of the plot. We figured we were approaching hero status and might even gloat a little too. Added to our inflated self-adulation was the thought that we had suffered through a terrible and unjust grounding.

Maybe Beverly will be there?

As we coasted to a stop on our bikes and parked in front of Burton's, I looked through the huge plate glass window with the name BURTON'S DRUG STORE printed across it. The whole crew, minus Beverly much to my dismay, was there waiting for our triumphal entry … and in a festive mood. Catching a reflection of myself on the glass, I stopped, adjusted my shirt and patted down my hair. I wanted to look good. The stage was set, the props were in place, and it was curtain time. Now the actors of this true to life drama, Bubba 'n me, needed to step forward and do our part. A-a-a-h yeah … we were ready … our moment of glory was at hand. The crew was loud and the jukebox was blaring "Great Balls of Fire." Someone had located the volume knob on the back of the machine and Jerry Lee Lewis was singing at the top of his lungs whether he knew it or not. The pool table was crowded, lots of people milling about and a certain buzz of excitement was in the air. As we walked through the front door, a rush of cool air from the air conditioning hit us like a wintry blast. *O-o-o-h that feels so good,* I thought. *Just like the reception we are about to receive.* Bubba 'n me stood a little taller and threw our shoulders back going into our look-at-me strut, smiling, and all set to hand out gracious "hellos" and "hi's" to everyone. I looked over my shoulder at Bubba and he was beaming like a proud, brand new father. The pride in what we had done was overwhelming. Why … I bet that Charles Lindberg didn't feel as much pride during his ticker tape parade in New York City for his historic transatlantic flight as we did at that moment in Burrton's Drugstore.

About the time I expected applause from the crew and a hero's welcome, I heard John announce loudly to the group gathered around the jukebox, "And here they are, ladies and gentlemen, straight from Sullivans Island, South Carolina, live and in person at Burton's Drug Store by popular demand." Then he paused for effect, swung his arm out to us and said, "May I present to you the *grave robbers*!" On cue everyone jeered and yelled, hissing and booing all at once.

"Grave robbers, grave robbers," they chanted in unison, pointing their fingers at us.

"Do what?" I couldn't believe what I heard but understood immediately the implication of what they said. I waited for their assault to calm down then I held my hands up and tried to reply. "Rob? Eah, we found…"

Too late. There were too many of them and obviously some planning went into this sneak attack. The crew laughed as Bobby threw in his two cents worth, "Do y'all like playing with the dead? Did y'all go swimming with him?" More jeers and laughs.

Tommy Wade took his best shot, "Hey, did you break off some parts and use 'em for bait." The crew roared on that one.

I tried once more but knew it would be useless. "Hey fog brain," I yelled to no one in particular, "we actually helped the police …"

I was shouted down again. This time by Jimmy Wearing. "Helped the police do what? Pick the crabs off the body." The crew let out a collective "U-U-U-G-H" on that one.

I was in disbelief while Bubba stood back with his arms folded staring, saying nothing. These were our friends, our classmates, people we had shared the big ruler treatment with and planned all our schemes and had suffered with at school over the years. This was the crew … but … I'd seen them like this before and they could be brutal. There was no use trying to fight them. They were a quick-witted bunch and were out to have some fun at our expense. Bubba, however, was taking this ribbing much too seriously and was as pissed off as I've ever seen him, giving Tommy Wade the wicked evil eye and slowly inching his way toward the loud mouth, frog-faced Tommy. And when I saw Bubba quicken his pace toward Tommy I sensed real trouble and not wanting to be a part of Tommy Wade's butt-cutting or an out right free-for-all, I decided to play peacemaker in the midst of all the crew's laughing and carrying on.

I intercepted Bubba just in time and Tommy Wade was darn lucky I was there to hold Bubba back. He would have beaten Tommy like a redhead stepchild.

"Easy, Bubba. Easy. Let's go. We don't need all this. C'mon."

I half held Bubba by the arm, easing our way toward the door but not without sending a parting shot, "You guys are crazy, you know that … you're whacko!"

More hoots and hollers and face-making. Raymond Neilson yelled, "Where y'all going? To lunch with Lumus and Bull Perry? What ya gonna eat, an arm or a leg?"

I'm sure the crew got a big laugh out of that but we were already on our way out the door. As we stepped outside, in one second, we went from the Artic to hell. The heavy heat jumped on us and felt like the proverbial gorilla on our backs. But the *real* heat was coming from under Bubba's collar. I was disappointed. Bubba was mad. He was still upset by being put down by Tommy Wade and was about to vent his anger. It's a good thing Bubba knew, or more than likely it was accidental, about venting because if he didn't he might have exploded from pent up frustration. I knew my friend well enough to just stand back and listen, which I did.

"That dog gone stupid idiot … that dummy … that Tommy Wade is a u-u-u-h … a u-u-u-h …"

I was standing there thinking, *Come on. Come on. Spit it out.* He was searching hard for the right word then he finally yelled out, "He's a jug butt! Yeah, he's a jug butt if there ever was one. Tommy Wade the jug butt! He's …"

I broke in. "A jug butt?" I said incredously. "Where'd you hear that one?" don't tell me on TV … HA!"

"N-a-a-w it wasn't on TV. I heard one of the teenagers the other day. It was that Burbage girl. She was yelling out of the car window at some guy. Called him some other names too."

My tactic had worked again. When Bubba got highly upset, I would listen and then try to get him to talk about other things, anything to help get his mind off whatever was bothering him.

Bubba was still upset but had calmed down enough to talk "Man, what's with those guys?" he said banging his hands down hard on his handlebars. "I thought they were our friends?"

"I don't know? Must be jealous that you and me did something that they didn't do. That's all I can figure," I surmised. "And that Tommy Wade … what a jack leg."

"Yeah, I'm gonna jerk a knot on that little twerp's head next time I see him. Maybe I'll beat him up good and throw him in the creek."

"A-a-a-w, he ain't worth all the trouble. The heck with them people."

"Y-e-a-h, you're right. The heck with 'em." Bubba paused then smiled and said, “What does Mrs. Brown say, “What come around, go around.”

I smiled, as I looked at Bubba. I was surprised. “So you remember me telling you what Mrs. Brown said, huh?”

“T-h-a-t-‘s right, Catbird. That Mrs. Brown is a smart lady. And what the crew is doing will come back to bite ’em in the you-know-where. Just you wait and see. By the way, where we going?” he asked.

“To see Lumus.”

“Lumus! What for?”

“Come on. You’ll see. I’ve got another brilliant idea.”

“Yeah right,” he said, “brilliant should be your middle name. BA-HA-HA-HA-HA!”

The hoopla on the Island following the news of a body being pulled from Miller’s Creek was an event of immense proportions and magnitude. Nothing this exciting had come along since the last mayoral election when Sambo announced his candidacy, sending the local politicians into a maddened frenzy. It had begun as a joke, a statement of rejection aimed at the present mayor and his non-accomplishments, but turned serious when the conspirators realized the true worry and anxiety it caused the mayor and his group of cronies. *Everyone* on the Island loved Sambo, the mayor included, and in his political nightmares the mayor envisioned himself turning over the reins of government to a smiling, hand-waving Sambo, decked out in his trash-stained “HARVARD” sweatshirt with a Falstaff beer in one hand and his handwritten acceptance speech in the other, which read, “All right, buddy. All right!”

The jokesters decided to play it to the hilt and went a step further placing a huge banner on the side of “Ol Blue,” Sambo’s rolling office, which read “Sambo for Mayor … He Will Get Rid of All the Trash”. The mayor, being the astute politician he was took no chances, and sure enough he found a loophole in the qualifications necessary to run for office and Sambo’s name was deleted from the list of viable candidates. It was revealed that Sambo wasn’t a natural-born resident of the county thus eliminating him from a race that he was never officially in. When someone asked Sambo how he felt about not being able to run for mayor he simply shrugged his shoulders, smiled, and said, “That be OK with me. I’s dinna wanna deal with dem folk anyway. I’s too busy collectin’ da trash. All right, buddy.”

The news of the dead body spread faster than that of a bad hairdo at the prom. Locals called the police station every five minutes wanting to know who it was and how did it happen. They stopped by the station with the same inquiries wanting the details, and offered their help. Was it a murder? An accident? A suicide? Was he stabbed or shot? The questions, as numerous as the seagulls, came in waves separated by a few minutes of peace. The rumors would soon start, and then the theories, until it was all balled up into one big unanswered mess. Finally, Chief Perry suggested to Lumus that they leave the station and meet back there in the evening when things calmed down and then they could talk without interruption. Lumus readily agreed.

Lumus and the Chief sat on the bench under the oak later that evening enjoying a slight breeze and a cold Coke.

"Lumus, let's go from the top and run through what we got. OK?"

"Sure 'nough."

"Well, we have an unidentified male, forty something, floating around in Miller's Creek, no weapon, no motive, no witnesses, no nothing." The Chief looked distraught. "Shucks, we don't have anything but a body. Now I'm assuming, and you correct me if I'm wrong, but I don't think by any stretch of the imagination that he drowned in that creek?"

"I'm with you, Chief. No, no way he drowned in the creek. I mean there's a remote possibility but highly unlikely. What would he be doing in Miller's Creek to begin with … swimming? I seriously doubt it. No, it doesn't make sense to me."

"Then he had to have been dumped there? Right?"

"Yeah. Either that or he could have killed himself right there and fell into the creek. But I don't think so."

"You reckon he was killed right there and just dumped in the creek?" the Chief theorized out loud. "Or killed somewhere else and taken there?"

"Hard to say. What I'm more concerned about is motive. Why was this guy killed in the first place?"

"Tell you what, Lumus. I'm gonna call Roy White over at the coroner's office, he owes me a favor, and see if they'll do an autopsy first thing in the morning. We'll get some X-rays and a dental impression done too. You got any other ideas?"

"Not really. Roy White, huh? That's your old fishing buddy … ain't it?"

"Yep, good man. It's probably the only way we're going to get an ID on the body. Man, those crabs really did a number on him and whatever else lives in that creek."

Lumus took a big swig off his Coke draining the bottle, letting out a long "A-a-a-h." "Chief, that'll take awhile. Meantime I've got a lead on who our man might be. It's not much but something. I'll follow up on it. And by tomorrow I should know more."

"Already? Eah, you've been busy. What you doing, Lumus. Bucking for my job?"

Lumus chuckled and said, "O-o-o-h no Chief, uh-uh. I'm not after your job, that's for sure. What I did was check around for anybody that might have been away for a while and this one fella, Thomas Poe, … he lives down at Station 12, hasn't been accounted for and hasn't been seen in the last week. It could be something? You never know?"

"Poe?" The Chief scratched his head. " Poe? Oh yeah. Works in the city, kinda quiet guy. Divorced last year, wasn't he? You've seen him, Lumus. Remember? He drives an old, blue Dodge, all beat up. Was it parked at his house?"

"Yeah, come to think of it, it was. I saw it in the driveway."

"Anyway, follow up on that and keep me posted." The Chief pushed himself up and with a smile rubbed his stomach. "I'm heading for the hill. The little Mrs. is cooking some fried chicken, fresh corn on the cob and a squash casserole. You wanna come by for a bite? Some mighty good eating."

"Thanks Chief, but I'll pass and tell your better half I say 'hello.'" I'll follow up on that Poe fellow and let you know something tomorrow."

"Good night, Lumus, check with ya tomorrow." A long pause. "Got some homemade apple pie for dessert."

"Maybe next time." Lumus smiled. "Good night, Chief."

The next afternoon while Lumus was nosing around Thomas Poe's place looking for anything out of the ordinary, Chief Perry received word from the coroner's office that Thomas Poe had died from a single gunshot wound to the back of the head and the deadly bullet came from a .45 caliber pistol. There was something strange about this particular slug, something odd, that Roy White and his crew couldn't quite explain. It came from a very old gun like an antique they thought but, and this was the puzzling point, how could a gun that old be in working condition? Roy made a mental note to check with Chief Perry on that.

Chief Perry immediately called Lumus on the radio and told him to come to the station. They huddled under the fan seeking some kind of breeze and relief from the heat.

"Lumus, I just got word from Roy White. By the way, did you find anything at Poe's?"

"Nothing at Poe's. What did Roy say?"

"The cause of death was a pistol shot in the back of the head."

Lumus allowed himself a grin before answering "Chief, I had an idea that might have been it but I didn't want to say anything and get everyone all riled up and then it turn out to be something different. I noticed a hole at the base of the skull when they pulled him out the creek." It was a statement of fact, not braggadocio.

"Well Lumus, that narrows it down to either murder or suicide. Me … I'm leaning towards murder."

"Me too, Chief. It doesn't fit that someone shoots themselves in the back of the head on the bank at Miller's Creek. Why not do it at home or in the car? Yep, I'm with you but I'll check the tide table and go to the landing at low tide and scout around for a weapon and a spent casing just in case."

Chief Perry, looking anxious, was up and headed for the door in more of a hurry than usual.

"Where you headed?" Lumus asked.

"Run those damn kids off the hill before one of 'em breaks his neck. The other day that O'Toole kid was sliding down backwards on one of those bread racks, you know the plastic ones Newman puts the bread in."

"So what, all those kids use those now … they've graduated from cardboard."

"Yeah, but he was standing up."

"A-a-a-w don't worry about them, Chief. Next thing you know they'll be sliding down on their heads."

"You're right, Lumus. But I'm still going up there and scare the hell out of 'em." The Chief paused and reflected. "You know Lumus, … you know what I think? … I think those kids get a kick out of me chasing 'em?" He gave Lumus a big grin on the way out. "Check with ya about suppertime?"

"Yeah, see ya then, Chief."

Lumus wasn't a trained detective, far from it. And for all intents and purposes wasn't even a trained policeman. What working knowledge he possessed in the area of police work evolved from his on-the-job-training and what he gleaned from Chief Perry, which was mostly in the area of human relations on how *not* to act at times. His technical training was minimal.

A great deal of his ability to perform his duties as a police officer, and for that matter as a human being, came from the training he received from his favorite pastime of sailing. There he practiced common sense and patience. With the Poe case he knew he had a murder victim on his hands and he knew he had to ID the body and then find the motive behind the death. The identifying of the body might take a while but that would be the easy part compared to finding a motive. Deep down all Lumus felt he needed was a starting line, a point where he could say "Go" and take off, and the rest would fall into place. But where was that starting line?

Meanwhile, Bubba 'n me were as happy as pigs in mud with our newfound freedom. Two restrictions within a few weeks were too much for even our well-trained and disciplined young minds to handle. Being locked up in a house was a mental strain on me. Physically it was like a short vacation but not being able to talk with people, to form and express my ideas and to exchange thoughts with others, the whole human mental process, was a stifling and frustrating situation for me. It led to frustration, an emotion I had a hard time dealing with. Even though our captive period had only been two days it felt more like two months and now the freedom felt great. It was even better than the *apology* of sorts I received from my parents who were not the type to give in to apologizing, especially to one of their own that they had unfairly punished. I felt like saying I told you so, but being out of the house felt so good … no not good, but GREAT! … so great that my anger at having been unjustly punished vanished. And I had also gotten over the grilling from the crew at Burton's. Wow! I was free again! And freedom sure has a perception of its own. Like my Mom used to say, "There's a silver lining in every dark cloud."

Bubba 'n me nearly wore the rubber off the tires on our bikes those first couple of days. Up and down the Island we went, going nowhere in particular, just going, moving, and checking things out. Maybe we suffered from Attention Deficit Hyperactivity Disorder, the modern day ADHD, and didn't know it. Shoot, if that were true then we could have used it as an excuse every time for our misbehavior, which led to so much trouble, and it could have gotten us out of being punished. But, alas, we were stuck with our own actions and we were responsible for them. How unfair can life be for two squirrelly twelve-year-olds?

Thinking out loud I mentioned to Bubba that school started back the day after Labor Day, only a few weeks away. His response was not what I had in mind.

"Devlin, what are you trying to do? Ruin a perfectly good day by talking about school."

"Eah, don't get all bent out of shape. It was just a thought."

He turned serious and almost yelled although I was only five feet from him, "Well, keep those kind of thoughts to yourself, OK! I don't feel like hearing about school, not now."

School was not Bubba's cup of tea, far from it. He struggled academically and his behavior was troublesome at times, which I was partly to blame for, sometimes egging him on to do something that I was afraid to try. The crew also knew that Bubba could easily be persuaded to take on some daredevil bet or be tempted into doing something stupid, while we all sat back and watched another tragedy unfold. It was almost like a modern day soap opera and Bubba was the leading character, the one who usually ended up getting caught and punished. I believe my friend acted this way in school partly because of a an impulsive type personality and at times, I'm sure, he felt backed into a corner and figured he had to make a choice of going along with the crowd and feeling accepted or turning his back on us and doing the right thing. Bubba would much rather be part of the group than anything. We all felt that way. Don't misunderstand what I'm saying. By no means did Bubba have a lock on getting into trouble … no-siree. The crew and I were often in hot water at school along side Bubba. So, in the end, we shared in the punishments, taking our medicine without complaint … mine being double trouble.

We were instructed, not taught, by the Order of O.L.M. nuns at Saint Angela's School in Mt.Pleasant, a new facility with spacious classrooms and new desks. There was no air-conditioning or lunchroom … only new classrooms and a chapel. It was completed in 1956 replacing the one- room brick building next to the Rectory of Saint Angela's Church at Station 12 where one teacher had taught two grade levels simultaneously, about forty squirming first and second graders. No wonder Sister Vincent never smiled and seemed to always have a bad disposition about her.

For many years I had heard or seen the anagram "O.L.M." following all of our teachers' names. Sister Mary Agnes, O.L.M., did this or did that. Sister Caroline, O.L.M. taught here or there. I never knew what the "O.L.M." stood for and never questioned it until the expansion of my little mind by the "teachings " of the nuns of "O.L.M." themselves led me to seek an answer. And where better to find the answer than in my own family from Sissy, our official future-nun representative.

I caught her in the midst of her favorite pastime preparing another of her classroom setups complete with desks, chairs, a chalkboard, and the ever-present crucifix hanging in the front of the room.

A particular, but not necessarily true story goes that the parents of a non-Catholic boy of frightful behavior and slack academic habits had enrolled their troublesome son at St. Angela's School in hopes of straightening him out. After only a week at school he showed immediate improvement and never gave an ounce of trouble studying diligently and becoming a model student. When asked if his turnaround was due to the strict demands of the nuns or the atmosphere of the Catholic regime he answered in a most serious manner.

"Oh no, it wasn't that."

"What was it then?"

He answered sincerely, "When they sat me down that first day in class and I looked up and saw that man hanging from a cross I knew they meant business!"

His understanding may have been flawed but no one could argue with the results.

I approached Sissy cautiously trying to be serious, which I was, but her perception of me was all-different. "Can I ask you something about school?"

"About school? You want to ask *me* something about *school*?" She looked like she was going to faint.

"Yeah, school."

"As long as you're not joking or up to some trick." She put the look on me. "Sure, what is it?"

"What does "O.L.M." after the nuns' name mean?"

"Oh that? That's easy. It stands for the name of their Order, their special group. It's Our Lady of Mercy … O.L.M."

I almost laughed but knew better to do that in front of a future nun. I might get a few whacks on the butt.

"Our Lady of Mercy," I repeated in disbelief with emphasis on "Mercy."

WHOA! Where'd that come from? I thought. Mercy? *Somebody must have made a mistake.*

There has never been a more erroneous title given to a group of people in the history of education or any other field for that matter than labeling those nuns as people of "mercy." The word was not in their vocabulary much less their thoughts. The only mercy they showed us was in not taking our lives.

When I relayed my discovery to Bubba he laughed and then commented, " Humph … that's a joke. They ought to be called O.L.P. … Our Lady of Pain."

I only thank God we were able to laugh about it.

A wooden ruler of the twelve-inch variety was the favorite weapon of choice used by Our Ladies of Mercy to administer their expressions of intimidation upon us. It was fairly small, handy and if handled properly was capable of inflicting enough pain to get and hold a student's attention and it could occasionally be used, when a teacher found the time, as a pointer during classroom instruction. Our palms had become calloused and our knuckles were hardened like steel over the years from the many reminders to pay attention or abide by this rule or that rule. Shoot, they must have had about a hundred of them. Bubba 'n the crew and me had taken so many whacks collectively that the structural integrity of the rulers at Saint Angela's had literally reached their breaking point. At first, when a ruler snapped during attitude adjustment time, we smirked and let out an occasional giggle while Sister "Whoever" continued to whale away with the remainder of the ruler, frustrating her even more. She would fret and stomp around looking for another ruler, all red-faced and bewildered looking. Sister Ann Marie got so flustered one time after breaking a ruler on Bubba's knuckles and then not being able to find another ruler that she grabbed the nearest textbook and let the grinning Bubba really have it. But by this time it was a done deal, the battle was over, as far as we were concerned when the ruler broke. We won that one. The misbehavior continued, the punishments continued, and to our enormous glee the breaking of the rulers continued. So Sister Roberta, the principal, who was not exactly of rocket-scientist mentality, but had enough sense to figure out that if the rulers were breaking then she would replace them with rulers that would not break, simple enough. That dreadful day arrived as we hid crouched behind a big oak tree near the parking lot and the Sisters came rolling in, packed tightly in the blue station wagon we had affectionately named "The Blue Goose." For weeks rumors had flown concerning the big rulers Sister Roberta had threatened to buy for every teacher (we had a spy in the front office) with orders to whack away and "see if you are strong enough to break one of these." Rumor had these rulers the size of a baseball bat with sharp nails sticking out the end but we weren't concerned with some silly rumor. We just wanted to see the real thing for ourselves. And we did that morning when Sister Rosalind, the strongest of the O.L.M. ladies, strained to lift the bundle of wood from the trunk aided by Sister Ann Marie, the next strongest. We weren't of potential rocket-scientist mentality ourselves but we knew trouble when we saw it and we saw it in the form of those huge, long, thick pieces of wood called rulers …well, they did have numbers on them. They looked like something Julius Caesar's troops might have used to slaughter the Gauls. Oh boy! Now we wished the old rulers had never broken under the pressure. In my mind was the question: *Who is going to be stupid enough to mess up and receive the first big-ruler treatment?*

It did not take us long to find out. That very morning Randy Dawson who was dumb enough to take the bet but not stupid enough to take the dare had the honor and for a measly fifty cents pushed Sister Rosalind, who didn't need much of a push to begin with, to the limits of restraint. And when he finally refused to quit turning in his desk and talking to the very quiet Mike Hartnett who wanted no part of the big ruler, Randy received markings that he carries with him today. Randy, smiling and grinning, approached Sister Rosalind upon her demand with his hands out, ready for the usual slap on the hands. Uh-uh, not today or tomorrow. No more raps on the hands anymore. To Randy's utter surprise and ours too, he was ordered to empty his pockets, bend over, and grab your ankles because it was you're-butt-is-mine-time. And, let me tell you, the little O.L.M. ladies of St. Angela's took Sister Roberta's challenge to heart and were trying their best to break a big ruler. They could lay the lumber!

Corporal punishment was quick, to the point, and over in a minute. And then we were off to find more mischief to get into. Instead of learning a lesson from our mistake and subsequent punishment we carried only a stinging backside from the experience, which disappeared along with any recollection of why we had been paddled in the first place. However, leave it to sister Roberta to come up with another form of punishment. One designed for those die-hard rebels who did not seem to be fazed by the big ruler treatment. It was "mental punishment," which in the end proved to act as a deterrent and benefit at the same time. A-a-a-h, the genius of Sister Roberta.

This mental punishment, which involved academic work like doing mathematics tables or memorization of lengthy poems or spelling lists, was a long drawn out affair and took place after school. We dreaded these sessions mostly because they required mental effort and sustained concentration. We never once gave a serious thought that these mental exercises could possibly be beneficial in any way but in the long run we should have been performing these types of "punishments" all along sharpening our skills and improving our memorization process. For normal misbehavior, like excessive talking in class or not doing your class work or disrupting class, the punishment might be staying in at recess and completing your assignment or just sitting there doing nothing for fifteen minutes. For more serious infractions, like being disrespectful toward a teacher or constant disruption of class or fighting, you would receive a request from the principal to stay after school, which you gladly accepted or the punishment would automatically be doubled plus a phone call would be made to your parents.

And this is where my friend Bubba suffered mental anguishes far greater than any physical pain he had endured from a paddling. It's true if his behavior had been what the teachers asked then he would not have to face the dreaded after-school detention but he seemed to be on the hot list of troublemakers along with me and three or four others who led the daily parade into the after-school detention room. We had permanent, reserved seating in Sister Ann Marie's room, front and center with an unobstructed view.

There were no paddlings, no knuckle rapping, no type of corporal punishment. To the outsider it may have looked like a piece of cake but the mental demand was almost overwhelming. Upon entering Sister Ann Marie's room you were usually handed a poem to memorize word for word, no exceptions allowed. The poem was not some three or four verse no-brainer that a third grader could memorize in a few minutes. Rather it was something along the lines of Kipling's, "A Tree," something to occupy even the smartest minds in our class, which I thought was ironic because the smart kids were never in detention. The poem was to be memorized in its entirety, verse by verse, word for word, and had to be recited to Sister Ann Marie verbatim before you were allowed to go home. I was blessed with the ability to memorize whether it was words or numbers, therefore I did not have that difficult of a time with the poems and was usually on my way home after thirty to forty-five minutes of hard concentration.

But poor Bubba.

He had a heck of a time memorizing what day it was and this assignment was way out of his league on the concentration scale. He surely would have preferred the big ruler treatment, anything other than trying to memorize a long poem, which held no interest for him. He tried his best but for whatever reason he was always the last to leave detention sometimes not getting home until 5:00 or 5:30. After one such lengthy stay and repeated failed attempts at reciting his poem, Sister Ann Marie jokingly suggested that Bubba get a cot and set it up in his classroom on his days of detention so he could sleep right there and never be late for school again. Bubba failed to see the humor in that remark nor did he cotton to my suggestion that he not get any more detentions and that way he would not have to worry about staying after school.

Bubba's response was, "And how am I supposed to not get any more detentions … kill all those nuns?"

He received no more suggestions from me.

29
THOMAS POE

I was tip-toeing across the back porch on my way outside. I was like a cat burglar. Quiet as a dead mouse. I could hear the rattling of pots and pans and the slamming of cabinet doors in the kitchen. It was my mother. Too busy, I hope, to notice me slipping out.

Hey, I'm getting pretty good at this, I thought. Not a board squeaked. *Now open the door r-e-a-l easy like and ZOOM ... I'm outta here.*

I pushed the screen door ever so gently.

E-E-E-K … a tiny, tiny squeak from the rusty spring.

"M-i-k-e!"

I froze.

"You hear me? Be back here by 12:00. I need you to watch over the girls," my mother yelled from the kitchen and then stuck her head around the corner. "I've got to go to Mt. Pleasant and run some errands … OK?"

A disgusted, "Yes Ma'am."

"Let me hear that again, Mister," she said like only my mother could say.

Way more cheerful, "Yes Ma'am," I answered like only I could answer.

Durn. I almost made it, I thought as I headed for Bubba's. *I know ... I'll put some oil on that spring.*

Bubba was just coming off his back porch when I came up the driveway.

"Eah! What ya doing?" asked Bubba."Where you headed?" He was picking up his bike.

"Nothing much, just came over to see what you're doing."

"I wanted to get out the house for awhile. Tell ya what … how about let's go for a ride," he suggested. "See what's going on."

"OK," I said, "let me get my bike … meet ya out front."

"Eah, I know what we can do." Bubba said suddenly all pumped up. "Let's go see if old Bruno wants to race. We haven't done that in a long time. Come on, that'll be fun."

Bruno was the Kimbrell's dog, a big Boxer, who loved to chase us on our bikes. We didn't know if he would bite us or not because we never hung around long enough to find out. But he sure looked mean and had a nasty bark. I was tired of racing Bubba all the time and didn't have anything else to do so I thought, *what the heck.*

"Sure why not."

Old Bruno was in his usual spot … half asleep … in the shade under an oleander bush.

"Br-u-u-u-n-o-o, where are you," Bubba chanted, drawing the attention of the now awake Bruno. He cut his eyes up at us and began to slowly rise, ready for the chase. We were about twenty feet away. We needed the head start because he was fast.

"Br-u-u-u-n-o-o, come out wherever you are," Bubba said challenging Bruno. "Bet you can't catch us." Bubba edged dangerously closer.

Old Bruno waited until we were within striking distance and then he charged, barking and growling like crazy. For whatever reason he seemed extra mad today. We took off and pedaled hard, pumping our little legs like pistons.

"See ya later, Bruno," Bubba yelled back at the fading dog. "You're to-o-o slow."

"Hey man, this ain't fun no more," I said as I coasted up beside Bubba. "Either Bruno is getting old or we're getting faster. Remember how he used to almost catch us?"

Bubba looked back again and Bruno was still running after us. "Yeah, but old Bruno don't know that. Here he comes. OK Devlin, let's really move … let's haul it. Ready. Go!"

I stood up and pumped hard, my legs moving in perfect unison. Bubba did the same as we put some distance between us and the barking Bruno. I sat on my seat, quit pedaling and began to coast. And then I heard Bubba scream.

"What's wrong," I asked, "looking back."

"W-H-O-A! Mike! Hey, come here quick … my chain's slipped off." Normally that was no big deal, a chain coming off the sprocket, but at a time like this it definitely became a concern.

A quick glance and there was Bubba coasting along, losing speed fast, and Bruno closing like a missile, growling with bared teeth.

"Hang on, Bubba. I'm coming!" And so was Bruno, closing the gap quickly between him and Bubba. Today, unfortunately, we just might find out if Bruno would bite.

I pulled along side Bubba who was looking at me and then looking at Bruno and then back at me. Bruno opened his big mouth and was about to take a bite out of Bubba's leg.

"Jump on my bike … on the seat." I yelled, … "I'll stand up."

Bubba jumped off his bike shoving it aside and with his feet barely touching the ground (maybe they didn't?) launched himself onto my seat, all in one quick motion grabbing hold to me while I pedaled with all I had.

Bruno gave it all he had too but giving it all I had we left him in the dust. I learned a valuable lesson in life that day … and it was that if you have enough incentive you can prevail when times are tough. I definitely had more incentive than old Bruno because you see I was the one about to be bitten. That was plenty of incentive.

"PHEW, man I'm pooped," I said as I slowed to a stop a couple of blocks later. "That was too close."

"Yeah, bet you are. But that was neat the way you picked me up … just like on TV … in the Westerns when …"

"I know, I know," I said cutting Bubba off … "when the cowboy jumps on the horse."

"How'd you know that?" Bubba asked.

I rolled my eyes at him and then said, "Eah, wanna try it again?" I teased and yelled, "Here Bruno-o-o-o."

"No, no way … hey, don't call that dog … I've had enough of Bruno. Mike, I really think ol' Bruno would have bitten my leg off if you hadn't saved me. Thanks, man."

"Eah, you're welcome, my friend. And just think all this time we thought Bruno was just playing."

"Shows you how smart we are," said Bubba and then we both laughed. It was mostly a laugh of relief.

We had to wait until Bruno went back to his resting place before we retrieved Bubba's bike and then we headed up the Island. Shoot, I only had a few hours before I had to be back home and baby-sit. On the way toward the business district we came across the Reilly's dog, Snowball, a feisty, pure white Chihuahua who charged us with the same vigor as Bruno even though he was about one-tenth the size of Bruno. He was furiously barking that irritating, high-pitched bark or yap that grates on the nerves. It reminded me of Mary Rogers at school when she went into one of her whining episodes.

"Go away, Snowball. We don't want to fool with you," I yelled. "Go away… you hear?" He would usually leave after being talked to like that but for some reason he was being a pain in the bee-hind today. He continued to bark and chase after us. After the race with Bruno we didn't feel like messing with some small time mutt like Snowball. However, the more we ignored him the more he barked and the braver he got until he was snapping at Bubba's heels, ready to pounce. And pounce he did! He jumped and bit at Bubba's shoe getting instead a mouthful of shoelaces and bit down hard, not letting go.

"What the …?" Bubba couldn't believe what he saw. Lifting his foot, Snowball came off the street too, locked onto Bubba's shoelaces. Poor snowball's teeth had become entwined in Bubba's shoelaces but we didn't know that. All we saw was this little dog biting down on Bubba's shoe with grim determination.

"Mike, can you believe this," Bubba chuckled, "I'm being attacked by the "monster dog" Snowball. Watch this." Bubba lifted his foot again and swung Snowball around. "Durn, he won't let go … stupid dog." Bubba held up his leg with the still growling Snowball locked into Bubba's laces, dangling in the air.

"T-h-a-t's right, Catbird," I said, "this time you're on your own." I pedaled ahead. "See ya l-a-t-e-r."

"Eah, wait up," yelled Bubba, "what am I gonna do with …"

I looked back and Bubba was coasting along with his leg raised and shaking it with Snowball, growling like a mad dog, hanging on for dear life. Bubba made a close pass at a group of garbage cans, and gave a gentle swing of his leg toward the garbage can knocking the hanging dog into it. Bubba wanted Snowball to hit just hard enough to knock loose the gritty little Chihuahua, not to hurt him. I might have known Bubba's luck. He was forever getting caught. It didn't seem like he could get away with anything. Because at that very second Mrs. Reilly poked her head out the door just in time to witness Bubba banging Snowball into the garbage can and dropping to the ground. She came flying down the steps screaming at Bubba to stop and claiming she saw what he did to her poor little Snowball.

"Come back here, Bubba O' Toole! You hear me! Come back here this second! I'm gonna get Bull Perry on you … you just wait and see!" was the last thing we heard her yell.

Man, what a day with these dogs, Bubba thought, *no more for me.*

As I leisurely pedaled on I heard this voice behind me scream, "Eah, wait up."

Within a minute my friend was at my side, grinning broadly.

"What you so happy about?" I asked.

"Guess," he said.

"No more dogs?" I said and Bubba let out a loud, "BA-HA-HA-HA-HA!" Then he said very quietly, almost in a whisper, "Right."

Bubba 'n me came across Lumus at Chippy's gassing up the police Jeep. We pedaled hard for more speed, slammed on brakes in the gravel turning our handlebars sideways so as to go into our infamous gravel-slide, timing our slide perfectly, coming to a stop not five feet from Lumus.We were smiling, feeling good about life after getting off restriction.

"Hey there boys! How ya doin'? Free again, huh?"

"Yes sir," Bubba yelled and smiled, "and we aim to stay that way. Right Mike?"

"Yep, for as long as we can. That being grounded is for the birds."

"Eah, I got a question for y'all."

We were all ears.

"What's worse than one wild Irishman let loose on the Island on a bike?"

"I dunno?" we answered together.

"Two!" There was a pause and when Lumus started to laugh we joined in.

"So … you boys doing OK?"

We really didn't have to say a word to explain how we felt. Our body language was oozing with good feelings.

"Great Lumus," I said, "we're doing great."

Shoot, if it hadn't been for Lumus we would probably still be grounded and I wanted him to know that.

"Lumus, I want to thank you for finding that body. If you hadn't we would have been grounded for life." I glanced Bubba's way. "Right, Bubba?"

"Yeah… uh-huh … that's right." He hadn't even heard me.

He was eyeballing the shapely figure of Julie Owens, nineteen years old and a real "looker," going into her father's grocery store and who could blame Bubba. She was beautiful and built like … well, I heard one of the adults put it rather succinctly, "She'd make a grown man cry." She was wearing a pair of pink short-shorts so tight she had to be poured into them, and a low-cut tank top advertising her endowment.

Lumus noticed me noticing Bubba noticing Julie and said with a friendly smile tinged with fatherly advice, "Later boys, later, when you get a little older."

Bubba snapped back to reality when I punched him in the ribs. "Oh yeah … later. That'll be nice. What later?"

I ignored Bubba and was curious about the body that was found in the creek. "Who's the dead man, Lumus? Anybody we know?"

"Don't know for sure yet but as soon as we find out, you boys will be the first to know."

"For real, Lumus!" *Wow! He's gonna tell us first about who the dead man is,* I thought. *Maybe we can help him find out who the man is. Get to do some police work.* Shoot, I was excited about just the possibility of helping the police solve a case, maybe even a murder case? "Hear that Bubba? Lumus is going to …"

Bubba had drifted off again. His only interest was Julie as he stared at the store hoping for her to exit so he could ogle at her again. And when she came out she stopped, glanced across the street, and gave a big wave and smile. "Hi boys, how ya'll doing? … Hey, Lumus." Bubba, his elbows resting on the handlebars, tried desperately to return the wave, but lost his balance and fell over the front of his bike falling onto the pavement like a drunk.

Lumus couldn't hold back a small laugh. Me? I laughed so hard I almost fell off my bike while Bubba picked himself up and checked himself for injuries, trying hard to maintain some degree of dignity. "Eah, I gotta go," said Lumus. "When we find out who that guy is we'll let you know. Keep your noses clean … and Bubba … look out for them pretty women. They can be dangerous."

Lumus wheeled off with The Drifters top song, "There Goes My Baby," playing on the small transistor radio dangling from the mirror. Their soulful sound cut through the humid air and as I sang along with them I was tempted to do a little dance right then and there. And I probably would have, but Bubba was the only available partner … Bubba with the two left feet.

Why couldn't Beverly be here? Right now. We could dance. I was thinking out loud. My mother told me that thinking out loud and talking to yourself were signs of old age. *Twelve years old and getting old. "Humph. Dag gone ... I better slow down.*

"What's today?" I asked as we were riding back down the Island.

"Wednesday. Why?"

"Wednesday!" I whistled. "Great day. It's almost the weekend. You going to the movies Saturday, aren't you?"

"Yep."

"You got any money?"

"Nope."

"How you gonna get in?"

"Sneak in … how else?"

"I should have known. You and Sharpe I bet? You know, y'all are gonna get in trouble …just wait and see."

"Mike, let me tell you something. There's only one way we're going to get into trouble and that is if we get caught which ain't gonna happen as long as ol' Harvey's working. That guy can go to sleep standing up. Ever see that?"

"Yeah, he puts his hand on the side of his face and props himself up and just goes right to sleep. He never has checked my ticket. Eah, maybe you and Sharpe got something good going there?"

"T-h-a-t-s right, Catbird. And don't you get any ideas, OK? You just go ahead and pay like always."

"All right, all right. I was just thinking …"

"I know what you were thinking so just don't think it any more, OK?"

"Eah, I heard ya. Don't get all excited; you might fall off your bike again."

Bubba smiled but not at my remark. He was remembering why he had fallen off his bike earlier.

"Let me ask you this, Mr. Sneaker-In. How do you plan on buying popcorn and a Coke and stuff? Gonna sneak in on that too?"

"Oh no. I thought I'd borrow some money from you."

"Fraid not, my friend. You better think again."

Bubba looked dejected but only for a second then he grinned from ear to ear and said, "Let's go crabbing."

I wondered how long it would take him to figure that out.

"Bingo! Look, I've got to baby-sit this afternoon for a few hours but the tide's not right until late this afternoon …right?"

"Yeah … real late," Bubba said. "So here's what we do. I'll get us some customers while you baby-sit and get the lines together. How's that?"

"T-h-a-t-s right, Catbird," I said slowly and happily.

We pedaled a little faster and with a little more enthusiasm. We were going *crabbing*.

It hadn't been ten minutes since we talked to Lumus about the murder and already I had forgotten about wanting to help him with it. Well, not completely forgotten but my mind was on going crabbing and making some money. Sister Roberta had often fussed at us about something called attention span or something like that. Maybe that was what she was talking about?

Lumus and the Chief had no problem with their attention span. They were focused. And determined to first identify the body and then seek out a motive. Lumus was already thinking ahead.

That evening Lumus and the Chief, Cokes in hand, sat on the bench outside the station again going over all they knew about the dead body hoping that by talking it out they might strike a nerve with each other and spark something new which would get them going in the right direction.

Lumus' summary was getting old, even to himself. "White male, about forty years old, shot in the back of the head, old pistol, .45 caliber, body dumped in Miller's Creek. Ain't much to go on, huh Chief?"

"Nope, ain't much. Ain't much at all, Lumus. We should hear something back on the dental impressions tomorrow. Here's what I'd like for you to do. Call Dr. Brandenburg." Paul Brandenburg was the local and only dentist on the Island and served half the Island's residents. "And see if that fellow … what's his name … the one you been checking on …"

"Poe," Lumus said, "Thomas Poe."

"Yeah, Poe. See if he just might be a patient of Brandenburg's and if he is then run a comparison of his dental records with the X-rays Roy White has. Maybe they match and we catch a break."

Lumus flashed a grin: "I'll be on it like a mockingbird on a June bug, first thing in the morning. But you know, Chief … there's something else bugging the fool out of me …"

"Yeah, I know, I know," the Chief said, "motive … what's the motive?"

Lumus and the Chief's adversary, Dr. Steven Jenkins, had been busy too. And he also was a determined man. Determined to cover all bases and leave "those two Island country bumpkin cops scratching their empty heads."

Steven Jenkins had made it a point to be busy … a little more active in places he went … about the Island more than normal but not so much as to arouse any unnecessary suspicions. He did this because he knew the Island was small and a hotbed for gossip and rumor and by taking an extra shopping day or by checking the mail three times a week rather than his normal two he might overhear an opinion or some gossip regarding the recent finding of a body, which would help him get a feel for where the authorities were in their investigation.

His confidence got a shot in the arm when he overheard a conversation in Owen's Grocery about a week after the murder.

Two of Gertie's Girls were in open discussion while they snooped and shopped. He had never met any of these infamous ladies personally nor did he care to but, information regardless of the source was information and these ladies were full of it. Steven had spotted them when they first came into the store. He hadn't given them any thought, thinking they were just two old ladies out to do some shopping. Then he overheard the word "dead" in their conversation. That got his attention. So he trailed them, staying as close as he could without arousing suspicion. As he fiddled with groceries on the shelf, he listened.

"Who do you think that dead man is that Lumus and the Chief found?"

"I don't know but I have my suspicions."

"Well, who then? Tell me because I want to see if it's the same person I'm thinking about."

"You won't say anything to anybody if I tell you, will you?"

"Oh no, this is just between you and me."

Steven breezed by the gossipers, whose antennae sensed another person's presence and immediately they clammed up, holding up jars of jelly as though they were conducting an inspection.

"Afternoon, ladies."

A speedy "hi" and "hello." They quickly put the jelly back on the shelf giving Steven a cursory glance. They wanted to get back to talking.

Steven set up a listening post behind the bread rack performing his own inspection of different brands.

"I think it's that Wilburn fella, the one that lives over near Middle Street. He's always complaining about the noise from all the cars or the kids playing or somebody hammering or God knows what. He says his neighbors … and Betty told me this too … make noise at night slamming the doors at their house. He's always mouthing off about something. He can't keep his big mouth shut."

"N-a-a-w, it ain't him."

"It's gotta be! Ain't nobody meaner than him. Why last month I heard he cussed out Sambo for rattling the trash cans. Yeah, more than likely it's him. Somebody got tired of all his stuff and let him have it."

"N-a-a-w, it ain't him, I'm telling ya."

"Well, how can you be so sure? To me he's a prime candidate for being shot and dumped in the creek."

"I know it ain't him because I just saw Mr. Wilburn in the Post Office this morning and he wasn't dead. He was alive as you and me standing here."

"O-o-o-o-h." A long pause. "In that case … well, u-u-u-h … do you think the Chief and Lumus can catch whoever did it?"

There was a slight chuckle. "Are you kidding? Those two couldn't catch a cold swimming naked in the ocean in the middle of January. Do you know they don't even have bullets for those guns? Shoot, Moses on foot with just his stick would have a better chance than Lumus and Bull Perry." They both shared a laugh on that one.

"They're that bad, huh?"

"Yep. Bull Perry's been here for what ten years? And he hasn't even caught one kid on the hill yet. You think he's gonna catch a murderer? Fat chance. If he does I'll personally buy him two dozen of his favorite doughnuts. And Lumus …" She rolled her eyes. "Humph. Forget it. Let's get outta here … my feet hurt."

Returning home Steven Jenkins reflected on the events of the past week going over in his mind any lingering doubts about any evidence he might have overlooked: was the car clean of fingerprints or any other materials that could place Thomas Poe in my car, could anyone have seen me that night, did anyone hear the shot? But the fact that the police had not visited him and the public's perception of the police's ineptness assured him that he was worrying for nothing. He figured that by the time Lumus and Chief Perry got around to him as a suspect, if they ever did, he would be long gone.

The banking business had been tricky but money can buy silence and with the extra cash from the sale a portion of it had gone to the right person who assured Steven that "your business is strictly confidential." Upon his banker's recommendation Steven's "retirement funds" were resting safely in a Zurich bank, account number unknown except to Steven. The Swiss, he was comforted to know, were very good at this sort of special banking.

There was one more piece of important business to be taken care of but it could wait a few days.

"Enjoy yourself." He told himself. "Late breakfasts, more TV, the beach … It's over. You did it."

That's what he thought and he constantly told himself to relax but no matter what he did or where he went he could not shake the image of Thomas Poe's slumping head.

Early the next morning Lumus received a return call from Dr.Brandenburg's office. It was not the greatest break in the world but it was all Lumus needed. It was a start. Thomas Poe had been a patient of Dr.Brandenburg and "yes" they had a recent set of X-rays on file and "yes" Lumus was welcome to them.

Why not go by Dr.Brandenburg's, pick up those X-rays, take them to Roy White at the Coroner's Office and let him make the comparison?

Everything went smoothly except Roy White was not at his office so Lumus left the X-rays there and enjoyed a leisurely ride back to the Island, especially taking in the spectacular view from the top of the Cooper River Bridge, a monstrous two-lane structure perched some two hundred feet above the Cooper River, connecting Mt. Pleasant and Charleston. Lumus could clearly see the Island and its silent features, feeling like a bird in flight looking down even though the Island was several miles in the distance. By the time he reached the causeway and took in a closer view of the Island he wondered, *Why would anyone want to live anywhere else?*

Lumus spent the rest of the afternoon or what was left of it performing the unenviable task of taking care of the office paperwork, a job he hated and a task which Chief Perry conveniently ignored. The Chief was napping in the back room.

Late that afternoon Lumus decided to spend the night at the station rather than go home.

After his dinner of a greasy burger and fries, Lumus went outside and plopped on the bench. The phone rang later alarming Lumus who was half napping under the oak tree. He caught it on the fourth ring.

"Hello, Lumus here."

"Lumus, hello, it's Roy White. Sorry I missed you this morning … damned meeting and I've been so busy all day I don't know which end is up. I didn't catch you napping under the oak tree, did I?"

"How'd you know?" Lumus snickered. "But I was only half napping."

"Is that all y'all got to do out there in paradise?" Roy joked. "Well, maybe I shouldn't say that now, seeing that you got a real case on your hands."

"To tell you the truth Roy, we don't know what we got on our hands just yet. Hoping you might help us out."

"Lumus, I know you didn't expect to hear from us so soon but Angie said you seemed a little anxious this morning about getting these results back and anyway, we got a real break on identifying your man."

Lumus almost jumped through the phone. "What kind of break, Roy?"

"Well, as it turns out, the deceased still had his college ring on. Seems he is a Citadel graduate, Class of 1934."

"But Roy," Lumus interrupted, "I don't understand. There were a lot of graduates in that class, weren't there?"

"Yep, but like I said we got a break. This graduate just happened to have his name inscribed inside his ring. Get a pencil out or something to write with. You ready?" A slight pause. "Thomas Edward Poe was his name," he said slowly. "Help you any? Oh, by the way, I checked with the records people over at The Citadel and they verified his attendance and graduation."

"Oh great, thanks Roy. That's a tremendous help! You just don't know. We were leaning toward this guy but couldn't nail down anything solid, just some hunches. This is great! Thanks so much, Roy."

"Hey, you're welcome, Lumus. Anytime and tell that fat ol' boss of yours to quit eating so many doughnuts and to call me next time he goes fishing."

"Will do and thanks again." Lumus hung up and turned toward the back room.

Chief Perry who was supposedly napping in the back entered the room yawning and tugging at his underwear stuck in a big crack and then he plopped in the chair at his desk.

An excited Lumus, thankful for the official ID of the body, and ready to get started with a full investigation, sat down across from the Chief. "Chief, would you believe … "

"Y-e-a-h, it's Thomas Poe, right?"

Lumus nodded. The Chief added, "And next time tell Roy White I'll take him fishing if he brings the doughnuts." Then he smiled at Lumus.

"Oh yeah, right," Lumus stammered, "but how'd you know? A-a-a-w, never mind. And Chief there's something else. Your wife called earlier and is looking for you and said if you aren't home by 7:00 she's throwing your dinner out to the dog."

"Damn, Lumus!" The Chief jumped from his chair like he'd been stuck with a needle. "Why didn't you wake me up?" He raced to the backroom, reappearing instantly while slipping on his hat.

"Are you kidding? I want to live long enough to help you solve this case." They both chuckled. The Chief was halfway out the door, waving goodbye. "See ya in the morning, Lumus."

"Good night, Chief."

Bubba 'n me were lucky to get orders for three dozen crabs on such short notice but our faithful buyers were dying for some fresh crabmeat. Mrs. Kelly wanted two dozen, said she had company coming and had to make some devil crabs, and Ms. Kingman needed a dozen. I wondered if Ms. Kingman really believed eating crabs would make her live longer? N-a-a-a-w.

It was a creepy almost scary feeling going back into the same creek again where ten days earlier a body had floated up to us from out of nowhere. Bubba was extra quiet from the minute we approached the landing and so was I. We looked to each other for assurance that everything was OK but each of us received a blank stare. Our fears were imaginary but you could not convince me of that. If I didn't need the extra money I would not have gone crabbing in Miller's Creek on that day. Maybe another time when the newness of what had happened had worn off a bit. But … here we were.

Could it happen again? Would it happen again? And what if it did? I asked myself, beginning to worry. *What would I do?*

As we drifted down the creek, my imagination got the best of me and I envisioned an underwater cemetery managed by ghoulish creatures of human design but outfitted with gills so they could breathe underwater. They were short and green and their half-fish, half-human bodies were decaying as pieces of their flesh fell off and were sucked away by the current only to be replaced by new green skin. And they decided when to release another body to the outside world from the line of dead people lying on the bottom of the creek all around them. Was today the day they let another one go? What if they let two go? Or three? Or four?

"Eah Bubba, you wanna try down by that little creek on the right?" I was obviously trying to steer us away from the sewer pipe and to relieve myself of thoughts of ghouls and dead people.

"Yeah, that's good." Bubba was up front about his fears and knew what I was thinking. "I don't want to go over there either," he said pointing across the creek toward the sewer pipe. "Unless you want to?"

It was somewhat tempting because we both knew the sewer pipe was a hotspot for the crabs and that by *not* crabbing there it would take longer to fill our order but, on this day, it would have taken more than the prospect of catching crabs quickly to lure us anywhere near that pipe. And sure enough by crabbing upstream and in unfamiliar territory we ended up on the slow boat to China as we occasionally pulled in a crab, waited, checked the lines and would pull in another a few minutes later only to repeat the slow process all over again. But neither of us complained, not once, because the reality of what we encountered ten days ago was still fresh in our little minds and who knows if there was another body over there? The slower pace inadvertently taught me patience, an area of my life I was definitely lacking in, and it made me more appreciative of what we were doing, borrowing from Mother Nature without any cost to us. Also without hurrying and rushing I had more time to think, something I enjoyed doing except for when I was in school.

I wonder who that man is? How did he die? Wonder if Lumus found out who he is?

I was quiet for a long time and enjoying the crabbing and Bubba's company when he spoke up. "I bet you're thinking about that dead man and who he is?"

"Yeah right." I was surprised. "How'd you know?"

"Because I was too. But you gotta remember I'm the one who is gonna grow up and be the police chief on the Island and solve *all* the cases. Tell you what, Mike. If you keep thinking about that dead man and figure out how to find out how he died and all, I'll make you my assistant, like Lumus is, and we'll catch all the bad guys."

I smiled at such a thought. Bubba the police chief and me as his assistant. "Just like the Cisco Kid and Pancho, huh?" My imagination was really running wild today.

"No, man, like The Three Stooges. U-U-A-H-H ... KNUCK-KNUCK-KNUCK." Bubba was gritting his teeth and turning his lips up at the corner of his mouth while rolling the proper four fingers, moving his arm back and forth bent at the elbow, then slapping one palm onto the other fist, all with wide open eyes, exactly like Curley. He was getting pretty good at being a Stooge.

"Instead of being the police chief why don't you get Tommy Wade and "Stinkey" Johnson and y'all take the place of The Three Stooges. Shoot, with those two and yourself y'all wouldn't even have to practice any routines. Y'all could just act natural and go right on TV. A-HA-HA-HA!"

It was my small attempt at humor on an otherwise humorless day and Bubba understood what we both needed. He threw back his head and roared with laughter, over and over sending out his best "BA-HA-HA-HAS" across Thomas Poe's silent and beautiful grave. Getting this first day in the creek behind us was a relief but knowing that we had run up on a dead person in Miller's Creek could never be totally forgotten. Like all bad things it would fade from our memory but a piece of it was lodged in permanence always to be remembered.

As soon as we hit the three-dozen mark Bubba yelled, "That's it, let's go!" And I agreed wholeheartedly. He pulled the anchor and we left for home.

30
HELPING OUT

Mrs. Kelly was one of our favorite customers, always upbeat, friendly and extra generous with the Kool-Aid, cookies, and smiles. Sometimes she even gave us a tip like my father used to earn while rowing the boat as a teenager, which I thought was nice of her, and having a little extra money didn't hurt either. She had retired years ago but still had a lot of the school teacher in her and liked to challenge us to a word game or present us with some type of riddle to solve, usually of the homemade variety dealing with the locals. I enjoyed the riddles more than the word games, which reminded me too much of schoolwork. I don't know what Bubba thought; however, he seemed to enjoy the Kool- Aid and cookies most of all … I think?

"Mrs. Kelly! Mrs. Kelly!" I yelled from the porch. "It's Bubba 'n me."

Bubba was bent over the basket, giving the crabs his final inspection so I thought.

"Eah, what you doing?" I asked. Bubba was waving his hands over the crabs. "Blessing them crabs?"

Bubba looked up. "What?"

"Are you blessing the crabs? The way you're waving your hands and all?"

"No, can't you see? I'm conducting a symphony, Einstein. Now leave the maestro alone."

"A symphony?"

"Yeah, if you'd be quiet for a second you could hear the music. S-s-s-s-h … listen. Hear it? There go the violins and if you listen real close you'll hear the horns come in." He cocked his head close to the basket, cupping his ear. "Hear 'em … now."

"Have you gone nuts? I think you've been in the sun too long."

"N-o-o-o …just watch." Bubba leaned over the basket, took his hand and moved it in a conductorly manner waving it just over the crabs' heads back and forth. All the crabs moved this way and that way, their extended claws moving in and out while their feelers moved to the sound of Bubba's imaginary music. And their beady little eyes diligently followed each movement of Bubba's hands. The faster he moved his hands the faster the crabs moved and when he slowed down so did the crabs. It was one heck of a symphony all right. The Crab Philharmonic Orchestra conducted by Crabber Bubba while he hummed the tune to "Dixie."

I yelled again real loud over the music from the symphony. "Mrs. Kelly!" I practically screamed in Mrs. Kelly's face as her shadow appeared on the other side of the screen door.

"Hold your horses! I'm coming, I'm coming."

"Oops, sorry Mrs. Kelly I didn't mean to yell when you were right there so ..."

"That's OK Mike, all is forgiven as long as y'all brought me some nice fat Jimmys like last time."

"Oh yes Ma'am. Two dozen fat ones." Actually there were twenty-five crabs. I slipped in an extra because she always gave us free Kool-Aid.

She reached in her apron pocket producing three quarters, placing them in my hand with a wide smile and she turned to leave as though she were in a big hurry. She was, and rushed off without saying a word. I didn't even have time to get a "thank you " out of my mouth.

Durn! No riddle or Kool-Aid?

As quickly as she left she returned, wiping her hands on her apron. Then she pulled her hair out of her face and put her hands on her hips.

"Couldn't let those cookies burn, now could I? Kool-Aid and burnt cookies? That wouldn't be so good, huh? You boys wouldn't drink a little Kool-Aid and eat some fresh chocolate chip cookies, would you?"

The hungry look in our eyes gave us away.

"Oh yes Ma'am," Bubba said immediately, "that would hit the spot." My eyes were wide open and I was nodding my head.

"Why Bubba, you're so sweaty. Looks like you've been conducting an orchestra?"

Bubba 'n me turned instantly and looked at each other with puzzled expressions, not saying a word.

"Hold on. I'll be right back." Mrs. Kelly ran back in the house again.

Bubba glanced toward the door to make sure Mrs. Kelly was gone. "Mike, how did she know about me and the crabs and the music and ..."

"I dunno know. Maybe she just knows stuff before it happens like one of those psychos... uh ... psychies ... no ... u-u-u-h ... help me out. What's the word? You know what I'm talking about."

"N-o-o-o, I don't."

"People that know things before they happen. In school one time Sister Ann Marie mentioned one who ..."

Mrs. Kelly came whirling onto the porch and said, "Psychic is the word you're looking for Mike. Someone with extrasensory perception or powers who can foresee the future and sometimes even read other peoples' minds." She set down a tray of warm chocolate chip cookies and a cold jug of our favorite … grape Kool-Aid.

"Yeah, that's it. Are you a ps… psy … psykit, Mrs. Kelly?" I asked.

"You mean a psychic. And no I'm not anymore than y'all are."

"Well, what about Bubba and the symphony he was conducting? How'd you know about that?"

"Oh that? Oh, I heard y'all talking through the screen door. I didn't mean to be eavesdropping on your conversation. I just overheard y'all. Both of you get a little loud every now and then … you know?"

"Not me," Bubba said, "it's Devlin who's loud. I'm the quiet one." Mrs. Kelly stepped back, hands on hips and looked at Bubba and said, "Yeah sure and I'm the Easter Bunny." She told us to help ourselves to the cookies and then asked if we were enjoying our summer?

"Yes Ma'am,"we answered, nodding our heads with mouths full of cookies.

"Y'all been behaving yourselves?"

"We always behave, Mrs. Kelly," Bubba said, "you know that."

"You do?" Her head rocked back and her eyes, big brown ones, opened wide. "I heard some wild rumor about Sambo being thrown from the garbage truck not too long ago down there near your house. Any truth to that?"

"Down by our house, huh? Well, you see … u-u-u-h … the truck kind of … well …" I was beating around the bush in hopes Mrs. Kelly might change the subject. Then she interjected, "Hah, that must have been a sight … Sambo falling off the truck. He wasn't hurt seriously, was he?"

"Oh no," Bubba said, "he just got bruised up some, nothing real bad."

"Yeah, and just a little cut on his arm, that's all," I added.

Durn. We done gone and told on ourselves again.

Mrs. Kelly studied us for a moment and said, "Seeing that we've already had our word game for today how about a riddle?"

"Yeah, great," I answered eagerly. Bubba nodded his head and put on his serious face.

"OK ready? Here goes. If I were you and you were me, where would we be now and what would we be doing?"

"Would you repeat that, please?" I asked.

"Sure," she said.

I was racking my brain trying to get the jump on Bubba. Somehow he always solved the riddles before me.

Too late. Before Mrs. Kelly could get a word out Bubba blurted out, "That's easy, we would be standing on your porch talking to you and you would be here selling us crabs."

"Right, Bubba! Right! That's good, real good and so quick too! You must do really well in school … in your grades I mean … you solve all the riddles."

"U-u-u-h … yes Ma'am … I … uh … do real good in school."

I thought at least he's being halfway truthful this time. I remember when someone gave him the same compliment and Bubba said that he made the Honor Roll. Shoot, he couldn't even spell "honor" and the only roll he ever made was down the hill.

Mrs. Kelly continued, "And I'll tell y'all something. If I were selling those crabs I'd charge at least fifty cents a dozen because I hear that's what the boys get for them in Mt. Pleasant." There was a short pause. "Just something for you boys to think about next time you're on restriction. Not that y'all will ever be on restriction again." Mrs. Kelly looked upward and rolled her eyes. "Check with me next week … OK?"

"Yes Ma'am," we said together. She turned and went inside.

We grabbed an extra cookie and got on our bikes. We rode in silence for about a block, both of us thinking about what Mrs. Kelly told us.

"That was nice of Mrs. Kelly to let us know we can get more money for our crabs," I commented. "Don't you think so?"

"Humph! I think we just got gypped by Mrs. Kelly. That's what I think."

"Yep … maybe so?" I smiled at Bubba as I rubbed the extra quarter between my fingers in my pocket, our tip.

We were on our way to Burton's when we passed a familiar sight. It was Pappy Lewis edging his way inch by inch with the help of his cane tapping on the ground in front of him heading towards Chippys to have his daily fill of beer. His distinctive straw hat and slow shuffle were an Island fixture. At the rate he was moving it would take the aging Pappy an hour to cover the three blocks to Chippys and the humidity was really high. Already he was sweating so I thought, *Why not help him out?*

I turned around calling for Bubba. "Come on, let's see if Pappy wants a ride to Chippys?"

"D-o-o-o what?"

"Come on. Let's see if Pappy needs a ride. It won't take but a few minutes. Look at that poor old man. You wouldn't want him to die out here in this heat before he got his last beer … would you?"

"Well, when you put it that way … no … I guess not."

We coasted to a stop beside the aging, wrinkled man, startling him somewhat.

"Who's that?" He peered hard through his glasses, the Coke-bottle kind. Even with the help of those glasses I don't believe Pappy could see more than three feet in front of him.

"It's me Pappy, Mike … Mike Devlin." He edged up to me and put his face real close to mine like he was examining some important document and affirmed my identity.

"And Bubba! Over here, Pappy," Bubba yelled announcing his whereabouts.

"Yeah, oh yeah, hey. How y'all doing?"

"Good Pappy, real good. You doing all right?"

"Yeah," he drawled, "for an old man I guess I'm doing OK."

"Look, it's kind of hot out here and we were wondering if you might want a ride up the Island?" I asked. "You're going to Chippys aren't you?"

Pappy's eyes lit up with thoughts of sipping on a cold beer sooner than he had expected. "Yep, sure am. I'm headed in the right direction, I hope?" He paused and looked around. "Yeah, that would be nice. You got a car?"

Bubba quipped, "Yeah, Pappy we got two of 'em but they're the kind that you pedal."

Pappy leaned over and squinted at Bubba's bike and then mine. "Well, that's fine with me … if you can tow me somehow? Anything beats walking in this damn heat."

"Tell ya what, Bubba. Why don't I set Pappy in your basket and let his legs just dangle over the front and he can hold onto the handlebars?"

Bubba screwed up his face … he was thinking. "Y-e-a-h, I guess that'll work and you can carry his cane."

"Hear that, Pappy? I'm gonna put you in Bubba's basket and you can just sit there. It's only a few blocks. Think you can handle that?"

"Oh hell yeah! Let's go!"

"All right … just stand right there … and don't move. Bubba, pull up right behind him … easy … there you go. No, no. Pappy, turn around." I touched his frail shoulders to adjust him and there was nothing but a thin layer of skin and bone so fragile I thought for a second he might break if I tried to pick him up. Pappy's weight and age must have been about the same … both around ninety.

"OK Pappy, lift your arms and I'm gonna pick you up and put you in the basket … all right?"

"Let's do it," exclaimed Pappy who was eager to get to Chippys and have a cold beer.

"Need some help?" Bubba asked extending his hand.

"Yeah … just kind of help set him down easy." I was right. Pappy couldn't have weighed much more than ninety pounds soaking wet with rocks in his pockets.

"Easy … there you go" Pappy was situated, sitting in Bubba's basket gripping the handlebars and smiling.

"Bubba, he's not too heavy, is he?"

Bubba smiled and said, "Man, I've carried groceries heavier than this."

"Hah? What you say?" Pappy asked turning to find Bubba.

"Nothing, Pappy. You ready?"

"Let's go … I'm thirsty!"

I led our small parade up Central Avenue twirling Pappy's cane like a baton … dropping it twice …then I decided to use it like a drum major and pointed it skyward and pulled it up and down while I hummed a drum beat to match my movements. Bubba and Pappy were engaged in conversation about something and it must have been funny because Pappy was smiling the whole time. Either that or he was scared to death and putting up a good front.

The stares we received from passing motorists were mostly those of acknowledgement. The locals knew Pappy and they knew Bubba 'n me and figured out rather quickly what was going on … the obvious clue being that we were headed in the direction of Chippys.

Bubba eased his bike over the last bump and into the parking area at Chippys and rolled to a smooth stop like he'd done this a hundred times.

"There you go, Pappy … we're here. We made it. Safe and sound."

"A-l-l right, Bubba. That was pretty quick. And you're a good driver. Now if I can just get out of this thing." Pappy was already trying to wiggle out of the basket.

I was feeling pretty good about Bubba 'n me helping Pappy out. I mean we didn't exactly help an old lady across a busy street but helping an old man get to his beer a little sooner … well, that ranked right up there as far as I was concerned.

Then I heard Pappy yelling."Damn it. I'm stuck!" He was squirming and turning, trying hard to free himself.

I rushed to him. "Easy Pappy … I'll get you. Hold the bike still, Bubba."

"Eah, I'm trying but …"

"Pappy, you got to sit still for a second … OK?" I made a quick assessment and sure enough Pappy was wedged in the basket like a sardine.

"Here you go, Pappy. Hold on and I'll have you out in a jiffy." I grabbed a hold of his arms and pulled upward but he was stuck too tightly. Then I grabbed his legs and tugged on them.

Pappy immediately yelled," O-w-w- e-e! That hurts … it hurts my hip. The bad one."

"Sorry, Pappy." I backed off and thought for a second, "Maybe if two of us … one on each side got hold and kind of pulled at the same time?"

"Bubba!" It was Pappy looking for Bubba only two feet away. "I want a beer … a Schlitz. Can you get me one?"

"Not now Pappy. I'm holding the bike … remember?"

"Oh … oh yeah … I forgot." Pappy squinted his eyes real tight and found me." Mike, can you get me a beer?"

"You mean right now, Pappy?"

"Hell yes, I mean right now. What'd ya think I meant? Next week? I might die right here in this basket in this heat when there's ice-cold beer only thirty feet away. Wouldn't that be somethin'?"

"Yeah, that would be pretty bad … pretty bad I guess." I paused and tried to think.

"Let me try one more time and then I'll see about getting you a beer … OK?"

"No, no, go get the beer and then try. Can you just do that for this poor old man?"

After such a plea how could I resist? "You got any money, Bubba?" I reached down into my pocket. "I have a quarter … I need a dime."

"Here ya go." Bubba handed me a dime and smiled at me shaking his head back and forth.

"Be right back. A Schlitz … right?"

"Yeah … a nice cold one."

"What in the name of heaven are y'all doing with Pappy out there?" It was Mr. Bollinger, the bartender peering through the window.

I looked around before answering and thank goodness the place was practically empty. All we needed was for four or five ex-military retirees running outside and trying to pull poor Pappy from the basket.

"We gave Pappy a ride and he got stuck. We'll get him out in a few minutes. But he wants a beer … a Schlitz." I laid the thirty-five cents on the counter. "Is that enough?"

I could tell from the frown on Mr. Bollinger's face what he was going to say.

"That's enough but I can't sell you any beer … you're underage."

"Yeah, I know I'm not old enough to buy beer but it's not for me. It's for Pappy and he's just right there." I turned and pointed. "Couldn't you for once …"

"Nope. No way. I could be in big trouble."

Discouraged and knowing I wasn't going to be able to buy a beer, I said, "Yes sir." I picked up the money and walked outside.

"Here's your dime, Bubba. Mr. Bolinger wouldn't sell me a beer. Says I'm not old enough."

"Well … I am by God!" Pappy shouted still lodged securely in the basket.

"You OK, Pappy?" I asked. "We're gonna get you out of there in a minute."

"I'm OK but I'd feel a lot better if I had a cold beer. You hear me? I want a beer!" he bellowed as he squirmed around trying to get out of the basket. "Y'all see this?" Pappy was showing us a balled-up fist. "If I don't get a beer soon then somebody is gonna get some of this and it ain't gonna be pretty. I want a beer! What in hell does an old man got to do?"

"Yes sir." We answered together. It was a good thing Pappy couldn't see us. We were grinning big-time, about to explode with laughter and we surely didn't want him to see us laughing at him because then we might have gotten some of what he was offering up and we didn't want that to happen.

"I want a beer, damn it! And I want it right now!"

"Hang on, Pappy … just hang on. I know how to solve this." Bubba barely had the words out his mouth when he began wheeling the bike, Pappy and all, through the door into Chippys stopping at the bar.

"What the …?" Mr. Bollinger's eyes bugged out at the sight of Pappy sitting in a basket on a bike demanding a beer.

"And make sure it's good and cold … you hear me? Where are you Bollinger?" Pappy was looking all over for Mr. Bollinger who was standing right in front of him.

I pulled Bubba aside and asked him if he thought maybe we should just go and leave Pappy right there? We had done our duty and Pappy seemed happy? Why not leave?

"My bike," Bubba said, "that's why."

"Oh yeah," I said, "forgot about it."

"Plus we'd probably get grounded again for leaving an old man stuck in a basket. And you, Mike… it'd be double trouble for you."

I agreed and after huddling again we decided that Bubba would call Lumus who would know what to do.

"What if Bull Perry answers?" Bubba asked terrified at the thought.

"Then hang up, Einstein."

"Oh?"

Lumus was Johnny on the spot and when he arrived and saw the problem he turned his head to hide the grin, which was quickly turning into a laugh. Old man Lewis drinking beer from a bike basket. Shucks, the old timer looked so content Lumus almost didn't feel like bothering him.

"Mr. Lewis, Mr. Lewis, over here Mr. Lewis. It's me … Lumus Mc Farland."

Pappy took a big swig of his Schlitz, looked in Lumus direction and said, "Lumus! Hey,
how are ya? Kind of early for the police to be drinking ain't it?"

"Yep, a little early for that. Look, I'm going to try and get you out of there, OK?

Lumus gently grabbed Pappy by the arms and gave a tug. More of a test than anything. Pappy hollered. This time, he claimed, his arm hurt.

"Yeah, he's in there pretty good. Bubba, why'd you squash this man in here like this?" Lumus jokingly asked?

Bubba laughed and pointed at me. "Devlin did it. Not me."

"Just kidding boys. Help me roll him outside. I've got an idea,"

Lumus said as he walked ahead of us and went to his Jeep. He returned carrying a small plastic bottle.

"What's that?" Bubba asked reaching for the container.

"Suntan lotion," said Lumus smiling. "We're gonna grease up Mr. Lewis real good and slide him right out of there."

The first couple of attempts were unsuccessful so Lumus really scooted the lotion on Pappy's pants soaking 'em through to the skin until it was dripping on the pavement.

"Why don't y'all get me a six pack and wheel me down to the beach and I can get a tan and drink beer while checking out the ladies?" Pappy said with a big grin.

We all laughed. I hoped that when I was as old as Pappy I would still as good a sense of humor as him.

"Mike, go get Mr. Bollinger … will ya?" Lumus said. " I know what to do now."

With Mr. Bollinger and myself on one side and Lumus and Bubba on the other we carefully lifted up Pappy and the bike and ever so gently turned them upside down being extra careful not to drop our precious cargo on the concrete. Gravity cooperated and Pappy slid out of the basket like a newborn babe.

"Where's my beer?" Pappy exclaimed. "And thanks for the ride, Bubba." He then slowly plodded back into Chippys.

"Thanks, Lumus," we said together, "you saved us again."

"That's OK but if y'all keep this up I'm gonna have to start charging you." He laughed and waved as he took off in the Jeep.

"Well … what now Einstein?" Bubba asked as we pedaled away.

"L-e-t-'s see … we can stop by Ms. Kingman's and see if she needs a lift? A-HA-HA-HA"

"Eah, whose bright idea was that anyway? To give Pappy a lift?" Bubba asked giving me the look.

"I don't know … wasn't me. Eah, I know. Let's go to Burton's … I'll buy the Cokes."

I just remembered I had an extra quarter.

31
THE ROCKS

There comes a time in our lives when we take things for granted whether it is a loved one, our job, our health, our good fortune or maybe even our very existence. Most people take for granted the positive aspects or natural beauty of the place where they grow up no matter what type of geographic setting they might come from. Whenever I went to the mountains I would just stand and look at the spectacle before me for hours and marvel at the wonderment and beauty not to mention the enormity. The mountain people who lived there looked at me like I was crazy because they grew up amongst the mountains seeing them every day and thought nothing of the grandeur before them. I was just like the gawking tourists who came to our magnificent Island in hopes of seeing the Atlantic Ocean for the very first time. Many times we would see people just standing on the beach and looking at the ocean, not swimming or walking, just standing and staring. I never could understand what they were doing? Now I know.

The beach at Sullivans Island … our beach … it is a beautiful expanse of sand and ocean. And it had always been there. We, Bubba 'n me and the crew, had taken it for granted for so many years always assuming it would be there at our disposal, never taking the time to really see it in its proper perspective or to appreciate it for the hours of fun and enjoyment it gave us. And its allure was wrapped up in its own beauty.

Now that we were a little bit older and our mental awareness was beginning to catch up with our physical growth spurt we came to a somewhat more mature understanding of what a unique and wonderful place the beach was and how lucky we were to have such a gift only minutes away. Maybe it was not a conscious effort on our part to be thankful for the beach and all it offered, maybe it was the maturation process coming into play? Whatever it was that alerted our senses made us thankful for our beach. We were lucky.

At the entrance to Charleston harbor there is a set of two jetties, the north and the south jetty. Both jetties were visible from the beach, situated no more than a mile offshore. However, the north jetty curved and headed toward land while the south jetty was straighter forming a barrier, which spread from the entrance to Charleston harbor out toward the ocean. The distance between the two jetties was no more than a quarter of a mile providing ample space as a shipping lane for the huge freighters that visited Charleston on a daily basis. About a half mile off shore, the north jetty disappeared as though it dove into the ocean never to rise again, but in reality it ran under the water and resurfaced on the beach at Station 20, forming the area known by Islanders as "the rocks." These huge, granite rocks ran up the beach for about a hundred yards, like the back of a dinosaur, all the way into the sand dunes stopping at the beginning of an overgrowth of small trees and shrubs on the Island. These enormous rocks filled with decades worth of barnacles and oyster shells were piled one on top of the other and were about ten feet in width and eight feet tall.

From a very early age one item that *always* accompanied us when we went to the beach to swim was our faithful friend the inner tube. Practically every kid on the Island owned one. These were not some pretty store bought types with Donald Duck or Minnie Mouse logos plastered all over them but were old car tire tubes that had been discarded for one reason or another. Many times Bubba 'n me in need of a new inner tube would ride our bikes around the Island searching out debris piles, especially during springtime cleaning, in hopes of finding a throwaway tube. People usually threw them out because of a small hole, which was easy to patch. We simply put a patch on it from our small tin kit and pumped it up.

When you went to the beach you might forget your towel or ball or something but you never … ever … left your inner tube at home. What were you going to relax on and paddle around in the ocean or ride the waves or play kick fight until the backs of your arms were red and raw from paddling and rubbing against the rubber all day?

The kick fight episodes were loads of fun and a great way to relieve any pent up feelings or frustrations. A wonderful tension reliever. Too bad the adults didn't get involved. They seemed to need the relief more than us kids. The object of this game was to dump your opponent using only your feet and because I had big feet I got pretty good at this game early on in life. People with small feet were at a distinct disadvantage and those with tiny little feet didn't have a chance at all. And God help you if your opponent had a really rough day at school or things weren't going good at home and they took out their anger on you.

I must have dumped my sister, Sissy, a thousand times but she always came back for more and I obliged her. Shoot, she was way bigger than me but I had a secret plan. I would look over at her and picture Sister Roberta sitting on that inner tube in her nun outfit, habit and all. Yep, I figured if Sister Roberta ever did go to the beach she would wear her nun outfit, looking like a misplaced penguin. Sissy never had a chance.

It was Billy Scott who stretched the limits of imagination when it came to the use of an inner tube and in doing so innocently enough transformed the rocks into a summer playground of fun, fun, fun and girls, girls, girls! It seems that his uncle worked at Charleston Air Force Base and had access to discarded inner tubes from the wheels of the huge cargo planes much the same way we picked up our smaller inner tubes on the Island. Many a time we had watched the low flying gigantic planes descending for landing at The Air Base in Charleston but not once in our wildest dreams did we think we would ever be floating around in the ocean on one of the inner tubes from their wheels.

When fully inflated a tube stood seven feet tall and was six feet in diameter. It took two people just to roll it to the beach while six of us together could sit on it comfortably.

The previous week had passed in the blink of an eye and by Friday afternoon I had done all my chores mainly mowing my yards … my college yards I called them and was now ready to play. Bubba was home resting after a vigorous workout with the TV and The Three Stooges. We planned go to the beach the next day. Go early and stay all day. Of course, we would take a mid day break and head to Burton's for a Coke and a pack of crackers.

The next morning our game plan was to head to the rocks and mess around there but if there was not anything going on there then we would ride our bikes on the beach, if the tide was low, to Breach Inlet. Eventually, we would end up back at Burton's and see what the crew was up to.

We hadn't been at the rocks very long talking with some local crabbers who had a couple of keepers and were working hard on catching a mess when we heard yelling and screaming coming from the foot path at Station 20. It sounded serious like someone was in trouble, really loud screams and yelling. And out of nowhere we saw the black monstrosity rolling out the end of the path, turning slightly and heading our way. It was the giant inner tube out of control with Billy and Sammy Scott chasing it and just a yellin,' "Whoa! Whoa!" Then they spotted Bubba 'n me and hollered, "Help! … the inner tube…" They were pointing at it. "Mike! Bubba! Help! We can't stop it!" And on it came. Right toward us.

It was on the open beach now and rolling at a good clip added by a westerly tail wind and was headed for the rocks loaded with barnacles and super sharp oyster shells growing from the edges like curved razor blades.

Billy was going bonkers hollering and screaming and trying to give instructions all at once. "The rocks! The oyster shells! Stop it. Mike! Bubba, y'all stop it!" He looked back and yelled at his tired brother. "Sammy, come on hurry up!"

Sammy had given up, stopped and sat down, breathing heavy and was watching the inner tube roll toward the rocks with Billy in hot pursuit. I had the same feeling as Sammy. I stood and watched except I wasn't breathing heavy. I thought, *Eah, what can I do? What can anybody do? It's gonna hit the oysters shells and probably pop ... more like explode?* I stood and watched in amazement at how fast that thing was going, picking up speed by the second. Gee whiz, that thing must have weighed a hundred pounds and as fast as it was moving only an idiot would try to stop it. *Ain't no body in their right mind gonna get in the way of that thing,* I thought.

And that's when Bubba fulfilled my thoughts and decided he was going to stop it, all by himself. Oh no! I couldn't believe what I was seeing. He was lining himself up in the path of this oncoming, huge, rolling mass of rubber, which was ready to steamroll anyone or anything in its path. Bubba bent his knees, lowered his shoulders, and kept his head up with his arms outstretched assuming a textbook linebacker stance. He looked like Sam Huff, the ferocious linebacker of the New York giants, getting ready to put a world of hurt on somebody. Only problem was Bubba was getting ready to get a world of hurt put on him but he didn't know it. He grunted and growled like a mad dog, swinging his arms back and forth and then to our utter amazement he charged the oncoming tube. Billy, realizing the danger in what Bubba was about to attempt, stopped and yelled, "N-o-o-o, Bubba … n-o-o-o!"

I couldn't bear to look but I did. He was my best friend and if he were going to die right in front of me I figured it was only polite to watch.

Before I could finish half a Hail Mary, Bubba made contact with the massive tube but only for a nanosecond. He did not even have time to close his arms around it before he was knocked into next Thursday. WHUUM! The contact sounded like a cannon going off and poor Bubba was the projectile.

He went flying straight backwards and his butt, thank God, making contact with the beach first, sliding a few feet, then the rest of him followed. He lay flattened with only his pride hurt, while the uninjured tube was detoured toward the sand dunes where Billy was finally able to slow it down stopping it beneath a tall dune in a smooth area where it came to rest like it was at home. And that's where we left it.

Bubba still cringes each summer when we tell newcomers the story of how the giant tube came to rest beneath a tall sand dune and inadvertently became our beach trampoline. Poor Bubba stayed in a daze that day but felt better when we assured him that he was a hero for taking on the tube and saving it from going into the rocks.

"Yeah, some hero I am, huh? That was the dumbest thing I've done in a long time … I think?"

"T-h-a-t-'s right, Catbird," I said grinning, "that was dumb … u-u-u-h" I corrected myself quickly. "I mean you are the hero, the hero for the whole rest of the summer."

Bubba just looked at me and laughed and then said, "Thanks for helping me. And believe me I won't do anything that stupid again."

Billy, the daredevil of the group, had been looking at the tube, looking at the dune, looking at the tube again.

"Eah, do you guys see what I see?"

And before we could answer Billy was on top of the ten-foot dune eyeing the possibilities.

"Yeah, oh yeah." I said. "We could use it for a trampoline …maybe." I was thinking we could but some brave soul would have to try it out first and it certainly wasn't going to be me. One glance at Bubba who was still wobbly from his fight with the tube and I knew it wouldn't be him either. Our problem was solved instantly. Before Bubba 'n me could urge Billy to jump on the tube and see if he would bust his butt, he leaped into the air and landed squarely on one side of the tube and was propelled straight up like a rocket and then floated to earth landing safely in the soft sand.

"Oh man, that's neato!" Billy yelled. "WOW!"

He was grinning big time and quickly got up to try it again. Once I saw Billy didn't die I literally jumped at the chance and was up the dune and then leaped onto the waiting tube. It really had some bounce to it. We were soaring like seagulls. Sammy joined us and up into the air we went, landing in the sand and then raced up the hill to go again and again … Oh man! What fun! Bubba, still smarting from his collision, stood off to the side just watching and rubbing the back of his head.

"Eah, we're going high enough to do a flip … aren't we?" It was Billy seeking some kind of reassurance because I could tell by the look in his eye that he was going to try a flip regardless of what we said.

"Oh sure. You go so high big brother you could probably do a double flip."

"Shut up, Sammy," I yelled. "What ya doing … trying to kill your brother?"

"Eah, I hadn't thought of that. Billy, maybe you could do three flips … what ya think?"

"Sammy, just shut up … will ya," Billy said, "and let me concentrate on doing this one flip … OK?"

We watched anxiously as Billy edged closer to the jumping off point.

"I'm gonna do one of those flips like they do in the Olympics where they stretch out and land on their feet with outstretched arms," announced Billy.

This boy was either real brave or real stupid. Maybe a little of both? We thought for a second about talking him out of trying it because we were afraid he might get seriously hurt and we didn't want to have to break up the fun to take home an injured jumper. Our curiosity outweighed our protests. He looked down and not only stepped off the dune but jumped into the air in an attempt to get more height for his downward descent.

Billy didn't disappoint us, landing squarely on two feet placed together with outstretched arms, bowing to the applauding audience of three … it was a "10."

"OH WOW! Come on, Mike. You try it."

I'm thinking, *Ain't no way. I want to live long enough to kiss Beverly Ann.*

"No, no, not me." I said apologetically. "Uh-uh."

"C-h-i-c-k-e-n, you chicken."

"Just call me Rudy," I said. "Ain't no way I'm gonna bust my butt doing some stupid flip."

"Bubba, how about you. Do a flip?" Billy said as he launched himself into the atmosphere.

"Fraid not, I ain't that stupid."

The giant tube frightened Bubba. I knew it because when he was afraid of something he would back away and not say anything, and right now he was twenty feet from the tube and silent.

Billy and me and Sammy jumped and bounced until we could barely climb back up the dune, however, Billy was the only flipper in the group that day.

That week news of the big inner tube at the rocks spread and by next Saturday there was a crowd of anxious kids at the rocks, our crew among them, ready to take the jump off the dune and join the fun. Billy obviously was there showing off for the rookies, springing high into the air doing his flip and later that day dazzling us all with a backwards flip, which we gazed at in amazement. The air was filled with "O-O-O-H-S" and "A-A-A-W-S," except for Bubba who commented, "That should be easy for Billy. That's how he lives his whole life … backwards." I sensed a hint of jealousy but kept my big mouth shut. Bubba had yet to try even one jump.

Sammy, John, Robert, Jocko, Carl, Rusty, and Stinky, most of our crew, were there but more noticeable were the girls and more noticeable than them was the obvious improvement in the size of their breasts, which seemed to me to be a lot bigger than I had noticed the previous summer.

I wondered, *Did girls' boobs just get bigger all of a sudden ... like all at once ... BOOM ... and there they were? Or did they grow real slow?* And another question I kept to myself: *How come some girls had big ones and some still had small ones?*

I didn't know so I sought out an expert in these matters who would have all the answers. I poked Bubba in the ribs and whispered, "Eah, do the girls' boobs seem bigger to you this summer or what? Last summer they were kind of small and now they look so much bigger. Do they just …"

Bubba interrupted me, "Mike, just look will ya?" He was smiling as he looked in the direction of the stacked Leslie Wildering. Then he looked back at me with wide eyes and said, "Now what do you think? Huh? You're a kind of smart fella. Figure it out."

In our minds Bubba 'n me had begun to explore the mysteries of the opposite sex but only in *our minds.* Oh, we had talked a little bit about girl stuff occasionally on our beach walks but neither of us had any real experiences to talk about …not yet anyway. So on this day we stuck to looking at the new shapes before us … and I kept wondering.

The giant tube had served us well as a makeshift trampoline, and in the future would still be used for jumping on, but its real purpose was to be put into the ocean and used like any other inner tube except on a grander scale. Instead of one voyager it took on six and at times as many as eight. Its maiden voyage was into a rough sea of five-foot waves coming in periodic sequence aided by an east wind. The object was first to get on the tube, no easy task in a rough sea, and once on try to stay on the tube when the waves came crashing down. We were having a blast, yelling and screaming just before we would take on a mouthful of seawater when the whole tube would be flipped by a huge wave. When our feet touched the ocean floor we would crouch with bended legs, push off with all our strength, springing up like flying fish popping to the top, immediately looking around counting heads, making sure none had drowned. Then we swam after the tube, which was usually being taken toward shore by the waves. And then it was back out again … and again …and again. We spent hours at a time in the ocean without a break.

The newness of the big inner tube wore off for some of the crew but not for Billy and Sammy and me, it only got better. We jumped from a higher dune we found down the beach, doubling our fun, and through a lot of persuasion we coaxed Bubba into trying a jump, which he did and promptly busted his butt. Him and that tube just didn't seem to get along. We got a huge laugh at Bubba's expense when he jumped and did not land squarely on the tube's upper surface but rather he landed more on the side and he shot out sideways in a flash, landing face-first in the sand. He swore off jumping for the rest of the summer.

We took it in the ocean every chance we got, especially when it was rough and the waves were big. We were counting the days until late summer and early September, which was peak hurricane season in hopes of a storm approaching the coast. Then we would take the giant tube out and really have some fun. Even though Bubba stayed clear of the tube on land, he rarely missed a chance to get on it when it was in the ocean.

I asked him about that and he said, "Why would you ask me

something so dumb? Couldn't you figure it out, Mike?" He stopped and gave me a dumb look, one meant for the way I was acting. Then he said, "Look … if I fall off of it and land on the hard ground it's going to hurt … right?"

I nodded.

"And if I fall off of it in the ocean then I land in the water … and not get hurt … don't ya see?"

I shrugged my shoulders feeling a little bit stupid for not having figured that out myself. So I replied, "Eah, it makes sense to me."

It was a hot Saturday and most of the crew was at the rocks. With a strong east wind blowing, big waves, and rough, it was the perfect day for going out on the tube. Of the six on the tube that day there was a special passenger … Mandy Miller from Mt. Pleasant. She was special or maybe different from all the other girls in a physical way. Bubba 'n me might have been inexperienced when it came to the opposite sex but we weren't blind. And anyone with normal vision could tell that Mandy was not only endowed, she was truly endowed to the point of being blessed. To put it mildly she had a set of headlights that couldn't be missed by even a blind man. They were mounted high on her chest and stuck straight out like they were frozen but even Bubba 'n me, in our limited knowledge of girls' anatomy, knew that wasn't possible, not in all this heat. They surely would have melted. When she came walking up earlier that day at the rocks I saw Sammy look in her direction and say, "H-e-r-e *they* come. Mandy Miller." But only loud enough for the boys to hear.

I was lucky. I was on the tube that fateful day along with Bubba, Rusty, Susanne and Linda and of course, Mandy.

Whether by design or not Mandy's bathing suit top continuously flopped open caused by the movement of the tube in the rough water exposing the fullness of her young chest muscles. This went on repeatedly and each time her bathing suit opened wide so did six watchful eyes as we three boys followed the motion of Mandy and her bouncing boobs. It wasn't a long exposure but plenty enough to arouse the attention of three curious twelve year olds.

Time froze for me and I could hear The Shirelles singing away: "Just one look … that's all it took … just one look, o-o-h, o-o-h, o-o-h… just one look …"

I think Bubba gave me a knowing wink on the second eyeful of Mandy but I wasn't sure? Maybe he was blinking his eyes? He didn't want to miss a thing. All I know is that the boys were praying for more waves to keep bouncing us around, while Mandy, sweet innocent, young Mandy, acting like nothing was happening, smiled away having a good time bouncing up and down, especially down.

Bubba 'n me and Rusty were so enthralled, so excited, about what we were seeing that we blocked out everything around us. A whale could have surfaced beside us and we wouldn't have noticed it. This was better than no homework, staying up late *and* chocolate shakes at the Milk Bar all rolled into one. A wave would take us up and then down into the trough. Mandy would go up and then her top would go down, way down!

I was so oblivious to anything around me that I didn't notice the huge wave, a six-footer, suddenly bearing down on us that by the time it crashed on us there was no time to react. The tube flipped. Mandy was sitting directly across from me and the impact of the wave knocked her already loose top completely off presenting open acknowledgement of what lay beneath the fabric of her top. In an instant I was on her, cushioning my fall with outstretched arms and open hands that innocently found their way to the treasure of Mandy's unmasked breasts. Instinctively, I squeezed the firmness for a second, which to me seemed like an hour. We went under the water for a second and popped back up like corks. I was blushing when I got to the surface but before I could apologize to Mandy, who was adjusting her top, she smiled at me and said, "It's OK."

To me it was more than OK … it was super … it was great. It was an unbelievable feeling. But my good old Catholic upbringing reared its ugly head and right beside it was Mr. Guilt. And my thoughts turned quickly from sensual pleasure to utter damnation. That feeling of pleasure was wrong and it was a sin. And I tried hard not to show my mixed emotions but Mandy probably had a clue as to my boyish naiveness and excited mind when I said, "Yeah, they're OK."

Checking out the girls' flopping breasts while they jumped up and down on the inner tube and occasionally sneaking a peek when their tops slipped out of place was one thing but putting my hands on them was all together an unforgettable experience.

Going home that day I told Bubba what happened with Mandy on the tube.

"Well," he said, "according to what we've been told at school by the wonderful Our Ladies of Pain, I figure your hands will rot off soon … you lucky rascal."

I understood his reference to the nuns' attitude toward touching a female body part and how my hands would probably turn an awful green color and slowly rot until they dropped off but I was puzzled about being called "lucky."

"No hands. Lucky … whatta you mean?"

"Well, I was thinking. You see, Mike, with no hands you'll never have to worry about going blind."

"Going blind?" Now I *was* confused. "What in the world are you talking about?"

"You know …with no hands … no …" he made a small up and down gesture with a cupped hand.

"O-o-o-h." I nodded and laughed a soft laugh. "Y-e-a-h." Then I stared off into the afternoon sky, beautiful and light blue. Lost again thinking about Mandy.

"Hey you!" Bubba yelled. "Wake up!"

I jumped. "What?"

"Mike," and a most serious look came across Bubba's face. " I'd like to ask you just one question … OK?"

"Go ahead, my friend." I had a feeling what was coming. "Fire away."

"How did they feel?" Bubba's eyes opened wide and his forehead wrinkled in anticipation. "You know … Mandy's boobs?"

"Unbelievable, Bubba. Unbelievable."

"Unbelievable? What do ya mean?"

"What I mean is that you wouldn't believe how good they felt … unbelievable." We both shared a huge smile.

32
LUMUS

It was yard cutting time for me and time for Bubba to flop in front of the TV where lately he spent a lot of his spare time between the beach and going in the creek. Cutting yards was hard, sweaty work and I prayed often while laying out the smooth, even, rows that I wouldn't have to do this for the rest of my life. Today, however, I had other things on my mind after the experience of touching Mandy Miller's breasts and when I got home I was determined to talk with my father this evening about some questions I had about the opposite sex. I had been thinking about this particular talk for a quite some time but I suppose the incident with Mandy Miller brought it to my consciousness. However, I was filled with great trepidation. My father who was an understanding and kind man would listen to me. I knew that. But … a talk about girls and sex and all that stuff. I don't know?

My father was in his usual spot in his favorite chair by the lamp with the newspaper after supper, a routine that rarely changed. I had thought many times before about asking my father about girls but never could seem to find the courage to actually ask him. Why I don't know? But somehow I knew I would tonight. There was something on my mind and had been for quite a while that needed an answer so I approached my father with a lot of built up anxiety and a little fear.

"Hi Daddy, how you doing?"

My father brought the paper down slowly and looked at me, not with surprise but more out of concern. "Hi Mike, what you know good? Yankees won again I see."

"Yeah." I paused. "Yeah, they sure did. U-h-h … what you reading about?"

"I'm reading about the new Federal Courthouse they plan to build in Charleston. Supposed to be a huge thing. You heard about it?"

"N-a-a-w, I don't read the paper much. Just the sports page." I paused again. "Daddy there's something I'd like to ask you."

"What's that, son?" He pulled the paper down again and folded it in his lap.

I couldn't get the words out. I couldn't bring myself to ask my own father about girls.

"When we going fishing?" I piped up. "I'm tired of catching crabs … I wanna catch some blackfish."

"O-o-o-h, I don't know exactly. Let me check the tides. Maybe we can go this weekend or next, OK?"

"Great … yeah … that would be great," my voice trailed off. "Think the Giants can beat the Yankees?" I asked without much conviction.

"They should. They have the better pitchers and good hitting. Don't you think so?"

"Pitchers … who?" I answered looking down "What pitchers?" My father was looking at me earnestly.

He put the paper aside, stood up, and looked around eyeing the girls who were miraculously being quiet, absorbed in a "I Love Lucy" episode on TV.

"Come with me for a minute," he said, "I wanna show you something."

I followed him into his bedroom where he took an old gilded picture frame from the dresser and handed it to me. In it was the picture of a young boy about my age and an older man standing together with an old car as a backdrop, both with serious expressions on their faces and wearing odd looking clothes.

"Know who that is," he asked pointing to the young boy?"

"No sir, but that old man looks a lot like Grandpa."

"Right, that's him and the little fella there with the funny looking pants is me."

"Yeah? You sure were little, Daddy."

"Yep. And that's why I'm showing you this. All of us adults were little at one time. Just like you. Well, you're not so little now. We had to grow up too, you know? Well, I not so sure about Bull Perry. I don't think he was ever little." He chuckled and I did too knowing he sometimes joked about Chief Perry.

"Mike, everyone goes through the pains of growing up and I can tell there's something on your mind that you want to talk about. Correct me if I'm wrong. Isn't that so?"

I didn't know what to say. "U-u-u-h … kind of Daddy but … I … uh …"

"Look, it's OK if you don't want to talk about it. You don't have to unless, of course, you are in some kind of trouble that I need to know about. That's not what it is … is it?"

I felt much more at ease and figured what the heck so I just blurted it out. "It's about girls, Daddy."

"Girls!" he exclaimed. "Oh boy! Son, if it's advice about them you need then you've probably come to the wrong person. Shucks, I'm surrounded by five of 'em every day and they're driving me nuts." He laughed and rubbed my hair. I grinned.

"Sorry Mike, I was just kidding." He paused, placed the picture back on the dresser, smiled, and asked, "What's on your mind, son? If I can help I will."

"Well Daddy, it's like this. I … uh … I … have been lately kind of … uh …"

"Been thinking about girls and their … how you say? … their body parts let's call them."

"Yeah, that's it. Their body parts." I grinned but wasn't near brave enough to say anything about me actually having touched some of these body parts. "How did you know?"

"Like I told you. All of us go through growing up and I went through the same thing that's probably troubling you."

"What I want to know Daddy, is it wrong to think about a girl's body parts. Is it like a sin and all?"

"Son, what I'm about to tell you don't you ever say anything about it at school around the Sisters … OK?"

"Yes sir."

"Mike, if it was a sin to just think about a girl's body parts then we would all end up in hell, including your father here." He paused just long enough for me to interrupt.

"But that's not what the Sisters at school teach us."

"Yeah, and that's why I just told you not to say anything about this at school. Look, it's not the thought that's a sin but what you do with that thought that could lead to a sin. Are you following me?"

"Yeah …kind of … I guess?"

"Try to look at this way. It's … u-u-u-h … what we call temptation and it's all around us … it's everywhere."

"O-o-o-h, you mean like how the devil tempts us? We learned that at school too."

"Yeah, that's it. The devil tempts us and when we give in to him and do something wrong we sin."

"Oh, I see. When we really do something is when we sin."

"Yeah, you've got it. You're a smart young man." He paused. "OK back to your question. What was your question?"

"A-a-a-w … you already answered it." My father had answered part of it. The other part I would have to figure out on my own. The part about actually carrying out an act and enjoying it. But that could wait until another day.

"Anything else, Mike? I wanna get back and enjoy that peace and quiet while I read the paper."

"No sir … and thank you Dad."

That night before falling asleep I went over in my mind the conversation I had with my father and finally realized that even though

I had been thinking about girls' body parts, Mandy Miller's boobs in particular, I mean who couldn't, I didn't think I had actually sinned. Those were just thoughts. And besides, I didn't intentionally grab them that day at the beach, it was an accident. But it did feel good. That was the point at which I became confused: Was that a sin? Accidentally doing something wrong that felt good? Oh boy. I was tiring myself out thinking about all this stuff. Maybe tomorrow I would ask my father about that?

After a restless sleep filled with visions of inner tubes and bare chested girls, I got up and dashed out the door skipping breakfast and anxiously headed to Bubba's. I had serious business on my young mind.

As I grabbed my bike I told Mollie,"Ain't got time for daydreaming about girls and all that stuff, huh?"

I pedaled into Bubba's backyard, stopping at the back steps, placing my foot on the second step and started yelling. I was in the clear to yell because his parents weren't home otherwise Mr. O' Toole would stick his head out the backdoor and tell me to quit yelling and "come knock on the door like a mannered person does. *Why go to all that trouble when I can sit here and yell?* is what I thought. However, I never revealed that thought to Mr.O'Toole who was a nice man, but you didn't want to get on his wrong side. All he ever heard from me was, "Yes sir."

I yelled again. Louder. No answer. I screamed. Bubba finally appeared zipping and fixing his pants.

"Oh sorry," I said apologetically. "Didn't mean to rush you in the middle of your business."

"Yeah, it's kind of hard to just get up and go. What ya doing?"

"I'm going to the police station. Gotta see Lumus. You wanna go?"

"I guess so… but … what about you-know-who?"

"Bull Perry? Ah come on. We'll just take a chance he's not there. I got some good stuff to tell ya about those Isle of Palms girls."

"Yeah, I'll ride with ya but first I gotta drop the crab net off at the Scotts. Won't take but a minute."

We found Sammy Scott in the dirt driveway at his house tying down a boat with a piece of rope.

The Scotts were creek people who practically lived out of Miller's Creek sustaining themselves on crabs, fish, and shrimp in the summer and oysters and clams in the winter. It looked as though Sammy was getting ready to go in the creek? Mr. Scott's car was in the driveway with a twelve-foot aluminum boat sticking out the back window of the car or what was left of the back window. Apparently the window had been knocked out and the boat picked up and shoved into the car?

We sat on our bikes just gawking, scratching our heads in wonderment.

"What in the world?" Bubba said quizzically. "Mike, would you look at that. Holy mackerel. A car with a boat in the window." We pedaled up closer for a good look.

"By the way Sammy, here's your net … and thanks."

"Oh hey, guys. Just throw it over there. Y'all catch any crabs?"

"Yeah, a few. Sammy. How did you get the boat there by yourself?" I asked sitting on my bike with folded arms in a distinct judgmental position. "It's kinda heavy, ain't it?"

Sammy nonchalantly went about his business of tying the rope to the bumper securing the boat.

"Oh that? We put it there. Me and Tommy," pointing at Tommy Wade in the front seat of the car, ducking down real low trying to hide from Bubba, the incident at Burton's fresh in Tommy's mind.

Bubba smiled and while still on his bike rolled over to the open window giving Tommy the double bad eye.

"Hello Tommy," Bubba asked, "How ya doing?" It was a question that came out in the form of a threat.

Tommy was trapped and knew it.

"Got any more smart remarks to make about Mike and me finding a dead body … huh, jack leg? Remember?"

When Tommy was scared he stuttered and right now he was real scared. "H-e-e-e-y Bu- bu-bu-a. N-o-o-o-o, I-I-I-I-I don-don-don- don't ha-ha-ha- have any (he blurted out) th-th-th-thing t-t-t-to sa-sa-sa-sa-say."

"You better not, you babbling jug butt. Just shut up." Bubba backed off smiling.

"Yeah, uh-uh … I see y'all put the boat there, Sammy. But why?" I asked out of curiosity. "Don't ya'll have a trailer?" I looked around the yard.

"Oh? Someone borrowed the trailer and we wanted to go crabbing and didn't have no way to get the boat to the landing so we knocked out the back window and just slipped it right in … nice fit, huh?"

"Yeah, real good fit," Bubba said, "Real good."

I nodded my approval.

Mr. Scott's old car was getting older fast. It already had dents and scratches all over it from encounters with Sammy. No seat belts and now no back window. What was next? I suppose it was a progressive destruction until the car ended up with no wheels.

"What's your father gonna say when he sees the window out?"

"A-a-a-w nothing, he probably won't even notice. Well, we gotta go. Remember no man waits on the tide." He cranked the car, backed out, and headed slowly for the landing, which was just down the road behind their house.

"Yeah right," Bubba remarked, see ya later. You too Tom-tom-tom-tom- Tommy."

I had a sudden thought. Sammy would never have to learn how to back a trailer down to the water when he wanted to launch a boat. For many people that was a tricky proposition and many never learned the certain skill needed to back a trailer. What an ingenious kid. Of course, he'd need to learn that the correct saying was, "The tide waits for no man."

I also thought Bubba was a little rough on Tommy who all of us knew was all talk and a big chicken. So I mentioned it to him. "Bubba, you were kind of tough on Tommy there, weren't you?"

"Tough? Huh, he ain't seen nothing yet."Bubba's face reddened and his steely eyes took on a mean look so I quickly changed the subject.

"That Sammy. He's something else, ain't he? A boat in the car. I paused and pedaled ahead a little bit hoping to get the jump on Bubba and then yelled, "Race ya to the church." And we were off.

We were going to the police station to see Lumus. It didn't occur to us that Lumus had other business to attend to other than fooling around with two hyper kids who had nothing better to do than get in his hair. But we liked Lumus. He was different than most policemen because he actually talked to us and even joked around a little bit. But Lumus also had a job and responsibilities to take care of.

He had been busy the last few days. Real busy. He had helped pull some tourist's car from the sand, written up four speeding tickets, and rescued two cats, one from the top of a telephone pole and the other from an open drainage pipe.

All in the line of duty I reckon. Besides, Chief Perry wasn't about to try and rescue any cats, Lumus thought. *Guess that's what they pay me for?*

However, not all of his efforts were of the small-town Mayberry variety. The previous summer he had put an end to a string of petty robberies from vacant beach houses using an old police trick Chief Perry taught him about night patrolling. He patrolled the side and back streets with his headlights off giving no warning to any potential crook other than the sound of his car's engine that he was approaching. In the wee hours of the morning he surprised a robber coming out of a front beach home, stolen goods in hand, who made a run for it and gained a sizeable lead in a souped-up '57 Chevy. The speedy crook was no match for Lumus and the lumbering old Ford. Lumus did manage, however, to keep the suspect within sight but was losing ground fast. Thinking quickly, Lumus took a gamble. Realizing he couldn't run this guy down in a month of Sundays, he called the night operator on the Ben Sawyer Bridge and told him to open the bridge …" NOW!"

And when the over confident thief made a left turn at Chippys he had made his first and last mistake by accidentally boxing himself in. Lumus had him cornered from the rear and the open bridge offered no escape in front of him.

Later Chief Perry asked Lumus," How did you know that the robber would try to leave the Island on the causeway?"

"Easy. Because he didn't live on the Island."

"How'd you know that?"

"First of all, if he lived on the Island he would have known about the bridge and not gone that way and second, he would have been on foot. And besides, most Islanders don't steal from each other."

Lately Lumus had been taking care of his normal duties and throwing himself full tilt into the Poe investigation. He decided he needed a break.

He had just polished off a double cheeseburger and order of fries from the Milk Bar and a big slice of Grannie's apple pie. He kicked his feet up and leaned back … "A-A-A-H."

He was dozing, not able to completely get Thomas Poe off his mind. *What was the reason for his death? Hate? Jealousy? Robbery?*

"Lumus, you there?" I was yelling, my nose pressed against the screen. "Lumus!"

"No, He's not. He's trying to take a nap." Lumus yelled. "He's tired."

Lumus grudgingly rose from the comfort of his chair and pushed open the screen door. "Hey, what's all the commotion? Y'all didn't find another body now did you? I sure hope not?"

Bubba was glancing around nervously and said, "No. No more bodies. How you doing, Lumus?"

Bubba then snuck a quick peek inside. "Where's Chief Perry?"

"Chief? Oh … he went to Mt. Pleasant. Why? You want to see him?"

"Oh no … no. I was just checking … you know …"

"Yeah, I understand," Lumus said. "Look boys, just because Chief is the meanest man on earth doesn't mean you have to be afraid of him." He chuckled and we gave a slight grin, not quite sure how to take the remark. "Actually, the Chief went over to the print shop to pick up some Wanted Posters."

"Of the murderer, you mean?" I exclaimed loudly. "Y'all already know who it is?"

"Well no, not exactly … not of the murderer. The posters are of the two most wanted desperados on the Island." He paused and gave us a serious look. "You and Bubba. We're going to put 'em up on the wall in the Post Office right beside Trigger Bert."

"Oh Lumus, you're too much," Bubba said hopefully. A long pause. A forlorn look. "You are kidding, aren't you?"

"A-HA-HA, had y'all going there for a minute, huh?"

"Yeah, you sure did," said Bubba with relief.

"Don't scare us like that," I added. "We've been in enough trouble lately."

"Well, what brings y'all here? Thought y'all would be out crabbing.

What's wrong? Business slow?"

"N-a-a-w, business is good," Bubba answered. "And it would be a lots better if Mike here would listen to me. But you know how hard headed them Irish can be sometimes."

I ignored Bubba and eagerly interrupted. Since this morning I'd had something on my mind that I wanted to ask Lumus.

"Lumus, we came by to see if you need any help with the murder case. It is a murder case isn't it?" I wanted to at least have my facts straight if I was going to help solve the big case. "Bubba 'n me are real smart when we have to be and we could …"

Lumus held up his hand to cut me off. "Well," Lumus said hesitantly … "let's just say Mr. Poe didn't drown accidentally … OK?"

"You mean he drowned on purpose?" Bubba asked.

I nudged Bubba in the side. I didn't want Lumus to think we were complete rookies when it came to police work. "No, he means that he didn't drown at all. Right, Lumus?"

"Yeah, something like that."

Bubba nodded consentingly. He always did that when he wasn't quite sure about something. He did it a lot in school.

"I've been thinking, Lumus. Why would anyone kill somebody from the Island?" I asked. In my mind we were all good people, except Mr. Grunting and maybe old man Griffith who was a grouch, but no one so bad they should be killed.

"That's what the Chief and I are working on now. We're trying to find a motive."

"A motive?" Bubba asked. "What's that?"

Another poke in the side and an exasperated look.

"A motive? It's the reason you do something. Like what's y'alls' motive for catching crabs?"

"To get money," Bubba said quickly.

"There you go. That's what me and the Chief are working on."

"What?" Bubba said. "Making money?"

"No," I said impatiently. "Bubba," and I really gave him the look, "let me do the talking … OK?" I was afraid he was going to blow the whole idea of him and me helping with the case. Then I added, "Just be quiet … will ya!"

"Eah, I'm just trying to help, Sherlock."

"I know but …"

"Back to your question, Mike. I don't think we need any extra help with the case. At least, not now. Too many cooks can spoil the stew. You understand, don't you? Besides, aren't you and Bubba kind of young to be doing police work?"

Right away I felt discouraged that we couldn't help. Shucks, I figured Lumus and the Chief needed all the help they could get even if it was from two kids, two smart kids at that. But I wasn't leaving just yet …not without having my say-so.

"Yeah, Lumus we are kind of young but we aren't stupid. And we have lived here a long time and know a lot of people and what goes on and besides, nobody would suspect Bubba 'n me of snooping around and …"

I think Lumus butted in just to shut me up. "OK, OK, tell you what … but no promises. If we need someone to help or do some legwork or something, we'll keep y'all in mind. Fair enough?"

"Great! Yeah," I said, "that sounds great." We weren't out of the game yet.

"*Now* can I return to my nap?"

"Thanks, Lumus," I said. And remember we know a lot of stuff about the Island."

"I bet you do."

We hopped on our bikes and were leaving when Lumus took one parting shot. "Bubba!" he yelled. "Been fighting any inner tubes lately?"

Bubba grinned and waved off Lumus while I waved a goodbye with thoughts of catching a murderer.

Bubba rode up beside me and said, "Now tell me all about those Isle of Palms girls that you never talked to … BA-HA-HA-HA-HA!"

33
THE INVESTIGATION

"Hello, Mrs. Poe. This is Lumus Mc Farland with the Sullivans Island Police Department."

It had taken Lumus some time to track down the whereabouts of Thomas Poe's ex-wife. He made a long distance call.

"How are you?" A pause. "Fine, just fine, thank you. I'm calling from Sullivans Island and … well … I'm afraid I have some bad news. And I'm not exactly sure of the best way to go about this so I suppose I'll just get to the point… Yes Ma'am … It concerns Mr. Poe. Again I apologize about being so blunt about this but I don't know any other way to approach this. Two days ago we discovered a body and late yesterday afternoon we positively identified it as Thomas Edward Poe … Yes Ma'am. Here on the Island. That is your ex-husband? Yes Ma'am, for sure. I would have called sooner but it took a little legwork before I found where you live …. Yes Ma'am. Your neighbor Mr. Williams remembered your maiden name and well …. What's that? Oh yes, we're sure it's him.
We have his Citadel ring … he did graduate in 1934?" *Pause.* "Oh, in the top of his class … what an honor. We're also doing a backup check on his dental records as a precaution." *A long pause.* "Yes, Dr. Brandenburg."

The shaky voice on the other end turned to small sobs. Lumus knew it was time to get off the phone. He had completed this unpleasant task.

"Mrs. Poe." He paused searching for the right words but knew instinctively there were no right words at a time like this. "I realize this is a trying time for you. My sympathies go out to you and your family." *Pause.* "Yes Ma'am, I understand and I won't keep you but another minute." *Pause.* "Yes, we made contact with his brother. Yes, in Ohio." *Pause.* More crying. "I've talked to Warren Poe and he's letting Mc Swain's Funeral Home in Mt. Pleasant handle all the funeral arrangements."

He listened for a second. "Yes, Mc Swain's. The funeral is Wednesday." *A long pause.* " Right. Good. I'll talk to you on Friday if that's OK with you? I'm sorry to be the bearer of such bad news and if there's anything we can do, don't hesitate to call. OK …. sure … goodbye."

Oh man, Lumus thought as he placed the phone down and stared at the ceiling. *I pray I don't ever have to do that again.*

The day of Thomas' Poe's funeral Lumus and the Chief met at the station to plan some kind of strategy for the investigation of Thomas Poe's death.

"Well, Chief. Let's hope we can finally get going and make some headway on this case."

"Yeah, let's hope so? By the way, Lumus …" A pause for a big bite into a fresh glazed Grannie's doughnut. "You're going to see Mrs. Poe tomorrow. Right?"

"No, on Friday. She told me she would be here until Saturday clearing up some legal stuff and all. I didn't think it would be right to go barging in right after the funeral. You want another Coke?"

"No thanks." Chief wiped clean his mouth with the back of his hand. "Do you think she can help us?"

"I don't know, Chief. But she sure can't hurt us and she's our only lead right now."

"Lumus …" Another pause as he reached for the sixth and last doughnut. "Didn't the newspaper say something about Mr. Poe having a sister besides the brother in Ohio?"

"Yeah," Lumus said lifting the lone napkin in search of a doughnut, "but the sister's deceased. His brother is supposed to be at the funeral, according to Bobby Dawson over at Mc Swain's. Bobby said he'd call me today and let me know something for sure."

"As soon as you hear something let me know," the Chief said ambling toward the door. "And Lumus when you talk to this brother. What's his name again?"

"Warren."

"Yeah, whatever. Grill him real good before he gets out of town. Know what I mean?"

"Gotcha, Chief. Where you headed?"

"Gotta run a couple errands for the little lady. Then it's my day to patrol."

"Check with ya later," Lumus said, "And Chief …"

"What?"

"Stay off that hill, please."

Funerals and death were not to Mary Helen Poe's liking, especially when they took her away from home, which included a five-hour drive. Her daily routine had been upset, a routine, which had become comfortable at best. Life at home when you're forty-one could be a nightmare but her mother had been more than supportive since the divorce and the fact that the girls spent nine months of the year away at school made the transition easier for both. Besides, it was a temporary situation. She would be moving on soon. As for poor Thomas … well, she had mixed feelings of sincere grief and a sense of relief that he was out of his personal misery.

She thought it quite ironic that one of the constant sources of disagreement in their marriage had been the issue of whether there was life after death or not. Thomas believed strongly in another world, spiritual in essence but very real. He could never explain his feelings completely, which added to the fury of Mary Helen's argument that when you're gone, you're gone … that's it. Now only Thomas will know for sure and that fact kind of irritated her. That Thomas found out sooner than she but considering the price he had to pay it was better this way.

Those were her thoughts as she crossed the Savannah River into South Carolina with the girls dozing comfortably, Jean in the back … the smart one … the intellectual … never gave a moment's trouble even as a baby.

Joan, her favorite in the front … the rebel … the instigator … Smart too but not on a level with Jean by any stretch. They had, so far, handled the death of their father extremely well but she knew the real test was yet to come … the funeral and the burial. She hoped they would hold up.

Bury Thomas. Meet with the lawyer and head back home as soon as possible. Let Warren worry about the rest.

Mary Helen drifted in and out recalling the good times with Thomas in their younger days: dancing on Folly Pier, the long walks on the beach at night when they revealed their hearts and minds to each other, the plans, the laughs. Where had it all gone? And … so fast?

And *now ... here I am ... going to bury him and ...*

The Platters, singing from their souls on the Mighty TMA, Charleston's only rock station brought her back to reality with "Smoke Gets in Your Eyes." She knew for sure that she was getting close to Charleston.

And that policeman from the Island ... Mc Farkin, Mc Far..., Mc Farland ... he wants to meet with me. I don't have time for some small town cop. If he calls, he calls ... if he doesn't all the better.

All Mary Helen wanted to do was get in and out of town as quickly as possible.

"Hello Chief, this is Bobby Dawson at Mc Swain's Funeral home. Long time, no talk to. How are you?" A pause. "Is Lumus there?"

"No Bobby, Lumus isn't here right now. How's business?"

Bobby gave Chief his pat answer. "Dead … real dead."

Chief always got a chuckle out of that. "Yeah, if business was alive and kicking you wouldn't make any money, would you?"

"Nope, not too much. Be kind of hard to bury them live people." They both chuckled.

"Lumus called the other day wanting some information on the Poe family. So I'll just give to you. OK, Chief?"

"Yeah sure. We're working on the investigation now and whatever you got will be of help."

"All right. But we don't have much, Chief. Thomas Poe's next of kin is his brother, Warren. He's a housing contractor from Cleveland. Went up there right after the War and hit it big with some government contracts. Anyway, he'll be here until Sunday and is staying at The Brookgreen Court in Mt. Pleasant. Seems like a nice enough fellow." *Pause.* "What's that, Chief?"

"Yeah, he's by himself. I guess you know the ex-wife is here … Mary Helen Poe. She still uses her married name. Lives in Florida with her mother. And the two kids came with her. They're staying at The Colonial House Motel and will be here until Saturday. That's all I have. Wish I had more. Hope it helps you some?"

"I do too. And thanks, Bobby. Tell your old man I say, "Hello."

"Sure thing, Chief. I suppose it's too early to have any real leads in the case? Everybody's talking about it."

"No real leads yet. But we're working on it. Thanks again … will do and the same to your family … bye."

Chief Perry clutched the dusty handle of the radio microphone and called Lumus.

An old Island rite of passage marking a young male's passage into teen-hood involved taking "The Ride." It was a silly thing to do, was absolutely unofficial and non-sanctioned, and had no common sense value whatsoever. Plus it was dangerous. Those were more than enough reasons for Bubba 'n me to give it a try. Even though Bubba 'n me weren't officially of age, we couldn't wait to perform our manly duty and prove we were ready to begin our teenage years like so many other Island boys before us by doing something foolish.

There was no designated day or time to take "The Ride" or anyone to train you, to advise you, or help you. You just did it.

All of us Island boys knew the terms of "The Ride" having heard the legendary tales told over and over by the older teenagers. The terms of "The Ride were simple: The unspoken rule was that the participant had to ride half the length of the Island on a bike while being towed behind a car with a rope attached to the bumper with the driver of the car having no knowledge of your being towed behind them. One minor stipulation, however, was that you must be towed through the business district giving the business owners and their patrons the opportunity to be ample witnesses to serve as proof of your ride. Therefore, a midnight ride, ala Paul Revere would not qualify.

In recent years the driver who had unknowingly participated more times than anyone else in this ritual was the frail and fragile Sergeant Henry, eighty-six years old with fading eyesight thus making it almost impossible for him to see anyone behind him. Shoot, Sergeant Henry had trouble seeing anyone in front of him. He also was a favorite to ride behind because he rarely reached the speed limit of thirty-five miles an hour, which became a built in safety feature. Bubba 'n me pretty much knew his schedule of going to the Post Office or grocery store during the week and Chippys on Fridays for his weekly fill of beer and then back home. Our bikes were ready. All we needed was some rope. I borrowed our anchor line from our borrowed boat while Bubba borrowed some more rope from Ms. Kingman's ever-shortening clothesline. We camped out one morning around the corner of Sergeant Henry's house and waited for the nearly blind old man to appear and head out on one of his trips to the business district.

It wasn't long before Sergeant Henry came hobbling down the steps, his eyes squinting in the bright sun heading to his car and presumably to the Post Office. His jingling car keys mingled with the chirping birds made for a catchy musical melody as he slowly shuffled down the walk. I'm sure he held onto the keys so he wouldn't forget where they were. His memory was failing at the same rate his eyesight was and his hearing was extremely poor. Other than that he was in great shape.

I don't think he would have seen Bubba 'n me perched on our bikes no more than twenty feet behind the car had he been looking for us, as he felt and fumbled around the car door searching for the handle. Our ropes were in position, one end tied securely onto the back bumper, and the other end dangling over the handlebars of our bikes.

"The Ride," "The Ride!" We were really going to take "The Ride" up the Island and through the business district. I was excited to be involved in what seemed like more of a grown up situation, an ordeal that had a purpose to it and would prove something other than the immature escapades of past years. This undertaking involved our very manhood, our rank in the hierarchy of teenagers and the crew. It seemed like yesterday, even though it had been over two years, since Ryan, my brother, came home bragging and strutting around like a peacock after he made "The Ride." He still liked to brag that he did it behind Mrs. O'Brien's car, one of the known speed demons on the Island. He claimed that she went almost forty miles an hour.

Sergeant Henry took forever to get in the car and locate the ignition switch, finally finding the right key after repeated close-up looks at the keys only inches from his eyes. At first I thought he was going to eat the keys when he brought them up so close to his face.

I noticed Bubba was tying his rope around the handlebars with double knots, nice and tight.

"Eah, what ya doing?" I asked, thinking maybe I had missed something. "With the rope?"

"What's it look like?" He gave me that look and began to launch into his Three Stooge Curley act when I raised my hand in protest and shook my head from side to side.

He said, "I'm tying the rope so it won't squeeze my hand when I'm holding on," sneaking in a quick "KNUCK, KNUCK." Then he added, "That'll give me two free hands. See."

"That's kinda dangerous, ain't it? What if you want …"

Before I could finish my warning, Sergeant Henry fired off the big Buick. It roared, spit smoke, coughed, spit some more smoke, and did not move an inch. It was in neutral. I saw Sergeant Henry hunch over the steering wheel, stare down at the column, and then pull on the gear stick. And with a loud CLUNK the car was in gear and we were off.

The only responsibility we had was to sit, enjoy the ride and be ready to work our breaks, when necessary. The first place where we would need our brakes was at a stop sign about a half block from Sergeant Henry's house. We prepared ourselves lining up our feet on the pedals but should have known better as our driver didn't slow down even a little bit and zoomed right through the stop sign. I guess he didn't see it?

We quickly adjusted to the task at hand and put to rest any fears or apprehension we previously imagined as we coasted up the Island waving and grinning at the locals who had pulled over when they recognized Sergeant Henry's dark blue Buick approaching in the other lane. It was like a funeral procession as the oncoming traffic, protecting themselves from any collisions, pulled over and stopped while the blind man with two young boys in close pursuit drove toward the business district. Oh, it was fun! And with all the cars pulling over and with a top speed of maybe twenty-five miles per hour we felt safe, secure and a little bit cocky. Oh yeah, we thought we were the cat's meow.

"Eah, watch this."Bubba showed off his no-hands skills. "YA-WHOO! I'm flying!"

Trying to outdo Bubba, I maneuvered around so I was sitting backwards and guiding the bike with one hand.

"Ain't nothing to this. And Ryan told you how scary it was and all … he was just trying to scare ya."

"Yeah, guess so. Eah, try this." I put my feet up on the handlebars and leaned back.

"A-l-l right!" Bubba yelled, "Here we come!"

The really fun part would be coasting through the business district while everyone stopped what they were doing to look at us and we would wave and feel good because we completed part of an old Island tradition.

We were no more than a half a block away from glory when something went drastically wrong. As we closed in on the business district, instead of stopping at the grocery store or the gas station or anywhere in the business district Sergeant Henry kept right on going. He turned left at Chippys on the corner and headed for the causeway and Mt.Pleasant and now, for whatever reason, he decided he was in a hurry. He goosed the old Buick and it responded with a mighty surge and a cloud of smoke. I hung on for about a hundred yards but when his speed got to about thirty-five I chickened out and yelled at Bubba as I let go of my rope and coasted to a stop. Bubba, sensing the situation, was frantically trying to untie his double knots but the strain and the tautness of the rope made it clear the knots could not be untied, at least, not by the rider. Just as Sergeant Henry was heading off the Island onto the main causeway, he stomped down on the gas again and sent a steady stream of black exhaust smoke all over Bubba who cursed, screamed and prayed all in the same breath. Bubba looked back at me as to say his final good bye to an old friend. All I could see were two big, white eyes and a pitiful face. The only timely advice I could think of at the moment was for Bubba to stop so I screamed, "The brakes … hit the breaks!" I don't think my fading friend heard my fading words. The only thing I could make out from him was a dim "O-O-O-O-H NO" as he unwillingly raced across the causeway.

Well, I thought, *if Bubba survives this then he can have the bragging rights for the all time top speed gained on "The Ride."* They must have been going close to fifty miles an hour when they approached The Ben Sawyer Bridge. WHOOSH … UP and WHOOM … DOWN! They were over the bridge in a flash. Like a roller coaster and onto the Mt. Pleasant side. That was the last I saw of Bubba but I think I heard him yelling?

A thousand thoughts all at once rushed through Bubba's brain.

Oh man, what am I gonna do? Bubba thought. *He's going faster and faster ... what do I do? Don't panic. Just keep this bike from crashing.* Bubba did everything in his power to keep the bike straight behind the speeding car. Ho*w can I untie this durn rope? ... if I had a knife I could cut it.*

*Oh God! Th*e thought hit him like a ton of bricks. *What if Henry is going to Charleston? Or worse yet ... what if he gets in a wreck?* Bubba knew they were going at least fifty miles an hour but it felt more like a hundred. The wind was whistling a steady tune, Bubba's eyes were watering, and the telephone poles were zipping by like they were toothpicks. And the oleanders were a green blur. It was low tide, he could smell it, and then he had an idea: *It's my only chance. I'm gonna die if I stay on this bike. Oh God, I'm sorry about putting the ex-lax in the sisters' milk and ... SPLATT ... a bug right in the mouth. Oh man, now the bugs ...what next?*

There was a spot near Simmons Seafood where the road curved somewhat, not much, but Bubba knew it would be his only chance of escape. Sergeant Henry would have to slow down some there. *Surely he will?* The curve was coming up fast. That's where he decided to make his move. Going into the curve, Bubba very gently turned the handlebars to the right in the direction of the marsh, grabbed the rope with his left hand and pulled with all his strength so as to get a run, then he could coast for just a second or two and get ready to jump. Surprisingly the force pulled him even with Sergeant Henry who glanced out his passenger side window. Bubba could have sworn Sergeant Henry waved at him and gave him a quick wink. At that instant Bubba made the leap of his life. Aided by the speed at which he was traveling, he was thrown almost to his intended target, however, he landed a few feet short onto the shoulder of the road, took one big bounce and landed face down in the safety of the soft pluff mud. Scratched and bruised and muddy but still alive.

Bubba knelt in the mud and watched as Sergeant Henry drove right on dragging his bike into Mt. Pleasant.

Within minutes Lumus, who had been alerted by the ever-watchful group at Chippys, found the mudded Bubba standing on the causeway, dazed a bit but all in one piece.

Lumus couldn't help but smile at the sight of Bubba. "You all right? Man, you're a sight for sore eyes."

Bubba quickly launched into an explanation."Lumus I can explain everything." Bubba was more worried about getting in trouble again than about broken bones. "It was part of a …"

"Calm down, calm down. I know. You and Mike took The Ride. Right?"

"Yeah, how'd you know?"

"I saw y'all behind Sergeant Henry at Station 21."

"Oh?"

"Come on. Hop in. We'll track down Sergeant Henry and pick up what's left of your bike."

"Thanks, Lumus," said Bubba as he brushed himself off. "Thanks, a lot."

"You're welcome," said Lumus.

Bubba paused, looked back up the causeway and got into the Jeep thankful to be alive, then mumbled to himself: "Wait till I get my hands on that Devlin … hit the breaks he says … humph!"

It was the day after Thomas Poe's funeral. Time for the Chief and Lumus to begin in earnest the investigation of his murder but they had a problem, a big problem.

"Lumus, we don't have a darn thing to go on. No murder weapon, no witnesses, and no motive." They were at the station, late in the evening. The Chief was in his chair scratching his crew cut with a serious look on his face. He leaned over as though he were going to tell Lumus a secret.

“So let’s try this. You talk with the ex-wife and I’ll see what I can get out of the brother. Then if we have time, we’ll double back and I’ll talk to the ex and you can follow up with the brother. What ya think?”

“Sounds good to me, Chief,” said Lumus leaning back in his chair.

“Right. That way if we miss something we’ll be checking on each other.”

“That’s good, Chief. Two heads are always better than one. Oh yeah, don’t know if I told you or not? But I’m meeting Mrs. Poe later today.”

“No, I didn’t know. What’s the rush?”

“Well, I was going to meet her Friday but she told me that she had to get back to Florida as soon as she could and wanted to know if we could meet today. So …”

When Lumus had first contacted Mary Helen Poe on the phone she had seemed polite enough considering the circumstances. Emotionally he wondered about her. Had the divorce gone peaceful enough that she would be cooperative or did she still have it in for her ex? Was the divorce one of those messy affairs with each party greedily going after everything in sight, leaving a bad taste in Mrs. Poe’s mouth?

They planned to meet in the adjoining restaurant of the motel over coffee. It was a quiet place and big enough if they needed some privacy to talk. As she appeared, Lumus seated at a corner table, rose to met her. She was not at all what Lumus had envisioned. She was tall and slim like a model and even walked like one but not near young enough to be one. *The growing bags under the eyes gave away her years, probably hard years*, Lumus thought.

Lumus wasn’t much for small talk knowing that Mrs. Poe would be leaving soon so he decided to jump right in and try to answer the one question that had been bugging him from the beginning of the investigation … What was the motive for Thomas Poe’s death? He questioned her about her finances, her lifestyle when she was married to Thomas Poe, her hobbies and interests. Everything he could reasonably think of that might, just might shed some light on an otherwise dark trail and lend any kind of clue as to the motive behind Thomas Poe’s death. But from the start the short quick answers with no show of emotion, gave Lumus the feeling that this was not going to be a productive meeting. And so far he was right. He had put into question form the statement that she must really be sad or depressed over the happenings of the last week: the death of her ex-husband, the funeral, and having to come back to the Island under such dreary circumstances. Expecting a “Yes, it’s quite hard” type reply, Mrs. Poe very straight faced said, “No” and continued to stir her coffee.

She was not uncooperative or arrogant or unfriendly. She answered Lumus’ questions but offered very little information, instead resigning herself, to answering no more than was necessary. It was a non-committal conversation at best. "Yes, no, I don't recall" were her replies. It was a type of interview that left Lumus wondering.

Lumus got the impression that she felt bothered by the whole affair, the death and all, so rather than risk alienating her by pushing her he decided to cut his losses and hope for a better day.

Condolescences offered and goodbyes rendered, Lumus left scratching his head.

Hope Chief made out better with the brother.

Lumus felt so down after his encounter with Mrs. Poe he stopped by Grannie's and loaded up on doughnuts even buying a dozen of the new "Special," jelly-filled doughnuts. He needed a pick-me-up and what better than a pound of sugar. *Chief will help me with these, I'm sure.*

The Chief was waiting with cold Cokes in hand. He had heard Lumus round the corner at the church and reminded himself to tell Lumus to get that dog-gone muffler fixed.

"Chief, I can't explain it. Talking to that woman was like … like talking to u-u-u-h…u-u-u-h … a-a-a-w …" Lumus said gloomily. "I don't know. She was …"

The Chief realizing Lumus' frustration offered, "A statue. Right?"

"No, not exactly. She talked back but there was no emotion. None at all. It was more like discussing a business affair or the weather. I got more reaction from Susie up at Grannie's than this lady."

"Did she tell you anything useful at all? Anything?"

"No, not that I remember. And that's what's so frustrating. Maybe you can talk to her and get some kind of information or reaction from her?"

"From what you tell me I don't particularly want to talk to her. Tell you what, let's put her on hold a minute."

The Chief paused while he reached for another jelly-filled. "Lumus, these are good. You got 'em at Grannie's?"

"Yep, on special too."

"Look Lumus, you were 0 for 4 today with Mrs. Poe, OK. Don't fret about it none. Tomorrow's a new day and if whoever killed Thomas Poe is still on this Island we'll find 'em. O.K?"

"Y-e-a-h Chief, you're right. I guess I was expecting too much. How about the brother? Anything there?"

"Nice guy and was depressed as hell about the whole thing. But I think we got a small break. We talked a long time about him and his brother growing up on the Island. It was your normal upbringing nothing outstanding but later on, as a teenager it seems, Thomas picked up a hobby that he pursued until it turned into a full time passion and also into quite a financial sum. Turns out our dead man was a dedicated coin collector. It's not much of a lead but it's something. And that's what I want to check with you about. Besides being non-committal did Mrs. Poe happen to mention anything at all about a coin collection or anything else about anything of value that her ex owned that might have been in his house?"

Lumus paused and thought for a second, got up and paced the room. "Nope, not a word." That's kind of strange, don't you think? What if I talk to her again?"

"N-a-a-w, won't do any good. From what you told me, she doesn't much care. All she wants to do is go home. Can't much blame the woman in a way?"

"Yeah, guess so," Lumus said dejectedly. "And besides, if need be, I can always call her."

"Tomorrow Lumus, here's what we do. We go sniffing around for a coin collection. We'll go through Poe's house and if nothing comes up there we'll go to the banks and see if he kept it in one of those safety boxes. This could lead to something. You never know?"

"Chief, I was just wondering. Do you think maybe Mrs. Poe has this coin collection?"

"H-u-m-m … that's a thought, Lumus.One way to find out. Call the lawyer who handled the divorce. I think it was Dickie Hopkins? You know Dickie, don't ya? The golf nut … guy plays more golf than Sam Snead …he'd know."

"Yes sir." A perked up Lumus said, "Tomorrow for sure." The sugar was kicking in.

Chief Perry had done his share of worrying over this case too. Only he did his fretting at home. He didn't want to present to Lumus a sense of despair or show the slightest chink in the armor. He also had some definite ideas about the case that might prove useful. Now was the time to act.

The next morning Chief Perry called Warren Poe on a hunch with a couple of follow-up questions and then called Lumus immediately. "Lumus, meet me at the station as soon as you can. And don't stop for doughnuts. I already got some."

Lumus barely stepped into the office and the Chief was off and running."Lumus, have you called Dickie Hopkins yet?"

"No. But I'll get right on it."

"Never mind. Don't need to. At least, I don't think so?"

The Chief was excited about something thought Lumus *or he had too many doughnuts again.*

"I talked with Warren Poe this morning and really tried to pin him down him about Thomas' coin collection. He assured me that his brother would *never* part with that collection come hell or high water. Said he loved it more than he loved his wife. He also said he always kept it at home. How about them apples!" The Chief was smiling and excited and rightfully so. They finally had *something* to go on. Not much but *something*   "Whatta ya say we go looking for a coin collection?" said the Chief. "We'll start at Poe's house."

Lumus grabbed his hat and followed the Chief out the door. "Now we're getting somewhere, Chief." It was Lumus' turn to smile and get excited. "Yes sir, now we're getting somewhere!"

34
THE FISHING TRIP

I laid in bed half awake staring at the ceiling. The rising sun filtering through the green curtains presented a medley of odd shapes and forms dancing on the ceiling extending to the far wall, most of them looked like fish to me. They jumped and swam from the ceiling back to the wall as the curtain was swayed by a gentle breeze. And I caught every one of those fish smiling and laughing the whole time while my father gave me a huge smile of approval.

As I woke from my imaginary fishing trip I felt something in the room, a slight wind blowing through the open window. *Breeze? Wind? ... Oh no!* I jumped out of bed and raced across the room, stuck my head out the window and checked the top of the tall pecan tree for movement of its leaves. Mollie was on my heels and jumped up resting her front paws on the windowsill.

"WHEW, Mollie." I rubbed her head. "For a second there, I was scared."

Thank goodness. My worst fears were relieved because the breeze came from the south, not the dreaded east wind, the enemy of all fishermen. The southerly breeze might bring heat from the Gulf but at least the ocean would be calm and we could go fishing without the worry of rough waters.

I was excited and keyed up. I was going fishing today and not with just any old body. This was special. I was going fishing with my father! It was a Saturday, cloudless, no rain in the forecast and with the slight breeze, the ocean would probably be flat as a pancake, a perfect day for going to the jetties. But old worrywart me had to be certain. I didn't want any surprises, especially from the weather, to ruin our day. So I dressed quickly, yelled for Mollie and we were out the door. I jumped off the back porch landing softly in the dew-filled grass. It felt good … wet and cool like a washcloth on my face in the morning. I also felt the humidity; it would definitely get hotter later in the day, a good sign. The fish seemed to bite better the higher the humidity. Just to double check on the wind speed and direction, I took a quick bike ride to the front beach and examined carefully the movement of the always reliable sea oats lined up on the tops of the dunes. Yep! The gentle breeze was from the south as the sea oats swayed softly to and fro. The dance they performed was a slow waltz as they moved slowly in step with their partner one way and then back the other.

My father would be up soon, have his usual cup of coffee and meet me in the backyard under the chinaberry tree where the boat was kept and where I would faithfully be standing guard, waiting for the greatest fisherman in the world. We had spent the previous evening preparing the boat, a sixteen- foot wooden Halsey, powered by a thirty-five horsepower Johnson motor, a huge red monstrosity that must have weighed a ton and in the words of my father "ran like a sewing machine." It was more than enough horsepower for our short run to the north jetties just off the Island from Station 20. These were the same jetties my father rowed out to as a teenager and he knew all the good spots for catching fish.

Going through the ritual of preparing for a fishing trip was half the fun, getting everything gathered and placed in the boat. The other half was pulling in the numerous black sea bass, called blackfish by the locals, which grew up to about twelve inches in length and weighed anywhere from two to five pounds. We considered a "keeper" to be about eight inches long, and my father always had the final say-so on what was a keeper should I be in doubt as to the captured fish's status …freedom or not? On trips nowadays I never argued or whined about having to throw back a freshly caught fish. That would be childish behavior. However, in my early apprenticeship as a fisherman my father definitely cut me some slack and I sometimes brought home what I thought were whoppers until the head was cut off in the cleaning process and suddenly that big ol' fish didn't look so big any more. When that would happen I guess I'd get a look of surprise on my face, and my father knew I was learning and would tell me, "That's OK, Rusty can eat that one." Rusty was the neighborhood cat that never missed a free meal and regularly showed up on time when we started cleaning fish. And these fish were some of the best eating to come out of the ocean, sweet tasting with very few bones and plenty of meat. Just ask Rusty … he'll tell ya.

And the one thing I loved about going fishing with my father was that we *always* caught fish. Sometimes not as many as we would have liked to, but we never got skunked mainly because there were plenty of fish at the jetties and my father knew those rocks like the back of his hand. You just needed to know *where* and *when* to fish for them. My father's theory was that if we anchored and didn't get a bite within a couple of minutes it meant we weren't on them … meaning a school of them. Rather than sit and wait for the fish to hopefully come to our bait we would pull anchor, my job, and go in search of the fish. Keep moving until we got on 'em, then catch all that would bite and when they slacked off, move again. At the end of a good day with a bountiful catch and after a lot of moving from spot to spot, the anchorman was pretty well worn out. But that was also part of the fun of it: participating and being helpful.

Like my father used to say, "Mike, there is a difference between going fishing and catching fish. We are going to *catch* fish. Always remember that."

Without doubt, the most gratifying part of these trips to the jetties or crabbing in Miller's Creek was being with my father and knowing that he took what little spare time he had and spent it with me. I felt wanted and appreciated for helping in little ways like with the anchor or holding the boat at the landing. I did my small part but felt big on the inside. That's what made any outing with my father so very special.

My father was running a few minutes late this morning so I rechecked everything in the boat, making sure the supplies were in their rightful place. The anchor line was coiled and in the bow of the boat nestled snugly with the anchor, the oars were in place laying along the sides of the boat, along with their counterparts the oarlocks. In case of an engine breakdown we would row home. The net was back by my father's seat, and my hand lines, up by the front seat, were rigged out properly with my small tackle box nearby with extra hooks and sinkers. It wasn't a real tackle box but rather a discarded cigar box of Uncle Schroeder's, which suited me quite nicely and held the few extras I might need. It was cardboard and a bit frayed and worn and the top was held together with tape. I made a mental note to check with Uncle Schroeder when we got back and get another tackle box from his endless supply. A big, mesh laundry bag, the kind with holes in it, was in the middle of the boat and was used to keep the fish we caught. And it was appropriately called a fishnet bag. Now all we needed to do was fill it with fish. When we were anchored it hung over the side of the boat holding our catch assuring that the fish would remain fresh rather than dry out in the sun if we placed them in the floor of the boat. And each time we moved the boat to try another spot my father would yell, " Fish up!" And I would scramble to haul in the bag, counting each fish every time to make sure none had escaped.

Today my father was going to fish for the elusive sheepshead using his experienced cane pole rigged with a special leader and the exact size hook needed to hook into its small rounded mouth, while I fished for blackfish with my trusty hand lines. The sheepshead was a crafty customer. Along with the flounder, which was more of a creek dweller, they were considered two of the toughest fish to land requiring tremendous patience and expertise. Also, knowledge of their habitat and the correct time to fish for them was essential. But the wait was worth the effort. They were delicious eating and you had the honor of having outsmarted and landed a fish that not many people were capable of catching, especially the sheepshead. The sheepshead derived its name not from any resemblance to the head of a sheep as the name implies but because its broad, incisor, teeth were similar to those of a sheep, almost human in shape and configuration.

I circled the parked boat again and again carefully checking and rechecking every item in the boat memorizing its place and anticipated use. Like my father had told me, "If you get out on the water and need something there's no hardware store right there for you to pull into and get what you need." I figured it was better to err on the side of caution. The only element missing and the most vital for me was the bait I would use, which was shrimp and it was still in the freezer and wouldn't be taken out until right before we left. That way it stayed frozen and hard for a while longer which made it stay on the hook longer until old Mr. Blackfish came along and tried to eat it. The blackfish loved shrimp but rather than pay the high cost at the seafood market my father and I would head to Miller's Creek with a cast net and a plastic bucket and within minutes have enough shrimp for several fishing trips. This was where my father demonstrated Job-like patience teaching me the age-old technique of casting a net. Shoot, I scared more shrimp in those early days than I could catch in a lifetime.

Now Mr. Sheepshead was a finicky eater and wouldn't just eat just anything. Uh-uh, he didn't like shrimp nor would he bite on a piece of squid no matter how tasty it looked. There was only one bait he would go after. There had to be a fiddler crab on the hook if you hoped to land the slick and shrewd sheepshead. The fiddler crab was a miniature version of a blue crab, a super miniature version. It had two claws, one was large, the main food gatherer and defensive weapon while the other was tiny and used mainly to help place food from the larger claw into its mouth. The movement of their claws, one claw up and the other moving back and forth, as they sat motionless in the marsh resembled those of a violin player thus earning the little crab the moniker of a "fiddler."

And that's we called them … fiddlers.

The fiddler lived in the mud usually on the edges or near the banks of the marsh, its home a small burrowed out hole. They lived in communities of thousands and built their homes about a foot apart giving the marsh floor the appearance of Swiss cheese, only brown in color. They ranged in size from one half to an inch in length and no bigger around than your pinky finger. The fiddler had to be equipped with sonar-like hearing because no matter how quietly I tried to sneak up on them and capture them as they sat by their holes playing their violins they would invariably dart back into their hole and safety before I could even make an attempt at grabbing them. They weren't fast runners in the open ground but they were quick sprinters. If they played baseball all of them would be shortstops.

The dominant male was equipped with a larger-than-normal claw and if strategically placed on a kids' fingertip it could cause pain similar to a weak bee sting. I tried to avoid the fiddlers with the big claw but was not always successful.

There was a certain talent and strategy involved in catching the fiddler. They were not willful or voluntary partners to being placed on a hook and dangled before the hungry eyes of an eight-pound sheepshead. Some fishermen deployed the slow tedious method of going into the edge of the marsh with a small bucket and a short flat stick and digging up each fiddler individually. A stick would be inserted into the soft mud about ten inches deep and the fiddler was pried from his home while the fisherman made a quick snatch of the terrified resident as it scurried for safety toward a neighboring hole. A good fisherman would need forty to fifty fiddlers when fishing for the sheepshead so this process of bait gathering was not only time-consuming but could be frustrating because you weren't assured of a nabbing a fiddler at every hole. Mr. Fiddler might have been out running errands or visiting a neighbor's house when you called. Sometimes when we were riding across the causeway and the tide was low I'd point out a fisherman in the edge of the marsh laboriously bent over with a stick in his hand in search of bait. My father would chuckle and say, "Wonder if he'll get home in time for supper tonight?"

On occasion determined fishermen who refused to leave the marsh without sufficient bait and admit defeat to the elusive fiddler would lose track of time and end up with plenty of bait but to their dismay they would miss the tide.

My father knew from experience a much better way to catch fiddlers rather than prying them up one at a time and had devised a really neat plan for catching them. Well, I thought it was neat because it involved me helping him. What he would do was scout out a large open expanse where thousands of fiddlers would congregate so thickly that we couldn't walk without crushing them. These areas were not common in the marsh's edges but were usually found along a shoreline with sand. My father would place me at one side of the group caught in the open and upon his command I would corral the fiddlers like a cowboy herds cattle into a pen, running from side to side waving my arms and yelling. I really liked the job of fiddler-herder, especially the part of helping my father, and most of the time the terrified fiddlers cooperated running into the steady clutches of my father waiting with a bucket. His tough hands with what seemed like bite-proof fingers would quickly snatch a handful and put them in the bucket like a soda jerk scooping ice cream to make a sundae except he was a lot quicker with his scoops. The first time I tried scooping up a handful I quickly learned that there was more to it than just grabbing them. I was imitating my father and grabbed a handful of runaway fiddlers but was too slow in releasing them. A reluctant old male clamped down on my finger and wouldn't let go regardless of all the shaking and screaming I did. A hungry old "Chinaback". That's what my father called that felon that day as he pulled its claw apart and rescued me … a Chinaback. The colors of their shell ranged from a beautiful deep purple to a bright red with a repetitious design. Some had green and black mixed in but the purples and reds always stuck out in my mind … they were beautiful, Chinabacks.

We had gathered fiddlers the evening before from the back marsh taking advantage of a super low tide due to a full moon. They were snug and secure in their new home, an old coffee can, and some had already dug new holes in the mud and sand in the can from their home terrain. I checked on them and they looked safe and secure and happy as they ran around visiting their friends in their new neighborhood. If they only knew the trial they would be put through that day they would surely be trying to find a way out of that can. Even though I was put in charge of making the last minute check of the boat and its supplies I'm sure at some point my father had done his own check, not leaving to chance our well-being in the ocean in the hands of a twelve-year-old. That was OK with me. I was happy to help in any way I could.

My father appeared, gave me a big smile, and said, "You ready?" as he tossed me a pack of frozen shrimp. The only thing bigger than my smile was the excitement that ran through me as I answered, "Yes sir, let's go *catch* some fish."

The boat landing was a short ride of about eight blocks. Time enough for my father to thank me for loading the boat and to assure me that we would catch plenty of fish. He was in silent thought and I was all smiles. He rested his muscular arm out the open window, flicking ashes from his ever-present Pall Mall and exhaling a steady stream of white smoke, looking very much the part of Captain-of-the-car and Captain-of-the-boat. Each time we went fishing my father would casually ask why Bubba didn't come with us. I would shrug my shoulders and answer, "I don't know." Because every time we went fishing I invited Bubba.

My father expertly backed the trailer into the edge of the water being careful not to submerge the trailer in the salt water, which prevented it from rusting away so quickly. And together we launched the boat. As I held onto the bowline with the boat in the water while my father parked the car and trailer, I thought about why Bubba didn't come with us. He had been invited on many occasions but politely turned them down offering no real excuse. And I had no answer.

I was really excited now that we were in the boat and getting ready to get underway on our short trip to the jetties. Waiting for the motor to fire off was like being at a big football game between two rivals, anticipating the kickoff. The tension mounted until I felt like hollering out loud.

Finally, my father put the big Johnson in gear and gunned it. The ball was now in the air. Instead of hollering, I dutifully assumed my lookout position in the bow and delighted in the sights all around me trying hard not to miss a single smell, sight or thought. I pointed out the huge pelicans that flew so close to us I could almost touch them. The dolphin were plentiful making their way toward the creeks behind the Island in search of breakfast. Their air holes said "hello" as they broke the surface and their tail waved "goodbye" on their downward descent. And the ever-present squawking seagulls were overhead occasionally swooping down low taking a quick peek into the boat to see if we had any extra food for them. "Not today. Get outta here!" I yelled shooing them away. My father never failed to laugh at the gulls and me.

We made the turn at the end of the Island, the westernmost point, and went through part of the harbor on our way to the jetties, no more than a three-mile run. The sun was up spreading its warmth across the water like Grandma's quilt on a cold winter's night. Both of us shaded our eyes with a hand. We were looking directly into the rising sun as we glided across the smooth ocean. My father responded to the glassy ocean surface with a knowing smile and gently pushed the throttle to full speed, the powerful Johnson responded with a steady hum. The diving gulls and pelicans in the distance made ripples that flowed in perfect circles, disturbed only by the speedy Halsey sliding across the ocean carrying a happy boy and a generous, caring man.

Our conversation was limited due to the roar of the motor and the wind whistling in our ears, which drowned out everything but our thoughts. I never questioned my father about what he was thinking on those memorable boat rides but I remember clearly how delighted I was to be going fishing with him and what a good feeling it gave me. Many a time on those fishing trips I vowed one day to have my own boat and take people fishing with me. And to *catch* fish.

Our familiar and trusty spot was easy to locate. So easy I would point it out to my father who would smile and nod his head as we approached it. Like he needed help finding *any* spot at the jetties. Shoot, he'd been fishing these waters for over forty years. Our spot was twenty yards from the last protruding rock perpendicular to the beach, on the Charleston side of the submerged jetties. The silhouetted rock was easy for me to remember because it was in the shape of an old man's face complete with a beard. The submerged rocks ran to the beach resurfacing at Station 20 forming "the rocks," the gathering spot of the crew. (It was amazing how one set of rocks could have provided so many wonderful memories for an Island boy.)

There was an unspoken progression in the ranks of boatmanship that had been carried on in the Devlin family for generations similar to military promotions from private up to the rank of general. I started out in the ranking system as a beginner, a mere spectator, who went along with my father at a very young age just for the ride. I was maybe five or six years old then. My duties were minimal, if any at all. I think my father was pleased if I didn't get seasick during those early outings and stayed out of the way. I didn't disappoint him and was lucky that I had a natural feel for the sway and bounce of the not- so-always-calm ocean. And I helped a little by being his "gopher" and retrieving this and that so he wouldn't have to walk around in the boat. I was small and nimble. Many of my friends weren't so lucky: even though they desired very much to go out in a boat, they weren't able to simply because of their propensity for seasickness.

From a beginner I advanced to the participant stage a couple of years later when I was given a handline and allowed to fish on my own. This was a formidable stage when I learned how to bait a line, tie knots, put together rigging consisting of a sinker and hook, and to take my catch off the line by myself, which at times could be a tricky undertaking. This stage was a continuing effort that really never ended but rather became more advanced over the years until the day came when I owned my own boat and became the captain like my father who had gone through this same process as a youngster.

Now that I was twelve and developing a little bit of muscle I was given anchor duty, which consisted of putting out and pulling in the anchor upon the request of my father. The natural habitat of the blackfish and sheepshead was a rocky area where their food source lived, and anchoring on top of these rocks could be an expensive ordeal. The configuration of a sand anchor with its pointed ends didn't lend itself to the cracks and crevices in the rocks and it constantly got hung up and on many occasions lodged so tightly that the only way to freedom was to take a knife and cut the anchor line. Replacing a few feet of anchor line wasn't a big deal but buying a new anchor … well, that was different. Money was not plentiful in the Devlin household and my father, being the thrifty man he was, tired rather quickly of buying a new anchor only to lose it on the next trip to the jetties. So he simply found a cheap but adequate substitute, a concrete cinder block, which were plentiful and could be found in any junk pile on the Island. Our concrete block anchor was the kind with two big openings where the line could be run through and tied securely and if it got hung up, which rarely happened, then we just cut it loose and tied on our spare concrete block.

My father maneuvered the boat into position allowing for the pull of the strong current and slight wind, and on his signal I lowered the anchor, being extra careful not to inflict my sensitive hands with rope burns as in the past. Upon my father's OK I tied us off and eagerly grabbed for my handline. We were positioned on the edge of the rocks but my bait had to be in the rocks where the fish fed. A short cast, a flip of the wrist sent my handline dead on target. The object was to find the rocks on the bottom, which was no more than ten feet down and continuously bounce the sinker up and down enticing the fish and keeping the sinker from becoming hung up in the crevice of the rocks. I had to be alert because a blackfish would take the bait and be hooked and before I could pull him to the top he would dart under a rock and now the whole rigging would have to be cut free plus losing the fish, and valuable fishing time was lost while I rigged out another line. In later years I solved the problem of wasted fishing time by making extra riggings the night before and when a quick blackfish outsmarted me and I was forced to cut him loose, I pulled up my line and quickly tied on another rigging.

I bounced my sinker a few times and BOOM- YOW I felt the hungry blackfish hit and I tried not to be overly excited because I had learned from experience I could possibly have a dreaded toadfish on my line. So I gave one hard pull to set the hook and began pulling the line in hand-over-hand letting the line coil at my feet while peeking over the side of the boat in anticipation of seeing a monster fish because this one felt pretty heavy.

" WHOA! Daddy, look!" I held up two blackfish on the line. One on the top hook and the other on the bottom hook and both were keepers. My first double ever and you would have thought I'd just pulled in the world record the way I was carrying on, yelling and hollering. I was so happy. I was grinning from ear to ear. And my father shared this moment with me by flashing a big smile of approval and asked me if I would teach him how to do that … catch 'em two at a time. Most important of all I knew that my father was happy because I was happy.

The blackfish must have been hungry that day as they continued to bite and I obligingly pulled them into the boat, took them off the hook and put them in the laundry bag hanging over the side. I was old enough to know the difference between a keeper or one that had to be thrown back but occasionally I would consult with my father when in doubt just to be sure. And if it wasn't a keeper he'd say, "That one's not big enough for Rusty. Throw him back and you can catch him next summer." Therefore, the small ones that were going to be thrown back and given their freedom innocently acquired the name of a "Rusty Fish." Sometimes I'd pull in one of questionable size, look at it carefully, wondering whether to keep it or not and my father sensing my indecision would say, "Rusty Fish, huh?" Overboard it went. Sometimes he would " MEOW" and smile when he saw me pull in a particularly small one and I would laugh and toss the little fella overboard and tell him "he'd better get home" and that I'd be back next summer to catch him again.

What wasn't a laughing matter, however, was the toadfish problem, or should I say nuisance, and a danger on top of that. The infamous toadfish lived in rocky areas so whenever we fished at the jetties we had to deal with these nasty creatures. These fish were useless from a human standpoint … they were ugly fish, they were inedible, and were capable of swallowing a whole hook. It was a hideous looking creature, half fish, half toad, with a rounded head like a frog and bulging eyes on top and a body that narrowed down into a thick tail. It was brownish in color and had two rows of teeth that were capable of serious damage with jaws so powerful they could bite through an inch of stainless steel. Well, not that strong but strong enough that you did not get your fingers anywhere near their mouth. Trying to remove a hook that one of these fish had down his throat using a pair of pliers was nearly impossible and so dangerous that I got to the point of cutting the line and tossing both overboard. And no matter what kind of bait you were using they would go for it. They were definitely not picky eaters.

My uncle who was from Columbia and came to the coast often to fish and shrimp became so frustrated with these awful fish that he invented a "flipper" whose sole purpose was the removal of the dreaded toadfish. It was a simple device. A piece of steel about a foot long bent at one end to form the handle and bent back about an inch at the other end leaving a small opening where the hook could be placed. The small end would be placed around the hook, which is down the throat of the fish, the other hand would take hold of the fishing line and pull one way while the flipper would pull the other way until the fish was dangling in midair. And then with a quick flip of the wrists the fish was flipped off the hook. This invention of Uncle Johnny's in 1959 worked so well that my father often urged his brother to make some of these flippers and sell them. Uncle Johnny said that he did not have time for such foolishness and besides nobody would buy the stupid things anyway. The squeamish fisherman who didn't want to handle a slimy fish could also use the flipper, for instance, to take a blackfish off the hook. The only person I ever saw in our boat use the flipper to take a fish off the line other than a toadfish was a cousin of mine … and *she* was from Greenville.

I was having fun pulling in fish after fish. We must have been over a school of blackfish because this was too easy and it wasn't due to my skills as a fisherman while my father labored at trying to land the elusive sheepshead. What made them so hard to catch was the configuration of their rounded mouth with the two rows of human-like teeth, which they used to their advantage. The sheepshead did not attack its prey in a rush like most fish. Rather it cuddled up to the dangling fiddler, placed its open mouth around it and ever so gently applied just enough pressure to crack the shell and then it sucked out the insides of the fiddler while the unsuspecting fisherman wondered when he was going to get a bite. I had caught as many fish as my father had put fiddlers on the line trying for what he said was a big sheepshead. Time and time again my father pulled his line up to find an empty shell at the end. He would patiently reach into the fiddler bucket and tell me that this was the one that was going to catch 'ol Mr. Sheepshead. I was more than content to catch my blackfish along with an occasional toadfish. But I was also carefully observing the every action of my father because someday I too planned to fish for sheepshead.

"PHEW-EE, Daddy. It's getting hot."

I took off my cap and wiped the sweat from my face. The morning sun getting up higher and higher, doing its job. And now I prayed for some wind, even a little breeze. The blackfish had acted like the crabs had done in the creek … bite like crazy for a while and then all of a sudden there was no activity … nothing. I hadn't had a nibble for quite some time but rather than get impatient or complain I took my father's lead and patiently dropped my line to the bottom and bounced it up and down and continued to fish.

My father glanced over at me and sensed my uneasiness at not catching any fish and my fighting the heat. "Just hang on a little bit longer. I'll have supper in the boat real soon." He grinned as he re-baited his hook for seemed like the hundredth time. "This ol' sheepshead is going to bite down anytime now."

Another aspect of the sheepshead that made it difficult to catch was that they did not travel in densely packed schools the way other fish did. They were more solitary creatures.

But patience paid off and sure enough within five minutes his cane pole suddenly bent like a ton of bricks had been tied to it. The pole doubled up and my father quickly worked his hands down the pole while attempting to get the fish off the bottom and away from the safety of the rocks, the only place where it could dive under and cut the line or hang it up. Under the boat went the fish and the pole, my father hanging on. "Gotta be a big one," he said. "A real big one."

I studied carefully every move my father made understanding that there was more than just luck involved in successfully landing a big sheepshead. The muscles bulged and tightened on my father's forearms while his huge wrists held firmly. If it came down to a battle of strength Mr. Sheepshead was going to lose. My father wore a plain white tee shirt, rounded at the neck, which accentuated his broad shoulders and well-defined chest and its color also reflected the heat. He had on his familiar khaki pants. And as I watched this battle of two experts I realized now why he always wore long pants. My father had worked his hands down the cane pole until he had a good grip on the end of the pole. With one hand he was controlling the fish and with the other he was going for the line. The leader wire on his cane pole was about four feet long and right now it was pressed tightly against his leg from the weight of the fish. And without protection that wire would slice deep into his leg. Anyone who has been around boats and fishing knows that a taut wire can cut through skin in a second.

Around the motor to the other side and back under the boat again. "Hand me the net, Mike." The sheepshead tried the same maneuver again but didn't know he was dealing with a veteran sheepshead fisherman and my father was waiting, net in hand. Pulling the fish up with his left hand, my father put the net under the water and in a flash the huge squirming sheepshead securely in the net was pulled in the boat. It happened so fast I never saw the fish until it was lying in the bottom of the boat.

"WOW! How'd you do that?" I asked. "That was so quick the way you netted him."

"Practice, Mike. Lots of lost fish and practice." He smiled and looked toward the anchor line. He didn't need to say anymore. We had what we came for. "Well, we got supper. You ready to head for home?"

I had caught my share of blackfish and it was getting hotter by the minute. Plus we had fish and a boat to clean when we got home: "Yes sir."

I looked back at my father in the stern and then at the anchor line and my father nodded while he sat down, fired up a celebratory Pall Mall, and grabbed hold to the black rubber handle of the pull cord. And with one swift pull from his strong right arm the Johnson came roaring to life. After pulling in the laundry bag with my catch of blackfish I pulled in the anchor and we looked around the boat satisfying ourselves that everything was in order and secure for the ride in. And we were off.

The big sheepshead with its distinctive black and white stripes was too big for me to pick up and put in the laundry bag so I let it lay on the deck of the boat. And on the ride in I stared at that fish and envisioned how someday I would have the know-how and patience to catch me a big ol' sheepshead along with some friend I took fishing with me. Maybe Bubba would go?

That evening the Devlin clan feasted on the sheepshead, hush puppies, French fries and cole slaw. As a side dish there were fried blackfish … I ate a whole bunch of them.

Those were some wonderful fishing trips with good and solid memories about love shared between a father and a son. They were burned into my mind and remain as memorable as though they happened yesterday.

35
HELPERS

Three days after Thomas Poe's funeral, Lumus, Chief Perry and Warren Poe gathered at Thomas' house to search for what Warren called "Thomas's baby, his real love," his coin collection. They searched high and low finding nothing of importance. Coming up empty-handed they waited until Monday and went to Thomas's bank and inquired about a safety deposit box. Thomas had none. "Never did," they were told by the bank.

After considerable thought and going on the little bit of information they had, Lumus concluded that the robbery of Thomas Poe's collection was the motive behind his death. It was more of an educated guess than anything, arrived at from the scant evidence he had at hand. But it was all he had to go on. He believed that the collection itself was targeted specifically and was not part of some thief just breaking in and randomly seeing what he could make off with and then killing Thomas Poe when things went wrong.

However, there were other questions troubling him: Was the deceased killed by someone Thomas knew? Or was this the case of an overzealous owner trying to protect his property without regard for his own life? If that had been the case someone could easily have ended up dead.

The robbery of the coin collection specifically, Lumus thought, *had to be the motive. It had to be!* It was the only theory Lumus had to go on until something else more concrete showed up. However, more puzzling and even stranger was the fact that when he had questioned Poe's ex wife, she failed to mention even the existence of such a valuable collection, much less how much her ex husband had treasured it. Surely she knew about the collection and how valuable it was. Why didn't she mention it? Was her omission intentional or not? Something didn't fit.

Like Lumus' Daddy used to say, "There's some smelly fish in Denmark" or something like that. He never was sure what that meant but he knew something wasn't right and it was going to take a lot of legwork and some luck to uncover any tangible evidence, if any at all.

Keep plodding, keep asking questions. Something will come up, Lumus told himself. *Who would want Thomas Poe's collection? And who would want it bad enough to kill for it.* He asked himself over and over. It had gotten to the point where it consumed his thoughts so thoroughly he was having a hard time thinking of anything else … like food. His growling stomach reminded him that he hadn't eaten all day. He pulled into Grannie's for another sugar fix with the same blank look he'd had since talking with Mrs. Poe.

Something else that perplexed him was that Chief Perry didn't want to follow the trail of the lost coin collection. The Chief believed that the shooting was the result of a robbery gone sour and that was it. He did not believe the coin collection was the premeditated target of the robber.

"Whoever ended up with that collection will pawn it off somewhere Lumus, and we'll never see it. I guarantee you that."

"Lumus! You awake?" Shirley yelled, standing behind the counter at Grannie's, wiping her hands on her apron, patiently waiting for the comatose Lumus.

Startled, Lumus flinched. "Yeah … yeah, I guess." Lumus was staring at the jelly-filleds, lost in thought.

"What's wrong? Bull Perry working you too hard?"

"N-a-a-w. It's not him. It's the case … the Thomas Poe thing. We've been working …u-u-u-h… what's the special today, Shirley?"

"Fried apple fritters but you don't want them. Ain't sweet enough for the Chief," Shirley said without missing a beat, smacking on a big old wad of Juicy Fruit. She knew the sweet tendencies of every Islander. "So the case is giving you a fit, huh?"

"Yep," Lumus said moving a few steps toward the end of the glass counter. "It sure is."

"Well, it ain't often you have to solve a murder on Sullivans Island. How long has it been since someone was killed over her? Forty … fifty years?"

"I guess?" Lumus answered without much thought as he surveyed the choices beneath him in the glass case. "How about those chocolate things … right over there?" Pointing at the chocolate covered doughnuts with colored sprinkles on them.

"Good choice, the Chief's favorite … at least this week." Shirley propped her elbows up on the top of the counter and looked at Lumus. "What seems to be the big problem with the case other than you don't know who killed the guy?"

"Lots of things, Shirley. Stuff I can't tell you. You know … official police business."

"Oh.OK … But let me give you a little free advice, Lumus. Sometimes when you have a problem there are people right in front of you who can help but you just don't see 'em or you don't want to see 'em. Think about that sometime. And think about what you want to buy because I'm headed to the back to get those pies out the oven before they burn up. Be right back."

"H-u-u-m, fritters or chocolate covered?" Lumus mumbled to no one.

Part of Lumus' plan for investigating the murder was to visit the different Island businesses, like he was doing now at Grannie's, and kind of mill around and sometimes even shop where it was feasible and chitchat with the owners and customers in as much a normal fashion as possible. He didn't want to come across like he was questioning people giving them the impression they were part of official police business. That would excite folks and lead to all kinds of wild goose chases. He figured the Island locals, especially the old timers, knew more about what was happening on the Island than he did and it was possible some tidbit of information he acquired might be the small break he needed. Lumus' attitude was "you never know?"

Chief Perry gave Lumus that little extra smile when Lumus walked in the station with the familiar Grannie's box in hand.

"Your favorite, Chief." He placed the box on Chief's desk. "Dive in."

"Thank you, Lumus. Haven't had a doughnut … uh, let's see … since … yesterday? No, wait a minute … had a couple last night." He chuckled, grabbed two doughnuts and sat down. "OK, Lumus. Let's talk."

"You're welcome, Chief." Lumus settled into his favorite chair, kicked back, cupped his hands behind his head and tried to think and relax at the same time. Talking things out with the Chief helped clear his mind of small nagging doubts and wild theories that had him going in circles. The Chief sometimes asked more questions than he gave answers but invariably he was of help.

"Chief, are you still sticking to what you said the other day about Poe being killed during a robbery gone bad?"

"Yep, sure am. It's all we got and it's the only thing my little pea brain can come up with right now." The Chief rested his chin on his hand and stared at Lumus. "Whatcha got on your mind? I can tell something is bugging you and I know it ain't no woman problem."

"Eah, how you know it ain't a woman problem? You been checking on my love life?"

"No. Because if it was a woman problem you'd be walking around here in a fog mumbling to yourself and bumping into furniture and all that. You seem like you're thinking about something. Something you can't figure out, right?"

"Yep." (Pause.) "Chief, let's figure for the sake of argument that someone could have stolen the collection without any knowledge of its value … they just took it at random like you said. That could have very well happened … I'm not discounting that possibility. But there is another angle. Suppose they took it knowing its value or they wanted it for some other reason." Lumus paused and went into thought. *A-a-a-h, but for what other reason?* He felt like he was on to something but could not quite place it.

"OK", the Chief said looking at Lumus and waiting for him to finish. Lumus was looking at the Chief waiting for the Chief to help him out. The Chief knew a Mexican standoff when he saw one so he went for another doughnut, sat back and threw his feet up on the desk.

After a minute or two Lumus spoke up, "Well, what?"

"I'm waiting for you to tell me what that other reason was," the Chief replied grinning. "The one you were talking about a minute ago."

"That's just it. I don't know." A frustrated Lumus got up and walked over to the window and looked out, hands set firmly on his hips. "I'm not sure of anything." *I wasn't trained for all this,* he thought.

Lumus moved slowly to his chair, easing himself down with a deep serious look on his face and sat there deep in thought for a couple of minutes.

"Lumus!" yelled the Chief, "Wake up …you sleeping or just daydreaming?"

Startled but maintaining his thought Lumus jumped up quickly. "Thinking, Chief. Just thinking," he said slowly.

"Hear anything back on matching the bullet from Poe's body?" the Chief asked.

"Not a thing. Just that it's from an old 45. And how many of those are floating around?"

"Thousands, I reckon," the Chief answered. "After the War lots of soldiers kept their issue gun or had one as a souvenir. I've got one at the house myself."

"Chief, if we go looking for a murder weapon it could take until Christmas to check out just what's in this area. That's way too much ground to try to cover. Besides, we'd have to call in the State boys and I know you don't want that." Lumus was able to return to his prior thought. "Let me ask you this, Chief. What *kind* of person would want Thomas Poe's coin collection other than your everyday crook who happened to stumble upon it?"

"Well …" Chief was scratching his chin and rubbing his crew cut, a sign of deep thought, "Let's see … u-u-u-h … someone who was poor and wanted to steal it and sell it or someone who didn't know it was valuable and took it or …"

"No Chief, let's throw out that type person all together. *Exactly* what type of person are we looking for?"

"Oh, I see what you're getting at. A greedy person would be the type … like someone who knew Poe had the collection and wanted it for himself. Shucks, I'm just talking Lumus … I don't know. I really don't know."

Lumus bolted from the chair like he'd been shocked. "Be back later, Chief." He bolted for the door.

"Where ya going?"

"Gotta run an errand. Save me a doughnut."

Man! When that boy gets an itch he sure goes to scratching, the Chief thought, *wonder what he's up to now?*

The heat wave and humidity that had draped the Island for weeks was finally breaking. Relief was brought on by a Canadian cold air mass dropping our temperature from the oppressive mid-nineties, occasionally a hundred, down to the ninety-degree mark. Although the temperature only dropped a few degrees, the humidity level fell from the high eighties to a more reasonable fifty percent giving the cooler air a chance to be felt and making not only breathing easier but everyday tasks, like walking and bike riding. And accompanied by late afternoon breezes sweating was kept to a minimum.

The crew had gathered at Burton's after a day at the rocks playing on the giant inner tube and diving off the new diving board wedged in the rocks. This diving board was a springy two by twelve treated piece of lumber, brand new, and "borrowed" from a nearby construction site. It was about ten feet long and was capable of launching our frail bodies high into the air. Of course, you had to put some effort into it but any moron, even Tommy Wade, could get high enough to call it a dive.

Billy Scott was at it again doing flips and landing in the deep gully feet first, barely making a ripple as he entered the water. Bubba, the one who still refused to bounce off the big inner tube, couldn't get enough of the diving board and was a true challenger to Billy in the flipping department. Billy, however, was still the champion only because he could do a double flip successfully while Bubba when he tried the double made this tremendous splash when he hit the water like a descending whale.

I couldn't figure why Bubba wouldn't bounce off the inner tube yet he would fly high into the air off the board, performing swan dives, jackknifes, and flips so I asked him.

"What's the deal? Why won't you go off the tube?"

"Are you crazy? And land on that hard beach and break my neck. Besides, that tube and me don't get along," he said grinning. "Remember?"

"Oh yeah … it tackled you."

"T-h-a-t-s right, Catbird," Bubba droned. Then he looked around scouting the beach for girls. None were to be seen.

"Where is everybody?" I asked looking around at a nearly bare beach.

"At Burton's … I reckon," Bubba answered. "Let's head up there and see what's going on."

From the rocks to Burton's was no more than a five-minute walk when taking the short cut through the sand dunes. So when the beach activities slowed or there were not many kids at the rocks we would go to Burton's in search of the action.

As soon as we opened the door at Burton's we heard the crew from all the way in the back.

"Are so!" Loud.

"Are not!" Came the reply, only louder.

"Are so! Loud again.

"Are not I'm telling ya!" Really loud.

They were at it again. This arguing accompanied by yelling and screaming and finger pointing was something we hadn't seen or heard much about in past years but recently it had begun to creep into the ranks of our group. And just recently, this unique form of communication had reared its ugly head as an almost everyday occurrence. The majority of the crew were long-time friends since childhood. They had grown up together since kindergarten days and rarely argued notwithstanding your normal spats over ownership of a certain playtime article or who gets to go first in line. Those were expected outbursts and considered to be part of the growing up process. But arguing about senseless things or just arguing to be arguing? I wasn't sure where its place was in the grand scheme of things.

Bubba 'n me tried to steer clear of the arguments but sometimes they were unavoidable, like today when we walked in on one in progress. We figured there were more fun things to do in life than argue with someone over something that in the end didn't matter anyway unless, of course, it concerned the good name of the New York Yankees or the Notre Dame Fighting Irish football team … now that was different.

Staying out of arguments was easy for me. I just followed my father's advice: "Son, always remember. It takes two to argue so you take it from there."

It seemed to me that the older we got the smarter we got in relationship to our environment but not in terms of our relationship with other people. I thought, *God help us if this trend of arguing carries over into our adult life. No way I told myself. We were just going through some silly childhood phase or maybe the moon and the planets were out of line.* Little did I know?

"For the last time I'm telling you," Jocko shouted, "they aren't *real!* Can't you hear me?"

It was Jocko and John going at it again. I wondered if they were still arguing about whether Elvis was the king of Rock and Roll or Ricky Nelson. That particular argument had been going on for the entire school year.

The crew enjoying every second of this argument had gathered in a circle with John and Jocko in the middle. John, pointing his finger, yelled at Jocko. "How do you know so much about girls' boobs anyway, Jocko?"

Boobs? Wait a minute. Now they had my attention. My interest piqued and I moved in closer.

"I don't know that much but I'm telling you they aren't real. They have some kind of padded bra thing… like some …u-u-u-h, Jocko fired back. "You know …"

"Bra!" John yelled and almost laughed, "For your information they don't wear a bra under their bathing suits." The crew murmured their approval.

"Eah, I didn't say that. I meant they had some kind of padding." Jocko looked my way. "Devlin, what do you call them things girls stick in their bras to make their boobs look bigger?"

I shrugged and gave him a blank look. I didn't know the name but I knew what he was talking about because I had seen them one time in Sissy's room. But I definitely didn't want to get in the middle of this particular argument so I answered in a very serious tone, "Mantle batted .302 last year with forty-two home runs."

Jocko looked mad and waved his hand at me in disgust. "You knucklehead!" he yelled, "We're talking about girls, not baseball… Mantle's bee-hind. Whatta you call those things. Does anybody know?"

Bubba, returning from the soda fountain, yelled above the buzz of the crowd, "They're called falsies, you jack-leg." Bubba then bent over and whispered to me. "Mike, sometimes I think Jocko is almost as dumb as Tommy Wade and twice as lazy."

I nodded.

"Do you know how lazy Tommy Wade is?" Bubba asked grinning.

I played the straight man. "No. How lazy is he?"

"He's so lazy he thinks manual labor is the President of Mexico. BA-HA-HA! Get it?" He slapped me on the shoulder.

"Yeah. I got it. HA!" I gave him a big smile and an "A" for that one.

"Manuel labor. Eah, that's pretty good."

John wasn't about to give in to Jocko's firm belief that all the girls wore falsies and their boobs were really a lot smaller than portrayed. John was a proof man. Talk didn't mean much to him.

"Jocko, if you say they aren't real then what was that falling out of the top of Leslie's bathing suit at the beach today every time she bent over?" My imagination? Eah, I saw 'em and they were real. Weren't no falsies or whatever there!"

"Right, John. You're right." It seemed like Jocko was ready to admit defeat and then things could get back to normal. But he had a parting shot and took it. "But Leslie is an exception," he said.

"A what?" John asked. "Did you say an acception?" John thought he had said, "A-c-c-e-p-t-i-o-n and was about to question it.

"Yeah, you heard me!" Jocko yelled, moving closer to John. "An exception."

"You mean an exception … like an e-x-c-e-p-t-i-o-n?"

"That's what I said you jug-butt! An exception. You finally got it! Are you stupid and deaf?"

Jocko brushed back his Elvis wave, bowed up and tapped John on his chest, trying to be the intimidator. John stood his ground glaring at Jocko. Bubba looked at me and I looked at John and Jocko. Bubba had seen enough. And I had too. I stepped in trying to be diplomatic. "Guys! John, Jocko! Eah, let's argue about something else, O.K? Like maybe … u-u-u-h … baseball."

"Baseball?" John asked with his face all screwed up, "Why baseball?"

"Because … well … at least we know something about that." I gave John a big smile hoping he would agree. "How 'bout it?"

"Oh? … OK," Jocko said with a dumb look on his face, just standing there. He didn't know what to say next, but at least, they weren't in each other's face.

The guys would argue whether the sun was coming up tomorrow or not. Maybe they just liked to hear themselves talk? I paused and thought for a second. Then I remembered. I knew one sure fire way to get them going and get their minds off girls. I moved in closer slowly positioning myself in the middle of the group.

"I want all of you to know one thing and that is Mickey Mantle," I announced in no uncertain terms, "is the greatest baseball player alive today! Ain't another player good enough to hold his jockstrap."

"O-o-o-h boy! Here we go again with all that Mickey Mantle stuff again!" John was a die-hard Giant's fan and I knew I could count on him for an argument. " No way! Willie Mays is way better … hits for a higher average than Mantle …and he …"

"F-r-a-y-e-d not." Jocko was doing the dance. "Both of you jackasses are wrong." "Roberto Clemente is a better hitter than both of those two put together and a better fielder too."

"Ain't none of 'em good as Duke Snider," added Rusty always pulling for the underdog. "He's called The Earl of Flatbush in New York and he … "

"Who cares about Duke Snider!" John being a Giant's fan was naturally a Dodger hater. "He couldn't hit a bear in the butt with a base fiddle if it was standing next to him."

I had the fire going. Now to add the fuel. "And another thing, you bunch of Einsteins. Notre Dame is the best football team in the whole U.S.A. You hear me? The whole U.S.A. I'll tell ya how good they are." I looked toward Bubba and yelled, "Eah Bubba, if Notre Dame is the number one team in the nation then who is the number two team?"

"North Carolina?" Tommy Wade blurted out.

"North Carolina? You dummy, we're talking *football* here! Tell 'em, Bubba."

It was Bubba's turn to play the straight man and he rose to the occasion like he was announcing royalty. "Notre Dame's second team, of course."

When Bubba said that jeers and catcalls rained from the crowd. People then started arguing and carrying on, trying to yell above each other in a frenzy of loyal display for their favorite football team. It was summer and baseball was now in season but football, however, was in season 365 days a year and loyalties ran deep. I think I even heard The Citadel's name mentioned? They seemed to have forgotten all about the girls and their fake boobs.

Now that the crew was back to normal and good and riled up I walked away to a table in the back accompanied by Bubba.

"What'd you do that for?" he asked. "Got them all stirred up. Look at 'em ... yelling and screaming at each other."

"To get their minds off the girls, man. Did you see how mad Jocko was getting? Next thing you know they'd be fighting. When they argue about sports and stuff they just yell but girls ... that could lead to real trouble."

Sipping on a Cherry Coke with my best friend in the cool of Burton's Drug Store, no debts to pay, no real job to have to go to the next day, no kids to raise, no mortgage payments ... no real worries of any kind. I had the world by the tail, right? You'd think I would be happy as a pig in mud. But oh no, I had to find or invent something to fret about and the ol' worry bug was crawling around in my brain looking for a place to settle down.

That dead man in the creek. The thought of him would not go away. Who was he and who killed him? That was one worry and probably shouldn't have been, however, I had a natural thirst for solving problems and right now I was in the middle of the Sahara Desert with no water.

The other worry was Beverly ... Beverly Ann Johnson, my perfect girl. And I hadn't even as much as called her although she had kind of flirted with me a little bit near the end of school. This beautiful girl that I was enthralled with who had told me she would try to come over to the beach this summer and had even asked me where I hung out. And all I had to do was pick up the phone and call her. What was wrong with me? I wasn't sure what to do. I guess I was worried that she wouldn't want to talk to me much less consider being my girlfriend.

"Hey!" Bubba yelled and poked me. He could read me like a book. "What you worrying about now?"

I snapped back to reality and smiled. "Ah, you know. Same ol' stuff.

Except I was thinking about that dead man and all … and of course …"
"Beverly?"
"Yep."
"Don't worry about her. Everything will happen in due time if it's supposed to. It's beyond your control, and your fears of rejection stem from man's basic inferiority complex, which he inherited from his ancestors, the apes."
"*What* in the world are you talking about?" I asked very slowly. I could not believe how he was talking.
"I don't know," he said with a chuckle. "It's something I heard the other day on TV." He leaned back in his chair and let go a huge "BA-HA-HA-HA! BA-HA-HA-HA!"
I had to smile and immediately it took my mind off worrying. "You sure know how to cheer a friend up." And that wasn't the first or last time he brought me back to reality.
"Eah!" He slapped me on the shoulder and said, "With an old worry wart like you it's easy."
Bubba glanced toward the opening door and his eyes widened. "Great day in the morning! Look who just walked in."
I turned around in my chair and saw Lumus strolling past the crew and he was headed in our direction.
Bubba immediately took on the look of a guilty bank robber. "We done anything wrong today? Think, Mike, … quick, think! What did we do today?"
"Eah, I haven't done anything wrong. What about you?"
Lumus was at the table before Bubba could answer. "Afternoon, boys. How y'all doing? Mind if I sit a spell?"
"Doing good, Lumus." I said, "Here sit down." I pulled a chair out.
Bubba said hello and asked how Lumus was and then tried to act at ease but it was not working. He was the only person I knew who could be completely innocent of anything and still look guilty of everything.
"I'm doing pretty good," Lumus said, "pretty good. What's with the gang over there? What are they arguing about?"
"Oh … sports and girls and stuff," I answered. "Just a friendly little shouting match."
"Mostly girls," Bubba chimed in. "But they don't know what they're talking about. Why they don't know their bee-hind from third base when it comes to girls. Ever heard that saying, Lumus? … Bee-hind from third base?"
"No Bubba, can't say that I have. You know being around the Chief all the time I gotta watch my mouth and all."
"You mean you can't even say 'bee-hind?' Bubba asked with disbelief.
"Nope. I can't even say 'bee-hind.' Chief gets real mad. I think it

reminds him of his double wide bee-hind." Lumus was grinning that grin of his and now we knew he was teasing us.

"Eah," Lumus asked as he stood up, "you boys want a Coke? I'm buying."

I looked at Bubba and he looked at me somewhat surprised at a policeman offering to buy us a Coke. But seeing that we never turned down anything that was free made the surprise offer easier to accept. "Shoot yeah," Bubba exclaimed then had the nerve to ask, "but can I have a Cherry Coke?"

"Sure," Lumus said. "How about you, Mike? Cherry Coke too?"

"Can I get a Vanilla Coke instead?" Then I added, "please?"

"Coming right up." While Lumus headed to the counter for our Cokes I motioned Bubba closer and whispered, "What's he doing here? We aren't in trouble really … are we? You didn't do anything you haven't told me about, have you?"

"No … uh-uh," Bubba said shaking his head and then adding, "*Maybe,*" and Bubba turned his head to make sure Lumus was out of hearing distance, "he wants us to help him with the murder case? Remember we did offer to help. What ya think?"

"I don't know. But if we sit here long enough we'll find out … cool it. Here he comes."

Maybe he did want us to help him, I thought. *WOW! Wouldn't that be great!* Just the thought of helping made me feel antsy and excited and I visualized myself catching the murderer single-handedly after a chase over the Island and ending up in Miller's Creek where I hit him over the head with an oar, tied him up, laid him on my bike and took him off to the police station. I would be the local hero. And I could see it now: a picture of Beverly and me in the paper with the captured killer and the police and Beverly, yea Beverly at her hero's side with an admiring smile on her beautiful face. Maybe I could miss school for a while as a reward for nabbing the killer. Of course, I'd have to check with Sister Roberta on that possibility. That's when my fantasy came to an abrupt end … when I visualized Sister Roberta scowling at me.

Maybe we needed a break from crabbing and going to the beach and just didn't know it. Some kind of change of pace. Shoot, Bubba 'n me had about crabbed ourselves out and I know the crabs would be happy to get a break from the two little Irish pests while we put our energies into catching a murderer. And even the beach routine … it too was beginning to dull although the girls weren't, but with all the arguing and stuff going on I was ready for a new adventure. Yep, I was ready for a change but I was probably whistling in the dark if I thought Lumus, who had to get Bull Perry's OK, would let us help with the case.

Lumus returned and before he could set the Cokes on the table I blurted out, "Do you want us to help you with the case, Lumus? Bubba

’n me will help for free … no charge… right, Bubba?”

“T-h-a-t-’s right, Catbird,” Bubba drawled. “For free … n-o-o-o charge.”

Feigning surprise and opening his eyes wide Lumus eased himself into the chair and said, “Now, how did you know that’s why I came looking for you two? Y’all must be clairvoyant? I’ve been thinking about what y’all said about wanting to help and well ….you boys seem to get around the Island and know a lot of people and everything, know what I mean?”

“Hey, Lumus! What’d you call us? Clare… a … boyant?” Bubba acted offended but truthfully was fishing for an answer, not wanting to seem dumb because he didn’t know what that word meant.

“Oh that,” Lumus said, “it’s a big word I learned at the Citadel.”

“It’s clairvoyant” … Lumus spelled it: “ c-l-a-i-r-v-o-y-a-n-t.”

I chided Bubba because I halfway knew the meaning. “Eah, you remember Phil Osophy, don’t ya? Well, this is Clair Voyant. She’s Phil’s cousin. A-HA-HA-HA!”

“Oh, you’re real funny Devlin … KNUCH, KNUCK, KNUCK! … Does she have big you-know-whats like Shirley?” We both laughed recalling how we had put Tommy Wade on that day.

Lumus’ head was going back and forth taking it all in. “I’ve heard about this act before. Now I get to see it. Is it free?” We all got a good laugh out of that. It was one of the reasons we liked Lumus. He had a sense of humor.

“Bubba,” said Lumus, “a clairvoyant is like a psychic … someone who…”

“I know,” I interrupted, “someone who can tell the future.”

“Yeah. Hey, you knew all along,” Lumus said looking at me first and then at Bubba. “Didn’t ya?”

“No, not really,” Bubba replied. “You see, Mrs. Kelly taught me and Mike what a psycho is.”

I rolled my eyes giving Lumus a let’s-move-along-look. He nodded. “Yeah… good … Bubba …u-u-u-h that’s real good. Anyway I was saying. You boys move around the Island a lot and I need somebody to do a little job for me. It isn’t anything big or spectacular but something y’all might be able to handle. Still interested?”

“Sure,” we answered in unison. “Whatever you need.” We moved our heads closer to Lumus like we were in a huddle.

“OK. Here’s the deal but I won’t go into a lot of detail because … uh … well, because I won’t. Y’all are pretty smart so you can figure it out for yourselves.”

This was starting to sound complicated to me already and we hadn’t even gotten out the door. So I concentrated real hard and was all brains while Bubba was all ears.

Lumus continued, "Here's what I need and y'all will have to find it. This is kind of like a treasure hunt but there isn't any real treasure."

"Sure," I said nodding to Bubba. "What do you need?"

"I need to find out if there is anyone on the Island who collects coins … like someone …"

Right away Bubba interrupted: "I know someone who collects coins."

I can't believe I'm this lucky, Lumus thought. *I should have known these two knew everybody and everything that went on. I should have come to them sooner.* "Who Bubba?" Lumus asked anxiously, "Who?"

"Why that's easy, Lumus. Old man Finklestein. My Daddy says all the time that man will squeeze a nickel 'till the buffalo hollers. So he must have some other coins too."

Lumus head dropped and I heard a small sigh and a soft, "Oh boy."

"Yeah Bubba, that's good," Lumus said, "but that's not what I had in mind. I'm talking about a serious coin collector … someone who collects old and rare coins. Someone who is really into it and likes it a lot like Mike likes the Yankees." Lumus gave my Yankee's hat a friendly rub.

"O-o-o-h … I got it now. I understand. I've been hanging around that Devlin fella too long. Know what I mean, Lumus?"

"Yeah, I gotcha. Bubba, you better watch out for them Devlins." Lumus grew serious, placed his hands together and propped himself up with his elbows on the table. "Now I can't tell y'all how to go about finding this coin collector person but I'll give you a clue."

A clue. On boy. Just like in the movies. We would be on the case. I sure hoped it would be a good clue.

"If a person is a serious coin collector then he would subscribe to some sort of coin collector's magazine or newsletter or something like that. Something that would be sent through the mail. Some kind of mailing. And … and … sometimes … they just throw away some of the mail they get. Are y'all following what I'm telling you?"

"I think so?" I said.

Lumus looked at Bubba for assurance he was not sending two twelve year olds out on a wild goose chase.

"I'm with you so far," Bubba answered. "What you're saying is that people throw away mail. Right?"

"Yep.You got it." Lumus smiled broadly and stood up. "And that's as far as I'm going. Bubba, you can fill Mike in and y'all know where you can find the Chief or me. If you find anything let us know, OK?"

We both frowned at the mention of Bull Perry. "We'll let you know, Lumus. If that's OK?" Bubba asked. Lumus knew about our fear of Bull Perry, imagined or not.

"Yeah, yeah. That's fine. Just let *me* know. Gotta run. Enjoy your Coke and I'll see y'all around." Lumus made his way through the dwindling crew, about all argued out.

Bubba 'n me were tickled pink that we had been chosen to help with the case even thought I wasn't real clear about exactly what we were supposed to do? We decided to celebrate with another Coke when Tommy Wade with great trepidation approached our table. "Hey, what y'all doing? What'd Lumus want? Y'all in trouble?"

Bubba stood up, looked Tommy square in the eye, put his hands on his hips and spread his feet. "First of all, we're sitting here. Second, what Lumus wanted is none of your durn business and third, we're not in trouble but your bonehead will be if you don't get out of here in the next five seconds."

Tommy Wade didn't say a word, wheeled around, and was gone in three seconds. I glanced over when Tommy reached the group and his answer to them was a shrug of the shoulders.

"You're too hard on that boy, Bubba. Lately you've really been on his case. What'd he do to you now?"

Bubba pointed his finger at me and in a low shout said, "You got a short memory sometimes, Devlin! A short memory." Then he calmly said, " I should have beat him up good the first time he called me a queer."

"You mean he did it again?"

"Kinda but I can't prove it. Anyway … forget him … he's gone."

"Right, yeah. U-u-u-h … about the thing with Lumus. I understand what he wants but I'm not sure about where to look for it? Do you know where to look?" I asked. "That's the part I don't get."

"Come on fog brain, think!" Bubba paused and stared at me. "You know what your problem is? You think about that girl too much. Where do you think we look?"

"I don't know … at Beverly's house? A- HA-HA-HA"

Bubba rolled his eyes upward. "You don't ever quit do you?"

"Well, you brought up her name, not me … so …"

"So forget it. We look at the Post Office … where else?"

"You mean in the mail boxes. Now how we gonna do that?"

"No Mike. In the trash can. Didn't you hear what Lumus said? Haven't you ever seen people throwing away mail in the big trash can, the one by the table?"

"Yeah, yeah … oh yeah," I said. The light finally came on. "I'm with ya, Curley. KNUCK-KNUCK-KNUCK"

"Well good. Anyways, that's where we look. And it's more like this you moron, A-A-A-W … KNUCK, KNUCK, KNUCK." Bubba did it faster and with the finger roll and a silly grin.

"So what you're telling me," I said, "Is that in the middle of the day we're going to go looking through the trash can at the Post Office? I don't think they're gonna let us do that."

"Sure we can. Lumus wouldn't have asked us if it wasn't OK for us to dig through the trash."

"Let me ask you this … if that's the case then why doesn't Lumus do it himself?"

"Because Lumus is a policeman and all. And how would it look for a policeman to be digging through a trash can?"

"Then why didn't he get a trash expert, like Sambo, to do it?" I was joking but Bubba was serious and answered quickly, "Because Sambo can't read, that's why."

"O-o-o-h, I see but I still say they won't let us do it. Eah, let's go ask Mr. Keenan if we can and … I know … we can tell him we're collecting stamps and maybe we could find some good ones in the trash."

"All right, worry wart," Bubba said. "We'll ask him." Bubba glanced at the crew, looked back at me and asked, "Do you think we ought to tell the crew what we're doing?

"Are you kidding?" I declared. "After what they did to us about finding the body. Uh-uh. Let 'em wonder. Let's go."

The crew had argued themselves out and had moved to the dance floor in front of the jukebox. Jocko was on center stage. He was on a roll doing his spectacular Elvis imitation using a pool cue as a microphone and a chair as a stage prop. Three consecutive Elvis tunes were played on the jukebox and Jocko knew them all by heart, singing and swaying the hearts of young Island girls. Jocko, with his shock of black, wavy hair and dark sunglasses, looked so much like Elvis. Lumus should have stuck around for this show. We didn't, having seen it a million times. The crew screamed and yelled their approval when Jocko and Elvis broke into "Jailhouse Rock."

Halfway to the Post Office Bubba was still humming the melody to "Jailhouse Rock."

"Jocko's not too bad a singer," Bubba said, "Maybe he'll be a rock and roll singer someday."

"Yeah right! And I'm gonna grow up and be the pope. Look … when we u-u-u-h … get to the Post Office let me do the talking … OK?"

"Sure Pope Devlin. Just because my English," and he yelled, "ain't always right … you just go right ahead and do all the talking."

"Eah, I wasn't talking about your English, Bubba! It just so happens that Mr. Keenan and my father are good friends and I kind of know him too." I jokingly added, "Ain't nothing wrong with your English except you get "F's" in it."

"All right, Devlin. That's enough … I mean it!"

"OK, OK. No more about the grades, I promise."

We sat on our bikes in front of the Post Office. I was rehearsing the speech to myself, which I would present to Mr. Keenan hoping he would grant us garbage can rummaging rights. Bubba grew impatient and began rubbing his hands together very rapidly and making funny little noises, so ready or not I jumped off my bike and headed for the counter inside where Mr. Keenan did business. Bubba followed.

Our exit from the Post Office was as quick as our entrance.

"Have you ever heard of such a thing? Stupid! Idiotic! Federal property? Humph, it's trash. How can it be federal property?" I moaned. "And Lumus is counting on us. Durn!"

"Maybe Mr. Keenan didn't like the part when you told him your father wouldn't take him fishing anymore if he didn't let us go through the federal government's property?"

"A-a-a-w, whatever. Let's go."

Bubba got that glint in his eye, hopped on his bike and said, "Come on Pope Devlin … I's gots something to show ya." When he talked like that I knew *something* was coming. What? I wasn't always sure of. But something.

I followed him to the back of the Post Office where he stopped, got off his bike and with a sweeping hand and a bow pointed at a huge rectangular container. "Taa – dah … introducing to you, the trash keeper. Trash keeper, Pope Devlin." It was the trash bin, like a big dumpster, where *all* the Post Office trash went at the end of the day.

"O'Toole," I said smiling, "you are something else. How did you think of …"

"Have no fear, Paddy O'Toole is here."

"You mean Bubba?"

"Yeah, Bubba too! BA-HA-HA-HA."

I was thrilled at my friend's thinking about the trash bin but my joy was short lived. "Whoa!" I suddenly realized the time and had to get home and baby-sit. "Eah, I gotta get home. Tell ya what, let's meet at the cistern tonight at 10:00 and we'll go from there. And bring a flashlight."

Bubba was smiling. He knew exactly what I was thinking: "T –h –a- t –'s right, Catbird," he drawled slowly. "See ya then."

36
LUNCHTIME

A couple of days before our meeting with Lumus at Burton's I had been in the backyard by the shed, having just mowed the grass, and was putting away the lawnmower when I heard a rustle in the bushes along the fence. From the movement of the bushes it sounded like a trapped animal thrashing about, a big one making quite a commotion. Cautiously I moved closer and peered through the dense overgrowth. I barely made out a form, not of an animal but rather of a human, trying to part the tangle of wisteria and vines.

"Who's that?" I asked.

"Who dat say who dat?" came a reply.

"It's me."

"Who me be?"

"Me! Mike … Mike Devlin."

"Oh … there's you is. I thought I'd heared you," Mrs. Brown said clearing a small opening in the thick bushes. She poked her head through it. "Why ain't you say it you?"

"I did … I don't think you heard me, Mrs. Brown. How you doing?"

"Huh? What you say?"

I practically screamed, "I said how you doing?"

"O-o-o-h … fair to middlin' I reckon for an ol' lady… and you?"

"Doing real good … just finished cutting the grass."

"Yeah, I sees dat." She looked around the yard giving it a cursory inspection. "You's done a real good job."

"Thank you, Mrs. Brown. Your yard looks good too. Those goats been busy, huh?"

"Dat's right. Dem goats de does da job an I's ain't even haffa tell `em. Wish dem no count chillren was da same. Shucks, de ain't do nuffin' cept sit on ea butt all day … lets an ol' lady likes me tend to alls da chores. Ain't right I's tell ya … ain't right "

"Guess you thankful to have the goats, at least they keep the grass cut."

"Y-e-a-h. Amen, amen. I thanks an praise da Lawd fa dat."

I thought I heard her voice raise a note or two on "the Lord?" Time to go. I was too late.

"Mike?" She paused. "You is Mike ain't cha?" I nodded. "Whats I's wanna ax ya is when ya goes crabbin' agin could ya brungs me a dozen … dat be twelve ya know … of them big ol' Jimmies like I's seen ya takes to Ms. Kingman's house."

"Oh? … You want to place an order for a dozen crabs? Yeah sure, Mrs. Brown. I'll do that. Bubba 'n me are going this afternoon, I think?"

"I's don't knows nuttin 'bout no order. I's just wants twelve of dem crabs."

"OK. We'll bring 'em by this afternoon for you, Mrs. Brown, some big ol' Jimmies." She smiled and was about to say something when I said, "Well…I gotta go now, Mrs. Brown. Take care and I'll see ya later."

"OK But yous ain't gotta rush off." Her voice trailed off and she turned slowly. *"Guess talking wiff an ol' woman thru da fence ain't be he idea of fun,"* Mrs. Brown said to herself as she let go of the bushes.

I could sense Mrs. Brown had wanted me to hang around and talk to her but business came first and I had to find another order for crabs. It didn't make sense to go in the creek for just one dozen crabs. So I decided to check with Mrs. Kelly, one of our better spur of the moment customers and hope she wanted a dozen. And then I had to find Bubba, which should be easy. It was Saturday morning. And he would in his usual spot, glued in front of the TV.

"Hey Curley, get away from that TV," I yelled pedaling across Bubba's side yard. "We got crabs to catch!" I side straddled my bike and timed my jump from the bike perfectly, me landing on the second step leading up to the porch and the bike coasting slowly to a stop and gently falling, coming to a stop, resting against the hedge.

I heard the TV click off. Bubba appeared on the back porch hopping on one foot while trying to pull on his favorite crabbing shoe on the other, his Chuck Nelson black high tops.

"I didn't think we had any orders for today?" he said. "What's up?"

"I didn't either until a little while ago. Mrs. Brown wants a dozen and I went by Mrs. Kelly's and she said she'd take a dozen."

"You mean we're going in the creek for two lousy dozen," he said rather objectively. "Eah man, it ain't worth the trouble."

"Well," I hesitated, " that's true. But while we're out there I thought I'd catch a dozen for my mother, free of course, and I thought maybe you could catch a few for your Mom? What ya think? Besides, we ain't got nothing else to do right now and the tide's right." Bubba rubbed his chin for a second thinking. "Y-e-a-h, whatever. You got everything ready to go?"

"Yep, everything but the net. Sammy borrowed it the other day. We can run by there and get it on the way."

It was one of those perfect mornings, weatherwise. Not a cloud in the sky, not too hot and a breeze out of the east. The sky was a light blue that made it look so soft that you wanted to lie on it. Off in the distance I could hear the sound of a lawnmower engine as someone cut their yard. I was thankful that my week's work of grass cutting was done and I could go crabbing.

As we rode into the Scott's driveway we saw Sammy kneeling down next to his father's car with an open can of paint on the ground and a paintbrush in his hand.

"S-a-m-m-y how ya d-o-i-n-g?" I asked.

"Oh hey, guys. Pretty good. Y'all come for the net?" He pointed to the aluminum boat lying on the ground with the net lying on the seat. "It's over there."

"Sammy, I've been meaning to ask you something," Bubba said. "Is it true you were named after Sambo? BA-HA-HA-HA!"

Sammy retorted, "Yep …I sure was. And do you know what Sambo's middle name is?"

"No, what?"

"It's dummy."

"Oh really," Bubba said.

"And do you know how you spell it?" Sammy asked.

"Uh-uh, how?"

"You spell it "B-u-b-b-a." And a BA-HA-HA- to you. Why you come around here wasting my time, man. Can't you see I'm busy?"

Sammy was about to dip his paintbrush into the paint … pink paint at that.

"What ya doing?" I exclaimed in disbelief. "You're not going to paint …"

"Yep, sure am. My father grounded me 'cause I broke the back window out the car to haul the boat … remember?"

"Yeah, oh yeah. We saw that."

"Anyway he grounded me until I fix the car so I'm gonna fix the car. I'm gonna paint it for him. Make it look real nice."

"Pink?" Bubba asserted. "You gonna paint the car pink?"

"Well, it was gonna be red but the hardware store was out of red so I thought … hey, pink is close enough … so. Anyway it's better than this old blue color that's on it now."

"Does your father know about this?" I was curious and a little unbelieving at the same time. "I mean … you painting the car?"

"No but he will when he gets home." Sammy dipped his brush and ran a long streak down the side of the car door. He stepped back, took a look at his handiwork, ignoring the obvious brush marks and hideous color and said, "Looks pretty good … huh?"

"Yeah … r-e-a-l good," Bubba said shaking his head and staring at the pink streak down the side of Mr. Scott's car. "See ya later, Sammy." Bubba nudged me in the side grinning and said, "Eah, if you do a good job on the car then I might let you paint my bike."

We left the Scotts in disbelief and somewhat amused at Sammy's latest enterprise. "Bubba, would you really let him paint your bike," I asked.

"Are you kidding? I wouldn't let him paint my sister's wagon. A pink car! Humph … can you imagine? That boy ain't right, you know?"

The crabbing was going good. The crabs were biting fast and steady and within an hour we had all we needed, pulled the anchor and headed back to the landing. First we delivered to Mrs. Kelly who was her usual chipper self but cut short our word game because she was running late with her housework. But we did get some Kool Aid and cookies to munch on as we headed to Mrs. Brown, our first-time customer.

"Mrs. Brown," I yelled from the bottom of the steps "Mrs. Brown!" I looked at Bubba. "Sometimes you got to talk real loud," I told him, "she's a little hard of hearing." Bubba nodded.

Louder."Mrs. Brown! Hello, are you there?"

I tried again. No response. We waited, staring at the crabs.

"Let me try," said Bubba who then screamed at the top of his lungs, "Mrs. Brown! We got your crabs!"

"Whoa, boy! If she's there I know she heard that. Man, you can yell." I clamped my hands over my ears anticipating another yell from Bubba.

Still nothing. All we heard was the buzz of the flies. "She ain't hard of hearing, Devlin.That woman's deaf … if she's here."

I went up on the porch and beat on the door while peeking through a cracked pane. Mrs. Brown was standing in the kitchen drying dishes with her back to me.

"I see her … in the kitchen. Come here, look." Bubba walked up the stairs, peered through the glass into the kitchen and then gave me a blank look.

"She ain't there," he said. "You sure you saw her?"

"What? Let me see. I looked back in and Bubba was right … she wasn't there."

We stood for a minute scratching our heads wondering what was going on?

"Let me look again," Bubba said. He shaded his eyes from the glare, peeked in and then looked up quickly. "You ain't gonna believe this but there she is … right there in the kitchen."

Before I could say a word Bubba was through the front door on his way to the kitchen. I followed toting the crabs.

Mrs. Brown's front room was simple with walls that held old, faded photographs on top of peeling wallpaper. The room was full of old furniture, the kind that looked worn and comfortable. Her house had that same feeling. The kitchen was directly off the front room where Mrs.

Brown stood by the sink looking out the back window.

"Mrs. Brown," Bubba hollered. "Mrs. Brown, it's me Bubba … Bubba and Mike!"

"Mrs. Brown slowly turned around, somewhat surprised, and said, "Oh dare you is. I's been in da backyard, heared some folk callin' me an I's looks an looks but don't sees nobodies. You's been in da back directly?"

"No Ma'am. We've been out on the front porch." Bubba was talking real loud. "Anyway, we got your crabs."

"O-o-o-h good. Praise da Lawd! said Mrs. Brown as she peeked in the basket. Her smile of approval told us the crabs were of suitable size. "Could ya puts 'em right chere … by da sink fa me? I'd 'preciate it much."

"I got 'em, Bubba." Mrs. Brown directed me to dump the crabs in the sink. Said she was going to cook 'em up right here in the kitchen. Bubba 'n me couldn't help but notice a wonderful odor clinging in the air of the small kitchen. It came from a big cast iron pot on the stove. It was the familiar aroma of beef stew.

We made small talk for a few minutes about family, and crabbing, and the weather and then we ran out of things to say. I was looking at Bubba and he was looking at me. Mrs. Brown was looking at both of us. There were a few seconds of awkward silence then it dawned on me that maybe she wasn't planning on paying for the crabs thinking for whatever reason they were free? She certainly wasn't making any effort or acting like she was going to pay so I spoke up being as diplomatic as I could.

"Mrs. Brown, we have to be … u-u-u-h … going now. And I was … u-u-h … wondering if you … could … if you could pay us now?"

"Pays you what?" she said with a sincere, quizzical look on her wrinkled face.

I had my answer but she had *our* crabs. However, in her mind they were *hers*.

I tried my best to be polite. "For the crabs. You see, we charge money for catching them," I said almost apologetically. Bubba was really giving me the look with his hands on his hips just a shaking his head from side to side.

"You charge money fa da crabs? I's ain't neva heared of such a thing. You shoo?"

"Oh yes Ma'am, he's sure," Bubba said. "*Sure* screwed this up," just loud enough for Mrs. Brown *not* to hear.

"I's thought de was free likes da ones you gives Ms. Kingman an all."

"O-o-o-h, I see … you thought …oh no … you see we charge her too, Mrs. Brown. I'm sorry for the mix-up." I paused and thought for a second and said, "Gosh, I don't what to tell you."

"Well, I's can'ts expects to takes de crabs fa nuttin' … that wouldn't be right. By da way. How much he is, anyway?"

"Twenty-five cents a dozen … so it's just a quarter," I said hoping the misunderstanding was cleared up and now that she asked the price she was going to pay.

"Oh Lawdy! I's a poor old lady. I's ain't gots a dime to my name … be broke as a church mouse.I ain't gots no extra money." She smiled and I was ready to forget the quarter and leave, then she added, "A quarter you say? H-u-u-m … tells you what I'll do. How's about iffin I's feeds you two some of my special stew and sometin' sweet? Den we be even? Hows `bout dat?" She moved toward the big pot, lifted its lid, sniffed and then said, "I think this yhere stew be ready to be eaten, rights now."

From the delicious smell coming from the stove I was thinking we would be more than even. Bubba 'n me peeked into the pot of simmering stew. I knew I couldn't resist. "How about it, Bubba? Ready to eat?" We were hungry from crabbing and being in the sun and Bubba had been eyeing that stew since we walked into the kitchen so I knew what he would say.

"Bring it on, Big Momma," he said softly, " bring it on."

"What he say?"

"Uh … he said … after he eats he's going home to see his Momma."

"Dats good! Dats real good. Praise da Lawd! Now y'alls just sit yooselfs right chere while I's gets some plates an a bowel an … y'alls wants some cold tea?"

"Oh yes Ma'am, thank you." We were already seated at the rickety old table where thousands of wonderful home cooked meals had passed over the years.

Mrs. Brown dished up two plates of brown stew on top of homemade biscuits, brought us a big pitcher of ice tea, and a bowl of custard. With wide eyes we dove in like refugees.

Bubba was finished his stew and into the custard before I even finished the stew.

"Oh man, this is s-o-o-o good! And sweet, u-u-u-m-m. Devlin, you gotta try this. Here, eat some!" He was shoving a spoonful of custard in my face.

"Wait a minute, will ya. Let me finish my stew … OK?"

Mrs. Brown had sat down looking pleased at the sight of two hungry boys gorging themselves.

"Mrs. Brown, what is this custard called," Bubba asked, "it's so good."

"Oh that? That be my special … I calls it possum puddin.' My nephew brungs me four possums yestaday frum Awendaw. Eh calls me 'n say he only gots three but when he git chere eh have four. Eh say eh find one be dead on da causeway so he stop an picks him up. But don't you worry none a bit … he be fresh kill."

Bubba didn't say a word. He looked at me, set his spoon down, and then looked at the possum pudding and then at Mrs. Brown. His eyes opened as wide as saucers and he definitely had the look of a sick person. He clutched his stomach first, then his hands covered his mouth and he jumped up, and ran out the house.

"What wrong wit that boy?"

I was smiling because old hog Bubba had outdone himself again, gobbling up the stew in a hurry so he could be first at the dessert. A-HA-HA-HA! It was possum. A-HA-HA! Poor old Bubba. Eating possum.

"Oh nothing," I reassured Mrs. Brown, "he gets like that sometimes when he eats too much."

"Eh shoo need to learn some manner, dat boy. Dats fa shoo."

I nodded at Mrs. Brown's comment and discreetly tried to push my pudding away but the watchful Mrs. Brown caught me.

"Yous gonna eats yo puddin,' ain't ya? It be real good."

"I don't think so Mrs. Brown. I'm s-o-o-o full," I said rubbing my stomach. "Maybe next time." Just the thought almost made me sick. Besides, I needed to check on Bubba.I stood up and politely excused myself. I stopped at the door and looked back at Mrs. Brown who was clearing the table.

"By the way. Mrs. Brown, I was just wondering … what's in that stew? It was delicious."

A sad look like a shadow came over Mrs. Brown's face.

"O-o-o-h me … o-o-o-h me … dat was Matthew, he be my favorite."

I gulped hard and asked immediately, "Matthew who?"

"Matthew … da goat.He be my favorite. Yous seed 'em in da yard. He been da big brown one. He be reel old and he pass on this very morning, jas falls over dead in da yard. So I's makes a goat stew … nice an fresh. I happy that you …"

Mrs. Brown didn't have a chance to finish her sentence. I ran from her house clutching my mouth. I was feeling sick too.

"Oh Lawdy,dems some strange boys dere. Des eats and eats and then des runs an runs … I's don't know 'bout thems? Well … come on Mr. Jimmies … yous going in da pot."

37
A CLUE

After being denied permission to search the trash can in the lobby of the Post Office by Mr. Keenan, I returned home to baby-sit, which gave me some time to try and piece together what exactly it was Lumus was after. Why did he want Bubba 'n me to find something addressed to a coin collector? Did a coin collector kill that man? Or was it just some small clue he was working on? Or was it something entirely different?

Well, to me it didn't really matter why Lumus wanted us to help. Shoot, I was thrilled to death to get in on a real police investigation and have another adventure to be a part of. And it would give me the chance to show the crew that I could pull off something spectacular, something bigger and better than anything they had ever done. I was going to help catch a murderer. After the garbage truck flop and the ex-lax thing at school, which by the way we got severely punished for, it was now time to do something really cool and neat. It was time to stand up and be counted. That is if we found what it was Lumus was looking for. *Then* everything would work out great.

Bubba 'n me met that night behind the cistern and mapped out our plan for searching the trash bin at the Post Office. Getting in and out of it, we figured, would pose no problem for two kids who could climb almost anything. Our only fear was being caught in it at 10:00 at night, which we figured would be hard to explain. But we had talked our way out of trouble plenty of times in the past so, what the heck we thought, we would go for it. We agreed that the safest way to assure our secrecy was to crawl inside the trash bin and pull the top down so the beam from our flashlights wouldn't be visible to a possible passerby. And if we kept relatively quiet then we should be OK. At least, we didn't have to worry about being caught by the Island police.

My main concern was Mr. Keenan, the Postmaster. If he didn't want us in the trash can in the lobby then what would he do if he got caught us in the main trash can. That might be worth twenty years in a federal prison making little rocks out of big rocks? Could they hang us? Shoot, I don't know why I should worry. At 10:00 he was more than likely home sleeping like the rest of the Island.

That night we snuck into the trash bin with our flashlights and gently lowered the top. Then we rummaged through ankle deep, discarded paperwork in search of anything dealing with coins or coin collecting. We looked and looked for over an hour and came up empty handed. Unbeknownst to us, Lumus sat in the Jeep concealed behind a clump of oleanders about a half block away observing his helpers at work.

Yep, he thought, they're a couple of real go-getters. That's for sure.

For three consecutive nights Bubba 'n me snuck out and met at the Post Office and sorted through the junk mail in that hot bin with the top down. We felt like Thanksgiving turkeys going into the oven. All we found was the same kind of stuff over and over: flyers advertising everything from the new G.E. washer/dryer combo to Brly Creme hair tonic in a tube promising, a little dab will do you. There were discarded magazines on fishing, home repair, and pamphlets of all kinds but nothing pertaining to coins. Our initial enthusiasm began to wane so we decided to give it one more night then tell Lumus, "Sorry but …"

Hopefully, he would have some other job for us like riding around in the Jeep with him, especially on beach patrol, so we could look at all the pretty girls. That would get the crew's attention for sure and maybe Beverly would …

"Eah, Devlin! Wake up!" I was sitting down pretending to search through the trash and just about to doze off. "Remember what we talked about last night? We're gonna do this one more night, right?" His question came out more as a plea.

I was about as feed up with playing detective as he was."Y-e-a-h, unless you wanna keep on looking."

"Are you kidding? I'd rather smell a bear's butt for an hour."

"A what?" I exclaimed. "Boy, where'd you hear that?"

"On TV"

"TV? What you been watching?"

"A-a-a-w …it was on some cowboy movie the other night."

"Anyway, I take it that you want to call it quits too, right?"

"Yeah … this ain't no fun."

After we left the trash bin that night we seriously considered not going back the next night but we had agreed one more night wouldn't kill us and wouldn't you know … the next night we found something of interest. We were lucky that's all. It's like that last cast you make when you've had a bad day fishing and bingo you catch a whopper.

"Eah Mike, look at this. Is it any good?" Bubba held up a postcard size piece of mail from a magazine called "Coin World," offering a fifty percent discount if you subscribe now.

"I'm not sure?" I said, " it's about coins and it has an address on it … right?"

Bubba flipped the card over and looked."Yeah, right here."

"Yeah man, we'll keep it. Way to go, O'Toole. You got eyes like a hawk."

Bubba was smiling, not so much from finding *something,* but relieved that the searching and the nightly sneak outs were over. And so was I.

"Whatta you think?" he asked, "Is this what Lumus is looking for?"

"I don't know … could be? Eah, it's better than nothing. We'll take it to Lumus and see what he says. Let's get out of this mess."

"A-a-a-w … tell ya what. Why don't you … u-u-u-h … drop it by the police station tomorrow," Bubba said hesitantly. "I got some stuff to do."

"No man, you come with me … you found it and all."

"N-a-a-a-w … you take it."

"What's wrong?" I asked and then by the look on his face I understood. "Oh, I see. You're afraid of Bull Perry. That's it, huh?"

"Scared? Me? I ain't scared of Bull Perry… I'm terrified of him."

"OK … OK, scaredy cat, I'll go by myself and I'll let you know what happens. Oh, I'll take Mollie with me to protect me from the big bad wolf … A-WHOOL… A-WHOOL!"

Bubba grinned at me, threw his head back, and let out a big "BA-HA-HA-HA, HA!"

We were both relieved that all the sweaty work searching in the trash bin had produced at least something. We also learned that police work wasn't as glamorous as it was cranked up to be.

Lumus was in his usual hiding spot, watching: *Looks like they're leaving early tonight. Maybe they found something?* he thought. *I sure hope so.*

Returning home I carefully hid the mailing Bubba had found in my secret hiding place, a slit in the mattress underneath my pillow. No one knew about this hiding place except Mollie and me and she was sworn to secrecy. As I dozed off to sleep I wondered. *Could this little piece of paper possibly be of help?* I didn't know but I'd find out in the morning.

Bright and early I was anxiously out the door, on my bike and coming out the yard when there he appeared, silhouetted against the backdrop of the tree line of Back Street. He was moving so slowly he barely disturbed the dirt on the road, pedaling his rusty old bike, with no chain guard and tires so bald we called them "may pops." The basket on the front secured with bailing wire was just the right size for a twelve-pack of beer, however, on occasion I had seen eighteen piled into it. The aging loose fenders scraped against the wheels announcing the arrival of Herman Norris, the notorious town drinker and spy extraordinaire. He hailed me with his right hand and a wobbly head so immediately I knew something was up. Coasting to a stop he went into his patented story about spies, espionage and secret drop sites, which in my wildest imagination could have never found their way to Sullivans Island. Today's lecture concerned official briefings and meetings which, I'm sure, originated in Washington, D.C., at the FBI headquarters and had been relayed to

Herman by some top-secret code unknown to everyone except him. He had told me on numerous occasions that he worked for the FBI, and once when I asked to see his badge he mumbled something about he didn't carry it with him in case he got caught by the Russians so it wouldn't give away who he was. His being on a bike at age fifty and not entirely sober all the time didn't lend much credence to his claims of being an FBI agent but I, like everyone else, went along with his stories. When pressed about why he didn't have a car he said, "Don't need one. Only place I go is to Chippys." Thinking hard he added, "Sometimes I go to the Post Office."

"Why do you go to Chippys?" I asked already knowing the answer.

"To buy my beer," he said patting his stomach. "What you think for?"

And that's where he was headed this morning and by mid afternoon he'd be weaving his bike all over the road, barely able to pedal. And when that hand started waving everyone knew Herman was well into his pints. I tried to have a conversation once when he was like that but the more the hand waved the further his head dropped obscuring his already slurred words. It was an unconscious, unpracticed routine where he would raise his hand waving it the whole time and drop his head, from the weight of the alcohol in it I presumed. And at the moment when his drooping chin touched his chest he would raise his head up suddenly as though it bounced off his chest while his hand came down on the handlebar of the bike at the precise moment his head straightened up. Then he would invariably ask, "Ain't that right?" I agreed, not having a clue as to what he was talking about. Then it was back to the hand waving and mumbling and the falling head.

This morning he cornered me on the side of the road. "I see you running from Mrs. Brown's yard the other day." He eyed me cautiously like a trained spy. "What chasing you … the goats?" You ain't got to be afraid of no goat … he can't hurt you." He was smiling broadly.

"No Herman. The goats weren't chasing me." I thought for a second and said, "On second thought one of them kind of was but … anyway … what you doing up so early?"

"Who, me?" Herman answered. (*Who else am I talking to?* I thought.) "Oh, I got some real serious business to do. A killer loose on da Island. You heard, I know." He reached in his back pocket and pulled out his wallet. "Here, let me show you my badge." He eyed me again in a strange way like he was looking for something. "Didn't you ask me about it one time? Yeah, you see I remember. A good spy has to have a good memory. Right?" He fumbled with the wallet dropping it twice and almost falling off his bike picking it up.

"That's OK, Herman … I gotta get going."

"Where you going this early?" He was closer and I caught a whiff of his day old, alcohol stained, breath. P-H-E-W-W, it was strong. "U-u-u-h"… I lied … "to the store to get a paper for my father." I didn't want him following me to the police station. He was bad about tagging along with you, especially when he wasn't invited. Evidently, going for a newspaper didn't seem to interest him.

He threw his hand up, started waving it and went into a speal about how the FBI was gonna come down here, take over the case and catch this killer because the Chief didn't know nothing and Lumus was too lazy and … By the time he got to that part I was half way down the block.

Old Herman, I thought, *what a character. With his bike and beer riding around the Island and not a worry in the world. He was about as well known as Sambo but not quite. If he really was an FBI agent then the FBI had themselves one super undercover spy who would never have to worry about his cover being blown because he didn't have any cover to blow away. Everyone knew Herman worked for the FBI.*

Lumus and the Chief agreed that to try and track down the sale of every .45 pistol in the county, much less the State, was impossible without the help of many law enforcement people. And the weapon they were looking for was an older one, an antique practically, which made the task even harder, if that was possible. And what if the murder weapon was purchased outside the State? Going at it from that angle was like looking for a needle in the pluff mud. However, the break they needed was approaching the station at this very moment in the form of myself. Even I had no idea that the piece of paper I was about to deliver would turn out to be a huge break in the Poe case.

"Lumus! Hey Lumus!" I dropped my bike on the sidewalk. "You there?"

"Yeah, come on in." Lumus feigned surprise when he saw the mailing in Mike's hand. "Hey! What ya got there … something from the … Lumus almost slipped ... the …he corrected himself and said, "What's that?"

"Something we found … well, Bubba found it. We were looking in the Post Office's trash bin. I don't know if it's any help but …"

"Here, let me see," Lumus said eagerly taking the mailing. He glanced at the name of the company making the offer, "Coin World," however; his special interest was the addressee's name. It was mailed to a Dr. Steven Jenkins. He walked toward the desk thinking, trying to put a face to the name.

"Any help?" I asked anxiously. "That's kind of what you were looking for, isn't it?"

"Yeah, and I don't know if it's any help but it's a start." Even though he knew the answer Lumus asked anyway, "When did y'all find this?"

"Last night."

"Last night?" Lumus acted surprised again. "What you mean …last night?"

"Oh … we were in the trash bin out back of the Post Office the last few nights because Mr. Keenan wouldn't let us look in the trash can inside the Post Office."

"Well, y'all done a good job… real good." Lumus reached in his back pocket, pulled out his wallet and took two dollars from it. "Here, take this. You and Bubba go treat yourselves at Burton's."

"Thanks anyway, Lumus but you don't have to pay us. Remember we said we would help for nothing. Besides, we still got money from crabbing."

"A-a-a-w … take it. It's my way of saying "thanks" … go ahead."

"Oh … OK … And thank you."

Even though Lumus didn't demonstrate a show of emotion in front of Mike when he received the mailing with Dr. Jenkins' name on it, he was thrilled to have a lead to follow up on and the possibility that it could break the case wide open. The worst-case scenario he thought would be that Dr. Jenkins was a kind old man enjoying his coin collecting and retirement and wasn't capable of hurting a fly. Shucks, he probably teaches Sunday school at the Lutheran Church?

Now to find the Chief. Lumus glanced at his watch … 8:30. H-u-m-m? It only took Lumus one call to find the Chief. He was interrupting his boss' morning ritual, and he knew it, but he needed to talk with him.

The five booths lining the far wall in Grannie's Bakery were full of oversized patrons analyzing yesterday's happenings and solving all the world's problems while loading up on their favorite pastry and sipping coffee. It was the "Geritol crowd" and Chief Perry felt as comfortable with them as he did his with doughnuts. They swapped stories and told lies about everything from their golf games to the number of fish they caught. A new member of the group, and one of the youngest at age sixty-five, made the mistake one day when he went to bragging about his frequency of sexual encounters with his wife. There was a long pause in the conversation and then silence all around the booth. Most put down their coffee and stared into space trying to recall such wonderful times. The outspoken "youngster" looked around with true concern and bewilderment at the suddenly silent group. The elderly gentleman in the booth next to him tapped him on the shoulder and whispered, "Joseph, we don't have memories that good … to talk about … uh … sexual matters. You do understand, don't you?"

Lumus was at the station pacing in and out, sitting on the bench a minute or two and then back into the station. The Chief was late and Lumus' hands were tied without the Chief's approval about questioning Dr. Jenkins but when he heard the rumble of the old Ford rounding the curve by the Baptist Church he raced into the station, sat at the desk, and made himself look busy with some paperwork, glancing up as the

Chief strolled in. "O-o-o-h, there you are." Lumus said casually and then gathered himself explaining the mailing he had and how he obtained it.

"Here, let me see that," the Chief reached across the desk taking the mailing from Lumus "H-u-m-m, that's interesting. It just might be the start of something." He rubbed the stubble on his chin. "Could be, could be?"

"Chief, I know it isn't a piece of hard evidence by any means and a long ways from incriminating but there is a connection in a round about way. Know what I'm getting at?"

"Yeah, I sure do and I suppose you want to question this doctor … this …" He looked at the address … "this Dr. Jenkins?"

"Of course I do, Chief. I planned on going this morning and …"

"Hang on, Lumus. Just hang on a second. You can't just go barging in there questioning this man and giving him even a hint of an idea that he's a suspect until we can do some legwork and find out something about him. Shucks, you could spook him and if he really is involved in some way he would run and then where would we be? If he's innocent then no damage done. You understand what I'm saying?"

Lumus nodded and said, "Yeah… I gotcha. How about if I go by to see this Dr. Jenkins giving the impression that I'm questioning the whole neighborhood … no suspects … just looking around. Tell him it's stuff we have to do … be real casual about it? I could do that."

The Chief scratched his head and said slowly, "Y-e-a-h, now that might work. But you have to keep your questions real general. Nothing specific. Then I think you'll be OK. And whatever you do, don't scare him even if you halfway think he's our man. We don't want this guy running off like a scared rabbit. Just get the lay of the land. Remember you're questioning everybody in the neighborhood. It's all routine … that kind of stuff. Understand?" The Chief paused and received a look of agreement from Lumus. "Hate to rush off, Lumus but I gotta get back to Grannie's. I got a couple fish on the line that want to bet against the Yankees. Call if ya need me."

Another of Lumus' father's favorite sayings was, "Don't ever go bear hunting with a switch." When he first heard it, he was too young to appreciate such advice or even understand what it meant but now he knew its full implications. And so he went looking for something more than a switch before he questioned Dr. Steven Jenkins. He knew he needed information of any kind: personal, social, past or present. He would search until he found out all he could about Dr.Steven Jenkins before he met him face to face. He started by asking himself, "Now *who* would know Dr. Jenkins? Or who would know something about Dr. Jenkins? *Who … who*?"

Lumus parked in the corner of the parking lot in the shade under the tall Palmettos at the Post Office and waited. It wasn't long before Gertie

Evans appeared in all her gossipy glory with a disciple in tow, Pearl Walker, who was as good a back fence talker as any on the Island. Gertie was yakking away a mile a minute, shaking her bony finger in Pearl's face to emphasize a point of possible slander. Pearl didn't mind the finger pointing so much but seemed irritated that she wasn't able to squeeze in an opinion of her own.

Lumus timed his interception carefully, casually bumping into them just outside the door.

"Good morning, ladies." He tipped his hat and smiled. "How are you on this fine day?"

"Good morning, Lumus," Gertie said speaking for both ladies. "Just fine."

"Ms.Gertie … and you too Ms.Pearl … I was wondering if y'all could help me with something?"

"Be glad to," Gertie replied, "what's on your mind?"

"Well, there's this gentleman that lives on the Island who is kind of new to these parts and the rumor is that he wants to run for the vacant seat on town council in the next election. Anyway, Chief asked to get the rundown on this gentleman. You know, check on his character and all. Actually, I'm supposed to do that for all the candidates but there are so many and …"

"What's his name?" Gertie asked catching Lumus off guard.

"U-u-u-h … Jenkins … a Dr. Steven Jenkins." Lumus paused giving Gertie time to digest the name and hopefully regurgitate some helpful information. "He's been living here about two years I think?"

"One year," corrected Gertie turning to Pearl who was nodding her head.

"Oh … one year. OK. He's single … I believe?" Lumus had no idea and was just fishing.

"Widowed. His wife died six months ago … heart trouble."

"All right." This was going better than he hoped for Lumus thought. "I don't believe he works?"

"Nope.Retired. Came from some big hospital in Atlanta."

"Does he live alone?"

"Yeah, if you don't count the dog, "Dodger." He lives at Station 10, tan house with green shutters." Pearl's head was moving back and forth taking everything in hoping to sneak in a reply or two.

"Does he go to church?"

"Occasionally at Holy Cross Methodist," Gertie continued. "But he hasn't been in the last two weeks."

What doesn't she know? "How about his social life?"

"See him around and about but nothing special. Mostly keeps to himself."

"Well, thanks Ms.Gertie … and you too Ms. Pearl. That helps. Sounds like he would make a fine councilman." Lumus bid farewell, "Have a nice day, ladies."

Gertie motioned Pearl to come closer with her finger and whispered, "And Lumus thinks we'll fall for that bull of a story about running for council. I know why he was asking about Dr. Jenkins."

"Why?" Pearl asked.

"Tell you later Pearl but you have to promise you won't say a word to anybody."

Well, that was a good start. I just hope Gertie doesn't run her mouth to the whole Island about Dr. Jenkins being a suspect, thought Lumus on his way back to the station where he would work on a line of questioning for Dr. Jenkins.

Meanwhile Dr. Steven Jenkins felt better about things now that all his planning and preparations had been taken care of. He even felt confident. The Charleston paper had only run one small byline about the death of Thomas Poe and from what he could gather from Island gossip the local police were handling the investigation, which was good news in his eyes. As long as SLED, the State Law Enforcement Division, kept their noses out of it he felt he could rest easy.

These two local cops couldn't find their bee-hinds with both hands tied behind their back, he thought. *The Chief can't stay out of Grannie's long enough to lead an investigation much less start one. And that assistant of his ... he's a hick from some town called McClellanville. Remind me of The Keystone Cops. No, as long as those two are on the case I won't have to worry. Just a few more days and it will all be history anyway.*

I've got to make that call tonight he reminded himself when he heard a car coming up the drive.

Who in the world could that be this time of day? A quick peek through the window. Well, well, speak of the hick from the sticks himself. It was the Chief's assistant.

Dr. Jenkins waited on the porch and for the first time got a close up view of the gangly figure of Lumus as he got out of the Jeep and walked toward the porch.

Damn if he don't look just like Ichabod Crane in a police uniform, Dr. Jenkins thought, *a spitting image.*

"Hello," Lumus spoke to the figure through the screen. "Are you Dr. Steven Jenkins?"

"Yes, I am." He pushed open the screen door. " And you are Officer ...?"

"Mc Farland … Lumus Mc Farland. Sorry to come unannounced, Doctor. Hope I'm not disturbing anything?"

"No, no, not at all. Do come in. Get out of that sun."

"Thank you. I won't take up much of your time, just a few minutes."

Lumus stepped onto the porch instantly taking a mental picture of everything.

"Here sit down." Steven motioned toward a rocker. "I would invite you in but it's actually cooler out here in the breeze."

"Thank you. This is fine and the breeze does fell good."

"Would you like something cold to drink … ice tea or a soda?"

"No thank you but I appreciate the offer."

"And what may I ask brings you way down this end of the Island?"

"Well, Dr. Jenkins …The Chief, Chief Perry, and I are investigating the death of a Mr. Thomas Poe who lived here on the Island, a few blocks from here as a matter of fact. We found his body last week and we're more-or-less covering the whole Island questioning as many people as we can. Let me assure you that you're not a suspect or anything like that. This is just routine police work."

"Ah yes. I heard about that gentleman. Terrible … just terrible. Wasn't he shot and his body was found in the ocean or something?"

"The body was actually found in Miller's Creek and yes, he was shot. What I'd like to check on is whether you have noticed any strangers in the neighborhood or strange cars down this end of the Island late at night in the last two weeks?"

Dr. Jenkins paused as though he were thinking or trying to recall something." No, nothing out of the ordinary." Then he looked directly at Lumus trying hard to get a read on this country bumpkin masquerading as a policeman.

"How about on the beach," asked Lumus, "Any strangers or seedy looking characters hanging around?"

"No, none that I can recall. Not many people frequent this area of the beach. You did say the gentleman was shot?"

"Yeah, that's right." Lumus paused. "And for now we are treating it as a homicide."

"Did anyone hear the shot or shooting?"

"No, not a soul. No one including me and the Chief know much of anything." Lumus paused again gathering his thoughts trying to recall the sequence of his pre-planned questions. "Just a few more questions and I'll let you go." Lumus then asked, "Do you live alone, Dr. Jenkins?"

"Yes, my wife passed away six months ago and now it's just me and the dog … good old "Dodger."

Lumus appeared almost apologetic when he said, "I hope I'm not getting too personal when I ask this … but do you go out much, socially, I mean?"

"Not too much. I have a few friends I visit every now and then and we get together on occasion. No one real close. Now I do go to all the fish fries and oyster roasts put on by the Volunteer Fire Department. That sort of thing is a social outing for me."

"Again I don't mean to be prying and if you feel that I am then please … cut me off." Lumus paused and tried to be as relaxed as he could, "Do you have any special interests or hobbies, like golf or fishing?"

This time Dr. Jenkins hesitated at the out-of-place question wondering why he was asking about his hobbies. Sensing no real danger he answered, "No, just the beach and walking and … oh yea, I'm an avid reader … every day. Mostly I just hang around the house and enjoy my retirement."

Lumus began to push himself out of the rocker. "Well, I've taken up enough of your time and I thank you. I wish I could say you've been a big help but I'd be telling a lie." Lumus half chuckled attempting to lighten the mood.

"You're most welcome. Come anytime. If you see the car in the yard just come on in. If I can help in any way let me know."

"OK, and thanks again for your time." Lumus waved from the Jeep.

Back at the station Lumus sat and thought long and hard about his conversation with Dr. Jenkins. Two items kept popping up: *He didn't mention anything about coin collecting*, Lumus thought over and over. No*w that's strange. Did he forget or knowingly not say anything about collecting coins?* And the other thing was: *He asked if anyone heard the* shot? I think those were his words? H-U-U-U-M?"

38
A COLLECTOR

It was Friday afternoon and I had just finished mowing our yard. The tall, cold, glass of homemade lemonade and the shade were helping me forget the heat as I sat in the shade of the pecan tree with Mollie at my side. Her tongue was out and she was just a pantin.'

"You OK, girl?" She got up and headed in the direction of her water bowl.

I heard the screen door on Bubba's back porch slam and looked up as Bubba came tearing across the backyard, obviously excited about something.

Oh boy, I thought, *what now? Must be something he saw on TV?*

"Eah Curley," I yelled. "What ya running for? Tommy Wade after ya?"

"Yeah right. I wish ... that little twerp. It would be the last time he ever chased anybody. Eah, I got some news for ya. At least, something that might interest ya," Bubba said with a skirmish grin. I couldn't tell if he was serious or joking.

"What? What's going on?"

"Well, it's something I heard down at Burton's yesterday. Now, I'm not sure if it's true or not ... s-o-o-o maybe I shouldn't say anything ... because ... w-e-l-l-l ... I don't want to going spreading rumors and all. You understand don't you, Mike? You and me try real hard to be good boys and always tell the truth like our parents taught us and ..."

Bubba was hemming and hawing and I knew it. "Spit it out," I demanded. "What'd you hear?"

"O-o-o-o- K, it's about this certain girl you know who has blonde hair but I don't know if I should say anything or not?" He paused and just stood there looking at me.

I jumped up quickly and grabbed Bubba in a playful headlock and gave him a mild scroogie on top of his head.

"A-A-A-A ...WHUP,WHUP,WHUP (Bubba sounded just like Curly)... all right, all right." he yelled. "If you're gonna be that way about it."

I let go and made a feint toward him for another headlock.

Bubba backed up, his hands in the air. "I give, I give! KNUCK-

KNUCK-KNUCK!"

"So what'd you hear?" I asked sitting back down in the shade.

"A-a-a-w nothing much. Just that Beverly Ann will be at the movies tomorrow for the double feature, that's all." His arms were folded and he looked dead serious.

"Are you telling the truth or just making that up?" Information of such vast importance needed to be verified. *"Who* told you that?"

"Susan Huggins told me … that's who and she doesn't lie. Mary Rogers, Beverly and Susan are going together. Mary's Mom is dropping them off."

"Are you sure? Or you just trying to get me all riled up?"

"Yeah, man. I'm sure." Bubba held up three fingers imitating a scout and declared, "Honest injun."

"Eah man, you don't have to honest injun me … OK? As long as you're not kidding."

Then my mind was off and racing. Beverly at the movies. I was thinking, *WOW-EE! OH BOY, OH BOY, OH BOY! HALLEJUAH!* But I didn't want Bubba to know that I was that excited so as casually as I could I said, "Hey, that's great but guess what? I don't have any money. I spent my last two bucks on a tube for my bike. Durn! How am I going to the movies if I ain't got any money?"

"Easy," Bubba smiled and looked at me like I was crazy, "Sneak in."

"Yeah right. And if I sit with Beverly and she wants some popcorn or something what am I supposed to do then? Steal it?"

"Well …"

"Don't answer that." I sat down under the tree and rubbed Mollie's head for good luck and began to think really hard about where I could get some money by tomorrow. Then it hit me: "Got an idea … let's go."

"Where to?"

"Get some crab customers. I need some money, man. How about you, Mr. Moneybags? Got any money?"

"Nope, I'm broke too."

"Well, don't just stand there. Let's go."

Bubba seemed reluctant about going crabbing, he just stood there with a blank look, which wasn't like him at all. He loved the creek and going crabbing as much as I did.

"What's wrong with you?" I asked looking back. "Let's go."

I walked back toward Bubba as he explained: "It won't do any good to get any customers, Mike. We've missed the tide and it won't be right again until late tonight."

"Dag gone it!" My face and spirits dropped. "What?" But I was determined to make some money and meet Beverly at the movies. I sat back down under the tree and started thinking, rubbing Mollie's head again for good luck and then it dawned on me.

"What's the tide doing now?" I asked.

"Dead low. Why?"

"Perfect!" I proclaimed. "Yeah, that's perfect… low tide. Let's go! We gotta find some customers and I'll tell ya what we gonna do, Curley. Come on Mollie, let's go."

Either we were lucky or people really liked eating crabs as our stand by customers came through again: Mrs. Kelly and Ms. Kingman. Plus we had an open order policy with my mother and Bubba's mother, which brought our order to four dozen, which was plenty. But when it rains it pours and Mr. Barber flagged us down.

"Mike, Bubba when you guys go crabbing again get me another dozen, will ya? Those things are delicious."

"Sure thing, Mr. Barber. We're going in just a little bit. You want just one dozen?"

"Yeah, one dozen is plenty and Bubba I want to thank you again for helping me cook and clean that last batch. You've got me hooked. And make sure they're them big old Johnnies."

"Yes sir, Mr. Barber." Bubba said grinning but he didn't have the heart to tell him they were called Jimmies. "One dozen of big Johnnies coming right up."

Riding off I yelled back at Mr. Barber, "Hey! Mantle hit two more yesterday!"

He gave me a big smile and a thumbs-up.

Today we were traveling light for crabbers who needed to catch five dozen crabs. All we had was a basket for the crabs and two oars. Yet we planned on killing two birds with one stone. We launched our favorite boat, Bobby Graham's faded red one, which we had nicknamed the "Red Rocket," a satirical reference to the speed we made through the water when we paddled.

Miller's Creek was now littered with crab traps, so numerous we could hardly paddle the boat without hitting one with the oars but I was on the lookout for a special one. In my father's youth and up until I was very young, there were no crab traps in the creek. I often wondered what it would look like twenty years from now?

"Do you remember *exactly* which trap is Tommy Wade's?" I asked looking out over the creek at the many traps.

"Yeah," Bubba said motioning with his head as he paddled along, "It's the one over there with the blue marks painted on the cork. I'm sure. I saw him pulling it up one day and I remember the blue marking."

"Good, let's try it first and then work our way back. That way we can stick close to the marsh line." I smiled and thought, *Man, this should be some easy pickings.* Then a nagging thought hit me, one of guilt. *I knew what we were doing was wrong: Taking something that didn't belong to us. Then I thought just as quickly: What the heck, we won't do it but this one time. And shoot, nobody will miss these few crabs.* I wasn't completely comfortable with this rash justification for stealing but …

"Mike," … and Bubba had that worried look about him, "what if we get caught?"

"Eah, you sound like me now, Mr. Worry Wart. Look, the tide's so low nobody can see us from land even when we're standing up in the boat." I stood up to show Bubba and to reassure myself. "Looka here, can't nobody see us. And we'll be quick."

"OK," he said uneasily, "but I still don't like it."

"Bubba, you don't have to like it," I said. "Just help me, OK?"

I knew I was pushing our friendship to the limit but my desire to make some money and meet Beverly at the movies consumed me. And Bubba was right. I didn't like what we were about to do either except for the part dealing with Tommy Wade's trap.

"We gonna rob Mr. Scott's trap too?" Bubba asked. "It's the one right over there."

"No, uh-uh. Just these others. Beverly Ann is going to be at the movies, man. This is my big chance."

"Wrong again, lamebrain. You got two chances with Beverly … slim and none. And slim just left town," Bubba commented and then smiled. "Did you hear me?"

"Yeah, yeah, yeah. Maybe so. But at least I'll try. I'm … u-u-u-m … per… per … persis … what's that word? … persistent? Yeah, that's it. I'm as persistent as a hungry mosquito."

"Hey, hey! That's pretty good, Mike. Persistent as a hungry mosquito. Where'd you hear that?"

"Nowhere. I just made it up."

"Yeah! You oughta be a writer when you grow up."

"Right! That'll be the day. I'll be a writer when *you* become the Pope. A-HA-HA-HA!"

"Pope? H-u-m-m, does that mean I would be the boss of the nuns?" Bubba's eyes were sparkling. I wasn't sure what he had on his mind?

"Well … yeah … I guess so," I said.

"Oh boy! Those nuns would be in for some real trouble if I got to be the boss. You hear?"

"OK, OK. I believe you, Pope Bubba. Now let's get some crabs real quick like."

We paddled slowly up to Tommy Wade's crab trap and Bubba grabbed the rope, and began pulling while I stood up and glanced back toward the landing, keeping an eye out for any unwanted intruders. Bubba remarked that Tommy's trap must be full from the weight of it. And he was right. As he pulled it into the boat, it was slam full of crabs, lots of big Jimmies too. There must have been thirty or more in the trap but we didn't have time to count. Bubba quickly opened the slot and shook the trap like crazy while I continued to play lookout. In rapid order we raided three more traps taking turns shaking out the trapped crabs, and within thirty minutes we had more than enough crabs to fill our orders. After we cleaned out a trap we left the bait intact, closed the trap back, and dropped it back as close to its original spot as possible so as not to arouse any suspicion from the owners that someone had been messing with their trap.

On the way back to the landing, Bubba gave me his serious look and asked, "You don't feel bad about taking these crabs from somebody's trap?" Bubba was being upfront about what I had been thinking earlier. "I mean it's like stealing and all."

I could tell his conscience was beginning to bother him. And so to relieve his mind and sooth mine a bit I used the old "what somebody don't know won't hurt 'em" philosophy. Shoot, there was no sense in both of us feeling guilty.

"Bubba, you gotta look at it like this. Suppose the owner of that last trap we just got crabs from, came today to check that trap, how many crabs would he have gotten out of it?

"I dunno?"

"About how many did we get out of it?"

"About ten?"

"OK, then the owner would have gotten ten … right?"

"Right."

"All right. So if the owner comes tomorrow or the next day and checks his trap … are you with me?"

"Yeah."

"Then about how many crabs will he get out of that trap then? Eah, keep in mind how good the crabs are running now. About how many?"

"Ten or so, I guess," he said.

"Well? Then what's wrong with us taking these ten today? See what I mean? He was only going to get ten anyway… either today or tomorrow."

"Yeah … but …"Bubba answered, his mind not quite sure of my flawed but reasonable sounding logic. "But what if the owner showed up right now? What then?"

"Oh, if he showed up right now? Then we'd be in big trouble, that's what. We'd probably have to call in your friends to rescue us."

"Who? Bubba asked, "The crew?"

"No man, The Three Stooges … who else?" Bubba gave me a big BA-HA-HA-HA and I chuckled not at my joke but at the fact that I had a good friend who would risk getting into trouble with me over a few crabs.

As we approached the landing none other than Tommy Wade appeared rolling up on his bike with a basket in one hand and a paddle stretched across his handlebars. He stopped and watched us coast to a stop at the landing.

Oh God. I wondered, *How long as he been there? Did he see us?* Well, we were about to find out.

"See who's watching?" I said very quietly. (Sound travels over water for long distances.) "Up on the bank."

"Yeah, my good buddy," Bubba said sarcastically. "Think I'll throw him in the creek after I've filled his pockets up with rocks."

"Don't start anything, OK? I don't wanna see the poor boy get his crabs stolen and his bee-hind cut on the same day."

"OK, OK. I'll try to be nice." We came to a stop, lifted the basket of crabs out of the boat, set them on the landing, put the anchor up on the shore, and pushed the Red Rocket back out to rest.

"Hey!" Tommy yelled, "What y'all doing?"

"Oh nothing much," Bubba said, "Just been doing a little crabbing."

"Looks like y'all got a few?" Tommy said looking in the basket … "nice size too."

"Yeah we got lucky." Bubba 'n me each had hold of a handle of the full basket of crabs and were trying to make our way up the embankment and get out of there quickly before any more crab trap owners showed up. They would be able to put two and two together real quick and see that we didn't have a net or any bait yet our basket was full figuring the only way to get that many crabs was from traps. Tommy Wade wasn't that observant. Tommy Wade wasn't that observant about anything.

"I'm going to check my trap now. Haven't checked it in a week. Should be full … anyway I sure hope so."

"Should be really full," Bubba said winking at me. "Full of water," Bubba whispered.

"What y'all gonna do with all those crabs, Mike?"

"Sell 'em."

"Yeah, me too. I get fifty cents a dozen. How much y'all get?"

"We get fifty cents too," Bubba said in a gruff tone, "What'd ya think we got?"

"I don't know. I was just asking. I got to make some money so I can go to the movies tomorrow. Double feature and all," Tommy said genuinely excited about going to the movies. "Y'all are going to the movies, aren't ya?"

"Yeah, I think so?" I said. "Bubba, are we going to the movies tomorrow?"

"Movies? Oh yeah, we'll be there."

"OK, yeah … well … good luck," I said feeling a little bit sorry for him but not sorry enough to give him back his crabs. "See ya later, Tommy."

We walked at a brisk pace, never looking back, putting some distance between us and the unlucky Tommy Wade who was about to find out that his unlucky trap was not able to capture a single unlucky crab that day.

There's too much going on around here to concentrate on this Poe case. Way too much. Running the patrols, office work, and those durn kids on the hill again. And the calls for this and that. Chief Perry was thinking out loud while patrolling. *I need some quiet time. Some time for just Lumus and me to put our heads together and come up with some kind of plan for this investigation.* Turning onto Back street he passed the Devlin and O'Toole boys carrying a basket loaded with crabs. Without thinking he waved and smiled at the boys who did not acknowledge his hailing them. They had their heads turned.

Wonder what they've been up to? He rolled on by trying to think what to do next in the Poe case. *Looks like they've been in the creek?*

That evening after supper Chief Perry barely touched his pecan pie.

Doris had thought something was amiss because her husband had been unusually quiet from the time he stepped into the house. And when he didn't gobble up his favorite kind of pie she knew something was definitely wrong. "OK William, out with it."

"What? What are you talking about?"

"Whatever it is that's bugging you. That's what."

"Well … it's this damn Poe thing," the chief said as he stirred his coffee for the hundredth time. "I don't have time to sit down and talk with Lumus and come up with some kind of decent plan, Doris. Something concrete that will get us going. Lumus, despite what everyone says about him, is a helluva smart kid but I seem to be holding him back. And we're going nowhere."

"Well William, from what you say the only thing you need to do is go somewhere where just you and Lumus can sit down and talk. Somewhere where it's peaceful and quiet. It's that simple. Y'all put your heads together and y'all will come up with something."

"You're right, Doris. You're absolutely right." He then made a phone call.

Early the next morning Chief Perry was tapping on the front window of Grannie's, his nose smearing the glass as he looked inside for any kind of movement. It was 6:00 and thirty minutes before the scheduled opening time. It wasn't that he was hungry for a doughnut or two. He was here to meet Lumus and have coffee and go over the Poe case. Being early and beating the morning crowd would give them some quiet time together and, now that he thought about it, he might have a sweet roll or two. He finally caught Shirley's attention who, after giving him an exasperated stare, unlocked the door and let him in.

"Just can't stand being away from your friends more than twelve hours, huh, Chief?"

"You got me pegged, Shirley. Just had to come see you."

"Me? I was talking about the chocolate covereds." They both laughed.

"Help yourself, Chief. There's fresh coffee over there and I'll have a batch of glazed out in about five minutes." She headed to the kitchen.

"Thanks, Shirley," the Chief yelled to the back. "Lumus is supposed to meet me any minute now."

For the first time ever the Chief viewed an empty Grannie's. It was an almost eerie sight. Shucks, he even had his choice of where to sit. He looked around the room checking the location of each booth and tables carefully and decided on a booth in the back. That way if they were still here when the early bird customers arrived they would be out of hearing distance. As he eased himself into the booth he experienced a moment of transcendence while observing the quiet perfection of Grannie's. Everything was in order and in its proper place, right down to the pencil and pad used to take orders lying by the cash register and the pastries lined up neatly in the glass enclosed case. The only sound was the distant whirl of Shirley's blender thinning more dough. Heaven couldn't be better than this he thought. Fresh coffee, solitude and a room full of the best pastries ever made on earth. The sound of someone tapping on the window brought the Chief down from heaven. It was Lumus. Struggling to clear his belly from the table the Chief got up and went to the door turning the key letting Lumus in.

"Welcome to heaven, Lumus. What's the password?"

"Huh?"

"Just a little private joke. Come on in … I got here a little early. I figured by 6:30 or 7:00 this place might be getting busy. This way we can talk in peace."

Lumus looked around and asked, "Where's Shirley?"

"In the back. You want some coffee?"

"Is a forty pound robin fat?" Lumus said heading for the coffee pot in the corner. "You already got yours, Chief?"

The Chief held up his cup of coffee and gestured to Lumus. "Sit here, Lumus. I'll get us some doughnuts."

Chief Perry rested his chin on his folded hands propping himself up, looked earnestly at Lumus for a few moments, cleared his voice and began to fiddle with his coffee.

"Lumus, we've been on this case for how long now? Two weeks? I was thinking about it last night and to tell you the truth we aren't getting anywhere. It's like we're stuck in the sand spinning our wheels and … "

"But, Chief …"

"Wait a minute, Lumus. Let me finish. You see, we don't have the resources and manpower to really get out there and beat the bushes. You know what I'm saying? To turn over every rock and find this slug." He stopped and observed the pained look on Lumus' face. "Look, I'm not criticizing you or myself. It's just that we ain't getting the job done. Plus we got all this other stuff to deal with every day. Hell! Old lady Robinson calls me every other day to get her damn cat out the tree. Next time she calls I'm gonna shoot the sucker out the tree and tell her, "Well, here's your cat."

Lumus had a feeling what was on the Chief's mind other than shooting cats. "You're not considering calling in the SLED boys … are you?"

"I dunno? I've given it some serious thought. The only lead we have as we sit here is from two kids, which is a mailing they dug up in the trash. That don't look so good. You understand where I'm coming from, don't you?"

"Yeah, Chief but before you call in SLED, please hear me out."

"OK, go ahead. The floor is yours." The Chief leaned back, sipped on his coffee and then reached for another doughnut, carefully listening to Lumus.

"Chief, that Dr. Jenkins is hiding something. I know it. I mean I can feel it. I can't put my finger on it but … o-o-o-h … there's something that's not right. Help me out here, Chief."

"What you're trying to say is you have an intestinal sensory discernment."

"A what?" Lumus blurted out.

"In other words … a gut feeling."

"Yeah, that's it. Where'd you learn about a intestinal sensory … uh … whatever?"

"The War. That's where. How do you think I made it home in one piece." The Chief added, "What gave you that feeling, Lumus? I mean what made you feel that way … was it something he said?"

"No… no … not anything he said but more the *way* he said it. His mannerisms, the way he acted, I guess. What was strange was that he could not look me in the eye or even look at me when we talked. I know you've talked to people like that. It's like they're hiding something or afraid of something." Lumus paused and looked to the Chief for approval.

The Chief nodded. "Go on … I'm with ya."

"And when I asked him if he had any hobbies he didn't mention coin collecting and it's true we haven't absolutely established the fact that he collects coins but there is a strong possibility he does or did in the past. Right?"

"That's right … a good point." The Chief took a long sip of coffee. "Was he cooperative? Agreeable to talk to … or did he have an attitude? Was the man rude?"

"Oh no. He was the perfect gentleman and told me that if he could be of any help, just let him know. Of course, he didn't look at me when he told me that."

"Interesting, Lumus. You know you just might …"

"Excuse me for interrupting Chief, but there's one other thing and it could be something important or maybe nothing at all … see what you think. Toward the end of our little talk he asked me if anyone heard *the shot.* At least I think that's what he said if I heard him correctly. He might have said shots. But I didn't want to sound the alarm by confronting him so I let it slide."

"Good Lumus, you done right. Can you remember his *exact* words?"

"No, not really. He caught me off guard. It was so quick. The best I can recall is that he said, "Did anyone hear the shot or shooting?" Lumus was searching in his mind desperately trying to remember.

The Chief noticing Lumus' anxiety said, "Don't worry about it, Lumus. In court it would simply be your word against his even if it made it into evidence. From what you've told me you need to pay Dr. Jenkins another visit and this time try to get in the house for a better look around. Wait a few days, OK? And when you go back don't bring up the coin collecting. We can wait and see on that. And I won't call SLED if that will relieve your mind a little."

"Oh thanks, Chief. Thank you! Eah, we're gonna find whoever did this, believe me, and we don't need no help from those fancy SLED boys."

"Yeah, OK. If you say so. Look, I got to go check on a reported bonfire on the beach last night," the Chief said pushing himself away from the table. "Next thing you know somebody's gonna burn down the Island. Wanna go with me?"

"No, I'm going to the station and make some calls. I'll get up with ya later. How about lunch at Bessingers?"

The Chief smiled broadly. "Oh yeah. Best news I've heard today … you're on."

"Bye Shirley," they yelled together toward the kitchen. "See ya later!"

"Yeah, bye guys. Have a good one and leave the door open on the way out."

From what I heard they ain't never gonna catch no murderer," Shirley mumbled to herself. "Not those two."

Lumus regretfully called the State Law Enforcement Division, SLED, in Columbia for the fifth time in the last two weeks seeking any kind of lead on the murder weapon hoping against hope when the only information he could provide them with was the caliber of the gun. Lumus couldn't even give them a list of gun owners in the State. *Nope, that dog won't hunt*, he thought. *H-u-u-u-m. I w-o-n-d-e-r if …*

He had an idea, one that he had not run by the Chief and he wasn't sure if he should try it or not. But, he figured, what could I lose? So he decided to add one little tidbit to the mix, a name. And he gave his contact in Columbia the name of Dr. Steven Jenkins as a possible owner of an antique .45 caliber pistol to help narrow the search, but as positive as Lumus wanted to be, he knew it was a long shot, a real long shot. Time was moving on and the trail was growing colder so he decided to come up with a different approach to this whole case or he wouldn't have to worry about it, if and when, the SLED boys moved in, something he didn't want to happen.

He dropped everything he was doing, called the Chief, and told him he would be out on his boat until lunchtime. Lumus kept the twenty-three footer tied up at the marina just over the Ben Sawyer bridge, and when he really needed to come up with an answer to a difficult problem he launched the "Just Us" and sailed across the harbor, up the Ashley River to the Stono Cut and back. Usually when Lumus had difficult or puzzling questions he could talk it out with the Chief or find the answer by himself. But the question nagging him since the boys found the mailing with Steven Jenkins name on it was a tough one indeed. Maybe, just maybe, if he relaxed enough, the answer would come to him, so right before he got underway he stated the problem to himself for the umpteenth time letting it sink in, and then he put it out of his mind, dismissed it and let it go. He would then go about his business of sailing and enjoying the beautiful day ahead of him. "Forget it and let it come to you" was his theory, and unbelievably it had worked in the past. He desperately needed for it to work this time so he added a little prayer. The difficult question bugging Lumus was: "What kind of person collects coins?"

It was 3:00 in the morning when Lumus woke up from a dead sleep and sat up in his bed.

Coin collecting ... coin collecting ... Lumus thought. What kind of person collects coins? And the answer was right in front of him as plain as day. The answer was so simple.

A *collector* ... a *collector collects coins. That's it! That's it!*

39
HEARTBREAK

The Island movie theater had been open for about a year. It didn't have a formal name so we just called it "the movies." It had been a part of Fort Moultrie and sat abandoned for many years after the Army pulled out. Eventually it was cleaned up, refurbished, and opened offering the kids on the Island another place to hang out. To us it was everything: a meeting place for the crew, a place to have fun, a place to meet new people and, oh yeah, a place to watch a movie. Did we like going to the movies? You bet we did! But the movies themselves were not the main attraction. We had other things on our minds.

This gathering of our friends at the movies is where it all came together socially: peer approval, bragging rights, fashion display and hopefully recognition and acceptance from the opposite sex. However, peer approval above everything else was extremely important to us, especially at our influential age. None of us wanted to be disliked or shunned by the group. That would be so stressful it might bring on another zit … and God knows we didn't need any more of those dreadful things. The social setting of the movies was the perfect test for this facet of our lives. Because when our crew gathered they minced no words when it came to handing out approval or not. All one had to do was say something or do something and their opinion would be right there, up front and personal.

Bragging rights were exhibited whenever the opportunity presented itself. And if we didn't have something worthwhile to brag about then we usually made up something. But one had to be careful what he bragged about because it was directly subject to approval by our peers. If your friends never told you that you were "a liar" or "full of it" then you weren't much of a braggart. Shoot, people were always telling Bubba 'n me how "full of it" we were. But that didn't deter us one bit. We kept on bragging about something …

Fashion display was easy. We all dressed alike. Well, close to the same. Some kids wore more expensive clothes but didn't try to stand out in a crowd, not trying to bring attention to themselves thus subjecting themselves to the approval or disapproval of the always critical crew.

Acceptance from the opposite sex or seeking acceptance from the opposite sex was new to me. In previous years I had never given it much thought. The boys only sought acceptance from other boys. Now that we were seeking acceptance from the girls, we learned very quickly that this was a whole new ballgame. Shoot, we had stepped into another whole new world. And we didn't have a clue.

The diverse group of people who showed up at the movies made it a different setting than our hangout at Burton's where our crew dominated the scene. *Everybody* went to the movies: our crew, the teenagers, adults, locals, visitors, and young children. It was a hodgepodge of humanity, especially on double feature Saturdays or when they featured a hit movie like "Psycho" or "Ben Hur." Many parents took the liberty of using the movies as a babysitting service, dumping off their little ones at 1:00 and returning reluctantly that evening to pick them up after enjoying an afternoon of peace and quiet from the rigors of parenthood.

Inside the theater the different age groups flocked together in an unspoken code of behavior, which said that you sit with your peers or else there could be trouble. It was ironic how the youngest group, the little kids, sat way down front and moving progressively back came the next age group and so on until the very last row of the balcony was occupied by cuddling teenagers. I would learn later why the teenagers preferred the loneliness of the back row and all I'll say is that it didn't have anything to do with a better view of the movie.

Our group, the twelve-to-thirteen-year-olds, were allowed in the balcony but were still subject to the whims and fantasies of the older teenagers who occasionally flexed their muscle by forcing us to go get their popcorn and Coke or ordering us to shut up when we talked too much or got a little loud. These teenagers were a real pain because they weren't quite old enough to drive and go out on dates like their older friends and they didn't want to associate with us silly elementary school kids so they took out their frustrations of being trapped in their teen limbo-land on us. We learned to avoid them like the plague and set up our own little world on the far side of the balcony where we were free from their taunts.

The price of admission for the Saturday double feature was twenty cents, a bag of popcorn or a Coke cost a dime and all candies were a nickel. For the price of admission we didn't exactly view the greatest films of that era. Most were B-type productions of questionable quality. But we didn't care. Shoot, we weren't film critics …we were there to have fun. I recall movies such as "Pork Chop Hill," "Thunder Road," "The Blob," and "Flubber." The all-time disaster had to be "Godzilla in Japan," a subtitled affair so bad it was pathetic. In truth, it inadverntly turned out to be a pretty good comedy.

Bubba 'n me's main interest wasn't which movie was playing but rather which girls were going to be there. However, on this particular day I was concerned with only *one* girl. And I even put on a clean shirt and Bermuda shorts with a belt. I knocked the dirt off my tennis shoes, combed my hair into my best Elvis imitation, and checked my right front pocket making sure my hard-earned crabbing money was there.

The movie itself was of little importance. Half the time we didn't even know or care what was playing. The crew spent the majority of the day in the lobby, gathering in small circles, laughing and joking with each other like long-lost friends who had just been reunited. The reality was that we had just left each other no more than two hours ago from Burton's, but everyone seemed to come up with something different to talk about. We would socialize for a while and then go back to our seat only to return a few minutes later with some absolutely vital piece of information that we had just remembered it needed to be shared with the group. The whole day we went back and forth like yo-yos. The only time someone would settle in for the day was when he or she made contact with someone of the opposite sex and they ended up sitting together throughout the rest of the movie. And that's what I was hoping to do today … make contact with Beverly.

Bubba was somewhere in the theater, up to who knows what? He was on thin ice with the owner for earlier this spring being caught running a money-making scheme by sneaking friends in through the bathroom window for half price. The owner noticed a larger number of people in the theater than his receipts showed as paying customers. He knew the only entrance to the theater was through the front door or the bathroom windows, yet the windows were supposed to be locked. So he began a careful surveillance of the mens'room and his suspicions were confirmed when he noticed a heavier than normal flow from there. He staked it out making occasional pop-in visits between his job as the projectionist and helping in the concession stand in hopes of nabbing the culprits. By pure chance he happened in on Bubba struggling to free our well-rounded, chubby friend, Mike Hart, who was firmly lodged in the small half window looking like a beached whale. A stern warning was issued to Bubba and new locks were put on the window.

Bubba still believes his getting caught was an inside job instigated by Tommy Wade whom he believed squealed on him, which explained in part Bubba's animosity towards Tommy. I told Bubba, "I don't think the boy had enough sense to pull something like that off."

Bubba retorted, "Devlin, that's exactly how stupid people act."

I had already done a walk-through of the theater looking for Beverly, Mary, and Susan and not finding them returned to the lobby where I waited anxiously, pacing the lobby like an expectant father. Every thirty seconds I would walk over to the curtain draping the front door, slide it back a few inches, and peek out front in hopes of seeing Beverly and her friends arriving. I was hoping they would get here soon because "Shane" was playing today … a real bang-bang shoot 'em up Western … and I didn't want to miss any of the action.

I waited patiently while members of the crew came and went, many giving me the I know who you're waiting on stare.

Jocko and Stinky breezed by, heading to the concession stand, and Jocko yelled back at me, "Who ya waiting on, Devlin? The bride of Frankenstein?"

When they returned I told Jocko that if I was waiting on the bride of Frankenstein's grandmother she would look better than his girlfriend.

"Oh yeah," he said. "How's that?"

"Well, everybody knows your girlfriend is a dog and she ain't no Collie either," I said with a playful smile.

We could joke with Jocko in that manner because not only was he a free-spirit with a great sense of humor but also he had the most beautiful girlfriend in the world and he knew it. I think he took all the ribbing because he felt sorry for us poor losers when it came to comparison in the girlfriend department. But I was hoping to change that soon.

"Is that so? Guess next week I'll have to try and see if I can't upgrade Jo Ann to Bulldog status … HA-HA-HA!"

"See y'all later," I said.

"Yeah, later alligator," Jocko said. "I gotta get back to my dog."

Anxiety is not supposed to be a part of a twelve-year-old's persona much less his vocabulary. But that's what I felt as I stood in the lobby waiting for Beverly. The anxiety coupled with my constant worrywart attitude made me begin to sweat even in the cool of the air-conditioned lobby. A little at first then it increased until I could feel it all over my body. Durn! I checked my armpits and the stain was spreading, a droplet rolled down my cheek, and my much-attended-to Elvis hairdo was beginning to sag. Now instead of peeking through the curtains I was running to the bathroom every two minutes to check on my appearance. I looked like I had just come from a dip in the ocean. What would Beverly think? Would she even talk to a wet, sweating admirer?

"Hey, what ya doing down here all by yourself?" It was part of the crew … John, Andy, and Cathy. "Gee whiz, look at ya. Sweating like a pig. You're soaked, Devlin. You O.K?" John remarked, sincerely concerned about my condition.

I lifted my arm for a look and quickly put it down. "Yeah, I'm fine. I'm just waiting on someone." I kept my arms down straight attempting to hide the spreading sweat stains.

John pulled me aside. "You got the sweats, man." He paused and told Andy and Cathy he'd catch up with them in a few minutes. "You must be nervous about something?"

"The sweats? Whatcha talking about?"

"It's how you get when you get all nervous and worried about something like a girl. Are you waiting on a girl, Mike?"

"Yeah," I said, but I'm not sure she's gonna show up."

"A-a-a-w … that don't matter. Somebody said it means you must really care about her to be that nervous, but I ain't so sure about that because the same thing happened to me one time. I was all nervous and everything and started sweating a lot, just like you. Man, I sweated so much I was drenched. I lost so much water I almost fainted."

I felt relieved to know that someone else my age had gone through this. "Oh yeah," I said with a broad smile, "Who was the girl?"

"Oh, it wasn't no girl …it was my dog … he was sick."

"O-o-o-o-h, I see … I think?"

"Anyway good luck. Gotta go … talk to ya later."

Shoot, next thing you know I'd have the chills and then a fever? If this was any indication of how things were to be in my future love life, then I was beginning to have doubts about the whole deal. How could a twelve-year-old girl who I had never even held hands with make me feel this way? How would I react if we did make contact and I advanced to the point where I actually held hands with her and then somehow managed to kiss her? Would I sweat all the fluid out of my body and die? Calm down I told myself … you're at the movies on the Island and Beverly's not here … relax … calm down.

The onrushing Bubba and Billy flew by me bound for the concession stand or were running from someone. They saved me from sweating to death or from having an anxiety attack with their sudden appearance scaring the worry out of me. Knowing those two they were probably being chased.

"Eah, what's the rush?" I asked. "What y'all doing."

"Oh nothing," Bubba said looking back over his shoulder. "We put some ice down the back of Betty's blouse and she got mad, real mad." He was walking away as he talked, moving fast. "You haven't seen us, OK?"

"Yeah," Billy added, "you ain't seen us. Let's go Bubba before she shows up."

"All right, but I wouldn't mess with that girl. Y'all you could get hurt."

Betty Beastwick, better known as The Beast, was a she-man. She was tall with broad shoulders and short-cropped hair. And she was *real* strong. One time at the rocks we saw her grab Stinky Johnson by the neck and shake him like a rag doll just because he accidentally kicked sand on her while she was sunbathing. Shoot, none of the crew in their right mind, except Bubba and Billy, of course, messed with The Beast … uh-uh, not me. Her muscular arms and powerful legs only added to the mystique surrounding her true gender. Of course, we knew or were pretty sure the only thing feminine about Betty were her private body parts. None of us had ever checked or volunteered to try to check any part of her private anatomy or would in the future either. The only proof we would ever gather was from looking at her in a bathing suit, which was plenty of proof for me. We were taught in Religion class at school that God was perfect never having made a mistake and I believed that. Until w-e-l-l … when I met The Beast doubts began to creep in. In Betty's case I wouldn't say God made at mistake but maybe, just maybe, He was in a hurry the day she was created and possibly, just by some freak accident, some parts got mixed up. Something wasn't right. That was for sure. But any male with common sense didn't mess with her and if Bubba and Billy kept up their shenanigans there could be trouble. Me? I got along fine with Betty. I steered clear of her.

I was peering out the curtain again, still wiping the sweat when I heard heavy footsteps behind me.

"Hey you, Devlin!" I recognized the deep, husky voice of the approaching female. I turned slowly and it was Betty, red-faced and obviously on the warpath. She came strutting right up to me, stopped with her hands on her hips and looked down at me. I was thinking, *Geez, I'd sure hate to have to guard her in a game of basketball.*

She bellowed, "Have you seen your pal, Bubba, and that fog brain Billy?"

"U-u-u-h …"

She shook her fist at me: "Don't you lie to me!" Then she exhaled her hot breath on me, laden with the smell of popcorn and Ju Ju Fruits.

"U-u-u-h …" I figured I better tell at least half the truth. "Yeah, they ran by here just a minute ago. I think they went that way?" I pointed to the bathroom.

"Thanks. I'm going to wait for 'em to come out and teach both of 'em a lesson. You don't mess with Betty Beastwick and get away with it."

I'm thinking, *Yep you're right about that. Nobody wants to mess with a monster like you* but instead I asked innocently, "What'd they do?"

"Put ice down my back. They about ruined my new blouse. Look at this …those stupid idiots.

"Eah, maybe they like you Betty and that's their way of showing you attention?"

"Humph! I don't care if they like me or not because I don't like them. Wait till I get my hands on them." She paused, took a couple of deep breaths, and looked toward the men's bathroom. "Who you waiting on?" she said. It came out more as a demand than a question.

"Nobody." I answered too quickly and Betty pounced.

"L-e-t me think. Oh yeah, I know. That pretty little blonde. What's her name? U-u-u-h… Beverly something, huh?"

"N-o-o-o-o, actually I'm waiting on Marilyn Monroe. We have a date tonight."

"Hey, don't get smart with me or I'll give you some of what your buddy is gonna get." She shook her fist again in my face. "You been hanging around Bubba too long … that's what I think."

I dared a retort:"Yeah, I'm glad that's what you think, Betty." She didn't seem to hear me. She was heading toward the men's bathroom. I was praying Bubba and Billy weren't really in there.

I parted the curtain for a quick glimpse outside and I couldn't believe it. There they were. Mary and Susan getting out of the car. My heart did a little dance and I felt a tingle on my neck. At least, I had quit sweating but there wasn't time to check my hair so I patted down the top, slicked back the sides and smoothed the wave in front the best I could. I checked my shirt and shoes and peeked a look again through the side of the curtain.

As suddenly as my heart had risen it fell. All the way to my shoes it felt like. Mary and Susan were out of the car and walking toward the ticket booth. But there was no Beverly.O-o-o-h… no … it can't be. She wasn't with them. I kept looking and hoping my eyes had deceived me in some way and Beverly would magically appear in all her radiant beauty. It was not to be. Disappointment is one thing. I could deal with it but I was way past disappointment, closing in on despair. I had learned a long time ago that everything doesn't always go your way, but the heartache I felt was almost unbearable. I was a devastated twelve-year-old and so sad I felt like crying. Not wanting to make a public spectacle of myself, I did the next best thing. I ran and hid in the safety and darkness of the theater and pouted. Where is she? What happened? These questions managed to squeeze themselves in between the silent moans and groans as I buried my head in hopes of not being spotted by any of my friends. And, of course, I had no answers as to Beverly's whereabouts.

I sulked my way through the last half of "Shane" and then decided to go home. I didn't feel like being around the crew or Bubba or anyone. I wanted to be alone and sort all this out: Beverly not being here, the anticipation, the waiting, but most of all my feelings.

Bubba wasn't hard to find. All I had to do was listen for a minute and sure enough I heard the laughing and carrying-on coming from the left side of the balcony. He and Billy and Sammy were whooping it up as the short serial, "Flash Gordon," started with our hero, Flash Gordon, blasting off in search of Emperor Ming. I trudged up the steps and sat in the row right in front of them. I told Bubba that Beverly didn't show up and I was going home.

"Eah, I'm sorry to hear that. Are you sure?"

I managed a pitiful, "Yea … so I'm going to head on."

"Mike, don't leave. We're going skating at 6:00. Everybody's going. We'll have a good time," Bubba pleaded. "Come on and stay."

I understood his good intentions but felt so sad and let down and confused that I couldn't tell him how I really felt. I didn't know how I felt myself.

"N-a-a-w, y'all go. I'm heading home. Maybe I'll see you later at the skating rink?" That was a lie. The tone of my voice to my best friend, who knew me better than I sometimes knew myself, told it all.

"All right then," Bubba said. "Eah, you OK?"

"Yeah. I'm fine. I'll talk to you later."

"S-h-h-h, knock it off down there," some interested moviegoer demanded.

"Who said that?" Bubba commanded, looking around.

"I did, kid." A very large teenager named Puggy two rows over stood up and glared at us. "Are you going to shut up?"

"Yeah … oh yeah. Sorry. I'll be quiet … right now," Bubba pleaded as Billy and Sammy melted into their seats.

I was gone.

That afternoon I walked my bike home, which gave me more time to think and try to figure things out. But there didn't seem to be any easy answers and the more I thought about Beverly not showing up and how I had reacted made me worry that much more. What bothered me the most was not the fact that Beverly did not show up but how I felt when she didn't. I wondered about my reaction. Had I overreacted? And if so, why? I didn't know if I was in love or what. But one thing I knew was that it was a sickening feeling and I did not care ever to experience it again. Maybe I had my expectations set too high? Better than having them set too low, I guess. Shoot, I didn't know. So that night I laid in bed and thought it over and simply decided that it wasn't supposed to work out this time. Maybe next time.

And as I posed that question to Mollie, she pulled her ears back and smiled. It made me feel a little better as I dozed off to sleep.

The next morning after church I was in the midst of my least favorite task: cleaning up my room and making my bed, and generally sprucing up the area whether it needed it or not. Gosh, it had just been cleaned three weeks ago. What was the rush? What were we expecting, an attack of the giant germs? I bet other kids didn't have to clean their rooms that often. Those were some of the failed arguments I had tried with my mother who said that if I wanted to sleep in that room tonight then I'd better get in there and clean it up. Where else was I gonna sleep? I thought about the boat but Mollie and me in the boat didn't seem like such a good idea. The cot on the porch? Naw, I'd tried that last summer and the mosquitoes had a picnic. Not only did Mr. And Mrs. Mosquito and their family show up for the feast but I think they invited *all* of their relatives too. And I mean *big* mosquitoes. They were so big I overheard two of them arguing over which one was gonna throw their saddle on me and ride me home.

"Hey, look Moe, look Larry there's Mike cleaning his room … A-WHUP-WHUP-WHUP" followed by a "KNUCK-KNUCK-KNUCK-A-A-A-H!"

I turned around and there was Bubba's smiling face in the window.

"Grab the cinder block and come on in," I said referring to the cinder block right below the window that was used as a step.

"Eah, whatta ya think I'm standing on." In a flash he was through the window and lying on my freshly made bed, stretched out like he was at home.

I grinned and said, "What brings you over so early, Curley? Can't find Moe and Larry?"

"Eah, you're just jealous because you don't have two smart friends like Moe and Larry."

"You're right, absolutely right! And guess who my best friend is? Yep …you! So how smart does that make you?"

"H-u-m-m, guess I stepped into that one?"

"Yeah. At least you didn't step into something else." I gave Bubba a friendly poke on the shoulder and put up my dukes.

"Just came to check on ya. We missed ya last night." Bubba paused and got serious for a second. "Still thinking about you know who?"

"Y-e-a-h, some," I lied. Actually I had been thinking about Beverly all morning despite the promises I had made to myself the night before. I quickly changed the subject. "Did y'all go to the skating rink last night?"

"Yep, told you we were going. I mean, heck, it's right across the street. Oh man, I've got some good stuff to tell you. You should have stayed. You missed it all!"

"Yeah, what happened? Did you get kicked out of the movies?"

"No, I did not," Bubba answered emphatically." Almost but… anyway, we all went to the skating rink after the second movie. By the way, you missed a real humdinger of a movie, something called "Casablanco"or something like that. It was dumb. Anyway, Betty shows up at the skating rink and she's still mad about the ice thing at the movie so I figured hey, I ain't gonna have the beast after me all night so I got her off to the side and apologized to her and all. I told her I was sorry and didn't mean to mess up her blouse."

"Oh yeah. What did she say?"

"Oh, she was real nice and said everything was all right. She looked happy when I told her I was sorry and all."

"What about Billy. Did he apologize?"

"No and that's what I wanna tell you about. Not only did he not apologize but he kept picking at Betty and calling her big 'un and Amazon-lady and stuff like that. You know how mean Billy can be sometimes. Susan and I kept telling Billy to quit but he kept it up the whole night. It was bad and he thought he was being so cute skating around backwards and all calling her names and …"

"What did Betty do?"

"Hold on, I'm getting to that part. I kept telling Billy to knock it off and leave Betty alone but he just shoots me the finger and laughs and kept on messing with her. Of course, Betty couldn't catch him, not on skates, she's too slow, but I could tell she was slowly coming to a boil. You could tell because she got real quiet and didn't say much of anything the rest of the night, especially to Billy. That should have been his warning. Later on Billy was doing his little act. Twists and jumps and all. He was really showing off like he does at the beach on the inner tube. Anyway, he was strutting around real cocky like he was something else and then he went into his skating backwards routine."

"Backwards? I didn't know he could skate backwards."

"Oh yeah! He's good too. And fast. Well, he was flying along backwards and Betty saw her chance. She was over there by the stage. You know where it's kind of dark and off to the side, where Billy couldn't see her. So she timed it just right and snuck out to where Billy was headed when his back was turned, stopped, and got down on all fours like we do at school when we're gonna push someone over after you've snuck up behind 'em."

"Oh n-o-o-o. " I had my hands on top of my head anticipating a crash. "Did Billy run into her?"

Bubba smiled broadly."Oh man, did he." She was real low and Billy hit her at full speed. He went flying over Betty and landed on the back of his head half knocking him out. When his head hit the floor it sounded like a rifle going off … PHOW-YOW! And Betty jumped up and was on him like a mockingbird on a June bug. Poor ol' Billy, groggy and all, didn't have a chance and it got ugly real quick. I tell you, Mike it wasn't much of a fight if you could call it that. Betty grabbed his shirt and slapped him around telling him this one was for so-and-so name he had called her and this one was for so- and-so and … PWHEW! Man, it was bad …real bad. The whole time she was asking him if he was sorry. Shoot, Billy couldn't hear nothing and if he could have answered I'm sure he would have apologized ten times and because he didn't say anything it only made Betty madder so then she took to punching him. Billy never made it off the floor. Man, she beat him to a pulp. Jocko and me had to finally pull her off him."

"What about Betty? Did she get hurt any?"

"No, nothing. Not even a scratch. Only thing she got was tired from whipping up on Billy. When you see him you'll see what I'm talking about. Man, he looks bad, especially the knot on his head from the floor. Big as a plum."

"But you know, Bubba. If Billy had quit picking on her like you told him none of that would have happened. Right?"

"T-h-a-t-'s right, Catbird. But eah, that's not the real news. Got something neat to tell you."

"Better than the flying-Billy story?"

"Well yeah, for you anyway. You're not gonna believe this but I found out from Susan why Beverly wasn't at the movies." He paused for a long time. "You wouldn't be interested in that would you?" Then he grinned.

I grabbed Bubba in a playful headlock and grabbed his nose and threatened to pull it off if he didn't start talking right now.

"Let go so I can tell you. Does he do that to you, Mollie?" Bubba paused and gathered his thoughts. "U-h-h-h, let's see … Susan said that … no … it was Mary who … u-h-h-h …"

"Spit it out, tell me." I demanded, ready to choke it out of him. I was sitting on the edge of the bed about to pop from anxiety.

"All right, all right. Listen. Beverly never was going to the movies in the first place. Mary made up that part of the story because she knew it would get you to go to the movies."

"Me! Why me?"

"Come on, foggy. Why you think?"

"You mean …Mary? She wanted to see *me*?"

Bubba was grinning somewhat, while I was grinning from ear to ear. What great news! The relief I felt was greater than the disappointment of the night before and equal to the happiness of the moment. Oh me, oh my! This meant that Beverly didn't stand me up after all. And then it dawned on me. So that's why I had felt so bad yesterday. Deep down I felt rejected by someone I cared about but did not want to admit it or did not realize that was it. There was still hope. There was still a chance we would get together.

"Oh WOW!" I yelled, "Neato!"

"Neato? You mean you like Mary? Eah, she looks like an overweight toad frog."

"No, I don't like Mary but be easy on her, OK? She's got a great personality and she's pretty smart. She fooled both of us didn't' she?"

"Yeah, but that ain't saying a whole bunch."

"When did you talk to Mary? Last night at the skating rink?"

"Yeah, right after the flipping-Billy show."

"Eah, let's get going to the beach. Beverly might show up at the rocks today?"

"You don't ever give up, do ya, Devlin?"

"You know me. Never say die. Come on Mollie, let's go."

"Hey my friend, don't get too carried away. I've got some bad news too. Beverly won't be at the rocks today." Bubba held up his hands shutting me up. "I've already checked it out."

“Oh,” I replied softly, “OK. But eah, we can still go to the rocks can’t we?”

“Yeah, sure. But first of all we gotta go check on Billy. He’s home probably trying to remember what happened last night.”

40
DECEIT

September, 1919

The Great War was over. The Huns were defeated, giving hope to many that the world was now safe for democracy and America could return to normal.

Young Steven Jenkins was one of the many who hoped to realize his dreams. He waved back at his mother and brothers and sisters gathered on the dilapidated front porch to witness the only Jenkins to ever march off to college. The faded clapboard suitcase he carried down the dusty road weighed more that the few articles of clothing inside but he had to make a favorable impression on his fellow classmates. He had already said his goodbyes to his father the previous summer when they buried him in the family plot in the field beside the church and during those goodbyes he promised his father and himself that he would never fall over dead in the middle of a field on a hot day behind a plow. It did not matter to Steven that he was poor and had little or nothing in the way of material possessions. He had been poor all his life and never had much except the great love of a mother, which was equaled only by the strong work ethic instilled in him by his father. With those two blessings and the brains God gave him he figured he could make something of himself but not here in Eutawville, Tennessee, population … one hundred and fifty-two.

Becoming a schoolteacher had been his dream since he was a youngster, wishing to take after his favorite aunt. So late into the night under a kerosene lantern he read every book Aunt Harriet dropped by the house at the end of each term of school plus plowing through the extra textbooks she gave the family. She was a teacher over in Ridgeville and, noticing Steven's keen eye and love of the written word, encouraged him at every turn and assured him that he too could become a teacher if he applied himself.

At Peabody State Teachers College he did just that. He graduated with honors and with the love of his life, Peggy Kramer, whom he met his freshman year. They married that fall and encouraged by Peggy's dogged determination Steven gave up his plans to teach school and decided to study pre-med at the university in Knoxville. He thought why not? I can always go into teaching if this doesn't work out. He hit upon his true calling throwing his entire being into his studies. He never imagined learning could be such a wonderful experience. The only thing he loved more than going to classes was his wife and their son, Steven, Jr.

Upon completion of his residency at Baker Hospital in Knoxville, Tennessee in 1928, he decided to set up a general family practice in the small rural town of Beniston, Georgia, a thriving, little community where cotton was king and the potential for growth was unlimited. His overhead was low, the clientele was steady, and there was little or no competition. As a matter of fact, he was the only doctor in the county seat. His predecessor, a well- beloved aging country doctor, had passed away the year before while making a house call. The people of Beniston welcomed the young Dr. Jenkins and his now growing family with open arms and the feeling was mutual.

He savored the thought of making a nice living while helping the sick in the county, and not having to live under the pressure of a big hospital atmosphere had he elected to take up one of several offers to work in a place like Knoxville's General Hospital or Atlanta Memorial. Also, he could care for his patients on a more personal level foreign to the larger hospitals whose main attention and bottom line, as far as he was concerned, was the almighty dollar … "assembly line medication" is what he called it. His pre-Depression decision proved wise, if not downright prophetic, as he weathered the hard times the nation suffered with minimal discomfort yet steadily building his business during the years 1929- 40.

Marriage agreed with Steven and Peggy as the family grew to three children with Peggy assuming the unenviable role of mother, wife, housewife, civic volunteer, and supporter of her husband's career by accompanying him to the thousands of luncheons and seminars over the years. They were a solid couple known throughout the community for being dependable and ready to lend a helping hand.

While the larger cities, like Atlanta and Augusta, were learning to cope with the post- WWII building boom, Beniston moved along slowly but steadily like the tortoise in the race with the hare, with no delusions of grandeur, and so did Steven's medical practice. By 1958 a healthy but aging Steven decided to take in a partner to help take some of the load off and, he thought, in fairness to his many clients it was the right thing to do. He chose a young doctor who wanted to practice in a mid-size town, which Beniston had grown into, and who planned to stay for the long run. Two more years he told himself and he could turn over the business to his partner knowing it would be in good hands and then he could begin to take up fishing and enjoying the many surrounding lakes that dotted the Beniston area. Maybe even take a golf lesson or two? Travel some? In reality, however, he knew he would probably spend the majority of his time with his grandchildren whom he adored, which would be a whole lot more rewarding than catching a fish. But it would be nice to have such options.

Sometimes in life, circumstances, or fate, or as some might call it the luck-of -the -draw, can be as cruel and unforgiving as a force ever imagined by man and as uncontrollable as a nightmare. And Steven Jenkins was about to become personally entangled in a living nightmare and facing the age-old question, "Why do bad things happen to good people?"

Peggy became ill. The symptoms in the beginning were occasional dizzy spells but they were spaced far enough apart that they were not considered serious. Peggy, being the trooper that she was, wrote them off to improper diet and old age … maybe a little vertigo … and often did not even bother telling Steven about them. Rather than complain she would just go lie down for a while, rest, and when it passed, go about her business. But then she fainted … and fainted again … and again.

Steven insisted and Peggy agreed to some tests. After viewing the results of the blood work, Steven said a few prayers and without alarming Peggy called a friend in Atlanta, a heart specialist, and set up an appointment for his wife.

The treatment at Atlanta Memorial was thorough and professional but the diagnosis was deadly. The heart specialist broke the dreadful news to Steven as gently and truthfully as possible. Peggy's heart had simply worn out and barring a miracle her time was limited to maybe a year, maybe less. He was told to try and make her as comfortable as possible as the energy and eventually life itself would slowly be sapped out of her.

Only through sheer determination and the help of his children did Steven endure the next six months caring for Peggy who had gradually weakened by now to needing around- the-clock assistance. Tending to her wasn't the hard part because he loved her and felt duty-bound to do all he could for her just as she would have done for him were the roles reversed. The hard part was watching her waste away on a daily basis and knowing the pain and anguish she must have been going through.

And unbelievably, the worst was yet to come.

Steven was at work. It was a Monday morning, he recalled, because the mother had been frantic from the moment she arrived in his office telling the nurse over and over that her little girl's fever hadn't let up since Friday night and she wanted to see the doctor immediately. The two year old had a slight fever, a headache, and some stiffness in her neck. It was the flu season and with no history of blood or intestinal disorders in the family there was no reason either medical or otherwise for alarm. Steven had treated little Suzanne since she was a baby so his diagnosis of the flu was an experienced evaluation and with a healthy dose of penicillin, aspirin, fluids and rest, he felt she would be just fine. And "yes" he would do a follow-up call to make sure she was alright.

His office records proved that Mrs. Martin, his receptionist, made a follow up call that Wednesday but there was no answer and two other calls that day went unanswered. The penicillin prescribed by Steven could do little for Suzanne's condition and by Friday she was dead. Steven was absolutely devastated. He grieved, prayed, cried, and then asked questions. How could this possibly happen? That child was basically healthy except for a bout of flu. He treated her not ten days ago. How … how? And what could have possibly killed her?

Steven's reputation in the community was solid as a person and a doctor but things within Baby Suzanne's family were very different. Her father, a Cornell graduate, had met his future wife in college and upon his graduation from Law School and subsequent marriage they moved south to his wife's home state. His visions of taking over this small town with his mighty legal expertise and building himself an empire had not worked out. He was struggling to pay his monthly bills and it never dawned on him that his brash, Yankee disposition had anything to do with his struggles as a lawyer. To the people in Clarke County it had everything to do with whom they chose to do their legal work. He saw an opportunity and jumped on it but not without an argument from his wife who was more understanding of the ways of a small town and personally did not hold anything against Dr. Jenkins. Money would never bring back Suzanne and by suing Dr. Jenkins they could only ruin another life. A concerted effort at persuasion tempered with mild threats swayed his wife regretfully enough to swing the tide of battle in his favor. They sued Steven claiming gross negligence in a wrongful death suit that if successful meant the ruin of Dr. Steven Jenkins' medical career, not only in Georgia but nationwide, and personally it meant the ruination of him as a man.

The trial of Dr. Steven Jenkins, labeled the "Baby Suzanne Case" by the media, was to take place in the county seat in Athens, Georgia and so much media attention had been focused on the plaintiff's grieving and the painful suffering endured by Baby Suzanne, Steven's attorney wondered if they could get a fair shake anywhere in the state? However, the burden of proof lay with the prosecution, which could prove to be a daunting task seeing that no one, not even Steven himself, knew the cause of death … at least, not presently.

In his own defense and against the advice of his attorney Steven took the stand at the trial thinking, *What do I have to lose?* He sincerely believed that his original diagnosis was correct and reasonable according to the standards of law and the information he had to rely upon when making his diagnosis. From a legal standpoint the issue was: if Baby

Suzanne did not die from the flu then what did she die from? And if she died from something other than the flu then why wasn't she diagnosed with that particular ailment and treated for it accordingly?

Steven Jenkins' only hope was that the poor child died from the flu and he would be exonerated and found not guilty of negligence.

The prosecution was ahead of Steven and his well-intended attorney who in truth was relying on the mercy of the jury, which he felt was Steven's best chance, during which time the prosecution petitioned the court for the exhumation of the body in order to run more in-depth tests. The court allowed it. Following the additional testing and results, which would certainly doom Steven, his attorney fought bitterly the admittance of them as evidence but in the end Steven's case and life came tumbling down.

The expert witness for the prosecution concluded with reasonable certainty that Baby Suzanne died from bacterial meningitis caused by the Streptococcus pneumoniae. Meningitis symptoms include a high fever, severe headache and stiff neck and possibly a rash, nausea, vomiting and confusion. Meningitis does not cause the sore throat and coughing that accompany the fever and aches of influenza. Flu doesn't cause the stiff neck of meningitis. It was an invasive infection. The germ settles in the fluid of the spinal column and the fluid that surrounds the brain causing swelling in the brain and death. It made no difference legally that it was such a rare occurrence that only newly-discovered testing methods and expert testimony from a specialist revealed the cause of death.

Following the expert testimony and learning the cause of death, Steven sat frozen, staring into space looking back on his career remembering the day he left for Peabody State, the part-time jobs to support himself, the endless hours of studying, the sacrifices to build a clientele … and Peggy. Oh God, Oh God. What's happening?

He was levitating through the courtroom looking down on a hapless poor creature named Steven Jenkins sitting with his head lying on a table staring up at himself. Their eyes met and he heard a voice from deep inside say, "It's over, Steven … it's all over."

He thought he was dying. Then the word came loud and clear shocking him back into a dreadful reality: "Guilty … guilty … g-u-i-l-t-y." It echoed off the high Georgian ceilings onto the shiny hardwood floor and up through the clasped hands over his ears into his now conscious state of total disbelief and devastation.

The disbelief was soon replaced with bitterness followed by an attempt at acceptance generated by alcohol.

Everything he had worked for was gone …down the drain. All because of a once-in-a lifetime disease that appeared in his office on his call day resulting in the death of a child he thought had the flu. What were the odds? How could this possibly happen? Not in a million years

… a million years.

I didn't do anything wrong ... nothing, Steven thought. *Why should I have to lose everything? It's not one damn bit fair. All I did was ... the flu ... she had the flu. Damn it, damn it. And now my life is ruined for what? Doing my best? And poor Suzanne ...what did she ever do to deserve such a cruel fate?*

And when the reality of losing everything set in, he sought the help of a friend. His faithful friend and companion who was always there for him, never disputing his logic or offering unkind advice. No, the bottle never talked back. For a while it held all the answers, but like the liquid crutch that it was it soon ran dry and Steven had to make some really hard choices. It seemed as though all his options had vanished into thin air and he didn't know where or to whom to turn. He was lost like so many who have been dealt not one but two impossible hands in a row. He briefly considered using drugs. Maybe a slow death on drugs. Perhaps heroin? Certainly cowardly, but final.

Working in the medical profession was questionable at best but he gave it a try sending out resume after resume all over the country … yet it seemed that everyone had heard or read about the celebrated "Baby Suzanne Case" and recognized the name of Dr. Steven Jenkins. None dared hire him.

One of his closest friends advised him that if he ever wanted to practice medicine again he should consider moving to Europe. There were other fields of work he could keep in mind; however, his age and his desire to practice only medicine were obstacles that couldn't be overlooked and limited him severely.

Caring for his wife now became more of a burden only fueling the misery and pressure that began to close in on him. Recently he had words with Peggy, strong words, which later he regretted. He felt trapped and when the finances began to dwindle he knew *something*, God knows what, had to be done. He needed to get away, a respite, anywhere for a short time. A place where he could find some peace of mind and could think about what to do. His friend who had suggested moving to Europe came up with a better idea and recommended a former vacation spot that would be perfect for Steven. Small, peaceful, beautiful, with a nice beach, Sullivans Island, S.C.

"Go Steven, you'll love it and you need it. Stick around here much longer and we'll have to start taking care of you. Marianne and I will take care of Peggy and the house. Please, for your sanity, just go, OK?"

"Are you sure? I don't want to be a burden on anyone."

"Yeah, go ahead. And there are lots of nice Irish folks there. You'll feel right at home."

And so he went.

His friend had been absolutely right. The people on the Island were friendly and helpful like the good folks back in Beniston, offering him an unsolicited history of the Island and inviting him to several crab cracks. He learned quickly that if he ever needed information of any kind the place to hang out was the Post Office where the "talkers" met and dispensed data at an alarming rate.

The beach was a Godsend, a lovely clean stretch of sand and clear ocean water and not nearly as crowded, except on the weekends, as he envisioned it would be. Early morning and late evening walks proved to be the most settling and fruitful. At least he could think without distraction and he was beginning to piece together somewhat of a plan of action in hopes of dragging himself out of this pit of despair.

It was during this recuperative period when he met her, during one of his solitary beach walks. She was accompanied by two teen-age girls … her daughters, he presumed, from the interaction he witnessed. What attracted him was the manner in which she carried herself. It was somewhere between the elegant gait of a queen and the fearless strut of a runway model. Confidence. She brimmed with confidence. It was displayed by her youthful exuberance as she talked, laughed, teased and played with her children at the rocks on the beach, Steven's normal turning around point after his walk from the cottage.

He risked a "hello." Her response wasn't overwhelming. It was adequate, maybe a little guarded? *Motherly instinct*, he thought. *But hey, I'm a total stranger*.

Enjoyable small talk aimed at the weather, Island life, and raising children, revealed an open and seemingly sincere woman but something was troubling her. He could sense it.

Steven's attention was with her but his gaze was on the ocean. *What a pleasant woman and pretty too. Peggy ... a job ... the trial.*

"Are you O.K?" She couldn't help but notice the turn in the conversation. "You looked so worried there for a second."

"Yeah, I'm fine … just daydreaming. Got a lot on my mind."

"Do you live here or just visiting?" she asked

"Just visiting. My first time here and I love it. The beach and people and everything … so nice and peaceful. I assume you live here?"

"Yeah, I've lived here about ten years. My husband's family is from here. I'm an adopted Islander, originally from Florida. Where you from?"

"Ben … ah … Atlanta. Actually a small town outside Atlanta no one's ever heard of so I just tell everyone Atlanta."

"Know what you mean. When I'm out of town and I tell people I'm from Sullivans Island they say, "Where?" so I tell them Charleston and they go, "Oh I know where that is. I bet if I asked them to tell me where it is they wouldn't have a clue." She smiled and gave a small chuckle, which Steven took notice of.

He decided he didn't want to overdo his stay and the girls had been giving him the wary eye. "Well, it's been nice talking to you and thank you for being so nice to a stranger." He moved away a few feet.

"Oh think nothing of it. You're quite welcome and don't consider yourself a stranger anymore."

"Why thank you. Do you come to the beach often?" he asked beginning to walk away.

"Yeah, *lately* pretty much."

There it was again: the inflection in her tone, something *was* bothering her. *God, I hope it's not me,* he thought?

"Maybe I'll see you again and, oh goodness, forgive my manners." He practically blushed. " I haven't properly introduced myself: My name is Steven Jenkins."

"Well, Steven Jenkins, nice to meet you but there is no need to be so formal even though I do appreciate a person of manners. You're on Sullivans Island now. My name is Mary Helen ... Mary Helen Poe," she said with a big smile. Their eyes locked in concert for a long second, a silent gaze that spoke volumes.

"M-o-m, it's getting late, we gotta go," the girls sang in unison."M-o-m ..."

Somewhat startled Mary Helen flinched. "OK, OK ... I'm coming." She turned back to Steven and said, "Gotta run. Enjoyed talking to you. Enjoy your stay."

They waved goodbyes. Both hoped to meet again soon.

On his walk back to the cottage he couldn't get out of his head the way she said "*my husband*." Was it ingratitude? Remorse? Bitterness? *A-a-a-h ... I'm just wishing.*

All that evening Steven thought about her. He tried reading and watching TV but her face and her wonderful smile kept interrupting his thoughts. The gentle soothing tone of her voice, the way she moved and the cute curl of her upper lip, which gave her a permanent pose of confidence. Her eyes sparkled reflecting the green-blue waters of the Atlantic. But more impressive was the genuine interest she took in him. He hoped for two things: that she would be at the beach tomorrow and the other was that he was right about her sincerity.

"I don't care how you feel, Thomas." Mary Helen was cleaning up after breakfast and was emphatic about getting out of the house. "I'm going for a walk on the beach and you can take the girls to Mt. Pleasant. Just because you're depressed and all bummed out doesn't mean the rest of the family has to feel that way. Do you understand?"

Thomas rolled his eyes and said softly, "Go ahead, I'll take the girls."

About the time Mary Helen was making her way to the beach, Steven left the cottage with high hopes. He took the foot path directly to the beach, said a little prayer that she would be there, and began to walk. When he rounded the bend at Station 15, he strained to make out the figures casually strolling around the rocks and when he saw that walk, only Mary Helen's, he had to hold himself back from bursting into a full run. *Calm down,* he told himself, *you just met her yesterday.*

He gave a wave and unconsciously quickened his pace. Mary Helen reciprocated with a big wave and a friendly smile from afar and unconsciously began walking toward Steven. His steady pace matched that of his heartbeat. It wasn't love at first night. More like love at second sight. And he was so relieved to know that she felt something too, probably not as deep as his feelings, but there were feelings there, he could tell.

They walked to the Breach Inlet and back, about four miles, taking their time. Both wanted it to last. She talked of her failing marriage. He talked of his failed business. They talked about family, ambitions, plans and the desire to get from under their respective lifestyles. It was a common thread, which would soon weave a pattern of deadly deceit.

He admired her attitude, which brimmed with confidence. It was like she was stuck in a deep hole but rather than complaining about it she was trying to figure a way out and just from the little he knew of her, he figured she would find a way out. That attitude made such an impression on Steven and he thought that if he had adopted that approach right after the trial maybe he would be closer to a lot more answers than he currently was. He had been wallowing in self-pity far too long and was finally realizing it. He attributed his change in mood to Mary Helen. What a breath of fresh air she was!

Mary Helen was taken by Steven's maturity and straightforwardness. *No baloney with this guy ... he's to the point. And for a man his age he's in good shape. And handsome too. Who knows? His wife could pass away any day now and the door would be open.*

The affair began that day with an innocent handshake and a small quick hug as they parted. That singular touch set it off for him and her too.

"I'll see you in two weeks," he said. "Take care of yourself."

"That'll be great. You take care too and have a safe trip."

The affair took on serious overtones in the following months. At first they met on the beach, taking long walks providing a sounding board for each other. Holding hands led to an embrace, a kiss, and then the inevitable.

Steven's trips to the Island became more frequent as the romance blossomed. At home Peggy was slowly sliding downhill, now barely able to get out of bed. It was a nightmare that he prayed for both of them to awaken from soon.

It was following an afternoon of complete togetherness with Mary Helen when the innocent pillow talk led to a possible solution to all his problems. It was then that he learned of Thomas Poe's passion for collecting coins and his ownership of "The Standing Liberty" quarter collection. *What a coincidence. Or was it? Here I meet my soul mate and her soon to be ex-husband holds the final piece of the puzzle.*

Steven gave it a lot of thought and he planned and then he planned again and again until he hit on the perfect scheme: Peggy and he would move to Sullivans Island and Mary Helen would move to Florida. And he would take on a new identity … he would become Dr. Steven Jenkins, a retired heart specialist formerly of Atlanta Memorial Hospital.

41
PROGRESS

Chief Perry licked the last fragments of sugar from his fingertips, dropped his feet

from the desk, let go a loud belch, and fingered the radio handle.

"Lumus, what's your10-20? He waited. "Lumus, come in … where are you?" No answer. "Lumus!" he yelled into the microphone, "what's your 20?"

Lumus gently placed his hand on the Chief's shoulder and said, "Right here Chief."

Chief Perry jumped noticeably. "Dag gone you! You scared the hell outta me. What are you doing here anyway?"

"Stayed all night. I'm still trying to piece this Poe thing together. Just about time it starts making sense it falls apart." Lumus glanced at the empty doughnut box on the desk. "Save me one by any chance?"

Chief shrugged his shoulders.

"I really think I need to go see Dr. Jenkins, our coin collector and this time I want you to go with me. Let's make this visit *real* special."

"H-u-m-m …in other words you wanna double team him? Y-e-a-h … that sounds like a good idea. Put a little squeeze on him. When do you wanna go?"

"How about Saturday morning? That'll give me time to get my thoughts together and take care of some of this paperwork around here. It's starting to look like "Junk Mountain" in here. And you know Chief, tomorrow is the second Friday of the month."

"Yeah, yeah, yeah … your day off. I haven't forgotten. What ya gonna do?"

"Going sailing. I'm taking Caroline and we're gonna make a run up the Ashley, dock at the Harbor Restaurant, sit back and have a few cold ones and think of my favorite Chief." He grinned at the Chief. "If you need me today I'll be on patrol and then over at the marina for a while messing with the boat."

"All right, just keep your radio on, please. I'll call if I need ya."

"Sure thing. I'm gonna stop by Grannie's first, seeing that *someone* ate all the doughnuts … *again.*

"Lumus, you know, you ought to feel sorry for an old man like me whose only real pleasure in life is eating doughnuts," said the grinning Chief. "That's about the only enjoyment I have left."

Lumus thought for a second that there might be some truth to what the Chief said. "OK, you're forgiven this time," he replied. "See ya later."

"Yeah, enjoy yourself. I'll hold down the fort."

That afternoon Chief Perry was awakened from his catnap by a call from the Tennessee Law Enforcement Criminal Division in Knoxville.

"Would you repeat that, please." The Chief grabbed for a pad and scribbled down what he heard as proof that he wasn't dreaming. "Now you're sure … OK … and thank you very much."

He paused for a second to reflect.

"MAN-OH-MAN! Great jumping grandmas. We done hit the jackpot!"

He quickly grabbed the radio handle practically screaming, "Lumus, this is the Chief. Get yourself to the station on the double. You hear me. To the station on the double. Some good news!"

Lumus wasted no time swinging around on the causeway.

"10-4, Chief!" When the Chief said "on the double" he meant "on the double." *Oh Lord, I hope it's something good about the case?* Lumus thought as he roared to a stop, leaped from the Jeep, and ran for the office.

"What's the good news, Chief? Did my big raise finally come through?"

The Chief smiled appreciating Lumus' attempt at humor considering the stress Lumus had put on himself lately. "Sit down. Relax and listen up. It just might be our only and last break in this case."

Lumus slid a chair out from under the desk, turned it around and sat down so that his elbows were resting on the back of the chair and looked at the Chief with his full attention.

"A Lieutenant Kerr called. He's the guy you sent the request to two weeks ago in Knoxville and guess who happens to own an antique .45 caliber pistol?"

"Dr. Steven Jenkins," Lumus blurted out. "Dr. Steven Jenkins." He jumped out of his chair and slapped his hands together.

"How'd you know?" A somewhat disappointed Chief asked. He had wanted to break the big news.

"Well, I wasn't certain until you asked me but I knew that he was a collector since he had a coin collection. Then I thought, well, maybe he collects guns too being the type of person who collects things, a collector. But I didn't have any proof or anything to go on so it was just a lucky guess. What exactly did Kerr say?"

"Well, it seems that the young Dr. Jenkins, or should I say Mr.

Jenkins, did his residency in Knoxville from 1928-1931 and he purchased an Army surplus .45 and in Tennessee you have to register any gun bought there. Kerr said that he was just lucky and happened to stumble onto it because he was actually working on another case."

"Chief, that's great but …"

The Chief interrupted Lumus, "But where does that leave us, right?"

"Yeah, Chief you're worse than my Momma about reading my mind." He paused a second. "We have the slug and know that Jenkins bought a .45 a long time ago. Not having his gun to run a ballistic check doesn't put us any closer to him, not one bit closer. Right?"

"Bingo, Lumus. We have to get closer to Dr. Jenkins and that's just what we're gonna do starting right now."

"But …"

"Forget the sailing tomorrow, you hear me! I got a feeling we're gonna be real busy."

"What's the plan?"

"The plan? We're going to visit Dr.Jenkins, right now. That's what the plan is. Come on, I'll fill you in on the way over."

As much fun as Bubba 'n me had growing up on the Island we went through growing pains just like any other kids our age. Pain was inevitable. It went with pleasure is the way it was explained to me by Bubba. He said whenever I had pain, either physical or mental, try to imagine how good it was going to feel when the pain stopped.

I recall smashing a finger with a hammer trying to play carpenter once. "O-w-w-w! Man, that hurts. O-o-o-w-e-e." I shuck my hand violently as though the shaking would somehow magically cause the pain to disappear.

"Eah," Bubba said rather stoically because I was the one with the crushed finger, "you know how much pain you're in now, right?"

"Yeah, Einstein. I'm aware of that."

"Well, just think how good it's gonna feel when it quits hurting."

"Eah, that's great but what do I do now when it's hurting."

"You hurt … what else?"

"Where do you get all this mumble jumble from because I know you don't think it up all by yourself?"

"From the TV," he answered. "There's lots of good stuff on there."

"TV, huh? That invention is going to be the ruin of you if you don't watch out."

There was one constant pain, a real thorn in the side that we suffered from constantly. It originated from a group of teenagers on the Island who weren't old enough to have their driver's licenses and thus be off somewhere racing around or chasing after girls, doing the things teenagers are supposed to do. Their idea of fun in an attempt to rid themselves of frustration was to pick on anyone younger and weaker. They even smoked thinking that made them look cool and tough. Bubba 'n me were prime targets only because of our age and size. On occasion they drove their parent's cars using their beginner's permit racing around the Island tearing up the car if they could, trying hard to impress people. Generally, they were about three to four years older than our crew and we called them the big boys but they really were bullies. It wasn't all of them … just a select few, and they made life miserable for us younger ones. They were like snakes: you had to always be aware of where they were or you could get bitten.

Every now and then one or two of them would outfox Bubba 'n me, catch us off guard and trap us, steal our money and slap us around pretty good and then laugh at our futile efforts to fight back. We often discussed what method of punishment we would use when we grew strong enough to take them on in a fair fight.

"I'd like to punch 'em out in a big fight … a free-for-all. Those punks would be laid out just like in the Westerns on TV," Bubba said, "and I'd be standing over like John Wayne and be telling they better watch their step next time, Mister."

"Not me. I want to take 'em on one at a time and give 'em a good whipping. Maybe beat up five or six in one day. Show 'em who the boss is … Y-e-a-h."

"BA-HA-HA-HA," Bubba laughed. "What we should really do is get Sister Roberta and Sister Ann Marie to beat the hell out of them with their big sticks and then say a prayer over 'em."

"Yeah, good idea. And then we could get Sambo and Herman to help. Sambo could finish 'em off by whacking 'em up side the head with a trash can lid and then Herman could arrest 'em and lock 'em up in prison where they could make little rocks outta big rocks. That is if Herman could ever find his badge."

We both got a good laugh just thinking about it. In reality it was all pure fantasy, however, and we knew it because neither one of us had a mean bone in our body. But it sure made for some good, tough, man-talk.

Living just up the street was one of these bullies. His name was Roger Hollingsworth, tough guy. At least, he thought so. His buddies called him Holly, which he thought was neat. I told Bubba he was named after a tree and the only difference between him and a tree was that the tree had more sense. Whenever possible Bubba 'n me rode our bikes, which not only got us around the Island but was a means of avoiding and escaping the bullies who had long ago given up the immature act of riding a bike. One afternoon I had walked by myself to Junk Mountain in the Scott's yard and was going back home, when Roger surprised me and came racing across the road from his backyard and was on me in a flash. It was the usual demand. He wanted money knowing that Bubba 'n me crabbed to make money and we usually carried a few quarters with us. This wasn't the first time he had looted me but today it was going to be the last time as far as I was concerned. I quickly made up my mind that enough was enough. I was tired of it so I stood my ground telling him "No!"

He acted surprised and sneered, "Does no mean you don't have any money or you won't give me any money."

"It means I won't give you any money." If I had told him I didn't have any money he would have grabbed me and gone through my pockets so I decided if I was going to stand up to this bully it would be all or nothing. I recalled in past years when Roger and his buddies would corner Bubba 'n me, each one grabbing an ankle, turning us upside down and shaking us like rag dolls to get the change to fall out of our pockets …money I had worked hard to earn …so these guys could go buy cigarettes. No more!

O-o-o-h, I was scared all right. He was way bigger and stronger but I was a quick, wiry, ball of fire and I figured he would be overconfident in dealing with a skinny little twelve-year-old. Also in my favor was that I was fighting for a cause, something I dearly believed in and cared about and that made a big difference, in my mind at least. I figured he had to come to me and I knew from past episodes where he would go to first, my pockets. So when he made his initial thrust I quickly turned my back and hunched over pulling my arms close to my body. I was going to need them for grabbing so I made sure ol'Holly didn't pin me down. He grabbed me from behind and yelled something about giving me the money or he was going to beat me up and all that. I didn't listen and was almost smiling now because as soon as the scrap began the nerves flew away and I was relaxed and ready to go. It was just like the feeling after the first hit in a football game. And Roger made his first mistake when he grabbed me. He tried unsuccessfully to get into my pocket from the side while he held me with his other arm wrapped securely around my waist but I was bent over and jumping around enough so he couldn't get his hand in my pocket. I was squealing and squirming like a baby pig in a sack. Roger was determined too. He was hanging on desperately trying to get to the change rattling around in my pocket. We could both hear its distinct sound. Guess 'ol Roger thought he was in for a big payday? Not being able to reach in my pocket from the side, he decided to go over the top (his second and fatal mistake), and reached over my shoulder exposing his arm. Instantly I grabbed his wrist with one hand and his elbow with the other and squeezed with all my twelve-year-old might. I had the leverage and summoned all my strength for one big play and I pulled Roger onto my back and then all the way over. I flipped him just like I'd seen the wrestlers do on TV. But Roger didn't land on a soft canvas mat, uh-uh. He hit the ground hard landing on his back with a loud THUD and extremely wide eyes. And he did not jump up quickly. He laid on the ground for a few seconds, stunned both physically and mentally trying to catch his breath.

I think he was the most surprised person on Sullivans Island that day other than me. I took a couple of steps back, assumed a fighting stance with the meanest look I could conjure up, and glared at Roger. He dusted himself off, shot me a dirty look, and walked away mumbling something about I'll get you later you little twerp.

I breathed a little easier, looked up to heaven and said, "Thank you, God."

And after that encounter I never had trouble with Roger again. Never.

Bubba 'n me knew the murder case was still going on but we hadn't talked to Lumus since I gave him the piece of mail we found at the Post Office. Before we hit the beach we decided to track down Lumus and see how things were going on the case. We rode all over the Island in search of him and in avoidance of Bull Perry who earlier this week had run us off the hill for the umpteenth time.

"Why doesn't Bull Perry just come to our houses and get us or tell our parents about us being on the hill?" Bubba asked."He knows where we live."

"Eah, remember I told you once already. He could do that but it wouldn't be the same as catching us like when we were doing it. I think he wants to catch us in the act. If he went to our parents it would be like after the crime. Kinda like cheating."

"Well, isn't that what the police do. Catch the bad guys after they did something wrong?"

"Yeah, but this is different. It's kind of a game. O-o-o-h, it's hard to explain. It's not really a game, it's …" a long pause. "It's like this. If he doesn't catch us this time then maybe he can catch us next time. Does that make any sense?"

"Yeah, but he won't catch us because he's too fat."

"I know that and you know that but does Bull Perry know that?"

"I don't know *that* but I know *what*."

"What?" I asked. Bubba was confusing both of us.

"A-a-a-w, what the heck! Forget it. Let's go see how Billy is doing. It won't take but a minute."

"Uh-uh. No way," I said. "He looks terrible." I was in no rush to see Billy again. He was still on the mend after his beating from The Beast and stayed mostly in the house out of embarrassment, hoping that the crew wouldn't see his battle scars. After the other day I didn't want to see him again for a while, at least, until the bruises went away.

Bubba gave me a stern look. "Now what kind of good Christian are you, Devlin?"

"What ya mean? Just because I won't go see Billy."

"Yeah. T-h-a-t-'s right, Catbird. You know what the Bible says?"

"No what?" I replied.

"To visit the sick, that's what!"

"Yeah, that's right, Catbird! But it don't say one thing about visiting the beat up."

Bubba let out a "BA-HA-HA-HA-HA" and said, "You so funny, Devlin." He stopped his bike and said that we really should go and visit Billy. He paused, gave me a serious look and said, "After all he is our friend."

And Bubba was right. If I were laid up I'd want my friends to check on me so I gave in.

"A-l-l right then, let's go and see Billy."

We knocked on the back door and to our surprise Sammy answered. He was *never* at home unless he was outside guarding Junk Mountain.

"What are you doing here? In the house I mean?" It was Bubba who was just as mystified as me on seeing Sammy in the house.

"A-w-w-w, I'm on restriction. Been grounded."

"Oh yeah? For what?" Bubba asked as he brushed past Sammy heading towards Billy's room.

"Billy's not here if that's who you're looking for. He went to the doctor to get the stitches checked on."

"Oh, OK. What'd you get grounded for?"

"Nothing much. I was trying to help my father. Well, I was really just trying to do something nice for him after he got mad at me for painting the car pink and …"

"What'd you do, Sammy?" Bubba asked quickly. Bubba loved to hem-and-haw others but he couldn't stand for it in other people, not for a second.

"Well, it was kinda dumb and I …"(he paused)

"Durn Sammy. What'd you do?" Bubba asked rolling his eyes.

"OK, OK. I saw my Dad's beer in the refrigerator and knew he was going fishing the next morning and I know he likes cold beer so to make sure they were good and cold for him I put 'em in the freezer."

"How many was it?"I asked.

"The whole case," Sammy answered looking down, "all twenty-four."

Bubba grinned and remarked, "I'll bet they were nice and cold the next morning, huh?"

"Oh yeah, they were cold all right. Cold enough for a two day restriction. Took me almost an hour to clean up the mess in the freezer".

Bubba asked, "What happened to 'em?" He was smirking like he already knew the answer.

"They busted open. They like exploded and some of the stuff dripped down into the refrigerator and got all over everything, then my Mom got

mad. I won't do that again."
I just shook my head from side to side. "Was your Dad real mad? Never mind, don't answer that."

"Well, sorry to hear about your restriction and grounding and all and tell Billy we came by, OK?"

"All right. I'll tell him y'all came by."

See ya later." It was Bubba talking and edging toward the door ahead of me. I knew what was on his mind but I let him go. I pretended I was talking to Sammy giving Bubba some free time.

Once in the yard Bubba ran quickly to his bike, yelled that we race to Burton's and the loser buys the Cokes. I calmly picked up my bike, got on and rode off to Burton's, way ahead of Bubba who lost precious time putting the chain back on his bike that I had slipped off just before going into the Scott's house.

It was about the same time Chief Perry was getting his good news from Tennessee that Steven Jenkins made his phone call. He had given it a lot of serious thought and decided it was the right thing to do even though he and Mary Helen had agreed to no phone contact.

"Hello, Mary Helen. How are you?"

"Fine, just fine. You OK?" Before he could reply. "Steven, you know you're not supposed to be calling me."

"I know, I know. That's why this will be short, real short. Look, something's come up on this end and there's going to be a change in plans. We'll be leaving sooner than we expected."

"How much sooner?"

"We have to leave in two days. Whoa, hold on before you get all worked up. I realize it's short notice but believe me something serious has come up. This cop on the Island has been snooping around and acting real suspicious so I'm not going to take any chances. We've come too far to mess up now. Just be ready to leave Saturday afternoon. I'll explain everything in detail when I see you. I love you and miss you. I have to go, OK?"

"OK, I love you too. Please be careful and I'll be ready. Goodbye."

Steven Jenkins was going through his mental checklist now that plans had been finalized: pack light, go to bank and close out accounts, food for "Dodger" for the trip, gas up the car and don't forget the gun collection.

"Ha," he said to himself. "Guess Mr. Nance will hit the overhead when he doesn't collect the rent from me this month. Maybe I'll leave him a bad check on the dining room table. N-a-a-w, better not. The old man might have a heart attack."

Rather than feeling jumpy or nervous Steven felt calm, almost serene, surprising even himself, but the careful planning had paid off and with the locals on the case he had guessed correctly that they wouldn't be able to do much with a case like this. They didn't have the manpower or the mental power, as far he was concerned. His only real regret was that Thomas had to die. However, the only consolation was from what Mary Helen had told him about Thomas' deteriorating condition … maybe he was better off dead? Basically, he kept telling himself, it was Thomas dying or him living as a dead man. And when he met Mary Helen, Thomas' murder seemed totally justified because now he had a reason to live. He expected things to work out, but one thing he certainly did not expect was a visit from Lumus and the Chief.

He heard "Dodger" bark and then he heard the crunching oyster shells in the drive. He was surprised but didn't show it when he saw the patrol car roll to a stop.

Be nice and keep the conversation to a minimum. Find out what they want.

"Hello, gentlemen." He greeted Lumus and the Chief as they stepped out of the car. "How are you?"

"Fine," the Chief said, "Just fine. Hope we're not disturbing you in anyway? Mind if we come in for a few minutes?"

"No problem, come on in. I don't believe we've met. I'm Dr. Steven Jenkins," extending a hand to the Chief.

"William Perry, nice to meet you. All the locals call me Bull Perry. Maybe that sounds more familiar to you?"

"No", he lied. *Everyone knew Bull Perry. Up close he does look like a bull.* "Can't say that I've heard that one."

"You already know my number one and only assistant Lumus … Lumus Mc Farland." The Chief chuckled turning towards Lumus.

Steven was thinking, *Yeah Chief, use the old humor 'em a little trick to soften 'em up and then stick it to 'em. Who do these clowns think they're dealing with?*

"Yes," Steven said pleasantly, "patrolman Mc Farland was here just a couple of days ago."

Lumus nodded a "hello." Silence. A long pause.

"Oh, pardon my manners. Y'all come on in."

"Thanks," the Chief said, "don't mind if we do." Lumus and the Chief walked onto the porch with darting eyes looking for anything out of place.

Steven quickly took a seat in the same rocker he did two days earlier. "Sit down, sit down," he half ordered, "I assume you're here concerning your investigation in the death of Mr. … uh? What's his name?"

"Mr. Poe," said Lumus, "Mr. Thomas Poe."

"Yeah, poor Mr. Poe. What a shame."

"Dr. Jenkins", the Chief said, "I'll get right to the point about why we're here. Save you and me a whole lot of time. We would like to look around inside your house for a few minutes … with your permission, of course."

Steven responded calmly, "Look around in the house. What do you mean?"

"Just that," the Chief shot back, "look around in your house."

"Could you be more specific? I mean am I a suspect? Are you looking for something in particular or what?"

"Well, in a way you are a suspect. About all I can tell you is that new light has been shed on the case and we would like to nose around inside."

"Suspect or not I have my rights and I'm not so sure I want two strangers, even if you are the police, nosing around in my house."

"Yeah, that's correct and believe me, we are aware of your rights, Dr. Jenkins." The Chief decided to turn the screw a little tighter. "But we also have rights and if forced to will exercise the proper legal procedures to the fullest."

Lumus stood back not saying a word. He was carefully noting Steven's reaction.

Steven was irritated with this small town cop's tone and attitude. He decided to play his trump card.

"Chief Perry, you'll just have to go ahead and pursue your legal steps if you want to search my house. I don't have anything to hide, but my house is not open for a random search by anyone, not even the police. Do you understand?"

Still standing, Chief Perry placed his hat on his head, tipped the brim and said, "I understand completely. The next time we see you, which will be soon, we will come with a warrant in hand making things all legal like. Have a good day, Dr. Jenkins. Let's go, Lumus."

Steven didn't bother to get up. He sat and was planning his next move before the car left his driveway.

That evening at the station Lumus and the Chief huddled outside on a bench in the shade with a cold Coke.

"What ya think, Chief?"

"He's spooked all right. Let's hope he's spooked enough. Did you see Judge Harrison this afternoon about the warrant and all."

"Yes sir."

"And?"

"It's all taken care of. Sure hope you're right on this, Chief?"

"O-o-o-h, he's our man, all right. We'll just have to wait and see … just wait and see."

42
SURPRISE

It was Thursday. Where had the week gone? Shoot, where had the summer gone? There was only a week left before school started back and it seemed like school had just let out a few weeks ago. Just the idea of going back to school gave me a bad feeling. The thought of having to sit in a classroom all day was depressing. At school whenever I could, and without getting yelled at, I would sit and watch the birds playing in the giant oak tree just outside our classroom. I especially noticed the loud and boisterous Blue Jays calling and fussing with each other then playing a game of tag with the Mockingbirds. Sometimes I wished I were one of those birds. Free to roam with no real worries except for finding something to eat. But that wasn't really much of a problem because there was plenty of food on the school playground everyday if you could beat the greedy seagulls to it. And they didn't have to sit at a desk all day and study. Shoot, I'd rather take a whipping or even worse be put on restriction and put up with my four sisters all day than be stuck in a classroom with some Lady of Mercy on my back all day. At least on restriction I had Mollie to talk to and I could take a nap if I wanted to. There was no napping in school. Uh-uh. That was a BIG, NO-NO! I think our teachers listed sleeping in school as one of the mortal sins.

It happened one morning in Sister Roberta's English class. Jocko, who had been up half the night flounder gigging with his father, as hard as he tried, couldn't stay awake while Sister Roberta droned on about participles and adjectives. Being the keen observer of humanity that I was I sat and watched this particular drama unfold from the beginning. And by observing others at school I was learning that I didn't get into near as much trouble. Jocko's eyes would close and his head would slump, only to quickly snap back up an instant before he dozed off completely. He would force his eyes open sometimes using his finger and he would shake his head in some feeble attempt to shake away whatever it was making him want to sleep. I grinned for a second knowing he was fighting a losing battle and the end, or should I say the beginning, was coming soon, real soon. His struggle with his tired body went on for about twenty minutes and finally Jocko gave in to the demands of the Sandman, folded his arms into a pillow, gently lowered his head, and began to sleep the sleep of the dead. The crew had also been watching this scene play out and knew what was coming if he didn't wake up and sit up straight real soon. Sleeping in class was one of Sister Roberta's many pet peeves. Mike Hart did his best to awaken Jocko with a few well-intentioned pokes in the backside. Jocko merely let go a long satisfying moan as though he were getting a back rub.

Mike then threw up his hands as to say, "What do I do now?"

Mike didn't have to worry. Sister Roberta was on her way. She strutted over to Jocko's desk and stood over him with one hand on her hip and the other clutching her big ruler, the Slaying Board we called it. She put the evil eye on Jocko who was totally oblivious to anything Sister Roberta did. She stared so hard I thought she was going to burn a hole right through the unconscious Jocko who was in Never-Neverland. In a flash so quick we didn't even see her raise her hand, Sister Roberta slammed the big ruler down on Jocko's desk missing his elbow by no more than an inch. PA-YOOW! … a sound like a rifle going off. The whole class jumped like a flock of startled birds. *Man,* I *t*hought, *she sure is quick for an old lady. We sure could use her at point guard on the basketball team.*

Poor Jocko must have thought he had been shot. Awakened from a deep dream he came to life in a startle and yelled, "Oh no Ma'am. No Ma'am. No, it wasn't me, it wasn't me. I promise, it wasn't me."

"Oh yes it was!" Sister Roberta countered. "I stood right here and watched you. Right class?"

We all obediently nodded our heads.

"Oh it's you, Sister. Yes Sister. You're right … u-u-u-h … what was the question, Sister?"

"Mr. Thomas!" she yelled. "That's it for you! This is the third time this semester I've called you down for sleeping! I've told you for the last time if you want to sleep, stay at home! This is a school, not a bedroom!" She paused. "Up!" She motioned with the big ruler and Jocko prepared himself for a few licks but was completely surprised when Sister Roberta marched to the back of the room commanding Jocko to follow.

"Against the wall, Mr. Thomas."

Oh no, she's gonna get a gun and shoot him, I thought. *Naw, no way?*

The whole class was in suspense. This was a new one. We had no idea what was going on.

Bubba looked at me and formed a gun with his finger and thumb and began pulling the trigger, grimacing at the thought. I shook my head from side to side and mouthed a "NO." I paused and thought again and shrugged my shoulders. Poor Jocko looked dumbfounded. His eyes were wide open now and darting around the class searching for an answer.

"Just stand there … for the rest of the period," Sister Roberta ordered and walked briskly to the front of the room resuming the lesson. "Enough of this wasting time."

We all turned back around to learn about participles leaving Jocko standing against the back wall. I waited a couple of minutes and snuck a peek at Jocko. He gave me a big smile and a quick thumbs up. Throughout the period all the crew at some point snuck a peek at our rock-n-roll hero Jocko-Elvis. We thought for sure he wouldn't be able to stay awake and would go to sleep standing up and then fall down or slide down the wall and into more trouble. I think that's what Sister Roberta was thinking too?

Jocko eventually closed his eyes and I thought, *Uh-oh ... here it comes. He ain't gonna make it. There he goes. No, not Elvis. Oh me, my heart was sinking. Not the King of Rock-n-Roll.* But to my surprise and utter delight Jocko didn't slump to the floor or fall down. He just stood there like a statue for the remainder of the period, which was thirty minutes or more. At the end of class Sister Roberta approached Jocko who heard the rattling beads coming closer to him and slowly he opened his eyes. Sister Roberta stood with her hands on her hips, sizing up Jocko before she spoke. "Mister Thomas, I'd like to see you after school for a few minutes in my office."

"Yes Sister." Jocko smiled slightly. "After school."

"And it's not for punishment either. I want you to explain to me how you are able to sleep in a standing up position without falling down. I've never seen anything quite like it."

"Yes Sister."

The crew couldn't wait for recess so we could talk to Jocko. The unbelieving crew gathered around him demanding an explanation of how he could sleep standing up without sliding down the wall.

Cool as ever, brushing back his hair and cocking his head, Jocko smiled at us and said, "Easy. Easy, man. I wasn't asleep."

"A-a-a-w, come on, you were too. You told us this morning you had been up all night. And we saw you standing there with your eyes closed and you weren't moving." Bubba spoke for the group as we nodded our heads and affirmed what Bubba was saying with small "yeas" and "uh-huhs."

Jocko took his hand and smoothed out his wave of black hair again, checked his ducktail, and stated bluntly,"Eah, I might have looked like I was sleeping but I wasn't. I wanted to go to sleep but knew that if I dozed off I'd be in trouble again so I ..."

"You closed your eyes?" I interrupted. "How could you not go to sleep?"

"Well, I know you guys aren't going to believe this but in order to stay awake I tried praying."

Hoots and jeers rained on Jocko. Elvis praying? No way.

"Praying? Are you kidding?" Bubba shouted above the buzz, "you don't even know how to say the blessing before a meal."

Jocko held up his hands, shook his shoulders a-la Elvis and commanded,"Eah, hold it down a minute, OK." He looked over the crowd. "Let me finish. And by the way O'Toole I do *know* the prayer before you eat. Anyway, where was I? … Oh yeah, I started saying some Hail Marys just to keep awake and the next thing you know I was wide awake and had this kind of peaceful feeling, like quiet all around me. It was neat so I went ahead and said a whole Rosary. And the more I prayed the more peaceful everything was and the more awake I was. It was cool, man."

"Well, I'll be. If that ain't some story," John remarked. "I guess from now on we'll call you Father Elvis or how about Saint Jocko?" We all laughed.

"Eah, call me what you want but I didn't get into any more trouble, now did I?"

"Nope you sure didn't," Timmy said then asked, "What you gonna tell Sister Roberta after school?"

"Just what I told y'all, what else?"

Bubba looked at Jocko and asked, "Think she'll believe you?"

"Oh yeah! Sure she will."

"Yeah, and how do you know that?" John asked

"Because it's the truth and besides, those Sisters believe anything you tell 'em" and he stopped for effect, smiled and said, "if it has to do with prayer. Haven't you morons figured that out yet?"

Jocko paused looking around at the suddenly quiet group. "Well, sorry to leave you fine young gentlemen but the ladies are waiting. And Elvis here has got to go. See ya." He whipped a comb from his back pocket and ran it through his big wave of hair, then cut a seam down his ducktail in the back and strutted off, slipping the comb into his back pocket in one quick move without even looking.

That particular story about Jocko happened in the first semester of school. Recalling it now proved how fast time was going by. It seemed like it happened yesterday.

But I suppose time flies when you're having a good time. Shoot, before I knew it I'd be thirteen years old and then fifteen and twenty and …great day. I was getting old.

Bubba 'n me decided to make the best of what freedom we had left and had thought about going crabbing but decided not to. We had just about crabbed ourselves and the crabs to death. Bubba told me in a round-about way we should leave *some* crabs in the creek for other crabbers, especially for those people from Upstate who dreamed all winter about coming to the Island and catching a nice mess of crabs even if they didn't know beans about crabbing. I thought about it and he was right. The way he put it was: "Suppose you went Upstate to go hunting, like squirrels or something, and there were no squirrels left because two greedy little country fellas had shot 'em all and you hunted all day and never saw one. How would you feel, Devlin?"

He had a point but I still thought he was watching too much TV.

We had made some good money crabbing though and enjoyed the movies and the skating rink and Burton's. The beach was fun but it too was getting kind of old. The hill had been used so much there were only ruts left in place of where there was once slippery grass. And fewer of the crew was showing up at Burton's. Maybe it was losing its charm? It might be time to go back to school? Oh God. What a dreadful thought.

It was one of those lazy summer days when the birds were singing and the sound of the ocean blended perfectly with the slight breeze and blue Carolina sky. Bubba 'n me were on our bikes riding to nowhere, taking in the sights we'd seen a million times before. But somehow we always saw something different making each ride a new ride.

That was the magic of the Island … we could see one thing one day and the next day it would look entirely different … like it had disappeared and been replaced. It may have seemed like magic to us but in reality it was our natural maturation process at work. Bubba 'n mine's attitudes and perspectives were changing at an alarming rate. We just weren't aware of it. But whatever the reason it was fine with us … it made the Island an even greater wonderland. It would be many years later at the ripe old age of eighteen when my mother with her earthly insight told me, "that nothing is permanent." Looking back, and even today, that one pearl of wisdom explained so very much about life.

"Where to?" Bubba asked, hoping I had come up with some magical new place we could go to and explore.

"Let's go to the field and play some baseball. We haven't been there in a long time."

"N-a-a-w, it's too hot. I don't feel like running around."

"How about let's ride up to the Breach Inlet?"

"N-a-a-w, too far."

"How about the hill?"

"Nope, nobody there."

"Well, what *do* you want to do?" I asked running out of ideas.

"I know." Bubba said, "Let's go to the Point and mess around the old bridge for a while and then go to Burtons."

"The Point sounds OK but I tell you what. I'm getting a little tired of Burton's, especially that Tommy Wade and he's always there. That boy's getting on my nerves. He accused me of robbing his crab trap. Ain't that something?"

"Whatta ya gone crazy? *You did rob his trap."* Bubba was staring at me. "Remember? I was with you."

"What I remember is *you* robbed it, not me."

"Me? You mean us!"

"F-r-a-y-d not. I was just there in the boat. You shook the crabs out, right?"

"Yeah, but who was the lookout?"

"I was but I didn't rob it."

"OK, OK. All right," said a frustrated Bubba. "Next time Wade says something to you, send him to me. I'll take care of him."

"Why? What you gonna do?"

"I'm gonna box the hell out of him, kick him between the legs, and then run over him with my bike after I whoop him upside the head with a two-by-four."

"O-O-O-O-K then, *we* robbed the trap. Man, I don't want the boy to die. Gee whiz."

"Look out!" I yelled. Bubba sideswiped an oncoming car missing it by inches.

"Damn Yankees!" he yelled shaking his fist at the disappearing car.

"Boy, you better watch your mouth. What you been doing? Taking cussing lessons from Herman?"

"No, I heard it …"

I interrupted him, "Yeah, I know, on TV."

"Eah", Bubba asked, know the difference between a Yankee and a damn Yankee?"

I couldn't wait to hear this. "No, what?"

"A Yankee is someone who comes here, visits, and goes home. A damn Yankee is someone who comes here, visits, and stays … BA-HA-HA-HA."

"V-e-r-y funny, HA-HA," I answered in a sarcastic tone. "Guess you heard that on TV too?"

"Nope!" And he smiled. "Sambo told me that one … BA-HA-HA."

The Point was the very end of the Island, the western end closest to Charleston. The houses on the Point overlooked Charleston harbor offering spectacular views not only of the harbor but the jetties forming the harbor entrance and our southerly neighbor James Island, which was nestled in behind Fort Sumter where the first shots of The Civil War were fired. Most memorable were the sunsets in the winter over Charleston displaying a sky so streaked in orange and blues it was almost spiritual in its effect.

A bridge with trolley rails at one time connected the Island to Mt. Pleasant crossing the Intracoastal Waterway at the Point. When the new Ben Sawyer Bridge was built around 1930, connecting the Island and Mt. Pleasant to allow the passage of the taller vessels, a section of the old bridge across the Intracoastal Waterway was torn down. Right where the old bridge used to connect to the Island was now the boat landing and a favorite fishing spot for the locals who usually landed a few croaker or spot in the summer and maybe a trout or two in the winter. The tide was low so Bubba 'n me parked our bikes and like a couple of pack rats roamed over the oyster laden rocks looking for abandoned fishing rigs that had gotten hung up in the rocks and then were cut loose by a frustrated fishermen. They would fish on high tide and getting hung up in the rocks was a constant source of irritation. It had been years since we last purchased rigs from the store and today we were lucky finding about five nice riggings each. We checked out the fiddler population for future reference, caught three nice Jimmys with only a stick and threw 'em back, and then talked with Mr. Rowland, one of our favorite old Islanders. He was the unofficial resident-in-house keeper-of-the-boat-anding and an expert fisherman.

"Mr. Rowland," I asked, "where are the flounder biting?"

Mr. Rowland gave me the look, rolled his eyes and said rather distinctly, "Now how many times do I have to tell you boys that I'm not gonna tell you where the fish are biting."

"A-a-a-w, come on, Mr. Rowland" Bubba pleaded, "p-l-e-a-s-e."

"If I told you two, the whole Island would know within an hour and then I wouldn't have anywhere to catch fish. And especially that Norman Keenan. That old buzzard don't miss a thing."

"We promise, Scout's honor," we said even though we weren't scouts, "we won't tell anyone." It was a last-ditch effort at getting fishing information from the most tight lipped man on earth. "We promise. Right, Bubba?"

Bubba was nodding his head and hoping for a hint or even a clue as to the whereabouts of one of Mr. Rowland's favorite spots.

He grinned, shook his head and told us, "Let me tell you two boys something right now and I want y'all to listen real close …OK." He paused and stared upward as though divine inspiration was about to descend upon him. "My ex-wife was the last person I told where a good fishing spot was and she had promised on her mother's grave she wouldn't tell a soul and you know what? She blabbed it all over the Island that same day."

Bubba asked jokingly, "Is that why you divorced her?"

Mr. Rowland smiled and said, "T-h-a-t-'s right, Catbird" and then laughed.

We laughed too and waved goodbye as we headed to the rocks at Station 20, hoping the crew would be there. At least, that's where I thought we were going.

"Let's go to Burtons," Bubba suggested. "Get something to drink."

"No man, it's a good day for the beach and we only have a week left. Don't you think the crew will be at the rocks?"

"I don't know." Bubba shrugged, not showing much interest in the rocks.

"To the rocks then?" I asked.

"A-a-a-w, let's go to Burton's."

"Tell you what. You go to Burton's if you want to. I'm going to the rocks, OK?"

"All right, all right, OK. To the rocks, to the rocks," Bubba pedaled ahead, looked back and yelled, "Race ya to the church. Loser buys the cokes!"

Some of the crew were at the rocks diving off the board, some were bouncing on the inner tube and a few were swimming in the ocean, all having a good time. It might not have been a tight-knit group but they sure knew how to have a good time laughing and joking and cutting fool all the time just like at school. A quick survey showed no Tommy Wade and I felt relief because I detected a hint of truth in Bubba's earlier threats about what he would like to do to Tommy. Bubba wasn't that big or overly strong but I wouldn't want him jumping on me. He'd be like one of those little terrier dogs. Once they latched onto you, you weren't getting rid of 'em anytime soon.

I looked around and there sat poor, still beat-to hell-Billy Scott on a beach towel watching the action and wanting desperately to jump off the dune onto the big tube but had been advised by his family doctor not to strain himself because of dizziness he was still experiencing. And the stitches from the beating by The Beast were still in place.

Eventually *all* the boys made their way to the inner tube when the stacked girls from Moultrie School decided to do some trampolining. Up and down they went and so did the eyes of the crew following their flopping breasts. This was an activity the boys never got tired of, watching the girls bouncing up and down on that silly inner tube. I guess we were in the early stages of girl watching and didn't realize just how addictive it would become! This particular group of girls was from Mt. Pleasant and attended the local public school there, and had been coming to the rocks the last few weeks in larger numbers. We were fast becoming fans of theirs as they flew through the air. We had hopes of becoming much friendlier. And, as I glanced around. I noticed more and more boys showing up too. Bubba thought the girls wanted some good-looking boys to talk to, like us, because the boys in Mt. Pleasant were kind of "fruity" and ugly. At least, that's what he told me and I believed him. Shucks, we didn't care as long as the girls kept coming and kept bouncing on the tube. And the amazing thing was that they got along fine with the girls in our group, never arguing or complaining or causing trouble like the boys in the crew had been doing lately. That wonderful experience of life would come later in high school when we got our drivers' licenses and started dating and the backstabbing and petty jealousies developed.

We were at that wonderful age of innocence and didn't know it. And admittingly we boys might not have known our bee-hinds from third base when it came to the opposite sex but we sure were enjoying the view. Like the old saying goes, "Just because a dog barks at the tire doesn't mean he wants to drive the car."

Checking things out I looked toward the ocean and there he was appearing out of the surf like a walking whale. It was Tiny Mulhaven, all three hundred and twenty pounds and in a bathing suit. What a sight. It was hard to believe but since school let out for the summer Tiny had put on weight, especially in his belly region, which bulged out so far you could arrange a dinner setting for four easily on it. And when he walked he giggled like a bowl of Jell-O.

Most of us felt sorry for Tiny because of his weight condition except for Bubba who could find the brightest spot in the darkest cloud.

"Shoot, Tiny might be fat but look at all the food he gets to eat. Ain't nothing wrong with that." However, Tiny did have one advantage over us in that he was cross eyed and when he had to deal with Sister Mary Joseph, the cross eyed nun, they saw things eye to eye.

Tiny, however, at the moment, was in our doghouse for two reasons: We had not forgotten, nor would we ever, that horrendous expulsion of gas that he let go the last day of school. The crew had gathered and held court and had ruled that Tiny was in violation of the International Rules Governing Cruel and Unjust Punishment and Excessive Farting. He was mostly forgiven that infraction because it indirectly led to the early dismissal of school, but the other screw up was … well, he was banned from the new diving plank we had jammed into the rocks, which extended out over the deep gully. Tiny had broken our previous board like a matchstick, leaving us a wonderful, natural swimming pool but with no diving board. He accepted his banishment in a manly manner and didn't complain or pout. As a matter of fact, Tiny was a man of *few* words and *many* pounds. He waddled toward the inner tube to take in the views … I thought.

After ogling the girls for a few minutes, like the rest of us, Tiny made his way to the base of the sand dune, stared upward contemplating the situation, and decided he was going up the sand dune and join in the fun. Most of us scooted up that dune like a squirrel. Not Tiny. He lumbered with all his might up the hill like a baby elephant. Bubba remarked that by the time Tiny got to the top and came back down, he would have to go home. It would be time for lunch. I really thought he was just going to climb the hill and look around … no way would he try to jump on the tube, no way! No one else gave it a second thought that Tiny would jump on the tube, or they would have cleared the area. But when I saw him close one eye and stare down at the tube, I knew what was coming. Janice and Sallie, the female version of Mutt and Jeff, were sitting on one side of the tube chitchatting and flirting with the boys, as usual. Janice was tall and thin, the yakker. Sallie was short and quiet, the mousy type. They were too busy smiling here and there and waving at any boy who would look their way to notice the huge Tiny looming ominously above them.

Tiny on top of the hill, momentarily blocking out the sun, positioned himself on the edge, peered over and was cautiously calculating the angle of descent, while trying to build up enough courage for the leap of his life. He would close one eye, look, open the other eye while closing the other to get another look until he was satisfied he could hit the tube. Then Tiny leaped, more of a step, his leap being about three inches high but enough for him to begin his downward flight toward the tube and the unsuspecting victims below. Someone saw Tiny jump and screamed a warning as though some celestial body were falling from the sky but it only took a second or two for Tiny to hit the tube. His landing was perfect; his tonnage hit squarely on the tube with maximum effect, almost flattening the giant tube. The impact didn't bounce Tiny very far. Gravity prevented that. He kind of flattened out and rolled to the side lying on his back in the sand with a big smile on his face. But Janice and Sallie were suddenly launched like they were shot out of a cannon. WHOOM … Straight up and they were screaming! Everyone parted at the sound of Tiny's impact, looked up, and to their amazement saw two screaming, flying girls whose eyes were as big as saucers. They were in the air so long they had time to eat a ham sandwich and drink a glass of milk.

Tiny, watching the girls fly away, said, "OOPS."

Bubba yelled, "Look out" while I said a quick prayer.

"A-A-A-A-A-H," they screeched as they reached the pinnacle of their flight and then began their downward journey.

Janice was lucky in a sense. She found the softest landing spot on the beach coming to rest on top of Tiny and was engulfed in a sea of sweat and sand and fat landing on his enormous belly that was spread out like a platter of blubber. Tiny groaned and mumbled a "You're welcome" as Janice got up and said sarcastically, "Gee thanks, Tiny," not in reference to his acting as a landing pad but about his jumping on the tube. For Janice it must have been a terrifying ordeal to land in such an undignified place but it at least saved her from any serious injury.

Billy, sitting on his towel, decided to play hero and jumped up and made an effort to catch Sallie. No matter how small she seemed, down force and gravity can and did make her a lot heavier, which Billy soon found out. He was positioned with outstretched arms and bent knees and then WHUUP. He caught her all right … they went down in a heap with Billy on the bottom, hollering and screaming. His stitches had busted loose and he was holding his aching head with bloody hands sending red droplets all over his face. He looked a mess.

Meanwhile Janice brushed herself off and headed for Tiny with her fists balled up. He was still down wallowing around in the sand trying to get up, but he couldn't. Again the force of gravity had taken over. And Janice had the look that only an angry woman can have and it wasn't pretty.

"Uh-oh, here we go again," Bubba said, "another boy 's gonna get his butt cut by a girl."

We raced to get between the sprawled out Tiny and the charging Janice who definitely wanted a piece of Tiny and, believe me, there were plenty of pieces to choose from.

Three of us helped Tiny to his feet and thank goodness he had sense enough to leave. He didn't say a word, walked down to the rocks, picked up his towel and left. We never saw him on the beach again and from then on we referred to him as "Silent Tiny."

Sallie was OK and Billy loved the attention he was receiving from the girls for his heroic rescue of poor airborne Sallie.

"Billy," Bubba asked, "why in the world would you try to catch Sallie … what with all them stitches and all you got?"

"Well," Billy said almost in a whisper as he looked around to make sure no girls could hear him, "ever since my fight with Betty I've been trying to get back in good with the girls and I figured this was my chance."

"Boy, you must have been hit in the head by Betty a lot harder than you realized if you think you were in a fight with her."

"Oh yeah, what you talking about?"

"What I'm talking about is that was no fight, Billy. It was a beating, a whipping, a pure-tee butt-cutting, and you were on the receiving end of all of 'em."

All Billy could reply was, "Oh really."

When the excitement of Tiny's jump died down we realized just how hot and thirsty we were.

"Let's go to Burton's," Bubba suggested. " I wanna get something cold to drink. We can come back later maybe." Bubba began to walk away. "You coming, Mike?"

"Yeah, I guess so. I've seen about all the excitement around here I can stand for one day. Tiny jumping on the inner tube. Can you believe that? And Billy trying to catch Sallie, humph."

"Let's go this way." Bubba was headed toward the dunes. "It's shorter."

"I'm coming, I'm coming … wait up."

Most of the crew also ended up at Burton's where the cool air was a welcome relief on our hot skin, another reason we liked Burton's so much.

The pool table was taken so we grabbed a table near the jukebox and listened as Fats Domino sang about "a thrill up on the hill…"

Small groups were scattered about talking and laughing and joking around. The last couple of weeks everyone had been more civil toward each other, more friendly and nicer. I think we all realized our summer vacation was quickly drawing to an end and there wasn't time for arguing and all that stuff. We overheard Jocko telling Rusty about Tiny's jump and how Janice got mad and went after Tiny. They were laughing loudly. When the pool game was over Sammy came over and asked me to help him lift the table and drop it so they could get another free game. He needed more than my skinny little arms to help him so I asked Bubba to help but he didn't seem to hear me. He was focused on the front door watching it like a guard dog.

"Hey you, Bubba." I finally yelled, "B-u-b-b-a!"

"What?" he snapped, not wanting to be bothered.

I gestured for him to help me with the table. He told me he would be there in a minute but instead went back to eyeing the front door.

The heck with him, I thought so Sammy and I managed to lift the table and get a free game. With all that effort I reasoned I earned a game.

"Me and you, Sammy. Eight ball and no Calhoun Street rules." I was referring to the Catholic High School on Calhoun Street in the city. We considered them to be cheaters.

"OK, Devlin. Read 'em and weep," Sammy said chalking his cue. "You know you got two chances …"

"I know, I know … slim and none."

"Yep, and slim just left town. Just try to give me a game …OK … Devlin?"

I knew I better take careful aim because Sammy was a crackerjack pool shooter and if you missed you might not get another shot. I picked out my intended ball, an easy shot. It was the three ball resting right beside the corner pocket, and after that I would go after the seven up at the opposite end. I leaned over, took careful aim and a few practice strokes and was about to eliminate the three ball from the game when I caught a tiny glimpse out the corner of my eye of a tiny glint of unmistakable blond hair flash by. I looked up immediately and there she was … Beverly Ann Johnson, in person, standing at the soda counter and smiling at me.

Well, Sammy didn't get the chance to beat me again in pool. I quickly told him, "I quit," handed my stick to Bubba who was standing behind me smiling and I walked toward Beverly. I had no idea what I was going to say but was praying that whatever I said would come out OK.Maybe the right words would just come to me? I said a quick prayer. My fears were relieved as I strolled up to Beverly who spoke first.

"Hi Mike, how you doing?"

Don't just stand here looking at her. Answer her dummy, I told myself.

"Uh, fine, real fine. I mean just good… a-a-a-w, I'm doing good."

We both let go a small giggle at my shyness. Finally, I managed, "How you doing, Beverly?"

"I'm doing good too." She smiled broadly. "Actually I'm doing real good now that I'm finally home. I've been in Florida for four weeks with my parents. One of those vacations you have to go on. And I'm so glad to be home. How's your summer going?"

"Oh wow! It's been fun. Been doing lots of neat stuff. Did you hear about the dead man Bubba 'n me found in the creek?"

"Yeah, a little bit, not much. You'll have to tell me all about it."

"Well, let me tell you what happened. We went crabbing and …"

We ended up at a table and talked for two hours. I told her about finding the dead body. She told me about her cat and summer job at the cleaners. I told her about selling crabs, about the movies and skating. She told me about her vacation and Florida and her brothers and sisters. It seemed like five minutes had passed since we sat down when Beverly announced she had to go. Her mother, she told me, was picking her up at 5:00. We hit it off so good and I wanted to see her again but didn't know exactly how to go about it when I thought… what the heck … just *ask* her. Beverly beat me to it, "Will you be at the movies tomorrow?" she asked sensing my reluctance.

"Yeah, I go every Saturday. Bubba 'n me," I answered still not secure enough to ask if she would meet me there.

Beverly to the rescue again, "So I've heard. Would you like to meet me there?"

"Oh yeah, I sure would. That would be great!" I was so happy I could hardly talk.

"See ya about 2:00 then … OK?"

Beverly walked away. " Bye Mike."

"OK, 2:00. I'll be there. Bye Beverly."

This was incredible. No, it was more than incredible. It was GREAT. It was, OH- MAN!

When Bubba 'n me left Burton's I didn't need my bike. I could have floated home. I was going to meet Beverly at the movies. WOWEE! MAN-OH-MAN! It was a dream come true and to happen to run into her at Burton's like that was unreal, luck, God sent and a miracle all at the same time. As soon as I got outside my emotions took hold and I began a personal celebration of happiness. I started yelling and screaming and jumping up and down with a smile as big as Texas on my face. I looked like a cheerleader, only more animated and way more happy. My ecstasy must have overwhelmed Bubba because he simply stood beside his bike gawking at me.

"What's wrong?" I said. "You haven't ever seen anyone be happy before?"

Bubba edged closer to me, cleared his throat, and nodded his head toward the front of the store and then mumbled something. The only word thing I could understand was "look."

I peeked over my shoulder and to my total embarrassment was the crew standing behind the huge plate glass window of Burton's staring at me with open mouths.

John opened the door, poked his head out and asked in a sincere way, "Eah, are you all right, Devlin?"

"Yeah, I'm fine," I said and then my voice trailed off, "just celebrating at little … that's all." *It's OK to be happy about something and show it even if it was a girl,* I was thinking. *There's nothing wrong with that. But I'm not about to share that with the crew. Man, they will laugh me out of the county.*

I was hoping John would leave but he persisted, "And what are you celebrating, may I ask?"

"Oh nothing … just … u-u-u-h" … I was thinking fast for worthy excuse. "For uh … school starts in one week," I blurted out.

"Yeah right," John said as he rolled his eyes. "I really believe that."

"Well, if you must know then …"

Being the friend that he was John saved me the embarrassment of telling the truth in front of the whole crew and whispered, "All I can tell you Mike, is that having a girl friend ain't all it's cranked up to be." He smiled at me and then said, "Good luck and see ya later."

Thankfully he shut the door and the crew moved away from the window and went back to having a good time.

During my euphoria, and before John and the crew had interrupted me, something was bothering me. My concern was that Bubba, my best all time friend, wasn't saying much, nothing at all. As a matter of fact he was being extra quiet and not sharing in my happiness. Here was my greatest wish come true and my best friend not sharing this moment with me. I sensed something wasn't right.

"Bubba, I can't believe this. Beverly's meeting me at the movies tomorrow. I just can't believe it. It's so great, man. So great."

"I can," he said with that sly grin of his.

"You can what?"

"I can believe it," he answered reassuridly.

"Wait a minute. Whatta you mean, "You can believe it?" I asked. There was something about the way he said it that didn't fit.

Bubba grinned at me. "Just what I said I believe it happened."

"You mean … you mean to tell me that …" I thought for a second. "Whoa, wait a minute." I stopped and got off my bike. Bubba rode on. I was so overjoyed about meeting Beverly tomorrow I couldn't pedal and think straight at the same time.

Then it dawned on me. *How many times did Bubba mention going to Burton's today?*

"Eah, come here a minute." I waved him back. Bubba circled back and coasted to a stop.

"You mean to tell me … did you? U-u-u-h… did *you* set this whole thing up?"

"You'll never know, my friend," he said with a big smile followed by a thunderous, "BA-HA-HA-HA … you'll never know."

43
BREACH INLET

The Breach Inlet was a small body of water, about three hundred yards wide and no more than a quarter of a mile long, connecting Sullivans Island with the Isle of Palms. What it lacked in size it made up for in ferocity. It was a treacherous stretch of strong undertows with tides and boiling currents that ran so swiftly that even a ten-ounce sinker from a fishing line couldn't find its way to the bottom. It ran its course from the Atlantic Ocean to the creeks on the backside of the Island and the Isle of Palms. It was as though the Island and the Isle of Palms at one time were one piece of land only to be sliced and disconnected from each other by this fast moving body of water. The current was never-ending, either incoming or outgoing and each was just as powerful as the other. Anything or anybody who found its way into its deadly currents was lost forever, thus earning it the well-deserved title of "the graveyard of memories." Over the years many a memory of a love lost in the form of a letter or picture or some gift of sentiment had found its way into those fierce waters by the hand of some devastated lover attempting to drown memories that at one time in their life had been very precious to them. A few individuals looking for the only way out had plunged themselves into the dark recesses of its unforgiving memory never to be seen again.

It was a Friday nearly 2:00 in the morning and a visitor, Dr. Steven Jenkins, interrupted the stillness of the night at the Breach Inlet. He was alone and cautiously pulled into the small paved parking lot on the Sullivans Island side just to the right of the bridge after riding back and forth for the last half hour checking and rechecking to make sure he was alone. He had thought about stopping on the bridge and taking care of business right then and there but decided against it. He wanted to make sure that what he had to do was done correctly and thoroughly. No mistakes could be made. Besides, it was high tide and the fast moving waters were lapping against the seawall so he couldn't make a mistake.

He parked near the darkened end, cut out his headlights, and carefully scouted the empty lot as he stepped from the car remembering to leave the car open.

As he walked the few yards to the edge of the seawall, he could make out the sound of the swift moving current in the inlet, sounding like it was racing into the arms of its lover, the mighty Atlantic, which it had left just six hours before. He gazed into the darkness, thought about what he had to do, turned and began to walk back to the car. Just as he turned he heard steps behind him. Someone was obviously not trying to hide them.

Then he heard a familiar voice, "Good evening or should I say good morning, Dr. Jenkins."

Steven turned around quickly and stared at the figure silhouetted against the night sky. "You! What are you doing here?"

Lumus had emerged from beneath the corner of the seawall where he had been crouched for the last five hours. "I was just getting ready to ask you the same thing."

"Well," Steven said with as much confidence as he could gather, "I was out getting some fresh air. There's no law against that, is it?"

"No. No law against that, that's for sure," Lumus said and paused waiting for Steven to reply. When none came he added, "It took you long enough to get here. My legs were beginning to cramp."

Steven made a feeble attempt at a getaway by walking slowly toward his car acting as though this chance meeting was nothing more than an annoyance and he would be on his way.

"Dr. Jenkins, wait up." Lumus hustled up in front of Steven and stopped in front of him, blocking his departure. "Before you leave I have something here I'd like to give you." Lumus extended his hand with the search warrant in it. "Here, take it."

"What's this?" Steven asked. "Some kind of …"

"It's a search warrant," Lumus interjected, "that's what it is. Remember what Chief Perry told you yesterday? Surely, you haven't already forgotten?"

"Yeah, I remember but for goodness sake, man. Why give it to me here … now?"

"So everything will be legal and when we get to court some slick lawyer can't have our case thrown out on a technicality. We can't be too safe, now can we?"

"I don't understand? If you want to search my house then why are you serving a warrant on me *here*? And *now*? It doesn't make any sense. Get out of my way, I'm going home."

"Whoa there, Dr. Jenkins. Who said anything about searching your house? If you read what's in your hand you'll see that this warrant is to search your car, not your house." Lumus paused. "Shall we take a look?"

Steven stood hopelessly by the car thinking of a way out while Lumus recalled the Chief's words of advice, *"Be careful, Lumus. Be real careful."*

"First Dr. Jenkins, I want you to place your hands on top of the car, hold them there and take two steps backwards."

"For what?" Steven protested. "What are you going to do?"

"A little checking, that's all."

"Checking for what?"

"Anything that might harm me, that's what for. Now turn around or I'm going to turn you around myself. Understand?" Lumus motioned for Steven to turn around.

"There you go. Now spread your feet a little. That's it. Now hold it right there". Lumus placed his left foot on the inside of Steven's right foot and began his pat-down.

Lumus recalled practicing this drill at the Police Academy during training and used to laugh to himself thinking, *I'll never use this, not on Sullivans Island.*

"Why I've never heard of such a thing. There must be some mistake. I mean you can't do this. You have no right to look in my car or anywhere else. I won't allow it!"

Lumus sensed the desperation in Steven Jenkins' voice.

"Dr. Jenkins, I *am* going to search your car. We can do this the easy way or the hard way, the choice is yours. Do you understand?" Steven noticed Lumus' hand edging toward the baton on his right hip.

"What do you say, Doctor?" Lumus asked being careful to keep a safe distance from Steven.

"All right, all right." The second "all right" was barely audible. His tone was the sound of a man dying, his last breaths on earth agreeing with Lumus, and his eyes were closed. The light from the pole revealed a defeated Steven Jenkins. His memory flashed back to the dreadful days just after the trial recalling the despair and hopelessness he had experienced and then the wonderful turn of events: meeting Mary Helen and the chance to start his life over again. And now he was about to return to the nightmare. He could barely breathe, which was a relief to him and at that instant he hoped that all life would be sucked from him, quickly and decisively.

Steven Jenkins put his face in his hands and cried, "I can't believe this. I can't go back. No! I can't believe it." He was sobbing, the tears beginning to flow.

Lumus knew where to look and within a minute felt the distinctive outline of the steel barrel and instantly stopped and began to get a handkerchief from his back pocket. Very carefully he gripped the pistol and began to slide it from underneath the front seat being extra careful not to ruin any potential fingerprints. The pistol, the only remaining piece of evidence that could tie Steven to the murder, was Steven Jenkin's intended victim this night. It had been bound for the bottom of the Breach Inlet.

Steven Jenkins had a tough decision to make and he had only a few seconds in which to make it. He tried hard to clear his head and make a rational choice but the flood of memories and emotions was too much washing away the little bit of sensibilities he had left. Panic set in and the possibility of any sane thought was completely vanished.

When Lumus bent over to pull the pistol from under the seat, he lost eye contact for a split second with the accused. That was all the time Steven needed. He bolted for the bridge.

By the time Lumus set the gun on the front seat and gave chase, Steven had a sizeable lead, already he was leaving the parking lot and running onto the beginning of the bridge.

What a stupid thing to do, Lumus thought, *where does he think he's going?*

And then he realized what was happening. Lumus gave chase and raced hard closing the gap considerably as Steven approached the middle of the bridge. It didn't matter how close Lumus might have come. It would never be close enough.

Lumus stopped dead in his tracks and looked, not believing what he saw. Steven Jenkins, without breaking stride, leaped over the short railing into the swift and dark current of the graveyard of memories.

Lumus could only stand there and stare, calling out only once for Steven Jenkins because he knew it was hopeless. He never heard a thing, only the only sound of the rushing current. His diving in to save him was not a choice because he knew that if he did that then the Rescue squad would be dragging for two bodies in the morning.

Early that morning the Island's Fire and Rescue Squad did all they could to locate the body but the unrelenting currents in the Breach Inlet would not cooperate and trying to maneuver around the many sandbars became almost impossible. The more experienced members of the squad knew Mother Nature would take her course and eventually Steven Jenkins' body would wash up on either the beach at Isle of Palms or Sullivans Island if the crabs didn't completely devour him first.

Two days later, the decaying and bloated body of Steven Jenkins washed ashore on Sullivans Island near Station 30, about two blocks from the bridge.

Chief Perry and Lumus were at the station when they got news of the discovery of the body. They were more thankful than relieved that this particular job was over. As a form of celebration this called for Cokes and doughnuts all around.

"Lumus, do you think that Dr. Jenkins thought he could actually swim the Breach Inlet and get away?"

"No, no way," Lumus said immediately, "he was caught red-handed and knew it. He took the chicken way out. Poor guy."

"Well, let me ask you this, Lumus … it's been on my mind. You were obviously right about him going to Breach Inlet. How'd you figure that?"

"Well …" Lumus paused to lick the sugar from his fingers. "To answer that I'll have to backtrack a little. You see, I knew this guy was a coin collector so I asked myself what kind of person collects coins? The answer was a collector. You what I'm saying, chief? Besides collecting coins maybe he was a collector of other things too … like stamps, or butterflies or maybe *guns*? Then when you learned that he had owned a pistol at one time it occurred to me that he had to get rid of it. So I asked myself where would someone go to get rid of something like that? Where would they dump it so that no one would ever find it? And the only logical answer that kept coming up was Breach Inlet. Of course, your visit Chief is what set it all in motion. The only other possible place to get rig of the gun was the front beach so I checked the tide table and it was going to be a high tide tonight and had he thrown it into the ocean then when low tide came the gun would have been just lying on the beach. And if he hadn't shown up at the Breach Inlet we could have searched the house the next day and probably found it. But you know Chief, I knew he would try to get rid of it real soon because you spooked him pretty good on Thursday."

"Lumus, what I can't figure is why didn't he just throw it out the window of his car or stop on the bridge and throw it in?"

"Chief, that's something we'll never know … we'll never know. But there's one thing I do know and I'll bet ya a dozen glazed doughnuts that our bullet slug matches that pistol."

"O-o-o-h no! I wouldn't take that bet, Lumus. I'm not that stupid."

They laughed. Silence fell between them as they began to finish off the doughnuts.

Lumus was deep in thought, head back, staring at the ceiling fan moving slowly in its circular world. It almost put Lumus in a trance. He caught himself drifting off and then remembered what it was that had been bothering him.

"Chief, I've been wondering about one other piece of business that I can't quite figure out?"

The chief wiped the corner of his mouth with the back of his hand, looked over at Lumus and said, "And what's that?"

"What about the coin collection … the one that belonged to Thomas Poe?"

"You mean the one we never found?"

"Yeah, what do you suppose happened to it?"

"Well Lumus, I've given that some thought too," said the chief as he leaned back, folded his hands behind his head and put his feet up on the desk. "And to tell you the truth I don't think we'll ever see that collection. It's probably somewhere a long way from here."

"You reckon the doctor got rid of it?"

"Yep … that's what I think … it's long gone."

"Well, now that the case is solved I guess we go back to chasing the crew off the hill and hanging out at Grannie's … huh?" said Lumus with a slight grin.

"About chasing those kids off the hill, Lumus. I've been meaning to have a little talk with you about that. See I'm getting older and what I think we should do is …" The chief's voice trailed off as he looked over at Lumus who was sitting in the chair, oblivious to the world, fast asleep.

"And like I was saying, I'll be at Grannie's if you need me." The chief left the room as quiet as a cat. He believed a man should never disturb anyone in the middle of a good nap.

Lumus slowly opened one eye and watched the chief get in his car and leave.

I'm not going to get stuck chasing that durn bunch of kids off the hill. Uh-uh … I didn't sign on for that job. Now I think I'll take a real nap.

A huge grin came across the face of Lumus as he fell off to sleep.

44
THE RECORD

Beverly and I were at the movies sitting in the last row, deep into the second movie, "Thunder Road" … I think that's what was playing? My mind was obviously elsewhere, racing from one thought to another. The only answer that came from my inexperienced little mind was, "What do I do now?" I had managed enough courage to slowly slide my hand toward hers, little by little while pretending to watch Robert Mitchum outrun the police again, and then finally place it on top of hers. After much effort I was able to interlock our fingers in probably the clumsiest romantic move ever made by a twelve-year-old. But the beautiful Beverly came through again, responding with a slight squeeze of her smooth thin hand and a smile. I gazed through the flickering light from the film room at Beverly's face and thought how beautiful she looked and how OK everything in the world was at that moment. Then came an unintended touching of the shoulders setting off a desire I'd never felt before making me want to grab and hug her but even as inexperienced as I was with the opposite sex, I knew that wouldn't be too smart. But when she gently pulled my other hand from the bag of uneaten popcorn and stared into my eyes I knew what that meant. And I was scared. I reached down deep and summoned all my young manly courage and decided it was time for our first kiss. I surprised myself and didn't rush or seem too eager, hoping not to make a flop of this tender moment. Our heads inched closer and closer, I could feel her sweet breath, until we were at the moment of ecstasy and then …

"Hey sleepyhead. Wake up. It's 9:00 …what are ya gonna do … sleep all day … get up!"

I bolted straight up and gazed strangely at Bubba who was standing at the foot of my bed. He was grinning like a jackass eating briars. "You heard me … get up," he said as he sat down on my footlocker.

"What the ..?" I was rubbing my eyes in disbelief. "You? How'd you get in here?" I asked in a half awake voice. When it finally dawned on me that I wasn't at the movies with Beverly, I plopped my head back on the pillow, moaned, and stared at the ceiling

"Through the door," he said, "like most people … BA-HA-HA-HA."

I had wanted to sleep late. It was one of my last chances of the summer. Pretty soon I would be dragging myself out of bed early … Monday through Friday getting up and getting ready for school in pursuit of an education. Yeah right. In mine and Bubba's case it was more of a war of attrition with Our Ladies of Mercy and trying to stay one step ahead of them, which to this point had been impossible. They must have received secret government training from the FBI or someone, the way they kept a watch on us spoiling our plans before we could get them off the ground. For every episode of mischief we had pulled off, five had been foiled in the planning stage. I would definitely have to check with secret agent Herman and find out if any of the nuns at St. Angela's were on the government payroll.

I yawned and stretched, finally coming to life. "And Mollie," I asked, "Where is she?"

"Mollie? I let her out. She's in the yard. Eah, guess what? They found another body."

"Who did?"

"The Rescue Squad and Lumus and Bull Perry."

I smiled, rubbing the sleep out of my eyes fully realizing that I wasn't at the movies with Beverly and here was my best friend waking me from a special dream to tell me the news of the day. I should have been mad but I realized it wasn't important because no matter what Bubba did, it was hard to stay mad at him for more than a minute.

"What body? What are you talking about?"

"A body. You know like a dead person. It washed up on the beach at Station 30. Some lady walking her dog found it. Wanna go check it out? I'll even ride down to the police station with you. We can find Lumus and see what's going on."

"Wait a minute there Curley, how do you know all this. About the body and all?"

"Oh, the body? Herman woke me up this morning just like I woke you up and he told me all about it."

"Get outta here. Herman … humph. He wouldn't know his bee-hind if someone handed it to him."

"Naw, just kidding. I saw it on TV."

"You and that TV, huh? Tell you what. You can go check on it if you want to … I'm not. I'm gonna read about it in the paper tomorrow, maybe. And eah, it ain't got nothing to do with us anyway."

Bubba shrugged his shoulders at my lack of interest in the dead body.

"Tell ya what," I said, "I got a better idea."

"Yeah what?" Bubba perked up immediately like always when I said I had a better idea.

"Tell ya later. Let me wake up and get something to eat and I'll be over in about twenty minutes, OK?"

"Aw right but hurry up. I'll be waiting. See ya later, alligator."

"After while crocodile. Oh, let Mollie in, will ya?" I yelled at the departing Bubba.

I called for Mollie when I heard the screen door slam and she came running across the room and leaped on the bed greeting me with luscious kisses. Actually they were licks but I never told her that.

I lay in bed and thought how fast the summer had gone by. School started back in barely three days, the day after Labor Day, and our time of freedom would be over. Our long-awaited summer vacation had come and gone like a passing jet. For a moment I felt sad thinking I had to go back to school, sit in class, study and do homework but something went off in my mind and I quickly remembered all the fun we had the last three months: crabbing, the beach and the giant inner tube, helping Lumus with the murder case, and, the best of all, finally getting together with Beverly. *Shoot,* I thought, *I should be celebrating, not lying here thinking about the drudgery of school.* "Right Mollie?"

I made a decision right then and there, a positive one too. I jumped up, slipped on my shorts, grabbed my hat and headed for the kitchen. Right away I noticed something different. It hit me like a ton of bricks, the silence that is. It was eerily quiet. No one was there. No yelling, no screaming or wild Indians running from room to room and around the kitchen table trying to scalp each other. Where was everyone? Was I still dreaming? Was Bubba's visit a dream? This was strange.

Man, this is like the Twilight Zone ... it's so quiet, I thought. *I better get out of here before I end up stuck forever in some outer dimension.*

Then I remembered. Oh yeah. My mother was taking my dear sisters to Mt. Pleasant for a little pre-school shopping, and it would be little because of the lack of money. Ryan and Sissy must be at work.

Before I finished my cereal I finished laying plans for a spectacular end to my summer. I had the prefect idea. Now all I had to do was to get Bubba to go along with me, which shouldn't be hard to do, I reasoned, as Mollie and I raced off the porch into the yard.

Bubba was in his backyard fiddling with the lawnmower. "There you are, Devlin. Looka here a minute. You know about these things."

"Eah, you aren't gonna cut the grass now are ya?" I asked because I had big plans for us.

"N-a-a-a-w, not really. I was just fooling around. Actually I'm trying to find a way to break this thing so I won't have to cut the grass this afternoon." Bubba paused, looked at me, and then looked down at the lawnmower with a scowl on his face.

"Don't like that lawnmower, do ya?" I asked already knowing the answer. I was attempting to get some conversation out of Bubba before he took a hammer to the lawnmower.

"No, I don't. Me and him don't get along." He stopped again and said,

"How do you do it? Cut all those yards all the time, Devlin. Don't you get tired?"

"Yeah sure I do but …" I was bending over the lawnmower pointing at the sparkplug and the wire connecting to it. "See that wire there … the distributor wire? Right where it connects onto the spark plug. Just loosen it so there's no contact and ol' blue or green or whatever color this thing is won't run anymore. It won't even crank."

You'd have thought I'd given Bubba a million dollars. He lit up like a Christmas tree, bent over and asked, "Which one? This one?" He had the spark plug wire between his fingers.

"T-h-a-t-'s right, Catbird. Now separate the little steel piece at the bottom so it's real loose and kind of put it back on the spark plug. Yeah, that's it. You got it."

"You sure?"

"Yeah, but don't tell your father I told you to do it if you get caught, OK?"

"Get serious, man. Have I ever told on you before?"

"Let's see," I said rubbing my chin and looking up at the sky. "Remember back in kindergarten that time when …" I smiled at my friend knowing that all secrets were safe with him.

"Holy mackerel, Devlin. You mean that's all I had to do earlier this summer to not cut the grass?" Bubba exclaimed as he pulled on the starter cord and got nothing, not even a sputter.

"Yep, but what about the grass? I mean it'll just grow and grow if you don't cut it."

"So?" Bubba stated, hands on hips looking down at the disabled lawnmower. "Eah, that grass could grow until it covers the house. I don't care." He looked around. "Enough of this grass stuff. What's up? What's on your mind? You been pacing around here like an ol' worrywart. I know you're thinking about something.""

"We are going crabbing." I looked at Bubba and said no more.

After a few seconds Bubba said, "And …then what?"

"This time is going to be different. Well, for a different reason. I'm not going too fast for you, am I?"

Bubba didn't catch my sarcasm. He just nodded his head.

" This time when we crab we are going to set a record for the most crabs caught on Sullivans Island using hand lines, not those stupid traps. We are going to catch the most crabs ever but … we will need some help." I paused and looked at Bubba to see if he agreed with me. His grin said, "yes."

"To be able to pull this off we are going to need some help. And the best person I could think of is Captain Al."

"Why Captain Al? How can he help?"

"I'll explain all that it a minute."

Captain Alfred Huggins was the father of one of the crew, Susan. He was our mentor of sorts who often advised us about many worldly matters. Not that we always took his advice but he was free to give it and we enjoyed hearing him give it. He dispensed his worldly wisdom much like birdseed: he threw it out there for the taking if you so desired you gobbled it up. Plus Captain Al loved going crabbing. For some strange reason when I mentioned the Huggins' house Bubba smiled, suddenly perked up, and was on his bike, ready to go.

The Huggins' house was one of those great old two story structures built by the federal government when Fort Moultrie existed constituting what was known as Officers' Row, a splendid group of houses set side-by-side, about fifteen in a row.

Riding over to the Huggins,' Bubba asked, "Let me get this straight, Devlin. You want to go crabbing and see if we can catch the world's record for the most crabs caught using hand lines. Right?"

"That's what ..."

And he cut me off. "Well, we can't do that because in the first place we don't even know what the record is ... even if there is one?"

"Wait a second! Will you listen to me? It's not the world record we want to set, OK! It's the Island record ... the most caught by anyone on Sullivans Island."

"L-o-o-k out!" Bubba yelled as Sambo and Mr. Nick made the corner coming *real* close to us.

"Sambo, how you doing?" we yelled in unison waving at him.

"A-l-l r-i-g-h-t, buddy." He waved and gave us a big smile. "All right!"

"What were you talking about, Bubba? Oh yeah, the record. Eah, all we got to do is find out from one of the old timers on the Island what the record is. Shoot, somebody must know. Like ... u-h-h-h ... Mr. Mc."

"Mr. Mc Daniel?" Bubba asked doubtingly. "That old codger."

"No. Mr. Mc Laughlin ... the real old guy. He's gotta be the oldest person on the Island?"

"Humph, are you kidding. He's so old he can't even remember his own name."

"I don't know about that? He's pretty smart."

"Smart? How you know that?"

"Well, you don't live to be no hundred years old being a dummy," I said with a slight chuckle.

"Yeah, that's right, Devlin," Bubba said grinning, "I never looked at it that way. But how old do you think he really is? He ain't a hundred is he?"

"I don't know but I'll put it this way. He showed God where to put the dirt ...A- HA-HA."

Bubba grinned and said, "Eah, how about Ms. Kingman, bet ya she would know."

Captain Al Huggins, long time Island resident, was a small, wiry, bespeckled, man. He was full of life and energy often pulling off strange off-the-wall stunts, things we would never think of. One time he faked that he was dying and laid on his deathbed moaning and groaning as Bubba'n me sympathically stared at our dying friend. Then he jumped up suddenly, and asked us in a rather serious tone what we were doing in his room. We stood there startled and speechless. Then he burst out laughing. But there was no one with a bigger heart than Captain Al. Bubba 'n me had gotten to know him through Susan with whom we went to school. We had become endeared to her quick wit and carrying on like a ham just like her father. She clicked with the crew from day one. Captain Al, a term he didn't mind us using, was in reality a captain in the Merchant Marines and had been all over the world ten times and often held us spellbound with his tales about Indonesia and the Philippines or South Africa and Japan. There wasn't a port he hadn't been to and he brought back an interesting story from each one. He loved crabbing and had repeatedly asked if he could tag along with Bubba 'n me on our next trip. Now would be a good time to have an extra veteran crabber along, seeing that we would be going for the record, *whatever* it was. (Later in life it occurred to me that Bubba 'n me were the *sons* Captain Al never had because of the way he treated us, always with respect and concern for our well-being but at the same time keeping things light and enjoyable. And he was full of love for life and people.)

We enjoyed his company and funny stories plus we needed a car, as I explained to Bubba as we rode over to Captain Al's house, to haul the extra equipment we would need if we wanted to set the crabbing record. We figured we should take at least two regular- size trashcans and our two trusty straw baskets to put the crabs in, two nets, and eight hand lines with extra chicken necks in reserve. Oh, and plenty of cold Cokes and some cookies. And on this particular trip we would be crabbing off the beach because of all the stuff we had to carry with us, the extra cans and all. Crabbing from a boat was out of the question considering all the extra stuff and three people unless we had a twenty-foot boat.

Sure enough Captain Al was right where we thought we'd find him. On his front porch in his favorite red chair with his coffee, newspaper, and familiar Salem dangling from his lips.

We rode up the sidewalk and stopped at the bottom of the steps. "Hey Captain Al!" We yelled together. "How you doing?"

Somewhat startled, he flinched and waved, "Hi Mike, hi Bubba." Smiling, he paused, looked down, took a huge drag off his coffin nail, (my father's term,) and slowly raised his head exhaling the smoke skyward and said in a serious tone, "Not so good, guys … not so good."

He had a sad look about him.

"What's wrong?" Bubba asked. "You sick?"

Captain Al stood up, brought himself to full military attention, saluted, and looked at us very seriously. "Did y'all hear about the body they found on the beach this morning? Up at Station 30?"

"See! Told ya so, Devlin," Bubba said turning to me and nodding. "I saw it on TV."

"It was a doctor," Captain Al said. Bubba was nodding. "His name was Dr. Steven Jenkins, at least that what Bull Perry said and you know if he said it then it's right. Well, he was my doctor for my skin allergy. Yeah, he was a dermatologist. I' ve been going to him for a year for this darn skin thing I have and last week he promised me that he would take care of it once and for all. It's driving me crazy … all the time, scratch, scratch, scratch." Captain Al demonstrated as he talked. He was going in circles like a dog chasing its tail scratching at his arms and his back. "Well, let me tell you, that no good rascal didn't help me one bit. As a matter of fact, it got worse and I got tired of paying him over and over for nothing so I came home, got my gun, and went back and shot him, right there in the office. Shot him dead. Then I dumped him in the ocean. He won't mess with me any more, that's for sure. Heh, heh, heh. Hope they don't find the bullet hole and catch me?"

Bubba 'n me turned and looked at each other. There was a noticeable silence. We began easing our bikes back down the sidewalk, not sure about all of this. We were ready to leave.

Captain Al got about half way down the steps and burst out in laughter: "A-HA-HA-HA-HA! Really had you guys going there, huh? Oh boy… gottcha good then …huh?" He continued to laugh, rubbing his hands together real fast, turning his head from side to side, looking up and making funny little sounds, acting just like Bubba had been for the past couple of months except Captain Al added a little dance, a jig, for emphasis.

Ah huh, so this is where Bubba picked up that little routine of his," I thought. Then it dawned on me, *And I bet Bubba wasn't over here visiting Captain Al either ... h-u-m-m?*

Turning off the laughter like a spigot, Captain Al got serious and nonchalantly asked, "What brings y'all over this way?"

"Captain Al," I said, "you sure fooled us again." He grinned and took a drag on his smoke. We breathed a sigh of relief.

"We came by to see if you wanted to go crabbing with us? We're not just going crabbing like regular old crabbing. We're gonna do something special."

"Yeah," Captain Al's interest peaked, "Like what?" he asked.

"Shoot, Captain Al, we're going for the Island record today … see if we can catch the most crabs ever caught. You wanna go?"

“Great, great. Oh yeah, I’d love to go. What time? But one other thing, Mike. What *is* the record?”

Bubba spoke up, “U-u-u-h ... we really don’t know for sure Captain Al, but we’re working on finding out.”

“About 2:00, tide will be right then,” I said, “and don’t forget your sun lotion and your skin cream.”

“You mean 1400 hours, right? Yeah, u-u-u-h ... tell y’all what I’ll do. I’ll bring my lines and a net and ... what else should I bring?”

“A-a-a-h, nothing else. That’ll be good. We have everything else. Oh, you might want to bring some extra chicken necks in case you want something to chew on,” Bubba said jokingly.

Captain Al was gazing up at the clouds with his hands almost together looking through them as though he were taking a celestial reading. “Yeah sure,” he said, “extra chicken necks to chew on. That’s all?”

“T-h-a-t-s right, Catbird,” Bubba said as we pushed off. “See ya later.”

“Catbird? Where’d you get that?” Captain Al was smiling broadly. “Catbird! Dag gone you, Bubba. You always coming up with something.”

When I looked back Captain Al was standing on the sidewalk rubbing his hands together, making a whining noise, with his head cocked to one side doing his little dance.

We were headed home to get all the crabbing stuff together. We were excited about going for the record and were psyching ourselves up for the title match. The Championship ... the match of the Century ... Jimmies vs. us! If my father had anything to do with it he would have placed the Jimmies as seven point favorites. But Bubba ’n me were confident we were not only going to cover the spread but slaughter them.

Bubba was bouncing up and down on his seat and jerking on the handlebars. “I’m ready,” he exclaimed, “Captain Al done got me all fired up.” He paused for a second and said, “Eah, what about that story. Shooting the doctor, that was weird.”

“A-a-a-w, just adult humor,” I said, “that’s all. You know how Captain Al is.”

“Yeah, I know. But do you think he’ll bring some extra chicken necks to chew on? BA-HA-HA-HA-HA.”

“Eah, he probably will.” I chuckled to myself at the thought of Captain Al gnawing on a raw chicken neck. Then I remembered something: “How about let’s stop by the police station and invite Lumus to the crab crack ... won’t take but a minute.

“OK, as long as you know who isn’t there.”

We rode a few blocks in silence enjoying one of our last morning rides seeing that school would start soon.

“How you and Beverly doing, Mike? Gonna get married anytime soon?” Bubba was giving me that teasing smile.

"Yep, as a matter of fact real soon. Yes sir, we're gonna go right up to the church and do it. Big decision but a man has to … what do you say, "cut bait or fish." The only thing I have to decide is who is gonna be my best man."

Bubba smiled hopefully.

"Nope, not you. Sorry Mr. O'Toole. It's gonna be either Tommy Wade or Sambo."

"Sambo, take Sambo!" Bubba yelled loudly. "If not Sambo, then Herman."

"HA-HA," I laughed. Give me a break, will ya? We're doing OK. That reminds me I have to call her today. Something about a party next weekend."

"Party huh? Can I go?" Bubba asked.

"I don't know? You might steal my girlfriend away, lover boy."

"N-a-a-w, you don't have to worry about that, my friend."

"T-h-a-t-s right, Catbird and I think I know why."

"Why?" Bubba asked giving me a serious look. "What you talking about, Devlin?"

"Eah, do *you* think *I* think that you've been going over to the Huggins house to visit Captain Al? I might be dumb Catbird, but I ain't stupid … huh, Susan?"

"A-a-a-w, you don't know nothing. Forget it. I don't want to talk about it. Race ya to the station" and he took off. I knew then that I had guessed right about him and Susan. It brought a smile to my face, one of those solitary, good feeling type smiles.

We were both relieved to see only Lumus' Jeep parked in front of the station.

"Lumus, Lumus, you there? Lumus." We were yelling from the sidewalk sitting on our bikes. "Hey! It's us!"

Lumus appeared with a big grin and said, " Who's that? The Dillinger gang? Thought you guys were in jail?"

"Not us, Lumus. Uh-uh. We done been in jail enough this summer," I answered, and truthfully never wanted to go to jail or be put on restriction again the rest of my life.

"What kind of trouble y'all got planned for today?"

Bubba answered, "A-a-a-w, not much. Thought we might rob Grannies and give all the doughnuts to Chief Perry. You know? Try to get on his good side maybe?"

"Hey, good idea. Just don't get caught robbing Grannies. The Chief might think you're trying to steal his doughnuts then it would be double trouble, right Mike?"

I grinned at Bubba and said, "T-h-a-t-s right, Catbird. Double trouble."

"Suppose y'all heard about the body washing up on the beach?"

Lumus asked and then sat down on the bench. "Up at station 30. It was on TV."

"Yeah," I said, " but we didn't pay no mind to it." I glanced at Bubba and he was nodding his head, resting on his handlebars with a toothpick sticking out his mouth.

"Well, maybe y'all should have because this dead guy is the one who killed Thomas Poe … the man y'all found."

"No kidding?" I asked. We'd had enough dead man jokes for one day.

"We're ninety-nine per cent sure. Gonna run a test on the bullet that killed Mr. Poe with the gun we found in Dr. Jenkins car and if they match up … then it's case closed."

"A doctor? He was the dead man?" Bubba asked. "Lumus, we know who …"

"Bubba, shut up!" I yelled. I knew what he was thinking. "Captain Al was just joking. Good grief, he was kidding us … OK?"

"Captain Al … Mr. Huggins? What's he got to do …?" Lumus asked looking at me.

"Nothing Lumus. Believe me it's nothing really. Forget it." I gave Bubba a dirty look and he just stared back at me.

"Look, we came by to see if you want to come to a crab crack today?"

"Oh yeah, where?"

"In Bubba's backyard." I looked at Bubba for approval. He nodded and stuck out his tongue at me making a face.

"H-u-m-m? What time? I've got patrol duty this afternoon."

"O-o-o-h, about 6:00 or 7:00."

"Yeah, that sounds good. Tell you what. I'll try my best to get by … and thanks."

"Great. See ya then, we hope. Gotta go."

"Where y'all rushing off to so fast? Hold up there … I've got some good news for y'all. Chief Perry and I were talking just this morning and we wanted to give y'all something special like a gift or something for helping with the Poe case. After all, the mailing y'all found got us onto Steven Jenkins and helped break the case so we came up with an idea. Well, it was mostly the Chief's idea. Are ya'll ready?"

Ready? We were on pins and needles waiting to hear what Bull Perry would give us.

Yeah, yeah!" we practically screamed.

Ok … so here's the deal: y'all can slide on the hill for a week without anybody bothering you. Not me or the Chief or anybody. How's that sound?"

"H-u-m-m … that sounds pretty good," Bubba said leaning down on his handlebars, "but what about our friends, them too?"

"You mean yawl's group. Whatta you call 'em … the gang?"

"No," I said, "the crew. We ain't no gang."

"Oh, excuse me." Lumus said smiling. "The crew. Yeah, the crew is included."

"Gosh thanks Lumus," I said haltingly, "thanks … but we gotta get going and catch the crabs for tonight" We jumped on our bikes. "And hey. We're gonna catch the all-time record for the Island."

Bubba was over his pouting spell after I had told him to shut up and he asked Lumus, "Do you know the record for the most crabs ever caught on the Island?"

"Gosh Bubba I haven't the slightest idea. You probably need to ask one of the old timers like … u-u-u-h … Mr. Rowland or Ms. Kingman. They might know."

"Oh, OK. Thanks Lumus … see ya."

Lumus thought, *Record for crabs ... humph. What will they come up with next? I don't think I want to know.*

Bubba 'n me rode in silence for a couple of blocks. Every now and then he would look over at me when I wasn't looking at him. Then he stopped his bike and stood cross-legged over it and asked, "Eah Mike, you thinking what I been thinking?"

"I think so." I looked at Bubba and then cast my head down, shaking it. "We done messed up big time, huh?"

"T-h-a-t-'s right, Catbird!" Bubba looked at me earnestly. "Sliding on that hill without the chance of Bull Perry chasing us wouldn't be no fun at all …now would it? Durn!"

Bubba was right. The fun would be taken out of it but thank goodness it was only for a week. "Eah, do you think we ought to tell the crew?"

Bubba paused for a second, thinking and then said,"N-a-a-w, it would only ruin their fun too and besides they probably wouldn't believe us anyway."

"You're right." I replied. "Shoot, let's go crabbing."

We gathered all the stuff we needed in pursuit of "the Island record." We had about come to the conclusion we would establish our *own* record by catching a huge mess of crabs being careful to count 'em, Bubba's job, and then mention to the widow Elliott how many we caught and have her swear she wouldn't tell anyone. That way the word of our catch would be spread all over the Island in no time and we would be the official record holders.

I borrowed Katie's little red wagon and we loaded it down with two trashcans, nets, a cooler, and crab lines. The basket on Bubba's bike was full and he had one of the straw baskets over his head, peeking through the cracks to see where he was going. We looked like part of Moses' troupe leaving Egypt.

Captain Al was standing in his yard, puffing on a cigarette, pacing back and forth nervously glancing at his watch as we rode up.

"What the heck! You think you guys got enough trashcans there?

What'd y'all do, rob Sambo? And y'all are late. Look here." He was pointing at his watch. " It's 1405 hundred hours. Y'all would never make it on my watch. No sir, I'd have to write you up." He started to rub his hands together when I said, "Here Captain Al, take this and put it in the car, please," handing him a straw basket. "Thanks."

Then he started laughing. "I wouldn't really write y'all up, you know that."

"Hand me the cooler there, Bubba, and then we can put the nets on top of everything and get to crabbing."

Bubba went into his ritual of cocking his ear toward the ocean and said, "S-h-h-h … hear 'em?" By this time I knew my cue. "Catch me … catch me … catch me if you can," I sang. And we laughed.

Captain Al was trying to follow our conversation and count on his fingers at the same time and got all mixed up. "Now dag gone it. See what y'all made me do?"

"What?" We looked at each other. "What? You all right, Captain?"

Captain Al's eyes opened wide and he put his finger up and shouted, "Oh yeah, I remember" and took off running to the house. He reappeared shortly carrying a Styrofoam cooler, a big white one.

"You're not gonna put crabs in *that*, are you?" Bubba asked shaking his head back and forth slowly. Even us rookies knew not to ever put crabs in a Styrofoam cooler. The crabs could eat right through the Styrofoam. We had seen enough of our brethren from the Upstate pull that stunt and end up chasing crabs all over the beach.

"No, no, that's to keep the beer cold." He laughed rubbing his tummy. "See." And he opened the cooler showing us cans of beer with ice on top.

"But we can't drink beer, Captain Al," Bubba protested, "We're too young."

"I know, I know … it's for me!" Then he went to rubbing his hands.

We had chosen a seldom-used spot that day on the front beach for crabbing in order to try and set the record. It was late in the summer and the harbor waters had warmed up considerably since June almost catching up to the temperature of the hot humid waters of the creeks. We were gambling that the rocks at Station 12 would be full of crabs, especially on the incoming tide, and regardless of Captain Al's watch we were on time because now that we knew better, we planned on being at least a half hour early allowing for setup time and rigging lines and so on. The harbor was smooth and there was a hint of breeze out of the east. And we were lucky because we were the only crabbers this day at Station 12.

Captain Al was excited as a kid with a new toy checking under the rocks for an easy crab or two he could capture with just a net, so Bubba told him to go for it while we got the lines out and began tying the chicken necks on them. Within three minutes Captain Al came walking back grinning and said, "Any time you slackers want to help me catch some crabs then come right on." He had four keepers in the net. *Oh boy,* I thought, *that's a good sign. If he can catch four that fast then they must really be here today.*

And they were!

The drop off right next to the rocks was like a black hole where thousands of crabs must have lived, either that, or there was a crab convention going on, and we were dropping the bait smack dab on top of 'em. Captain Al was so busy he didn't even have time to rub his hands together and dance his jig. The other side of the rocks was just as busy where Bubba was working four lines stopping only to empty his net in the tall trashcan pulling in multiple catches one after the other. Me? I was helping with a line here and there and netting a few and giving Captain Al a break when he went to his cooler for another cold Pabst Blue Ribbon. When Bubba needed a break, then I took up the slack there. Usually crabs will bite good for a while and then slack off until another group comes along. Not this day. They wouldn't quit biting and we wouldn't quit pulling 'em in and throwing 'em into the trashcans. It was like assembly line crabbing. I had never seen or experienced anything like it, that day or since. For nearly three hours it was constant action as we filled every container we had, even emptying Captain Al's Styrofoam cooler of empties, lining it with a towel, and then filled it with crabs.

Bubba lost count of the crabs at somewhere around one hundred but assured us that when we got back he would carefully count each and every one as though they were money. We began to cram more crabs into the trashcans until we finally agreed enough is enough. Plus we were hot and tired and still had a huge task ahead of us ... cooking all these crabs.

Captain Al helped us unload at Bubba's and promised to come back as soon as he went home and showered and cleaned up a little.

Bubba ran over to Captain Al as he was backing out the drive and I overheard him ask, "Is Susan coming?"

I was fiddling with the crabs, washing 'em down and when Bubba walked by I said, "Bet she *is*?"

He grinned and said, "Gimme that hose."

And I did. I sprayed him from head to foot before he could wrestle the hose from me and spray me. It was truly a ceremonial cleansing of both body and soul.

It was a beautiful evening for a crab crack. A steady breeze had picked up keeping the mosquitoes at bay and the pesky flies drawn by the smell of the crabs. With so many crabs we were overwhelmed and we were afraid they might die before we could cook all of them. After we got Bubba's pot boiling we borrowed a wash tub from my yard and a huge tub from the Scott's off the junk pile being careful to scrub it out real good before cooking with it. It wasn't long before we had three roaring fires and boiling waters. Two sawhorses had been set up and a four by eight piece of ply board was set on top of it for our table, which we covered with old newspapers. Paper napkins were taken from our kitchens along with plenty of butter knives, used to crack the claws. Small pots were filled with water to be used to rinse off the bodies of the crabs after the lungs (known as the deadman) and the guts had been discarded. You would dip your crab in the pot and give it a couple of vigorous swishes. An experienced crab-eater would have already pulled the claws off and would have them stacked in a pile in front of them. Eating a few claws then eating a few bodies gave the palate a sensation that screamed for more. We were under the huge oak tree in Bubba's backyard sharing the shade and getting everything ready for our guests who would be arriving soon. Well, they weren't really guests. It was family and friends and we had told them to be ready to eat crabs late that afternoon. I guess they believed us because about 6:00 Bubba's mother and father bellied up at the table and dove in, followed by my parents, my sisters and Ryan and a couple of his buddies. Captain Al, Mrs. Huggins and Susan showed up later. Lumus, true to his word, stopped by for a while and ate his fill and then returned to work. The surprise guest of the evening was Sambo.

He came lumbering up the road from Back Street, stopped by the oleander bushes, sniffed the air and said, "Got thems crabs, huh buddy?" We waved him in. And could he eat crabs! Bubba 'n me cuddled up next to this happy man and watched him eat, and eat and eat … at least, three dozen. *We* might have set the record for the number of crabs caught but *Sambo* had to be the undisputed crab-eating champion of the world. He thoroughly enjoyed himself and with his big smile made the day.

Of course, the adults had the luxury of washing down their crabs with a cold beer or two. It was Cokes for us kids. My little sisters were running around chasing each other with open crab claws, screaming when someone got close, ready to put the pinch on 'em. Bubba's sisters joined with the Devlin kids and last we heard they were going to play tag. I noticed Billy keeping a keen eye on Sammy every time Sammy got anywhere near the fire. There was no telling what Sammy might do? Billy assured us that he wouldn't let Sammy burn anything down. The adults milled about eating and sipping on their cold beers and chitchatting, all having a good time. Captain Al and Mrs. Huggins were enjoying the company as much as the meal. After a few beers Captain Al went into his little routine and was really putting on a show with his hand rubbing and dancing his jig. It was especially cute when Sarah, my three-year-old sister, tried to imitate Captain Al. Everyone got a laugh out of that.

We let one fire burn on well after the last crabs were cooked. The fire illuminated the leafy oak tree giving the leaves the appearance of twinkling Christmas lights. Someone brought a pack of hotdogs for those, usually the younger children, who didn't care for eating the crabs. The hotdogs were placed on the end of a coat hangar and cooked over the fire. Before the evening was over they would be replaced by marshmallows making for a hot gooey dessert.

And Bubba was in hog heaven and well he should be. He just about set all this up by himself and was quite the host catering to the needs of everyone there: cleaning off piles of crab shells and left over pickings, bringing more crabs and fetching beer from inside. And when Susan told him how proud she was of him for all he had done he purred like a kitten.

Later in the evening the Scotts wandered over and ate their fill and from the looks of the huge pile of scraps in front of them they might give Sambo a run for his money. We fed everyone and still had dozens of crabs left.

"What we gonna do with all the leftovers?" I asked my father. "Look at all of 'em."

"Share 'em," he said.

"With who?"

"You and Bubba figure that out."

Bubba 'n me huddled up and, as usual, came up with a plan. And when I told my father that we were going to give some crabs free of charge to our customers he just grinned at me and gave me a thumbs up. We loaded up a couple of baskets of crabs, hopped on bikes, and were ready to take off when my mother asked, "Where y'all going?"

"Make some deliveries. We'll be back in a little while. Let's go, slowpoke," I yelled at Bubba who was staring lovingly at Susan. "Time's a wasting."

"Yeah, yeah, I hear ya … always in a hurry … you know that?"

"Well, we got to go to Ms. Kingman's and Mrs. Kelly's and Mrs. Kimbrell's and Ms. Brown's and …"

"Don't forget Mr. Barber," Bubba reminded me as we pedaled off. It was our way of saying, "Thank you, for the business this summer."

"Eah, Bubba. Did you remember to count the crabs like you said you were going to do?"

Bubba gave me a forlorn look and then looked down and stared at the ground and mumbled something I couldn't understand … like he always did when he messed up.

"Aw come on! Don't tell me you forgot. Just like you always do in school." My plea that he hadn't forgotten sounded more like a scolding and Bubba reacted.

His head popped up quickly and he grinned. "Not this time, my friend. I counted each and every one right down to the last one." Then he just looked at me …

"Well, how many was it?"

"I don't think I'm gonna tell ya. Eah, pull in here. Let's go to Mrs. Kimbrell's first. No, I'm not gonna tell ya until you take back that remark about me always forgetting in school."

I really wanted to know how many we had caught so as sincerely as I could sound I said, "O.K., O.K., I'm sorry about you always forgetting in school and me making a smart remark about it" I paused to see if he caught on to my sarcasm.

Bubba threw back his head and let go a loud, "BA-HA-HA-HA and added, "Devlin, you so funny! I don't know what I'd do without you around. You are the best friend and …and by the way we caught one hundred and eighty seven crabs … do you believe that?"

"WOW! One hundred and eighty seven crabs! Now that has to be some kind of record. No wonder we have so many left over" … I was astounded … *one hundred and eighty seven,* I repeated to myself over and over. *We are the champion crabbers.*

"Let's hurry up and get these delivered so we can get back to the crab crack," Bubba urged. "I want to see Susan before she leaves."

"Yep, ain't nothing like a girl to get you moving. Let's go!"

School started in two days which meant the end of our trips to Burton's, long bike rides, fun at the beach, the movies and messing around in the creek. But it was the beginning of another adventure for me. My first love, my first romance. Beverly and I were now officially boyfriend and girlfriend. The relationship was cemented by the fact that we held hands together at the movies and I called her on the phone five times a week. We talked for hours on end … mostly about nothing … and loved every minute of it. I couldn't be happier.

And Bubba seemed happy too … he and Susan, that is. I can see them now laughing and joking and looking at each other in that special way. Those were wonderful times, unforgettable times.

"Eah, just look at those people eating crabs and laughing and carrying on and having a good time," I said to Bubba as we sat on our bikes out on the dirt road beside his house. I paused for a few seconds and reflected about living on the Island, then said, "You know we're pretty lucky living on the Island and getting to go crabbing and to the beach and all that stuff. Y-e-a-h, we're pretty lucky."

"T-h-a-t-'s right, Catbird," Bubba answered with a big old grin and then added, "but you know what? …"

Bubba was rattling on about going back to school or something … whatever but I didn't hear him as I was distracted by what I saw directly beneath my bike. There was the remnants of the infamous hole we had dug back in June to wreck the garbage truck. For no explainable reason I became lost in thought. Instant memories flooded over me … the truck in the hole, the inner tube at the beach, the ride on The Ben Sawyer Bridge, crabbing in Miller's Creek, finding the body, the hill and Lumus and Bull Perry chasing after us. All these happenings flashed before me in a kaleidoscope of images so clear and vivid that it felt like a dream. But then I smiled because I knew it had all happened. My focus returned to the hole as Bubba was practically yelling at me.

"Eah, wake up, dream boy! Eah!! You hear me!" He paused and then said, "Are you O.K.?"

It felt as though I was awakening from a dream. I felt groggy and answered in a dull tone, "Yeah, yeah. I'm O.K. I was just … a-a-a-w … never mind."

"No, go ahead," Bubba said, "what were you going to say?"

"Well," I hesitated for a second … "I was just looking at what's left of the hole we dug … it's right there" … I pointed. "And I was thinking about …"

"Uh-oh … you were thinking," Bubba joked, "now that's a bad sign. And …" There was a pause. Bubba was waiting on me to speak.

"I was thinking how stupid we were to have taken that bet and gone to all that trouble. All that planning and digging the hole … all that stuff and for what? That was dumb, dumb, dumb. Those days are over. You hear me?"

Bubba took in what I said, reflected for a second, pushed himself up straight on his bike and with folded arms said, "You got that right, Catbird." He was smiling and then added, "but you know what? In two days from now we start back to school. You thought about that?"

"Yep, and that's O.K." I paused and looked at my best friend to check his reaction. "You know why?"

"No. Why?"

I grinned and said, "Because there will always be next summer."

"Eah, that's right!" Bubba yelled, "and then we can go to the beach and to Burton's and …"

I drifted off again deep in thought with pleasant feelings: Yep, I was a lucky boy, and I was thankful that I had the freedom to roam and play on such a wonderful and natural playground called Sullivans Island. I was also thankful for my understanding parents and my good friends with whom I shared that summer. And as I sat on my bike I will never forget the sound of laughter that drifted over Bubba's backyard on that summer's night on Sullivans Island in 1959.

45

STILL CRABBING

July, 2005

It's 6:00 A.M. I'm sleeping and the phone is ringing. I reach for it, half get it and drop it clanging to the floor.

"Damn! Hang on, hang on!" I yell into the phone from the bed, "I'm coming."

I get the phone to my ear and that all too familiar voice rings out: "Wake up, sleepyhead! Them big ol' Jimmies are crawling around in da creek, just waiting on somethin' to eat."

"Yeah, yeah …I hear ya … I hear ya," I groaned, "I'll have the lines and boat ready. You got the net and basket? … And eah, don't forget the beer …See ya about 9:00."

"Sure thing … BA-HA- HA-HA-HA …"